THE
WIZARD

BY GENE WOLFE FROM
TOM DOHERTY ASSOCIATES

THE WIZARD KNIGHT
The Knight
The Wizard

THE BOOK OF THE SHORT SUN
On Blue's Waters
In Green's Jungles
Return to the Whorl

THE BOOK OF THE NEW SUN
Shadow and Claw
(comprising *The Shadow of the Torturer* and
The Claw of the Conciliator)
Sword and Citadel
(comprising *The Sword of the Lictor* and
The Citadel of the Autarch)

THE BOOK OF THE LONG SUN
Litany of the Long Sun
(comprising *Nightside of the Long Sun* and
Lake of the Long Sun)
Epiphany of the Long Sun
(comprising *Caldé of the Long Sun* and
Exodus from the Long Sun)

NOVELS
The Fifth Head of Cerberus
The Devil in a Forest
- Peace
Free Live Free
The Urth of the New Sun
Latro in the Mist
(comprising *Soldier of the
Mist* and *Soldier of Arete*)
There Are Doors
Castleview
Pandora by Holly Hollander

NOVELLAS
The Death of Doctor Island
Seven American Nights

COLLECTIONS
Endangered Species
Storeys from the Old Hotel
Castle of Days
*The Island of Doctor Death
and Other Stories
and Other Stories*
Strange Travelers
Innocents Aboard

can fail to revel in the sheer profligacy of invention and the exhilaration of the prose." —*Locus*

"*The Knight* ranks among Wolfe's most enjoyable and accessible books, and it leaves the reader eager for the concluding volume." —*San Francisco Chronicle*

"With *The Knight* and its sequel, *The Wizard,* Wolfe takes his fantasy in a new direction that should appeal to a wider audience. . . . *The Knight* is a success."
—*Rocky Mountain News*

"Another triumph from the greatest writer in the English language alive today. *The Knight* is astonishing: deep, involving, humane, and absolutely original."
—Michael Swanwick

"*The Knight* by Gene Wolfe will open a portal that invites many new readers to discover his works." —Robin Hobb

"Gene Wolfe has written a fine, carefully crafted novel, filled with mythic adventure and populated by fantastic creatures." —Brian Herbert on *The Knight*

"Wolfe's version of Faerie is both allusive and elusive, beautiful, and fatally glamorous."
—Tad Williams on *The Knight*

"An absorbing meditation on honor and manhood that's not only Wolfe at his literate best, but romantic, charming, and exciting to boot." —Delia Sherman on *The Knight*

"In this dazzling return to form, Gene Wolfe manages to create heroic fantasy in a truly different fashion."
—David Drake on *The Knight*

"Wolfe is a wizard. In *The Knight,* he resurrects the Epic Quest from a graveyard of hackneyed abuse and imbues it with all of the original energy and wonder of Malory or Ariosto." —Jeffrey Ford

THE
WIZARD

BOOK TWO OF
THE WIZARD KNIGHT

GENE
WOLFE

A TOM DOHERTY ASSOCIATES BOOK
NEW YORK

This is a work of fiction. All the characters and events portrayed in this book are either products of the author's imagination or are used fictitiously.

THE WIZARD: BOOK TWO OF THE WIZARD KNIGHT

Copyright © 2004 by Gene Wolfe

Illustrations copyright © 2004 by Gregory Manchess

Edited by David G. Hartwell

A Tor Book
Published by Tom Doherty Associates, LLC
175 Fifth Avenue
New York, NY 10010

www.tor.com

Tor® is a registered trademark of Tom Doherty Associates, LLC.

ISBN-13: 978-0-765-35050-3
ISBN-10: 0-765-35050-5

First edition: November 2004
First mass market edition: September 2006

Printed in the United States of America

0 9 8 7 6 5 4 3 2 1

Dedicated with love and respect
to Lord Dunsany, author of
THE RIDERS

"You asked to become a knight, not an expert on knighthood. To train you further would make you into a scholar, not a fighting man. What remains for you to learn you must learn by living and doing."

—YVES MEYNARD,
The Book of Knights

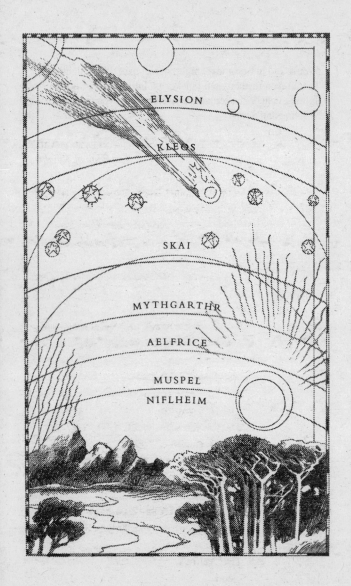

B*en*,

I was not going to put in another list of names, but I thought what if he does not get the first part? So here is another. If you got the first half of my letter, you will remember who Disiri is, and Bold Berthold, and a lot of the others. But I have put them in anyway just in case.

Not every name is here. I am sure I missed a few, and some don't matter.

ABLE	This is what they call me here. It is really the name of Berthold's brother, whom Disiri switched for me.
AELF	The people Kulili made.
AELFRICE	The world under Mythgarthr, where I am now.
AGR	Marder's marshal.
ALVIT	The valkyrie who carried me to Skai.
AMABEL	The woman who saved Payn when his mother died.
ANGRBORN	The giants of the ice country (Jotunland).
ARN	One of Garvaon's archers.
ARNTHOR	The king. His father was a human king, but his mother was a water dragon. Setr was his brother.
BAKI	The Aelfmaid who healed me with her blood.

BEEL	The ambassador Arnthor sent to Jotunland.
BERGELMIR	One of Ymir's parts that lived. The kings of the giants come from him.
BERTHOLD	The man who took me in after I got to Mythgarthr the first time.
BORDA	The captain of Idnn's bodyguards.
BORGALMIR	The right head of one of Schildstarr's friends.
BYMIR	A giant I killed with a spit.
CLOUD	The best charger anybody ever had.
COLLE	A baron of Celidon that I freed.
CROL	The herald who helped me when I met Beel's party.
DANDUN	Another baron of Celidon that I freed.
DISIRI	The woman I love and the girl I love. Both.
EGR	One of Beel's upper servants. He was in charge of the baggage train.
ELYSION	The world where the Most High God lives. It is above all the rest.
ERAC	One of Arnthor's own knights.
ESCAN	The Earl Marshal.
ETELA	A slave girl owned by a smith in the town of Utgard.
ETERNE	The Mother of Swords.
FARVAN	My puppy.
FENRIR	He is as bad as the Giants of Winter and Old Night ever get. He bit off the arm of an Overcyn I used to know and liked a lot.
FIACH	A warder in the dungeon under Thortower.
FOLKVANGER	The Lady's house. You would not believe how big it is, or how nice.
FORCETTI	Marder's town, near Sheerwall Castle.

FRIGG — The Valfather's queen and Thunor's mother. She is a beautiful quiet lady everybody loves.

GALENE — A woman I found begging in Kingsdoom.

GARSECG — This is just a name Setr used sometimes when he made himself an Aelf. He was nice to me.

GARVAON — The knight who taught me how to fight with a sword.

GED — A warder in the dungeon under Thortower.

GERDA — The woman Berthold loved.

GILLING — The king of Jotunland.

GRENGARM — The dragon I killed. His picture is on my shield.

GYLF — He was really one of the Valfather's dogs, but he let me keep him for quite a while.

HAF — One of the boys who tried to rob me.

HALWEARD — The steward Marder sent to Redhall.

HEIMIR — Gerda's son. He was human but it could be hard to remember.

HELA — Gerda's daughter. She said she was dumb because she was way too smart to say she was smart.

HERN THE HUNTER — People call the Valfather that sometimes when he hunts with a pack of dogs like Gylf.

HROLFR — A forester who used to work for Escan's father.

IDNN — Beel's daughter. Not big or strong, but she had more guts than most men.

IRONMOUTH — One of Smiler's knights. He was a fine swordsman and the best wrestler I ever saw.

IRRINGSMOUTH — A northern port the Osterlings wrecked.

ISLE OF GLAS	Not really an island, but the top of the tower Setr built in Aelfrice. There were trees and grass on it, and a pool that went to Aelfrice.
JOTUNHOME	The secret country of the Angrborn women. I have never been there.
JOTUNLAND	The Angrborn country, north of the mountains.
KEI	One of Arnthor's knights. He was a fine jouster.
KINGSDOOM	The capital of Celidon.
KLEOS	Michael's world, between Elysion and Skai.
KULILI	A person who knit herself out of worms. She could unravel and scatter, which made her hard to catch.
THE LADY	Her father was the Valfather, and it could be hard to believe that somebody so good could know so much and have so many angles.
LAEMPHALT	This was the name Toug gave to the white stallion Beel had given me.
LEORT	The Knight of the Leopards.
LER	An Overcyn. He was the sort of friend you do not have to talk to, and some people thought we were brothers.
LIS	Etella's grandmother.
LLWCH	One of the toughest knights the Valfather had. They said his sword leaped like fire, and it was true.
LOGI	The smith who owned Etela, Lynnet, and Vil.
LOTHUR	The Valfather's youngest son. You had to like him, but you always felt you could not trust him.
LOTHURLINGS	The people west of the sea.
LYNNET	Etela's mamma.

MANASEN	One of Arnthor's own knights.
MANI	The talking cat who followed Gylf and me from the ruined cottage. He was almost as slick as he thought he was, and a pretty good friend.
MARDER	His dukedom was the northernmost in Celidon after Indign's was dissolved.
MIMIR	No matter what I say, you will call it a magic spring. Drinking from it brought back certain things you had forgotten.
MOONRISE	Svon's mount.
MUSPEL	The world the dragons come from.
MYTHGARTHR	The world that belongs to people like us. From highest to lowest: Elysion, Kleos, Skai, Mythgarthr, Aelfrice, Muspel, Niflheim.
NERTHIS	An Overcyn who lived in Mythgarthr. She was the queen of wild animals and made trees grow.
NIFLHEIM	The lowest world, where the most low god is.
NOTT	She is one of the nicer Giants of Winter and Old Night. Night in Mythgarthr belongs to her.
ORG	He was an ogre, and might have been the last in Celidon. I want to say he was a man-shaped snake but hot instead of cold, but he was really more like a gorilla.
ORGALMIR	The left head of Schildstarr's two-headed friend.
PAPOUNCE	The upper servant in charge of Beel's servants.
PARKA	The lady from Kleos who gave me my bowstring.
PAYN	The Earl Marshal's chief clerk.

POUK	A sailor I hired in Irringsmouth.
QUT	The leader of the men-at-arms at Redhall.
RAVD	The knight who paid me to guide him.
REDHALL	The manor that used to belong to Ravd.
SANDHILL CASTLE	It was way down on the southern border of Celidon and belonged to Leort's father.
SETR	He was half human but a dragon. He just about took Aelfrice, and I am sure that what he really wanted was to conquer Mythgarthr.
SIF	Thunor's wife. She was beautiful, and her hair was always what you remembered best. It was incredible.
SKAI	The Valfather's world, where the Overcyns are.
SKOLL	The last knight to bear Eterne before me. He was killed by Grengarm.
SMILER	This is what we called the Dragon Prince. The dragon was Grengarm. His people were the Lothurlings.
STONEBOWL	One of Smiler's chief ministers.
SVON	When I first met him, he was Ravd's squire; later on he became mine. I left him in the forest because I was afraid I would kill him.
THIAZI	Gilling's minister and wizard.
THOPE	Marder's Master of Arms. He was good, brave, wise, and tough, from what I saw of him.
THRYM	The captain of Gilling's guards. He was the biggest Son of Angr anybody ever saw.
THUNOR	The Valfather's oldest son, and the model for knights. There were times when I was very, very glad he was on our side.

THYR	The first peasant girl.
TOUG	The peasant boy I took to Aelfrice when I was trying to dodge some outlaws.
TOWER OF GLAS	The skyscraper palace Setr built in Aelfrice.
TYR	Even Thunor said he was the bravest Overcyn.
ULFA	Toug's sister. She was a little older.
UNS	A farm boy who took in Org and went to work for me.
URI	A Fire Aelfmaid. Setr made her my slave, like Baki.
UTGARD	Gilling's castle. The town around it was called Utgard, too.
VAFTHRUDNIR	A giant famous for wisdom.
THE VALFATHER	The King of Skai and the model for kings.
VALT	Leort's squire, and a good one.
VIL	The blind slave who was probably Etela's father.
VOLLERLAND	In old books this means Jotunhome.
WAR WAY	The main road between Celidon and Jotunland.
WELAND	He made Eterne and became King of the Fire Aelf.
WESTERN TRADER	The ship I left when I met Garsecg.
WILIGA	Once she was the Earl Marshal's lover.
WISTAN	Garvaon's squire.
WODDET	Just about the only friend I made in Sheerwall.
YMIR	The first giant.

YOND   The squire who threw himself down on me
        when they were trying to kill me.
ZIO   The Overcyn who helped Weland. He has a
        lot of names.

THE
WIZARD

CHAPTER ONE

I'M A KNIGHT

Some of this part I saw myself, Ben. But not much of it. Mostly it is what various people told me. I am not going to stop all the time to say who told what, since you can figure it out as fast as you read. Mostly, it was Toug.

Uns, bowed at all times, bowed still lower to Beel. "Toug here sez Master's dead, Ya Lordship. Got Master's horse 'n dog, ta. Show 'em ta ya, Ya Lordship, hif ya wants ta see 'em. Don' t'ink he means no harm, Ya Lordship."

Idnn asked, "Do you believe him?"

"Can't say, m'lady. . . ."

"You'd say more if you dared," Beel told Uns. "Say it. You won't be punished."

"He believes hit hisself, Ya Lordship, dat's all. He ain't lyin', hif ya know what I mean, Ya Lordship. Mebbe 'tain't so, jist da same."

Mani, seeing Gylf prowling beyond the sentries, sprang from Idnn's lap and scampered off to pay a visit.

"I understand." Beel nodded. "Speak, lad. I'll no more punish you than this poor fellow who brought you."

Toug did, telling his story to Beel and Idnn as he had told it to Uns the night before.

When he had finished, Beel sighed. "You yourself saw the griffin?"

Toug stood as straight as he could, feeling it was what I would have done. "Yes, sir. I mean, yes, Your Lordship. I saw Grengarm, too, only not up close. But I saw him."

"Did Sir Able say you were to have his horse, his dog, his saddle and saddlebags, and so on?"

"No, Your Lordship. He—he . . ."

"Out with it."

"He said that when I was a knight I'd have a shield, Your Lordship, and to have a griffin painted on it. And he told me what you have to do to be a knight, the kind he was."

Idnn smiled. "Are you going to do it, Toug?"

Toug wanted to shrug, but did not. "I will, Your Ladyship. I know it's going to be terribly hard."

"You'll try, just the same."

"Yes, Your Ladyship. I—I won't always be able to, Your Ladyship. I know that. But I'll try harder next time, if there is a next time."

Idnn's smile widened. She was extraordinarily pretty when she smiled. "You won't always be Able?"

"No, Your Ladyship."

"But you'll try. You sound like him already. You would sound more like him if you said *My Lord* and *My Lady*. You're not one of Father's retainers. Not yet, at least."

Beel cleared his throat. "You wish to become a knight?"

"Yes, My Lord. It's what I'm going to do."

"Perhaps. Will you fight beside us when we overtake the Angrborn who robbed us?"

"Tolt him 'bout hit, Ya Lordship," Uns put in.

"Yes, My Lord. But I don't have much to fight with."

Beel nodded. "I have fallen into the habit of saying we need every man and every woman. Now I find I must say that we need every lad as well. I want you to find Sir Garvaon. He's teaching archery. Tell him I said he was to arm you in any way he could."

"Yes, Your Lordship!" Radiant, Toug turned to go.

Idnn called, "Wait, Toug. You haven't been dismissed."

He turned back, flushing. "I'm sorry, Your Ladyship. I mean no offense."

"Of course you didn't." Idnn's smile lingered. "I just wanted to say we're poor now, Father and I."

Not knowing what to say, Toug wisely said nothing.

"You find us sitting under a tree. But when we first spoke with Sir Able it was in a silk pavilion. We think the Angrborn near now. We hope to overtake and engage them today or tomorrow, and if we beat them, we will be rich again. I don't mean that the gifts Father was bringing to King Gilling will be ours. But we'll have our own things back, and we brought a great deal—horses, money, arms, jewelry, and so on. We've few arms now. Not nearly enough for everyone. But if we win, I'll give you a shield. It will be my gift to you, and it will have a griffin on it."

Not long after that Garvaon told Toug, "I've got nothing to give you. We haven't so much as a bodkin to spare. What about this hunchback of Sir Able's?"

"Got a stick 'n me hatchet what I cut hit wid." Uns displayed them. "Plenty fer me, sar."

"That isn't what I meant. Can you give the boy anything to fight with?"

Uns considered. "Cut a stick, mebbe."

"Do it." Garvaon turned to Toug. "I have no weapons to give. None. If you can make something for yourself, even if it's just a quarterstaff like Sir Able's hunchback has, you must do it."

Garvaon glanced up at the darkening sky. "When the battle's joined, some will fall. More may drop their arms and run. If you don't, you can pick up something."

"I will."

Garvaon's hard, middle-aged face softened. "Try to stay out of harm's way. Get a bow, if you can, and arrows."

Toug nodded.

"And be ready to rise early and ride hard. We're close. We riders will have to hold them 'til those on foot catch up, not that they'll be much use. You have Sir Able's horse."

Toug nodded, and Uns said, "Got me mool."

"So you'll be with us. If you can't keep up, try to hurry those on foot. They're women, mostly."

Toug resolved to outride Garvaon if possible.

"We've got sixty-two men," Garvaon was saying. "We lost a few along the way. Of those, forty are mounted and decent riders. Twenty-seven women, not counting Lady Idnn, who'll lead them. Our scouts have spied on the Frost Giants, and there seem to be—"

"That doesn't matter," Toug said, and left him.

It was nearly dark when he and Uns selected a sapling from the little stand along the wandering steam that marked the eastern edge of their camp. Uns felled it with three mighty blows, working by feel as much as by sight; and they trimmed the top and cut away such small limbs as remained.

After that, when Toug was making a bed on the ground from pine boughs and blankets from my saddlebag, Gylf brought the other saddlebag. Opening it, Toug found a big single-edged knife with a handle of plain black ivy root. It had been wrapped in rags and tied with strips torn from those rags. Toug bound it tightly to the end of his quarterstaff.

They were awakened before dawn. Like Uns, Toug got hard bread for his breakfast, which he washed down with sips from the stream. The rising sun found him trotting north with the others, shivering mightily in the morning chill, with his short spear in the lance-rest and Idnn's cat half in and half out of one saddlebag.

The cat troubled him. It had not thrust its head and forepaws out of the saddlebag until Idnn and her marching women were a league behind. Toug felt, on the one hand, that he should take it back, on the other that everyone— himself included—would assume that he had shrunk from the fight.

Garvaon rode ahead, half a long bowshot from the tail of the column, where Toug and Uns rode side by side. Garvaon would not see him if he turned back, but someone surely would, and would raise a shout.

What could a cat do in a battle with giants? The cat would be killed, and it was Idnn's. He would be killed, too. What could one boy do? Nothing.

He had wanted to make one of a Free Company once. He and Haf had declared themselves outlaws, and lain in wait for someone weak enough to rob. Their chosen victim had been a younger boy, who had beaten them both. What could he, a boy who could not even rob a younger boy, do against giants?

As much as the cat.

Bitterly, he recalled his resolve to ride faster than Garvaon and reach the enemy first. Now he wondered whether he would reach them at all. Would he not panic and run at the mere sight of a giant?

The white stallion that had been mine slacked its pace. "Goin' ta be trouble," Uns said loudly enough to make himself heard over the hoofs of three score horses.

"What?" Toug looked around at him.

"We're gittin' ta far ahead. Them walkin' won't ketch up 'til hit's over."

Toug shrugged. "What good would they be anyhow?"

"How 'bout us?" Uns' grin looked sick. "Bet I kills more giants dan ya."

"You're scared," Toug said, and knew it was true.

"Ain't!"

"Yes you are. You're scared, and badly mounted. You can't fight on a mule."

"I kin try!"

Toug shook his head. "You'll just get yourself killed. I've got an errand for you that'll save you. See that cat?"

"Ain't hit Lady Idnn's?"

Toug nodded. "It must've crawled into my saddlebag to

sleep, and if it stays where it is, it'll get killed. I want you to take it back to her."

Mani ducked out of sight.

"Won't!" Uns declared.

"I'm ordering you to."

"I ain't ya man." Uns pounded the mule with his heels, and drew ahead of Toug by half its length.

"I'm a knight," the words startled Toug himself, "and I order you to. Take it back to her!"

Uns shook his head, refusing to look.

Furious, Toug drove his heels into the stallion's sides and lashed its withers with the ends of the reins.

And the stallion bolted.

To Toug it seemed that someone had thrown the whole column at his head. Before he could catch his breath, they had left the War Way and were galloping over rolling brown grasslands, he bent over the stallion's neck and clutching the pommel, the stallion stretching nearly flat with every bound, neck out, mouth slavering, and the bit in its teeth.

And Mani triumphant on Toug's back with his claws deep into Toug's shirt and thick, tangled hair.

When the stallion was blown, they stopped at last.

"Now that," Mani announced, "was more like it."

Toug gaped at him as well as one can gape at an animal clinging to one's head and back.

"The thing for you to do," Mani continued, "is to kill all the giants yourself before anybody else shows up. Then you can be sitting on a pile of bodies when Sir Garvaon and the rest get here, and have a laugh on them."

"You can talk!"

"Indeed I can." In order to converse more comfortably, Mani sprang from Toug's shoulder to the rather large space Toug left in my war saddle. "I'm choosy about those I talk to, that's all."

Toug shook his head in bewilderment.

"There's old Huld, whom I used to belong to. She's dead, but I still talk to her. There's Sir Able, my newer owner. If I say he's dead too, will you start crying again?"

Thinking he had lost his wits, Toug shook his head.

"Then there's Lady Idnn, my current owner. And you, now. Were you afraid she'd worry about me?"

The white stallion had stopped to graze, but Toug scarcely noticed. "I didn't think animals could talk."

"You're responsible for your own mistakes," Mani told him, "in this life and the others. It's one of the rules that never change. But you don't have to worry. Lady Idnn told me to ride on the baggage, what there is of it. She was concerned for my safety, which does her credit."

Toug managed to say, "You didn't."

"I did not. No order given a cat has legal force, you understand. Under the law, each cat is a law unto himself or herself. It's one of the principal differences between cats and dogs. If she'd told her dog to do it—I mean, assuming she had one. Do you understand?"

"No," Toug said, and felt that he had never been more truthful in his life.

"Obviously, she does *not* have a dog." Mani sounded apologetic. "I would never associate—"

He was interrupted by a bark, sharp though not loud. Toug turned in the saddle to see Gylf trotting over the hill they had galloped down a few seconds ago.

"Except Sir Able's old dog," Mani continued smoothly, "as I was about to say. Sir Able was a noble knight, and Gylf and I have a working truce. We're sworn enemies. Yet enemies who often find it more useful to work for the common good, though he tries to take more than his share."

"I don't understand how a cat can talk," Toug explained.

"Nor do I understand why the others cannot." Looking

pleased with himself, Mani smoothed his whiskers with a front paw. "Gylf tries with very limited success, I ought to have said. Are you going to take my advice regarding the giants?"

"That I kill them? I couldn't, and I don't even know where they are."

"I do. So does Gylf, I'm sure."

Gylf nodded and sat down in the long, dry grass.

"When we were up there," with a wave of his right paw, Mani indicated the hilltop, "I could see a farm away to the north. There were giants around it, as well as a sizable herd of horses and mules. Don't you think that's them?"

"It certainly sounds like them," Toug admitted.

"Then you need only—"

Mani was interrupted by galloping hooves. A young man in a mail shirt and steel cap was cresting the hill.

CHAPTER TWO

IS DAD DA CAD?

Isn't that Sir Able's dog you have?"

"Why do you ask?"

"It is. I'd know him anywhere. Hello there, Gif old fellow! Remember me?"

Gylf snarled.

"Lady Idnn said the boy who said he saw Sir Able die had his horse and dog, but that's not his horse."

Toug said, "It's the one her father gave him."

"Ah! That explains it. You're the boy."

"Do you call yourself a man?"

"Certainly!"

"If you're a man, so am I." With heels and reins, Toug

edged the lame white stallion closer to the newcomer's black. "Do you want to fight mounted or on foot?"

"You want to fight me?" The stranger did not sneer, but seemed very near it. "You'll be killed."

"Mounted? Or afoot?"

The sneer appeared. "Mounted, then."

The butt of Toug's crude lance caught the newcomer full in the face, knocking him from the saddle. Gylf was on him in an instant, and both his arms could not keep Gylf's fangs from his throat.

"No," Toug shouted. Gylf, who had been growing bigger and darker, shrank again and backed away.

"Danks." The newcomer sat up and spat blood; much more streamed from his face and neck. "I yield. I—I ask dad you nod leave me widout a 'orse in dis wilderness. I've no more righd do Moonrise—" He spat again.

"Get up, and give me that sword," Toug said.

Less than steadily, the newcomer did.

Toug handed it back to him. "You can keep your horse, your sword, and whatever else you've got." Struck by a new thought, Toug added, "Except food. Give half of it to us."

The newcomer nodded. With one hand on his bleeding nose, he opened a saddlebag and emptied it of twice-baked bread, a cheese wrapped in a white cloth, beans, and dried meat. Unwrapping the cheese, he drew a gold-chased dagger.

"You don't have to cut that," Toug told him. "Keep it and give me the meat, half the bread, and half the beans."

The exchange completed, Toug stowed his loot in the saddlebag that had held Mani. "Now tell me who you are."

"My dame's Zvon. I'm Zir Able's 'quire, or was. He's really dead?"

Toug nodded. "What are you doing here?"

"Lookin' for him." For a moment it seemed Svon wanted to say more, but he spat blood instead.

Toug decided that his nose was broken. "Why weren't you with him when I was?"

"Wish I'd been. I'd died wid him. Wanded do."

"Only you didn't." Toug dismounted. "Sit down. I'll bandage while you talk. Got anything for bandages?"

Svon did, a spare shirt they cut into strips.

"He 'bandoned me," Svon said while Toug was winding a bandage about his nose. "He's angry wid me, an' I don' blame him. I was angry wid myse'f."

"Uh-huh." Toug was trying to get the bandage tight.

"Wish he'd bead me but he din. Stamped off indo da forest an' lef' me wid his servand. Derr'ble fellow."

"Have you seen my cat?"

"Whad?"

"My cat," Toug repeated. "Well, it's really Lady Idnn's cat, but I was keeping it for her, a really big black cat with green eyes. Have you seen it?"

"No," Svon told him. "Din zee a cad."

"Gylf'll know. Where'd the cat go, boy? Back to her?"

Out of Svon's line of sight, Gylf shook his head.

"He went into the forest by himself?" Toug asked Svon. "Sir Able, I mean."

Svon nodded. "He jus' walked 'way an' lef' us." For an instant he seemed to hesitate. "You know 'im well?"

Toug stopped his bandaging to consider the question; neither the dark sky nor the rolling gray-brown grasslands proved helpful. At length he said, "I didn't know him very long, but I feel like I knew him better than I know most people. We talked a lot one time, and we were hunted by outlaws once, or anyway I think they were hunting us before we went to Aelfrice. And . . . There were some other things. I couldn't talk for a while, but he fixed that."

"He's wiz'rd. You know dad?"

Toug shrugged. "I heard my sister say he was."

"Si'der's righd. Duke gave me do 'im for pun'shmend, I

s'pose. Anyway Zir Able cursed me afder 'e lef'. Lef' 'is zerv'nd an' me, I mean. 'Is Graze gafe me do Zir Able, bud Zir Able gafe me do a 'vis'ble mon'der."

Toug froze in the act of tearing another strip from the shirt. "What?"

"'Vis'ble mon'der. Id's dere bud you har'ly efer zee id. Don' bel've me?"

"No," Toug said shortly.

"I'm dellin' da drud."

"Are you saying that there's a monster we can't see here with us now, listening to what we say?"

Svon winced as a bandage was applied to his neck. "Dad dog was goin' do kill me, wasn' he? Guf or w'atefer da name is. Zir Able's dog."

"Sure."

"He's durnin' into somedin' elze w'ile he'z doin' id. You mus'a zeen id."

Toug said nothing.

"I dink I could'a held off a ord'nary dog. Efen a big dog. Den he s'arded do change."

Svon waited for Toug to speak, but Toug did not.

"You wand do know w'eder we god a mon'der wid us? Da answer's yes. Bud dad isn'd my mon'der—isn't da mon'der Zir Able gave me do. Id's your mon'der."

Toug stared at Gylf, then looked back to Svon. "I want to know about yours. Why isn't it here?"

"'Cause I been ridin' hard. Id can'd drafel fas' as a fas' horse. But w'enefer I s'op, jus' for a day, id finds me. I dried do go home w'en Zir Able 'bandoned me. Did I dell you?"

"I don't think so." Toug was inspecting his work while wiping his hands on what remained of the shirt.

"We'd been dravelin' nord," Svon explained. "Zir Able was do dake a s'and ad a moundain pass. When he 'bandoned me, hiz zerfand zed he'd keep goin', dad he's zure Zir Able'd come. I doughd Zir Able'd given up on da whole idea. Id wasn' 'zactly drue, bud wha' I zaid."

"Was his name Pouk?"

Svon twisted around to look at Toug. "How'd you know?"

"Was my sister with him? My sister Ulfa?"

Svon started to shake his head, but was dissuaded by his nose. "Dis hurds."

"Sure, but I can't do anything about it. Was she?"

"No. Id'd been jus' Zir Able an' me, an' da zerfand. And da mon'der, an' dad dog. I doughd id had s'ayed wid de servand, w'ich was fine wid me. I dind wan' do be remin'ed of Zir Able den. I hadn't lef' him, he'd lef' me, an' I was goin' home. If he wanded me, he'd send for me. Dad's how I was dinkin'."

Toug nodded.

"'Fore long I had da mon'der wid me." Svon swallowed. "I douched id once. I dink I douched a arm, an' id was like douchin' da pigges' znake in Mythgar'hr."

"Or a dragon," Toug suggested.

"Dad's id. Dad's id 'zac'ly. Hod. Dad's w'en I knew I had go back. I'd been pressin', you know? Dryin' do go fas', bud nod so fas' I'd wear oud my horse. For a w'ile I was keepin' ahead like dad, bud 'fore lon' id's back. We're in da moundains an' dere's pig churls dere, churls dad live in caves. You mus'a zeen dem."

Toug shook his head. "Do you mean the giants? I've never seen one."

"Da Angrborn? Not as pig as dad. Just fery pig. Dink a' da piggesd you efer saw, den a man, oh, dis much pigger." Svon's hands showed the increase, a cubit or so.

"I see."

"I give dem gif's an' gained deir frien'ship. Or doughd I had. Zoon as da s'ars came oud, dere's one 'round my camp. I'd hear an' shoud do go 'way. He'd grund an' zeem do go, bud 'fore long he'd pea pack. Da mon'der caughd an' killed him. I heard him die, drashing 'round, an' afder dad I heard id crackin' bones." Svon fell silent.

"So you rode hard after that."

Svon nodded, not moving his head much. "Up 'fore da zun an' off. Jus' now I overdook Lady Idnn, who's leadin' a pardy on food. She dol' me her fader was up ahead wid men-ad-arms, an' dere's a boy—man, I mean. A man wid him who'd zeen Zir Able die. I'd 'splained dad I was lookin' for Zir Able. I never found da baron an' his men-ad-arms. I—I dried do cud across where da road made a wide zweep."

"So did I," Toug said.

"Bud I caughd sigh' a' you, an' rode over here. You're da one Lady Idnn dol' me 'boud?"

"Yes," Toug said miserably. "Yes, I'm sure I am."

"You zaw him die? You zee his body?"

Toug shook his head. "He fell into the sea."

"Here? Dad's nod poss'ble!"

"You don't know what's possible." Toug stalked off after his horse, caught it, and mounted. "You just think you do." Memories of Disiri and the griffin had come rushing back. "Things you think aren't possible happen every day. Did Lady Idnn tell you we were going to fight the giants?"

"She did." Svon had risen, too, much more slowly. "You can'd coun' on me for fighdin', I'm 'fraid. I—I'm priddy weak jus' now."

"Do what you can." Toug felt sure it was what I would have said. "I'm going over to have a look at them. Then I'm going to find Sir Garvaon and Lord Beel and tell them—"

He stopped as he caught sight of Mani, who had emerged from the tall grass to stand regarding him. "Excuse me," he said. "I'm going to have to leave."

"Is dad da cad?" Svon wanted to know as Mani jumped high enough to get his claws into the skirt of Toug's saddle. "Lady Idnn zaid she'd los' one. You goin' do dake id back?"

"Not now. I'm just going to make sure he's all right. You can go back to the road. Whatever you want."

Left alone, Svon took a water bottle from one of his saddlebags and sat down again. The twice-baked bread was hard and dry, but not without flavor. Sips of water made it possible for him to eat and even enjoy it, and the cheese Toug had left him was better than good. The wounds Gylf's teeth had inflicted seemed to burn, and his nose (still oozing blood into its bandage) hurt worse. For a time, eating and sipping cool water provided a welcome distraction.

When he had finished, he took off his steel cap and studied his face in the polished metal. Noblemen rarely had broken noses, although knights often did. It was one more indication that he would never claim his father's lands. As a knight, he might get lands of his own. Not his father's broad and smiling acres, and nothing like his castle. A little manor house somewhere, with farms to pay him rents. It would be better than hanging on as someone's dependent. Drilling his brother's men-at-arms.

It's not an ax, Olafr. (His own voice spoke in his mind.) *Put your thumb here, parallel to the blade. Parallel means in line with it. No, you don't have to remember that. I mean, you have to remember about your thumb but not what parallel means. Remember what I told you about your thumb, and remember you mustn't cut wood with your sword. Take good care of your sword, and it will—*

A manor would be better. Much, much better.

Pain made him shut his eyes. It was childish to cry. He managed to stifle the sobs, but the tears came anyway, overflowing bruised and blackening eyes. His handkerchief was already sopping with his blood. He found what remained of the shirt, and though it was bloodstained too, dabbed at his eyes with it.

He had thought himself handsome once, and he would never be handsome again; but he would cheerfully have consented to be hideous, if only the pain would stop.

I should have brought wine, he told himself. Then he remembered that he had, and had drunk it, too.

Moonrise, who had been peaceably cropping grass, raised his head, ears up and forward.

Svon resumed his helmet, got to his feet, and loosened his sword in its scabbard. *Thrust at his groin to make him lower his shield, then thrust at his face.* But the rush of the outlaws—

It was only the boy come back, Sir Able's new servant or whatever he had been, with his knife lashed to his stick and the cat (absurdly) riding his shoulder, and the monster dog at his horse's heels. Svon jogged to Moonrise and picked up the reins, but the boy—Toug?—dismounted.

"There's a farm that way." He pointed. "It's not very far. The giants have stopped there, and I'm going to sneak over to see if I can find out what's going on. After that we'll have to find Sir Garvaon and Lord Beel, and bring them here. I want you to look after the horses while I'm gone."

"No," Svon declared. "We can hobble dem."

"But I want—"

"I'm comin'. An' if you've god a man's good sense, you'll go for riders an' led me do de spyin' 'lone."

Later, when the hulking farmhouse was in sight, Toug whispered, "There's supposed to be a old man here. A blind friend who's looking for Sir Able."

CHAPTER THREE

A GREEN KNIGHT FROM SKAI

Dis is Ber'hold, My Lord," Svon told Beel. "Doog here found him."

"You found him," Toug declared.

"You dold me he was dere, Doog. If you hadn'd, I wouldn'd haf known 'bout him, or known wad do make of him wen I came acrozz him."

Beel asked, "What happened to your nose?"

Svon managed to smile. "Doog broke id for me, My Lord. We had a dispude, w'ich he won."

"Svon won the second one."

"Wid words," Svon explained. "Ad blows Doog besded me, an' was gen'rous in vicdory."

Berthold spoke then for the first time since they had dismounted. "He's not no bad lad, Toug ain't. Recollects me of my brother. Got many men, sir?"

Garvaon snapped, "Say *my lord*, fellow."

"About sixty," Beel told Berthold.

He sucked what teeth remained to him. "Might be enough. Good fighters?"

"They'll have to be." Beel looked grim.

"I'd fight. Only I can't see."

"Your tongue may serve better than any sword. Are they going to stay the night? It will give us time for those of us on foot to come up."

"No, sir. They come to our farm and seen Master Bymir's gone. Sir Able—Svon and Toug know him— killed him for us. Only the others didn't see. We drug him out with two yoke and dug where the ground's soft, and put a haystack on top, you know. The women hid, and I said he's gone and left me to look after the stock. I can't feed you unless he says. Well, they took it, sir, like I knew they would. While they was eatin' I made off 'til this Svon got me. Only they ain't going to stay. They'll move on directly."

Garvaon started to speak, but Beel motioned him to silence, saying, "How do you know, Berthold?"

"They'd of had me unload the mules, sir, and the pack horses. They never said nothing about it, only talked about killing me, and that's when I snuck off and went looking for Sir Able, hoping he might be around yet."

Beel looked at Toug, who shook his head.

"You're a friend of his?"

"Aye! He was going to get us out, me and Gerda. It was him that killed Bymir. That's Gerda come to stay with me, sir, 'cause Sir Able's going to take us out when he's back from the big castle up north. Only he ain't come yet."

"We've come," Garvaon said somewhat self-consciously, "and that may be good enough."

"I do hope, sir."

A distant sentry shouted, and Garvaon muttered, "They're going," and was on horseback before Toug had time to ask what that might mean for them.

It had seemed best to wait until the Angrborn were clear of the farm, with its fences and pigsties. Then Garvaon ranged his riders in a broad crescent, strongest at its ends, that would envelop the Angrborn while leaving a slender and closing route of escape to the north. The objective (as he and Beel had explained at a length that Toug found wearying) was not so much to kill the Angrborn as to separate them from the pack animals. It was hoped the Angrborn would abandon their booty once they realized they were nearly surrounded. Svon was at the center of the crescent, with Toug on his left and Uns on his right. Privately Toug wondered whether Svon was capable of fighting; with a flash of insight he realized that Garvaon had put him there for his mail and helmet—that Garvaon hoped the giants would take him for a knight.

"Where's Zir Able's dog, Doog?" Svon's words were snatched away by a cutting wind. "We may need him."

Although he agreed, Toug shrugged. "I don't know."

"Whis'le for him, can'd you?"

Toug whistled loud and long, without result.

Uns waved. "Wear da big house is, mebbe,'n da barn. I seen da lady's cat. Mousin' in da barn, I reckon."

A trumpet sounded, and the crescent surged forward, some riding too fast, others too slowly. "Keep line! Keep line!" Svon shouted. Few obeyed—or even appeared to understand what he meant; he left his place, cantering up the crescent to restrain the impetuous and urge the laggards forward.

Their ragged advance seemed to take hours. Toug nerved himself for the fight a dozen times, his states of readiness never lasting for more than three of the white stallion's strides. Then (and it was much too soon) the Angrborn came into view. The trumpet blew the charge. Toug leveled the lance he had made from my knife and a sapling, tucking its butt under his arm, and clapped his heels to the stallion.

The next three or four minutes were a pandemonium of dust, noise, and confusion he was never able to recall with clarity. A pack mule ended his charge, the stallion crashing into it so that both fell amid thrashing hooves and rattling goblets the size of soup tureens. While he was scrambling to his feet, a sword as long as a weaver's beam flashed over his head, red already with someone's blood.

He must have found his lance and caught the stallion, because he was mounted again, bruised and badly shaken.

The Angrborn roared, horses and mules shrieked, and men shouted, bellowed, and groaned. An Angrborn rose before him. Perhaps he rode toward it; perhaps he thrust at it with his rude lance; perhaps he fled. Perhaps all three. The image remained in his mind, bereft of fact.

Abruptly, there was a servingman in the saddle behind him. The reins were snatched from him, and they were riding away, streaming from the fight with twenty or thirty more; my knife was crooked on the end of Toug's staff, crooked and dripping, a drop striking him in the face as he raised his staff and the stallion dropped to a weary trot.

He twisted and snatched the reins, wanting to say they were running but must not, that they had to fight again and win; but the servingman hit him on the ear, knocking him into a night in which there was no more fighting.

When he was able to stand, he saw scattered, frightened men with bows. There was no dooming cloud of arrows, nothing that would fit the descriptions of battles he had heard. An arrow flew now and then, as a lone bird flies at twilight, a faint singing in the empty air.

To the north, the lofty figures of Angrborn were making off through a field of millet, man-high millet that betrayed the presence of the animals they drove by frantic, irregular motion. An arrowhead of gray geese passed over animals and giants, three birds on one side of the leader and two on the other, creaking like rusty hinges as they rode a cruel wind. Their arrow seemed more warlike and more apt to be effective than those shot by the men with bows. The giant king was letting fly geese from the ramparts of his castle, Toug thought, a castle like the one he had seen when griffin fought dragon above the clouds, although doubtless larger.

Almost idly he looked farther, shading his eyes, to where two—no, four pinpricks of scarlet appeared along a range of brown hills. Darker against the darkling sky, a mounted man bent as if plucking something from the grass. He straightened, and held a light smaller than the blossoming scarlet that made his mount sidle away. Rising in the saddle—an act scarcely discernible at such a distance—he cast the lesser light west, a spark arcing high against the cloud banks.

A moment later, he wheeled his mount south, toward Toug. Driven by the wind, the crimson lights raced as fast as he; a breath, another, and the pungency of smoke.

Hardly a bowshot away, the Angrborn halted and seemed to confer. One pointed. Garvaon was galloping toward them sword in hand, with Svon keeping pace and soon outreaching him. Toug began to run, shouting he knew not what and waving to the men behind him until a brawny arm scooped him up and plumped him down on the withers of a loping mule.

"Ya ain't got nothin'." Uns' head was below his own. "Ya ain't got no sword nor nothin', 'n dey'd kill ya even if ya had dat sword ya talk about."

Mules and horses were streaming toward them through the millet, animals driven as much by the thunderous shouts of the Angrborn as by the fires the Angrborn feared. Struggling to control his own mule, Uns relaxed his grip, and Toug slid off, rolled, and sprang up.

He found no dropped weapons, but he ran forward, dodging left and right to avoid panicked animals and buffeted by the loads they carried. He had nearly reached the nearest giant when a great dark beast sprang upon it— Toug glimpsed fiery eyes and a ravening maw. In a moment the beast was gone and the giant lay dead at his feet.

There was a knife in the giant's belt, a knife with a wooden hilt as long as Toug's forearm and a blade twice the length of the hilt. He drew it, and though the grip was too big for his hands, it narrowed at pommel and guard enough for him to grasp it as he might have gripped a quarterstaff.

Smoke left him weeping and coughing. When he could see again, what he saw was a knight in green and gold reining a gray taller than any horse he had ever seen.

"Is that you, Toug?" The knight slung his shield on his back and removed his dragon-crested helm. "Who hit you?"

"Sir Able!"

More smoke wreathed us as I helped him into the saddle. "Watch that sword, buddy. Better hold it crosswise."

Coughing, he did. "I got this from a giant," he gasped, "and Lady Idnn's promised me a shield."

When we were clear of the smoke, I said, "One of the hardest things a knight's got to learn is how to use his weapons without hurting his horse. Master Thope told me that, but knowing it's one thing and doing it's another."

Toug craned his neck. "Have you killed some giants?"

"With my sword today, you mean?" I slowed Cloud to a walk and had a look at the battle. "Not a one. But Gylf's probably done for a couple."

Idnn and her women had come up by the time Toug said, "Isn't the fire going to kill everybody?"

"I doubt it," I told him. "The battle's drifting out of its way, and there's a storm brewing. From the smell of the wind, I'd say a snowstorm. We've still got work to do."

We did it, but it would take me longer to write about everything than the fighting took—rounding up the mules and pack horses in the snow. We spent the night in the big house that had been Bymir's, with fires roaring in every fireplace and most of us as near one as we could get. Toug found me in the barn, where Master Egr and his muleteers were unloading, feeding, and watering their charges.

"I—I wanted to talk to you, Sir Able. Can I?"

"May." I stepped away from Cloud and looked down at him, trying not to grin. "Okay, you may if you're willing to work. Are you?"

"Sure! Anything."

"Only you're tired and your face hurts."

"Svon's hurts worse, and he's been doing a lot."

"Which hasn't included unsaddling his horse and seeing that it has water and corn. Not so far, anyhow."

"He's been helping Lord Beel and Lady Idnn."

"That's good." Reaching up to the level of my eyes, I ran the comb along Cloud's back; when I got to her tail I handed the comb to Toug. "Know what this tool is?"

"No, sir."

"It's a currycomb, the comb you use to groom a horse's coat. If I had a squire he'd take care of my mount—not because I don't think it's important, but so he could learn to do it. When he was a knight himself, he might not have anybody to care for his horse."

"You have a squire, Sir Able. It's Svon. He told me."

I shook my head. "If Svon was my squire, he'd be here, seeing to Cloud."

"He's afraid of you. That's what I think."

"There's something else here of which he ought to be a lot more scared. Does Uns know about it?"

"The visible monster? I don't know, sir."

"Tell him next time you see him. I'm going to teach you how to take care of your horse now. Are you ready to learn?"

Eyeing my charger, Toug nodded. "Can you talk while I'm doing it?"

"Sure. Are you scared of Cloud?"

"A little bit. He's so big."

"She. Size has nothing to do with it. A vicious horse is terribly dangerous, even if it's small. A gentle one may hurt you by accident because it's so much bigger than you and so much stronger. But it isn't likely. The man you told me about—the one who hit you—is more dangerous to you than I am. This's the same kind of thing."

Hesitantly, Toug nodded again.

"The first thing you have to do is take off the saddle and saddle blanket. His saddle tires your horse as long as it's on his back. If you've ever lifted one, you know why. The saddle blanket will be wet with sweat, so it comes off too. If he's hot, or outside in cold weather, you ought to cover him. Anything clean, dry, and warm is okay. In here, I don't think we've got to do that."

"I understand," Toug said.

"Good. A horse doesn't think like you do, but a good one hears your thoughts better than you hear his. You've got to listen hard, and your listening starts with knowing your horse gets thirsty, hungry, cold, and lonely just like you do. If you know that, your horse will know you know it from the way you act. If you don't know it, he'll know that too."

"Sir Able, you—"

"The difference will show up in little things, most so small you may not see them. Battles are won or lost because of small things. You want to ask a question?"

"You were dead, Sir Able. I mean, we thought you were."

I shrugged. "What does it matter? I'm here, breathing the same dusty air. Do you think I'm a ghost? If you want me to, I'll stick my finger so you can see it bleed."

Toug shook his head.

"That's good. I'm alive, Toug, just like you. When we ate tonight a couple of dozen people saw me eat. Eating is proof. Ghosts can't do it."

"I didn't know that."

"You do now. Is it this mail with gold in the rings? I got it when I got Eterne." I touched, but did not draw, my sword. "Her scabbard was on a belt fastened to this. I took sword, mail, and all. What would you do after you had taken off the horse's saddle and saddle blanket, and covered him if he needed it?"

"Take off the bridle," Toug said. "Water him and get him something to eat, if I could find anything. That's what I did with your old horse when I had him."

I nodded. "After that?"

"That's all."

"After that you should look at his feet. I want you to lift Cloud's right hind leg now, so you can check on her hoof. I'll hold the lantern."

Toug did, looking like he thought Cloud's hoof might blow up.

"You don't have to worry. She's used to having her feet checked. She knows you're doing it because you want her to be okay. Any stones in there?"

"No, sir. Is it all right if I ask where you got her?"

All around us, horses and mules stirred and stamped, and muleteers laughed and swore. At length I asked, "Is the shoe wearing out?"

"No, sir."

"Are the nails loose? Any of them?"

"No, sir."

"Good. Take a look at her left hind hoof."

Toug did.

"By now you must think I'm not going to answer. I am, but I was thinking how to. The Valfather gave her to me, but that doesn't tell you much. Have you ever looked at a pool and seen Skai reflected in the water? The clouds, the sun, the birds, and so on?"

"Lots of times. This foot is all right, too, sir. Only who's the Valfather?"

"Some people in your village pray to Disiri. Your sister told me."

"Yes, sir. Are you going to get her out of Utgard?"

"Your sister? Sure. That's one of the reasons I came back. Look at Cloud's right front hoof."

Somewhat less hesitantly, Toug lifted that foot as well.

"When I talk about Overcyns, I don't mean Disiri or her people. How many Overcyns do you know?"

"Well, there's Thunor . . ." Toug hesitated. "And the Thunderer."

"They're the same guy. Name some more."

After a long pause: "Mother says Nerthis."

I laughed. "Now you've got me. I never heard of him."

"It's her."

"Let's have some more."

"I don't know any more, Sir Able. But this foot is all right, too. I'll look at the other one."

"You've heard a great deal of swearing since you came in here, and that may be as good a way as any to find out who men ought to revere. What names have you heard?"

"Uh . . . Frigg. And Forcetti? Is that an Overcyn, sir? I thought it was a place."

"It's both. The city was named for the Overcyn, because

people hoped for justice there. Is that all? You don't seem to have been paying much attention."

"Fenrir and Sif, sir. And the Wanderer."

"Nice going. The Wanderer is the Valfather. Now pay attention. You saw Skai reflected in a pool. But that pool and everything around it, all our world of Mythgarthr, is the reflection of Skai. Lord Beel gave me the white horse that we left behind when we climbed on the griffin. Maybe I told you."

"Yes, sir."

"The Valfather gave me Cloud, just like that. You look sick. What is it?"

"Your horse, the one I had until that man knocked me off. I—nobody's taking care of him, unless he is."

"I see. He's still your horse, Toug, even if he was stolen from you."

"He isn't really mine, Sir Able. He's yours."

"I'm giving him to you. I just did. The muleteers are supposed to be caring for all the horses, but if he's here I want you to find him and make sure he's been cared for. Tie him next to Cloud. Make sure his tether's plenty long enough to let him lie down, and make sure he has clean straw."

Toug started to leave, but stopped. "You did all those things for Cloud before I got here, didn't you? Looked at her feet and everything."

I nodded.

"I thought so. If I'm going to be a knight, I have to see about the man who knocked me off, too, don't I?"

I nodded. "Sooner or later."

"I want to do it before I sleep. I will if I can, as soon as I've seen to Laemphalt."

As Toug vanished among the milling animals and men, I called, "Wash his legs when you've seen to his hooves. Warm the water."

Some time after that, when I lay on the floor in what

had been Bymir's front room, Mani left Idnn to stretch on
my chest. "Are you awake?"

Gylf raised his head to look at him, but did not speak. I
said, "Yes. What is it?"

"Do cats ever get to Skai?"

I thought awhile. "Maybe. The Lady of Folkvangr's got
four. How'd you know I'd been there?"

"Oh, I know such things."

I thought about that, too, and since I had been more than
half asleep when Mani came, the thinking took a while.
Finally I said, "I won't try to make you tell. I know you'd
ignore an order. But if you won't tell me, I won't answer
any more questions."

"I probably shouldn't."

"Then don't." I yawned. "Go away."

"I have important news."

Gylf yawned, too, and laid his head between his paws. I
said, "What is it?"

"Why should I answer your questions if you won't answer mine?"

"You didn't answer mine," I reminded him. "Go away."

"I wanted to. It's a delicate matter."

"Better not to touch it. You cats are always knocking
over cups and stuff, and I've got to sleep. We won't ride
early unless I'm up with the sun."

"It was my old mistress who told me, you see." Mani
paused, studying my face. "Surprised you, didn't I?"

"Of course you did. She's dead."

Mani grinned; his teeth, which were white and as sharp
as heck, looked red because of the firelight. "So are you,
Sir Able."

"Hardly."

"I won't argue—it's beneath me. Is it a nice place?"

"Skai? Very."

"Maybe I'll see it someday. This isn't. I mean, it's nice
sometimes. But in general . . ."

"It isn't," I muttered. "No argument."

"You can't have been there very long."

"Twenty years or so."

"You only rode away a few days ago."

I sat up, catching Mani and settling him in my lap. "Tell me how you talked to your mistress, and I'll tell you a little about my time in Skai." Looking at Toug, who lay with his eyes tightly closed, I added, "I'll tell you some anyway. Nobody can cover twenty years in a conversation."

"You must be explicit," Mani hedged.

"Okay. I will be."

"If you'll tell me about the cats there, I'll give you my important news too. But you first. Agreed?"

"No, because I don't know much about them. Suppose I tell you everything I know. Will you say it's not enough?"

Mani pressed an inky black paw to his inky black chest. "Upon my honor as a Cat, I will not. That is the highest oath I have. But you have to tell about Skai as well."

"All right. Time is different there, just like it is in Aelfrice. I'm not a learned man, but it seems like time runs really quick in Skai. A month there is a few hours here, or less. Something like that."

"That's not like Aelfrice."

"I think it is," I said. "Time goes slow there. Toug over there spent a few days in Aelfrice, or that's what he thought. But it had been years here. The rule seems to be that time runs down, slower and slower as you get deeper and deeper. Skai's the third world, Mythgarthr's the fourth, and Aelfrice the fifth."

"I knew that. How did you get to Skai?"

"A nice girl named Alvit brought me. The Valfather collects heroes more or less as some men collect armor. His daughters and some princesses get them for him, princesses who've died nobly and been picked by the others. Alvit's one of those. The Valfather accepted me and gave me the cloud-colored mount you probably saw me riding today and my shield, with some other stuff. Is that enough?"

"No. What did you do there?"

"Feasted, sang, told stories, practiced the arts of war, and fought giants, the Giants of Winter and Old Night."

"Lady Idnn fights giants, too," Mani said proudly. "She put an arrow in the eye of one today."

"Hooray for Lady Idnn," I glanced at her across the cavernous room, "but the Frost Giant she blinded was nothing like the giants we fought. Let me tell you about a raid I went on. It's always cold and gloomy where they live, and that time it was windy, too. We took refuge in a cave."

"So would I," Mani declared.

"I'll bet. It was a big cave with five small ones branching off from it. They were all dead ends, and empty. We made a roaring fire in the big one and slept comfortably enough, with one or another keeping watch."

"I would have gone scouting. You never know what you may find."

"Exactly. I had the last watch, so I was up before the others. When my watch was over I woke them up, and I thought I'd have a look around. There was a range of hills to the north, and I climbed one. It was your lying on my chest that reminded me of all this."

"Do tell."

"I will, and I'm telling the truth, no matter what you think. When I got to the top, I saw a great big face to the west with its eye shut. The beard was like a forest, the mouth was like a pit, and the nostrils were like a couple of tunnels. I looked downhill, and saw my friends leaving the cave. I saw, too, that it wasn't really a cave at all, but the glove of the giant I was standing on."

Mani licked his left paw thoughtfully.

"I doubt that you believe me, but there's more. Want to hear it?"

"Go ahead."

"Our leader made himself bigger when I told him. Bigger and bigger until he was as big as the giant I'd climbed, and his hammer and helmet and everything else that was his grew with him. Seeing him, the rest of us made ourselves bigger too. I hadn't known I could, until he did it. But when he did, I understood how it was done and did it too. I couldn't make myself as big as he was, none of us could. We could make ourselves very big, just the same. And we did. I won't tell you the rest, because you'd never believe it."

Mani completed the licking of his left paw and licked his right for a time, and at last said, "Tell me about the cats. As much as you know."

"They belong to the Lady of Folkvangr, just like I told you. She's one of the Valfather's daughters, I think the youngest, and she's . . . Well, nobody can say how beautiful she is. There aren't any words for it."

Mani grinned. "I noticed you choked, just thinking about it."

"The first time you see her you fall on your knees and draw your sword, and lay it at her feet. I did that, and I saw a lot of others do it, too."

"Touching."

"She smiles and makes you get up, and tells you very sweetly that she understands you'd die for her, and swears she'll be your friend always."

"That happened to you?"

"To all of us. It was a wonderful, wonderful moment. I'd be tempted to say the most wonderful moment of my life, if it weren't for a moment that was even more wonderful. But honestly, Skai's full of wonderful moments. May I tell you what it's like?"

Mani's voice smiled. "I wish you would, Sir Able."

"I saw a cat at Sheerwall that had been born crippled. It had to hop like a rabbit, more or less."

Mani nodded.

"Now imagine every cat was like that. And after years

and years something happened to you so you could run and jump the way you do. How would you feel?"

"I suppose I'd go mad with joy."

"Exactly. That was what Skai was like. Our lives in Mythgarthr had been bad dreams and now we were awake and the sun was shining, and those dreams had no more power over us. Do you want to hear about Folkvangr?"

"Yes, if that's where the Lady's cats live."

"Folkvangr is a beautiful hall in the loveliest of all meadows. Sometimes it's near the Valfather's castle, and sometimes it's far from it. They both move, but in different ways. There are gardens, and the meadow is the best garden of them all, always full of wildflowers. There are towers, rotundas, and courts, and a thousand hives filled with great golden bees that never sting anybody. There are special places for dancing and games, for singing, for talking and teaching, and for practicing the arts of war, both inside and out. You're forever finding something new there, and it's always something good. Secret stairs leading to rooms full of books and instruments you've never seen anyplace else, or windows with beautiful views you never knew were there."

"It certainly sounds like a place I'd like," Mani said thoughtfully. "Are there only four cats? It must be a very big house for four cats."

"I only saw four," I told him, "but maybe there's more. Even though I lived there for years, I didn't see everything, and it's possible nobody could see everything, even if he lived there a thousand years. Did I tell you that the Lady and the Valfather swap heroes?"

Mani shook his head.

"They do. The Lady's the Chief of the Choosers of the Slain. Some are brought to her, and she keeps a few. But she lends to her father sometimes, and sometimes he lends her a few of his. I was lent to her for a while."

"What do her cats do?"

I smiled just thinking about it. "Hunt in the meadow and sleep in the sun. Wander through her hall for purposes you'd understand a lot better than I do. They're her friends and messengers. On great days they draw her chariot."

"Male or female?"

"Both, I think, and that's all I know about them."

"No, it isn't," Mani declared. "What colors are they?"

"Two tabby, one black-and-white, and one all black like you. Now it's your turn to talk."

"You're aware that cats see ghosts?"

I shook my head. "I'd never even thought about it."

"Seeing ghosts," Mani explained with satisfaction, "is one of the many areas in which cats are superior to you, and seeing ghosts was one of the chief functions I performed for my late mistress. Dogs also see ghosts at times, as do some birds. Cats, however, are far superior to either."

Gylf growled softly.

"He knows it's true. It goes along with our nine lives. Once you've been dead, it seems very natural to see ghosts."

"That's interesting."

"Isn't it though," Mani purred. "Now, dear owner, we must go outside. My news requires it."

CHAPTER FOUR

TOUG'S MIRACLE

This is convenient," Mani said, "but not comfortable. Walk that way, toward the big barn. Would it be possible for me to get into your cloak with you, kind master?"

I shut it around him. "I thought you were Idnn's now."

"I am indeed," Mani explained. "Lady Idnn is a person of distinction. Thus I'm her cat whenever it's advisable. I'm your cat as well, however, just as I was. A cat can't have too many friends in these wild northlands."

"I see."

"Not my mistress's ghost, I hope, since I don't see it myself. But I did, earlier. She's been hovering around us ever since we left her house, hoping to do us some good turn. Now, having gained information she believes may be of value to— Are you aware that your dog is following us?"

"Of course." I turned to look at Gylf, who glanced behind him. "I know," I said. "Don't worry about it."

Bracing his legs against my arm, Mani stood up to see over my shoulder. "Something's going on between you two."

"Nothing important, but you said your mistress's news was. What is it?"

"A friend of yours has been hurt."

"I'm sorry to hear it." I stroked Mani's head with my free hand. "I don't have many."

"And another friend, knowing you could help her, is refusing to ask you to."

My hand shut on Mani's neck. "Is it Disiri? Tell me!"

"It isn't, I promise you. Another friend."

"A woman." I pulled the hood of my cloak up. "I've forgotten so much, Mani. Who is it?"

"One of those red Aelf girls. I forget her name, but they're pretty well interchangeable anyway."

The barn was as dark as the gut of a tar barrel. "This way," Mani said. "Up in the hayloft. There's a ladder."

"I know. I slept up there. It seems so long ago."

"Your dog will have to stay here, I'm sorry to say." Mani did not sound the least bit sorry. "He can make himself useful by watching for intruders. Don't worry about me, I'll ride on your shoulder."

"I'm not worrying about you," I whispered. "I'm waiting for the intruder. Talk about something else."

"In that case I'll go up." Mani climbed to my shoulder. "And make sure she's still alive."

From the hayloft, someone called, "L-Lord?"

I was listening to the squeaking of feet in the new-fallen snow outside, and did not reply.

Slowly, almost silently, the big barn door swung, and a vertical bar of starlight appeared. Toug slipped through, and I caught him by the shoulder, making him squawk.

"If you want to be a knight, you mustn't scare so easy," I told him. "It helps not to shut your eyes tight, too."

"I didn't mean any harm, sir."

"I never thought you did, and a talking cat's bound to make anybody curious."

"It wasn't that. I knew Mani could talk. He talked to me, and I think he talks to Lady Idnn. It was you, talking about Skai. It sounded so wonderful. I wanted to stay with you and learn more if I could."

Above, the voice whispered, "Please, L-Lord Able . . ."

Mani leaped, hitting the logs of the wall with a thump. After a few seconds, he called, "I think her back's broken."

"I can't help her," I told Toug, "but you can. This is why you were awake when you should've been asleep, and why you followed us. Go up and heal her."

As Toug mounted the ladder I told Gylf, "I'm going back in for a minute. You can come with me or wait here."

"I'll come," he rumbled.

We returned to the house and found a cup, and a big lamp made for Bymir. Outside, its flame fluttered in the wind, and I had to shield it with my hand.

"I want you up there," I told Gylf when we regained the shelter of the barn, "and the hole Toug went through won't be big enough. See the big one where they throw hay down?"

"Yep."

"Put your forelegs on the edge and jump a little, and you ought to be able to get up pretty easily."

Gylf said nothing.

"The giant who owned this place stuck his head through there. So it's around twice my height." To see it better, I held up the lamp. "Say half a rod and a bit more. Still, it won't be too hard for you."

"Can't jump that high." Gylf would not meet my eyes.

"Maybe if I go up first, and call you?"

After a long moment, Gylf nodded.

Climbing the ladder without spilling oil from the lamp was anything but easy; yet I managed it, mostly by balancing myself, releasing the rung I held, and grabbing the next. It was a relief when Toug reached down and took the lamp.

"There's an Aelf up here," Toug said.

"I know. It's Baki, isn't it?"

Mani peered over the edge. "That's right, Sir Able, and she's suffering terribly. She's most grateful to my mistress and me, but we've done all we can."

"She wants you," Toug added.

"She can't have me," I told him as I climbed into the loft. "I was hoping you'd fixed her by now."

"I don't know how!"

Somewhere beyond the lamplight, Baki moaned.

I found her and sat on the straw beside her. "She's in pain," I told Toug, "and you're wasting time. Kneel here."

He did.

"Run your fingers over her. Gently! Very gently!"

"I can't do this."

"Yes, you can. That's the point. You're a god to her. Not to me and not to Mani. But to her you're a god. This world of Mythgarthr is a higher world than hers."

Toug tried, and nothing happened.

"Think her whole. Healed. Imagine her healthy and well.

Jumping, dancing, turning cartwheels. She did all that before this happened. Think about how she used to be."

Toug tried, eyes tightly shut and lips drawn to a thin line. "Is anything happening?"

"No. It won't happen gradually. When it happens, it'll be over before it starts, and you'll know. You'll feel the rush of power that did it."

"L-Lord," Baki gasped.

"I can't help you," I told her, "but Toug can and will. Have you got faith in Toug? You've got to, or die."

"You . . . drank my blood, Lord."

"I remember, and I'd repay you if I could. I can't help you now. Toug has to do it."

"Please, Toug! I—worship you. They will kill me for it, but I will worship you. I will sacrifice, burn food on your altar. Animals, fish, bread." Baki gasped. Her upper half writhed. "Every day. A fresh sacrifice every day."

"Who do you swear by?" I made it as urgent as I could.

"By him! By Great Toug!"

"Not Setr?"

"I renounce him." Baki's voice had to a whisper. "I renounce him again. Oh, try, Toug! Try! I'll build you a chapel. I'll do anything!"

"I am trying," Toug said, and shut his eyes again.

I bent over Baki. "Renounce him by both names, now and forever. Believe me, he can't make you well."

"I renounce Setr called Garsecg! I renounce Garsecg called Setr. Always, always, forever!"

"Your mother is . . . ?"

"Kulili!"

I laid my hand on Toug's shoulder. "She's a thing in your mind, and you can trust me on this. She's a thought, a dream. Have you got a knife?"

He shook his head. "Only my sword."

"I do." I took out the little knife that had carved my bow,

and handed it to him with the cup. "Cut your arm, long but not deep. I'll hold the lamp so you can see what you're doing. Your blood will run down to your fingers. Catch it in this. When it's full, hold it so Baki can drink it."

Shutting his eyes, Toug pushed up his sleeve and made a four-finger cut.

"Hold it for her. Say Baki, take this cup." I steered it to her lips, and she drained it.

Toug's eyes opened. "I did! I did it! Sit up, Baki."

Trembling, she did. Her coppery skin was no longer like polished metal, and there was a new humanity in her smile. "Thank you. Oh, thank you!" She made obeisance until Toug touched her shoulder and told her to stand up.

"I wish Gylf had seen this," I said, "but he's heard it, and maybe that's enough."

Rising, I went to the wide hole in the floor through which Bymir had poked his head. "Here, Gylf! Get up here."

Something huge and dark sprang from below, leaving mules and horses plunging and squealing. When it gained the loft, its weight shook the whole barn. Swiftly it dwindled, and was a large brown dog with a white blaze on his chest.

I scratched his ears and sat down again; Gylf lay beside me, resting his massive head on my knee.

"I'm going to have to explain a few things," I said. "Most especially explain to Baki why I couldn't help her after what she'd done for me. I don't like explaining, so I'm going to make you do it yourselves as far as possible."

Baki said softly, "I don't understand about Gylf, Lord."

"I don't think Gylf understands either. Do you, Gylf?"

Gylf shook his head, an almost imperceptible motion.

"He doesn't, so I'll explain that. But you understand a lot that the others don't, Baki. You must explain it now."

"Must I tell them of Setr, Lord?"

"You must tell them a lot more than that." I waited for her to speak, but she did not.

Toug said, "Who are all those people you talked about? Setr and Kulili, and the other one."

"I don't believe we mentioned Grengarm," I said, "but we might easily have included him as well."

"I renounce him, Lord."

I shrugged. "I know you do, but he's dead so it hardly matters. Who made you?"

"Kulili, Lord."

Toug said, "Kulili *made* her?"

I glanced at Baki, and Baki nodded.

"I don't understand that at all."

"Mani's mistress made him, too. Or I think so. Do you want to tell us about that, Mani?"

"I would if I could," Mani declared, "but I can't. I remember being a kitten and nursing, but I doubt that helps."

"Could you talk then?"

There was a hush that seemed long. At last Mani said, "Of course I could."

I nodded. "There are elemental spirits, spirits like ghosts, though they've never been alive. Can you see them?"

"Certainly."

Cloud spoke in my mind. *So can I, Rider. The men who were here are coming back with lights. Do you care?*

No. Aloud I said, "Kulili's the group mind of creatures who are largely unaware of their individual existences. Does that seem strange, Toug?"

"I don't even understand what it means."

"Let it pass. You're a group mind, too, and it may be better if you don't think about it. Kulili was thousands of creatures, but she had no friends. She made the Aelf to keep her company, shaping bodies of vegetable and animal tissues and chaining elementals in them to speak and think. They're long-lived."

Toug nodded reluctantly.

"Much longer-lived than we are. But short-lived as we are, we're immortal. Our spirits don't die. It's not like that for the Aelf. Dead, they're gone completely."

I spoke to Baki. "Is that why you embraced heresy?"

"No," she said.

"Why did you? You have to tell me that. I don't know."

As Baki drew breath, Toug said, "I still don't understand about Gylf, and I'd like to."

"You will. Maybe you know that there are seven worlds. This is the fourth."

Toug nodded. "Mythgarthr."

"Right. Baki, start with the creation of the worlds."

"Do you think it is really . . . ? All right. The High God made them. First He made servants for Himself, as Kulili did later. Then He gave them their own world. It was a reward for things they had done for Him. There was some evil in it. I don't know why."

I said, "It had to differ from Him. Since He's perfect, anything that differs must be wrong some way. Go on."

"They did not like that, so they collected as much as they could and put it into a place He made under theirs. Now we call their world Kleos, the World of Fair Report, because it is so nice. The world under it is Skai."

"Where you were?" Toug asked me. "It didn't seem evil. It sounded wonderful."

"I spoke of the Giants of Winter and Old Night."

"I said evil," Baki continued, "but I should have made it clear that much was merely badness, imperfection. It was all one thing at first, a giant named Ymir, alone, violent, and miserable. Some servants of the Highest God surrendered their places in Kleos and went down to kill him. They did, but they could never go back."

For half a minute, perhaps, all of us were silent. The

voices of muleteers floated up from below, with noises made by horses and mules. The flickering light of the muleteers' lanterns shone up through the hatch and the cracks in the floorboards. I got up and went to the hatch. "You're worried about the uproar," I called down. "You don't have to be. They're over their fright, and it won't happen again."

"I don't understand," Toug said when I sat down. "What does killing a giant have to do with making her well?"

"Baki?"

"The servants of the High God have His ear in Kleos."

Seeing he was expected to speak, Toug said, "All right."

"Those who left no longer had it. They had to ask their brothers to intercede. They multiplied, and their children knew no other place. Their brothers became their gods."

Mani touched my arm with a tentative paw. "What about the giants up there, Sir Able? Where did they come from?"

"From the body of Ymir. When Ymir died, pieces of him still lived. Ymir was vast beyond our imagining."

"The Highest God made another world below Skai," Baki told Toug. "It is where we sit talking now. Mythgarthr, the Clearing Where Tales Are Told."

I said, "The Overcyns, by which we mean our own gods in Skai, needed a place to throw what remained of Ymir, you see. That was the plea they made their brothers, and they promised they'd cleanse their own world of evil as far as they could, casting it into Mythgarthr, with the rotting flesh of Ymir, his blood, and his bones. We call his bones rock, his flesh earth, and his blood the sea."

"That's horrible!"

I shook my head. "The living giant was horrible, as those parts that lived on are horrible still. A dead man is horrible. Have you ever seen one? Not a man newly dead, but one who has begun to decay?"

Slowly, Toug nodded.

"But a dead man returns as trees, grass, and flowers.

So with Ymir. It's useless to condemn the evil he was. That is gone. The good he has become remains. If we won't bless it with our lips, we must bless it in our hearts every time we see a sunrise or a flowering meadow."

"You said the Lady lived in a meadow," Toug reminded me. "A meadow where flowers bloom all the time."

"So I did. We call those flowers stars."

Baki said, "You know how our race came to be, but I do not know how yours did. If you want Toug to learn it, you must tell him."

"I know," Mani declared. "The giants—not those you talked about, but giants like the one who built this barn—were oppressing the cats. Men were made to help the cats."

I smiled. "And where did those lesser giants come from, wise cat?"

"From Skai."

"Correct."

Mani looked pleased with himself. "I knew that had to be right, because it's the only place they could have come from, and there were giants there already."

"A long time after the death of Ymir one of the Overcyns coupled with a giantess." I spoke so softly that Toug had to lean forward to hear. "I don't know how long that time was, thousands of years for them, and I think it likely that it was more than thousands. The Overcyn was Lothur. Some say he's a son of the Valfather's."

Mani said, "His father must have been some Overcyn."

I nodded. "Unless he was one of the group that left Kleos, which some allege."

Baki said, "Will you tell us the name of the giantess?"

"You know it already. Angr's kids, the Angrborn, were not strong enough to resist the Overcyns, but the Overcyns didn't want to kill them, because they were their relatives. To rid Skai of them, they sent them here."

Toug said, "What about us? How did we get here?"

"The Most High God raised us from the animals. Does that sound horrible?"

Mani said, "Well, *I* certainly don't think so."

"Neither do I," I told him. "You're innocent, always, and often brave and loyal. No one who has known Gylf as I have could be ashamed of being related to him, though there have been many times when he must have been shamed by us."

Toug exclaimed, "But he's a magic dog!" At which Mani shook his head.

"We will talk about Gylf later," I told Toug. "In fact, I hope Gylf will talk for himself."

Gylf looked at me like I had sold him out.

"We're talking about Baki now, and how you healed her. Or if we aren't, we should be. How did Aelfrice come to be, Baki? You must know."

Toug said, "You said we were raised from the beasts. Like they grew up and became us. But you didn't say why."

"Because the Most High God willed it. Do you think He discussed the matter with me? He discusses His decisions with no one."

"He must have had some reason."

"No doubt, but we can only guess. Mine is like Mani's—we're to preserve Mythgarthr from the Angrborn. They're cruel for cruelty's sake, and destroy for the sheer love of destruction. The animals He put here don't do such things, and He may have hoped that if He gave us reason and the power of speech we'd serve as a check on the Angrborn. As we do."

"But we do those things sometimes, too." Toug looked at Baki for confirmation, and she nodded.

"We do. We build houses and barns as well. How do you think the Angrborn learned to do those things?"

"By copying us?"

"You got it. Way too often, we turn around and copy them." I turned to Baki. "You talk."

She cleared her throat. "First I would like to thank Toug again for healing me."

Toug muttered, "You don't have to."

"I want to. I also want to thank Sir Able for bringing you and teaching you to do it. You would not have if he had not urged you. I know that.

"As for the creation of Aelfrice, it is obvious, surely. It is a dump for the refuse of Mythgarthr." Baki sighed. "If you spit upon me, I will be honored by your attention."

I said, "You still resent us, though you reject Setr?"

"I suppose I do. While we remained elemental spirits, Toug, we could do little harm. Do you think spirits, ghosts, and all such all-powerful?"

"I guess I did."

"You were wrong. But once Kulili had given us bodies we did all sorts of harm—there, and here. She remonstrated with us, and we turned on her and drove her under the waves. We wanted to be free, and to us that means free to do what we want, judged by no one and nothing."

"I wouldn't judge you," Toug said miserably.

"You must! You are our gods! Try to understand."

Toug could only gape at her.

When several seconds had passed, Mani said kindly, "The gods of each world are the people of the next one up. That's Skai for us, and us for Aelfrice."

I added, "Aelfrice for Muspel, the sixth world."

Baki signed again. "You know all about it." There was resignation in her voice.

"Not all. No one knows all there is to know about a thing except the Most High God. The Valfather once told me that if anyone ever learns all there is to be learned about anything, it'll be found that he or she is the Most High God and always has been. You renounced Setr and accepted Toug. What harm can my knowledge do after that?"

"I am ashamed for my people. For the Fire Aelf."

"Their shame's no worse because I know. Do you want to repay Toug for healing you? Tell him."

Mani added, "If you don't, we will."

Baki shrugged. "There is not much to tell. You know we can visit your world?"

Toug nodded. "The Queen of the Wood did."

"And your kind can visit our Aelfrice?"

He nodded again. "I've been there."

"We saw you up here, and saw how rarely you heeded our prayers. How foolish you were, and how cruel. We visited the world below our own. It is a beautiful place, a place of fire, and there are wonderous beings there, beings powerful and wise. We proclaimed them our gods."

"You can do that?" Toug's eyes were wide.

"We did. We prayed to them, sacrificed our own folk on their altars, invited them to come to Aelfrice to aid us in our struggle against Kulili."

Toug said softly, "Your mother."

"Our mother, yes. We were trying to kill her, as we had for centuries. The gods from Muspel were to help us in that, forging a unified plan."

Toug shivered.

"But it wasn't all of you, was it?" I said. "It was only you Fire Aelf at first."

"We were the leaders, and we followed Setr."

"And Grengarm?"

Baki raised her eyebrows. She was squatting in the straw with her knees pressed to her breasts; yet it seemed that she was about to flee.

Toug said, "Did you know that Sir Able killed Grengarm?"

"No." When no one else spoke, Baki repeated, "No. . . ."

"You weren't among those who danced for him here in Mythgarthr," I said. "Where were you?"

"It was hard for him to come here." It seemed she spoke

to herself. The yellow fire in her eyes was smoky. "Some of us still prayed up, even after we worshipped them. It was a triumph for him that he could get here at all."

"The Osterlings sacrificed us to the dragons," I told her, "casting the victims into the Mountain of Fire. I saw their faces screaming in Grengarm when I killed him."

Toug said, "I won't ask about Gylf anymore. I know you don't want to talk about that."

"Not now," I told him. "Later, perhaps."

"But I want to ask about Grengarm and the other one. Why is it they're so much stronger? Stronger than we are, and stronger even than people like her?"

"The Aelf," Mani purred.

"You worshipped them," I reminded Toug. "Don't you even know their name?"

"They're supposed to be great. They could do anything. She doesn't seem like that."

"Baki," I told him. "Her name is Baki, and she's your worshipper, the only one you've got. The least you can do for her is use it. Would you explain, Baki, why Toug finds you so disappointing?"

"We were never meant to be your gods," Baki said. "Have you ever built a house?"

Toug shook his head.

"But you must have seen all the things that are left over when the building is done, the odds and ends of wood, the warped shingles, and the cracked stones."

Slowly, Toug nodded.

"We are what was left when the Highest God finished building your world. What He piled together and buried."

"It's getting late," I said. "We should sleep, all of us, and now that she's whole, Baki will want to go home."

Mani said, "I love this. I could do it all night."

"I'll bet, and sleep all day afterward. But Toug and I will have to ride, and Gylf will have to run. We may have to fight, too." I turned to Baki. "How were you hurt?"

"I was scattering the mules for you, Lord. Uri and I found twenty or so. When we tried to scatter those, they broke into two groups. She followed one, and I the other. One of the Angrborn came for mine."

I nodded.

"I should have run, but I tried to scatter them. He caught me and threw me on the rocks."

"I'm sorry. Terribly sorry."

Toug added, "But you're all right now?"

"Better than ever!" Baki smiled, then grew serious. "It was a long time before Uri found me. I wanted her to take me to you, Lord, so you could heal me. She would not do it. She carried me back to Aelfrice, and came back here to find one of the new gods to do it."

Toug looked at me, but I said nothing.

"Then she said the new god was dead, and nothing could be done. But I saw you up here . . ." Baki sighed. "It took a lot of searching, Lord, but I found you and came as close as I could."

I stood and blew out the lamp. "Go back to Aelfrice. Tell Garsecg I haven't forgotten my promise."

"But, Lord—"

"Do what I told you." I turned to Toug. "We've got to sleep, or we'll be good for nothing in the morning."

CHAPTER FIVE

CONFIDENCES

Much later, when we lay in the crowded house that had been Bymir's and he sensed that I, too, was awake, Toug whispered, "Will you tell me one more thing, Sir Able? Just one more."

"Probably not."

"Why wouldn't you heal Baki yourself?"

At length I said, "You told me Lady Idnn had promised you a shield. Has she given it to you?"

"Not yet," Toug whispered. "There hasn't been time to paint it anyhow."

"You'll have to remind her," I told him, "and both of us have to sleep."

Obediently, Toug closed his eyes; but as soon as he did, he saw sunshine, waving grass, and distant vistas of mountain and plain. He opened them again at once; but there was only darkness, and the flickering firelight.

"This is better," I said. I was standing beside the cloud-colored mount I had come back on, and the wind that whipped the plumes on my helmet sent her mane and tail streaming across the sky.

"Where are we?" Toug asked. His own mount, Laemphalt, was cropping grass some distance off.

"Most people think there's only one world on this fourth level," I explained.

"Isn't that true?" Toug took a step toward me and found that there was a shield strapped to his arm, a shield rounded at the top, with a long tapering point at the bottom, such as knights use. Its background was green, like that of my own shield, and on it was a white griffin with wings spread wide.

"The highest level, and the lowest, have only got one," I said. "The rest have several. This is Dream. It's on the midmost level, with Mythgarthr. Cloud brought us here."

She looked up at the sound of her name, and her head and back were as white as the whitest clouds, but her feet and legs remained as dark as storms. Gray were the mane and tail streaming from the hilltop in the warm wind of Dream.

"She's a magic horse . . ." Toug said, and his mind was filled with wonder.

"She's not a horse at all," I told him, "and a good one.

She's as wise as a woman, but she's not like a woman, and it will be well for you to understand her."

"She can take you from world to world?"

I nodded solemnly. "Can your horse?"

Toug shook his head.

"What of the horses of Aelfrice?"

Toug thought before he spoke. "I don't know about those, Sir Able. I've never seen one."

"There aren't any. I don't mean you'll never see an Aelf on horseback. For that matter, Uri and Baki rode some of the horses and mules they scattered. But any horse ridden by an Aelf, here or in Aelfrice, will be one of ours, a horse taken by the Aelf as a man or a woman may be."

Toug nodded. "I think I understand. Are you going to tell me about your dog now?"

I shook my head.

"You don't have to. You could tell me later, or not tell at all. I already know he can talk like Mani."

"Yes," I said, "and no. He can speak, but not like Mani. Mani speaks because he's a freakish combination of spirit and beast, though the spirit and the beast do not belong together. Gylf speaks of himself—of his nature. He has a spirit, of course, and an animal body. But they are parts of one whole. Can you write, Toug?"

Toug shook his head.

"You may learn someday. When you do, you'll find out that your hands speak just as your lips do now, and that the things they say are a little different. Still, you're one whole, lips and hands."

"You're saying he talks like we do, but Mani doesn't."

"Close enough." I raised my voice. "Gylf! Here boy!"

Toug looked around and caught sight of a running animal far away. It grew smaller as it approached, until a panting Gylf threw himself down at my feet.

"We were talking about you," I said. "When I go back to Skai, will you go with me?"

Gylf nodded.

"That's good. But maybe it won't be allowed. Or you may want to stay here awhile before you join me there. In either case, you'll belong to Toug. Is that understood?"

Slowly, Gylf nodded again.

"I want you to talk to him. I won't make you, but I ask it. Just to Toug. Will you speak?"

There was a long silence. At last Gylf said, "Yep."

"Thank you. Toug wonders how you change size. Will you tell him?"

"Good dog."

We waited, and at length he added, "Dog from Skai."

Toug exclaimed, "You had him before you went there!"

"I did. He was given to me by the Bodachan. Their reasons for making me such a gift were good but complicated, and we'll leave them for another time. Do you know the Wild Hunt?"

Toug nodded. "It's when Hern the Hunter hunts up in the air, like a storm. I'm not sure it's real."

"Hern's the Valfather. It's one of his names."

Toug gulped. "I heard him when I was little. The—his horse galloping across Skai, and his hounds."

"Then how could you not be certain it is real?"

"I thought maybe I dreamed it."

"You're dreaming this," I told him; and although Toug considered the matter for a long while after he woke, there seemed to be no adequate answer to it.

"I've talked about the Giants of Winter and Old Night. When I did, you must have thought them human-shaped, like the Angrborn. I think I told you about one wearing a glove, and if you hadn't thought them like us before, you'd surely have after that."

Toug nodded.

"Many are. Others are not. There's one with a hundred

arms, and more than a few who have or take on the shapes of animals. Fenrir's the worst. You've got to understand that there's no big distinction among the kinds."

Reluctantly, Toug nodded again.

"Ones or two at a time wander away from their sunless kingdom to steal and kill. When they do, the Valfather hunts them down, sometimes alone, sometimes with his sons or men like me, or both. But always with his hounds, who course them and bring them to bay. You heard them, you said."

Recalling how frightened he had been, Toug said nothing.

"It sometimes happens that one of the bitches of that pack gives birth before her time. The exertions of the hunt are too great, and the pup is dropped. It doesn't happen often, but it happens. Once in a hundred years, maybe."

"Isn't that thousands of years in Skai?"

"Right. When a puppy is dropped like that, or lost some other way, it may fall or wander down into Mythgarthr. Then someone finds it, helpless and alone, hungry and cold. He can kill it then, if he wants to. He can leave it to starve. Or he can take it in as the Bodachan did. Feed it, and keep it alive. If he does, he'll have his reward eventually."

"You mean when the Valfather comes to get it?"

"You're pale. Would that be such a terrible thing?"

Trembling, Toug nodded.

"I guess you're right. But a wonderful thing, too. If he finds the hound he lost loved the man who saved it, do you think he'll hate that man? That's not his way."

"I hope not," Toug said fervently.

"It isn't. It's the sort of thing the giants do, not the sort of thing Overcyns do, and it's sure as heck not the sort of thing the Valfather does."

When minutes had passed, Toug said timidly, "It's really beautiful here."

"Beautiful and terrible. Have you noticed how bright the colors are?"

Toug looked around, and it seemed that he looked with new eyes. "Yes," he said. "I hadn't paid any attention, but they are wonderful, like you say."

"They are yours, and if ever you give them up this will be a land of blacks and grays. But that's not what I brought you here to tell you. Nor did I bring you to explain Gylf."

"Where is he?" Toug looked around.

"Where he was. I brought you so I could tell you about the Valfather." I sighed. "He's very kind and very wise, and in his kindness and his wisdom he's a man who stands on two legs—his wisdom makes him kind and his kindness makes him wise. I told you I'd been in Skai for twenty years, even though it seemed a few days to you."

"It was hard to believe," Toug mumbled.

"I guess it was. It wasn't exactly true, since years are things of Mythgarthr; but twenty years takes us as near the truth as we're likely to get. After twenty years the Valfather spoke to me privately, something he hadn't done since I came. He began by asking about my first life, and he saw that even when we talked about my battle with Grengarm, I recalled very little. The mead of his hall has that effect, and it spares us a lot of pain. He asked me then whether I wanted those memories restored, and I said no. The Valfather is wiser than we are."

Slowly, Toug nodded.

"From the way I had answered him, he knew there was something more, and he asked whether I'd go back to your world if he let me. I couldn't remember Disiri, but I was haunted by her name and the feelings I got when I said it, and said I would."

I stopped talking; but Toug did not say anything more though minutes passed, only watching the clouds of Dream fly overhead, and a castle like a star that flew among them.

"We went to the spring Mimir," I said at last. "I drank its water and remembered you and Gylf, and a lot of other things. I visited myself, watching myself drink water in the ruins of Bluestone Castle. Afterward the Valfather laid his condition on me. You're a god to Baki and all the Aelf. You know that now."

"They don't like us being gods, and I don't blame them."

"Nor do I, because the fault is ours. There's evil and folly even among the Overcyns; but it's less, much less, than ours." I stopped again to think. "Baki sacrificed herself to me. Did we tell you?"

"I don't think so."

"She did. I drank her blood and was made well. That should have showed me how things stood, but it didn't. I didn't want to believe I was a god to anybody."

"I understand," Toug told me fervently.

"In the same way the Aelf have refused to be gods to the world below theirs, preferring to give them the worship they owe you. But that's not the point. The point is that the Valfather bound me not to use the authority that is mine. I was not to return as an Overcyn from Skai."

"You mean you have to act like one of us?" Toug asked.

"No. I mean I have to be less than one of you. I no longer have the authority of Mythgarthr. That can never be mine again. My authority's that of Skai. I swore not to use it, and if I break my oath I have to go back at once."

Poor Toug could only gape.

"I think it better if you know." I tried to keep my voice level. "From time to time I may need you—need somebody who can wield the authority of Mythgarthr for me, the way you did tonight. You need to understand why I need you."

Toug swallowed.

"In the meantime, you're not to sacrifice to me unless I ask. Neither are you to treat me differently in any way."

"N-no, sir."

"I'm glad you understand. Don't tell anyone. This is only a dream, after all."

"Uns is coming, Sir Able. See there?" Toug pointed; Uns' bent figure was only just visible as it topped a rise, hurrying along crabwise, but making good time for all that.

"We must go," I said, and the green hills of Dream, crowned with poplars and drooping cypress, were visible only as the reflection of the sun in water.

Toug blinked and sat up. The fire was scarcely more than embers. Cloud stood over Uns' twisted form, her noble head bent until their lips nearly touched. A moment more and Cloud had faded to mist and was gone.

Toug rose and put more wood on the fire, then knelt by me. "Are you still going for my sister?"

"I'm sending you," I said.

"I have the right to raise others to knighthood," I told Beel's followers. "If anyone doubts me, let him challenge me now."

Nobody spoke, though faces were turned toward Garvaon.

"I wish I could say I have lands to give as well, fair manors to bestow on such knights as I make. I have none, but Lord Beel has most nobly offered to make up the deficiency."

The watchers murmured, their voices less forceful and distinct than that of the wind. I raised my hand, and they quieted down.

"There are those who become knights in the great castles of the south," I continued. "There's a ritual bath, at which three knights stand near to counsel them. From dark to dawn they watch their arms. There are banners, prayers, and songs, and there are ladies in silk to watch it. We have a lady here, but she wears leather, and a quiver on her back."

Toug turned to look at Idnn, and saw that everyone else was as well. Her head was high, her eyes as bright as those of the big black cat on her shoulder.

"When the ceremonies are done, and the knight-to-be has been properly admired and gossiped about, a carpet is spread before the giver of the accolade. The knight-to-be kneels on it, and for that reason those who are knighted this way are called carpet knights."

Crol laughed, but fell silent almost at once.

"There are knights of another kind, too. Those who've watched the weapons of foes instead of their own, knights who get the accolade because all who know them know they're knights already, brave and honorable and skilled at arms."

A bar of sunlight raced across the plain, and was gone.

I had spoken loudly enough for everyone to hear; now I let my voice fall. "Come forward, Svon, and kneel."

Svon advanced, neither quickly nor slowly. For a moment that only seemed long he stood, before dropping to his knees. Maybe it was the wind that made his eyes water.

Eterne sprang from her jeweled scabbard into my hand, and I no longer stood alone. A score of knights, old and grim or young and gallant, stood with me. A woman who was not Idnn screamed among the onlookers.

The long black blade touched Svon's right shoulder, then his left. I said, "Arise, Sir Svon."

Svon stood up, looking dazed; Eterne shot back into her scabbard, and the phantom knights vanished.

I said, "Toug, step forward, please."

Proudly, Toug took his place beside Svon. His clothes were those of the village boy he had been, but on his arm was a beautiful green shield bearing a white griffin.

"Here stands a squire, Sir Svon. Will you have him?"

"Gladly," Svon answered, "if he will have me."

"Will you serve this knight loyally, Toug? As your father once served me?"

"I swear it!" Toug's voice was loud, and possibly for that reason cracked as he spoke.

No word of mine summoned Cloud. With Gylf at her

heels, she cantered through the onlookers to stand before me.

I mounted. "I'm going south, taking Uns and two more. I promised Duke Marder I'd take my stand in a mountain pass, and have yet to do so. When you free my servant from the Angrborn, send him to me. He'll know where to find me."

That night Toug hoped to dream as he had when we slept side by side. No such dreams came to him, but the warm pink tongue of a cat instead.

He rolled onto his back. "Hello, Mani. What is it?"

"Come with me," Mani said softly; and when Toug rose he led him from the camp to a place not greatly different from any other on that haunted plain, save that Idnn was there on a little folding stool, with another such stool before her.

"I need to speak with you, Squire," she said, "you and I have not been great friends until— Sit, please. I brought that stool out here for you."

Toug bowed and sat. "You gave me my shield and made me your friend as long as I live."

She smiled, a smile just visible in the moonlight. "That was courteously said."

"I don't know anything about manners. How to talk to a lady or a nobleman like your father, or any of that. I just said the truth."

"Sir Svon can teach you."

"I know, but he hasn't had time yet."

As though she had not heard him, Idnn said, "He has beautiful manners, when he chooses."

"The wise know how to be polite," Mani informed Toug, "but the wise know when to be polite as well."

"And do not choose to be courteous always," Idnn finished for him. "Sir Svon is brusque with me, Squire, unless my father is at my side. Why is that?"

"He hasn't told me."

"Of course not. I know I'm not beautiful—"

"Yes, you are," Toug told her; Mani purred approval.

"Beautiful women don't have noses like mine!"

"There were women and girls in our village, and there are your women and girls here, and most of the slaves the giant had were women. But when I try to think of somebody else like you, the only one I can think of is Queen Disiri, and you're a lot nicer than she was."

"You met her? Sir Able introduced you or something?"

Toug nodded.

"I'd love to. Do you think he's coming back?"

"I don't know."

"Address her as 'My Lady,'" Mani whispered; and Toug repeated, "I don't know, My Lady."

"But you could guess, Squire, if you were made to?"

"I don't think so," Toug said slowly. "He said to send his servant when we rescued my sister. I don't think he'd have said that if he were coming back."

Idnn nodded reluctantly.

"And he made Sir Svon a knight. Sir Svon used to be his squire, but now I'm Sir Svon's squire. Sir Svon's being a knight means you've got two, like you did when you had Sir Garvaon and Sir Able."

"Have you heard what Sir Garvaon said about that?"

Toug shook his head, and drew the cloak she had given him more tightly about him. "No, My Lady. I haven't."

"Garvaon said Sir Able thinks this will make Sir Svon or break him, and you, too. He thinks Able may come to Utgard to see how well you acted. Or how badly."

"That's wrong," Toug said, surprising himself. "I mean he's a knight and he knows a lot, My Lady, but I don't think he knows Sir Able as well as I do. He's not like that."

Mani asked, "May I speak, Lady Idnn?"

"Later." She picked Mani up, stroking his head. "I want to hear Toug now. What's Sir Able like, Toug?"

"I don't know a word for it," said Toug, who thought he did, "but he wouldn't test us like Sir Garvaon says. He knows already. He knows we can do it, or anyhow he knows Sir Garvaon and Sir Svon can."

"Two knights against a castle full of Frost Giants?"

"Sir Garvaon and Sir Svon and all of us," Toug amended. "You, My Lady, your father, Mani, Org, and everybody else."

"Org?"

"I shouldn't have said that. I'm sorry."

"It's just that it's a name I've never heard."

Mani's voice was melted butter. "If you will allow *me,* Lady Idnn, I can set your mind at rest concerning the entire matter, presently or privately."

"Please let him, My Lady. That way, I can say I didn't tell you."

"Org is a terrible man one rarely sees," Mani explained. "He's larger than a mule, silent, and lives on human flesh—"

"You're making this up!"

"I, My Lady? I assure you, no one is less inclined to prevarication than I, your most worshipful Cat."

"You know you are, Mani. You're fibbing!"

"Squire Toug's eloquent protestations have given away my little game, I see," Mani said stiffly. "I shall proffer no more unneeded details. The facts you require, My Lady, are these. Org is a servant of Sir Able's, one normally seen to by the hunchback. Before he left, however—prior to his brief yet gracious speech elevating Sir Svon to knighthood—he instructed Org to remain at Sir Svon's side, obeying Sir Svon as if he were Sir Able himself. I thought that I, with the hunchback and Sir Able's dog, was the sole witness to the conversation, but Squire Toug knows of it, clearly."

"I saw it." Toug wished the ground would swallow him. "I saw it and asked Sir Svon, and he said I'd better know but not to tell anybody."

"He's awfully handsome, isn't he?" Idnn's eyes shone.

Toug gawked.

"Sir Svon, I mean. He broke his nose fighting giants, and it will probably be crooked when it heals, but one must expect scars on a bold knight. Blue eyes . . ." She sighed. "He has a cleft chin. Did you notice, Squire?"

Toug managed to say, "Yes, My Lady."

"My praise is not to be repeated. You realize that, I'm sure. Both of you."

Mani said, "Most certainly not. Your Ladyship may rely on me absolutely." To which Toug added, "Me, too."

"I've had Mani's opinion of Sir Svon already. If you want to hear it, no doubt you will. You may hear it even if you don't want to. But I'd like to have yours. I realize you've been his squire for only one day."

When Toug did not speak, Idnn added, "You must've formed some estimate of his character just the same."

"I knew him before."

"So you did. I won't tattle, on a maiden's honor."

"And I," Mani announced, "speak to you and Lady Idnn alone. And to Sir Able, but he isn't here."

"A lot's what Sir Able told me," Toug said, "but he's right. I know he's right."

"About Sir Svon?" Idnn was clearly interested. "Better and better. What did he say?"

"Well, he's proud. Sir Svon, I mean."

"Anyone with half an eye can see that."

"He ought to be a nobleman, but he's a younger son, and then his mother died and his father married again. They're just trying to get him out of the way, really. He looks down on everybody, even the king, because he feels like everybody looks down on him, and he's got to learn—this's what Sir Able said when we talked one time."

"I understand. Go on."

"He's got to learn it's not all looking up or looking down. He said people keep hurting Svon because they think he needs his pride humbled. He said he'd done that, too. But Sir Svon's been hurt so much already that it only makes him worse and I shouldn't do it anymore."

"Have you humbled him, Squire?"

Toug looked around him, at the frigid northland night and the distant lights of the camp. It was time for a good solid lie, he knew, and he lied manfully. "I said something, My Lady. Only I took it back, after. I don't think he's forgotten; but I don't think he's mad anymore, either."

CHAPTER SIX

UTGARD!

The wall and towers of Utgard could be seen for a full day's ride before they reached them, and neither was as Toug had expected. The base of the wall was a range of mountains, or at least seemed so, low mountains but steep. From it rose a second wall of fitted stones, in which the stones were larger than cottages. Atop that rose a palisade of trunks so great as to make the stones look small. The towers beyond the wall were blue with distance—and immense, so wide they seemed squat, and often topped by spidery scaffolding, half walled. The men on them looked as small as ants; but when Laemphalt had trotted another league, Toug realized they were not human beings but giants.

"No wonder our king wants to make friends with them," he told Laemphalt. "We could never beat them, not in a thousand years, or even stop them from doing anything."

Svon turned in his saddle. "If you can't talk like a man, be quiet."

Toug nodded. "I'm sorry, Sir Svon. It slipped out."

"I killed one of those creatures a few days ago, and I'd like to make it a score."

At the head of their column, Master Crol sounded a trumpet and shouted, *"We come in peace!"* Privately, Toug hoped they would be received the same way.

The plain on which they had heard so many mysterious sounds and seen ghostly figures at dawn was given over to farms here, for the most part; and poor farms they seemed to Toug, although his father's fields had been scarcely fertile enough to feed his family. There were giants in these fields; but the reapers were human slaves, and mostly women.

"Look at that fellow." Svon pointed. "He doesn't know what he's about."

Toug touched his heels to Laemphalt until he and Svon rode side by side. "He's blind, Sir Svon."

"He is? How can you tell from here?"

"He's a man. See his beard?"

"Of course. What does that have to do with it?"

"The giants blind their men slaves," Toug explained. "Berthold told me. Didn't you see him?"

"Yes, and he was blind. But he's old. I thought . . ."

"They burned his eyes out. They do it to all the men."

Something frightening came into Svon's face.

Toug gulped. "They've got my sister. I told you."

"Yes. But your sister won't have been blinded, will she? The women at the farm were all right."

"They weren't all right, they just weren't blind. We're supposed to free Sir Able's servant, and find his horses and baggage, and send them to him. My sister was with Sir Able's servant, and he will have been blinded by now."

"It may be impossible. I hope it isn't, but it may be."

"Sir Able . . . He knew about these things, Sir Svon."

Reluctantly, Svon nodded.

"He knew you could do it. I told Lady Idnn after the battle, and maybe I—"

Svon had raised a hand for silence. "You told Lady Idnn? Did she ask about me?"

Toug nodded. "She wanted to know a lot about you. She likes you, Sir Svon."

"We'll have no more such talk as that!"

"No, sir. I'm sorry, Sir Svon."

"I'd be a landless man, if it weren't for her father's generosity. As it is, I own a manor I've never seen. She's the daughter of a baron, and you might circle Celidon without finding a fairer woman. She'll wed the heir to a dukedom."

"There can't be many of those around here," Toug said practically.

"Her father, and all of us, will return to the king when we've delivered his gifts, I'm sure."

Toug nodded, hoping Svon was correct.

"She was interested in me? She asked about me?"

Toug nodded. "She likes you, Sir Svon. I know what you said, but she does."

"An unproven knight."

"Can I say something? You won't get mad?"

Svon's smile was grim. "Try it, and we'll see."

"When Lady Idnn looks at you, she sees what the rest of us see, not what you see when you think about yourself."

"Which is?"

"A noble knight—one whose father's a nobleman. His mother was noble, too. A handsome knight with blue eyes and yellow hair and the kind of face women like."

"A knight dependent on her father's pity."

"Nobles reward knights," Toug insisted. "That's what they're for. You earned that manor fighting giants. You say you're a untried knight, I guess because you've never fought another knight. But which is harder, fighting another knight or fighting a giant? I know which one scares me most."

Svon smiled. "My nose buttresses your argument. Though I was no knight when you broke it, I admit."

Up ahead, Angrborn had blocked the head of the column, where Beel and Idnn rode. They had spears taller than many a tree, bare bellies like hairy sails, and beards as long as Toug was tall.

Garvaon rode back to join Svon and Toug. "The king's guards, did you hear that? No armor, and turn as quick as four yoke and a plow. His Lordship wants them to take us to their king. They want to kill us and take the mules. Or so they say. I'd like to see them try."

A richly dressed man who had followed Garvaon exclaimed, "Utgard! That's Utgard up there. I've heard about it all my life, but I no more expected to set eyes on it than the bottom of the sea. I'm going to make sketches."

"It's big all right," Garvaon conceded.

"Big, and full of Frost Giants. Seriously, sir knight, if you were to kill those up ahead, a hundred more would be on us before we'd gone half a league."

Svon said, "You're right, of course. Have we met?"

"Only briefly, I'm afraid. I know you've been meeting a great many people. I'm Master Papounce."

They shook hands, Svon stiffly. "Toug is my squire—"

Like an echo, someone farther ahead called, *"Toug!"*

"The only retinue I possess, at present."

Toug shook hands too, and Papounce said, "You've a good, strong grip. Going to be a knight yourself before long."

"I hardly know how to be a squire yet."

Garvaon edged his mount near enough to touch Toug's shoulder, a quick rough slap. "Somebody wants you."

"Here's a serving girl to fetch you, I believe," Svon added as one of Idnn's maids clattered up on a coarse pony that had begun the trip in the baggage train.

The maid did her best to curtsy in the saddle. "It's Lady Idnn, Sir Svon. I mean, it's not her shouting, but it's her that wants him, sir, and—and—oh, I don't know. But Lady Idnn says won't you lend him, I don't know what for."

"In which case we must find out. Come along, Squire."

Toug sensed that Svon was trying to sound grim, but that the prospect of conversation with Idnn made it difficult.

The king's guards had been joined by two more by the time Toug and Svon reached the front of the column. One of the newcomers overshadowed Beel and Idnn like a beetling cliff. "Anything you say must be heard by us," he rumbled.

"I can't stop you from listening," Beel told him, "but it is a thing no gentleman would do."

The Angrborn said nothing, frowning and leaning on a spear longer than a lance.

"King Gilling wants my daughter's cat," Beel told Svon. He rolled his eyes to indicate that there was no accounting for the whims of kings. "The cat Sir Able gave her."

Mani mewed loudly to indicate the cat intended.

"I don't know why he wants it," Beel continued, "or how he came to hear of it. But that's what he says, or rather, it's what this officer of his says he says."

The looming Angrborn took one hand from the shaft of his huge spear. "Hand it over!"

Addressing Toug, Idnn said, "He won't promise to give Mani back, or even promise not to hurt him."

The giant reached for Mani, and Svon's sword cleared the scabbard.

"Gentlemen! Gentlemen!" Beel raised both hands. "This is a diplomatic mission. You, sir—I am Lord Beel, a baron of King Arnthor's realm. May I ask your name?"

"Thrym." The hand had been withdrawn.

"We need to explain to these men," Beel indicated Svon and Toug, "what they're to do—what Toug's to do, and why he's to do it. Then we'll give you the cat, and you can take it to King Gilling, having accomplished your errand."

He wheeled his mount to speak to Toug and Svon. "Under these circumstances, my daughter is reluctant to hand her pet over. Understandably, as I'm sure you'll agree. She wanted to take it to His Majesty herself, and Thrym agreed. But she has been traveling, as we all have. I'd greatly prefer she not appear at court until she's bathed and dressed. Let her appearance bring credit to our nation, not disrepute."

"She could never bring disrepute," Svon declared.

"*I* said," Idnn put in, "that in that case King Gilling could wait until we were to be received. We would put a gold collar and some nice perfume on Mani—"

Mani sneezed.

"And I would exhibit him to King Gilling. This—this great lump of a royal officer wouldn't hear of it."

"His instructions are to bring Mani to his king at once," Beel said mildly.

"Yes! And leave us out here cooling our heels."

Beel spoke to Svon. "Thrym here would have allowed Idnn to carry Mani—that's her cat—to the king. I wouldn't permit it. I suggested that one of her maids do it."

Idnn snapped, "Absolutely not!"

Beel nodded. "Now that I've given the matter more consideration, I'm inclined to agree. At any rate, Squire Toug is the only substitute Idnn will accept. I described Toug to Thrym, and Thrym indicated that he might accept him, too." Beel turned to the giant. "Here he is. He's Sir Svon's squire, as I told you. Would he be acceptable?"

"If he don't piss himself."

"You don't have to go," Svon told Toug. "I won't order you to."

Beel said, "You'll permit it? If he goes willingly?"

"No horse," Thrym rumbled. "I walk. The king walks. You can walk too."

Toug nodded and dismounted.

Idnn held out Mani. "This is very brave of you."

Toug took him, putting him on his shoulder. "Would Sir Svon have done it?"

Svon said, "In an instant."

"Of course you would." Idnn smiled. "But I won't allow it. Mani doesn't know you well at all. Toug and I are the only people here Mani knows and likes, and it's going to be frightening enough for him even with a friend present. He's a big cat and a strong one. What if he were to scratch King Gilling's face? What would become of our diplomacy then?"

"Would Sir Garvaon?" Toug asked her.

She seemed surprised by the question; but after a moment she said, "Yes. Yes, I'm sure he would, if I asked him."

"So am I," Toug told her. "What about Sir Able? Would he go?"

"Yes. Absolutely."

"Then so will I." Toug looked at the gigantic Thrym, twice the height of the tallest man. "Shouldn't we start? We're keeping your king waiting."

Their walk across the plain consumed hours. The wind snatched dust and snow from the fields, and the green cloak Lady Idnn had given Toug seemed powerless to keep it out. Mani rode his windward shoulder and pressed a warm and furry side against his ear, which was a great comfort; but even Mani trembled in that wind.

With every step (and the steps came very fast for league after league, since Toug had to trot to keep up) the lonely train of horses and mules behind them shrank. A huddle of clumsy houses bigger than barns appeared before the monstrous wall; beyond these houses yawned a gate like the mouth of a colossal face, one to which a portcullis of close-set bars thicker than old trees gave teeth.

"Take a good look," Thrym rumbled.

"I am," Toug told him. "I've never seen anything like this."

"'Cause you may not see much after." Thrym's laughter was deeper than the notes of a kettledrum, and so cruel Toug shuddered. "We don't see your kind with eyes here. Your kind don't see us much, neither."

"You blind your slaves." Toug swallowed. "I talked to one a little. That's what he said, and he was blind."

"The men we do."

"But I'm not a slave, yours or anyone's. I'm Sir Svon's squire. Mani's not a slave either. He's Lady Idnn's cat."

"Animals we don't," Thrym conceded; and Toug felt Mani relax a trifle.

There was a dry ditch before the wall, a deep ditch so wide that it seemed a natural chasm, with tumbled boulders in its black depths. Over it arched a bridge of massive timbers dark with tar; it creaked and cracked beneath Thrym's weight.

"Don't worry about that," Thrym rumbled. "We're good bridge builders. We have to be. You worry about me. What's to keep me from taking the cat, stepping on you, and kicking your body into the moat?"

"Nothing, sir. Only I hope you won't."

"What about that toy sword you got?" Thrym halted to let Toug catch up and pointed to Sword Breaker. "You stop me with that?"

"No, sir."

"By Ymir's blood, you've got that right. Let's see it."

Toug drew Sword Breaker and handed it to Thrym, hilt first as courtesy demanded.

"Not even sharp."

"No, sir," Toug said again. "Sir Svon won't let me have a sharp one because he's afraid I might cut myself. But I'm his squire, and a squire ought to have a sword."

Thrym shook with laughter.

The greatest of all the towers was reached by steps so high that Thrym carried Toug up them, gripping the back of the stout homespun shirt his mother had sewn for him and dangling him like a doll while he clutched poor Mani, and Mani clutched him with every claw.

"We're ready to fight you. See?" Thrym set Toug down and gestured toward the steps they had just surmounted. "How're your men going to do on those, huh? Need a ladder or something. We'll come down them handy enough, and you ain't going to like what we do."

Thinking that he did not like what the Angrborn did at any time, Toug said, "I certainly wouldn't want to fight you on these, sir."

"Huh. How about that bridge we crossed over?"

"Nor there," Toug conceded.

"Built to burn, and fires ready laid to start it. Soon as you get on we throw a torch. Think you'll get off quick?"

"Yes, sir."

"You won't. You little hotlanders breed like red ants, so there'll be a thousand more pushing to get on from behind. The bridge'll burn, and you with it."

"We haven't come to attack you, sir," Toug said humbly, "but to make peace, if we can."

"You tell King Gilling."

The reeking throne room was every bit as huge as Toug had expected; yet its vaulted stone ceiling seemed low for the hundreds of giants who filled it with an indescribable din of laughter and shouts, stamping, and rattling weapons.

"That's the king over there." Thrym pointed to the far end of the immense room, where the crowd was thickest. "I'm goin' to get close as I can. You follow after, and mind you don't lose the cat."

Toug did his best, dodging giants.

"Wait!" Mani whispered in his ear. "What does he want with me?"

"I have no idea," Toug muttered. "I thought you knew."

"All cats are brave."

Toug ducked between the legs of one of the Angrborn.

"And I am counted brave even among cats. Still . . ."

Mani was interrupted by a roar. *"Thrym!"*

"Yes, Your Majesty!"

"Where is it, Thrym?" The question was deafening. "Didn't you get it?"

One of Thrym's hands closed on Toug, and he was lifted high into the air. Thrym's rumble sounded less impressive here. "I got it, Your Majesty."

Over the heads of twenty or thirty giants, Toug could see—on a high throne of gold on a dais so lofty that the hooked spikes of his iron crown seemed almost to scrape the vault—a king so large and so fat that the Angrborn about him, monstrous though they were, looked childlike.

"Bring it here, Thrym." The king's voice was neither particularly deep nor particularly high; what it was, was loud, so loud that it seemed a storm spoke. "What's that holding it?"

"He's the cat's servant, may't please Your Majesty. The hotlanders thought it oughta have somebody to look after it, somebody it knows. That sounded right to me."

"Fetch my table!"

A lean Angrborn standing beside the dais thumped the floor with a golden staff, a dull noise that made Toug think of Death knocking at a door. *"The king's table!"*

Four blind men carried each leg. They were guided by a woman who steered them by voice and touch. Briefly her eyes met Toug's—at once, she looked away.

"Now then," the king said when Toug had been lifted onto the table. "You must tell me about this magical cat, little fellow. Can he talk?"

"Yes, Your Majesty," Toug said, and felt Mani's claws sink into his shoulder.

"Then make him talk to me."

Mani shook his head, his whiskers brushing Toug's cheek.

"I can't, Your Majesty," Toug said. "No one can make a cat do anything."

The king laughed, his belly an earthquake, and the other Angrborn joined in his laughter.

"If he likes you," Toug explained, "he may talk to you. But I'm sure he'll never talk with so many people present. That isn't his way."

The king leaned toward him, his round, sweating face like a millstone. "Is he your cat?"

"He's Lady Idnn's cat, Your Majesty. She wanted to bring him herself, but her father wouldn't let her." Toug took a deep breath. "He didn't think she was dressed well enough for court, Your Majesty. I'm not either. I know that. But with me, we hoped it wouldn't matter as much."

King Gilling was silent a moment, and then he said, "A nice tunic. So you wouldn't be ashamed to appear before me."

Toug nodded. "Thank you, Your Majesty."

The king turned to the Angrborn with the gold staff. "A nice tunic, Thiazi. One of the slave women can run him up one. A gold chain, if you've got one small enough. Whatever else seems good to you."

Thiazi bowed. "Your Majesty's wish is my only will."

Toug ventured to say, "Lord Beel has beautiful presents for you, Your Majesty. He's waiting outside the wall. All you have to do is let him in, and he'll give them to you."

"Waiting with this Lady Idnn?"

"Yes, Your Majesty. And Sir Svon—that's my master— and a lot of other people."

"I wish to speak to this Lady Idnn. If her husband won't let her see me, her husband must be dealt with, Cat."

"My name's Toug, sir, and his name's Mani." Toug spoke softly in the hope of giving no offense. "And Lord Beel's not her husband, he's her father. Lady Beel's dead, I think. And I'm sure he'll let you see her. See Lady Idnn, I mean, when she's dressed up and everything."

"That is well." The king smiled. "We need to ask her where she got this cat, don't we, Thiazi?"

Thiazi bowed. "Indeed, Your Majesty."

"Oh, I can tell you that," Toug said. "She got him from Sir Able. He used to be Sir Able's cat, and Sir Able gave him to her."

CHAPTER SEVEN

HELA AND HEIMIR

Sumpin' worryin' ya, sar?" Uns was struggling to turn poles and a tarred canvas from Bymir's barn into the semblance of a pavilion, assisted by Blind Berthold.

"A thousand things," I told him.

Gerda looked up from her cooking. "We're in your way, ain't we, sir?"

I shook my head. "No. Not at all."

"If you'd want to ride ahead tomorrow, sir, and tell us where to meet up with you . . . ?"

I shook my head again.

"Org ain't hit, sar? Ya worried how Sir Svon might be takin' care a' him. So'm I, sar. Org ain't bad like they say. On'y he ain't good, neither,'n do take handlin'."

"No," I said. "Can I give you and Berthold some help?"

Uns looked shocked. "Us got hit, sar, 'less ya think us ain't doin' right."

"You're doing better than I would, I know." I seated myself on the ground and stared into the flames. Gylf lay down beside me.

"'Tis the boy." Gerda's tone was that of one who knows. "Young Toug. I'm worried 'bout him too, sir."

"You don't have to listen to this," I said. "You have work to do, all of you. I realize that. I have work to do, too, and I've been trying to do it. Thinking, not worrying. We thought very little in Skai, or at least I didn't think much. The Valfather, the Lady, and Thunor were very wise, and that was enough for us. We served them whenever we could, and ate and drank and jousted and sang when we couldn't. Now there's nobody to think except me, and one of the things I've got to think hard about is whether the Valfather foresaw it."

I picked up a stick, snapped it, and tossed it on the fire. "I'm sure he must have. The real question is whether it affected the restraints he laid on me when he let me come. And if it did—I think that it must have—how."

"Too much thinkin' leads to drinkin'," Gerda warned me.

"Too much worry, you mean. Too much circular thinking in which the mind turns around and around, shaking the bars again and again. Yes, it does, but I try not to think like that. I try to think as the sea flows. I miss it, by the way, though I doubt the rest of you do."

Gylf laid a paw in my lap.

"I'll tell you what I was thinking about in a moment, it's no secret. Let's dispose of Sir Svon and Toug first."

Bold Berthold, having finished staking the poles of the makeshift pavilion, came to sit beside Gylf, feeling his way with a peeled stick.

"You're concerned that the Angrborn may kill them, and so am I. But if I'd stayed, Toug would have remained my captive and Sir Svon would have remained my squire. Those outcomes were certain, not problematic. Once, long ago . . . Though it is not long ago to you. Once Sir

Garvaon told me I was a hero, the sort of knight men sing about."

Berthold said, "Aye."

"That's the sort of knight Sir Svon longs to be, and Sir Svon's right, because it's the only sort who should be called a knight at all. I don't mean that songs must be sung about every brave knight. There'll always be many whose greatest deeds no one knows. Before I made him Sir Svon, Svon charged a score of bandits, sword in hand. He killed some, and the rest beat him senseless and left him for dead. No song will be made about the bruised and bleeding lad who woke and saw Sir Ravd's body torn by wolves, who routed the wolves with Ravd's broken lance and buried Ravd alone in the forest. Yet he deserves a song, and I'm giving him a chance to earn one. A chance to feel pride in himself, not just in his ancestors.

"Toug's a peasant who wants to become a knight, and will become a knight if he's given room to grow. Uns, you know him better than Berthold or Gerda do. Am I wrong?"

"Dunno, sar." Uns, who had been straightening a pole the ropes had pulled out of line, paused. "Dere's Pouk ta, ain't dere? Dat was wit you at da farm?"

I nodded. "The Angrborn have him."

"You was dead set on gettin' him free."

"I was. I am. He was my servant, and a good one. I've sent him rescuers, and I feel they'll succeed."

Gerda said, "That's not what was worryin' you, sir?"

"No." I looked up from the fire. "First and always, I was thinking about Queen Disiri, as I always do. When the Valfather's mead had washed me clean of every other memory, I still recalled her name. She won't come to me. Therefore I must go to Aelfrice to seek her, as soon as I can."

" 'N me wit ya," Uns declared.

"Perhaps, but I doubt it. Time runs more slowly there. Have I told you?"

Berthold said, "My brother did, sir. He'd been took, or thought he had, and when he come back I was old, though I had my eyes. Dizzied sometimes, like now. But him! He wasn't but a lad like when he was took, though he did talk high."

"Why was he taken, Bold Berthold? Do you recall that?"

"To talk for Aelfrice up here's what he said. 'Cept he never did."

"I've wondered about that."

"You know 'em, sir," Gerda ventured. "There was that one come to you when we was under the tree, me and Bert. I said you shouldn't trust her, but you said you had already."

"Uri."

"That was her, sir. You knew her."

"Yes. I know her and Baki fairly well, I'd say. I used to think I knew Garsecg, too, and better than either of them. But I know better now, and know Garsecg's no Aelf."

Gylf said, "Wow!," but they thought it a mere bark.

"He's a demon," I explained, "a dragon in human form."

"Ya goin' ta kill him, sar?"

I shook my head. "No, Uns. Not unless I must. But we're drifting away from the riddle of Berthold's brother, and that riddle's one of the things I've been considering. Do you still want to hear about those?"

Berthold said, "I do, sir, if my brother's in it."

"Of course. Your brother couldn't recall anything that happened to him in Aelfrice."

"No, sir."

"Then we have three mysteries. First, why could he not remember? Second, why was he taught fair speech? And third, why has he not spoken?"

Gerda asked, "Don't you know the answers, sir?"

"Not all of them. The second we can all guess easily, I

believe. He was taught to speak well so he could deliver the message he had been given effectively. Uns, you've a sound head. Can you enlighten us as to the other mysteries?"

"W'y he coont remember, sar? Dint ya say dat first? Dey magicked him. Dey's handy wit spells, all dem Aelfs."

I nodded. "I'm sure you're right. But why do it?"

"Somebody give him a message," Berthold muttered.

"Yes."

"He never said who 'twas, 'cause he didn't know."

I nodded again. "I think you must be right. The sender wished to keep his identity secret, and his message as well."

Gerda pushed one of the forked sticks that would support her cooking pot into the ground. "Then he hasn't said what they told him. He's forgot it."

Berthold's groping hand found my arm. "Somebody here."

I looked down at Gylf, who raised his head, sniffed, and seemed puzzled. "You heard him?" I asked Berthold.

"Aye, sir. I do."

"There's a breeze." I rose, my hand on Eterne. "He must be coming upwind. That's why Gylf hasn't caught his scent." I stalked away, downwind, with Gylf at my heels.

Berthold and Uns were sleeping soundly when we returned, but Gerda had stayed awake and sat warming her hands. "It's good for somebody to keep watch," I said as I sat down, "but you can go to sleep now. I'm going to sit up, and Gylf wakes at the least sound."

"You didn't find him?"

I shook my head.

"I kept listening, sir. I thought if you killed him he'd cry out, most like. My ears ain't what they was, and I worried you'd do it so quick there wouldn't be no noise."

"I never saw him," I confessed.

"Somebody out there, though, wasn't there?"

I nodded.

"One of them giants?"

I shook my head. Gylf, who had seen him, had described him to me.

"A boy like that Toug?"

"No, a big man. As I said, I never saw him, but I heard him run away. A big man can move very quietly as long as he doesn't have to run, but when he runs there's not much he can do to silence the noise his feet make."

"Your dog couldn't run him down?"

"I'm sure he could have, but I wouldn't let him. Do you remember when he caught you in the hedgerow?"

"Won't never forget it."

"Uns wanted to know what was troubling me. I said there were a thousand things, I believe." I smiled. "That was a slight exaggeration, but one of them was the memory of Gylf's catching you. I saw your chain, and there was a moan in my mind. Almost a scream."

"I'm used to it, sir."

"We'll have it off as soon as we can find a blacksmith, I promise you, though that may be a long time. But the thing that has been troubling me tonight wasn't your chain but that moan." After a moment I added, "It wasn't me who moaned. I feel sure of that."

"If it was in your head, sir . . ."

"It had to be me? No. It didn't, and it wasn't. So who was it?"

"I don't know, sir. I didn't hear it."

"I was recalling it as well as I could and trying to decide whose voice it might have been. I had just about settled on my answer when it struck me that it could have been Berthold who Gylf found. Had you thought of that?"

Gerda stirred the fire.

"Berthold's past his prime, and blind, but still strong for

a man his age. And no man I know is less liable to give way to fear. He'd have fought, and Gylf would have killed him. The man who ran from us was younger and much stronger."

Gerda did not speak.

"There are men who should be killed. There are many more who must be killed, because they will try to kill us. But I'm not sure the man who ran from us—this very large young man I did not see—belongs to either group."

"You think he's mine, sir. You think it's my Heimir."

"I don't think anything. It struck me it might be."

"I don't know, sir. Really I don't." She wiped away a tear. "I feel like it is, like he's come back to me, or I've come to get him, sir, or however a body might say it. But I don't know, sir, it's all in my heart. I ain't seen him nor heard him nor nothing."

"We'll let him come closer next time, if there is one."

"That's good of you, sir. Sir?"

"What is it?"

"If it is . . . You wouldn't hurt him?"

"Of course not. Would he hurt me?"

Gerda hesitated. "He might, sir, if I wasn't with you. I can't say. He's hungered, most like."

"So are we. There's not much game here."

"Farther south, sir, south of the mountains—"

I shook my head. "I must take my stand at a mountain pass. We won't go south of the mountains for a long time."

She smiled. "I know you won't let us starve, sir. Not even if he's with us."

Someone big lay on a bed of fern in a low cave; for a fraction of a second, I felt his hunger and his loneliness. I looked up. Cloud was watching me, her head and dark eye scarcely visible. Hoping she could see it, I nodded.

"You said you'd decided about the moan, sir. The moan when you first seen me. What was that?"

"It was when I saw you were chained." Smoke drifted

into my face; I fanned it away and moved a little to my left. "You probably think I imagined it."

She shook her head. "Not if you say you didn't."

"I didn't. I know the flavor of my thoughts, and that wasn't one of them. It wasn't you either, and it wasn't Gylf. I can't say how I know, but I do. There was someone else there, someone I couldn't see. I'd been shadowed by the Aelf, and I thought it most likely that it was Garsecg." I paused. "Garsecg is not an Aelf, but he had pretended to be. I'll tell you more about Garsecg some other time, perhaps."

Gerda nodded. "Now you've changed your mind, sir?"

"I have. You said you saw an old woman with me."

Gerda's nod was timid.

"I think that was Mani's mistress. You must have seen Mani. A large black cat."

"A witch's cat, sir, if you ask me."

"Yes, though he's Lady Idnn's cat now. The witch is dead but still earthbound. When Baki writhed in the hayloft, his old mistress's ghost told Mani to bring help to her."

"You think she's haunting us, sir?"

"I doubt it. I'd guess that she went to Utgard with Mani, though I don't know. Lie down. Try to sleep."

"If that's all that was troubling you, sir. I was hoping there was more I could help with."

I laughed. "I doubt it, Gerda. Some Aelf were going to sacrifice a beautiful woman in the griffin's grotto. Who was she and what became of her?"

"Ler! I don't know, sir."

"Very tall. Milk-white skin and black hair." My hands shaped the figure of an invisible woman. "If you don't know who she was or where she went—"

"I swear I don't, sir."

"I believe you. In that case, tell me this. Why would the Aelf offer one of our women to Grengarm?"

"Why, I've no notion, sir. Do you?"

"Maybe. Grengarm was a creature very like Garsecg,

yet Grengarm seemed real here in Mythgarthr. Remember Toug? He was from Glennidam, a village where they worship the Aelf."

"That not right, sir. Nobody ought to do that."

"None of us should, at least. I don't think it would be terribly difficult to explain why the people of Glennidam do, though it's wrong just as you say. A better question, one I thought of much too late, is why the Aelf let them."

Gerda's face showed plainly that she did not understand.

"You mentioned Ler, mother. Suppose that Ler, with the Valfather and Lothur, were to appear before us, sacrifice to you, and offer you their prayers. What would you do?"

"I—" Gerda looked baffled. "Why—why I'd say there was some mistake or maybe they were making a joke."

"Exactly. But the Aelf, who should say the same, do not." I watched the moon rise above the empty landscape.

At last Gerda said, "I guess they like it, sir."

"Lie down," I told her. "Go to sleep."

When the moon had risen high enough for me to make out the mountains, I got up and saw to the tethers of our mounts. Those of Berthold's horse, and Gerda's, were still tight, as was that of Uns' placid brown mule. Cloud's had never been tight, and I removed it. Already bedded down, Cloud nuzzled my face and brought to my mind the image of a wild boar, huge and savage, rooting on the other side of the little river.

I nodded, slung my quiver behind my back and strung my bow. Parka's string sang softly beneath my fingers, the songs of men reaping and the songs women sing to children with heavy eyes, songs of war and songs roared in taverns, songs of worship sung at altars when blazing logs consumed whole oxen and Overcyns with horned helmets and hair like fine-spun gold appeared in the smoke—all these and many more blending into a single anthem of humanity, to which certain birds piped an accompaniment.

* * *

"Good pig!" Gylf licked his lips. "Want him?"

I said I did.

"Long way. I'll drive him."

Before I had taken two strides, Gylf was out of sight. In the blind dark under the trees, I reflected on the few, poor remarks I had directed to Uns, Berthold, and Gerda, and their questions and comments. Then, for a hundred cautious steps or so I whispered Disiri's name.

Gylf had located the boar; his snarls and the angry grunts of the boar rode the soft night wind.

Jotunland, I thought. This's Jotunland. Empty and cold and a little too dry.

Bold Berthold had spoken of digging deep wells, wells whose fearful construction required months, wells that failed even so in dry years, of carrying bucket after weary bucket into the fields, and of vicious fights between Angrborn over access to wandering brooks that never reached the sea.

So that was another puzzle. Large and strong as the Angrborn were, they might have lived anywhere. Why did they choose to live here?

Had the gods of Skai indeed driven the Giants of Winter and Old Night from the sun? Or had those Giants chosen their abode? Knights like Svon and Garvaon and Woddet had never driven the Angrborn north of the mountains, surely.

The snarling hound and the angry boar were nearer now, and I had reached a strip of moonlit water. Somewhere along here, Gylf would drive the boar into the shallows, then out again onto the other bank, if the boar still lived.

If Gylf had dodged the boar's slashing tusks up to that point. An arrow here might end the hunt, or as good as end it. I nocked a shaft and relaxed for a second or two to look up at the moon. It was beginning to snow, even while the moon still shone, so that the silver light seemed wrapped in mist, beautiful and threatening. We had traveled slowly, and would travel slower still tomorrow; and though we had not been comfortable, we would be less comfortable still. Who would want to live here?

The boar, obviously. But I knew the boar must die.

There would be meat tomorrow. Meat not only for Gylf and me, but for Bold Berthold, Gerda, and Uns. Meat even for the hulking young man who had crept so near our camp. The young man (call him by his name, I told myself, he has one) his suffering mother had named Heimir in the hope endearing him to the Angrborn, the young man who lay starving in his cave in the hills.

A man of his size, a man who might weigh half as much as Cloud, would require a lot of food, food difficult to find in this barren land. True Angrborn were even larger and could eat only because slaves worked their farms.

Dog and boar were nearer now; I heard saplings break, an angry *pop-pop-pop* my ears accepted as a single sound.

Quite suddenly it came to me that King Arnthor would have been wiser to send the Angrborn bread and cheese. Then that Lord Beel's embassy was doomed, that the Angrborn could never stop raiding the south for slaves because the Angrborn would starve without slaves—that no Angrborn could grow or kill enough for himself, a wife, and a child or two. They were too big and needed too much.

One never saw their wives anyway.

The boar broke cover and the arrow went back to my ear and sped away. The boar, black as tar in the moonlight, snapped at its shoulder, splashed through the shallows to midchannel, turned to defy Gylf, fell to its knees, and rolled on its side. The water carried its body a step or two from the point at which it had died, but no farther.

Gylf emerged from dark undergrowth. "Good shot!"

"Thanks." I unstrung my bow and slung it behind me. "Did he hurt you?"

"Never touched me." Gylf waded into the water to drink.

Skinning and gutting the boar took an hour or so. I cut off the head and forelegs (one of which Gylf claimed) and got the rest up on my shoulder. Our return was slower than our departure had been, but the distance was not great.

"Talking." In order to speak, Gylf had let the foreleg fall. Instinctively, he put a paw on it. "Hear 'em?"

I shook my head.

"Don't know her." He picked up the foreleg and trotted forward.

She rose as Gylf approached the fire, and for a moment I felt she would never stop rising—tousled blond hair that hung to her shoulders, a lean face that seemed all jaw and eyes, a neck as thick as my thigh, wide sloped shoulders and high breasts half hidden by a scrap of hide. Arms thick and freckled, fingers tipped with claws. Long waist, broad hips under a ragged skirt, and massive legs with knees so skinned and bony that I noticed them even by firelight.

"Hello," she said in a voice deeper than a man's. "Are you Sir Able? Hello. I'm Hela, her girl. She said it would be all right. Is that food?"

Gerda stood too, her head below her daughter's waist. "You're not mad are you, sir? I—I shouldn't of, I know. Only she—she's still . . ."

"Your child."

"Yes. Yes, sir. My baby, sir." This last was said without a hint of irony.

Uns sat up and goggled at Hela.

Berthold had clambered to his feet and was groping with both hands. "Hela? Hela?"

Hela took a step backward, although she was a full three heads the taller.

"Bert won't harm a hair of you," Gerda told her softly.

"Hela." A groping hand found her. "I'm your father, Hela. Your foster father. Didn't Gerda never speak of me? Bold Berthold?"

I laid the boar's body on the ground beside the fire.

"You were gone 'fore I got to Bymir's, and Bold Berthold that was, was gone too. Blind Berthold now. It's what they did. But the same that was, Hela. The same as loved your ma long ago."

She crouched and embraced him.

"Ah, Hela," Berthold said softly. "Ah! Ah, Hela!" There was no tune to these words, yet they were music.

"Maught us cook a bit a' dat, sar?" Uns was at my side, holding green sticks.

"I'd think you'd want to go back to sleep."

"I'se main hungert, sar." When I hesitated, he added, "Won't take but wat ya let me."

"Take all you want. Will you cook some for Berthold?"

"Yessar. Glad ta. Fer her, ta, sar,'n she'll want a sight a' feedin'."

"She will, I'm sure. But she can cook it for herself. If she is to eat with us she must work with us, and it will be better if we make that clear from the start."

"Fer ya, ter, sar. Be a honor fer me, sar."

"If Hela can cook her own meat, so can I." I unslung my bow, sat down before the fire, and accepted a stick. "Cut me some of that pork, will you?"

"Yessar. Ain't slept, has ya, sar?"

"No, and I should. I will when I've eaten something."

Yet when Uns, Berthold, and Gerda slept once more, and even Gylf slept, lying upon his side and snoring, and of all those with me only new-come Hela remained awake, squatting at the fire with a piece of pork twice the size of my fist on her stick, I sat up with her, questioning her now and again, and often falling silent to consider her replies.

"I'm not a maid of my tongue," she said, "to prattle pretty words and please men's ears. If I were, I'd soon be snug in a house, with hags and slaves like this fresh father to wait on me, and an ox for supper when I wished it." She laughed, and I saw that her teeth were twice the size of mine. "But

I'm as you see. As you hear, sir knight. What Frost Giant would be hot to take me to wife? They like their own, stealing into their beds from Jotunhome. Else southern maids of poppet size, with clever little hands and honeyed lips. 'Oh, oh, you are so great! Ravish me!' So I sought men my size in the Mountains of the Mice, and found them, too, served as maid serves man, and was paid in blows."

"Did they drive you out?" I asked her.

"Hunted me, rather. You noted my knife?"

I nodded.

"He did not." Hela laughed loud and deep. "In the south, they say, there are some called men who pale at sight of naked steel. Fops and fools! 'Tis not that knife that takes life."

"How old are you, Hela?"

"Sage enough to know a cat from a catamite. Are you troubled that I've come running to Mother, sir knight?" She took her meat off the stick, sampled it, wiped her mouth on her arm, and licked her fingers.

"No. You were hungry. No doubt I'd do the same if I had a mother to run to."

"We watch the War Way, Heimir and I." Hela returned her stick and the gobbet of meat it held again back to the fire. "Some give us something, sometimes."

"You did not beg of me, when I came up it."

"Didn't see you, sir. How many horses?"

"Pack horses, you mean? I had none."

"What would you have given us, sir knight?" She smiled; although it was not a pleasant smile, I sensed that it was as pleasant as she could make it. "Not even beggars work for nothing."

"Nothing is what I would have given you. Would you have robbed me?"

"A knight? With horse and sword?" She laughed again. "No, not I! Nor Heimir. Small stomach he'd have for such a fight! It's reavers returning we like best, sir knight, with sulking slaves tied tight as sausages, and heifers and horses to drive before them." Hela's voice rose to a whine. "Bless you, true Angrborn all! Blessed be Angr, true mother who bore you! Many a smile you'd have from your mother, for many a morsel you've won down the War Way. One morsel for me from you, great men? A bit for my brother? No more than you'd lose in a tooth, my masters." High already, her voice rose again. *"Morsel for me! Bread for my brother! Charity for children's the kindness of heroes!* So we bawl, and follow to steal if they let us." She shook her head.

I said, "That's no life for a girl. Not even for one as big as you are, though there are hundreds of beggar maids in Kingsdoom from what I've been told. What are you going to do now, once you've eaten?"

"Follow you, sir knight, as long as you'll feed Momma and me. Dig for my dinner, if it's digging you want."

She shook her head again, more vehemently, and I turned mine to look behind me. Gylf woke with a low growl.

"I can milk and butcher and churn," she said quickly, "and bear more than your mule. Try me. And if—you've no wench with you? Don't you shiver, sleeping?"

Thanks to Cloud, my inner eye glimpsed a shadowy figure larger than a man—with a rope between its hands.

From the night surrounding our little clearing, Uri's laughter showered us with steel bells. "Here is a hot wench if he wants one, one who will not take the whole blanket."

"What's this!" Hela stared into the darkness.

"Your victim's slave." Uri stepped into the firelight. "Lord, there is a great lout behind you—"

"With a rope, thinking to strangle me." I nodded. "His sister's been my protector twice."

Hela turned from Uri to stare at me. "You knew he was there? By Ymir!"

"So did Gylf. I doubt that he'd have gotten his rope around my neck."

"Nay, nor wished to. What's this?"

"An Aelfmaiden."

"Are they all red?"

Uri said, "None but the best, and we like it better than pink with brown blotches."

"Call your brother," I told Hela. "He's probably as hungry as you were."

She rose and held up her stick, with its gobbet of pork smoking and sizzling. "Heimir! This's for you!"

He was larger even than she, with shoulders that made me think of Org, and so thin every rib showed. His massive jaw, broad nose, and owl eyes promised brutal stupidity.

I motioned for him to sit. "Eat something. Gerda will be glad to see you."

Hela offered her stick. He took it, stared at the meat, and at last pulled it off and ate.

"You told me why you left the mountains," I said to Hela, "but not why your brother did."

"He'd left our old home with me, sir knight. He left our new one to be with me. You think him thick."

I said nothing.

"It's solemn truth he's slow of speech. Slower than I, though I'm slow enough for two most times."

Uri said, "I would call you a babbler, rather."

"You're the knight's slave? Slaves need a smoother tongue, or soon come to grief."

Uri turned to me. "Have you ever had to feed me?"

"No," I said.

"Or pay me?"

"No."

"Yet we have served you faithfully? Baki and I?"

"You're wondering how much she told me. Very little."

"Is she dead?"

"No," I said again.

"What happened?"

"We talked about you." I measured my words. "Why

you hadn't told me her back was broken and asked me to help her."

Hela giggled, a sound like a small avalanche. "That silenced her, sir knight. Black thoughts to raze her red face. Tell me true, are they underground? It's what Momma's gossips told me."

"They're from the world under ours. I wouldn't call it underground."

"Why doesn't she go there?"

"Would you," Uri asked, "if you could mount to Elysion?"

Hela's hard face looked troubled. "What's that?"

"Where the Most High God reigns." Uri rose. "You want me to retire to Aelfrice. Very well, I will go. But Lord, if you must feed this gross slattern—"

"I want you to go, too," I said to Uri, "but not back to Aelfrice. I want you to go to Utgard. Toug should be there by now, and so should your sister. Bring me word of them."

"I will try." Uri shot Hela a parting glance. "She and the lout will beggar you in a week."

"I hope to beggar myself. Go."

Uri vanished into the night.

I took the meat from my own stick and began to eat it. Hela asked if she might have another piece, and I nodded.

When she had finished cutting it, she said, "You're going to the mountains?"

"Yes. To take my stand at a pass. It's the sentence Duke Marder passed on me, and I must do it before seeking the woman I love."

"They love us not, that live there."

I swallowed the last bite of pork and lay down, wrapping my cloak around me. "They don't like me either. We'll face them together, if you're willing."

For the first time Heimir spoke, addressing his sister. "Sleep. I watch."

CHAPTER EIGHT
MANI'S OWNERS

Two slave women visited Toug in the turret room to which the king had sent him, one carrying a heavy gold chain and the other a tunic of black batswing. Both knew Ulfa.

"She's my sister," Toug explained. "I'm hoping the king will let me take her home. The man who came with her, too."

"Pouk," the taller of the women said.

"Yes, Pouk. He's Sir Able's servant, and Sir Able would like him back. The king must have a lot."

"It's not a bad life," the taller woman said; and the other, "It could be worse."

"I'll free you, too, if I can," Toug promised them. Both looked frightened and hurried out.

"I didn't mean to scare them," Toug said as the huge door banged shut.

Mani was composed. "Magic has a way of doing that."

"I didn't say anything about magic." Toug resumed his examination of the room. Among other things, it held a bed slightly smaller than his father's house in Glennidam, four chairs with rungs he would have to climb in order to sit in them, and a table upon which half a dozen people could have danced.

"There's a sandbox over here," Mani remarked. "That's hospitable of them."

Slowly, Toug nodded. "We're going to live here awhile. Or they think we are."

"If I were to offer a guess, you'd say I cheated."

"No, I won't."

"All right." Mani paused for dramatic effect. "My guess is that there is a chamber pot under that bed for you, and it's five times too—"

"What's the matter?"

"That picture." Mani was staring up at it with eyes wide. "He's gone."

"The man in the black robe?"

"It wasn't a man, it was a Frost Giant." Mani climbed a chair back as he might have climbed a wall, and sprang to the top of the table.

"I didn't know the giants painted pictures," Toug said.

"I doubt that they do. They don't seem to do much that they can get slaves to do for them."

"They're blind."

"Not the women, and many women are very artistic." The tip of Mani's tail twitched. "My mistress drew wonderful pictures when her spells required them. Magic and art have a great deal in common."

"You said those women were afraid of magic," Toug argued, "when there wasn't any for them to be afraid of."

"Little you know."

"Are you just going to sit and stare at that picture?"

"It's like watching a rathole," Mani explained. "There are ratholes in the wainscoting, by the way."

"I wouldn't have the patience."

Mani looked superior but said nothing.

"Did you recognize him?" Toug inquired.

"The Frost Giant in the picture? No."

The top of the bed was higher than Toug's chin, but by grasping the blanket and jumping he climbed onto it. "I did." He swung his feet over the edge.

"Who is it?"

"I'll tell you if you'll tell me why the king wants to see you."

"That's easy. My former mistress told him he ought to."

Toug's eyes widened. "Did she tell you that?"

"No. I haven't spoken to her since she told me about the Aelf with the broken back. But who else who knows about me could have talked to him? Now whose portrait was it?"

"She's a ghost? That's what Sir Able said."

"Correct. Fulfill your part of our bargain."

Toug swung his legs, kicking the side of the mattress. "Why would she want him to talk to you?"

Mani's unwavering gaze remained on the painting. "At the moment I've no idea, but that question was no part of our bargain. Who was it?"

"We should know after we've talked to him. Are you going to talk, Mani? He won't like it if you don't."

"Then I'd better, and this is the last time I make any such bargain with you. I thought you honorable."

"I am," Toug declared. "It was a picture of—"

The door opened, and a black-robed Angrborn so tall that the room seemed small entered. "It's of me," he said. "My name is Thiazi, and I am our king's primary minister." His voice was low and chilling.

He pulled out one of the chairs and sat. "Our king is dining. He'll send for you when he is finished. I thought it would be best to settle matters between ourselves first."

On the table, Mani had turned away from the empty frame.

Thiazi studied him. "Which of you is in charge?"

"He is," Toug said. "Only I don't know whether he'll talk to you. Sometimes he doesn't talk to people."

Mani's voice purred. "I always talk to magic workers. I am in charge, as my servitor told you. As to settling matters, what matters have we to settle?"

A frosty smile touched Thiazi's lips. "You will tell me when you'd like me to pet you?"

"I will tell you if I would like you to pet me. It's a privilege I accord to few, and seldom to them. Is that one? Am I to let your king stroke me whether I like it or not?"

"It might be wise. He's fond of animals."

"If he is fond of cats, he will understand."

Thiazi smiled again. "You wish no help from me in this matter?"

"I *require* no help from you in this matter," Mani said deliberately, "nor in any other. On the other hand, tangible gestures of goodwill are always appreciated and are usually reciprocated. How can we serve you?"

"In several ways. Are you aware that your party has slain thirteen royal Borderers?"

"We were robbed when I was not present to prevent it."

Thiazi nodded. "By the Borderers, of course."

"They did not identify themselves."

Toug interrupted. "Those were the king's men?"

Thiazi looked prouder than ever. "They were sons of Angr, our great ancestress, in royal service."

"But . . ."

"They took the goods you were bringing to Utgard. Of course they did."

Mani said, "Acting on the king's order?"

"Your party appeared warlike. Do you deny it?"

"Yes," Mani said. "Certainly."

"You had armored horsemen and bowmen. You've reasons to present, I'm sure, but they were there. We—His Majesty—wished to determine how strong you really were."

"Acting on your advice?"

Thiazi waved Mani's question away. "The experiment might prove of interest. It proved much more interesting than we anticipated. His Majesty's Borderers overcame your fighters with ease and carried off your valuables."

"We got them back," Toug said grimly.

"Exactly. We had hoped, you see, that your leader would return to his king for more gifts. That would have been profitable, though not enlightening. What happened instead was that a green horseman appeared among you."

"How do you know?" Mani asked.

Toug said, "We didn't kill all the giants. Some ran."

Thiazi nodded. "I have spoken to them. More to the point, I was watching you in my crystal."

Mani said, "I'd like to see it."

Thiazi accorded him another frosty smile. "You shall, little pussy. You shall."

Toug said, "Do you want to know if Mani and me fought your Borderers? I did, and he didn't. If you think you ought to do something to me for fighting the people who robbed our king, I can't stop you."

Thiazi shook his head, regarding Toug through narrowed eyes. "You think me a sadist. I inflict pain when duty demands it. I neither object to it nor enjoy it, but do my duty. Have you watched your friend toy with a mouse? When you have, he may no longer be your friend."

"Cats are cats," Toug said. "I never thought he looked like a cow."

Mani smiled, which he did with his mouth slightly open. Thiazi might not have seen it. "We're interested in the green horseman. You have other armored horsemen among you."

Toug said, "Yes, sir."

"Are their names secrets you may not divulge?"

"No, sir. Sir Garvaon, sir. He's the senior knight. And Sir Svon. I'm Sir Svon's squire, sir."

"Sir Garvaon is the green horseman?"

"No, sir. That's—"

"Can't you see they'll slay him?" Mani hissed.

"I hope not, little cat. We'd rather honor him. Your king sends you because he wishes our king his friend."

"He didn't send Mani," Toug said, "he sent Lord Beel and Lady Idnn with fine gifts."

"While His Majesty," Thiazi continued, "desires the friendship of the green horseman, whose name is . . . ?"

Toug said nothing.

"Oh, come now. Perhaps I should explain the political situation. His Majesty's father was king in his time. A wise king, as his son is, but one who insisted his commands be executed promptly and with a will. He was king, after all, and those who forgot it did so at their peril."

Toug nodded.

"He died, alas. His son Prince Gilling succeeded him, becoming our present majesty. You," a forefinger longer than Toug's hand indicated Toug, "stand at the brink of manhood. His Majesty's situation was the same. Young and inexperienced, he was thought weak. Distant lords rebelled. When we went east, rebellion broke out in the west. When we went west, the east broke out afresh. In the mountains of the south, Mice plotted to bring low the pure get of Angr. Partiality toward your kind was out of the question. The loyalty of many was doubtful or worse. We dared not lose a battle, and any trivial act that might support the lie that His Majesty favored you would've been disastrous. Thus he treated you with utmost rigor. He had to."

Mani asked, "Are things so different now?"

"Oh, indeed." If Thiazi had caught the irony in Mani's question, he ignored it. "The realm has been subdued. The rebels are dead, and their sons and sires. Their strongholds are in the hands of vassals of proven loyalty. I myself— someday I may show you Thiazbor and Flintwal, but no words of mine could describe them."

"If the king wants to be nice to us, he could let Lord Beel's people into Utgard," Toug suggested.

"As he will, when he's made his point." Thiazi smiled. "After we have decided just how they are to be treated. You are helping us with that, and I have come—I speak frankly—to suggest how you might best do it. You're loyal to your king, so you indicated. You fought our Borderers to recover your king's goods. You challenged me to punish you for it."

"Well, no—" Toug began.

"Your king desires His Majesty's friendship. Thus you serve your king best if you please His Majesty."

Slowly, Toug nodded.

"His Majesty has human slaves. You have seen them."

Toug nodded again. "I need to talk to you about those."

"You shall."

Mani yawned. "This doesn't concern me."

"The connection will become apparent, pussy. Our king's slaves serve him well. He treats them better than he might, and they're conscious of their honor as royal chattels. Not infrequently there are disturbances in remote locales, in the south, particularly. The Mice in the mountains and others. He has trusty servants who might act, yet he must hesitate before dispatching them. What if a fresh rebellion were to break out? And would not their absence encourage it?"

"I understand," Toug said. "You want us to do it."

Thiazi smiled. "It's really rather simple, isn't it? If slaves, forced to serve, serve well and loyally, would not friends, valiant horsemen attached to His Majesty by bonds of gratitude, serve better? He has gold to give, lands, slaves, fame, the encomia of a king. All that the valiant desire."

"I'll tell Sir Svon when I see him again," Toug said, hoping he would indeed see Sir Svon again.

"What of the green horseman? Won't you tell him, too?"

"If I see him."

"It can be arranged, perhaps. Do you know where he is?"

"No," Toug said. "He went away."

"But you, pussy. You are wise."

Mani opened his eyes. "Who are we talking about?"

Thiazi's huge hand found Toug's shoulder. "Tell him!"

"It's Sir Able, of course."

"Ah!"

"They weren't sure," Mani explained. "Now they know."

"We consulted my crystal," Thiazi leaned back, smiling, "and were shown a speaking cat. Neither His Majesty nor I could guess how a cat could bring the green horseman into His Majesty's service, but we resolved to do all we could. On my advice, His Majesty left the ambassador and his train without the walls and dispatched an officer to obtain the cat."

Thiazi's forefinger nearly touched Mani's nose. "You." The finger was withdrawn. "His Majesty's officer succeeded, and you, Squire, confirmed in His Majesty's hearing that it was a speaking cat. Furthermore, you informed us that it had been given to this Lady Idnn by a horseman." Thiazi paused. "No mean gift, is it? A speaking cat! He must esteem her."

"I'm sure he does, sir," Toug said.

"You will wish to discuss his regard for her with His Majesty." Thiazi rose. "And to decide how you and this cat will persuade him to enter our service. His Majesty will ask you that, I feel certain. It would be prudent to have an answer ready. Wash your face, too, and dress yourself in the clothing I provided."

When the door had shut, Toug slid off the bed, found the batswing tunic, and put it on, tossing the torn and terribly dirty shirt his mother had sewn for him into a corner. "I'd like to know how long I've been away," he muttered.

"From your home? Don't you know?"

Toug shook his head. "A lot was in Aelfrice, and things go slow there, Sir Able says. Only my sister Ulfa wasn't in Aelfrice, so maybe she can tell me."

Mani looked bored. "Still think she's here?"

"Remember when the king wanted his table for us to stand on? Blind men carried it, with a woman bossing them."

"Certainly."

"Well, that was my sister." When Mani said nothing, Toug added, "What's the matter? Don't you believe me?"

"Of course I do. I'm merely digesting the information." Mani's eyes flew wide, two shining emeralds. "You require experienced, wise, and subtle guidance, young man."

"Yes, but there's nobody like that here."

"Wrong. I stand before you. We must free your sister."

Toug nodded.

"We must also reunite Sir Able with his servant, and recover Sir Able's belongings—his horses and goods."

Toug nodded again.

"Nor is that all. We must assist Lord Beel in securing peace, and my mistress and your master in overcoming whatever impediments may separate them. You agree?"

"You bet I do."

"What else? Anything?"

"I'd like to meet some girls."

Mani smiled, displaying fangs too large for an animal his size. "I know the feeling. What about returning to your home in whachamacallit?"

"Glennidam." Toug had gone to the door. Its latch was higher than his head, but he reached it without difficulty. "This's locked."

"I expected no less. Want to go back to Glennidam?"

"I'd rather stay with Sir Svon and learn to be a knight, but I'd like to help my sister get home if she wants to."

"Well spoken. Now, are any of these mutually exclusive? Suppose, for example, that we make it possible for your master and my mistress to disport themselves as they think fit. Would it interfere with your learning to be a knight?"

"I don't see how."

"Nor do I. Did your sister recognize you?"

"Yes, I'm sure she did. We sort of looked at each other for a minute, if you know what I mean."

"Certainly. That being the case, why—"

"What's the matter?" Toug asked.

Mani gestured toward the frowning face of Thiazi in the painting. "He's back."

Reluctantly, Toug nodded. "Do you think he hears us?"

"I'm sure of it." Mani dashed across the table and sprang onto the windowsill.

"Be careful!" Toug called, but Mani had vanished.

"See what you did?" Toug asked the picture. "You and your magic! What if he gets killed?"

Mani's head reappeared over the sill. "This isn't bad at all. Are you a good climber?"

"Pretty good," Toug said doubtfully.

"Come on, then." Mani vanished a second time.

Toug dragged the nearest chair to the window, climbed it, and looked out. He had thought the turret room chill and drafty; but the wind beyond the window was colder, the bitter wind that he had braved all that morning. He drew his cloak around him and shivered before climbing from the chair seat to the windowsill.

He was just in time to see Mani ducking through another window, lower and well to his right. For a moment Mani's sinuous tail flourished over the sill of that not-too-distant window; then it was gone.

"Are you going to climb out there?" asked a voice Toug could not quite place.

Looking over his shoulder he saw a naked girl, a slender girl with a mop of uncombed hair floating over her head. The hair was red; the girl was red too, the gleaming, glowing red of new copper.

"I am Baki, Lord. I was dying, and you healed me."

Unable to speak, Toug nodded.

"You could not see well, up in the loft. There was just the lamp, and Sir Able kept the flame down. I suppose he was afraid we would set the barn afire." Baki smiled; and Toug saw that her teeth were not red but bright white, small, and pointed; her smiling eyes were yellow fire. "Cannot you change yourself into a bird, Lord? That would be safer."

"No," Toug said. "I can't do that."

"I may not be able to heal you if you fall, but climbing will be easier if you take off your boots."

"I know, but I hate to leave them here. They're not good boots, but they're all I've got."

"I can make myself a flying thing and carry them for you." Baki sounded pensive. "I will be terribly ugly. Will you try not to hold it against me?"

"You couldn't be ugly," Toug declared.

Smoke poured from her eyes. "This is a Khimaira," she said, "except that I am going to keep my face the same. They have awful faces, so I will not do that part."

Her slender body became more slender still, her long legs shrank and twisted, and her dainty feet turned to claws. Behind her arms were black wings, folded now. "Take off your boots, Lord," she said. Her face and voice were unchanged.

"Can you carry Sword Breaker for me, too?"

She could, and he removed his sword belt and handed that down to her. "It—it's a famous blade. I mean, it was Sir Able's once."

"I will be careful. There will be no danger for me, and none for Sword Breaker. But great danger for you. The ivy will help, but the wall is nearly straight. If you slip . . ."

"If it's bad I won't do it," Toug promised, and climbed out, flattening himself against the rough and freezing wall and finding purchase for his toes on a stout vine stem. Inch by inch he descended, moving far more slowly than Mani had toward the window Mani had entered. Wind whipped his cloak, and his new tunic seemed comfortless. When he was halfway there, a dusky thing spread wide wings and flapped from the window of the turret with his boots and sword belt. It rose, black against the sky—he could twist his head no farther, and it was lost behind him.

After that he was preoccupied with his own safety. The window was near. Very near, he felt sure, and he must reach it. Return was out of the question.

His fingers found the edge of a stone frame: it seemed too good to be true. One freezing foot was on the wide and (oh, blessedly) flat stone sill.

"As soon as you get in, I will hand these things to you," Baki said behind him. "It will make it easier for me."

He dared not look but muttered, "All right."

Then he was panting on the sill, gripping the frame with one hand, and he saw Baki flattened against the wall somewhat higher, his sword belt buckled around her neck, Sword Breaker and his knife hanging down her back, and his boots held by a finger and thumb.

"You can fly," he gasped. "You don't have to do that."

She smiled. "I did not like your seeing me so, Lord. Here. Take them."

Toug reached for his boots; as he touched them, she lost her grip. Lunging, he caught her wrist. Slight though it was, her weight nearly pulled him into the emptiness below.

And then—by magic, as it seemed afterward—they were inside, trembling and hugging, his boots lost. But alive! Alive! "I am s-so s-s-sorry," Baki said, and wept. "I nearly killed you. Al-almost killed you."

He tried to comfort her, as Ulfa had tried sometimes to comfort him. When her sobs had subsided to gulps, she said, "I knew I could if you could. I—I made my fingers more clawy. But I was not careful enough."

Toug nodded, wanting to say it did not matter, but not knowing how to say it.

"I want to be like you. The other half."

He did not understand. When she began to change he jumped, more frightened than when it seemed both must fall.

Obscured by swirling smoke, her coppery skin turned pink and peach. "Do I look right now, Lord?"

"You—you're . . ."

"Naked. I know. We do not wear clothes." She smiled. "But I am the other half. This is what Queen Disiri did for Sir Able to m-make him love her, and I can do it too. See?"

Toug managed to nod.

"We will have to find clothes and boots. Here."

It was his sword belt. He buckled it on, then took off his green cloak and put it around her.

"Thank you, Lord. It is the wrong color, but I know you mean well."

"It's green."

She nodded. "Disiri's color. But I cannot go around this castle naked, though the men are blind."

"You still have red hair. Redheads look nice in green." His mother had told him that once.

"Do we? Then it will be all right. And I look . . . ?"

"You're beautiful!"

She laughed, wiping away the last tears. "But am I of your kind? Do I look right in every way?"

"Well, your teeth aren't exactly like ours."

"I know. I will try not to show them."

The room seemed to be used for meetings; it was funnel-shaped, with a flat-topped boulder in its center, surrounded by rows of benches as high as the seats of the chairs in the turret room. Its walls were hung with pictures, but these were covered with brown curtains; and even the bottoms of these were too high to reach.

Toug looked around at these things, then put them from his mind. "We ought to find Mani."

"You like Mani better?" Baki gave Toug a sly smile.

"No." He sighed. "But I'm taking care of him. That's why I climbed out on that wall—I didn't want Mani to get away. But he got away anyhow, and I nearly got us killed."

"You should not feel badly, Lord."

He sighed again. "You'd better call me Toug when other people are around. And I do feel bad. I've been trying to be like Sir Able, and look at the mess."

Baki smiled, keeping her lips tight over her teeth. "You are more like Sir Able than you know, Toug. Very well, we will look for the cat. Perhaps we may find clothes for me and boots for you along the way. Let us hope so."

Toug scarcely heard her. Something that was neither fog nor gray smoke was shaping itself above the great stone in the center of the room. For an instant he glimpsed eyes and teeth; they shuddered and disappeared. The light from the window, which had never been bright, dimmed, and the high, cracked voice of an old woman spoke.

CHAPTER NINE

THE FIRST KNIGHT

You have no lance," the Knight of the Leopards observed. His armor gleamed beneath his fur-lined cloak.

"No," I said.

"You will fight me with your sword alone?"

He was young, I thought—not much older than I—and had probably grown his thin mustache to make himself look more mature. "If I choose to draw it, yes."

"Is it licit to fight under such circumstances?"

"It is," I told him, "and I will not permit you to pass this place unless you fight."

The Knight of the Leopards looked troubled. "My squire carries ancillary lances. I'll lend you one. You may return it when we've ended our combat, if it has not been broken."

Cloud danced over the snow, eager for action, and I told her she had to stand quiet. "I do not ask it," I said aloud.

"I've observed that, but my honor demands that we engage on something like equal terms."

"Do you expect to make yourself as tall as the Angrborn? Or do you think they'll make themselves no taller than you?"

Crabwise, Uns ran to my stirrup. "Ya gotta take hit, sar. Ya be kilt."

"I'll be defeated," I told him, "not killed."

"My squire will lend it to yours," the Knight of the Leopards ruled. "Your squire may pass it you. We'll take our places after that, and begin when my herald sounds his clarion. Is that acceptable?"

"I have no squire," I explained. "Uns is my servant, not a squire."

"Have you no one but him, and those old people?"

"No," I said. "There are others you haven't seen."

"But no squire?"

I shook my head.

"Your horse appears somewhat light."

"Cloud is a better mount than yours."

The Knight of the Leopards shrugged, and turned in his saddle to address his squire. "What do you say, Valt? Would you prefer to give a lance to one of the lackeys and have him pass it to that cripple?"

Valt, a fair-haired youngster with a good, open face, smiled. "I'm not so proud as all that, Sir Leort." Touching his heels to his mount, he came forward until he could pass a lance to Uns, who thanked him and gave it to me with a bow.

"Now then." The Knight of the Leopards donned his helm; it was of spotted gilt and the crest was a rampant leopard.

I retreated a good fifty paces, with Uns clinging to my stirrup, and shaded my eyes against the glare from the snow. "He looks wonderful, doesn't he?"

"Nosar, not good as ya does, sar."

"He looks far better than I, Uns. See the pennants! He has a herald, his squire, two pages, men-at-arms, and a whole troop of manservants."

"Seven a' 'um, sar. Da sarvents."

I smiled. "You counted them."

"Yes, sar. But, sar . . ." Uns cleared his throat and spat. "'Tisn't him, sar. None 'tis."

The herald brought his clarion to his lips. I put on my helm, and couched the spotted lance Uns had passed to me.

The clarion sounded, ringing notes of blood and dust echoing and reechoing. There was no need to clap spur to Cloud; she charged as an arrow flies. For an instant that was brief indeed, the Knight of the Leopards was before me, broad shoulders, and lofty helm with yellow and black plumes streaming, bent low above his charger's neck.

The point of my lance missed purchase on that helm, and the point of the Knight of the Leopards struck the dragon on my shield and I was dashed from the saddle. It was the first time I had been unseated since Llwch did it.

For half a minute, perhaps, I lost consciousness. When it returned, the Knight of the Leopards was standing over me, offering a hand to help me rise. "Thank you," I said, and turning spat blood that unexpectedly but pleasantly recalled Master Thope. "I'm Sir Able."

"You may keep your spurs," the Knight of the Leopards told me. "And certainly you may keep your crippled servant and the old people. I don't want them."

Querulously, Berthold was asking, "Didn't he win? Didn't Sir Able knock him down?"

"But the rest I must have," the Knight of the Leopards finished. "Give everything to my squire."

I knelt. "I beg a boon."

The Knight of the Leopards turned back to face me. "What is it?"

"My spurs, which you said that I might keep, are solid gold. You may have them, with all else I have, and welcome."

"But . . . ?"

"I beg leave to keep my mount and my sword. I beg it for my own sake, because I love them both. But I beg it for yours as well."

The Knight of the Leopards appeared to hesitate. He removed his helm and handed it to Valt. "No," he said. "I leave you your spurs. To that I've pledged myself. And your servants. But I will have everything else, and certainly I will have that horse."

As he spoke, Gylf came to stand beside my shield.

"You won't have Cloud," I said, "even if I gave her to you, you couldn't have her. You couldn't ride her if you sat her saddle. Nor could you get into it or even catch her to mount."

"Hand the reins to me," the Knight of the Leopards said. "I require this mare of you."

"I wouldn't treat you so. As for this sword, if I were to give it to you, you'd throw it away. Or it would throw you away. That wouldn't be pleasant."

"I am a lawful knight. I had supposed you were one as well."

"I am."

He shook his head. "It appears otherwise."

"If I may tell you about something that happened to me first," I said, "I'll give you Cloud as you ask. Otherwise you'll have to catch her yourself. Will you listen?"

"Relate the incident."

"It will be short unless you pepper me with questions. Once the king I served sent me to the court of another king, a king who commanded many brave knights like yourself."

"Continue," the Knight of the Leopards said.

"I mocked their courage. I challenged them to choose a champion, saying he might strike off my head if he presented himself to me in a year's time and let me strike off his."

"You are a brave man if you indeed spoke thus."

"It took no courage. A knight came forth. I knelt, bent my head, and told him, 'Strike!' "

A slight smile played about the lips of the Knight of the Leopards. "But he did not."

"You're wrong. He had a good sword with good edge.

One blow clove this neck of mine and sent my head bouncing across the rush-strewn floor. I got to my feet, retrieved it, and tucked it beneath my arm."

"You expect me to believe this?"

"I told him about a ruined castle in which he was to meet me in a year's time. He came, and he found me there. Do you understand this story?"

"Hand over your horse and your sword," said the Knight of the Leopards, "with all else that is yours."

I nodded, unbuckled my sword belt, and gave it to him, with Eterne still in her scabbard.

"Is that gold I see in your hauberk?"

"Yes," I said, "every fifth ring is gold. It's the mail worn by Sir Skoll. There's no magic in it, yet the wearer is blessed." I pulled it off and dropped it at the feet of the Knight of the Leopards.

Gerda, who had been watching and reporting our actions to Blind Berthold, came forward. "For your mother's sake, you take that an' forget the sword an' go your way."

"My lady mother would not have such a woman as you for her scullery maid," the Knight of the Leopards told her.

"Take it back!" Heimir, nearly naked and bearing a very large club, stepped from the opening in the cliff in which I had ordered him to hide himself. Hela followed. The men-at-arms, who had been lounging in their saddles, readied their lances and rode forward, then halted, possibly because I had raised a hand to stop them, possibly only because they had caught sight of Gylf.

"Take it back!" Heimir repeated, and aimed a blow at the Knight of the Leopards that would have felled a bull.

"Heimir!" Gerda shouted. "Heimir, stop!"

There was an impressive hiss of steel as the Knight of the Leopards drew his sword. He tried to parry Heimir's next blow with it, however, which proved to be a mistake.

I caught Heimir's arm. "That will do. That's enough."

"Make him take it back!"

Hela said, "Heimir speaks for me, Sir Able. But if your foe will not," she smiled, "we may feast right royally here, my brother and I on them, and our mother and new father, with you and Uns, upon their beasts. Wilt join us in taking these birds," she nodded at the men-at-arms, "'fore they fly?"

I shook my head. "Sir knight—what's your name?"

"He's Sir Leort, a right noble knight!" Valt announced.

"Sir Leort," I said, "you must look Heimir here in the face and swear on your honor that your mother would welcome such a woman as Gerda into her service. If you do not, I cannot speak for the result."

Instead, the Knight of the Leopards dropped his broken sword, and so quickly and skillfully that anyone might have supposed he had done it a thousand times, drew Eterne.

Phantom knights thronged him. Their swords menaced his face, and their empty eyes spoke threats more daunting than any sword. Into their unnatural silence came the drumming of spectral hooves. Cries no living man had heard were borne on the cold wind. I laid a hand upon his shoulder. "Sheath your sword. Sheath it now."

He knelt instead, and held out the sword Eterne, her blade flat across his hands. I took it, and the phantom knights drew back. The jeweled scabbard and the sword belt lay in the snow. I brushed them to dislodge the snow that clung to them, and as Eterne shot into her scabbard every phantom vanished.

"I yield," the Knight of the Leopards said. "I beg you spare my life, and Valt's."

"You beat me," I said, but he shook his head violently.

"Can I kill him?" If Heimir had been taken aback by the phantom knights, nothing in his brutish face showed it.

"May," I said. "No. Or at least not yet."

"I have insulted your lady mother," the Knight of the Leopards declared bravely. "It was foolish of me, and I tarnished my honor by besmirching a woman who'd done me no hurt. May I speak with her?"

Heimir looked to Hela. Hela nodded; and Heimir nodded reluctantly as well.

Neither slowly nor swiftly the Knight of the Leopards walked to the sheltered spot where Gerda sat with Berthold, and knelt. "I spoke hastily, My Lady. Your son is angry with me, as he has full right to be. I have nothing to give beyond my apology—everything I brought from home belongs to the Knight of the Dragon now. But—"

"I don't want anything," Gerda said. "Nothing from you, though 'tis kind of you to offer."

"My sire has a manor in the south," the Knight of the Leopards told her. "Sandhill Castle is its name. It's neither large nor rich, yet it is snug enough. If you and your husband will come there with me, he will lodge, clothe, and feed you as long as you wish to remain."

Berthold rumbled, "You couldn't speak fairer than that."

"Do you want to go?" Gerda asked.

"We might have to."

"My invitation will never be withdrawn," the Knight of the Leopards assured them. He turned back to me. "Will you let me keep my spurs?"

"We have to think about this," I told him. "What is mine is yours. You won fairly."

"I've begged for quarter," the Knight of the Leopards replied. "I'm at your mercy. I only ask my spurs, and that you set a ransom my family can afford."

"It's nearly sunset. I'm hungry and so are my servants. Our animals are about starved. Will you feed us?"

"Gladly."

Visions of southern pastures filled my mind, rich fields of ripe green grass spangled with buttercups and crossed by purling brooks; but I said nothing of them, only, "Then we'll talk about this in the morning."

The wind was cold; but we had a roaring fire, with

meat, bread, and wine, and oats in plenty. One by one the diners fell away, retiring behind walls of canvas to wrap themselves in blankets and such dreams as visit weary travelers in a cold land, until only Hela (nodding over wine), the Knight of the Leopards, and I were left.

I looked up, calling, "Uri? Uri?"

There was no reply; the Knight of the Leopards said, "Is that one of your servants? I'll fetch him for you."

"Can you go to Aelfrice?"

The Knight of the Leopards smiled and shook his head. "I can. I should be there now and wish I were."

Hela looked up. "She's a her."

"Do you fear I'll kill you while you sleep?" I asked the Knight of the Leopards. "Or are you waiting to kill me?"

He shook his head again. "I'm not fool enough to think I could kill you."

"Then go to sleep."

He hesitated. "I'd hoped to have a word with you while the rest slept."

"I'll sleep soon's I finish this one," Hela told him. Her voice was thick.

"You must speak now," I said, "or not speak at all. If Uri won't come, I'll have to find a spiny orange without her, one that's tall and straight. I planted some in a time I've almost forgotten, and I'll see if any will serve."

"I have heard of that," the Knight of the Leopards said. "Men make bows of it, sometimes."

"I have one I made. If you'd let me keep Cloud and my sword, it would be yours. Maybe it's good you didn't."

"You purposed to let me defeat you." If hot irons had drawn the words, they could have been no more agonized. "I know you must have. Why did you do it?"

"I meant you no harm."

Hela looked up from her wine. "Hesh not like you."

The Knight of the Leopards nodded. "Truth from the

cup, my father would say. I'm young, Sir Able, but you are not like any other man I've seen."

"You're young."

"Four and twenty summers," he said.

"But I'm just a kid, no older than Toug. I forget it sometimes, and sometimes it seems to me that the Valfather, who forgets nothing, forgets it too."

"You owe me no boon," the Knight of the Leopards said, "yet I beg you to answer my question. When you have, I'll be able to sleep, perhaps."

Hela belched as horses do. "He don' never sleep."

"I'm troubled at times. That's all."

"If you'd prefer we spoke in the morning—"

I shook my head. "We've got other things to talk over then, or there are things I meant to talk over. You wanted to go into Jotunland. Why you wanted to go there is none of my business, but I'll answer your question, honestly and in full, if you'll answer mine first. Will you?"

"Certainly. I was knighted at nineteen. You'll say that's early, and it may have been too early. I don't know. Early or not, I was overjoyed. I felt—no, I boasted—that by my twenty-fifth year I would be famous, that hearing my name on every side, King Arnthor would send for me. War is constant in our part of the country. The nomads raid us and we raid them. I couldn't tell you how many skirmishes I've taken part in." The Knight of the Leopards shrugged. "Half a dozen arrows, and they run. If you're lucky, you may cross swords now and then. I've done it thrice and once I put my lance through a chieftain." He sighed.

"Long rides by night, in fear of ambushes that rarely occur. Longer rides under a sun—this is not the place to complain of it. Heat and thirst, sweat to rust your armor, and a scarf tied over your face to keep out the dust. What fame do you think I had from all that?"

I said, "None, I suppose."

"Exactly right. My mother had a letter from her sister at court. An embassy was going to Utgard, and a relative— distant, but a relative—would be in charge. I left next day." Frowning, the Knight of the Leopards stirred the fire. "I was too late at Kingsdoom, too late again at Ir- ringsmouth but gaining. I thinks he's only a day or two ahead of me. Now this."

"He is a week ahead of you at least."

"You know that?"

I nodded.

"Yet there might still be a name to be won."

"By diplomacy?"

"Against the Angrborn. I might best their champions or defend the embassy. They are lawless folk."

"In which case you could hardly expect their champi- ons to fight fairly."

"To fight fairly is to fight as well as one can, among other things. Why did you let me defeat you?"

"Hesh deep." Hela slapped the Knight of the Leop- ards' shoulders hard enough to shake him, then rose and stumbled away. Her voice came floating back: *"You wash out."*

"I'll explain. I warn you that you won't find anything interesting in my explanation."

"I doubt that."

"We'll see. I love Disiri, the Queen of the Moss Aelf. I have all my life, or anyway that's how it seems now."

The Knight of the Leopards did not speak.

"You don't believe in the Aelf. I've been to Aelfrice and she's been with me here. You'll say I should know other women. I couldn't love them, and nothing they did could make me stop loving her."

"You are a fortunate man," the Knight of the Leopards told me. "Most of us never find such love."

"Maybe you're right. Once I nearly forgot her. I was far away from her. Very far."

"I would think this would be far enough."

"This is near. That wasn't—it's where she can never go. I thought I was happy and others thought so, too. I had strong friends, and they wanted me happy and did everything they could for me."

An owl hooted and I heard Cloud stamp, ready to gallop.

"Something gnawed me. I woke up crying and couldn't remember the dreams. Here I don't sleep. Not like you do."

"Something was said about that earlier."

"Then I probably lied, but I promised the truth now. A wise friend saw I wasn't really happy, though I didn't know it. He returned to my mind a thousand things I'd forgotten."

"Were you on the Isle of Glas?"

Surprised, I looked up. "I have been. Why do you ask?"

"An old woman who used to tell me stories said that men there forgot their lives and were only happy and foolish."

"I know nothing about that," I said slowly, "but I've been there and I'd like to go back someday. When my memories returned, you see, I knew that what I'd thought was happiness was just oblivion. I could never be happy without Disiri."

"You're fortunate, Sir Able, exactly as I said."

"I'm glad you think so. Here I returned bound. I don't intend to talk about the restriction put on me by my friend. It's another restriction that concerns you. I gave my word to Duke Marder, swearing I'd go to these mountains, take my stand, and hold the pass against every other knight 'til ice floated in the harbor at Forcetti."

"Or your arms were forfeit."

"Right. With helm, mail, and shield gone, I couldn't

hold the pass. I'd promised to fight, but not to fight well. You unhorsed me—"

"She's here." The Knight of the Leopards pointed. "I never knew a horse could walk as silently as a doe."

Cloud came to me, lowering her head for me to stroke.

"Does she understand what we say?"

"More than a child, but less than a woman. But she understands us better than a woman would, and beyond that I can't say. I'd planned to give her to you. My sword too. The sword is the ancient brand Eterne."

The Knight of the Leopards paled.

"It was too late when I saw I couldn't—that it was a coward's path I followed with a thief's conscience. How long 'til ice fills Forcetti's harbor?"

He shook his head. "No man alive knows less of ice and snow than I, Sir Able."

"That's the dead of winter. Six weeks. Two months, maybe. 'Til then no knight gets past me. Then I'll be free, and find Queen Disiri. . . ."

"As you hoped to do today."

"Right. I need a lance—a better one than the one I got from you, though I beg your pardon for saying it."

"My pardon will be gladly given, if you will tell me what ails mine."

"They're ash or worse, and too long. Is it by breaking his lances that a knight gets glory?"

"In part, it seems."

"In other words, they're lances made to break. I don't want glory. I want victory, and spiny orange."

The Knight of the Leopards fetched Cloud's blanket, and I my war saddle. While I was tightening the cinch, he got her bridle, but I waved it away.

I swung into the saddle, and we galloped up a hill of air. When we reached its summit, we stopped. I whistled, and Gylf ran up it to trot at Cloud's heels.

CHAPTER TEN

OATHS AND ILL MEWS

A naked girl." Ulfa looked Toug up and down.

Toug nodded.

"Did I say you hadn't grown since the last time I saw you? I know I did. Ymir! Was I wrong!"

"I didn't expect it either," Toug assured her, "and we don't have to have clothes. She's hiding, and she can keep on hiding. But if she could get clothes she could talk to people—it's pretty dark already because of the snow, and it'll be night before too much longer."

Ulfa nodded wearily. "Winter days are short up here."

"So we don't have to, but it'd help. Boots for me would help, too. And I've got to find that cat."

"King Gilling's cat."

"Lady Idnn's. Only maybe he's really Sir Able's. Cats don't like to tell you about this stuff."

"He's not—" Ulfa searched for a word. "Outgoing? Not as chatty as you might like him to be, this cat."

"Oh, he talks a lot."

"A talking cat."

Toug nodded. "That's why the king wants him, or part of it. We're supposed to be in our room and Thiazi's watching, so he must know we're gone. Have you got any clothes besides what you're wearing?"

"Upstairs." Ulfa gestured, and Toug trotted after her.

"You've got nice clothes yourself," she said when they had started climbing a stone stair whose steps were far too high. "What happened to your nice warm cloak?"

"Baki's got it now," Toug explained. "Lady Idnn gave it

to me. She said if I fought well when we fought the giants, she'd give me a shield with the white griffin on it. And she did, only it's back with Sir Svon. When she gave it to me, she gave me this too. She said somebody who was going to be a knight shouldn't shiver."

"It's always cold here. I suppose you've noticed I'm dressed in rags?"

"They aren't that bad," Toug declared stoutly.

"They're the best I've got. Why don't you get your friend Lady Idnn to give this—this naked girl—"

"Baki."

"This Baki some clothes?"

"She might," Toug said thoughtfully. "Only all the rest of us are outside the walls. When Mani— Mani's the cat."

"The talking cat." Ulfa looked back at him.

"Yes. When Mani talks to the king, he's got to get him to let them in. Or that's what I think." He looked up the steps into darkness. "Aren't there any torches?"

"Just cressets. It's a basket of iron straps you can burn things in. If this castle weren't stone, we couldn't use them. And there aren't many of those, because the giants can see in the dark and they don't care if we fall off."

"I see," Toug said.

"Which means you don't. All our men are blind, so they don't care that there's no cressets either. Are we going to have to go back down to give my clothes to your girl?"

"She'll come up with us, I think."

Ulfa stopped to look behind her, and he bumped into her in the darkness. "Sorry!"

"I don't see her," Ulfa declared.

Baki's hand slipped into Toug's. "You might not," Toug said. "Or Mani either, if Mani didn't want us to see him."

The three of them went down a dismal hallway that would have been as dark as the stair if some of the doors along it had not been open; at the end Ulfa opened the door of a room larger than Toug had expected. In it, two narrow beds had been pushed together to make a wide one. Ulfa tossed fresh wood on the embers in the little fireplace.

"This isn't so bad," Toug said.

"Most aren't this nice. Pouk can fight."

Nodding, Toug went to the window and put his head out. The turret in which he and Mani had been confined was visible far below and to the right, with an umber flag standing out straight from a pole on the roof.

"You'll catch cold." It sounded like home.

He turned back to Ulfa. "I will anyhow, I guess."

"Here." In quick succession she handed him a woman's linen shift, stained but serviceable, a gray wool gown with holes under the arms, and a short cloak that might once have been bearskin, although most of the fur was gone.

"I don't have shoes," Ulfa told him, "and I don't have stockings I can spare. Pouk might be able to give you a pair of boots." She considered. "But I don't know and I'm not about to give away his things, not even to my brother. Or he might be able to get you some."

"I really appreciate this," Toug said. He held up the gown. "I'm afraid this will be too long."

"Then she'll have to hem it. This girl—I thought you said you and the cat were the only ones they let come in."

Still looking at the gray gown, Toug nodded.

"Then where did this girl come from? Is she one of us?"

"She followed me, I think. She was hurt and I helped her. Sir Able told me how." Memories of long rides through snow and freezing wind returned, and he added, "This was down south, just this side of the mountains."

"You want me to help you find her now?"

There was a soft knock. Toug said, "That's her, I'm pretty sure."

He opened the door and handed the clothes out to Baki. "She'll come in when she's dressed."

In a moment Baki did, smiling as she returned his cloak.

Ulfa stared at her. "I thought you said my gown would be too long."

"She's gotten taller," Toug explained.

Baki made Ulfa a curtsy. "Thank you for sharing your clothing with me."

Ulfa was looking at Toug. "This's your—your . . . ?"

"My friend, that's all."

"There's a lot going on here that I don't understand," Ulfa said. A stubborn set to her mouth reminded Toug of their father.

Baki said, "There is so much that I do not understand either, Ulfa. You are Toug's sister? That is what he says, and your faces are like."

Ulfa nodded. "I'm three years older."

"More than that. Why are you in Utgard?"

Toug said, "You were at home the last time I saw you."

Ulfa nodded. "Do you want the whole story? It won't take long."

Baki said, "I do."

"All right. A knight called Sir Able came to our house in Glennidam." Ulfa sat down on a stool near the fire. "Do you know how many women would kill to have your red hair?"

"Certainly. I know Sir Able, too. Much better than you do. Did you want to marry him?"

Ulfa shook her head.

"Of course you did." Baki smiled, not quite carefully enough to hide her teeth. "Why else would you chase him?"

Ulfa turned back to Toug. "You wanted me to dress your girl. I've done it. Do I have to look for your cat, too?"

Toug considered. "I don't think so. For one thing, Mani's looking for you, so the best thing might be for you to go on doing what you'd do usually, so he can find you. If he does, tell him we'll be back soon."

"Tell your cat that."

Toug nodded. "He won't talk to you, and probably he'll

pretend not to understand. But he will, so tell him. Talk to him exactly like you would a person."

Baki giggled, a brass cymbal tickled with fingertips.

"Meantime you two will be looking for him."

Toug nodded, and Baki said, "Yes. We will."

"Listen here. You look for my husband, too."

Toug stared. "Are you married now?"

"Yes. His name's Pouk. I told you."

"Sir Able's servant," Baki explained.

"I don't know what he looks like," Toug said.

Baki said, "I do."

Ulfa ignored her. "Not much taller than I am, big nose, tattoos on the backs of both hands." For a moment, Ulfa smiled; it was the first time Toug had seen her smile since he had found her. "You said you wanted my story."

Baki said, "But you did not tell it."

"No. No, I didn't. I will now. I met Sir Able. This was when he took Toug away."

Toug himself nodded.

"We were all terribly worried about him, but my father wouldn't let me look for him, and he couldn't go himself and leave my mother and me alone. So I left after they'd gone to bed. I had money from some outlaws Sir Able and my father killed. It wasn't a lot, but I thought it was. I buried half in the woods. I took the rest, just walking you know, with a long stick."

"You could've been killed," Toug told her.

"That's right, but I could've been killed at home, too. There was a man who tried to rape me, and I got his sword and just about killed *him*. Except for that, it wasn't too bad."

Baki cocked an eyebrow. "You were not in love?"

"I thought I was. I didn't say I wasn't in love, I just said I didn't expect Sir Able to marry me. He was a knight, and I'm a peasant girl. Or I was then.

"I asked about him everywhere I went, but it was years

before I struck his trail, north along the War Way with a squire and a war horse and the rest of it. Sometimes at inns and where they'd stopped the people mentioned a manservant, too."

Ulfa fell silent; to start her again, Toug said, "Pouk."

"Yes, and I was interested in that because I was hoping Sir Able would hire me. I was a servant or a barmaid when my money ran low. He knew me, it seemed to me he'd liked me, and a servant—a woman who was willing to work and willing at night, too, you know what I mean—might be able to find out what he'd done with you."

She smiled again, bitterly. "I used to imagine you starving in a dungeon. You're thin, but I wouldn't call you starved. What did he do with you, anyhow?"

"I don't think we ought to get into that right now."

Baki said, "What we must do right now—so I think—is tell each other exactly what we want most. What each hopes to do. I am going to make a rule, that each of us must name one thing and one only, the one thing that concerns—"

Toug said, "Won't they all be different?"

"I am coming to that. Before we name it, every one of us must swear we will help the others. I will help you and Toug, Ulfa. But you must help me, and not Toug alone. Toug must swear to help us both."

Ulfa said, "I don't know about swearing," and meant that she was not sure whether she should swear or not.

Baki interpreted it as she chose. "I do. Each of us will swear by those over us whose claim to our allegiance is sanctioned by the Highest God. Hold up your hand, Toug."

Toug raised his right hand.

"Repeat this after I say it. 'I, Toug, as I am a squire and a true man, do swear by those who are in Skai' . . ."

"I, Toug—" Something took Toug by the throat, but he gulped and pressed on, his voice stronger and stronger at each word. "As I'm a squire and a true man, do swear by those who are in Skai."

" 'By the Valfather and all his sons, I swear, and by the Lady whose name may not be spoken.' "

"By the Valfather and all his sons, I swear." For a moment it seemed to Toug that Sir Able had drawn Eterne; tall figures stood in the corners of the room, gleaming shades of dust and firelight; and he felt their eyes upon him.

Ulfa said, "Well? Are you going to swear or not?"

"And by the Lady whose name may not be spoken." By some small miracle, the draft from the window bore a faint perfume—the scent of lilacs far away.

" 'That all that lies in my power shall be done for my sister Ulfa and my worshipper Baki, that they may achieve their hearts' desires.' " Baki smiled as she spoke.

Toug saw her teeth as clearly as he had ever seen Mani's, and the yellow gleam of her eyes. "That all that lies in my power," he repeated, "shall be done for my sister Ulfa . . ."

Ulfa smiled too, and her smile warmed him as much as the fire she fed; the shadowy watchers were gone.

"And my worshipper Baki, that they may achieve their hearts' desires."

"Your worshipper Baki?" Ulfa asked.

"Because I cured her," Toug explained hastily.

"Now it is your turn, Ulfa. Shall I repeat it?"

Ulfa shook her head. "I, Ulfa, as I am by rights a free peasant of Glennidam, do swear by those that are in Skai—"

"By the Lady now," Baki whispered urgently.

"By the Lady whose name may not be spoken."

"As by the Valfather . . ."

"As also by the Valfather and his sons, that all that lies in my power shall be done for my brother Toug and his worshipper—"

"You must say 'my worshipper,'" Baki whispered urgently.

"I didn't heal you!"

Baki sighed. "Begin again."

Ulfa looked to Toug, who nodded urgently. "If I've got to," she said. "I, Ulfa, as I am by rights a free peasant of Glennidam, though at present a slave of King Gilling's, swear by those who are in Skai, by the Lady who mustn't be named, and by the Valfather and his sons, that all that lies in my power shall be done for my brother Toug and my worshipper Baki, in order that they may achieve their hearts' desires. Will that do it?"

"It will. I, Baki, as I am a true Aelf of the fire—"

Ulfa gasped.

"Do swear by those who are in Mythgarthr, by Toug and by Ulfa, and if he excuse the impertinence by Sir Able himself, that all in my power shall be done for these sublime spirits of Mythgarthr Toug and Ulfa, that they may achieve their desire. So swear I, Baki, who does by this oath and others renounce the false and deceitful worship of Setr forever."

Ulfa stared. Toug said, "Who's Setr?"

"Of that we shall speak presently. First we must name the one thing we most desire. You swore first, and thus should speak first. Or so I feel. Will you dispute it?"

Toug said, "Well, we were going to look for Mani. . . ."

"For this woman's husband, too," Baki said. "For Pouk. But finding neither can be your heart's desire, surely. Your heart is larger than that."

"I need time to think."

Ulfa said, "Are you really an Aelfmaiden?"

"Of the Fire Aelf. Would you see it?"

Ulfa nodded. A moment later, she caught her breath.

Toug looked up. "What is it?" Ulfa was on her knees.

"You have seen more," Baki told him. She helped Ulfa rise. "It was very wrong, what you were doing. I am greatly honored, but honors one does not deserve are only crimes by another name. In my heart I kneel to you."

"I—I . . ."

"Have no need to speak, unless you will speak first. Will you? Or is your brother ready?"

"I'm not," Toug said.

"I didn't know." Ulfa gulped. "My old gown. It's not even fit to wear."

"But I wear it proudly," Baki told her, "and believe we shall have better by and by."

Ulfa gulped again, and bowed her head.

"Now we will have your heart's desire. Please. Name it. Toug and I have sworn to do all we can to help you."

"We just want to get out of here." Ulfa spoke so softly Toug scarcely heard her. "Pouk and me. We want go back to Glennidam. Or anywhere. Help us to get out, both of us."

"We will," Baki told her. "Toug? Your desire?"

"This isn't it." Toug tried to keep his voice steady. "I have to say something else first."

"Then do so."

"I want to be a knight. Not just a regular knight. It would be wonderful to be a regular knight like Sir Garvaon or Sir Svon. But what I truly want—this isn't my heart's desire, not yet—is to be a knight like Sir Able. I want to be a knight that would jump on the dragon's back."

Neither woman spoke, although Ulfa raised her head to look at him.

"I'm a squire now." Toug squared his shoulders. "I really am, Ulfa, and probably I'll be a knight sooner or later unless I get killed. So I have to learn fast. I know that if I wait 'til I'm a knight and try to be like Sir Able then, it won't work. I have to start before I'm knighted."

Baki's voice was just above a whisper. "Even so things may go awry, Lord."

"I know. But if I don't start now, they won't ever go

right. Well, Lord Beel and Sir Svon want me to get King Gilling to let them in here, into Utgard, so Lord Beel can be a real ambassador like our king wants. So that's my heart's desire. I want to do my duty."

"Bravo!" exclaimed a new voice. Mani was seated on the gray stone windowsill, as black and shiny as the best-kept kettle, with a gray winter sky behind him and the winter wind ruffling his fur.

"Bravo!" Mani repeated, and sprang from the windowsill, and then, with a bound that would have done credit to a lynx, onto Toug's shoulder. "I bear glad tidings." He looked at the women with satisfaction, his green eyes shining. "You shall have them in a moment, but first I'd like to hear the rest of this."

"Yes." Toug reached up to stroke him. "What's your heart's desire, Baki? You've heard ours."

"Do you really wish to hear it, Lord? Recall that you have sworn to help me get it."

He waited for Ulfa to speak, but she was gaping at Mani, and he said, "We can't, unless we know what you want."

"Not consciously, perhaps. The politics of Aelfrice are complex, but I must talk about them if you are to understand my heart's desire. My race, whom some of you worship, was brought into being by one we name Kulili. She created us to love her, but we came to hate her and rebelled against her, and at last drove her into the sea. We are of many clans, as perhaps you know."

Mani said, "I do."

"I am of the Fire Aelf, and we Fire Aelf hated Kulili more than any. We led the advance, and we were the last to retreat. When she disappeared into caverns beneath the sea, it was we, more even than the Sea Aelf, who urged that she be extirpated to the last thread. This though we saw her no more, and our land no longer spoke with her voice."

Toug, who could not imagine a being of threads, opened his mouth to ask a question, but closed it without speaking.

"We and others followed her into the sea and fought her there, when she could retreat no longer. I am a maid and not a man. Will you believe that I, too, fought?"

Mani said, "Yes," and Ulfa, "If you say it."

"I do. I did. 'Spears of the maidens!' we shouted as we joined the melee. 'Spears of the Fire Maidens! Death to Kulili!' I can voice those cries, but I cannot tell you how faint and weak and lonely they sounded under the dark waters. We charged her sharks as we had been trained to charge, and after a moment or two we few who still lived fled screaming. You, Lord, would not have fled as I did."

Toug said nothing.

"You would have died."

"Continue." For once Mani seemed subdued.

"In the days after that terrible day, our king tried to rally us. Many would not come, fearing we would be asked to fight again. It was a year before the assembly was complete, and it was complete then only because it was inland. There were many—I was one—whose spirit would have failed if they had been asked to venture within sight of the sea.

"Our king spoke of those who had died, first praising his bodyguard, of whom three-fifths had perished, then our clan in general. We had been one of the most numerous. We were fewer than any, and he told us so. 'We cannot fight her again,' he said; and we whispered when he said it, and sighed deep, and few cheered. Then he revealed his plan—a plan, he said, by which we might yet triumph.

"We no longer paid reverence to this world of Mythgarthr and you who dwell in it. You, we felt, were dull and sleepy and stupid, unworthy gods who no longer credited us even when we stood before you. There was no help to be had from you, he said. I doubt that there was anyone who did not agree."

Ulfa looked at Toug, her eyes full of questions.

Mani smoothed his whiskers with a competent paw. "We're their numina, you see. I am a tutelary lars in animal form myself, a totem. My images confer freedom, and what's always essential to freedom, stealth."

"Yet there were others who would help us gladly," Baki continued. "He had summoned them. Among them was Setr. For a time our king continued to rule, relaying the commands of Setr. With Setr and the rest to lead us, we stormed Kulili's redoubt again, and were defeated even as we had been defeated before. Not all our tribes fought, and some sent only a few score warriors. Such were the Bodachan and others. Setr said this was the reason for our defeat, and we believed him. We would not fight again, he promised, until every clan was ready to fight as we had."

Baki paused, and Mani asked, "He would compel them?"

"Exactly. He set out to make himself ruler of all, and to that end built the Tower of Glas, so lofty that its summit is an isle of Mythgarthr. He built it, I said, because that is how we speak. But we built for him, and he drove us like slaves." Baki held out her hands. "You would not credit me if I told you half what these have done."

"I would," Ulfa said.

"Our king was no more—crushed between the jaws of a monster of the deep, Setr said. He would not permit us to choose a new king, then said we had and that we had chosen him. When the Tower was complete he made us Khimairae to guard it. Have you ever seen a Khimaira, any of you?"

"I haven't," Mani told her, "and I'd like to."

In a moment, the old gray gown was off and lying like dirty water on the floor, and Baki wreathed in smoke. Her flesh darkened as if in fire, hard and cracked; her ears spread, her mouth grew and her teeth with it, becoming hideous fangs. Her feet and hands turned to claws, and she spread leathern wings.

Mani stood on Toug's shoulder with every hair erect and hissed like two score serpents.

The Khimaira hissed in reply; the sound was ice on ice, and held the chill of death. "Thuss I wass, and thuss I sstayed. I hated my form, yet did not wish to change. Such was Setr's hold on me."

Again smoke poured from her eyes. When it retreated, it left a long-limbed Aelfmaid with coppery skin. An Aelfmaid, she snatched up the gray gown. When it had passed over her, she was a human with flaming hair, fair to look upon.

"Sir Able made me renounce my oath to Setr," she said, "and returned me to the lithesome shape you saw. Yet my oath bound me still. First, because my rejection had been forced. More signally, because I feared him. I served Sir Able, and called myself his slave. This I do even now."

Toug nodded.

"And yours, for gratitude and love of you. Setr I fear, but I shall strike the thing I fear. You would be a knight. Learn from me."

"I'll try," he said.

"And so my heart's desire."

The sound of horses' hoofs drifted up from the bailey, and Mani sprang to the windowsill to look.

"It is simply said," Baki continued, "but will not be simply done. Or I fear it will not. I would bring Sir Able to Aelfrice and have him lead us against Setr."

Mani turned to stare at her, his green eyes wide.

"And you and your sister are sworn to aid me."

Toug looked to Ulfa (for he felt his heart sink), and Ulfa to Toug; but neither spoke.

"Little cat, you wished to see a Khimaira. You have seen one. Are you satisfied?"

"The Khimaira," Mani told her, "has seen *me*. That is what I wanted, and it has been accomplished. I knew you were no common girl. Now you know that I'm no common cat."

Baki made him a mock bow.

"My good news has been taken from me," Mani continued, "and my fate has supplied only bad news to replace it. Which would you hear first?"

Ulfa said, "I have no hold over Sir Able."

"Then you must gain what hold you can," Baki told her.

Toug said, "He doesn't owe me anything."

"He sees himself in you, and that may be enough. Cat, you have taken no oath, and I know cats too well to imagine you will submit to one. But will you help us?"

"I've strained every sinew at it already," Mani told her sourly, "and there isn't an Overcyn in Skai who could say why. Will you hear my news? I myself greatly like the good, but you'll want to spit my ill news from your ears."

"It said the good news wasn't true anymore," Ulfa muttered. Wearily, she rose from her stool.

"Not so," Mani told her. "I said that it was no longer news. It was that King Gilling has graciously consented to Lord Beel's embassy. He and my mistress and all the rest—your master, Toug, and so on—have entered this castle. You heard their horses, if any of you were paying attention. You can see them now by looking out this window."

Toug went to window to look, and Ulfa joined him. "It's very grand," she whispered.

"You should have seen it before it was looted," Mani told her complacently, "as I did."

She stared at him, and then at Toug; and her expression said very plainly, *Cats can't talk.*

He cleared his throat. "Some can. It varies. I mean, Mani's the only one I know, but he can."

"He's going to use that power," Mani said, "to remind you that we've gained your heart's desire. Our mission was to get His Prodigious Majesty to admit our company, and we have done it."

Slowly, Toug smiled.

"I include you because you accompanied me, and because I am large-hearted and generous to a fault. In my wanderings, I chanced upon the king and his great clumsy wizard."

"Thiazi."

"Exactly. I spoke, and they were amazed, the king particularly. Do you think you've heard me talk? You haven't heard me talk as I talked then. I was eloquent, diplomatic, and persuasive. Most of all, I was forceful, concise, and succinct. Gylf used to say I had a thin voice. Used to upbraid me for it, in fact. You recall Gylf."

Toug nodded.

"He should have heard me when I spoke to the king. I doubt there's a courtier in Thortower who could hold a candle to me. I explained that King Arnthor had sent us not as enemies but friends, to help him govern—"

"Toug . . ." Ulfa gripped his arm. "I—the cat's really talking, isn't it? I haven't gone crazy?"

"Sure he is, and he wouldn't talk with you around unless he liked you. Don't get all upset."

She pointed. "I saw a—a thing. Just now. Just for a moment. All those grand people down there were getting off their horses and it was over by that wall, and it was almost as big as the giants, only it wasn't one. It was horrible and the same color as the wall. It moved and disappeared."

"His name's Org." It was the best Toug could think of.

"I'll protect you from him," Mani told Ulfa. "You need not fear Org while I'm around. He's a simple sort of fellow, though I admit I don't much care for him myself. Simple and good, once you set aside his appetite for human flesh."

"You persuaded the king to let Lord Beel and his party into Utgard," Baki prompted Mani. "That is your good news, good because it was the desire of Toug's heart. You said you had ill news too. What is it?"

"Ill for you," Mani told her. "Ill for Toug and his sister, and not only because they've promised to help you. With your consent, I will say something else first, something cheering. I think it will gladden their hearts."

Baki nodded, and Mani spoke to Ulfa. "You're the king's slaves, you and your husband? You belong to him?"

She nodded wordlessly.

"One who's already persuaded the king in a large matter might well persuade him in a small one too, don't you think? When the opportunity is ripe, I shall suggest to King Gilling that you and your husband—with the horses and so forth—would make a trifling but entirely welcome gift to Sir Able. Wouldn't that get you your heart's desire?"

"You—you'd do that?"

"Mani." His voice was firm. "My name is Mani."

"You'd do that for us, Mani? For Pouk and me? We'd be in your debt forever."

"I know. I would. I will, at the appropriate moment." He surveyed the two human beings and the Aelfmaiden, his eyes half closed. "This brings us to my ill news, which you had better hear. King Gilling contemplates engaging an army of bold men—human beings as opposed to his Angrborn—who would serve the throne beyond the southern borders. Beyond the present borders, I should say. These men, these stalwart soldiers of fortune, if I may so characterize them, would not be slaves. Far from it! They'd be liberally rewarded, and heaped with honors when they were successful. In time their commanders, having proved their loyalty to His Prodigious Majesty, might even hold fiefs south of the mountains."

Mani waited for comments, but none were forthcoming.

"In short, they would conquer Celidon for him. It would become a vassal kingdom, paying an annual tribute in treasure and slaves. His Majesty hopes to enlist Sir Able to organize and lead this army."

CHAPTER ELEVEN
THE SECOND KNIGHT

Nobody wid him!" Uns reported, cupping his hands around his mouth. "Not nobody a-tall 'cept fer his horse, sar!"

"But he's a knight?" the Knight of the Leopards asked. He glanced at me, expecting me to show more interest; but I was fitting a head that had been a dagger blade to the short lance I had shaped, and did not look up.

"Gold armor, sar!" Uns shaded his eyes to peer down the pass. "'N a gold sun onna shield, sar!"

"This I must see," the Knight of the Leopards muttered, and scaled the rocks as Uns had.

Heimir came to sit by me. "You don't like me."

I shook my head. "You're wrong."

"I'm too big."

"How can a man be too big? He can be too big for this or that purpose, perhaps. Too big to get through a narrow door or too big to ride a donkey. But nobody can be too big or too small in general. It would be like saying a mountain is too small, or a tree too tall."

"You like my new father better." It was a challenge.

"I love Bold Berthold, and I love your mother because he does. Loving is different. Do you like me, Heimir?"

"Yes!"

"And I like you. Why should we quarrel?"

I offered my hand; Heimir took it, and though his was twice the size of mine he did not try to crush it.

"I'll fight him for you," Heimir said.

"You can't."

"Yes, I can. I'm not a good talker." Heimir nodded his own affirmation. "Hela says so. But I'm a good fighter."

"He's alone, Heimir. There may come a time when I'll need you to fight for me, but this isn't it. This is my time, the time I've waited for."

Heimir was silent; then, as if uncertain of what to say, he muttered, "I'll get your horse."

"Cloud is getting herself," I told him.

A long bowshot above us, Uns knelt and caught the hand of the Knight of the Leopards, helping him up. Panting, the Knight of the Leopards thanked him.

"Glad ta, sar." Uns pointed. "Thar he be, sar. Not trottin' like wen I first seen him."

"He doesn't want to tire his charger," the Knight of the Leopards murmured. "It may mean that he knows Sir Able's here, or at least that he knows someone's here. But what's a lone knight doing riding into . . . ?" The words trailed away.

"How'd he know, sar?" Uns peered as if the answer were on the pennant fluttering at the end of the newcomer's lance.

"We see him, surely he sees us. He's wearing his helm."

"Yessar. Dem do make hit hard ta see, I be bound."

"I didn't mean that. Did you see him put it on, Uns?"

Uns sucked his teeth. "Don't hit go da regular way?"

"I'm sure it does." The Knight of the Leopards looked thoughtful. "Have you seen his face at all?"

Uns shook his head. "Had hit on first he come, sar."

"Sir Able has a helm."

"Yessar, he do, sar." Uns was more puzzled still.

"You must have handled it, cleaning it or taking it when you unsaddled his horse. Was it heavy?"

"Oh, yessar. 'Twas dat heavy I like ta dropped hit."

The Knight of the Leopards nodded. "So is mine. That's why we don't wear them constantly. When danger's constant, we wear the little helm—the helmet, as it's called. It's generally an iron cap with a cape of mail to de-

fend the neck, and we wear it because it's much lighter
and still gives a good measure of protection. The helm,
weighing three or four times as much, is put on just before
battle, and only then. You say this knight's worn his since
he came in view?"

"Yessar. I'se dead sure a' dat, sar."

"Because he doesn't want us to see his face? It's the
only reason I can think of, but who could he be? And
why's he trying to hide it?"

"Wal, sar, dat's sumpin else p'cular 'bout him, ain't hit?
'Sides bein' alone like he is."

"He's not alone. Look down there, just coming into
view. Isn't that man leading another horse?"

Uns studied him. "Got a spear, ta, I'll be bound, sar.
Ain't he one a' dem squires? Like ta ya Valt? Dere's more
behind, ta, mebbe."

"This is going to be interesting," the Knight of the
Leopards muttered; and more swiftly than he should have,
began the climb back down.

"Know ye!" his herald proclaimed, "that this pass is
held by two right doughty knights. They are my master,
Sir Leort of Sandhill, and Sir Able of the High Heart." He
stood in the middle of the War Way with his clarion posi-
tioned to display the seven leopards of its pennon; and if
the Knight of the Golden Sun or his great fallow horse impressed him, there was nothing to show it.

That knight leaned forward in his war saddle. "Am I to
choose the one I engage?" His golden helm rendered his
voice hollow and almost sepulchral.

"That is your right, Sir—?"

"I choose Sir Able," the Knight of the Sun declared, and
wheeled his mount to make ready.

I was in the saddle before the Knight of the Sun
reached the point from which he would charge. The
Knight of the Leopards caught Cloud's bridle. "Do you
know who he is?"

"No. Do you?"

The Knight of the Leopards shook his head. "It might be well to refuse until he names himself."

"What if he refused, and rode forward?"

"We'd engage him together."

"Winning much honor." I shook my head, and spoke to the herald. "He waits your signal. So do I."

The silver notes of the clarion sounded. I couched my new lance and readied my shield, things I had done in Skai a thousand times. In the moment—the empty split second before the head of my opponent's lance struck my shield—I wondered whether the Valfather watched. Certainly he would know of this before an hour passed.

My lance struck the golden sun, and the shock seemed an explosion. Cloud staggered under the impact, and the knight to whom that shield belonged fell horse and all.

I turned Cloud, reined up, and removed my helm.

The herald was bending over the Knight of the Sun. "Yield you, sir knight?"

"No." He struggled to free his leg from the weight of his charger. "I claim gentle right. Let me rise and rearm."

"It will be accorded you," the herald said. The fallen charger regained its feet and limped away.

Its owner adjusted his helm. That done, he rose—a man of great size—and appeared to search the ground for the lance he had dropped; the herald motioned to Hela, near whom it lay; she picked it up like a straw and returned it to the Knight of the Sun.

He bowed. "Fair maid, thank you. It was kindly done."

Hela colored but said nothing.

His charger came at his whistle; he mounted, vaulting into the saddle with the help of his lance.

I had returned to the point from which I had charged. "I myself rode a lame horse to battle once," I called, "but having no other I had no choice."

"Nor have I any," the Knight of the Sun told me.

"Your squire will be here soon." I pointed with my lance. "It appears he's leading a second charger."

"He has a second mount for me, as you say." The hollow voice from the golden helm was without inflection. "I have no choice but to ride this one."

The Knight of the Leopards joined us. "You've engaged Sir Able. If you will not yield, you must engage me."

"I have engaged Sir Able," the Knight of the Sun said. "When he yields, I will engage you if you wish it."

Catching his bridle, the herald drew the Knight of the Leopards aside. After a moment he shrugged and nodded.

I watched the herald while readying lance and shield. The fallow charger would be slower; its rider might be slower, too. If my lance found his chest, he would die.

The notes of the clarion echoed from the rocks, and Cloud was off like the wind.

We met as a thunderbolt meets a tower. The golden lance shattered on my shield. The point of my lance passed over the right shoulder of the Knight of the Golden Sun, and its shaft dashed him from the saddle.

With Hela's help, he rose, nearly as tall as she.

"Yield you?" The herald posed the formal question.

"Not I." He whistled again for his charger.

The herald glanced at me. I nodded and made a slight gesture, and the herald said, "You are accorded gentle right. Sir Able will wait until your squire arrives with a fresh mount and another lance."

"I thank Sir Able," the Knight of the Sun replied. "He is a true and a gentle knight, one whose courage and chivalry are not in question. My squire will not come. I will meet Sir Able's lance with my sword."

The herald looked at me again, and I motioned to him. In half a minute more, the herald was mounted and galloping south along the War Way.

"I have ordered my squire to come no nearer," the Knight of the Sun said.

"Yet he will come," I said, "with a sound mount for you, and a lance."

The Knight of the Leopards joined me, with Valt and Uns scarcely a step behind. "You understand this," the Knight of the Leopards whispered, "and I would understand it too."

"If I understood it, I might tell you. I understand only a little more than you do."

"His squire will come at your word?"

I nodded.

"Might it not have been wiser to have my herald fetch horse and lance?"

"He'll come," I said.

Uns looked at Valt, and Valt at Uns; but neither spoke.

The Knight of the Leopards persevered. "You know this knight. So much is clear from his own words."

"I do, though he didn't have this much gold the last time I saw him."

At length the Knight of the Leopards said, "Does he fear you'd slay him if you knew him?"

I shook my head and answered no more questions.

Excited, Uns scrambled to the top of a boulder and stood, bent still but as straight as he could manage. "Dey's comin', sar! Him 'n him 'n more. Oh, ain't hit da sight!"

Gerda tugged at my surcoat. "You ain't off my Hela for what she done, are you, sir? She don't mean no hurt."

I smiled. "He's a very big man, isn't he?"

Whether it was my smile or my words that reassured Gerda, I cannot say; but she smiled in return.

It was indeed a sight, exactly as Uns had said. Two heralds rode in front, each with his silver clarion, the left with a blazing sun on his blue tabard, and the right with the leopards of Sandhill on his. After them, the squire of the Knight of the Sun, a clear-eyed youth with flowing hair and a jerkin of black leather spangled with gleaming gold studs; he carried two golden lances, from each of which floated a blue pennon blazoned with the golden sun.

Behind him, a dozen men-at-arms rode single file, grim-looking men in gambesons of quilted leather and steel arming caps, some with bow and sword and some with lance, shield, and sword. Liveried body servants rode behind them, and behind the body servants, muleteers leading laden sumpters.

I watched as the Knight of the Golden Sun spoke with his squire, accepted a new lance, dismounted, and mounted the unwearied charger his squire had led. Then (as I had hoped) he removed his helm. "You know me." He said it loud enough for me to hear, though we were separated by a half bowshot.

"Greetings, Sir Woddet!" I called. When Woddet did not reply, I added, "It's good to see you again, and Squire Yond, and good of you to come so far to try me."

"I have not come to try you," Woddet answered, "but to prevail." He resumed his helm.

Our mounts met with a crash that shook the earth; both fell. My helm was lost, and I was pinned by the weight of Cloud's side. Woddet had been thrown from the saddle, and was first upon his feet, sword in hand. "Yield!" he cried. He stood over me with sword upraised.

"Now I claim gentle right in my turn," I said. "I've been downed. I claim the right to rise and rearm."

"Refused! Yield or die!"

As Woddet spoke, Cloud sprang up. Her flailing forefeet knocked him flat and would have killed him.

I rose and offered Woddet my hand. "You'd claim gentle right again, I know. And I'd accord it. Hela, give him back his sword, if you will."

Woddet accepted my hand. "On my honor, I've no wish to kill you, but you must yield—lance, horse, and sword."

Hela had dropped to one knee. Kneeling so, her head was below Woddet's own. She held out his sword.

Woddet grasped the hilt. "I beg it," he said. His voice was a whisper. "Yond and I saved you when they would've killed you, and I was your friend when you had no other. Yield to me now."

"I cannot," I said. "I have sworn to hold this pass 'til there's ice in the Bay of Forcetti. I will hold it."

"Sir Able . . ."

I shook my head and stepped back.

"Listen to me." There was despair in the voice from the gold helm. "Nothing I've ever done was harder than refusing gentle right to you. I pray that if I fall again you'll kill me."

"Not even those who see the face of the Most High God grant all prayers," I told him.

I drew Eterne, and eight phantom knights stood around me, four to my right and four to my left; the wind carried the thunder of hooves and the snapping of flags.

Woddet removed his helm and cast it aside. "You told Agr you'd been knighted by the Aelfqueen. I believe it now. Will these knights engage me too?"

"No," I told him, "but like Sir Leort and his men they will stand by to see that our fight is fair."

We met sword to shield and shield to sword; the first stroke from Eterne split the blue shield, the next struck the sword from Woddet's hand, and at the third he fell. Hela came to stand over him with her cudgel poised and death in her eyes. I wiped Eterne with a rag Uns brought before I sheathed her.

"He won't die," said the Knight of the Leopards when the moon was high and we sat side by side before the fire.

"He may," I said; and Gylf, who knew me better than I knew myself, groaned and laid his head in my lap.

"That was a grievous cut you made," the Knight of the Leopards continued, "and he's lost a lot of blood. But if the loss were going to kill him, he'd be dead already. Then the giantess would kill us both, or try."

I smiled at that.

It surprised the Knight of the Leopards, and he said, "Would you fight her? What honor in fighting a woman, even a woman as big as she?"

"Her mother's human," I told him.

"The old woman? I know it."

"The Angrborn are not loved. They hold no spirits."

The Knight of the Leopards shrugged. "Do we? Yes, I suppose we do. I saw them."

"When I drew Eterne?"

"When I did. I try not to think about it."

Some time passed, during which we listened to the wind whistle among the rocks. At last I said, "I may not heal Sir Woddet, but I may implore those who still dwell in Skai to heal him. Will you help me build an altar?"

We labored far into the night, piling stone on stone. Uns, Hela, two servingmen belónging to the Knight of the Leopards, Yond, and some of Woddet's men-at-arms helped. Heimir, awakened by his sister, went into the mountains, broke stunted pines, and brought the wood.

We sang then, a song of praise for the Valfather, and another for the Lady (whose name may be sung, although it may not be spoken); and when the last song was done, I cut the throat of the lame charger that had been Woddet's, hewed the head from the neck, and hewed the body to pieces while the shades of a score of fell knights watched sorrowing. We fed the whole to the flames.

When that was done the rest slept; but I sat with Woddet to see if he would be healed, and heard the gasps of one near death, Hela's sobs, and the whistling of the winter wind.

Then I slept, the first real sleep since I had returned

from Skai, and in a dream it seemed I was in Skai still, and the Lady smiled upon me.

Then that I was on Alvit's steed, charging up a mountain of cloud; I felt Alvit's lips on mine, and learned that death is both bitter and sweet.

Then that I was on the griffin's back and springing from it. My fingers slipped, and I fell into the sea.

Garsecg swam with me, and Setr was in Garsecg's mouth. I knew the battle was coming, and knew Setr knew it too; but this was not the time to think on battles; we gloried in the waves, the scour of the tides, and the strength of the sea.

I was a boy in a garden that stretched very far, searching for a girl who had hidden, and I searched trees and grottoes, looked behind bushes and in the waters of a hundred fountains. At last I turned and saw her behind me, and she was small and green and sweet, with eyes of laughing fire.

I woke at her kiss, and saw Woddet sitting beside me. "You're better," I said.

"I'm not the man I was." Woddet grinned. "But I think I will be in a month or so."

I sat up (for I had seen that the sun was high) and rubbed my eyes, saying that I had slept long and had many dreams. As I spoke, I heard a shout, and Uns came running to me, and Yond, Valt, Heimir, Hela, the Knight of the Leopards, and many others until at last Gerda and Berthold came, he with a hand on her arm, and there was a great babble of talk.

"What's this?" I said. "What news is there? Why didn't you wake me?"

Berthold rumbled, "I wouldn't allow it."

Gerda seconded him. "Let him sleep, I said."

"Your friend said the same," Berthold continued, "the other knight."

"Sir Leort?"

"Me," Woddet told me; and Uns, "Sar Woddet." Gerda said, "You've slept three days," and I goggled at her.

There was a lot of talk after that; I slipped out of the center of it, went to the stream, and bathed in icy water.

When I left it, blue and shivering, I found Gylf waiting on the bank. "Scared," Gylf said, and kissed my hand as dogs kiss, and that was best of all.

"I've failed," Woddet told me after the two of us rode out, saying we were going to hunt. "Have you ever failed?"

"You came to kill me?"

"No! To best you and bring you back to Sheerwall, but you would not yield."

"I remember."

A narrow cleft grew narrower still, and at last ended. We turned our mounts and began the ride back; and I said, "I remember you, and your sword over me."

"I should've struck." Woddet turned his head and spat.

"I'd rather we were friends."

"So would I!"

I smiled. "It's a long way from Sheerwall to these mountains."

"It's longer through the Mountains of the Sun," Woddet said, "but I went there and fought the Osterlings."

"And gained much gold by it."

Woddet nodded. "As you say. We looted Khazneh. Want to hear the whole story?"

"If you'll tell it."

Woddet dropped his reins on his horse's neck and looked at the rocks above us and the steel-blue sky above the rocks. "Well, it was only a day or two after you left. The king asked Duke Marder for five knights and fifty men-at-arms to help against the Osterlings, loaned for two years or 'til victory. Everybody was mad to go. You know how that is."

"I can imagine."

"So His Grace got us together and said he knew all of us wanted it, but any knight who went would naturally want the other four to be men he could trust with his life. He was going into the Sun Room, he said. You know the Sun Room?"

I searched my memory. "I'm sure I should."

"It catches the light from the east, and there's a hanging with the sun on it. We were to stay where we were and talk it over. Each of us was to decide on one companion he'd want with him, and go into the Sun Room and tell the duke. Only he wasn't to tell anybody else who he'd chosen."

I said, "Then I won't ask you."

"Anyway, I decided." Woddet cleared his throat. "I was one of the last, ninth or tenth—something like that. His Grace was sitting at the table with a parchment before him. He'd drawn devices on it for all of us. Mine was a menhir with a spear through it then. Maybe you remember."

I nodded.

"There was a gazehound couchant for Sir Swit, pards for Sir Nopel, and so forth. Everyone who was fit to go. His Grace had a cup of barley. When I came in, he told me he wouldn't have to put my seed where most of them were already, and he showed me his parchment. My menhir had four on it." Woddet paused, embarrassed. "None of the rest had more than two, and some didn't have any."

"Had I been there, I would have named you myself. You have good reason to be proud."

"Anyway, I named—the knight I'd decided on, and Duke Marder put a grain down, and then he had two. What His Grace did afterward was take the knights who had the most grains. The king had asked fifty men-at-arms, but we brought seventy, counting bowmen.

"The king had marched when we got to Thortower, but we hurried after him and came up in time for the Battle of Five Fates. We beat them there."

A light had come into Woddet's eyes that told me more than any description.

"Their horsemen were like wasps, but the longbows would drop a score every time they came. Those little horsebows don't have the reach of ours. We herded the Golden Caan and his elephants into the angle between two canals and charged him. He had the elephants out front, and they killed a score of us and took that many lances before they fell. I lost my sword and used my mace, and before you could saddle up . . ."

I said, "The men you killed would have killed you."

"I know."

We rode in silence after that, until I said, "Does your wound pain you?"

"Only if I move my arm."

"Could you wield your sword with your left hand?"

Woddet smiled, a little bitterly. "Not against you. Why do you ask?"

"Against someone like Heimir? To the Angrborn, these are the Mountains of the Mice, and there are many men here as large as he. I just saw one." I had taken my bow from the bowcase as I spoke; I chose an arrow.

"I told you I used my mace," Woddet said.

"Yes."

"I'd been practicing ever since I was a boy. Hacking away at a stancher of soft wood and so on. Sword, mace, ax, and war hammer. I suppose we all have."

"It isn't easy for a boy to become a man."

"I thought I'd become one a long time before that."

I said nothing, scanning the cliff tops.

"It was like practice. Blow after blow after blow. The head, the shoulder, the head again. Twice the sword arm. My mace had spikes on it—little ones as long as your thumb. I don't have it anymore." He reined up.

"I won't leave you here."

"You can if you want," Woddet said. "I can take care of myself."

I watched the cliffs; and when I did not speak, Woddet said, "That's when you understand what the practice means. That's when you grow up, and afterward you can't go back."

It seemed to me that I heard Disiri's laughter echoing from rock to rock.

CHAPTER TWELVE

BY COMBAT

Toug asked, "In here, Master Crol?"

Crol nodded. "With His Lordship and Lady Idnn, and Sir Garvaon. I can't tell you what they're talking about, but there's no reason you shouldn't knock. If they don't want to hear your news, they'll tell you so."

Pouk said, "Sir Able's th' one I wants." He seemed to be addressing an invisible being on Crol's shoulder.

"Sir Able," Crol remarked as Toug knocked, "is the one we all want. I wish we had him."

Svon opened the door. "There you are! We've got people looking for you. Where's the cat?"

Behind him, Idnn seconded his question. "Where's Mani?"

"The king's got him." Toug stepped inside and added, "This way, Pouk."

"Aye, mate."

Beel was at the head of a huge table, sitting with feet drawn up in a chair several times too large. "I'm glad to see you, Squire. Is that one of the king's slaves with you?"

"I'm Pouk, sir." Pouk spoke for himself, touching his cap and looking to Beel's left. "I'm a slave, sir, right enough. Only I was Sir Able's man, an' 'ud like to be again, an' this lad says it might be done for me an' Ulfa."

"He's blind, Your Lordship," Toug explained. "They blind their slaves, just the men." He had shut the door. Now he watched as Svon climbed agilely into one of the enormous chairs and bent to help Idnn climb into it as well.

"Furniture for the Angrborn, you see," Beel remarked dryly. "They wish to make us feel small, presumably. We, on the other hand, are determined to show we are fully as large as they—in spirit."

When Idnn was seated, Svon stepped onto the arm, and from it onto the arm of the neighboring chair.

"I don't think they have much little furniture, Your Lordship," Toug ventured. "I mean, tables and chairs and things for us. They gave Mani and me a room with furniture like this, too. I'll tell the king they should have smaller things for us, and he might do it. He likes Mani."

"He's safe?" Idnn asked.

"I don't think the king will hurt him, and the others will be afraid to as long as the king likes him."

Beel said, "Take a chair yourself, Squire."

The seat was as high as Toug's chin, but he jumped and pulled himself up. Pouk climbed up as agilely as any monkey.

"We'll be presented at court this evening. Though we've little finery left, we must wear what we have. I'm glad to see you're better dressed than when last I saw you."

Toug explained.

"Thiazi is the king's chief minister?"

"I think so, Your Lordship. He said he was."

Beel sighed and turned to Idnn. "You see where we are. We must ask information of that kind from Sir Svon's squire."

She smiled and shook her head. "You'll know a hundred times more in a week, Father."

"I had better."

Garvaon said, "You and Wistan are to be clean and wear your best clothes."

Toug nodded. "I will, Sir Garvaon."

"Your master and I are to wear full armor. That was what we were discussing."

"I'll clean and polish everything," Toug promised Svon. Pouk offered to help.

Garvaon cleared his throat. "You squires will do your best, I know. But since when do knights wear mail to court?"

Idnn said, "This isn't how things are at our own king's, Toug. A knight at court wears ordinary clothes. The best he can afford, of course, and he wears a sword. But no armor. Armor's for war or a tournament."

"I think it may be because of things I told the king, My Lady." He looked at the knights. "I meant no harm."

Svon said, "I'm sure you didn't. What did you say?"

"How brave you are and what a skillful knight, and Sir Garvaon, too. It was while we were with Ulfa—"

Beel interrupted. "That's the second time I've heard that name. Who is she?"

"Me wife, sir." Pouk sounded apologetic. "Only me wife, an' a good woman."

"She's my sister, too, and she was with Pouk when they got caught and brought here. They got married after that."

Idnn said gently, "You mustn't be ashamed of your sister or your brother-in-law, Squire. Fortunes rise and fall, and the best people are often in the worst straits."

"I'm not!"

She smiled. "I'm glad to hear it. Glad, too, to hear you've spoken to the king. Was Mani with you?"

"Oh, yes, My Lady!" Toug tried to convey that Mani had spoken to the king as well.

"We must talk more about that—a lot more. But first, will you explain why you've brought your brother-in-law?"

Pouk touched his cap. "To serve you, ma'am. You don't know th' ropes, none o' you. Was it your father said so?"

Idnn smiled again. "Yes. It was."

"Well, ma'am, I do. Me wife, she does, too, an' more from th' woman's angle, if you take me meaning. She cooks, she does, an' serves an' all. I scrubs floors an' carries an' does heavy work as needs doin'. An' they don't no more notice us than you'd a fly, ma'am. So we hears an' knows, an' knows th' whole rig an' could take you anywheres."

"I see."

Pouk laughed. "So does she, ma'am. You keep on doin' it. I hope for th' gentlemen here likewise."

Beel said, "You'll be a useful friend, clearly. What can we do for you?"

"Get us out's all. Me an' Ulfa." Pouk's voice became confidential. "Th' lad's goin' to try, an' him an' me, we hope you'll try too, sir. Like mebbe the king'd be in a mood to do a favor? You might ask him for us, sir, sayin' you needed somebody to help. When you went home, why we'd be on board natural as anything."

"I will certainly consider it," Beel said slowly.

"I hopes you will, sir."

Svon reached from chair to chair to touch Pouk's arm. "What did my squire tell the king? Were you with him?"

"No, sir. That I wasn't."

"It was just Mani and me," Toug lied, "and the king and Thiazi. The king wants Sir Able to fight for him. But I know Sir Able has this friend—she's a friend of mine, too—who'd like him go somewhere else, and—"

"Where?" Beel inquired.

"I can't say, Your Lordship." It was hard to speak. "I'm sorry, but I just can't."

Beel raised an eyebrow. "You're sworn to secrecy?"

Unable to meet his gaze, Toug let his own rove over the

walls. "I can't tell, Your Lordship. Or not now. If—if you could meet her. If you could, it might be different."

Idnn's voice was more gentle than ever. "She is here?"

"I don't know, My Lady. Really, I don't."

"She might be here in Utgard at this moment, but she might not? Is that correct?"

"Yes, My Lady. That's it."

"She has been here? You've seen her here?"

Toug swallowed, his mouth dry. "Yes, My Lady."

"Today, since you yourself passed the walls only today. Do you love her, Squire Toug?"

"Oh, no, My Lady! I like her, I like her a lot, and . . ."

Beel said, "You owe her a great favor."

"No, Your Lordship. But . . ."

"She owes him one," Idnn murmured, "and he's as young as I, and finds her gratitude sweet. We'll delve no further in this, Father, if you'll take my advice."

"I shall," Beel declared, "after one more question. Would this friend enlist Sir Able against King Arnthor?"

"Oh, no, sir! It's nothing like that."

"Then we shall tease you no longer," Beel declared. He glanced at Garvaon and Svon, and added, "Is that understood?"

Garvaon nodded, and Svon said, "Yes, Your Lordship."

"Hoping that King Gilling would not wrest Sir Able from your friend, you praised my own knights? Is that correct?"

Something had stirred in the corner behind Toug's chair. Afraid to look, he said, "Yes, Your Lordship."

"I think you've done well," Beel said. "We'll find out tonight."

"Lord Beel!" Thiazi's voice was like a great drum. *"His daughter, Lady Idnn!"* His golden staff pounded the floor; and Master Crol sounded his clarion as Beel and Idnn

marched arm-in-arm into a banquet hall so vast it might
have held the entire village of Glennidam, with half its
kitchen gardens, barley fields, and meadows.

There was suppressed laughter as the Angrborn seated
at long tables to left and right caught sight of them.
Gilling, enthroned upon a double dais at the far end of the
room, was a colossus in the smoky firelight.

Beel addressed him boldly. "Your Majesty, my daughter
and I come in friendship. In more than common friendship, for we bring to you across forest, mountain, and
plain the friendship of our royal master Arnthor. He
salutes you, a fellow monarch, and wishes you peace in a
reign of countless years crowned with every success."

Gilling spoke as a distant avalanche might speak. "We
thank King Arnthor, and welcome you to Utgard."

Idnn's lilting voice filled the hall as larks fill the sky.
"Our king entrusted us with your gifts, Your Majesty, many
gifts and rich. We proved unworthy vessels. We were
robbed, and saved only a pittance of the precious cargo."

That was the signal. Garvaon and Svon entered side by
side in helm and hauberk, leading laden mules. Behind
them, Wistan and Toug leading two more, and after them
Crol, Egr, and Papounce, with the fifth, sixth, and seventh
mules.

The voice from the throne roared again, filling Toug's
imagination with boulders that leaped like stags and trees
smashed to kindling. "Come nearer. Are these the intrepid
knights we've heard so much about? Who's the little fellow with the tree on his shield?"

"That is our senior knight, Sir Garvaon, Your Majesty,"
Beel replied.

"What about the other one, with the swan?"

"Sir Svon, Your Majesty."

Mani appeared on Gilling's barrel of a knee, grinning.

"These little animals, these ponies or whatever you call
'em, are they carrying stones?"

"Your Majesty's penetration astounds us," Idnn answered. "Many of these things are indeed set with precious stones."

"Really?" Gilling leaned forward, his perspiring face touched by a smile that made Toug like him less than ever. "Diamonds? Pearls? That sort of thing?"

"Yes, Your Majesty."

Idnn had smiled in return, and Toug saw Svon and Garvaon stiffen as dogs do when they wind a partridge.

"Not only diamonds and pearls, Your Majesty, but rubies, moonstones, wood opals, bloodstones, sapphires, fire opals, emeralds, jade, jet, cat's-eye, and many another."

Gilling's smile broadened. "Two cat's eyes you've given us already, fair lady. We confess we like him almost as much as he likes you. Though now we come to think on it, his description of you was something wanting. Are you veracious as well as beautiful?"

Idnn curtsied in acknowledgment of the compliment. "We women are not famed for it, yet I strive to be."

Beel said, "If I may speak to my daughter's character, Your Majesty, her honesty rivals that of her patroness, and her wisdom the Lady's. Pardon the partiality of a father."

Thiazi's gold staff thumped the floor. "Neither that false slut nor the witch her sister find favor among the sons of Angr, Southling. Remember where you are!"

The color drained from Beel's cheeks. "Your Majesty, I had forgotten. Slay me."

Gilling chuckled. "Do we need your permission for that, little man?"

The Angrborn roared with laughter, and Toug (who would have liked to think himself too brave for it) trembled.

"Let us turn to safer topics," Gilling roared when the laughter had subsided. "A safer speaker, too. One safe from our royal self. Are you prepared to uphold the reputation for honesty your father gives you, Lady Idnn?"

"I'm glad Your Majesty asks no wisdom, for I've scarce

a thimbleful of that." Idnn, who had smiled the whole time, was smiling still. "But honesty I have in good measure, full cup and running over, whenever Your Majesty has need of it."

Gilling's finger, as wide as Idnn's hand, stroked Mani's sleek sable head. "First we'll have you prove what you say. Diamonds and pearls. Jade. Let us see what you bring."

Idnn went to Svon's mule, and Svon hastened to assist her in opening the pack it bore.

"A ring, Your Majesty." Idnn held it up; its flashing stone was the size of a cherry, and the ring would almost have made a bracelet for her. "It is woven of wire drawn from pale eastern gold, with your royal name worked in our own red sea-gold, a ring so cunningly wrought as to swell or decline to fit the finger on which you choose to wear it."

"Very pretty. What is that pink gem?"

"Rhodolite, Your Majesty. Or rosestone—so many call it. No woman can long resist the man who wears it."

Idnn had advanced toward the dais as she spoke. Gilling held out his hand, and she slipped it onto a finger.

"You are a woman, Lady Idnn. Tell us, is it true?"

"I scarcely know, Your Majesty."

Several of the watching Angrborn laughed.

"I never met a man who wore that stone 'til now."

Gilling was holding up his hand to admire the rosestone. "It's darker than we thought."

"It reflects the strength of the wearer, Your Majesty. Red if he is a full-blooded man of great strength, gray or white if his nature is cold."

Gilling chuckled again. "We should give it to Thiazi— that would test it."

The onlookers roared.

Idnn's presentation of gifts continued, with assistance from her father and the knights: a great platter, of pewter edged with gold; a gold basin; an oversized silver spoon, its handle rough with gems.

"Enough!" Gilling raised the hand that wore the ring. "My thanks to King Arnthor, who has been as liberal to me as his country has ever been to our people."

The merriment of the Angrborn shook the rafters.

"But we will see the rest of these fine things another time, when we in turn shall make gifts of them to those I find deserving. We would have livelier entertainment. Your knights have been described as masters of war. It made us catch our breath, for we had thought to find the masters of war here among the bold sons of Angr."

The bold sons of Angr cheered, and pounded their tables until Toug feared they would break them.

"So we'll have a trial of arms tonight. Your own king does it often, we hear, pitting one of his knights against another. Is that not so?"

Idnn answered bravely. "It is, Your Majesty. Our knights compete in tournament and joust, one with another."

Gilling smiled tenderly, stroking Mani's head. "You yourself have witnessed these tournaments, Lady Idnn? Your father likewise?"

Beel replied for both of them. "We have, Your Majesty, and can tell you much of them."

"But you will not." Gilling smiled again. "We'll tell you, for we are king here. Our first thought was to have these knights fight two of our champions. Schildstarr—"

A huge Frost Giant leaped to his feet with such violence that he sent his enormous stool spinning across the floor. "Schildstarr is ready!"

"And Glummnir—"

Another Angrborn jumped up with a wordless roar.

"But I soon saw that would not be fair. You agree, I hope, Lady Idnn?"

"Certainly, Your Majesty." For the first time, Idnn's voice held a slight tremor.

"As do I. Suppose King Arnthor were to send us two champions. We might then oppose Schildstarr and Glummnir to them, and no one could call it unfair. Agreed, kitty?"

Gilling looked down at Mani, but Mani gave no sign of having heard him.

"This case is rather different. We have knights chosen not by King Arnthor but by chance. We must oppose them with champions we ourselves choose by chance. Your acquaintance with the sons of Angr cannot be great, Lady Idnn."

"No, Your Majesty. It isn't."

"We thought not." With a grunt of effort, Gilling rose, depositing Mani upon a shoulder that might as readily have held a panther. "Our magical kitty, for which we thank you again, likes to ride on our shoulder. As you see. Perhaps he rode on yours as well."

Idnn made a small, strangled sound. "He did, Your Majesty. That is quite correct."

"We thought so. Have you, yourself, ever ridden on the shoulder of a son of Angr? There's plenty of room, you see."

"No, Your Majesty. I—I would prefer not to."

The look Beel gave Idnn was almost savage.

"Nonsense. You'll enjoy it." Gilling grinned. "What's more, your view of our little trial by combat will be as good as our own. But first, chance shall choose our champions."

He looked around at the assembled Angrborn. "The lot will fall on those in presence alone. Anyone who fears to face these knights may leave now."

Not one stirred.

Gilling strode to the laden mules; it was all poor Toug could do to stand his ground.

"This little creature still labors under his entire burden." Gilling had halted at the last mule, which shied nervously. "Let us relieve it."

Thick fingers snapped the pack ropes like string, and

Gilling reached inside. "What have we here? Why this is prime! A dirk of useful size, with a hilt of gold? Is that correct, Lord Beel?"

Beel bowed. "Your Majesty is never otherwise."

"A sparkly purple stone of some sort on the pommel." Gilling held the dirk up. "All sorts of pretty gems on the sheath. Agates, or so we judge them, and tourmalines, and Vafthrudnir himself could not say what else."

"Red jasper, Your Majesty," put in Thiazi.

"We will allow it," Gilling declared, "and a dozen more, all pretty and some few valuable." He waved the dirk aloft. "He who catches this shall face the knights from the south."

His throw carried it so high it struck the ceiling, from which it fell like a comet. Every Angrborn sprang to his feet, and a hundred huge hands grabbed for it. (For a moment Toug felt that all those hands belonged to one monster, one beast with a multitude of heads and arms and glaring eyes.)

There was a mad scramble in which it seemed Beel's party might be crushed. Idnn would have fled, but Gilling caught her up like a doll and raised her to his shoulder.

Wistan caught Toug's arm, saying, "We'd better saddle their horses."

"Here's a nice brooch to hold whatever kind of clothes you fancy," Gilling announced as the two squires hurried out. "It's got a big bad bear on it, all worked in gold. Whoever catches it—"

Together the two squires found the stables, upbraided the blind slaves there for the way the horses had been treated, and readied Garvaon's charger and Svon's Moonrise. But when they tried to lead them into the courtyard, they were turned back by Thrym.

"No horses! They fight on foot. Those are the king's orders." Seeing the bowcase and quiver Toug carried, he added, "No bows neither."

Wistan argued, but Thrym shouted him down. "Take those rabbits away or I'll kill them. Them and you."

"I'm senior squire," Wistan told Toug hurriedly. "Take the horses back. Tell the blind men to unsaddle them, and get yourself back here as a quick as you can."

Toug did. The courtyard (when he was able to slip between the thick legs of Angrborn) was lit by a few torches in brackets, and seemed bright after the filthy darkness of the stable; yet it was badly lit in comparison with the great hall in which Gilling had received Beel, and the few stars that gleamed fitfully through the streaming cloud combed by Utgard's towers did less than the torches to warm it.

Gilling was standing in the center, with Idnn on his shoulder and Mani on hers. "—our borderers. We knew them, and they served us. You knew them as we did, many of you. Now they lie dead, slain by these two and their friends."

His listeners growled; and Toug felt, as he had in the banquet hall, that they were in truth but one great beast.

"They're good fighters," Gilling continued. "Don't be fooled by their size. As we were coming out here, Skoel and Bitergarm promised us they'd gut them like salmon. If they do, we're well rid of them. But if they don't, we mean to take them into our service."

There were angry protests, and Gilling thundered for silence. "We can use good fighters, especially little ones. How many of you want to serve the crown in the hotlands?"

No one spoke.

"We thought so." Gilling pointed to Beel. "Are the knights you brought us ready?"

Master Crol stepped forward. He was wearing his tabard, with Beel's arms embroidered on front and back, and had his silver trumpet tucked beneath his arm; even by torchlight his face looked white. "Your Majesty." He bowed. "Sir Garvaon and Sir Svon wish to protest the terms of combat."

For as long as it took Toug to fidget, Gilling glared; yet

Crol stood his ground. On Gilling's shoulder, Idnn, whose head was something higher than Gilling's own, stooped to whisper into his ear. He shook his head violently.

"They ask to be permitted—"

"Silence!" Gilling raised his hand. "You accuse us of cheating."

"No such thought crossed my mind, Your Majesty." There was a tremor in Crol's voice, slight yet noticeable.

"That we will not permit. Who brings the accusation? You yourself? The little fellow King Arnthor sent?"

"No one, Your Majesty. No one at all!"

Gilling smiled. "All of you, then. Let us explain. We could've pitted our best against your knights. It wouldn't have been fair, so we didn't do it. You saw us choose. Man to man, with the same arms. That would have been fair— fair to everyone. Man against man and sword against sword. Some of you deny that we're men."

In his heart Toug said, "Yes, some of us do, and I'm one of them."

"So we allow your knights armor to compensate for their small stature and puny strength. Now you want more. Well, you won't get it. Thiazi!"

Thiazi hastened to Gilling's side.

"Stand here. When you hold up your rod, both sides make ready. When you drop it, the battle starts. Is that clear?"

Crol took a step forward. "We seek Your Majesty's solemn assurance that there will be no interference by spectators."

Gilling's fist, as large as a man's head, struck Crol down. For a few seconds he trembled; then he lay still, his heavy, middle-aged body twisted, quartered lamiae and lilacs seeming to writhe upon his back.

"Heed this!" Thiazi raised his staff as if nothing had happened. "When I strike the ground, let the combat begin."

Toug whispered, "I brought your helm, Sir Svon." He held it out. "Don't you want it?"

Svon shook his head. His sword was drawn, its blade glinting in the torch light.

"You'll win," Toug whispered. "I know you will."

Svon did not reply; his eyes were fixed on Crol's body.

Gilling's voice echoed and reechoed from the icy stones, drowning the whistling wind. "Everyone prepared? Speak now, or Thiazi's staff comes down."

To Toug's surprise, Svon spoke. "To kill a herald is to cast aside every usage of war."

The watching Angrborn laughed, and Gilling joined them as Thiazi's golden staff struck the stones.

Skoel and Bitergarm lumbered forward, Skoel wielding his huge weapon with one hand, Bitergarm swinging his with both. Shoulder-to-shoulder, Garvaon and Svon advanced to meet them. A moment later, Svon's shield blocked a blow that knocked him to his knees.

Up came Skoel's enormous sword again. It descended, and its stroke would have split a warhorse.

It did not split Svon. He darted forward. When he sprang back, his blade dripped blood from half its length.

Leaping onto Toug's shoulder, Mani whispered, "The weak must close if they can, while the strong have to try to keep them off. Strange battle, wouldn't you say?"

Toug surprised himself. "They're like oxen fighting flies."

"Sir Garvaon's cut his opponent's hands. That's good! Garvaon's a shrewd fighter."

Though Mani's mouth was at his ear, the Angrborn were making such a din that Toug had scarcely heard him. He kept his own voice down. "Shouldn't you be with the king?"

"Lady Idnn was waving her arms and knocked me off. I'll go back when this is over. Look! Garvaon's down!"

Garvaon was, and for a breathless moment Toug felt sure Bitergarm was about to hack him in two; he turned instead, facing about to aid Skoel as the stone turns in a mill.

The swords of the Angrborn slashed and slashed again, rising and falling like the flails of threshers. Svon's shining blade—the oiled brand Toug had polished that very morning—flickered and flashed forward.

Bellowing and cursing, the watching giants crowded closer; Toug and Mani climbed hay bales stacked on a wagon. "The ugly one's trying to get behind him," Mani remarked.

"They're both ugly." Toug strove to sound confident.

"The real ugly one."

The real ugly one was Bitergarm, and he continued to move, however ponderously, to his left, forcing Svon to edge left and left again as he fought Skoel. As Toug watched, horrified, Svon came too near a spectator, who gave him a shove that sent him stumbling toward Skoel.

Biting into Svon's shield, Skoel's blade swept him off his feet and sent him flying. The watching Angrborn tried to move aside but were not quick enough. Svon struck the legs of two, and was kicked under the wagon.

With Idnn weeping on his shoulder, Gilling lumbered into the center of the dim courtyard once more. He raised both hands for silence, and the laughter, cheering, and cursing of the watching giants faded. Wistan was on his knees beside Garvaon. Belatedly, Toug realized that he belonged with his own master, who might still live; he scrambled down.

A hand larger than any human hand plucked him from the bales of hay and raised him higher than he had been when he had stood on them.

"Here he is, Your Majesty. His servant had him." The voice was Thiazi's.

"I—I was keeping him for you, Your Majesty." Toug gulped, wondering whether the king would believe him, and whether it would matter if he did. "He was running loose, and I was afraid he'd get stepped on."

Idnn, still on Gilling's shoulder, held out her hand. "Give him to me, Squire. I'll take care of him." Her face was streaked with tears and her voice despondent, but that voice did not quaver.

"I don't want to throw him."

Idnn gestured. "Thiazi? Is that your name? Bring them over here, Thiazi."

Thiazi did, and Idnn received Mani, who mewed pitifully.

"Now put Toug down," Idnn said.

Thiazi lowered him, but maintained his grip.

Gilling's roar filled the courtyard. "All right, we've had our fun. Bitergarm! Skoel! Come here."

They came, the first licking a gaping wound in his hand, the second wet with his own seething blood.

"You've borne yourselves like heroes," Gilling told them, "and heroes you are. Now, all you sons of Angr, what will you say to these two? Let's wake the crows!"

The Angrborn cheered until they were hoarse. When the cheers were beginning to fade, one of the iron brackets that held a torch fell with a crash and a shower of mortar; Toug, who saw and heard it, saw too that its torch had gone out, although he paid it no more heed than the Angrborn.

"Silence now!" Gilling raised both his hands. "In celebration of our victory—"

"Your victory is not yet!" The voice was Garvaon's. His helmet was gone, and a bloodstained rag wrapped his head; as he spoke, he cast away his shattered shield. His left hand drew a long dagger with a wide guard.

Toug, still dangling from Thiazi's hand, raised a cheer. For a time that was in fact brief though it seemed long, his was the only voice, the cheering of one half-grown squire dangling beside the knee of a giant. Then Wistan joined his voice to Toug's; and Idnn, still seated on Gilling's shoulder, where she held Mani, cheered, too—the wild shrieking of a woman hysterical with joy: Svon had emerged from under the wagon to stand beside Garvaon. The right side of Svon's face was bruised and bleeding, his right eye swollen shut; but his sword was steady in his hand.

The air darkened as a torch behind Thiazi went out.

Beel had joined the cheering, and Garvaon's archers and men-at-arms, who had come so far and fought so hard, and the servants who had become archers and men-at-arms, too, because there was nothing for it but to fight and no one to fight but them. Papounce, in the fine slashed doublet of scarlet and blue he had brought to wear at court, was standing over Crol's body red-faced and shouting; and Egr, usually so silent and reserved, was capering and yelling like a boy.

Their cheers were overridden by the hiss and clang of steel on steel, and a new voice murmured, "My Lord Thiazi." It was husky, yet distinctly feminine. Toug craned his neck to see a woman taller than any he had seen before standing at Thiazi's right hand. Like most of the giants, she was nearly naked; and indeed, her fiery hair clothed her more than the rags she wore; unlike the giants (whose limbs were thicker than even their towering height would suggest) hers were as spindly as heron's legs, so that she appeared to stand on sticks, and to gesture from shoulders scarcely wider than Toug's knees.

"My Lord Thiazi, this is an evil place at an evil time."

"You . . . ?" He glanced swiftly at her, then looked away. "You're no true daughter of Angr."

She laughed—coins shaken in a golden cup.

"Not I, but only a fool who thought she might deceive you. Though I have seen them in Jotunhome, poor creatures—women like dray horses with faces like dough. Thank you."

Thiazi dropped Toug and took off the long cloak he wore. The impossibly tall woman accepted it and draped it over her shoulders.

"You'll be ravished," Thiazi muttered, "if you're seen."

"Will they think me a slave woman?"

It appeared that Svon must die, and Toug heard no more. It seemed to take an hour for Sword Breaker to clear the scabbard, another for his feet (clumsy in the overlarge boots Pouk had found him) to carry him into the fight. He gripped Sword Breaker with both hands and clubbed a knee as high as his chin with all his might, saw a beam of steel and felt the hot gush of his own blood.

And it was dark, snow swirled past his face, and there were more swords out than Skoel's and Bitergarm's, more swords than Garvaon's and Svon's, and his pain was terrible but distant. Once he watched a dark thing strike one of the last torches. And once he saw a lance-long blade descend and raised his arm, knowing that Sword Breaker could never break that sword, which would carry all before it with a blow like a falling tree. Something dark that seemed transparent (for he could make out what might have been a giant's wrist still) closed on the wrist of the hand that held that sword, and something else circled the giant's neck, blurring it. And under all the shouting, and all the rough music of blade on blade, he heard the sickening snap of breaking bone.

A giant fell, nearly crushing him; he thought it was Bitergarm until he saw the fallen crown.

"It seemed like there was another giant," he told Pouk afterward, speaking though the bandages and pain when he and those still living were barricaded in the keep. "A giant the other giants couldn't see any better than I could, and he was on our side. Was that Org?"

"There you have it," Pouk declared. "What do you need me for, shipmate?"

"I didn't think of it then," Toug confessed. "I didn't think of it until a long time after, not 'til Sir Svon got me to look for Lady Idnn. I guess Org was traveling with us the whole time we were riding here, but I never saw him."

Pouk chuckled. "He's not easy to see, shipmate. Not even for me, that knows th' rake o' his masts."

"Oh, Thunor!" Toug felt he could have bitten off his tongue. "I didn't mean to—to make fun of you."

Pouk cackled. "Think I'm blinded? Heard you say it."

"You aren't!"

"Not me, mate. Had to act so, just th' same. One eye's blind enough. See it?"

Toug nodded, and then, not certain that Pouk could in fact see, said, "Yes. Yes, I do. It—it's white."

"Aye, like sp'iled milk. Ulfa says that. Pouk Deadeye they call me."

Toug nodded again.

"An' t'other's squinty. Have a close look."

Toug did. "It's white, too—no, it's a real eye. I mean an eye to see out of."

"Thought I was blind, though, didn't ye? Here, I'll open it wit' me fingers."

Pouk's eye looked white and blind—and then, abruptly, a lively brown.

"You're rolling it up."

"An' there ye have it, matey. They'd a whole crew o' us, an' him that was blindin' complainin' o' the work, an' some gets blood-pizonin' when they blinds 'em, an' dies. So I says, don't have to worry wit' me, mate, an' I shows him like I showed you. I'm blind already, I says, 'n he passes on by. I was that happy. Aye! Never so happy in me life." Pouk's laugh was a joyous crow. "Drink? Why, drink's not nothin' to it!"

"I'm happy too," Toug told him. "I'm happy right now."

"You're a good hand. A stout hand, matey, an' mebbe I kin show Org to ye someday."

"Would he try to hurt me?"

Pouk considered. "Not wit' me 'round. Wit'out, well, I dunno. Best to keep a sharp watch."

"Mani tried to tell Lady Idnn about him once—"

Toug was interrupted by Svon. "We're meeting in the hall. All of us except the guards. That way."

Emptied of so many Angrborn, that vast hall felt almost friendly. There was food and drink everywhere, and though much of the food was half eaten and much of the wine and beer spilled, Pouk and Toug helped themselves before going to an immense fireplace where a crowd of humans and Angrborn were gathered about the towering figure of Thiazi.

"Are you the last?" Beel asked.

"Think so, sir," Pouk said. "Mebbe one or two more."

Beel cleared his throat. "Lord Thiazi and I have been conferring. Sir Svon, are these all you can find?"

"Yes, Your Lordship. Possibly Sir Garvaon may bring more. I don't know."

Svon looked for a stool, and finding none seated himself on the hearth. There were bandages on his face and arms, and Toug sensed that he was bone weary.

Beel seemed to sense it, too. "Your wounds must pain you, Sir Svon."

"Not so much, Your Lordship."

"If you'd prefer to go elsewhere, someplace where you might rest . . . ?"

"I'm resting now, Your Lordship. Sir Garvaon's squire and—and others washed my bruises and salved them."

"As you like, then." Beel looked around at the giants. "I am speaking first because we are more numerous. It means no more than that."

Toug felt the gentlest of taps upon his shoulder. He turned to see a red-haired girl holding a very large cup into which she stared demurely. "Drink," she whispered.

Suspicious, Toug lifted her chin; her eyes were yellow

fire. Her lips shaped words: *"My blood in wine, Lord. It will heal you."* Toug nodded, accepted the cup, and carried it to Svon. Kneeling, he presented it.

"So our status has not changed," Beel was saying. "I am here as our king's ambassador."

Svon drained the cup, nodded curtly, and set it down.

"Lord Thiazi is his king's chief minister. Our lands are not at war."

Beel glanced at Thiazi, who nodded agreement.

"King Gilling lies in his bedchamber," Beel continued, "and I pray that he is resting comfortably, and that he will recover. Lady Idnn is nursing him with two of her maids, together with five women . . ." Beel paused, and groped for words. "Attached to this castle."

"Me wife's there," Pouk whispered.

"In this grave situation, Lord Thiazi's wishes and ours are identical. We would preserve the king's life, steady his throne, and find the traitor who stabbed him. Lord Thiazi."

Thiazi stepped forward. (Toug, seeing the two together, decided that Thiazi was three times Beel's height.) When Thiazi spoke, his voice was deep and reverberant. "I am His Majesty's trusted minister. The Sons of Angr present knew it already, and you Southlings know it now. In His Majesty's absence, I act for him. When he's indisposed, as at present, only I can act for him. Does anyone dispute that?"

He glared at the watching Angrborn for as long as it took Toug to draw breath; when none spoke, at Beel's party.

Garvaon entered, alone, and after a moment's hesitation, sat down next to Svon.

"During the melee an Aelf woman appeared," Thiazi said. "She warned me that His Majesty was at risk and urged me to spirit him away. I've friends among the Aelf." He appeared to wait for someone to object, and studied his hearers while he waited. "None, surely, are better friends than she. When I reached His Majesty, he had fallen.

Stabbed by an unseen hand. We were able to get him inside and into his bed."

A frosty smile played about Thiazi's lips. "Lord Beel and I have taken counsel upon this attempted assassination. Lord Beel fears that one of you Southlings is the traitor."

"A traitor to King Arnthor," Beel explained, "who would never countenance this cowardly attack."

Thiazi nodded. "I, on my part, fear that the traitor is one of our own people. There was rebellion in Jotunland not long ago. It may be that there is rebellion again. Thus our barred doors. Our people, I hope, do not know that the king has been wounded. The assassin may think him dead. If so, he may reveal himself within a day or two. In either case, ignorance works to our benefit. With your help, I shall maintain it as long as possible."

Svon cleared his throat. "May I speak, My Lord?"

Thiazi nodded.

Svon rose. "You suspect one of us."

"No." Thiazi shook his head. "Your own lord does. I concede that he may be correct, though I consider otherwise."

"The more reason then for me to say upon my honor as a knight that I did not strike your king. You practice magic, My Lord. So I've been told."

"I am an adept, as it is called."

"Cannot your arts reveal the assassin?"

Thiazi frowned. "I have attempted it without success. In a moment or two, I intend a further attempt."

"I speak of magic, of which I've scant knowledge." Svon hesitated. "I was once Sir Able's squire, and I was knighted by him."

"I did not know it and am glad to learn it."

"Before we came into this hall to give your king our king's gifts, I learned that your magic had told him that to secure his crown he should take Sir Able into his service." Svon looked to Garvaon for confirmation, and Garvaon nodded.

"I believe he matched us as he did because he wanted to see whether we might be substituted for Sir Able. If that was the test, we could be."

"I'll be blunt." Thiazi stooped to the woodbox, and picking up a log twice the size of a man, tossed it on the fire, where it raised a cloud of sparks and ash. "The spirit I spoke to did not indicate you or your fellow."

"Sir Garvaon."

"It had nothing to say about either of you. I offer no criticism of your valor or your skill. They are inarguably great. Nor do I accuse you of stabbing His Majesty. I say simply that in my judgment you cannot be substituted for Sir Able. This I told His Majesty plainly when he proposed the ill-starred trial of arms in which you took part."

Svon nodded. "I agree, and want to suggest that someone be sent to bring Sir Able here. It is what your magic showed we should do, and I think your magic correct. I volunteer to go."

Thiazi addressed Beel. "If the test shows him to be guiltless . . . ?"

"No," Beel said. "Or at least, not until after the wedding."

CHAPTER THIRTEEN

THE THIRD KNIGHT

The clouds had sailed above me in scores of fantastic shapes, and I had not known them for the lands of Skai; yet they had told my fortune as well as they could.

I shut my eyes and wished those prophetic clouds and that kindly sky back, but all that I saw was darkness. Only in my imagination: the Valfather's flying castle. Eyes open, I saw the stars. If clouds were the mountains and meadows of the Overcyns of Skai, weren't all these stars the country of winged people like Michael? No, because the stars had been the wildflowers in the Lady's meadow. . . .

"Lord?"

I was sleepy enough to believe for half a minute or twelve that the word had been addressed to somebody else.

"Lord?" A winged figure bent above me, blotting the stars. Its wings dwindled; its muzzle melted into a face.

"A Khimaira? What has a Khimaira to do with me?"

"I am Uri, Lord. There is a plot, and I have flown here to tell you of it."

I sat up and found that Gylf was on his feet already, not quite showing his teeth, but near it.

"If you will hear me out, Lord, and ask no questions until my tale is done, it will go faster."

I nodded.

"Garsecg you know. He taught you. You think he lied, feigning to be one of the Water Aelf. It was not feigning, though he dwells in Muspel. The Sea Aelf have welcomed him and made him greater than their king, calling him Father. How then is it false for him to wear their shape?"

"If I am not to question you," I said, "it might be best if you don't question me."

"As My Lord wishes. Vile, I remain your slave." Uri knelt. "As I am Garsecg's. Indeed, I serve My Lord because Garsecg will have it so. My Lord recalls that when Baki and I were ill on the Isle of Glas, My Lord left us in Garsecg's keeping. As Setr he had us serve you, saying that we who had been his slaves were to be yours. We were not to tell you of his gift, for Garsecg does good in secret when he can."

"You've asked no question," I remarked, "and I ask you none. I've got a comment, though. You haven't obeyed him."

"If he punishes me, I will bear it, or try. If you punish me, I will do the same. I disobey because the matter is deadly, and one that Garsecg himself, though the wisest of men, cannot have foreseen. I will not ask whether he has been a friend to you, you know your answer. Nor will I ask whether you swore to fight Kulili for his sake. You did, and though I do not know it as well as you yourself do, Lord, I know it well enough."

I groped for Eterne, and found her. "He summons me."

"No, Lord. He does not. Did I not speak of a plot? It is my sister's."

Gylf growled, "Get to it."

"I serve no dogs," Uri told him, "not even you."

"Worse!"

She sighed, and there was more despair in her sigh than speech could express. "Now we know what your dog thinks of me, Lord. You may agree, knowing I betray my sister."

I wrapped the blanket about me, for the wind was cold.

"Baki plots to send you against Garsecg. To that end she has stabbed King Gilling, who lies near death. And to that end she has enlisted Toug and his sister. The witch's cat helps too, I would guess from malice. Now my tale is done. Lord, will you give me your word that you will never slay Garsecg? Or try to?"

"No." I lay down and studied the stars.

"Did you not give your word to Garsecg, as I said? To war on Kulili? Alone if need be? Upon your honor?"

"I did. Does he summon me?"

"No, Lord." Uri's voice sounded faint and far away. "He fears you too much for that, Lord."

We were too many for one fire; but Woddet and Yond, and the Knight of the Leopards and Valt, ate at mine, with Hela, Heimir, Gerda, Bold Berthold, and Uns, who had made it. When venison was on my trencher and wine in my flagon, I said, "I have news. It may mean a lot or a little to us—I don't know. Neither do I know it's true. It was told as true, no pledge of secrecy was asked, and it would be wrong not to share it. Believe it or not, as you choose."

The Knight of the Leopards asked, "When came this news?"

"Last night." I forked meat into my mouth on my dagger.

"We must set a better watch. My men were our sentries."

"I don't say they slept," I told him.

Woddet looked from one to the other. "Who brought it?"

"Do you have to know? It'll mean useless argument."

"No argument from me," Woddet declared.

Hela swallowed a great gobbet of meat. "He trusts not the bearer. Do thou, most dear knight, trust me?"

Woddet flushed. "I do. Though you lack gentle blood, you are a true maid, I know."

"As for blood, I have seen thine. You think my lineage foul. Does Sir Able here, a wiser knight, think it foul, too? I am of the blood of Ymir, Sir Able, for so my ancestress Angr was. Did you not tell me once that blood has drenched your sword arm to the elbow? That foul blood?"

I nodded, for I had told her things that had happened in Skai. "Say fell blood, rather."

"You are kind." She turned back to Woddet. "Dearest knight, as I am a trusty maid I counsel you to ask nothing, save you stand ready to credit any answer. Fell blood? Fell swords are here. Which swordsman would you see fall?"

"None." Woddet smiled ruefully. "What is your news, Sir Able, if it will not provoke strife?"

I sipped my wine, put down my flagon, then sipped again. "We agreed that if the Angrborn march south we'd resist them together, even though you and Sir Leort are my prisoners."

Woddet and the Knight of the Leopards nodded.

"This news may bear on it, if it's true. In fact it may bear on it if it's false, if it's believed. It is that the Angrborn king has been stabbed and lies near death."

Bold Berthold did not raise his blind eyes, but his voice was warm. "Who did it?"

"The sister of the person who told me. So she said."

Gerda ventured, "A slave woman?"

"Yes, but not King Gilling's or any other giant's."

Hela said, "You know her, sir knight. Your voice speaks louder than your words."

I nodded.

"I have no sister, and am glad of it. Sisters are talebearers always. You know her and are her friend. What think you? Would she do a deed of blood? Strike a throne?"

"She might," I said slowly. "If she were provoked or desperate, she might. If a particular youth were threatened, for example. If she had a good reason."

"I have one more question." Hela grinned, revealing crooked teeth in a mouth the size of a bucket. "Ere I ask, I give you thanks for suffering me as you have. If 'twas for Sir Woddet's sweet worth, why fiddle-de-day. Suffer me you did. Why did her sister hasten here, taking her news to you? Do you know?"

"I see I've got to tell all of you more than I'd like to. As a reward I'll have Hela's counsel, or anyway I hope so. If her counsel's as pointed as her questions, it'll be worth a lot."

Uns nodded and edged nearer to hear.

"There is a man called Garsecg. Not a human man. Will we all agree that Hela's sire was no human?"

"I am," Heimir declared. "I'm human just like you."

"I haven't denied it." I tried to make my voice gentle. "But Hymir was not human. However good he may have been, or brave, or generous. Nor was this man Garsecg human."

I waited for more objections, but got none.

"He befriended me. I owe him a lot. I think that he acted as he did to recruit me—as he did—against an enemy, one I wouldn't fight if I had a choice."

The Knight of the Leopards asked what troubled me.

"You know about the woman I love. She's where Garsecg is, and I wish I were with her now."

"Go to her then!" the Knight of the Leopards exclaimed. "Are you the only man in Mythgarthr who doesn't know the tale of the knight and the tumbrel?"

"I've sworn to stay until midwinter. I'm also bound by an oath sworn to the greatest and best of men. It's only by his grace that I'm as near her as I am."

"Now say, sir knight, think you more of your honor than your lady?" Hela's smile held something like pity. "Think well before you answer."

"For one smile from her, I would throw all honor in a ditch," I said. "Yes, and stamp on it. But I couldn't ask her to marry a dishonored knight."

Trying to understand, the Knight of the Leopards said, "You value her honor more than your own. You would die to preserve it."

Woddet began, "Now see here, how does this—?"

"We'll talk of that when the time comes. Let me finish. The lady is where Garsecg is. The person who came last night said her sister wanted to get me to fight him. She wanted me to bind myself not to."

"Deeper and deeper," Hela muttered. "Would this paltry cup were half so deep." She held it out, and Woddet poured more wine for her.

Old Gerda asked, "An' did you swear, sir?"

"No, mother. I've given oaths enough already. I want to be with the woman I love." I sighed. "If I fight him, it's possible she'll try to kill me. I'd welcome it."

"We wouldn't," Berthold rumbled.

"Wounded though I am," Woddet said, "I may throw my parole to the winds and kill you myself, if you won't get to the point. The King of Jotunland is sorely wounded. Isn't that what you said? What has that to do with us?"

"Do you think they may blame my cousin for it?" asked the Knight of the Leopards.

"We've had raids by no more Angrborn than we could count on our fingers," I explained. "By twenty at most, and more often by fewer than a dozen. It was these raids that your cousin hoped to persuade King Gilling to stop. Berthold, you were captured by Angrborn. How many were there?"

Bold Berthold fingered his beard. "Eight they was, when the outlaws sold me to 'em."

"What about you, Gerda? How many took you?"

"Lard an' Lovey, I can't say, sir, it's been that long."

"Twenty?"

"Oh, bless you, sir. Not half so many. Five it might a' been. Or six. Some was kilt, sir, for our men fought. So comin' or goin', sir? Comin' they might have been ten."

I nodded, and spoke to Woddet. "Suppose King Gilling dies? Might not his successor—we know little enough about Gilling and nothing about the successor—send a hundred?

"Berthold, Gerda. What about five hundred? Would you call that an impossible figure?"

Bold Berthold only shook his head, whether in denial or bewilderment. Gerda said, "Well, sir, I never seen that many all to onest, but when I think back on them I seen one time or the other, it's hundreds. More'n that, even."

"Hela? Perhaps I should have asked you first."

"As to their number? Five hundred I would think no very great figure. We have frequented this road, my brother here and I, and seen fifty one day, and twenty the next. Look up, you bold knights. What flies above?"

"Geese," the Knight of the Leopards answered her, "but they are too high for any arrow of mine."

"How many?"

"Thirty, it might be."

"Forty," Woddet offered.

"Forty-three and their leader, making forty-four in all. Forty-four that the three of us see now, for brave Sir Able will not look. How many geese do you suppose there are in all the world, knights? Hundreds?"

No one spoke while Hela gulped half her wine, coughed, and drank the rest.

At length I said, "Let us say one hundred and no more. Could we stand against a hundred? We three, and Gylf, and the men who follow the leopards, and those who follow the sun? And Hela, Heimir, and Uns? Would we?"

The silence grew until the Knight of the Leopards said, "Would you, Sir Able? Would you lead us? Answer truly."

I told him, "I've sworn to hold this pass."

"A rider on a blown horse, Sir Leort!"

The Knight of the Leopards cupped his hands around his mouth. "Just one?"

There was a lengthy pause, during which Woddet, Valt, and Yond hurried over.

"Just the one, sir!"

"Coming from the north?" Valt inquired of everyone and no one. "Do the giants ride horses?"

Yond shook his head. "They're too big."

The Knight of the Leopards silenced them with a gesture. "How do you know his horse is blown?"

Woddet snorted.

"She's tryin' to get it to trot, sir!"

The Knight of the Leopards opened his mouth, then shut it again, staring at Woddet while Woddet (his honest face a mask of confusion) stared back at him.

"A woman?" Valt muttered.

The Knight of the Leopards whirled. "Fetch my horse!"

North of the pass the War Way angled down, descending the mountainside in a score of breakneck curves. The Knight of the Leopards took them all at a gallop, and many a stone, dislodged by the flying hooves of his spotted warhorse, dropped down an abyss of air.

The last twist of that coiling road was behind him when he caught sight of the rider; when he did, she (topping a rise on a drooping palfrey dark with sweat) was so near that he nearly rode her down. She screamed, and seeing the shield he carried burst into a flood of tears.

He dismounted and lifted her from her saddle, holding her as he had when he was no older than Valt, and she a pretty child with flashing eyes and raven locks.

Pure white was the tabard of the herald who brought the Black Knight's challenge to me, and the charge on it was a sable. "My master," he announced to our own herald, "would pass into the north. His affair is urgent," he paused to smile, "and his purse heavy. Here are twenty pieces of broad gold, so that your own master stands aside."

"I am acting for Sir Able of the High Heart," our herald responded stiffly. "My master, Sir Leort of Sandhill, abides with him until his ransom is paid."

The Black Knight's herald lifted an eyebrow the breadth of a stem of clover. "Should you not be galloping south to attend to it?"

"Another is seeing to that. You will, I take it, see to your master's? Our brother left this place days ago. It is too late, I fear to ask him to act for you."

"He need not." The herald of the Black Knight held up the purse he had proffered a moment before, jingling it so the mellow chink of gold on gold could be heard through the deerhide. "My master pays his ransom in advance."

The herald of the Knight of the Leopards shook his head.

"Will you not examine them, so as to give report to this Sir Able you speak of?"

"You know my master's name—Sir Leort of Sandhill. I have declared that I act for him who overmatched him, Sir Able of the High Heart. I would know your own master's name and that of his manor, for with so much gold at his command he cannot but have one, before we speak further."

But speak further they did, with that overcareful avoidance of rancor characteristic of heralds, before the herald of the Knight of the Leopards returned to me.

"His master he styles the Black Knight," the herald explained, "and will not name him. Nor will he state his master's business, nor denote his castle."

I stroked my chin.

"A manor I called it, though I'd seen the broad pennant. I hoped to sting him, but it availed nothing."

"He is a knight banneret?"

"Or greater. He offers twenty gold pieces." The herald cleared his throat. "I examined them. He insisted on it."

I waved the gold aside. "He may not pass. Tell his herald . . ."

"What is it, sir?"

"That if his master wishes to ride north, he must engage me or go by another road." I paused. "I was thinking of Sir Woddet's herald. What was his name?"

"Herewor, sir."

"He left four days ago. Did they meet him on the road?"

"They did not. He may have met with mishap, sir. Let us hope they came by a different way."

"We must ask them when the fighting's over. Your master has not returned?"

"No, sir. Should I send a hobliar after him, sir?"

"I doubt that it's needed." I cupped my mouth as the Knight of the Leopards himself had not long before. "Sentry! To the north?"

"Your servant, Sir Able!" The sentry's mailed arm caught sunlight as he waved.

"What do you see of your master?"

"Ridin' slow with the traveler!"

I nodded and waved.

"Tell the Black Knight I'm ready to engage him."

The herald was visibly unhappy. "I must speak before you do, Sir Able. First the gold—"

"I don't want it."

"Twenty pieces of eastern gold, broad and fair, every one of them. I bit two, sir, and they were soft as leather. The head of some caan on every one."

"Does Sir Woddet know him? Or any of Woddet's party?"

"I don't know, sir. Shall I ask?"

I nodded; Uns, who had come up while we were speaking, said, "I'll do hit, sar. Right smart ta."

"I'll go with him in a moment, by your leave, sir," the herald said, "Sir Woddet may not like talking to such a hind. But first, sir, I must tell you this Black Knight fights to the death and only to the death. He accords no gentle right, and thus—" The herald took a deep breath and plucked up his courage. "You're not bound to engage him, as I see it. To fight to the death is war, and no proper trial of arms."

I smiled. "Sir Woddet was of this knight's mind also. Does that not seem strange?"

The herald began to speak, thought better of it, and hurried away.

Cloud took three steps forward, and I saw in my mind's eye my own image charging with couched lance. "Nope," I whispered, "nor should I tire you like this with my weight." I dismounted, and side by side Cloud and I advanced until the Black Knight's herald was in plain view, and the Black Knight also, waiting a long bowshot off beside his black charger.

"He has a skull for a crest," I explained to Cloud. "That's a human skull."

Gylf, who had followed us, grumbled, "Cat pride."

"It's boyish," I agreed. "We should get on well."

"To scare you."

"Of course. Only I'm not scared. Do you remember how I told you not to interfere when Sir Woddet and I engaged? You're not to interfere in this either. Would you like me to have Uns chain you up?" I turned to whisper to Cloud. "You're not to treat this knight as you treated Sir Woddet."

In my mind, Cloud stood riderless, her head down.

The Black Knight's herald was waving. "Sir Able! My master is ready to engage. Are you?"

"Soon, I hope!" Uns and our own herald were returning. As I watched them, I caught sight of Idnn and the Knight of the Leopards. I waved, and both waved in response, she with a white scarf.

"Dey'll aw talk, sar." Uns arrived first, breathless and panting. "'Cept fer him 'n he won't look me inna face."

"I see." I had a hand on the pommel and a foot in the stirrup. "What do the others say?"

"Nothin', sar. On'y dey say hit 'n he won't."

"They know nothing of a Black Knight, sir," announced our herald. "So they say, and I credit them. Sir Woddet surely knows, but he'll no more tell me than Uns here."

I mounted. "I'll ride to that rock that crowds the road, and turn. When you see me lift my lance, I am ready."

Awaiting the signal, I searched my memory. The Black Knight was known to Woddet; that was certain. Woddet had ridden untold leagues to defeat me, so that I would not have to face the Black Knight. Woddet was a friend, but who was this knight he'd feared would kill me? I tried to recall the knights at Sheerwall. I could remember only the knights who had been my companions in the Lady's hall, the knights in the Valfather's castle. Sir Galaad, Sir Gamuret . . .

No. Woddet had been willing to kill me if necessary to keep me from fighting this Black Knight.

Clarion and trumpet sounded, their clear, shrill notes echoing from snowy rocks. I couched the lance I had shaped from spiny orange and heard above the thunder of Cloud's hooves the whistle of wind in the carved dragon on my helm.

The Black Knight's point, directed at the eye slits of that helm, dropped at the final moment, striking my shield with force enough to stagger Cloud. My own point struck the pommel of his saddle, and the black charger was overthrown, crashing to the roadway.

I reined up, dismounted, and gave Uns my lance. The Black Knight lay motionless, and I noticed (in the way you notice a hare between two armies) that the skull had broken, losing part of an eye socket.

Then our herald was kneeling beside the Black Knight and asking again and again whether he yielded.

The black charger struggled to its feet; even with its pommel half torn away, its war saddle held the Black Knight still, though he drooped in it so that he was sure to fall. I tapped the herald's shoulder. "Enough. He's wounded or dead. Let's help him if we can."

Woddet and Hela were at my elbow by then, Woddet with eyes wet with tears. The three of us lifted the Black Knight from his saddle and laid him on the frozen roadway. Although he could scarcely talk, Woddet managed, "Will you remove his helm, Sir Able? Or should I?"

I shook my head. "Will you, Hela? A favor to us both?"

She did. "He is not slain, good knights. See his eyes flutter? Life stirs still." The Black Knight's face was pale as death, and his hair and beard were white: Woddet and I fell to our knees beside him. Berthold was groping the fallen knight with his stick. Hela told him, "He is as old as you, Father, and a noble face."

His herald began, "Know you that my master is none other than—"

The Black Knight completed the thought in a voice stronger than anyone could have expected. "Duke Marder of Sheerwall."

"Your Grace." I bowed my head. "I did not know."

"Nor were you meant to, Sir Able. Are you landless still? And penniless, too?"

"Yes, Your Grace."

"You need not— Sir Woddet? What are you doing here?"

"He rode ahead of Your Grace," I explained, "fearing I might kill you."

"You overcame him." Marder tried to sit up, and with

Hela's help succeeded. "I wished to test you, Sir Able. To see if you could be tempted, mostly. You passed both tests." He coughed. "I myself failed the second, alas."

"Your lance bid fair to split my helm," I told him. "You dropped the point."

"Of course, of course. I wanted to test you, not blind you." Marder caught sight of Berthold, and his face fell. "I beg pardon, sir knight. I did not intend to offend."

"Ain't but a poor man, sir."

"All these people." Marder looked around in some confusion. "This—this toplofty maid. And over there, the biggest man I've ever seen."

"My brother, Your Grace, and by Your Grace's leave a true man, though not supple-tongued. Yonder stands another noble knight, Your Grace, good Sir Leort of Sandhill."

Uns whispered in her ear.

"This trusty servingman has named the maiden with him, that I may make her known to you, Duke Marder. She is Lord Beel's lady daughter, called Idnn."

Idnn herself came forward, smiling and offering her hand to Marder. "We meet rough, Your Grace. Let's not meet wrong, too. We are Idnn, Queen of Jotunland."

CHAPTER FOURTEEN

UTGARD AND THE PLAIN

The hour was just past dawn. "Small enough there can't but one get in at a time, Sir Svon," the sergeant said as he hurried along, "an' I've three bowmen there an' two swords."

Nodding, Svon limped after him, with Toug in his wake. The men-at-arms held drawn swords; the bowmen had arrows ready. All seemed vastly relieved by Svon's arrival. When the sergeant threw wide the iron door, Toug understood. That doorway would allow two knights to stride through abreast, or let a mounted knight to ride through with head unbent; but the Angrborn in the freezing passage beyond it had to stoop, and looked too big to enter. His great, bearded face was like the head of a war drum, scarred, pocked, and dotted with warts; his nose had been broken, and his eyes blazed. Seeing him, Toug drew Sword Breaker.

"Who is your king?" Svon demanded.

"Gilling." It might have been a war drum that spoke. "Gilling's true king, blood a' the right line a' Bergelmir."

Although Toug had been watching his eyes, fascinated and terrified, he could not have said whether he lied.

"So say we all," Svon told him. "Enter, friend."

"What about the rest?"

"Tell them to return tonight."

"I'm Schildstarr. Tell the king."

"His Majesty is sleeping," Svon replied stiffly. "Do you wish to enter—alone—or do you not?"

"I'll tell 'em." Schildstarr took a step back. "You better shut this door."

It swung shut with a clang, and two bowmen heaved the great bar into place.

"Did their king really marry Lady Idnn?" The sergeant whispered, although it seemed impossible for Schildstarr to overhear even if he had crouched with an ear to the door.

Svon nodded, his face expressionless.

"By Thunor!"

"She's nursing him," Toug ventured, "with slave women and her maids to help, because it can't be easy to take care of someone as big as he is. I feel sorry for her—we all do."

Svon told him, "Fetch Thiazi." Toug lit a torch in the guardroom and hurried away.

The knee-high steps of the lightless stair that led (through stone enough for a mountain) to the upper levels seemed interminable; the pulse in his wound and the labored scrape of his boots mocked him with his own fatigue.

After a hundred steps or more, he heard feet other than his own, and though he told himself that it was the echo of his own steps returned from the upper reaches of the stair, he soon realized that it was not. Someone or something was descending, moving lightly from step to step.

The air grew colder still, and though he drew the thick cloak Idnn had provided around him, it had lost its warmth. Seeing Mani's emerald eyes on the step above, he guessed what those eyes portended. "It's her, isn't it? It's the witch."

"My beloved mistress," Mani announced solemnly.

"That's what you call Lady Idnn."

"Queen Idnn is my beloved mistress too," Mani explained. "My loyalty to both is boundless."

A voice from the dark asked, "Would you see her?" It might almost have been the voice of the wind outside, had it been possible for that wind to make itself heard.

"Yes." Toug leaned against the wall, wishing he could sit. "If we've got to talk again, that might be better."

An Idnn who was not Idnn descended the stairs, more visible than she should have been by the smoky light. "King Gilling is a beast." The false Idnn spoke as winter speaks. "He must not possess me—that I have come to tell you. I bring Sir Able, and Sir Able may save me."

"Sir Svon would," Toug offered.

"So would you. You have not lain with a woman."

Toug shook his head. "Not yet."

"You speak truth. Is he truthful, Mani?"

"Oh yes!"

"I've seen it," Toug explained. "I—know what to do."

"You have not seen King Gilling receive a bride. He will lie upon his back, his member standing."

Hesitantly, Toug nodded.

"Disrobed, I will love it as if it were a dwarfish man. I

will draw staring eyes and a smiling mouth. I will anoint it with sweet oils, cozen and kiss it, beg its love. Gilling will reply, speaking for the dwarf I kiss. Erupting it will bathe me in semen, and I will praise and kiss the more, saying how happy it has made me and begging it not to go."

"Lady Idnn will not do that." Toug spoke as confidently as ever in his life.

"If I do not, or show disgust by any word or act, I will die," the false Idnn told him. "I will not be the first to perish so, you may believe. Do you think she cannot bear him a child?"

Toug managed to say, "I don't want to talk about this."

"His semen will violate her. When she grows big with child, know you how big she will grow?"

The false Idnn began to swell. Toug shut his eyes but found he saw Idnn still, her body monstrous, misshapen, and surmounted by a weeping face. Unseen hands stripped away her clothing and opened her from breast to thigh. He pressed his hands to his eyes to shut out the blood; she writhed behind their lids, trembled, and lay still.

When he came to himself, he found he was sitting as he had wished, sitting on the cold and dirty floor of a landing, rocking and weeping.

"It hasn't happened yet," Mani told him; and Mani's voice, not normally kind at all, was kinder than Toug had ever heard it. "It may never happen."

"It won't," Toug declared through his tears. "I won't let it. I'll kill him. I don't care if it's murder, I'll kill him."

"It isn't. Now pick up that torch, and puff the flame before it goes out." Mani sprang from the last step to the landing, and to Toug's surprise rubbed his soft, furry side against Toug's knee. "It's murder when I kill another cat, except in a fight. It would be murder for you to kill, oh, Sir Garvaon or Lord Beél, except in a fight. But King Gilling is no more like you than Org."

Suddenly frightened, Toug rose. "Is he down here?"

"Org? Not that I know of."

"But that's what happened, right? When Sir Svon and Sir Garvaon fought the giants. Org was there, and he was pulling down the torches so the giants wouldn't see him."

Mani yawned, concealing his mouth with a polite black paw. "Certainly."

"And he . . . Did he hold them from behind, or something? Was that how the knights won?"

"I don't know. It became a riot in the dark."

Toug scrambled up the step from which Mani had jumped. "I've got to get Thiazi. Sir Svon wants him."

"Then get him, by all means. May I ride your shoulder?"

Toug held out his free arm. "Come on."

When they had climbed another score of steps, Toug asked, "Was it Org who stabbed the king?"

"I don't know who it was," Mani told Toug. "I didn't see it happen, though I wish I had." After another step, he added, "I doubt it. Org breaks necks, mostly, from what I've seen. You might not think anybody would be strong enough to wring the necks of these giants, but he is."

"The king was stabbed. Stuck deep, so a sword or a big dagger."

"The king killed Master Crol," Mani said thoughtfully.

"I know." Toug struggled to the top of another step. "This would be easier if there was something to hold on to."

"I'll speak to them."

"Org's supposed to do what Sir Svon tells him. Somebody told me that. I think it was you."

"It may well have been."

"Killing Master Crol wasn't fair. It wasn't fair at all. So why shouldn't Sir Svon tell Org to kill the king?"

"I see no reason at all," Mani conceded. "However, he did not. I was eavesdropping, you see, when Svon gave Org his instructions. No mention was made of the king."

"It's not nice to listen in when other people talk."

"Though I hesitate to disagree, I must. I often find it

pleasant, and at its best it can be quite educational. A cat who keeps his ears open learns a great deal."

Toug climbed farther; he was nearing the floor he wanted and their talk would soon be at an end. He stopped, waving his torch to brighten its flame. "I think you ought to tell me everything. I need to know a lot more."

"About what Sir Svon told Org?" Mani sprang from Toug's shoulder and stretched. "Well, it was while Sir Svon—"

"About what you and the witch are doing. She wants me to kill the king. If I do, we're going to be in a lot more trouble here than we are already."

"She wants you to save Queen Idnn," Mani objected. "That's rather a different thing."

"But she wants Sir Able to come back. She told Thiazi."

"Whom we're supposed to fetch? Didn't I hear that? I assume Sir Svon wants him, since he sent you."

Toug would not be deterred. "She told him the king ought to hire him if he wants to stay king, and that sounds like she's on the king's side."

Mani smoothed his whiskers. "I doubt it."

"Doesn't she tell you?"

"She confides in me from time to time," Mani said stiffly. "However, she has not confided that. I was to accompany Sir Able and his awful dog. I was to serve Sir Able to the best of my poor ability, as I have. Sir Able gave me to Queen Idnn, and I transferred my loyalty to her without a murmur. She in turn gave me to her royal husband, another step up the social scale. You agree?"

"But you're still the witch's," Toug declared bitterly.

"Certainly." Mani sprang up the next step. "Oh, I see. You're afraid I'll tell King Gilling you plan to kill him."

Toug, who had not thought of that, gaped.

"I won't, of course. The point you fail to grasp is that

I'm a loyal friend. If someone tried to kill him again in my presence, I might interfere. Or not. It would depend on the circumstances."

"It was a scene of indescribable confusion," Idnn had told us the previous evening. "You can't understand what happened if you don't understand that. The torches had gone out, or most had. Sir Svon and Sir Garvaon were fighting the champions His Majesty had matched them against, and others, too, because others had joined the fight. Some were fighting each other, drunken quarrels and settling old scores. His Majesty straightened up as if in a fit. He threw his head back and shook. That's when we knew something was terribly wrong. He bent double, and we slid off his shoulder. A moment later he was lying at our feet. His minister came, and we supposed our screams had brought him, but he told us afterward that an Aelf had said our husband was in danger." Idnn paused, searching my face and Marder's. "He wasn't our husband then. Have we explained that?"

"No!" The Knight of the Leopards could keep silence no longer.

I said, "Proceed, please, Your Majesty."

"It was horrible. Thiazi told us to look after him and disappeared. He'd gone to get people to help carry him into the castle, but we didn't know that. We stood beside him and shouted, trying to keep the rest from stepping on him. Our father came, and Thiazi with a litter and slaves to carry it. They were blind—blind men, and we want to put a stop to it. But they were blind and it was dark and everyone yelling and fighting, and the blind men and Thiazi rolled him onto the litter and they carried him away, with us trying to guide them, and we thought he was dead."

Gerda said gently, "You haven't eaten nothin', Queen

Idnn, when that deer haunch is awfully good. And there's onions! Onions is a real treat up here."

Idnn pecked at her food dutifully.

Watching her, I wished I could paint. The rocks behind her caught the dying light, and she in her diamond diadem and black velvet, with Duke Marder's aged face to her right and the Knight of the Leopards in his leopard-skin pelisse to her left, would have made such a picture as artists dream of.

Woddet whispered, "Are we going there?"

"I believe I am," I replied. "I would not compel you."

"If you go, I go."

"And I," the Knight of the Leopards declared.

Marder looked up from his plate. "We must comprehend the situation. Do you, Sir Able?"

I shook my head, and Marder spoke to Idnn. "Do you know who struck the blow?"

"No." Idnn laid aside the silver-mounted dagger she had produced when we sat down, a bite of venison still impaled on its point. "We were on his shoulder. Some of the . . . of our folk were fighting, and he was commanding them to stop when he was stabbed from behind. It was dark, very dark, though a few torches were still lit."

"That's the key," Marder said. "If we're to help you, Your Majesty—and I for one will do everything in my power—we must grasp it. Questions cannot but seem impertinent, yet I must ask them. Will you forgive me?"

"Certainly." Idnn's fingers warred in her lap.

"We must know, and I am a friend no matter what answer you make. Did you yourself stab him?"

She looked up, her hands extended to the sunset clouds of purple and gold. "Lady of Skai, witness our innocence! If we have done this thing, strip us of all favor!" Slowly she lowered her hands, stared at the palms, and held them up to Marder. "We will not ask whether you've cut off a woman's hands, Your Grace. You have not, we're sure. But if our husband's blood is found on these, you may cut them off and welcome. Or have the headsman do it."

Marder nodded. "I understand, Your Majesty. It had to be asked, though I expected no other reply. Another now, repellent as the first. Who do you think the assassin might be? I understand that you did not see the blow struck and can offer no proof. But have you no conjecture?"

"None, Your Grace."

From the other side of their fire, Hela gave me a significant look. "Sir knight?"

"Yes." I cleared my throat. "Your Majesty, I must speak. Hela there knows all that I intend to tell you. Sir Woddet and Sir Leort know but a part, as do these others save His Grace, who knows nothing of it. Will you hear me out?"

"Gladly," Idnn said, "if it will cast any light on our husband's misfortune."

"It may cast more darkness," I told her. "I'm afraid it will. This chief minister, is he trustworthy?"

Hela muttered, "Is anyone?"

Bold Berthold rumbled, "My stepdaughter talks too much truth, Sir Able. You can trust me, but no Frost Giant can."

Idnn nodded. "Just so. Our husband trusted Thiazi, and we would guess that he was right to do it—Thiazi wouldn't betray him. But he's a son of Angr's. We're a human woman."

"He told you that one of the Aelf had told him King Gilling was in danger?"

"So we said."

"Then I believe I'll trust him in that, at least. An Aelf-maiden came to tell me that her sister had stabbed the king. I told Sir Woddet, Sir Leort, and some others, though I didn't tell them that this woman is of the Fire Aelf. Her name's Uri, and I know her pretty well. Her sister's name is Baki. I know her too."

Hope shone in Idnn's eyes. "This is news indeed!"

"If it's true. I don't trust it."

Marder shook his head ruefully. "Coming from the Aelf? Neither would I." He turned to Idnn. "A new question, Your Majesty. Can the king speak?"

"When we left him, no."

"Then we cannot know whom he believes struck him down, though that would be a most useful thing to know. What of this Thiazi? What does he say?"

"That it was one of our people, one of the Angrborn. There were rebellions when my royal husband ascended to the throne, which a dozen claimed. Most of his reign has been spent putting them down. Thiazi believes a rebel has tried to win by stealth what he could not win by war."

The Knight of the Leopards said, "What of you? What do you believe?"

Idnn sighed. "Let us say first that Thiazi's an adept. His art confirms his opinion, thus we give it great weight."

"Lying spirits," Marder muttered.

The Knight of the Leopards would have spoken, but was silenced by Idnn's upraised hand. "Second we must tell you, Sir Able, that we, too, have been visited by a messenger. We'll speak of that when we're alone.

"Third we should tell all of you that our noble father believes that one of our party struck down our husband. He's loath to say it, but he's our father and we know it's what he believes. He's sick with worry, and we must give weight to his opinion. Our father's a knowing man of wide experience, and an adept himself."

Idnn paused to smile at me. "Lastly, we must give some weight to what Sir Able told us. We'd give it more if he gave it more himself."

"As for me," Marder said, "I give most weight to your own opinion. We have what? The Aelf, the Angrborn, and Lord Beel's folk. Which do you favor?"

Idnn sighed. "None. We—it's one reason we fled."

"We will give you escort to your father's castle or to King Arnthor—wherever you wish to go."

Idnn's eyes flashed. "Do you imagine that we'd abandon our wounded husband? Never! We come in search of aid for him, for knights with the courage to ride to Utgard. Will you come, Sir Able? If you'll come he will live and we triumph. We know it!"

"I can't," I said, "'til there is ice in the Bay of Forcetti. Until then, I have to hold this pass. I'm sorry."

Marder's hard blue eyes searched my face. "What if I release you?"

"I'd go, of course, Your Grace. Do you?"

Marder shook his head. "I'd intended to when I came here—it was part of my purpose. Now I must hear more."

"Then ask," Idnn told him. "Have you any notion how hard we've ridden these past days? Or the dangers we've escaped? For Sir Able alone we'd talk all night."

"He will not be alone," Sir Woddet told her.

The Knight of the Leopards: "Sir Able holds my parole. If he frees me, I'll go with him. If he won't free me, I must go with him."

Hela said softly, "My master has no men-at-arms save my brother, and not a bow save his own. Those the Black Knight brought outnumber good Sir Woddet's and Sir Leort's together. What does the Black Knight say?"

Idnn chewed and swallowed. "That he must hear more. Your Grace, we're learning how famished we are. Ask, and let us eat, and when you're done we'll lay aside our meat."

"Your Majesty, it was not my intent—"

"After that we'll sleep, for we've slept in our saddle these past three nights, and once we fell for sleeping. At sunrise we'll ride north again. Alone if need be."

"We need to speak of that, perhaps." Marder sipped his wine. "Sir Woddet and Sir Leort honor their paroles. I've given none, Sir Able, yet you have not bound me. I give you mine now. I shall remain your prisoner until my ransom is paid, set it as high as you will. Is that sufficient?"

I nodded. "It is, Your Grace, and if you'll free me from my vow, that'll be ransom enough."

Marder shook his head. "I want to know more. There's Sir Leort's question and some of my own. Your Majesty, how did you come to wed King Gilling? Why did you undertake so arduous a journey?"

The blade of Idnn's dagger paused halfway to her mouth. "Brave Sir Leort, you must pardon us. We had forgotten."

"I withdraw my question," the Knight of the Leopards said hastily, "and I regret most heartily any pain it has given you."

Marder said, "Yet we must have an answer. You wanted all my questions, Your Majesty, and now I have another. You cannot name the assassin. Still, it would give you pain even to voice your opinion. Why is that?"

Idnn laid down her fork. "Because so many innocent men may die. You have not been to Utgard, Your Grace?"

Marder shook his head. "No. Never."

"Our folk take slaves from the kingdoms to the south." Idnn's voice grew gentle. "This old couple we see—the woman is chained. Were they slaves in Jotunland?"

"I don't speak proper for a queen," Berthold rumbled, "but you've the right of that." Gerda whispered urgently, and he added, "Your Majesty's got the right of it."

"They blinded you, goodman?"

"Took my eyes. So they done."

"We have hundreds like him in Utgard," Idnn told Marder, "though all are younger and most much younger. It was dark, as we told you, but what is darkness to a blind man? And who had better reason to hate my royal husband?"

"I should not have pressed you for an answer," Marder confessed. "Let us talk no more of this. If the Angrborn came to think as you do, they would slaughter every man. Do all of you who heard Queen Idnn understand?"

"We'll say nothing," Woddet assured him; others nodded.

"We may be wrong," Idnn whispered. "We hope—oh, how we hope!—we're wrong." She paused to collect herself. "We slid from His Majesty's shoulder, as we said. We'd had Mani, but we must have dropped him. We carried His Majesty into the keep, where there were a few lights, and some slave women came with lanterns. We didn't know how badly he was hurt. We didn't even know whether he was still alive, and his blood was crawling everywhere."

I asked, "Where's his wound?"

"In his back."

Idnn laid aside her trencher and rose, and we with her; I had forgotten how small she was, and shuddered when I tried to imagine her in a crowd of fighting, yelling giants.

"Would you— Hela, is that your name?"

"Your Majesty's servant. Perhaps it would be more convenient for Your Majesty if I knelt?"

"No, stand. Stand, and turn your back to them."

Hela did. Rising on tiptoe, Idnn pushed aside the ragged hide Hela wore to show the place.

"On the right," I said, "under the shoulder blade?"

"Yes, that's it. That's it exactly."

Marder said, "Struck from behind by a right-handed foe. If one of us held the dagger, he'd have to be a tall man."

"A very tall man, with a dagger," I said. "I've never seen King Gilling, but I've seen Angrborn, and stabbed a few. They're much bigger than Hela."

Woddet said, "He could've been standing on something."

Marder shook his head. "Not likely."

"And yet," I said, "Lord Beel, who was there, fears it

was one of his party. He joined you, Your Majesty, while you were guarding the fallen king?"

Idnn nodded.

"He was with you, when you carried the king inside?"

"Of course. Our husband was talking then. He'd only been moaning before. He asked our father and Thiazi who had struck him. Our father said he didn't know, and Thiazi that he'd been stabbed by some rebel. We carried him upstairs after that—the slaves did, but we went with them. He was coughing blood, and each time he coughed I thought he was going to die. It was horrible. We were walking behind his litter then, and there'd be great clots of blood. They . . ."

Abruptly, Idnn sat again, and Marder, Woddet, the Knight of the Leopards, Blind Berthold and Gerda, Hela and Heimir, Uns and I resumed our places as well, permitted by her nod.

"We were going to tell you they seemed alive," Idnn said weakly, "but that wasn't really how it was. They were dying. Like—like jellyfish. Did we tell you we'd bandaged him? We had, and there wasn't much blood from his wound, but he kept coughing and coughing."

Marder said, "A sucking wound," and I nodded.

"We got him into bed, all the slaves and Thiazi and our father and we. He said to bar the doors of the castle, you understand. He was afraid the person who'd stabbed him would come in and . . . Finish. That was what he said. Finish.

"Thiazi went to see they were barred; the knights had followed our father in. Sir S-Svon and Sir Garvaon. They'd killed Skeol before the king was struck, and after that had just been trying to save their lives. They'd come up with him, with Master—with Master Papounce and others of our father's folk. Some were hurt, and we bandaged them."

I drank the last of my wine, poured out the lees, and put aside my flagon. "You wish us to return to Utgard with you. I will if I can, but maybe it'd be good for you to tell us about it. What can we do?"

Idnn raised her head. "Our father talked to our husband while Thiazi was gone. We were there and heard it, but took no part. He began by asking our husband whom he could trust, and when our husband said he could trust only Thiazi, our father assured him that he could trust us, saying we had been sent in friendship by our king and would never betray him.

"Our husband was grateful. He was weak, you understand. Very weak, but he thanked our father over and over. Then our father reminded him that Thiazi's magic had said the throne would stand secure if he took you into his service."

She looked at Marder, Woddet, and the Knight of the Leopards. "We don't think you know about that, but it did. Thiazi recited spells and looked into his crystal, and a spirit there said the king must get Sir Able to fight for him or lose his throne. He and Thiazi had told our father, and our father reminded him of it."

Marder asked whether the king had agreed.

"Oh, yes." Idnn drew her black velvet cloak about her more tightly; the sun had vanished behind the mountains of the west, and the wind promised snow. "He wanted our father to send for you, and our father promised he would."

"No one has come," Woddet said.

"We have come. We wed His Majesty next day. It seemed to us—we mean to our husband, our father, and we—that it would be best if the ceremony were witnessed by Thiazi, Thrym, and other Angrborn. We sacrificed to our Overcyns and the Giants of Skai. Only small sacrifices, three fowls and two rabbits, but they were all we had. Our husband . . ."

Marder said, "Yes?"

"He wanted to sacrifice twenty slaves. We were able to dissuade him, telling him that King Arnthor would never come to our aid if he knew we'd offered human beings."

"You hoped for help from Thortower?" Marder asked.

"Yes. Yes, of course we did. We do. We hope that when King Arnthor learns that we, a noblewoman of his realm, have become Queen of Jotunland, he'll send help."

"At last I understand," said the Knight of the Leopards.

"Understand also that silence is best," Marder told him.

I said, "Your father promised King Gilling he would send someone for help. He cannot have intended to send you."

"He'll be half mad with worry," Idnn conceded, "but he will soon persuade Thiazi to view us in his crystal, or view us himself in a basin—you may tell the rest about that if you wish. Then he'll see us here speaking to you, and that we're safe. Sir Garvaon and Sir Svon offered to go, but they were badly hurt. I was terribly afraid my father would let Sir Svon go. He isn't wounded as badly as Sir Garvaon and is younger. He has recovered remarkably. Their squires offered to go in their places, either or both together, but one's been wounded and they're only boys. So we went."

"And came through safely," I remarked.

"By the Lady's grace. We prayed—prayed ever so hard—that she'd let us live 'til our marriage was consummated, and she's given us reason to hope she's granted our prayer. You've been patient, all of you. May we try your patience a bit more? Sir Able, you hold His Grace's parole?"

"I suppose I do, but I'll free him of it whenever he wishes. I ask no ransom."

"Then free him, and we'll beg him to go to King Arnthor and tell him how badly we need his help in Utgard." Idnn turned to Marder and took his hand. "You'll go, won't you, Your Grace? Peace—a peace with Jotunland that will last—is almost within our grasp, and we'll bless you to the end of our days."

"You are a most excellent queen, Your Majesty."

Marder shook himself as Gylf would when he left a river. "So good, so beautiful and brave, that it's a great temptation to give you whatever you ask, no matter how unwise. Ten years ago, I probably would have."

He rummaged in a pocket of his jerkin. "Let us arrange lesser matters first. Sir Able, I have money in earnest of my ransom. You have given me fealty, have you not? You must obey my instructions. Take this and do not argue. We must ride tomorrow, and we should ride early."

The purse I had refused earlier landed in my lap.

"For the remainder of my ransom, you will have my favor as long as I live, and a seat in my council." He cleared his throat. "Now you're to answer yes. Are those things, with the foreign coins, sufficient?"

"Your Grace—" I began.

"I thank you for your most gracious acceptance," Marder told me firmly. "In return, I free you from your oath. You have held the pass indeed, but you have held it long enough."

Uns started to clap, but I silenced him.

"I ride north at first light in service to the Queen of Jotunland," Marder continued. "I take it that you, my loyal vassal, will ride with me?"

"Joyfully, Your Grace."

Woddet exclaimed, "And I with Sir Able, if he'll have me." To which the Knight of the Leopards added, "And I!"

Marder thanked them both. "As for your errand to King Arnthor, Your Majesty, my herald can perform it better than I could. I'll send him in the morning, south at the same time the rest of us go north. But I warn you, whatever help our king sends will probably arrive too late. Men will have to be collected and supplied. You yourself rode from Thortower to this point on the border of Jotunland, did you not?"

Silently, Idnn nodded.

"How long did it take you, Your Majesty?"

"Two months." Idnn's answer was so softly voiced that Blind Berthold cupped his ear to hear her.

"Before winter set in?"

She nodded.

"My herald must reach King Arnthor first. Preparations will not began until he does." Marder tugged his beard. "I told Sir Able once that he was to hold this pass until there was ice in the bay. The bay will be clear before we can have any hope of help from King Arnthor. We will have to settle this ourselves, and we'll need every sword for it."

Next day, still early of a dark morning, when Cloud was eating league after league of the Plain of Jotunland with a swinging walk that pressed every other animal in the column, and Heimir and Hela were loping at my right and left like the Valfather's wolves, I felt Thiazi's gaze. I touched spur to Cloud and drew Eterne; and so it was that Thiazi, looking up from his crystal, could report to Beel (and to Toug and Mani, who had just come in) that Idnn and I were riding north at the head of an army.

CHAPTER FIFTEEN
GIANT'S BLOOD!

Toug sat on the stone floor of the guardroom and listened to Thiazi, Garvaon, and Svon argue with Schildstarr. No one except Wistan paid the least attention to him; if they had, they might have thought him inattentive. Although he heard and considered all that was said, his eyes remained fixed on the darkest corner of the room.

"Won't stand," Schildstarr repeated stubbornly.

"Forever?" Thiazi's bass voice was smooth. "You're correct. It need stand only until His Majesty recovers."

"How do we know he's not cold?" Schildstarr leaned forward as he spoke, and his huge chair creaked under two tons of muscle and bone.

"You asked before," Thiazi said. "You know our answer. I am his chief minister. If he were dead, I would declare a year of mourning for our fallen king and hail a successor. If he dies, I'll do exactly that. He isn't dead, and by Geror's blessing may recover. You call yourself his loyal subject. Very well, he has need of you. Show your loyalty."

"Give me sight a' him and I will." Schildstarr sounded as intransigent as ever.

Garvaon said, "He's asleep. No man's wounds heal unless he sleeps. You must know that—I see your scars."

Schildstarr's laughter seemed to shake the walls. "Nae half a' 'em!"

Mani lay curled in the dark corner Toug watched, his luminous green eyes opening and closing; the shadowy figure behind him seemed Idnn at times, at others an ancient crone, and at still others both, or mere emptiness. And though the fire on the broad hearth had faded to smoke and ashes and the windowless guardroom was freezing, Toug was sweating. Beyond or beside his fear he wondered whether Wistan could see the witch, too, and decided he could not.

"I've questions of my own," Svon told Schildstarr. "We have answered yours. When the king wakes, we'll take you to him, provided he consents to see you. I'll answer one more, one you haven't asked but should. I think it likely that he will consent. Do you concur, My Lord? Sir Garvaon?"

"I do," Thiazi said; and Garvaon, "Yes."

"In which case you can do one of two things," Svon continued. "You can wait here like a sensible man, or you can leave this castle and return tonight with the others. You're not a prisoner."

Schildstarr snorted.

"You think we couldn't hold you, and no doubt you're right. But since we don't intend to try, it's neither here nor there." Leaning back in the oversized chair on which he sat cross-legged, Svon shaped a tower from his fingers. "You're the king's loyal subject. Does your loyalty extend to the queen as well?"

"King Gilling's nae wed."

"You're wrong. I won't try to prove it to you. You wouldn't accept my evidence, and there's no need since he'll tell you himself when he wakes. But when you hear it from his own mouth—as you will—will you be loyal to her? She's a human woman."

"One a' you little hotlanders?" Schildstarr rubbed his huge jaw.

"Yes," Svon said, "and your queen, whether you're ready to believe it or not. When you believe it—when you have proof of it—will you obey her?"

"Depend on wha' she wants, is my view."

Garvaon grunted and would have pushed his chair back, had chair and table been smaller. "You'll obey your queen if it suits you. Spoken like a true Son of Angr."

"You pick chains and lock 'em on you." Schildstarr's tone carried deadly hatred. "My folk dinna take to chains. Somebody else has got to do it."

"As you say. Someone does."

Thiazi raised a hand. "Enough!"

"I agree," Svon said. "We've need of friends here. We have plenty of foes already. I meant no insult, Schildstarr, and imply nothing. Do you know who struck down the king?"

Slowly the Frost Giant's head swung from side to side. "I was there. Close by, only I dinna see it. There's tittletattle noo. This one and that one, and some braggin's wha' I hear. Mebbe yes. Mebbe no. I don't know."

"Is anyone preparing to storm the castle?"

Cunning crept into Schildstarr's eyes. "There's talk. Tomorrow, mebbe. Why we come."

"Eighteen of you Angrborn?"

"Nineteen wi' me. Good fighters every one a' us. How many knights you got?"

"It's not we who have them, but your king."

"We have Angrborn, knights, men-at-arms, and archers enough to defend His Majesty's home against a determined assault," Thiazi told Schildstarr, "and defend it we will. My fear is that young bloods, foolishly contemptuous of those smaller than themselves, will assail us without reflection. That could ignite a new rebellion."

Schildstarr rose, a process that consumed some time. "You've nae a' us."

"That is not true," Thiazi told him.

"Nae muckle to eat, neither. Month's food?" He looked from face to face. "We might fetch some."

"Lord Thiazi. Sir Garvaon. Sir Svon." A slender woman dressed as slaves were had appeared in the doorway; a breath passed before Toug recognized her. "His Majesty has regained consciousness. He calls for the queen."

The corner Toug had watched was empty. Mani looked behind him and grinned.

Baki stepped hastily out of the way when Schildstarr and Thiazi hurried out, and curtsied to Svon, Garvaon, and Wistan as they passed.

Toug remained behind. "Is this a trick?"

Baki curtsied again, this time to him. "La, sir, and I am but a simple girl."

"He's really awake?"

"Yes. That is good for you, I think."

"It would be better for me if he died." For a moment, Toug was sick with fear. "I'm going to kill him, and since I am the man I am, I'll have to do it in a fair fight." The words came of their own volition, and the pitiful thing in him that cringed and wept was locked away. "That means a fight after he has recovered, a fight in which he has a chance to defend himself. I'm not looking forward to it."

"Lord Toug," Baki said, and knelt at his feet.

"Don't do that," Toug told her. "What if someone should see us?"

"I see you." Mani yawned. "I'm wondering whether you see yourself."

"Stand up, please." Toug took Baki's hand. "You wanted to bring Sir Able, so you could take him to Aelfrice because you can't fight . . ." He had lost the name, and groped for it.

"Garsecg, Lord. Setr. We can fight him, and fight those who cling to him still. But we cannot win that fight without someone like Sir Able. Or you."

Mani stepped in to rescue Toug. "What will Sir Svon say when he looks around for you?"

Toug gulped and nodded. "You're right. They're going to see the king. I better hurry."

He found Wistan waiting at the bottom of the stairs. "You were talking privately to that slave girl," Wistan said. "I stayed away, so I couldn't overhear you."

"Thanks."

"This is a funny place, isn't it?"

They began to climb as Toug agreed.

"There were a couple things just now." Wistan cleared his throat.

"Sir Garvaon and Sir Svon talking to that giant, you mean? I liked it better when we fought them."

"So did I." For a moment Wistan appeared to contemplate a change of subject. "Do you trust him?"

"No. Never. I'd sooner trust Seaxneat."

Wistan stopped. "Who's that?"

"A man I used to know. A thief."

"I see."

"A coward, too. I didn't think so then, because he talked so brave. Now I know he was trying to make himself believe it, but I believed him. I was a lot younger."

"I understand," Wistan said, and offered Toug a hand up.

Toug shook his head. "It wasn't really very long ago. It just seems like a long time. So much has happened."

They climbed for a minute or more; then Wistan said, "She's not bad-looking, is she?"

"Queen Idnn?"

"No, the redheaded girl." Wistan grinned.

"Oh. Baki."

"So many girls have dark hair. There's nothing wrong with that, but red hair or yellow hair makes a nice change."

Toug said nothing.

"There's all the freckles, of course. A lot of people don't like them, but I say what's wrong with freckles? She kept her eyes down, did you notice? Maybe not with you, but when I was in there, and our masters and the giants."

"No," Toug admitted. "Not with me."

"When they won't look you in the eye, it's because they don't want you to know what they're thinking."

"I didn't know that."

"So you know what they're thinking about. Only I wanted to say I'm not going to pick your flowers." Wistan mounted the next couple of steps.

"Don't try to pick that one," Toug told him.

"I won't. We're friends, right? We'd better be, since we're the only squires here."

This time Toug accepted the hand Wistan offered.

"But there's things I wanted to ask. Like, the voices. After everybody left? The two giants and our masters and me. So that left you and the slave girl."

Toug devoted his attention to the next step.

"I couldn't hear what you said, but I could hear voices—three people. One was you and one was the girl. There was somebody else with a thin, rough voice, too."

"What do you think the king will say?" Toug paused to catch his breath. "About Schildstarr and eighteen more?"

Wistan shrugged. "Another thing. I don't think this will bother you."

"I'm not bothered," Toug declared.

"There was something in the corner. Did you see it?"

"The king's cat."

"Is it the king's? I didn't know. It's a good thing you told me, I'll have to leave it alone. No, I meant something else, something in the shadow there."

"There are lots of things that live in shadows."

"You saw it, too. Was that the voice I heard?"

"Yes," Toug said, "what you saw in the corner."

Again, Wistan was silent for a time. Toug climbed as fast as he could, hoping to outdistance him.

"You were Sir Able's page. That's what I heard. Then when Sir Able made Sir Svon a knight, he made you Sir Svon's squire. Sir Able isn't like most people."

Toug agreed.

"There's something of that about you, too."

The rush of pride Toug felt was almost overwhelming.

"I'm your senior. If you won't acknowledge that, we can have it out right now."

"You were a squire before I was," Toug agreed.

Wistan nodded. "As senior squire I order you to tell me who the third voice belonged to."

"I already have," Toug said.

"The thing in the corner. Sometimes it looked like a woman. What was it?"

"A ghost, I think."

"What's its name?"

"I don't know."

"We gently born fight with swords." Wistan's voice was cold. "And we give others a chance to draw. Draw yours."

"I don't want to fight," Toug declared, "and I surely don't want to kill you."

"Coward!" Wistan's hand was on the hilt.

Toug took a step backward that put his back against cold stone. "I yield."

"I'd fight you," Wistan was furious, "and I'd beat you."

"I know it," Toug said. "I yield."

"You fought the Angrborn."

Toug nodded. "So did you. I know that, too."

"But you won't fight me?"

"No." Toug shook his head. "We may both have to fight the giants again soon. Can I keep my weapons? I swear I'll never employ them treacherously."

Wistan's grin was triumphant. "Hand them over."

Toug nodded and unbuckled his sword belt.

Wistan held out a hand. His grin widened.

"She's not a sword," Toug told him. "She's a mace. Sword Breaker's her name." He paused, caressing the hilt. "I'll give her to you, but I've got to tell you something. When Sir Able and I were boys, another boy and I tried to rob him. He beat us and took our weapons."

"You're lying! Sir Able's much older than you."

Toug nodded. "He is now, and when we met again he didn't remember me. Or if he did, he didn't say anything."

Wistan did not nod.

"Sword Breaker used to be his," Toug added as he handed her over. "He gave her to me. I told him I didn't deserve her, but I didn't say why. Maybe that's why I'm losing her like this."

Wistan was examining Sword Breaker.

"I hope you'll take care of her. She really was his."

"There's a cistern in the cellar," Wistan told Toug, "and they say it's so deep it's never been full. I'm going to drop this in there, the first chance I get."

Toug watched Wistan climb until he was out of sight.

* * *

Toug was refused admission to the king's bedchamber; but he argued so persistently with the giant on guard that Svon overheard him and let him in.

It was such a sight as he had never imagined, a room bigger than the biggest barn in Glennidam and rich as a casket of gems: the huge gilt bed, its surface higher than Toug's head, on which the king lay pale as his own sheets, propped by silk pillows the size of mattresses; the gold-embroidered bed hangings of crimson velvet (more cloth and richer cloth than Toug had ever seen) drawn back by massy chains of gold; Schildstarr (rough as a wolf, filthy as a cur, and thrice as big as anyone had a right to be) leaning over that bed as attentively as the best nurse; Thiazi, reserved and alert, his face tight with secrets; the resolute knights and the swarming slaves straining to see and hear.

A slave drew Toug aside. "He sez th' queen was wit' him inside the stuns'ls, only she warn't, 'cause these gals," the hand gripping Toug's arm tightened, "what kin see, they'd o' seen her, wouldn't they, mate?"

Toug managed to nod. "You'd have heard, too, wouldn't you? If the queen came in they'd say good morning, I'm sure, or something like that, so you men would know to kneel."

"Aye. That's so." Pouk's whisper declined until Toug could scarcely hear him, though Pouk's lips were at Toug's ear. "Under th' big bed, mate."

Toug nodded and edged nearer the vast bedstead, waiting for a moment when no slave woman was looking at him.

"You're a good friend," the king was saying; and his voice was the sound of that sad and weary wind which stirs the dead leaves blanketing the dead, warning of cold rain. "We'll remember," the wind moaned. "Remember. Remember . . ."

"Your Majesty must not tire yourself." That was Thiazi, like Schildstarr, bending above the bed.

"The question is who's to command, Your Majesty." The stern voice was Garvaon's. "We obey His Lordship. We're his men, and our men obey us. We obey My Lord Thiazi now because His Lordship has ordered us to. But if Schildstarr and the Angrborn he says he can bring us will obey only you . . ."

Garvaon let the sentence hang, but there was no reply from the king.

Schildstarr chuckled in a way that made Toug shudder. Still, no one spoke.

"Rum, ain't it?" Pouk whispered.

All eyes were on the king. Nodding, Toug ducked and stepped under the bed, where lips brushed his.

"Lord." Having kissed him lightly, Baki knelt.

"I wouldn't, if I were you." Mani sounded smug and knowing. "Females always make a lot of noise, even if you don't. Someone's bound to look under here then."

Toug, who wasn't certain he knew what Mani was talking about, sat on carpet so thick and soft that he felt he might sink into it. "Pouk said you wanted to see me."

"I do, Lord. Lord, that boy Wistan has the sword that is not a sword. Did he steal it from you?"

"He won it from me," Toug confessed. "He wanted to fight, because I wouldn't tell him about Mani and the witch. He thanks I should obey him as if he were already a knight, and I was his squire. He's not a knight, and I'm no squire of his. I wouldn't break my promise to Mani, and if I had told him about the witch it would have been something else. And something after that, doing his work for him or whatever, and I could see that, too. I told him about the witch and did it in a way that made him think he'd heard her when he'd really heard Mani."

Mani said, "It's almost the same, after all."

Baki nodded; her eyes were candle flames. "You did not tell him about me?"

"No. No, I didn't. I didn't tell him anything else, except that Sword Breaker had belonged to Sir Able."

"As did I," Mani said.

"He was going to push me and push me." Toug found that he was explaining to himself as much as to Baki. "Push 'til I was his slave or 'til I fought. If we'd fought, he'd have been killed or wounded—or else I would. He thought he'd beat me, and he may have been right."

Baki said, "I do not think that."

"Thanks. He—he's never lost a fight. That's what I think, anyhow. When that's how it's been for you, you keep pushing 'til you do. I used to be like that too. The funny thing is that nobody's a good fighter 'til he's lost at least one fight, and won one, too."

Mani said, "Well, you seem to have lost this one."

Toug shook his head. "I lost Sword Breaker, and I hate that. But I didn't lose the fight, because there wasn't any. I was dumb. I thought if I yielded he might let me keep my weapons and neither of us would get killed. I'll know better next time."

Baki said, "I will steal it back for you, if I can. We helped Sir Able like that."

"It wouldn't be honorable." Toug hesitated. "Wistan said he was going to drop it in the cistern, but he went up the stairs. I thought he'd decided to throw it into the moat. But it's outside the wall, and we don't have the wall, just this keep. Can you stop him from doing something like that? Dropping it in the cistern?"

"That would be the best thing that could happen, Lord. I could get it for you without theft. Anyone may pick up what another throws away. Let us see what he does with it."

Toug thanked her and meant every word of it.

Mani said, "Baki has things to tell you. So do I."

"Just one, Lord. I have mentioned my sister Uri."

"Was that the one who didn't want me to heal you?"

Baki nodded. "You know my heart's desire—it is that

Sir Able lead us against Setr. You promised to help with that, just as I promised to help you to do your duty."

"We've both promised to help Ulfa and Pouk get out of here," Toug reminded her, "and Mani said he'd help us."

"The keep's surrounded," Mani remarked somewhat dryly. "I could get out and so could Baki. None of you could."

"I didn't know that. Have the rebels laid siege to it?"

Baki shook her head. "They are only concerned for their king, and curious. Let me get to my news, Mani."

"I wouldn't think of preventing you."

"My sister Uri has been talking to Beel, who knows Sir Able is riding to aid you. Mani says you know, too, Lord."

"Yes. Thiazi saw it in his crystal and told us."

"He told Lord Beel as well, it seems. He is overjoyed. Now he hopes for a happy end to all his efforts, the throne secure, and peace between the Angrborn and Arnthor's folk."

"I don't see anything wrong with that," Toug said.

"Just this, Lord. My sister has told him I intend to take Sir Able from him and send him to Aelfrice. A brief sojourn in Aelfrice will mean a lengthy absence here."

Toug nodded.

"Lord Beel is determined to prevent it. If he learns that you and your sister have promised help, it will go ill with you." Toug felt Baki's hand on his, hot and as light as a butterfly's wing. "I do not think he will have you killed, or even get the king to. Sir Able and Queen Idnn would be sure to hear of it. But he will keep you from Sir Able, and send you into danger if he can."

Toug said, "Good."

"You have lost the weapon Sir Able gave you, and are smarting still. Sleep will cure it. You have been warned."

"I have," Toug said, "and to tell the truth, I feel I've gotten wonderful news. I need a battle cry, and Spears of the Maidens will be it 'til I get a better one."

"You ridicule me."

"Never. Never! Oh, Baki . . ."

Mani coughed as cats do. "Excuse it. Hairball. Let me give my news, and I'll leave you two alone. My mistress took the guise of my other mistress when she spoke to you on the stairs, remember? It seems she's become fond of it and has been wearing it to talk to King Gilling, and now he thinks Queen Idnn's here. And that's—"

Something dark, round, and wet fell with a plash on Mani's head, and he jumped backward snarling, every hair erect. "Blood! Giant's blood!"

A second drop, as big as a cherry, fell where Mani had been sitting. Bent nearly double, Toug hurried to the velvet ruffle that had curtained their assembly and ducked through.

CHAPTER SIXTEEN

INTO DANGER

Ah, there you are." Svon caught Toug by the shoulder. "By the Lady! What were you up to under there?"

"The king's bleeding," Toug gasped. "It's soaked the mattress and it's dripping through."

Ulfa heard him and called, "The stitches pulled out!" In a moment, Pouk and half a dozen other men had climbed the bed to furl woolen blankets thicker than carpets.

"They'll tend him," Svon said, drawing Toug to one side. "We should go to the battlements. Thiazi and Sir Garvaon are up there with Schildstarr." As they hurried out, Svon added, "I don't suppose you know where Sir Garvaon's squire is? He seems to have disappeared, and Garvaon's asking for him."

"I'll look for him." Toug hesitated, recalling things said upon the stairs. "I'd like to find him myself."

"Later." They started up yet another stair built for Angrborn. "Thiazi wants Schildstarr to show himself to the Frost Giants outside," Svon explained. "They haven't seen many of their own kind here since the king was struck, and some of them claim we're holding him captive."

Toug nodded and panted, his torn face throbbing under its soiled bandages.

"Schildstarr wants to tell his giants to come to the big doors—that they'll be admitted. It means we have to scrape together enough men to keep hundreds of others from forcing their way in."

"Wouldn't it be better if Schildstarr's giants came back to the sally port?"

"A thousand times, but Schildstarr won't agree to it. This is going to give him lots of prestige. He wants to milk it, and the king wants us to let him have his way."

"What will we do if the crowd gets in?"

Behind them Beel said, "We will do all we can to save my son-in-law's life, Squire. If they see how badly he's hurt, that alone may doom him by beginning a new rebellion. Still worse, they may kill him outright. A quarter if not half of them would be delighted to see him dead, and little courage is needed to murder a man who's gravely wounded already."

On the battlement, Schildstarr was addressing the crowd—about three thousand, Toug decided, and possibly more—gathered on the enormous stair that led up to the brazen doors of Utgard, and in the bailey at the foot of that stair. "Thiazi's tellin' you facts." It was like stones sliding from a mountain. "The king's sore struck, but he'll have me and mine wit' him night and day. My own to the door, every one a' you, an' nae one nae ours."

There was much more after that, but Toug soon found its hoarseness and hatefulness wearying, and shut his ears to it.

The sea of savage faces below and the dizzy abyss of freezing air filled him with sick dismay, and he jumped down from the crenel into which he had clambered to see them.

After that there was nothing to do but pull his cloak about him and heartily wish that he were out of the wind, in a room with a fire; the turret room where he had slept with Mani seemed a haven of comfort as he stood on the battlement.

"Have you seen Wistan?" That was Garvaon.

Toug shook his head. "Not lately, sir." Belatedly, it occurred to Toug that Wistan was securing Sword Breaker and my old sword belt, in a place where they would not be discovered by chance. Or taking them to the cistern. "Would you like me to find him, Sir Garvaon?"

"No, you'll have to run with my message yourself. I'll tell Sir Svon—don't worry about that. Go to the guardroom and tell the sergeant he's to pull the entire guard off post. Every man. Understand?"

"Yes, Sir Garvaon. Every man-at-arms in the guard, and every bowman. The whole guard."

"Right. They're to assemble in the big hall, and wait. Get moving."

Toug did, but Beel stopped him on the stairs. "You're overworked, Squire."

"I like to keep busy, Your Lordship, and this gets me out of that wind."

"No small consideration, I agree. Tonight you'll have various little tasks to do for Sir Svon. Polishing his mail and so on. Isn't that right?"

Wondering what Beel was about to ask, Toug nodded. "Yes, Your Lordship, all the things I do every night."

"Do you know where we're lodged? Where Queen Idnn and I were lodged before she became queen?"

"A floor above the great hall, Your Lordship. Left at the top of the stair. Is it the second door?"

Beel nodded. "Exactly. I must speak with you tonight when your work is done. Knock, and you'll be admitted."

"I will, Your Lordship." Toug turned to go.

"Wait. I won't order you to lie to Sir Svon. But there will be no need to tell him about this unless he inquires."

Toug agreed that there would not be, heartily wishing that he had never left the battlement.

Marder had decided that the largest tent, the pavilion he had brought for his own use, should be Idnn's; the lack of serving women was a problem not so easily overcome. Idnn agreed readily to be served by Gerda and Bold Berthold, but flatly refused to accept Hela and Heimir. "We fear them," she told me. "Call us cowardly. We know you fear nothing."

I shook my head. "I know you too well to think you cowardly, Your Majesty."

"We fear her wit and his lack of any. Brave as Thunor, you men say, and cunning as a Frost Giant. They are not all cunning as we know. But those who are, are slippery as eels, and your Hela is her father's daughter. Besides, she'd sell her virtue for a groat, if she had a jot of it."

I waited.

"Gerda can help us dress and her husband is better than a man with eyes—we don't have to worry about his seeing us dressing and he's too old for rape. But we don't think he can put up the pavilion by himself, or take it down either. Duke Marder's men put it up tonight. We don't want to have to beg help every night. You men say that women are always asking help anyway. And if that's not entirely true, it's not entirely false. Do you think we like it?"

I shook my head.

"Correct. Still, we're begging, just as we begged you to come to Utgard." The dark eyes that had flashed like gems softened. "It's easy, asking you. There's something about you that says even a queen needn't be ashamed of asking your help."

"That's good."

"So lend us Uns? Please? We ask it as a great favor, and only 'til we reach Utgard. You'll still have Hela and Heimir—or have you loaned Hela to Sir Woddet? But you'll have Heimir. Uns too, anytime you need him."

"I'm honored. You may have Uns, of course. Have him as long as he'll serve you, if you want. But I can't help being curious. His Grace brought eight servingmen. He'd lend you seven if you so much as hinted you wanted them. Why Uns?"

Idnn sighed. "Because he's yours, and closer to you than anyone else."

"You may have him, Your Majesty. But you're wrong about his being closest to me. Bold Berthold is closer, and so is Gylf." I laid my hand on Gylf's head.

Idnn smiled. "Berthold we have already, and dogs are not so easily borrowed. You'll tell him? It's only until we get to Utgard, as we said."

"Certainly, Your Majesty." I stepped back, expecting to be dismissed.

"Wait! Sit down. Please, good Sir Able, hear us out. The door is open—no one will think us compromised if we talk for an hour." Idnn's voice fell. "We must tell you."

"As Your Majesty commands." I sat on the carpet before Idnn's folding chair.

"We told you yesterday we'd had a visitor."

I nodded. "An Aelf?"

"No. One of our people. An Angrborn. You weren't long in Jotunland, Sir Able, yet you must have seen something of it. Did nothing seem odd to you?"

I shrugged. "A dozen things."

"We won't trouble you to name them. You saw our people, our giants, and their slaves?"

"Yes, Your Majesty. Of course."

"Giantesses?"

I cast my mind back; for me, it had been long ago. "I was in Bymir's house, but he had no wife and no children."

"His Majesty," Idnn told me, "has no children. And no wife but us. The wives and children of the rest are hidden. The girls will remain hidden throughout their lives, the boys 'til they are old enough to understand that they're hidden, and where they are hidden, and why. Then they're put out."

"If I were to ask where—"

"We could not tell you. There's a women's country. We call it Jotunhome; scholars say Vollerland, the Land of Wise Women. Because we're His Majesty's wife, we are ruler of Jotunhome. Not just Queen of Jotunhome, but monarch. They came on our wedding night, while our husband groaned and bled in our bed."

I suppose I nodded. "I see . . ."

"You don't. You don't even think you do—you're too wise for that. If we'd ordered a guard of women to come with us, running beside our horse as Hela and Heimir run beside yours, we could have had them. But we'd have been attacked, and we wouldn't be here." Idnn sighed. "They can fight, they say, and knowing how they live we know it must be so."

That night, when all the tasks Idnn had given him were done and everyone was asleep, Uns came to my fire. Heimir was asleep, his big body half covered by his bearskin. As Uns watched I saddled Cloud, whistled for Gylf, and galloped north across the night sky. All this Uns told me afterward.

"Be seated," Beel told Toug. "We need not stand on ceremony, you and I."

"I'll stand just the same," Toug said, "if it please Your Lordship. I'd be ashamed to sit in your presence."

"As you wish. You must be tired, though. The stairs of this castle would tire anyone."

Toug did not reply.

"My task is dangerous, but it shouldn't take long. You help Sir Svon, don't you, when he has charge of the guard?"

"Yes, Your Lordship."

"Thus the sentries are accustomed to obeying you. You know we fear an assault on this castle. Not a mere crowd hammering the doors and yammering to see the king. We've had plenty of that already. But a serious assault by rebels."

Toug nodded wearily. "I understand, Your Lordship."

"Have you ever seen a siege, Squire Toug? A proper one, I mean, directed by a king or great lord, with sappers?"

"No, Your Lordship. I haven't."

"I didn't think so. There are all sorts of engines that can be employed. Catapults, for example. Wooden towers on wheels, a mole, and so forth and so on. I've taken part in a siege like that." Beel laced his fingers. "We need fear nothing of that kind. His Majesty—I refer to my son-in-law—will have recovered long before such devices could reduce this keep. What we must fear is a sudden assault. Thus the guards. Thus I'm delighted that we have Schildstarr and his Angrborn, in spite of all the trouble they've given."

Toug, who wished that Schildstarr and his Angrborn were in Muspel, nodded loyally.

"Weak though we are, no assault can succeed without rams and scaling ladders—long ladders that can be put against our walls to let the attackers to reach the battlements and upper windows. Since the attackers would be Angrborn, such ladders would have to be very large."

Feeling he was expected to nod again, Toug did.

"Very large indeed, and strongly built. Have you a stick, Squire?"

"A stick, Your Lordship? No, Your Lordship."

"Get one. A stick about so long, eh?" Beel's hands measured the length of a war arrow. "If you're seen, you must feign blindness. A blind slave wandering that town beyond the walls should arouse no suspicion."

"Your Lordship wishes me to go out tonight to look for scaling ladders."

Beel smiled. "Will you do it, Squire?"

"When Your Lordship wishes it? I'll go at once."

"Not quite so fast as that, please." Beel raised a hand. "I not only wish to find these ladders, if in fact ill-intentioned persons among the Angrborn are preparing them, but to learn the identities of these persons."

Toug nodded. "I'll do my best, Your Lordship."

For a moment, Beel appeared troubled. "You're tired. It cannot be otherwise. Fatigue makes us careless. If you're careless tonight you may be caught and killed."

Toug stepped backward. "Queen Idnn left on horseback, Your Lordship, and she must have ridden through town, since we know she reached Sir Able. I doubt that it's dangerous."

"They may have been less well organized then."

Beel waited for Toug to speak; seconds ticked by, and at last Beel said, "Go then. Good luck."

Toug thanked him, and went out—stopping abruptly when he saw Wistan in the corridor.

"If you're going out," Wistan said, "I'm going in."

Toug shut the door behind him. "Why?"

"He sent for me." Wistan yawned and stretched. "Now get out of my way."

Toug's fist caught the side of his neck. A moment later Toug had seized his doublet. His forehead hit Wistan's nose with all the force he could give it. He jerked his left knee up, and when Wistan bent double, clubbed the back of Wistan's neck with the side of his fist. "I ought to kick you," he muttered when Wistan lay at his feet, "but I'll let you off this time. Next time, you get kicked."

The dark stair built for giants seemed less dark when he went down it and far less wearying. On the guardroom level, he found that the sentry at the sally port nearest the stair was a bowman he knew, and greeted him cheerfully.

"You still up, Squire Toug? It's gettin' late."

"Oh, the night's hardly begun." Toug grinned, and then, recalling Wistan, stretched and yawned. "I suppose I'll feel it in the morning, but when I said sleep Nott heard leap. How long have you been on post, Arn?"

"Just got here."

"That's good. I have to run an errand. When I come back I'll knock three times, and then twice. Like this." Toug demonstrated, rapping the iron door with his knuckles. "Let me in when you hear my knock."

"Yes, sir." The bowman refrained from asking questions.

"It could be a while, so tell your relief." Toug lifted the bar and tugged at the oversized iron door.

The passage would have been cramped for an Angrborn but seemed spacious to Toug in the moment before the door shut. In the dark it was neither great nor small, only forbidding. One hand he kept on the rough stones; with the other he groped the air, wondering whether his eyes could adjust to a dark so profound, and at last concluding that no eyes could. Too late, he recalled the stick Beel had suggested.

"If I'd had a stick," he told himself, "or a bow like Sir Able's, I could have beaten Wistan with it." It would not have been honorable, perhaps, but he found he no longer cared much about honor where Wistan was concerned. Wistan had a sword. Could it have been dishonorable to use a stick when the other had a sword? For two steps, Toug weighed the matter before concluding that it could not.

The enormous bailey seemed bright with starlight as well as white with snow. He had planned to lurk in the darkness of the passageway until he saw a chance to slip out unseen. There was no need. The snow, pristine in spots, was dented and rutted in others by the feet of Frost Giants; but the giants who had left their footprints had withdrawn to their beds, leaving the snow to him. It creaked under his rough, new, too-large boots so loudly that he expected to hear a sentry sound the alarm. There had been four at the bronze double doors atop the entrance stair—a man-at-arms, a bowman, and two armed servants. These were reinforced now by two of Schildstarr's Angrborn; but it seemed that no one had heard him, and with those doors closed and barred they had no way of seeing him. Pursued only by the hanging ghost of his own breath, he trotted toward the distant gate.

The guards who had saluted Thrym when Thrym had brought him to Utgard were gone. The gate, through which two score knights might have ridden abreast, stood wide open. Beyond the long black arch of the bridge across the moat, the clumsy overlarge houses of Angrborn (windowless or nearly) showed no gleam of light.

Panting, Toug stopped to study the sullen mountain that was Utgard's keep. Near its top, a crimson glow showed that some slave still fed a bedroom fire. For a moment he stood motionless, staring up at the tiny beacon, a constricted slit as remote as a star. It was eclipsed. He waved and waved again, and at last turned away, knowing his sister had seen him, that she too had waved, though he had not seen her face.

The houses of Utgard were three times the size of the biggest barns, built of planks overlapped and fastened with pegs or great black square-headed spikes; this Toug learned by running his hands over several when even by starlight he noticed their prickly appearance. Although bigger than many a manor, they huddled against the gaping moat like beggars' huts and were dwarfed to insignificance.

Unseen and seeing no one, he passed from house to house. Scaling ladders big and strong enough to hold the weight of Angrborn would require massive timbers. Scaling ladders long enough to let Angrborn attain the battlements of Utgard would have to be a bowshot long. Huge as the houses were, none could have held such ladders; he passed them with growing confidence, reflecting that he could return to the keep in another hour with his honor intact, and report to Beel next morning that he had searched diligently but found nothing.

A shadow, it seemed, flitted from one of the hulking houses to another. He blinked, and it was gone; yet he felt sure he had seen it. Less boldly, he moved to the next house and the next, then paused, pulling up the hood of his cloak.

The shadow moved again, a shadow much smaller than a giant—indeed, smaller than he. He flattened himself against a wall, grateful for the pegs that poked his back but broke up his silhouette. The shadow did not wholly vanish: he could see it, darker black, in the shadow of a house.

It moved, and something moved with it, something much larger, something even less distinct. An arm, a huge and twisted hand—

"No!" Toug shouted. "No, Org! Don't!"

The small shadow froze and he sprinted toward it. He glimpsed frightened eyes in a pale face and picked the owner of that face up without breaking stride.

At a noise from the house he passed he dodged down a new street, one so narrow it seemed impossible for Angrborn to walk it, then chose a new street at random and stopped to set his burden down.

"What was *that*?" The voice was a girl's.

"Org." Toug gulped freezing air. "He's a . . . I don't know. A kind of animal, I guess. He's sort of a pet of Sir Svon's. I—we . . . Who are you?"

"Well, I'm me. Etela." (Her head came nearly to his chin.) "You got eyes."

"I'll take you home. You'd better get inside before you meet Org again—he might not remember."

"Are you from the castle?"

Toug nodded.

" 'Cause you've got eyes 'n our men don't, 'less they're new. Not even then, mostly." Etela paused. "If you're one of the ones that have the king, I can tell you."

"Tell me what?"

"Well, 'bout the shovels 'n picks they're making. They done lots, 'n going to be hundreds 'n thousands."

"Is that what you came out at night for?"

"Uh-huh. Mama said tell you. Are you a knight?"

"No, but my master is. Where do you live, Etela?"

"Master's house. I'll show you." She set off. "I'm not 'fraid now 'cause you're with me. See how brave I am?"

"You wanted to tell us about the shovels."

"Uh-huh. Mama says they're going to dig 'n pile up dirt on the castle 'til they bury it."

"Nobody could do that," Toug objected.

"Well, it's what she says. Only nobody's s'posed to know. I'm scared of 'em, but I'm scared worse of that Org what tried to g-g-grab me."

Her teeth were chattering. Toug picked her up again and wrapped his cloak about her. "I'll carry you awhile, and we'll both stay warmer. What's your master's name?"

"Logi. Aren't I heavy?"

"You don't hardly weigh anything. How old are you?"

" 'Most old enough to get married."

Toug laughed softly.

"That's what Mama says. Because of the hair 'n getting big up here. It's a real long way to where I live. Are you going to carry me the whole way?"

"Maybe. Did you come this far tonight?"

Etela nodded. He felt the motion of her head.

"Then I think I can carry you back. We'll see. Maybe Org could carry us both. Be faster." She trembled, and he said, "I was just teasing, and I don't think Org would do it anyhow. Maybe for Sir Able or Sir Svon, but not for me."

"Was he going to kill me?"

"Sure. Eat you, too. Me and Sir Svon are supposed to feed him, but we haven't been doing it lately. There isn't much, and we've been busy. Sir Svon told him not to eat the slaves, but he's got to eat something, I guess. So that's something else to worry about. Getting lots of food quick. I don't know how we're going to do it."

"You don't eat people?"

Toug grinned. "Not unless they're cleaner than you."

"You shouldn't try to fool me. It's mean."

"All right."

"You got to turn up here at the corner."

"Which way?"

"Well, there isn't but one. What's your name?"

"Toug. Squire Toug, if you want to be formal, but you don't have to be formal with me."

The crooked, rutted street he had been following ended, and he turned left.

"Only you've got to be formal when you talk to Sir Svon or Sir Garvaon. Or Lord Beel. I mean, if you ever get into the castle you'll have to."

"Are you going to marry me?"

Toug halted in midstride. "I don't think so."

"Well, I do. When I'm bigger."

"It's not very likely, Etela." He began to walk again. "I'm not sure I'll ever get married."

"It is too, 'cause when Mama said I thought who'll it be 'n there wasn't nobody. But here you are, only you got to court me. Sing under my window, Mama says."

He smiled. "When you're older."

"Uh-huh, 'cause I haven't got windows at home." Pushing a painfully thin arm through the parting of his cloak, Etela pointed. "See that? That's the last house. Right up there. Go over the little hill, then it's where we live."

"Is that where the tools are? The picks and shovels?"

"I'll show you. Our forge's right on the house, like, 'n

that's good 'cause it's so hot, so it's a good place only there's not much to eat. Are you hungry?"

Toug shook his head.

"Well, I am. I'm real hungry. I thought maybe you thought Mama could give you something. Only Mama won't talk to you, most like, 'n couldn't give you a thing anyhow."

Feeling her shiver, Toug said, "You're cold."

"Well, it's always cold outside."

Toug had come to his decision, and he announced it. "After you show me the tools I'm going to take you to the castle. We haven't got a lot of food, but I can give you mine in the morning and find you better clothes."

"Well, I was hoping to get in." Etela sounded wistful.

"Sure. Pouk can find you clothes. Pouk's my brother-in-law, and he got me these boots. If Queen Idnn were here, she might—who's that?"

"Well, that's Vil," Etela whispered. "I guess he heard us."

CHAPTER SEVENTEEN

TOOLS

I feel the call of Skai every time we do this," I muttered. "What about you, Gylf? Don't you feel it?"

Gylf glanced up. "Yep."

"You've never been there. Not since you were small."

He did not speak.

"You could've come after me. But I suppose you didn't know where I'd gone. You thought I was dead."

"Yep."

"Now I'm back, no nearer Disiri, but nearer Skai than I ever was when I was with her. I just want to keep riding up and up too, closer and closer 'til I see the castle. I want to unsaddle Cloud there, and fill her manger until the corn runs over. Then I want to go into the hall and show you off, have a drink, and tell good lies about all we did down here."

"Are we?"

"No. But you'd like Skai. Love it, in fact. It's all plains and wild hills, and always changing. Look." Rising in my saddle, I pointed. "There's Utgard, black against the stars. See it?"

"Bad."

"I'm sure. But oh Thyr and Tyr, just look at the size of it! If ever I've doubted that our Angrborn are true sons of Bergelmir, I'd believe it now."

Prompted by my thoughts, Cloud began her descent.

"I swore I wouldn't use the power I was given there when I came back, but—"

"No?"

"You think I'm using it, don't you? Whenever we travel like this."

"Yep."

"I'm not. This is Cloud's talent, one of them. If I were to dismount, I'd fall."

"I don't," Gylf panted.

"No, but you can't ride." I reined up. "Look over there, the red light. That's a forge, I'll be bound, and they're still working. Why don't we hear the hammers?"

"I'll find out." Gylf loped off. Faint and far, I heard the wind rise; snow stirred at the feet of a group between Gylf and the glow of the charcoal.

When he returned he said, "Man and a girl."

"At the forge?"

"Yep."

I nodded. "The men have stopped work to talk to them? They're probably telling her to get to bed. Kids shouldn't be up this late."

* * *

"Not much of a fighter." The slave called Vil declared. "Where's your stick?" He had been feeling Toug's arms.

"I haven't got one," Toug explained. "I couldn't carry Etela and a stick, too."

The slave grunted. His face was thin, but his arms were thick with muscle. The hands that pinched and squeezed Toug felt as hard as iron.

"I should get back to my master," Toug said.

Without looking at her, another slave addressed Etela. "You goin' to bed like a good girl?"

"Uh-huh."

"Your ma's sleepin', or she'd been here botherin' us about you."

Etela looked doubtful. "Well, I hope."

Vil said, "We've got to make more."

Toug cleared his throat. "I've been wondering about that. What do you make here? Horseshoes?"

"It's mattocks now," Vil said. "Want to get the feel of one?"

"Yes, I'd like to find out what they're like." Toug sensed that the more eager to stay and talk he appeared, the more willing Logi's slaves would be that he go.

"Come along," Vil told him; and indeed Vil's grip on his arm left him no choice.

The forge was every bit as lofty as the house to which it was attached, dirt-floored and open at the side opposite the house, presumably so that horses could be led into it. There were no lights save the ruddy glow of burning charcoal, but a hundred candles could not have lit it as well.

"Right there," the slave said. "You like it? How'd you like to swing that all day?"

It was huge. Toug drew his hand back hurriedly. "It's still hot."

"Not all that hot." Effortlessly, the slave picked it up. "Hold out your hands."

"No," Toug said.

All three laughed.

"How you goin' to know how big it is if you don't feel of it?"

"Your hands are tougher than mine," Toug said. "If you say it's big, I'll take your word for it."

"Wait. I'll get you a cold one." Walking slowly but confidently, Vil went to the back of the forge and returned carrying a mattock whose blade was as long as Etela was tall, and whose handle had not long ago been a considerable tree. Toug took it, but quickly let its head fall to the ground.

"Think you could swing that?"

"He's real strong, Vil," Etela declared loyally.

"I'm not," Toug told her, "and not nearly as strong as your friends here. I wish I were."

"You come work with us," Vil said.

"I'm glad I don't have to. Is Etela's mother here? I'd like to talk to her."

"Inside. I'll take you." He led Toug and Etela to the back of the forge, past stacks of enormous picks and spades, and opened a door big enough for the largest Angrborn.

As they went through Toug said, "You're working late."

"Got to." The slave closed the door behind them and offered his hand. "Name's Vil."

"Toug." Toug took it, telling himself that any pain he suffered in Vil's grasp would be pain deserved, that a future knight should be as strong as any smith.

"Stout lad. You might swing a hammer yet."

Toug thanked him.

Vil's voice fell. "Got eyes, don't you?"

Here it was. "Yes," Toug said. "The Angrborn have never enslaved me. I can see."

"Tried to fool us."

"Yes," Toug repeated. "I should've known better."

"He's from the castle," Etela put in.

"One of King Arnthor's men?"

"I've never seen him," Toug confessed, "but I am."

"We were his people. All of us." Vil's empty sockets stared at something to the left of Toug's face, and a trifle lower, but his hand found Toug's shoulder.

"I was born in Glennidam," Toug told him.

"Never heard of it."

"It's smaller than lots of villages." Toug paused. "We kept the secrets of the Free Companies—gave them food and and beer and anything else they wanted, because they promised to protect us. Sometimes they just took it."

"You revered us," a new voice said, "because Disiri was kind to you, offering to hide your children when the Angrborn came."

"Baki?"

Someone stepped from a dark corner, in form a human woman with hair so red it seemed to glow in the dim light, and now and then leaped like a flame.

"This is a—a friend of mine, Etela." Toug gulped, drew a deep breath, and plowed on. "She'll be a friend of yours, too, I'm sure. Baki, this girl is Etela, and I've been taking her back to her mother. I'm going to bring her to the castle and feed her if her mother lets me. And this is Vil. He works here, and I'm sure he's a very good smith. Don't you like smiths?"

Etela said, "How come she hasn't got clothes?"

"I'm Baki's sister, and I love smiths." She was running her fingers down Vil's arm. "Smiths as hard as their anvils. Do you make swords, Vil?"

"Not—" His voice cracked. "Not good ones."

"I can teach you to forge a sword that will cleave the head of the hammer."

Toug drew Etela to one side. "Where's your mother?"

"Well, I think she's in the next room listening."

"Really? What makes you think so?"

"I just do."

Toug nodded. "Let's find out."

Leaving Uri in Vil's embrace, they hurried through the

kitchen. There was a fireplace in the next room, a little, niggardly fireplace by the standards of the castle Toug had left, but a large one just the same. The coals of a fire smoldered there, and two slave women slept in its ashes.

A third, a white-faced black-haired woman in a dress of black rags, sat bolt upright on a tall stool. In the firelight her wide eyes seemed as dark as sloes.

"That's Mama," Etela announced.

Toug cleared his throat. "I'm pleased to meet you, ma'am. I'm Squire Toug."

The seated woman did not move or speak.

"I found Etela in Utgard—in the town, I mean, all alone. Something might have happened to her."

Not knowing whether the seated woman heard him, he stopped talking; she said nothing.

Etela filled the silence. "Well, something 'bout did."

Toug nodded. "So I brought her back. But she was cold and she's hungry, and if it's all right with you I'd like to take her to the castle and feed her."

It seemed to Toug that the angle of the seated woman's head had altered by a hair.

"To your king?" Toug plowed on. "To King Gilling's. Maybe I can find some food for her and warmer clothes."

One hand stirred as the feathers of a dead dove might stir in a draft, and Etela hurried over. The woman seemed to whisper urgently, her whispers punctuated by Etela's *I will*s and *Yes, Mama*s.

Etela returned to Toug. "Well, she says we can, only we better go now 'n quick."

Toug agreed. He averted his eyes from the impassioned couple in the kitchen and tried to hurry Etela. Behind them, something had awakened; the timbers of the barn-like house creaked and groaned.

In the smithy two slaves were shaping a mattock, one gripping the red-hot iron with tongs while the other hammered it, sensing its shape (it seemed to Toug) with light taps of the hammer. Toug and Etela dashed past; and if the pair at the anvil heard them, they gave no sign of it.

"What did your mother say to you?" Toug asked when they were trotting down the street.

"Go fast!"

"I know, but what else?"

"Master's up," Etela panted. "If he heard you—"

The rest was lost in an earthshaking roar from behind. Toug turned long enough to catch sight of an Angrborn as wide as he was high, with three arms. Scooping up Etela like a puppy, Toug ran for all he was worth but was jerked off his feet by his cloak. For a moment that seemed an eternity, he struggled to withdraw his arms from the slits and prayed that it would tear and free him. Two more hands closed about his waist.

The Angrborn spoke. (Or might have believed he spoke.) All Toug heard was the voice of a beast, snarls that would have sent the biggest bear that ever walked into panicked flight. He shrieked, and could no more have repeated what he had said afterward—what he had promised Org or any Overcyn who would send Org—than he could have repeated what Logi had said to him.

It was effectual, whatever it was. A black shape left a shadow less dark and took Logi from behind.

Toug was dropped or thrown or both, and struck the snow-covered ground with force enough to leave him stunned. When he had recovered sufficiently to get to his feet, Org and Logi were grappling, Logi with a dagger as long as a sword, and Org with a scaly hand locked on Logi's wrist. Toug had never seen Org's face clearly before that moment; he saw it then and would have recoiled in horror if he had not known it for the face of their defender.

"Run!" Etela was tugging his arm.

He shook his head as the point of the dagger crept nearer Org's throat.

"Run! We gotta run!"

"I'm a knight. I can't run." He brushed Etela aside and threw himself at Logi, wrestling with a leg, then heaving at the ankle as a man would struggle to uproot a tree.

Org was struggling too, his free hand raking Logi's back and side so that blood and flesh rained down. A moment more, and Logi fell. He and Org rolled through snow, and though all Logi's hands circled Org's neck, so thick was that bull neck with muscle that Org fought on.

Until Toug drove the sword-long dagger he had snatched up into Logi's left eye.

Cloud and I might have cantered down to the top of one Utgard's towers. The thought amused me and for a moment I considered it. Cloud would have been safe there, but a less comfortable spot could scarcely be imagined.

Coming to earth outside the town and riding through it was liable to be dangerous; but I was tempted to do that as well. The safest course was probably to touch ground just beyond the moat and trot through the open gate, around the bailey, and so to the stables I had seen behind the keep. Rejecting that, we cantered a long bowshot above the highest spires, and down to the cobbles.

The rattle of Cloud's hooves awakened no dutiful groom. I dismounted and went in search of a clean stall. A horse nickered at my step. I found it—the white stallion I had been given in a time that seemed long ago.

The grooms, blind slaves, were sleeping behind the tack room. I woke them with the flat of my sword, filling the place with phantoms they sensed but could not see. When they were cowering in a corner, I addressed them. "There's not a horse in this stable that has water or corn, save one. That one horse—he belongs to an old friend—has water and corn because I watered and fed him. When I saw the way you'd treated him, I wanted to kill you. I still do."

They moaned.

"Your king is barricaded in Utgard. Is that right?"

"Y-yes."

"Thus you have felt yourselves at liberty to do as you wished, and what you wished has been to neglect the animals. Filthy stalls and empty mangers. Horses, mules, and oxen half dead of thirst. I'd pity you if you hadn't proved that you deserve blindness and worse. I'm going into the keep. You'll find my mount and my hound outside. Unsaddle my mount and care for her. Feed my hound and see that he has water. Is that understood?"

The slaves muttered assent.

"You're to clean every stall, and feed and water all the animals. I can't say how long my business with King Gilling will take. An hour, maybe. Maybe longer. No more than half the night though, and when I come back I'll check every stall to see if my orders have been carried out."

Leaving the stable I began the long walk around Utgard to the main entrance; then, finding the broad arch of a sally port sized for Angrborn, I entered its pitch black passage and pounded the iron door.

The archer who opened it looked at me with surprise. "Sir Able! I was expectin' Squire Toug."

"You really wanta hear what Mama said?" Etela asked as they hurried through the town.

"Yes," Toug told her. "I want to ask you about her too. Why she wouldn't talk to me and some other things."

"That's good, 'cause I wanna ask ever so much 'bout your face 'n the castle. You're going to tell me, aren't you?"

"I'll try," Toug promised. He had taken Logi's dagger and its sheath, and was carrying them over his shoulder.

" 'Bout Org, too. Will you answer 'bout him?"

"If I know the answer."

"All right, after Master was dead, you 'n Org talked. Only I was scared to get close. What'd you say?"

"He wanted to know if it was all right for him to feed from your master's body," Toug explained. "I said it was, but he'd have to look out for the Angrborn because they would kill him if they saw him. He said he'd take it someplace and hide it, and that way he could come back later and have some more. I said that was fine."

"He's not with us no more?"

Toug shrugged. "I don't see how he could be."

"S'pose somebody wants to hurt us?"

"I'll do what I can. I have this now." He indicated Logi's dagger. "So we're better off than we were. I got one of these before. It wasn't nearly as nice as this, and when my horse finally got to Utgard I stuck that one under the bed and forgot it. I won't forget this, ever."

"It's awfully big," Etela said practically.

"It's too big for me to hold right," Toug admitted, "but I think this handle's bone, maybe from one of the Angrborn or just from a big animal. Whichever, I ought to be able to cut it down and sand it smooth. It'll take work, but it'll be worth it. Now tell me, what did your mother say to you?"

"All of it? There's lots."

Toug nodded. "Yes, everything."

"Well, she said to go to the castle with you, only not to come back ever at all. To do whatever I had to, to stay with you. 'Cause you were my own kind of folks 'n the closer I got to my own kind the better it was going to be for me. She said get cleaned up 'n get pretty clothes if I could, 'n be extra nice 'n maybe you'd let me stay. Only if you said I had to go, don't do it, hide 'til you forgot."

"I won't make you go back," Toug declared.

"Well, all of you is what she meant."

When Toug had walked a score of paces, he asked, "What about her? Shouldn't we try to get her out, if we can?"

"She said don't come back for her, she's dead anyway." Hopelessness crept into Etela's voice. "It's how she talks.

Well, I mean when she does, 'cause sometimes she don't talk at all, not even to me. Only Vil will take care of her, he always does, 'n Gif and Alca will too."

"Is Vil your father?"

Etela shook her head. "My papa's dead. Only Vil likes Mama 'n me, 'n takes care when he can."

"Logi's dead too," Toug remarked thoughtfully.

"Uh-huh."

"I was wondering what would happen to your mother and the other people he owned."

"Well, I don't know."

Toug considered the matter for a minute or two, then pointed. "Look! That's the bridge over the moat. See it?"

"We'll be safe in there?"

"Safer than we are out here. What else did your mother say? You said there was a lot."

"Well, I forget. Be nice to you 'n make people like me, 'n go south where people like us come from, 'n tell 'bout the manticores 'n marigolds."

"About what?"

"The manticores 'n marigolds, only I don't know what they are. Mama used to talk 'bout them."

"What did she say about them?"

"I don't know. What are they?"

"You've got to remember *something*." Toug insisted. "What did she say?"

"On dresses, I guess, 'n a scarf. Mostly she'd just say the words. Manticores 'n marigolds, manticores 'n marigolds, like that. Don't you know what they are?"

"Marigold's a kind of flower," Toug said slowly, "yellow and really pretty. I don't know what a manticore is."

Unchallenged, they strode over the snow, across the bridge and through the gate. Etela halted for a moment to look up at Utgard, vast as a mountain and black against the chill stars of winter. "Well, I knew it was real, real big, only I didn't know it was as big as this."

"It's easy to get lost in," Toug told her. "You've got to be careful 'til you know your way around."

"Uh-huh."

"My sister's got a room way up high. Maybe you could sleep with her. I'll ask."

"With you," Etela declared firmly," 'cause Mama said."

"We'll see. Maybe you could help me take care of Mani. I'm supposed to do that, too, but like when I'm gone. Like now. Somebody ought to be taking care of him and nobody is, unless the witch will do it."

"A witch?"

Toug nodded. "Her name's Huld, and she's a ghost besides being a witch. I don't know if ghosts take care of anybody, really."

"There was a ghost where Mama used to live," Etela declared. "Only he was real scary 'n he took care of the house but not people. Mama said he didn't like anybody much 'n there were a whole lot he hated. I don't want to hear 'bout this witch 'cause I'll be scared tonight anyhow."

As he led her to the sally port through which he had left Utgard, Toug reflected that he had been frightened, and often badly frightened, ever since Able had forced him to accompany him into the forest. Always afraid, save for one or two occasions on which he had been too tired to feel fear or anything else.

"It doesn't make sense," he told Etela.

"What doesn't?"

"Being afraid all the time. Being afraid ought to be a special thing. You should be afraid just once in a while. Or maybe never. You used to sleep in that Angrborn's house, didn't you? With your mother?"

"Uh-huh. Every night."

"That would scare me. Weren't you afraid?"

"Huh-uh, it was just regular. It was where we lived."

"So I'm going to stop being scared, or try to. If somebody kills me, they kill me, and it will be all over. Only they're not going to make me scared all the time."

In the pitch darkness of the entrance, Etela whispered, "Weren't you scared when you killed Master?"

"Afterwards I was, but when it happened I was trying to do everything too fast—get this sword, and not get rolled on." With the pommel of the dagger he had taken from Logi, Toug tapped the iron door, three knocks followed by two.

Those two were followed by the grating of the bar, and a muffled grunt as the lone archer struggled with a weight that any of the Angrborn could have moved without difficulty.

The door swung back and Arn said, "There you are, Squire. Sir Able wants to speak to you right away."

Ulfa opened the king's door, and for a moment we stood staring. At last I said, "I know you, and you know me."

She shook her head. "What's your name, sir? I—I'd like to hear you say it."

"I'm called Sir Able of the High Heart."

She curtsied. "Your servant is Ulfa. Your servant is the wife of your servant Pouk."

"You made a shirt for me once."

"And trousers, and followed after you when you and your dog, with Toug my father, wiped out a Free Company."

I nodded. "I have to speak to you and Pouk when I have more time. Is he here?"

"I'll get him, sir," she said, and slipped past me.

The king's bedchamber seemed as vast as the Grotto of the Griffin, cavernous, its ceiling (painted with scenes of war and feasting) lost in the air overhead, its bureaus and chests, its tables and chairs like cottages. In its center, on a black-figured crimson carpet larger than many a meadow, the bed under which Toug had conferred with Baki and Mani seemed small until one saw the slaves waiting there, women

whose heads were well below the surface of the bed, so that
they had to mount ladders to serve the king, and walk upon
the blankets that covered him, blankets over a sheet that
might have served as the mainsail of the *Western Trader*.

Beside that bed, Beel stood upon the tapestried seat of a
gilt chain and spoke with Gilling, who sat nearly upright,
propped with immense pillows. Beel looked around at me
in surprise, and I halted and bowed. "My Lord."

"He's here," Beel told Gilling. "I'd don't know how
that's possible, but here he is."

Feebly, Gilling raised a hand. "Sir Able. Approach."

I did, climbing to a rung of the chair and from there to
the seat upon which Beel stood.

"How kind to us are our ancestors," Gilling muttered.
"They favor us, their unworthy son. Schildstarr came, now
you. The queen—do you know our queen?"

"I have that honor, Your Majesty. It was Queen Idnn
who sent me to you."

"She was here but a moment ago. A lovely girl."

I supposed that Gilling had been dreaming. "A beautiful
woman indeed, Your Majesty. You're to be envied."

"She's consulted the stars." Gilling sighed. "She divines
with stars and cards and by the flight of birds, for she is
wise as well as beautiful. Sir Able will save us. Sir Able,
she said, would come tonight. You are Sir Able?"

"I am, Your Majesty."

"There is no other?"

"No other known to me, Your Majesty."

"Nor to me," Beel said.

"It was you who slew our Borderers?"

"Had I known them for yours, Your Majesty—"

Gilling's huge, pale hand waved them away. "Forgiven.
Pardoned. We're beset by rebels."

"So I have heard, Your Majesty."

"Thus we say . . ." Gilling fell silent. His eyes closed,
and for a time that seemed terribly long there was no

sound in that vast chamber save the whispers of the slaves, a soft soughing like willows in a summer breeze.

"Beel . . ."

"I am here, Your Majesty."

"You said he was far away. So did Thiazi."

"Yes, Your Majesty. I thought it true. I have no doubt Lord Thiazi thought it true as well."

"This is Sir Able? He is really here?"

"He is, Your Majesty. He's standing at my shoulder."

"Come, Sir Able. Approach. Do you fear our touch?"

"No, Your Majesty." I stepped from the chair to the bed, finding it firmer than I expected.

Gilling's hand found me, and Gilling's eyes opened. "Helmet, mail, and sword. Have you a shield, Sir Able?"

"Yes, Your Majesty, and my lance, bow, and quiver, too. I can fetch them if Your Majesty wants to see them."

Beel said, "A forest-green shield, Your Majesty, with a black dragon on it."

"They said you were far, Sir Able. Only this afternoon we were told you were remote."

"I was, Your Majesty."

"How came you so quickly, Sir Able?"

"I have a good mount, Your Majesty."

"My queen told me you would come. She is wiser than Beel, though Beel is a good friend. She's wiser even than Thiazi. She read it in the stars."

"It's at her request I come," I said carefully. "Duke Marder is coming also, with two stout knights, Sir Woddet and Sir Leort, and a hundred men."

"Will you serve us, Sir Able?"

"I'll help you if I can, Your Majesty, for her sake and Lord Beel's."

Beel himself touched my arm. "Your Majesty, there is someone else here with whom we should speak before we three take counsel further. If your strength does not permit it, Sir Able and I can question him and report to you."

"We will let you talk," Gilling told him, "but we will hear him. Who is it?"

"Sir Svon's squire, Your Majesty. Thinking Sir Able still far away, I sent him out to scout the town for us."

"Toug?" I looked toward the door and saw him waiting there with a ragged girl, standing between Pouk and Ulfa.

Beel said loudly, "Come, Squire, I must present you."

Hesitantly, Toug advanced; the girl would have followed him, but Ulfa held her back.

With a hand up from me, he climbed the chair to stand on its seat next to Beel.

"Your Majesty, this young man is Squire Toug. He is the squire of Sir Svon. Sir Svon is the younger of the knights who accompanied me." In a whisper Beel added, "One knee!," and Toug knelt.

"You left this castle to spy out my foes, young man?" Gilling's voice was almost kind.

"To look for scaling ladders, Your Majesty, or battering rams. Anything like that. That was what Lord Beel said to do, and find out who had them."

Beel nodded. "Those were my instructions, Your Majesty. What did you find, Toug?"

"Neither of those, Your Lordship." At a slight gesture from Beel, Toug rose. "But they were making mattocks and shovels. Digging tools. They had a lot already, and from what I heard they were going to make a lot more."

Gilling's sigh was very nearly a groan. "Common tools for slaves, for farm labor. You found nothing."

I turned to Toug. "I'm not so sure. You said they had a lot already. What's a lot? A dozen? Twenty?"

Toug considered. "I'd say sixty or seventy shovels and thirty or forty picks. They were making mattocks when I was there. That's a thing like a pick, only a wide blade."

"We know what they are," Beel told him.

"There were eight or ten of those, and they were making another one when I was there, and—and, Your Majesty . . ."

Gilling's eyes opened, looking overlarge in spite of his vast pallid forehead and enormous nose. "What?"

"They weren't for slaves. They were way too big."

"They're going to undermine us!" Beel exclaimed.

Gilling's head rolled from side to side. "Their slaves would do that. They'll heap up earth and stones." His eyes closed again. "So we carried Aegri's isle."

Greatly daring, Toug said, "We could go out and get them, Your Majesty. Nobody's guarding us."

Gilling did not respond, and Toug turned to me. "Carry them back in here, or burn them."

I shook my head. "My Lord, I must confer with you. I realize how late it is, but we must talk and I must go. If I had more time, I'd talk to people separately—to Toug here, my servant Pouk, and Ulfa. To this Schildstarr, Lord Thiazi, and you. There isn't time. Let's get them together, if they'll come. Then I'll have to leave."

Beel nodded. "I'll see to it."

"Ulfa and Pouk are here already," Toug said. "So is Etela. Maybe you should see her too."

"Is that the girl?"

Toug nodded, and Beel said, "We're all here already, in that case, save for Schildstarr and Lord Thiazi. See whether they'll leave their beds for us, Squire."

CHAPTER EIGHTEEN

NIGHT

At the suggestion of the lean Angrborn called Thiazi, we met in a room in which the king sometimes entertained friends, a room rather larger than the banquet hall of the Valfather's castle. Richer too, and far colder, filled not with the trophies of the hunt and the shields of the brave, but with clumsy furniture that must have seemed massive even to the Angrborn, and a wealth of polished silver and pewter platters and cups, things lovely but overlarge, like the shelves that could scarcely hold them crowded and piled together.

"We've got to wait for that Schildstarr," Ulfa murmured at my elbow; I had not known she was there until she spoke. "Unless you need me, I'm going to get something for the girl. Toug says she hasn't eaten since yesterday."

I nodded.

"Would you like me to get you something, too?"

"No. But thanks. Please hurry back."

Pouk appeared at my other elbow. "You was wantin' to talk to me, sir? Might be a good time."

"The only time we'll get, I'm afraid. Our horses—that black charger Master Agr gave me. Where are they?"

"Horses is in the stable, sir. Them stablemen . . ." Pouk looked as though he wanted to spit.

"I didn't recognize them. The stable was dark, and I was in a hurry. I should have spotted them just the same."

"I go out when I can, sir, an' do what I can. Only I can't go often as I'd like an' can't do much. I fought them stablemen at first, but they got worse to show me an' you can't hardly fight a man what runs."

I murmured agreement, reflecting that Pouk, whose bad eye and squint had always made him appear blind, was blind now in fact. "You can't have gotten out there since the king was stabbed, I suppose."

Pouk chuckled. "Oh, I slips out just th' same, sir. Twic't, so far. I got a way."

"Good."

"Only t'other's gone, sir. Your traps, or most is."

"I understand." I had come to a decision. "I want to get you out, you and Ulfa both. I'm going to take Ulfa with me tonight, if I—"

"Bless you, sir!"

"If I can. I'm going to leave you here for the time being to look after my horses and get my things together, if you can. Find them, even if you can't move them. I'll be back with the duke and others before much longer, and next time I go you'll be with me."

Ulfa returned with a thick slice of dark bread, a lump of smelly cheese, and a wooden pannikin of what was probably small beer. She gave them to the ragged girl.

I leaned to my left to talk to Toug. "Is this another relative of Ulfa's?"

"No, Sir Able. I found her when I was out scouting. It's complicated."

Beel said, "We should hear it in any—"

An Angrborn entered as he spoke, a giant so big and ugly that for an instant I thought he might be one of the Giants of Winter and Old Night, followed by four more only slightly less hideous Angrborn.

"Yourself alone," Thiazi told Schildstarr firmly. "Your followers will not be permitted to stay."

He pulled out a chair and sat, and motioned for the four who had come with him to sit as well.

Wearily, Beel said, "We cannot have this."

"Then you'll nae ha' me."

"You think we can't drive you out. You're wrong. We can, and if necessary we will."

Schildstarr shook his head. "Fetch thy hotland lads and we'll go."

His followers protested.

"You're hot to fight shieldmates. I'm nae." He turned to Beel. "Count thyselves." He did, raising a thick finger for each man and woman as he pointed to Beel, Toug, Ulfa, Etela, Pouk, and me. "Half dozen. Fer me an' mine, Thiazi an' me? I'll nae stand for't."

"You have a point," Beel conceded.

"It's our king in the bed, an' our land you tread."

I said, "You're Schildstarr? I called this meeting, and I haven't a lot of time." I stood on the seat my chair and offered him my hand.

"You're nae hotlander," Schildstarr said when our hands parted. "Ne'er felt the like."

"You counted me among them," I told him. "You'd go, you said, if Lord Beel brought force. I'm here, so he has all the force he needs. But if you go without fighting, I'll go with you. I have to leave soon anyway."

"We stay."

"I want Sir Garvaon here," Beel said, "and Sir Svon. Refuse, and you have seen the last of me. You may call two more of yours, if you must counter us man for man."

Schildstarr shook his head, and Toug went to fetch them.

"Toug's been in the town this night," I told Svon, when they arrived. "I thought it too dangerous when I heard of it, but he says the danger was less than might be imagined—that King Gilling's foes weren't watching the castle. I can confirm that. I saw no one when I came here."

I turned to Toug. "You suggested we seize or burn the tools you found. They weren't guarded?"

"Only by the smith."

"His name?" Beel asked sharply. "Did you learn it?"

"Yes, Your Lordship." (I felt certain Toug was nearer exhausion than Beel.) "Logi, Your Lordship."

"Do you know him, My Lord?" Beel's question to Thiazi was nearly as sharp as his question to Toug.

"I have heard his name." Thiazi shrugged.

"You would not expect him to be a ringleader?"

"A smith?" Thiazi shook his head. "Hardly."

"Might talk." Schildstarr rumbled.

"If we had him here," Beel said, "I agree that means might be found to persuade him to speak. But he's not here, and I see no way to get him."

"Might come," Schildstarr rumbled, "if I try him."

"He's dead!" Toug burst out. "He chased us—chased Etela and me, and I killed him."

Schildstarr's laugh shook every ewer and cup.

Svon was grinning. "How'd you manage that?"

"He fell and dropped his dagger, and I stabbed him with it before he could get up," Toug said. "I need to talk to you about that when we're alone."

"You," Beel told Toug, "are a remarkable young man."

"Thank you, Your Lordship." Toug swallowed. "Except I'm not. Not really. I'm a really ordinary kind of young man, aren't I, Ulfa?"

She smiled warmly.

"Do you think we could go out and get those tools, Sir Able? Like I said?"

"I doubt it. What were the numbers? Sixty spades?"

"Yes, Sir Able. About that."

"And there were picks."

Toug nodded. "About half as many."

"I see." I paused to study Toug's serious, boyish face. "Did you handle any of them?"

"One of the mattocks."

"Could you have carried it back to this castle?"

Toug considered, then nodded again. "It was pretty heavy, but I think so. Not fast."

"No, not fast. Any of these Angrborn could carry more, of course. Let us say an Angrborn could carry four tools."

I paused to do the arithmetic, then turned to speak to Schildstarr. "You have more than these four, since Lord Beel suggested you bring two more into our meeting. How many?"

"Mysel' and eighteen mair."

I returned to Toug. "Let's say sixty spades, thirty picks, and ten mattocks—one hundred in all. Schildstarr and his eighteen could carry seventy-six, leaving twenty-four to be carried by twenty-four of us."

"We don't have enough men to defend this tower now!" Beel exclaimed.

"Right you are. Even if you stripped this keep bare we wouldn't have enough. If there's serious resistance—as there almost certainly will be—not nearly enough."

Pouk spoke up. "Me an' my mates could carry. There's more'n a hundred in our crew here."

I nodded. "Or we could use the horses from the stable. There are oxen there, too, so there are presumably carts as well. Schildstarr, you're shaking your head."

" 'Tis a brave lad, but nae gud. 'Twould be fight begun an' ne'er won." He leveled a huge finger at Garvaon. "Could you hold off a hunnert a' us? In the open, noo."

"We'd do our best."

"An' die."

Svon said, "If we went out, might not others rally to the king's side?"

"To me an' mine, it might be. Nae wi' you wi' us."

Toug said, "We don't really want those tools. Maybe we could burn them."

"We could burn the handles," I told him, "if our force made it that far. The heads are iron, aren't they?"

Toug nodded.

"They'd survive the fire, and anyone could easily fit new handles."

The girl on the other side of Toug tugged at his sleeve, and they whispered together. When he straightened up, he said, "Etela and me have another idea. Can I ask Schildstarr something?"

"Ask awa'."

"The place where they're making the shovels and the other tools belonged to Logi. That's what Etela says, and she did too. Her mother's a slave there. Only Logi's dead now, like I told you. Will they sell them? The slaves?"

Schildstarr nodded. "Aye."

Etela spoke up. "Well, it seems like the king's got lots of money."

Toug nodded. "It does, and Logi can't make any more shovels and picks and things now, so his slaves would have to make them. But they couldn't if you bought them and brought them back here."

Pushing out a lower lip as big and black as a burnt roast, Schildstarr raised his eyebrows.

"You could buy all the slaves," Toug added. "Etela's mother, too."

Beel said, "It might even be possible to buy the tools that have been completed."

I stood. "I got you together to make sure you wouldn't do anything rash before Duke Marder arrived—that you realized your limitations. I don't think I needed to worry, and I have to go."

"We should all go." Thiazi yawned hugely. "Back to bed. We should sleep on this and talk again in the morning."

"I need a word with Toug," I told him, "and another with his sister. May I have them?"

Mani climbed Toug's chair.

"I suppose, if Lord Beel concurs." Thiazi yawned again. "Toug is his, as long as he cares for the king's cat. Who's his sister?"

Ulfa said, "I am, Your Lordship."

"I see." Thiazi stood up. "Would you like to own your sister, young man?"

Toug stared; and Beel, watching him with some amusement, whispered, "Yes, My Lord."

"Yes. My Lord. Yes, I would."

"I'm acting for His Majesty during His Majesty's unhappy indisposition." Thiazi picked up his gold rod, which he had laid on the table when he had taken his seat. "As His Majesty's surrogate, I feel you should be rewarded for your activities on His Majesty's behalf tonight. In recognition of them, I present you with this healthy female slave. I'll have my clerk draw up a paper in the morning."

He asked Ulfa's name, and she curtsied and provided it.

"This slave Ulfa. You don't really need a paper, since Schildstarr and his friends can testify for you if a problem comes up. Which it won't. But we're trying to keep things neater than they have been in the past."

"Say, thank you, My Lord," Beel whispered. "Say thank you very much."

At the door of the sally port (separated by a wilderness of stone from the room in which we had met) I halted. "Sir Garvaon, Sir Svon, I apologize. To you particularly, Sir Svon. I must speak with Toug privately. Will you wait here? And you, Pouk, and your wife? I'll come back as quickly as I can. Maybe Sir Svon could hold Queen Idnn's cat."

"I will," Ulfa said, and took him from Toug.

The sentry opened the big iron door with a grunt, and Toug and I stepped out. "It was Org," Toug said as soon as the door closed. "I didn't say it up there because I know Sir Svon doesn't want people to know about him."

"I see. Org actually killed the smith?"

"No, I did. But Org saw he was chasing Etela and me and went for him. I said he fell down and dropped his dagger and I stabbed him, and that was all true. But it was because he was fighting Org."

I set off for the stable, motioning for Toug to follow.

"Maybe you're worried because Etela's sleeping in my bed for now. I know Ulfa is, but I'm not going to hurt her, and it's a real big bed."

"I'd hardly thought of it," I admitted. "I was talking

with Sir Svon and Sir Garvaon while you and your sister
were putting her to bed."

"Then I don't know what we've got to talk about, but
there's one thing I ought to tell and I should whisper it."

I stopped at the stable door. "Go ahead."

"Pouk isn't really blind. I mean, only in one eye, and he
was that way before."

"I noticed that myself." I felt suddenly that I was as
tired as any of them, and reminded myself that I could not
afford it—that I had a long ride ahead.

"You did?"

Gylf trotted up before I could reply. "There you are."

"At last. Is everything all right?"

"I bit one." Gylf yawned.

"He'll recover, I'm sure." I turned back to Toug and
asked how he had hurt his cheek. He was telling me all
about the fight in courtyard and the attempted assassination of King Gilling more or less as Idnn had, when iron-
shod hooves on the wooden stable floor interrupted us.
Cloud had trotted out to greet me, and for a second or two
we hugged, I with my arms about her neck and she
squeezing me between her neck and chin.

Toug patted her flank. "She's such a beautiful horse. I'll
bet you were worried about her."

"I was, but she could have told me if anything had gone
wrong. We don't exactly talk, but each of us knows what
the other's saying. Have I told you about that?"

"Kind of."

"Come with me." I led the way into the stable, followed
by Gylf and Cloud. Their footfalls mingled with the
scrape of shovels.

"This is the room where the stablemen sleep." I took a
stick from the fire and swung it until it burned brightly.
"We want light, and I think there must be candles or
lanterns here somewhere, even though the stablemen
don't use them."

"Right here, Sir Able." Toug had opened a cabinet; a large lantern of pierced copper held a candle equally large.

I lit it. "Thanks. I suppose they must use this when they have to light their masters' way, and we'll use it too." I tossed the stick back into the fire.

"I think I know what you want to show me."

"If I were a teacher, I'd have left that stall the way I found it," I told him. "I'm a knight, and can't treat a good horse like that. I got this so you can see that his stall's clean—it had better be—and that he has water and food."

We found the white stallion that had been mine, and Toug stared at him for a minute or more, holding the lantern high.

"He's dirty." Toug might have been choking.

"And thin."

"Yes. Sir Able . . ."

"I'm listening."

"We—everything was barricaded. They're plotting against the king. Nobody could go out. Lord Beel said so."

I took the lantern from him and hung it on a nail. "Lord Beel isn't a knight."

"I guess not."

"Neither are you. I expected you to say that."

"You said it, Sir Able. I know it's true, but I won't say it." Toug wiped his hands on his cloak. "There must be things to clean horses with around here somewhere. Sponges or rags or something. Water. I'll get some."

I shook my head. "You're a squire, and there are men here who've neglected their duty. Tell them what you want done, and see that they do it."

"You made them shovel this out, didn't you?" Toug stooped, and picked up a handful of clean straw. "What was it like before?"

"You wouldn't have wanted to see it. I have to go now.

Sir Garvaon and Sir Svon have been waiting too long already. So have your sister and her husband."

Toug nodded. "I'll see about Laemphalt."

"I want to say one more thing before I go. It's that you went out of this castle tonight."

"Lord Beel told me to."

"You risked your life and fought like a hero."

"Org—"

"I know about Org. Any of us who kills an Angrborn is a hero. Most men would have stood aside and let Org do the fighting. You didn't. But neither did you spare a thought for your mount. And you should have."

Toug nodded again.

"Pouk came out here from time to time to see about my horses, the horses he had when the Angrborn captured him. If he had not, things would have been worse than they were. Did Sir Svon ever attend to his own mount?"

"I don't know."

"Then he didn't." I sighed. "You'd know if he had. He was my squire, and Sir Ravd's. Neither of us trained him the way we should have. What about Sir Garvaon and his squire? I don't recall the squire's name."

"Wistan, sir. I don't know. I don't think so."

"Neither do I," I said, and left.

I was leading Cloud when I met the knights, Pouk, and Ulfa in the cold moon-shadow of Utgard.

"We thought we'd better have a look for you," Garvaon told me. "We were afraid something might have happened."

I smiled. "I'm okay, just tired. I guess we all are, Toug especially."

Svon nodded. "I'll keep that in mind."

Ulfa touched my arm. "Where is he?"

"In the stable, seeing to his horse. Pretty soon it will hit him that he ought to see to Sir Svon's. Maybe it already has." I paused. "You belong to him now. Do you feel you've got to have his permission to leave here?"

"You—you're . . . ?" Her mouth was open.

"I'm going to take you where you'll be free. Pouk, you agreed I could. Have you changed your mind?"

"No, sir!"

Dropping Mani, Ulfa kissed and embraced Pouk.

"The two of you will be back together soon," I promised them. "I hope so, anyway."

Svon said, "I came down because I want to ride with you. I know you said you met no resistance, but we may have to fight our way out, and you'll be burdened with this woman."

"You can't ride where we ride," I told him.

I lifted Ulfa onto Cloud's back and swung into the saddle behind her. So mounted, my eyes were not as high as the eyes of Schildstarr or Thiazi; yet I felt that I looked down on Svon, Garvaon, and Pouk from a great height— that Cloud stood upon an invisible tower, but a real tower just the same. I whistled for Gylf and watched him leap into the air, running toward the palisade of logs that crowned the curtain wall; and then (the palisade passed) toward a bank of somber winter cloud and the pale moon that peered around it.

Ulfa blew a kiss to Pouk, and he came forward and caught her hand and kissed her fingers.

Then I touched Cloud's flanks, and pictured myself (and Ulfa, too) on Cloud's back as she galloped across the sky. And at once it came to be, and the pennant on my lance, the green pennant the old captain's wife had sewn from scraps, snapped in the cold wind of Cloud's passage.

Ulfa moaned and shut her eyes, clinging with all her might to the high steel pommel of the war saddle. I wrapped my cloak around her, and turned to look back at Utgard as it dwindled and faded into night, becoming scattered points of light, a few stars in the general darkness of Mythgarthr.

* * *

Toug had run from the stable as Pouk kissed Ulfa's hand. He knew Ulfa was not looking; yet he felt it was his duty to wave, so wave he did, knowing his eyes had filled with tears. In his boyhood, Ulfa had held authority. He had protested that authority often and loudly, and acknowledged it only when he might have something to gain. As he had grown older and stronger they had come to blows.

Now he might never see her again; the past reclaimed in her face and voice was gone once more. So he waved, knowing she was not thinking of him, and knowing that his tears were soaking his bandage. Knew shame, but wept and waved still.

I whistled and Gylf ran up a hill of air. A few seconds more, and Ulfa and I followed upon a proud, long-legged mare as gray as cloud and as swift as the wind. Together we four dwindled into the south as swans dwindle when ice closes the marshes, great solid birds that seem too large to fly, seen only as specs of white against Skai, specs that wane and fade and are seen to be very small indeed.

"How—? How did he do that?" Garvaon spoke to everyone and no one.

Nobody answered, and Toug wondered momentarily whether Pouk would continue to maintain the pretext of blindness or confess that he, too, had seen Cloud canter into the sky.

A strange, high keening filled the courtyard, coming from everywhere and nowhere, a sound more lonely and less human than that of a dog howling on his master's grave.

"What's that, sir?" Pouk grasped Toug's arm.

"Org." The name had slipped from his lips.

Garvaon asked, "Who's Org?"

"Org isn't anybody." Toug sensed Svon's gaze. "I just meant Pouk was hurting my arm."

"We're all tired," Svon said. "Let's get to bed."

"But you saw it." Garvaon pointed. "You and Toug. You saw it just like I did."

"'With a lance of prayer and a horse of air,'" Svon quoted, "'summoned I am to tourney, ten thousand leagues beyond the moon. Methinks it is no journey.'"

Garvaon shook himself, the rings of his mail whispering. "He's crazy, the knight in that song. That's the whole point of the song. Sir Able's not crazy."

"We will be," Svon said softly, "if we talk about this."

He caught Pouk's shoulder. "You saw nothing, I know, but you heard us talking about it."

"Aye, sir. Only I ain't figured out yet what happened. I know Sir Able went an' took my Ulfa with him like he said, only I don't remember hearin' his horse go."

"It would be well for you to remain as silent regarding all this. I speak as a friend."

"Oh, I will, Sir Svon, sir. They'll ast me what's become o' Ulfa, though, I knows they will. All right if I say Sir Able's took her? They'll know he was here."

"Certainly." Releasing Pouk, Svon turned to Toug. "You haven't always been as discreet as I might like."

"I know, Sir Svon. But I won't say a word about what happened just now."

"See that you don't."

"Have you seen Mani, Sir Svon? Lady Idnn's cat? I mean the queen's."

"He's the king's cat now. You brought him here. What did you do with him?"

"I didn't, Sir Svon. My sister did. Only she didn't have him when she went with Sir Able."

"You'd better look for him before you go to bed," Svon told Toug; and when Toug went to search the shadows around the keep, Svon muttered, "I myself am going to bed, cat or no cat. Good night, Sir Garvaon. Pouk, you and I've been foes. I'm a knight now, and you're blind. If you harbor ill will toward me—"

"I don't, sir. Not I!"

"I would not blame you. Nor will I seek revenge, now or ever. I offer my hand." Svon held it out. "Let's hope we quit Jotunland alive together."

Pouk groped for Svon's hand, found it, and clasped it.

Garvaon said, "You were Sir Able's squire. You must know more about him than the rest of us."

Looking back at them, Toug saw Svon shake his head and heard him say, "I didn't learn a tenth as much as he could have taught me. I wish I had."

The three went under the pitch-dark arch of the sally port, and Toug saw them no more. He spat, clenched his thumbs in his fists to warm them, and leaned for a blissful moment against the rough stones of the keep.

"I could lie down right here," he murmured, "lie down and roll myself in my cloak and sleep. I'd freeze before the night was over, but I could do it." He yawned and shook himself more or less as Garvaon had, and set out for the stables. Mani was certainly capable of getting back into Utgard without help, and Toug decided that Mani was probably in their turret room that very moment, curled warmly beside a sleeping Etela.

In the stable, the slaves Able had awakened and set to work were just going back to the bed. As loudly as he could, Toug said, "Listen up, all of you! I'll be back tomorrow morning when I can look this place over by daylight, and I won't just be concerned about my own horse. Every horse you've got had better have food and water, a clean coat, and clean straw to lie in. Don't say you weren't warned."

Several muttered that they would attend to it.

"Meanwhile, I'm looking for a cat. A big—" Almost too late Toug remembered that these slaves were truly blind. "A big furry tomcat. He belongs to the king. Keep him if you find him, treat him well, and tell me when I come back."

They swore they would, and he returned to the keep more tired than ever. Long knocking got him inside at last. "I thought all had come back that was comin'," Arn said, and Toug explained that he was the last and told him about Mani.

No doubt Arn had promised to keep an eye out. As soon as he had begun the long jump-and-scramble up the too-high stairs, Toug could no longer remember. This part of the keep was practically solid stone, he knew. Solid stone with a few passages let into it. A few suffocating rooms like the guardroom, and stairs to dungeons dug like mines into the native rock. He felt the whole weight of Utgard around him waiting to crush him, a threat before which he ought to cower, and before which he would have cowered had he not been so tired.

"If the witch appears I won't even talk to her," he told himself. "I'll lie down and cover my head. If she wants to kill me she can."

But Huld did not appear, and the stair, which always seemed endless, and never more endless than it did that night, ended at last. The fire in the turret chamber was burning brightly; and though Mani was nowhere to be seen, Sword Breaker lay upon the wide bed next to the sleeping Etela, with the sword belt and dagger of human size I had bought in Irringsmouth.

"It's been a long ride and a cold one," I said, "but it's almost over."

Ulfa spoke through chattering teeth. "I wouldn't care if it were twice as a long, as long as it's the ride home." And then, "You'll bring Pouk? Bring him back to me?"

"Have you been a wife Pouk would want to come back to?"

"I think so. I've tried to be."

I said, "Then Pouk will bring himself if need be."

Only tossing black treetops were visible below; but Cloud was cantering down a slope. Gylf, who had gone chasing wild geese, was lagging and nearly out of sight. I whistled.

Ulfa said, "You know, I've heard that in the night, but I thought it was the wind."

"It may have been. See how it's blowing now. This wind whistles louder than I."

"But it isn't as cold as it was."

"Only autumn here. A storm's brewing."

"Is that Glennidam? The houses? Those little fields in the forest?"

"I think so, though it's possible I lost my way."

"Put your arm around me. Hold me tight."

I did, holding her as I had when Cloud first mounted into the sky. "Don't be afraid."

"I'm not." Ulfa sighed. "When I left—it seems like a long, long time ago . . ."

"It was."

"That's Glennidam!" She pointed. "There's our house!"

I nodded, and slowed Cloud to a walk.

"I used to think you and I would be married, and we'd come back here, a knight and his lady, riding together on one horse. Hiding myself in bushes beside the road to sleep, lying there with leaves and sticks in my face, I'd think like that so I wouldn't be afraid. It won't happen."

"No," I said.

"I wouldn't want it to, not anymore. I love Pouk and Pouk loves me. But this is close—as close as I'll get. We're going to have children. We want them, both of us do. When they're old enough to understand, I'll tell them about Utgard and how I left it, riding with you on this gray horse, between clouds like cliffs, and the moon so close I could touch it. They'll think I'm making it up."

A gust swayed Cloud, and her mane flew like a banner.

"They'll think I'm making it up," Ulfa repeated, "and after a while so will I. Hold me tighter."

I did.

"This is the moment of my life, the golden time."

Neither of us spoke again until Cloud's hoofs were on solid ground. I dismounted and dropped her reins, and lifted Ulfa from the saddle. She said, "Thank you. I can't ever thank you enough. I won't even try, but I'll tell about you as long as I live."

"Have I ever thanked you for the clothes you sewed for me? Or apologized for taking your brother?"

"Yes, and it doesn't matter anyway."

I turned to go, but she caught my arm. "Won't you come in? There'll be food, and I'll cook what we have for you."

"I don't want to leave Cloud outside in this."

"Just a moment. Please? Warm your hands at the fire before you go."

I hesitated; then nodded, seeing what it meant to her.

The door was barred. She led me to the back, to the door through which I had left the house long ago, and fished out the latchstring with a twig. The kitchen in which her mother had cowered was dark, though a fire smoldered on the hearth. Ulfa fed it fresh wood and knelt to puff the flames. "It seems too small!"

The autumn wind moaned outside as she opened a door to reveal two pigs, headless and gutted, hanging by their hind feet. "My father's butchering already. I can roast slices on a fork as fast as you can sit down."

Warming my hands as she had suggested, I shook my head.

"Sit anyway. You must be tired. I'll cut some bread—"

Gylf, who had followed us, said, "I'd like that meat."

Ulfa looked at him in some surprise. "Did you do that?"

I shook my head.

"I know that cat can talk. I've heard it."

The wind moaned in the chimney, stirring the ashes.

"Raw pork's not good for dogs. Not good for anybody." She threw wide the doors of a tall cupboard and found bones with a good deal of meat on them. "Ma was saving these for soup, I'm sure, but I'll give them to your dog."

There was no reply. I was already outside, and for a moment there can have been no sound in the kitchen save the creaking of the hinges of its door, which swung back and forth, and then (caught by a gust of wind) slammed shut.

One sunny afternoon I had jogged through this field on the same errand, a field full of barley. The barley was reaped now. I ran on stubble, my left hand clutching Eterne to keep her from slapping my thigh. *"Disiri? Disiri?"*

There was no answer; and yet I felt an answer had come: the leaves had spoken for her, saying here I am.

"Disiri!"

You can't find me.

I stopped, listening, but the leaves spoke no more. "I can't," I admitted. "I'll search the seven worlds for you, and turn out Mythgarthr and Aelfrice like empty sacks. But I won't find you unless you want to be found. I know that."

Give up?

"Yes, I give up." I raised both hands.

"Here I am." She stepped from behind the dark bole of the largest tree; and although I could scarcely see anything, I saw her and knew she was tall as few women are tall and slender as no human woman ever is, and too lovely for me to understand, ever, exactly how lovely she was.

My arms closed around her, and we kissed. Her lips were sweeter than honey and warm with life, and there was nothing wrong that mattered because there was nothing wrong we could not mend; and there was love as long as we lived, and love did matter, love would always matter.

We parted, and it seemed to me that we had kissed for centuries, and centuries were not long enough.

"You have the sword Eterne." Her voice smiled.

I gasped for breath. "Do you want her? She's yours."

"I have her already," she said, "because you have her. Know you why she is called Eterne?"

"Because she's almost as beautiful as you are, and beauty is eternal."

We kissed again.

"You're older," she said when we separated. "Your hair is giving up your temples."

"And fatter. I can forgive you anything."

She laughed. Her laughter was bells of delight. "Even a younger lover?"

"Anything," I repeated.

"Then I will have a younger lover, and he will be you."

The wild wind whirled about us, and I wrapped my cloak around her as I had wrapped it around Ulfa. "I could make myself younger, but it would be by the power of Skai."

"Really?" All the merriment of all the maidens was in her laugh.

"I'd have to go back then, honoring my pledge."

"Yet you ride among clouds."

"Cloud bears me up. I do not bear her."

Our lips met; when we parted we were lying upon moss. "The game is nearly over," she whispered. "That is what I came to tell you. Did you think it would go on forever?"

When Gylf found me, I was sitting alone, wrapped in my cloak and weeping. "I ate," Gylf said. "We ought to go."

I nodded and rose.

Cloud was waiting in the village street, her rump to the

wind. On her, I rose higher and higher until I was above the storm; but the wind blew hard even so and it was very cold. When at last we reached the camp in Jotunland I found I could scarcely dismount, and nearly fell.

"No more night riding," I promised, and Cloud nodded happily, and filled my mind with thoughts of sunlit cloud-mountains, mountains ever changing because they are ever new.

"Ya wanna blanket, sar?" The voice was Uns'. "I been keepin' ya fire goin'."

I nodded, and the truth was that I wanted a blanket and a fire badly; but I said, "You're supposed to be serving the queen, Uns. Not me."

"Her's sleepin', sar. Her don' want me. I'se sleepin', ta, most a' th' time. On'y I'd rouse 'n t'row onna stick."

"Thank you." I took off my helmet and rubbed my scalp with fingers stiff with cold. "But you must sleep. It's only a little before sunrise."

"Soon's I help wit' ya boots, sar."

Knowing that I should have removed them myself, I sat and let Uns pull them off; and while Uns was brushing them, I struggled out of my mail. "I need clean clothes," I said sleepily. "I can get some in Utgard, I suppose."

"Take 'um off 'n I'll wash 'um inna river fer ya," Uns declared. "Dry 'um at th' fire real quick."

The temptation was too great.

"Uns?"

"Yessar?"

"A woman told me my hair was receding, that it was leaving my temples bare."

"Yessar."

"It's true." Naked, I stretched myself on blankets Uns had spread near the fire and pulled them over me.

"Yessar," Uns repeated. "Looks nice, sar."

"But I was wearing my helmet, so it didn't look at all."

Seeing that Uns had not understood, I added, "It was dark, too. She can't have seen my hairline."

"Guess she seen ya some udder time, sar." Uns collected the soiled garments I had discarded.

"She must have, and must have seen me since I returned from Skai. One does not grow old in Skai, Uns."

"Yessar."

"No one does. I was there twenty years, and looked no older when I left than I had when I arrived. Now those years have overtaken me. Not that it matters."

"Nosar."

"What matters is that she's been watching me. I knew Baki and Uri watched from Aelfrice, as we watch Overcyns."

"Never seen none, sar."

"Those who look see them. We see what we want to see."

"Awright, sar."

"You're going to wash my clothes now?"

"Yessar."

"I wish you'd do me one more favor before you go. You unsaddled Cloud, didn't you?"

"Nosar. Not yet. Will, sar."

"Please do, and see to her needs. When you do, you'll take my bowcase and quiver with the saddle. I'd like you to open the bowcase and take the bowstring off the bow."

"Yessar."

"Bring it to me. If I'm asleep, put it into my hand."

No doubt Uns said, "Yessar"; for all his crudity, Uns was a good servant. Although he must have, I did not hear him.

CHAPTER NINETEEN
TOUG'S BOON

Mani heard Uns' breathing as he loosed Cloud's cinch, and his muttered words of reassurance to Cloud, and hunkered lower in my right-hand saddlebag. The saddlebags would be taken off, Mani reminded himself, and thrown down somewhere. There would be a shock (he braced himself), but it would be merely uncomfortable, not dangerous.

The scraping near his ear was the sound of my bow being taken from the bowcase. Was Uns (the muttered words had certainly been Uns') planning to shoot a cat?

No, because this new scrape was the bow being replaced, beyond question. That thump as the end of the bow struck the bottom of its hard leather case was unmistakable—unless it was really something else. Uns had not known what was in the case, and had taken it out to see if it was good to eat or play with. Finding it was not, he had sensibly put it back.

The thought suggested various occasions on which Mani himself had *not* put something back, and— Uns is lifting the saddlebags now. Here it comes!

But it did not come. The saddlebags settled into place Somewhere Else, where in place of Cloud's slow, grazing steps there was a faint, faint swaying. Mani shut his eyes tight and counted until he lost count somewhere between twenty and the other one, then risked a peek from under the flap.

Uns had gone. I lay under a blanket by a fire. This was as good as conditions were ever apt to be.

Untying the thong that held the saddlebag closed had
been the hard part of hiding in the bag. But Mani (who
was not inexperienced in these matters) had labored with
tooth and paw. Once inside, he had reached down to pass
the thong loosely through its loop. Now it was not even
necessary to pull it out. Raising the flap drew free the
thong. Half in the bag and half out, he had a look around.

The bags hung on a limb near the ground. A larger limb
held Cloud's saddle and bridle. Cloud herself was rolling
on her back in the manner of cats. Cloud, Mani reflected,
was an unusually fine animal and might well have a dash
of cat somewhere in her ancestry.

He leaped to the ground, flattened himself against it,
and waited for any sign that he had been seen. All quiet,
save for splashing some distance away. Fish jumping,
quite possibly. Large fish, and even minnows were very
good. Mani licked his lips.

More fires, and tents, on the other side of the tree. In this
tent, a tree-sized woman sound asleep, her breath heavy
with wine. Beside her, a snoring man with a blond mustache. Before the other, a shield tastefully ornamented
with spotted cats; in it, a dozen men asleep. One stirred,
and Mani left in haste. Black was surely the best of all colors. Assuredly, it was the best of all colors for cats. What,
he wondered, did white cats do? How could they live,
much less do their duty, when they were visible at night?

A sumptuous pavilion remained, which Mani felt certain was Idnn's. He entered boldly, found her asleep (and
the elderly maid at her feet also sleeping), and springing
lightly onto her bosom offered the traditional gesture of
love and respect until she woke.

"A thousand apologies, Your Majesty." He lowered his
eyes demurely. "I presume upon your affection, I know."

"Mani! What are you doing here?"

"Reporting, Your Majesty. When you left, you charged
me to observe everything, cautioning me that I'd have to

give a full account of all I'd heard upon your return. I've heard a lot, and given an opportunity to make an interim report, I seized it. There's much you should be apprised of."

"How did you get here? You can't possibly have walked this far."

"Nor did I, Your Majesty." Briefly, Mani considered the ethics of the situation. Ethics seldom concerned him, yet it seemed to him that this was one of those rare occasions when they had to be accorded weight. He cleared his throat. "My previous owner, the gallant knight for whom I still hold so much affection, carried me in a saddlebag, Your Majesty."

"Sir Able?" Mani had been hoping that Idnn would pick him up and stroke him, and now she did. "Mani, Sir Able's here—here in the mountains with us—not in Utgard. I spoke to him tonight."

"It is nearly morning, Your Majesty."

"All right, I spoke to him last night. Are you telling me he rode to Utgard and back in a night?"

"No, Your Majesty, for I do not know it."

The old woman stirred, and Idnn whispered, "Go back to sleep, Gerda. It's nothing."

"Your Majesty not infrequently doubts my veracity," Mani said stiffly. "Your Majesty is prone to discount my sagacity as well. I am, however—"

"I don't mean to insult you," Idnn declared, "and I didn't mean that you were nothing, only that Gerda should go back to sleep. But Sir Able—he simply cannot have gone to Utgard and returned with you as quick as that."

"Doubtless Your Majesty is correct." Mani's tone was no longer unbending. "Nor did I say he had, only that I rode in his saddlebag. As I did, Your Majesty. So riding, I arrived not long ago, and since my arrival have been seeking you. Famished and exhausted from a trip you yourself call lengthy, but seeking you and not my own comfort."

"There isn't a lot of food here, but I'll see that you have your choice of whatever we have."

"In that case, I may be able to provide Your Majesty with a quail or a partridge, and I would account it an honor for Your Majesty to accept any such gift I may supply. But I should warn Your Majesty that Sir Able was unaware of my presence in his bag. It might be better not to speak of it."

Idnn had not been listening. "How is my husband?"

"I am no physician—"

"But a shrewd judge of every matter brought before you." Having smoothed Mani's head sufficiently, Idnn tickled his chin. "How is he?"

"Your concern for him does you credit, Your Majesty. I am concerned myself. He has treated me with great civility, on the whole."

Idnn sighed. "I don't love him, Mani. I can't. But I'm his wife. To be noble is to do one's duty—"

"Indeed, Your Majesty."

"And to be royal is to do more. Knights serve their lord, and lords their king. But the king serves his people and his crown, or he is but a tyrant."

"A queen, Your Majesty—"

"Is a woman, and a woman, having half the strength of a man, must bear twice the burden. How is he?"

"Weak, Your Majesty, but stronger than he was when you left him. He has lost a great deal of blood."

"And endured a lot of pain. I know. Is he eating?"

"Soup, I think, Your Majesty. Broth."

"Does he speak of me?"

"With the greatest affection, Your Majesty. My former master explained to him that you had sent him to His Majesty, and His Majesty praised you to the skies, if I may put it thus picturesquely."

"He's awake then, and speaking."

"Happily so, Your Majesty." Mani coughed delicately. "He spoke of your wisdom, Your Majesty. Not of your wisdom exclusively, of course, for he praised your beauty as well. But he spoke glowingly of it. He— Here I can't help but be indelicate, Your Majesty, yet I think the matter important."

Idnn nodded encouragement, her nod just visible by the gray light filtering through the doorway.

"He compared your insight to that of his first minister, Lord Thiazi, Your Majesty." Mani purred. "He judged yours to be superior."

"I must thank His Majesty as soon as possible, Mani. He has paid me a great compliment."

"Indeed, Your Majesty. He likewise compared your acumen to your noble father's, again judging in your favor. That, Your Majesty, has a certain bearing upon my errand."

Idnn's hands left Mani. "I hope you're not about to tell me something to my father's discredit."

"Your Majesty is the best judge. Your noble father is eager that Sir Able enter your royal husband's service."

"I know it."

"A most impressive prophecy having assured him that your throne shall stand secure if Sir Able is your royal husband's vassal. Your husband wishes the same, for the same reason."

"I know all that," Idnn said brusquely. "Come to the point, Mani."

He made her a small, seated bow. "I am making every effort to do so, Your Majesty. I considered my preliminaries necessary. Doubtless you are also aware that your noble father designs the death of Sir Svon's squire."

At these words Uns, who had been listening outside the pavilion for the past minute or two, edged a little closer.

Svon woke Toug, shaking his shoulder. "I wish I could let you sleep, but Lord Beel wants to talk to us together."

Etela sat up. "And me. I'm going with."

"You need a bath," Svon told her.

"It's just charcoal from our shop." Etela tried to scrape her arm with a forefinger. "Smoke 'n stuff."

"You really do need a bath," Toug confirmed. "Clean clothes, too. My sister . . ."

"Left with Sir Able," Svon said brusquely.

Mute, Toug nodded.

"I wish we had her back. I wish we had Sir Able back, too. He won't return until he brings the duke, so he said."

"And my sister won't return at all." Toug got out of bed, found Sword Breaker, and looked around. "Where's Mani?"

"If you don't know, I certainly don't."

Etela said, "Put on more wood," and Toug did.

"You'd better be sparing," Svon told him. "There's only so much, unless we can go out and get more."

"Unless?" Toug looked around at him.

"I think something like that's what His Lordship wants to talk about. We won't know until we hear him, and we won't hear him until you're dressed."

Nodding, Toug turned to Etela. "My sister's gone, but Baki's still around, or I think she is. I know Pouk is, and he knows all the women. Find someone and tell them I said to give you a bath and see that you wash your clothes."

"I want—"

"Breakfast. I know. Say I said to feed you, too."

"To go with."

Toug took a deep breath. "When you're clean and wearing a clean dress, and you've had breakfast, you can come with me anyplace I go."

He and Svon left. As they climbed down the oversized stair, Svon said, "You're not really going to take her, are you? Any foray outside the castle will be dangerous."

Toug shrugged. "We may not be going anywhere, and if we are, we'll be gone . . ."

A heavy tread on the steps above interrupted. Both stopped and moved to one side.

"Gud mornin'. Wud you want me to carry you?"

Svon smiled. "Good morning, Schildstarr. I know your offer is kindly meant, but these steps don't really pose much of a problem for my squire and me."

"As you will. I'm for the lordlin'. An' you?"

"If you mean Lord Beel, the same."

"Stir stump, then. I'll not come for you." Schildstarr paused, then chuckled. "You sma' folk set us to work here. In our north country, we dinna fetch nor carry."

Still laughing, he preceded them, and they followed him as quickly as they could.

"Here's our dilemma," Thiazi told Svon and Toug. "As you just heard, we're sending Schildstarr and his men to buy the forge and tools, and to collect more of His Majesty's loyal subjects if they can. Lord Beel," he nodded toward him, "fears we cannot trust him. Perhaps I should not tell you that, since it may influence your own thinking. But I have no doubt you knew it before."

Svon nodded.

Beel said, "You're entitled to your own opinions, both of you, and I'd like to have them. Can we, Sir Svon?"

"I would not, Your Lordship. No more than we must."

Beel nodded. "Squire Toug?"

"I don't think he'd go against the king," Toug said slowly. "Only we're not the king."

"We act for him," Thiazi declared.

"But Schildstarr isn't sure we're honest about it. Or that's how it seems to me, My Lord."

"There you have it." Beel laid a leather bag on the table. "That's gold, a lot of it. I want you two—alone—to go into the town with it. Take no men-at-arms, and no archers. Just the two of you. Will you do it?"

Svon said, "Certainly, Your Lordship."

"Squire?"

Toug took a deep breath. "If Sir Svon goes, I'll go."

"Good. We've been hiding in here. You may think that's too harsh a word, but it's the truth. Hiding, and hoping His Majesty would recover and save us. And then Her Majesty, my daughter . . ." Beel paused, rubbing his forehead. "She left—rode to fetch Sir Able. That made it worse, for me anyway."

"To tell you the truth," Svon said, "I've been hoping for something like this."

Thiazi cleared his throat. That throat looked as long as Toug's forearm, and the clearing of it was like the noise of barrels rolled on cobblestones. "We can't hide, as Lord Beel calls it, much longer. There isn't enough food. We've told Schildstarr to tell everyone he meets that His Majesty is recovering."

Beel muttered, "They heard that."

"Of course they did. I repeat it to emphasize it. We also told him to buy food, if he can."

Svon nodded. So did Toug.

"Now I tell you the same things. If you speak to any of our sons of Angr, tell them His Majesty will be well soon. If you speak to slaves, as seems more likely, the same."

"We will." Svon nodded.

Beel added, "Buy food, if you can. Wagon loads of it. If Schildstarr brings more Angrborn we'll need tons of it. And in fact we need tons of it already, for Thrym and his men and for ourselves. To say nothing of the slaves."

"We'll get what we can," Svon said stoutly.

Toug added, "I think Schildstarr will, too. It's food for him and his men, a lot of it."

Beel nodded. "So far we've only asked you to do some of the things Schildstarr will be doing. But there's much more. No doubt you guessed."

Svon nodded.

"First, we need to test the waters. If we sent Sir Garvaon and his men-at-arms with you, the Angrborn would feel threatened. I have no doubt they would attack you."

"I agree," Thiazi declared.

"But one knight and one squire—don't take your lance, by the way. I want you to leave that here."

"I will, Your Lordship."

"Are clearly no threat. They've had ample time to grow used to the idea that there are humans in Utgard, friends of their king who are neither slaves nor foes. If I'm right, they should let you alone. I think you'll find I am."

Thiazi favored Svon with a cruel smile. "If Lord Beel's misjudged, you'll find yourself in a fight that will make you famous even if you lose. As you will. Will you still go?"

"Certainly, My Lord."

Beel spoke to Thiazi. "I told you."

"I know you did. I didn't believe you." He shrugged.

Svon rose, sliding from the seat of his chair to the floor. "Is that all, Your Lordship?"

"You're anxious to be away."

"Yes, Your Lordship. I am."

"There is one more item." Beel looked from Svon to Toug and back again. "Lord Thiazi tells me that under the laws of Jotunland the king can commandeer the slaves of his subjects if he has need of them. The slaves of this smith—Logi?"

Toug said, "Yes, Your Lordship."

"Assisted him in making the tools Toug saw. You are to sequester them, if you can, in the king's name, and bring them here."

Thiazi added, "Or kill them if you cannot."

Toug started to speak, then closed his mouth and waited for Svon; but all Svon said was "I will, My Lord."

Toug cleared his throat. "I ask a boon, My Lord."

Thiazi smiled as before. "To which you think yourself entitled, I'm sure."

"Yes. Yes, I do. You just gave me one, I know. You gave me my sister. That was really very nice of you, and I haven't forgotten."

"Yet you believe that you're owed another."

Beel said, "I will grant it myself, Squire, if I can."

"You can't, Your Lordship. Or anyhow I don't think so."

Thiazi leaned forward, both huge hands on the polished black wood of the huge table. "This is becoming interesting. Tell me why you deserve this boon, and I may grant it."

Toug filled his lungs. "When you gave me my sister, My Lord—and I'll never forget it—it was for going outside alone at night and finding Logi's forge, and killing him. Now I'm going out again, only in daylight. We'll probably be killed. Everybody here knows that."

Svon nodded and said, "I must speak to you privately."

"So I'd like the reward first, and because it may make it easier for me to do what you want us to do. I mean, get Logi's slaves, and bring them here."

"Go on," Thiazi told him.

"What I want is for you to promise that if we do, you'll set them free. All of them who come here and help the king. If you promise, we can tell them that you did and they'll do everything they can to help, and that may do it."

"Bravo," Beel muttered; and then, more loudly, *"Bravo!"*

"It's not a bad thought, Squire." Thiazi relaxed, with an amused smile at Beel. "I'd be disposed to grant it, if I could. Unfortunately, our law forbids the freeing of slaves for any reason."

"You tried," Svon whispered to Toug.

"However, I can offer another. One you may like as well or better. The slaves you bring here will be divided between Sir Svon and yourself. Sir Svon will have first choice, you second, Sir Svon third, and so on. Thus you shall each receive the same if the total is even, and Sir Svon one more if the total is odd."

"That won't make them help us," Toug muttered. "They don't want to belong to us."

"Oh, but it will. In time you and Sir Svon will return to Celidon, and they'll be free." Thiazi paused, and the cruel smile returned, "Unless, of course, you choose to sell them before you go. But you need not tell them that."

I sat up; and seeing Uns crouched by the fire to spread my shirt to the warmth of the flames, I said, "I've had the strangest dream."

"I got sumpin' I gotta tell ya, sar."

"In a moment, Uns. I want to tell somebody about this before I forget. We never dreamed in Skai. Did I tell you?"

Uns shook his head.

"We never did, and it never seemed odd to us that we didn't. At least, it never seemed odd to me." I found Parka's bowstring among my blankets and showed it to Uns. "I was listening to this before I slept. That might have had something to do with it."

"Wid not dreamin' in Skai, sar?"

"With my dream. I don't know why I didn't dream there. Perhaps the others did, though I never heard anybody mention it. The Valkyrie's kiss brings forgetfulness so deep that I never thought of Disiri. It seems impossible, but I didn't."

"Yessar."

"I was conscious of something wrong, you understand." I fell silent, lost in thought. "Exactly as I was conscious of something wrong in my dream. Years passed before I could put a name to it—before I remembered her face. That was when I went to the Valfather."

"Jist like me comin' ter ya, sar."

"My Valkyrie was Alvit, Uns. She'd been a princess and died a virgin, facing death with dauntless courage. I should have held her dearer than Disiri. I wanted to but couldn't."

"Yessar. Like ter see 'un someday, sar."

"Maybe you will. It isn't at all likely, but it's not impossible. What was I talking about?"

" 'Bout ya bowstring, sar, 'n ya dream."

"You're right." I lay down again and laid the bowstring on my chest. "My bowstring is spun of severed lives, Uns."

"Fer real, sar?"

"Yes. Of lives that are ended, and I think lives cut short. It may be only because most lives are."

"Guess so, sar."

"So do I, Uns. It's all either of us can do. Of lives cut short, whether for that reason or another. Maybe only because a woman cut them with her teeth for me. She may have ended the lives by that act. I can't remember her name."

"Don't matter, sar."

"She will remind me of it eventually, I feel sure. What I was going to say, Uns, was that whenever I let an arrow fly from this string, I hear them in its singing—hear their voices as they spoke in life. When I draw Eterne, all the knights who have held her unworthily appear."

"Yessar. I seen 'em, sar."

"Whether to affright my foes or encourage me, I can't say. Sometimes they fight at my side. Sometimes— judging, I suppose, that I have no need of their aid—they don't. Disiri saw to it that I gained Eterne. That I would have a chance to gain her, at least."

"Yessar." Uns had returned to his laundry, turning my drawers where they hung upon a bush, and feeding sticks and winter grass to the fire that dried them.

"She wanted me to win Eterne because she loves me."

"Yessar."

I sat up again, running my fingers along Parka's string. "Have you heard this, Uns? Have you, Gylf?"

Both nodded, Gylf more circumspectly.

"You have?"

Uns nodded again. "Kin I tell my news now, sar? Won't take mor'n a minute."

"And you'll bust unless you do. I understand. Okay, I'll listen. But you must answer a question afterward, or try to. Is the king dead? King Gilling?"

"Nosar. Gettin' better's wot he sez."

"King Gilling said that he was getting better?"

"Nosar. I mean, most like he done, sar, on'y 'twarn't him I heered. 'Twar that cat, sar. Ya cat, on'y if'n he's yorn, why ain't he here ter tell ya hisself?"

"He is," Mani announced with a fine flare for the dramatic. With head and tail high, he emerged from the shadows and bowed. "Your servant, most noble of knights."

"My friend, rather." Ignoring a low growl from Gylf, I opened my arms.

Mani sprang into my lap. "Your yokel spied upon me, Sir Able, and I have no doubt you would cut his throat for it if I asked. Certainly my royal master would hang him in chains, did I so much as raise my paw." Mani raised it, claws out, by way of illustration. "Would you prefer I forgive him?"

"Greatly," I told him.

"In that case I do." Mani's claws vanished. "You are forgiven, fellow."

"Tanks, sar!" Uns pulled his forelock.

I said, "A talking cat does not astound you, Uns?"

"Hit's a magic cat, I reckon."

"And you've seen a magic sword. Perhaps other things."

"That's so, sar, 'n hit come ter tell da queen lady I been workin' fer 'bout how her pa's tryin' ter git Toug kilt, sar. 'N I likes Toug 'n hope ya kin make him stop."

"I addressed Her Majesty before yourself because you had given me to her," Mani explained. "I felt you'd approve for that reason. She has influence with her father, and it would better for him to spare Toug voluntarily. If he's prevented by force—well, dear owner, he's King Arn-thor's ambassador. There's no getting around that."

I rubbed my jaw. "Is he trying to kill Toug? Or have him killed?"

Mani, who had decided his paw needed smoothing, smoothed it. "He is not. Your opinion of my judgment must be high, I know. We have known each other for some while."

"It is."

"In which case you will give weight to my opinion, which is that Lord Beel won't sully his honor with murder, whether by his own hand or another's. He thrusts Toug into positions of danger. The stratagem is not unknown."

"Why?" I lay down once more.

"He wishes you in his son-in-law's service because he believes he will keep the crown with you to guard it."

Mani waited for me to speak, but I did not.

"He believes this because my mistress, by which I mean by first mistress, has told him so. To be precise, because she told that long fellow Thiazi. You recall him, I'm sure."

"Yes, I do. Why did she say it?"

"She no longer confides in me as she used to," Mani said pensively. "Not that we are estranged. When one is dead . . ."

"I understand."

Mani condescended to address Uns. "I myself have been dead on several occasions. We are permitted nine demises, of which the ninth is permanent. Doubtless you know."

"Nosar, I dint. On'y I do now, Master Cat."

"You may refer to me as Master Mani, fellow. Though I am a cat, *cat* is not my name." Master Mani redirected his attention to me. "You asked why she prophesied as she did. May I hazard a conjecture?"

"Because it's true?"

"Certainly not. I would guess she feared that my master—by which term I designate His Royal Majesty King Gilling of Jotunland, to whom my royal mistress Queen Idnn, his wife, has given me—might do you violence otherwise. Thanks to her foresight, he is instead so-licitous of your life."

"More so than I." I shut my eyes. "You can hear my bowstring, can't you, Mani? Even now?"

For once Mani was silent.

"I can, there's one voice that cries out to me again and again. After I got this bowstring, I tried not to hear it. To tell the truth, I tried not to hear any of them. Now I have been listening, for that one especially. I hear it now, and I can make out a few words, and sobbing."

"Mebbe that queen ya like, sar? Could she be, like, passed across?"

"Disiri? No. Disiri is not dead."

For a half minute or more there was silence save for the crackling of the fire Uns fed and stirred; at last Mani said, "There is a room in Utgard, the Room of Lost Love."

I opened my eyes and sat up. "Have you been in there?"

Mani shook his head. "I've merely seen the door."

"You know where it is?"

"Lord Thiazi has a study. Very capacious, and nicely situated, in which he pursues the art. Other rooms open off it. I have been through all the doors but one, and that one is kept locked. I have climbed the ivy outside, but that room has no window."

"You'd like to get in."

"Perhaps." Mani's emerald eyes, which had been half shut, opened wide. "Certainly I'd like to look inside."

"Have you lost love, Mani?"

He sprang from my lap and vanished in the night.

"What about you, Uns?"

"Don' know a' none, sar, on'y I likes Squire Toug."

"So do I." I stretched. "I don't want him killed or maimed any more than you do."

"Then you'll stop it, sar? Tomorrer, like?"

"No. Mani told Her Majesty of Jotunland, while you eavesdropped. Is that right?"

"I never calt it right, sar."

"Naturally not. But you did. She may stop it. Or not. Surely she'll try. As for me . . ." I yawned. "Toug wants to be a knight." The song of the string had begun, and although Gylf laid a gentle paw upon my hand, I said no more.

Svon motioned to Toug, who shut Thiazi's door behind them. The vast hallway, always dark, seemed darker than ever; bats chittered high overhead. "That's a bad man," Toug said under his breath.

"That isn't a real man at all," Svon told him. "If you haven't learned it yet, learn it now."

"I know."

"Then act like it and speak like it. Their whole race is evil, though some are better than others. The worst are monsters far worse than beasts."

"Logi had three arms," Toug said pensively. "I haven't told anybody about it, but he did."

"There was once a knight named Sir Ravd," Svon said. He had begun to walk so fast that Toug had to trot to keep up. "Sir Ravd was sent to suppress outlaws in the northern forest from which you hail, the forest south of the mountains."

"I remember," Toug said.

"He was killed. I think Duke Marder thought the outlaws—the free companies, as they called themselves—would not attack a great and famous knight, though he had no comrade save his squire. If that's what Duke Marder thought, Duke Marder was wrong."

"I won't tell anybody you said that," Toug declared.

"I would say it to his face. I already have."

Svon took a dozen strides before he spoke again. "Sir Ravd died. His squire lived, though he had been left for dead. He returned to Sheerwall, eager to tell everyone how his master had charged foes so numerous they could not be counted, how resolutely and how skillfully his master had fought, sending scores to the wolves. How he, Sir Ravd's squire, alone and wounded, had buried Sir Ravd by moonlight, digging the grave with a broken ax, and heaping it with the weapons of the slain."

Not knowing what else to say, Toug said, "Yes, sir." He glanced behind him, for he felt unseen eyes on his back.

"They heard him in Sheerwall," Svon continued, "and they slandered him. Not to his face—they were not as brave as the outlaws, who had faced Sir Ravd and his squire too, and never flinched. But he found, this squire, that he had an enemy no sword could touch, rumors that dogged his steps."

Abruptly, Svon stopped and turned to face Toug. "I have tried to teach you in the short time we have been together."

"Yes, Sir Svon. I know you have, and I've learned a lot. From you and from Sir Able, too."

"This is my most important lesson. It took me years to learn it, but I throw it to you like a crust."

"Yes, Sir Svon," Toug repeated.

"We go into danger. You fought a Frost Giant and won. We may be fighting a score before noon. When we do, you may live and I may die."

"I hope not, Sir Svon."

"I've no wish to die. None at all. If we fight, I hope for victory. I'll do all I can to see that we're victorious. You have that mace."

"Yes, Sir Svon. Sword Breaker." Toug held her up.

"Where is the dagger you took from the Angrborn smith? You showed it to me—a dagger as big as a war sword. Have you still got it?"

"It's back in my room unless somebody took it."

"Bring that too. Bring them both."

"I will, Sir Svon."

"If I die and you live, Toug, you'll have to face a foe more terrible than the Angrborn, and more subtle. Whispers, sly smiles, sidelong looks. Do you understand me?"

"I think so, Sir Svon."

"You'll have to fight them, and you fight them by finding a battle to die in, and not dying. By doing that over and over, Toug."

"Yes, Sir Svon."

"You're a peasant boy? As Sir Able was?"

"We're not as bad as you think, Sir Svon."

"I don't think it." Svon sighed, and it came to Toug that Svon's sigh was the loneliest sound he had ever heard, a sigh like a ghost's, a sound that would haunt the cavernous halls of Utgard longer than the bats. "I was brought up by my father's servants, Toug. Mostly Nolaa and her husband. They were proud of me, and taught me to be proud of myself. It helped, and for years it was the only help I had. Has anyone been proud of you? Besides me?"

Toug gulped. "I wouldn't have been able to kill Logi if it hadn't been for Org, Sir Svon. He was fighting him first to protect us, and he did more than I did. Only you said I wasn't supposed to tell about him."

Svon smiled; it was not a warm smile, but it made him handsome. "I'm proud of you just the same. More proud, because you told the truth when the temptation to lie must have been great. I've lied often and know that temptation. Who besides me?"

"My sister, Sir Svon. Ulfa, when she found out I was a squire, and might be a knight someday."

"That's good, and Ulfa and I may be enough. Sir Ravd was never proud of me, and I was never as proud of him as I should have been. Here I feel I should order you to remember him, but you never knew him."

"I saw him, Sir Svon, when he came to our village and talked to people."

"Then remember that, and remember what I've told you about him."

They separated; but Toug, instead of going to the turret he shared with Mani and Etela, stood and watched Svon's back as Svon strode away down that lofty hall, a hall empty of all beauty and comfort, ill-lit by such daylight as found its way through the high windows on one side.

And it seemed to Toug that at its termination he saw a knight with a golden lion rampant on his helm and a golden lion on his shield—and that Svon did not see him, though Svon was so much nearer. Toug turned away muttering, "This whole keep's haunted."

Later, as he was starting up one of the endless flights of stairs, he said, "Well, I hope we don't have to fight at all. That we just get the slaves, and that's all there is."

Still later he added, "I wish Mani was here."

CHAPTER TWENTY

THAT WAS KING GILLING!

Summer in the midst of winter. Idnn sat upon a bench of white marble, delightfully cool, beneath wisteria; and though it was too dark for her to see the face of the young man beside her, she knew the young man was Svon. A nightingale sang. They kissed, and their kiss held a lifetime of love, throbbing and perfumed with musk.

For eons it endured, but ended far too soon. She woke, and held her eyes tight shut, and would have given all that she possessed to return for one hour to that dream—drew the blanket tight around her, and knew the febrile heat of her own loins, where something as old as Woman wept.

Gerda muttered in her sleep, turned, and lay quiet.

"Your Majesty . . ."

The voice had been real, not Mani's, not Gerda's or Berthold's, and certainly not Uns'. Idnn sat up.

A naked girl with floating hair knelt at her bedside. "Your Majesty. Your servant is Uri. Did you like the dream I brought you?"

Idnn caught her breath.

"I hoped it might entertain Your Majesty. Your servant Uri is a waif of Aelfrice, one who seeks to please you in every possible way and asks no more than a smile. One kind word in a year, but only if Your Majesty is so inclined."

Idnn did not feel capable of indignation, but mustered all she had. "Must we have a sentry at our door, even here?"

"Your Majesty does." Uri gestured. "There he lies, sound asleep beside his cudgel." She giggled. "I skipped over him."

Idnn swung her legs over the side of the bed that had been Marder's. "Rise. We wish to see you better."

Uri did, wand-slender and no taller than Idnn herself. "Shall I light the candle? Am I fair to look upon?"

"The sun's up." Vaguely, Idnn wondered what had become of her nightdress, then remembered she had brought none. "We will see you well enough in a minute or two."

"In sunshine? Your Majesty would scarcely see me at all." A flame sprang from the candle wick.

"You claim you are an Aelf?"

Uri bowed, spreading her hands and inclining her head.

"Your hair—it's very beautiful, but we have to admit it doesn't look human. May we touch it?"

"And more, Your Majesty."

Idnn did. "It has no weight."

"But little, Your Majesty, and so is stirred by every breeze. I am the same."

"Your eyes, too. You don't like to look at us."

"Your Majesty is a queen."

Idnn touched Uri's chin. "The queen orders you to look her in the face. You will not be punished."

Uri raised her head, and Idnn found herself looking into

eyes of smoky yellow fire. "You are what you say." A trifle light-headed, Idnn seated herself on the bed again.

"Would you like to see my true self, Your Majesty? I took this so as not to frighten."

"We would not have been afraid," Idnn declared stoutly, "but my servants may wake. Better that you stay as you are."

"They will not, Your Majesty, unless you wish it."

"Remain as you are, Aelf. What do you wish from us?"

"A smile."

"All right." Idnn shrugged. "You'll get it if you've earned it. Have you?"

"My dream," Uri began.

"We had no dream! What else?"

"Your servant Uri also brought a dream to Sir Able. It was of Glas, an isle well known to your servant. If he wants to revisit it, as I trust he will, he will have to remain in Mythgarthr. Thus, I hope to have him enter your husband's service and remain there. Does that please Your Majesty?"

"Certainly. If it's true."

"Thank you, Your Majesty. Your servant Uri also seeks to warn you of an ill-intentioned person who seeks the life of your royal husband. His Majesty has been stabbed. You, Your Majesty, were present on that sad occasion."

"Are you saying we stabbed him? You lie!"

Uri crouched, her hands raised as if to ward off a blow. "Your servant proclaims your innocence, with her own. Your servant has come to tell you the name—"

Something (afterward Idnn puzzled long over just what that something had been) drew Idnn's attention to the door of her pavilion; it stood open, though it ought to have been tied firmly with five golden cords—a discrepancy which at the time failed to disturb her. Through it, silhouetted against the sun, she saw a tall man with a staff. He wore a gray cloak and a wide hat, and he was walking toward her.

Their gazes locked, and she rose from the bed, naked as she was, and trembled until he stood before her. Naked, she knelt and pressed her forehead to the rich, uneven carpet of the floor.

"Arise, my daughter."

She did, slowly and hesitantly.

"Open your eyes."

"I'm afraid, Father."

"Do you think you must die if you behold my face? I am not the Most High. Look upon me."

It was a hard as anything she had ever done.

"Do you know my voice?"

"It is the wind, Father. I did not know it was your voice, but I have heard it many times."

"Look into my eye. Have you seen it?"

"Yes, Father. It is where the sun lives."

"I am . . . ?"

"The Wanderer." Her knees shook until it seemed she would surely fall. "You are King of the Overcyns."

"Am I to be so feared?"

"Yes, Father."

He laughed, and it was the laughter of a torrent.

"Y-you're displeased with me."

He laid his hand upon her shoulder, and strength poured from it to fill her. "Do you truly believe, Queen Idnn, that I am seen like this by those who displease me?"

"No, Father. I know you are not."

"Then what reason have you to fear? Is it because your husband is of the blood of Ymir?"

"Yes, Father. For that reason and many others."

"My own have wed the Giants of Winter and Old Night, Queen Idnn, and they us more than once. If I bless you, will you serve me? My blessing brings good fortune ever after."

She knelt, though not as Uri had, and the face that she turned up to him shone. "I'll do you whatever service I can, Father, now and always. With your blessing or without it."

He blessed her, giving her the blessing of Skai and the promise of a seat at his table, laying the hand that had held her shoulder upon her head and tapping her right shoulder and her left with his staff.

"Rise, Queen Idnn. You have a place with me always."

She stood. Weeping, she could not speak.

"I have a friend. I will not name him, because the name he bears here is not the name he bears among us, where he is Drakoritter. The dragon stands upon his helm, and coils on his shield."

Still weeping, Idnn nodded.

"I let him return that he might regain his only love. Help him, Queen Idnn."

She shut tight eyes from which the tears still streamed, and labored to bring fair words into the world: "F-F-Father. I-I-I am your slave."

Opening her eyes, she found that she stood alone in the pavilion that had been Marder's. Gerda slept still at the foot of the folding bed. Of the Wanderer, there was no sign. Nor was there any sign of Uri the Aelfmaiden, save that the candle burned with a long, smoky flame.

Wrapping herself in a blanket, Idnn went to the door. It was closed and tied so with five golden cords. She loosed the knots and drew back its bear-colored velvet. Uns lay across the doorway with a stout staff beside him. A bowshot down the slope of winter-brown grass and broken snow, beyond the dead campfires and the sleepers cocooned in whatever covering they had been able to find, green-robed spruce and white-limbed birch stirred in a dawn wind that repeated—once only—the blessing she had received.

Returning to her bed, she pulled the blanket from her maid. "Wake up, Gerda! The sun's up. Help us dress before Berthold and Uns strike our tent." The dawn wind, entering the pavilion, extinguished the candle.

* * *

Etela, clean and a little damp, was drying herself in the turret room. "Where you going?"

"Back into town." Toug tried to smile, and succeeded.

"What for?"

"To buy things. Lord Thiazi's given us money—that's Sir Svon and me. This castle's running short of everything."

"Coming with!"

"No, you're not."

"Am so! I know where everything is, the whole market."

"Put your coat on." Toug buckled on his sword belt and loosened Sword Breaker in her scabbard. "What if somebody were to see you with your gown sticking to you like that?"

"They won't. You've got the thing on the door."

"The bar." Toug picked up the dagger that had been the Angrborn smith's, and eyed it with disfavor. How was he to carry a sword as long as an ox goad? "It won't be there in a minute. I'm going, and it's too heavy for you."

"Wait up. I'll be really quick."

"You're *not* going. Lord Thiazi and Lord Beel said Sir Svon and me. Nobody else."

"Want me to show you how to carry Master's big knife?"

"How would you know?" Toug, who had taken it from its place in the corner leaned it against the bed.

"'Cause I'm smart. Watch."

Before he could stop her, she had drawn his dagger and ducked under one of the oversized chairs.

"What are you doing down there? Don't cut that!"

"I already have. This's really sharp."

"I know, I sharpened it. Be careful."

"This stuff's kind of worn, I guess. It's pretty soft." Etela emerged from under the chair waving a narrow strip of thick leather. "Now sit on the floor so I can do this."

"Do what?"

"Fasten on your sword. You'll see. Now sit!"

Reluctantly, Toug did. "I don't have a lot of time. Sir Svon's probably waiting for me this minute."

"We've already spent more time talking."

He felt a tug at the buckle of his shoulder strap.

"See, you've got this so you can make it shorter or bigger, and the sword's got a ring up here where Master tied it on his belt. You cut the thong, remember?"

Toug said, "Sure."

"Well, these chairs have big straps underneath to hold the cushions. So I cut a piece off the side, and I'm tying your sword on the buckle."

"Can you tie good knots, Etela?"

"I can *crochet!*"

The knot was tightened with a vengeance. "Now get up."

He did, and small hands made a final adjustment. "See? It hangs right down your back, slantwise so the handle's not behind your neck. Reach up."

His hand found the long bone grip he planned to shave smaller. He drew the sword, sheath and blade leaving his back together until the sheath fell with a slap.

"It's heavy, isn't it?"

Half an hour later, as he and Svon finished saddling, he remembered Etela's question and his answer, which had been a lie. "Sir Svon?"

Svon looked up from his cinch. "What?"

"I was wondering how long it took you to get used to wearing mail."

"I never have." Svon swung into the saddle as if mail, helmet, and sword weighed nothing at all.

"You haven't?"

"Not yet. I'm always conscious of it, and glad to get it off. Ask Sir Garvaon." Svon paused. "I'm glad to put it on, too. Are you afraid you can't mount with that war sword? Hang it from the pommel like your shield. Many men do that."

Toug's left foot was already in the stirrup; with a firm grip on the saddle, he mounted with everything in him.

"The weight wasn't as bad as you thought, was it?"

Toug shook his head.

Svon made a small noise and eased his reins; Moonrise trotted into the deserted courtyard, eager to be off. "You know what's a lot heavier?"

Toug hurried after them. "Your helm?"

"No. This burse." Its strings were tied to his belt; Svon shook it and it chinked melodiously. "If I were to lose my helm or my shield, I'd go on without them. Lose this, and who would trust me afterward?"

"I would."

Svon laughed. "Nicely spoken. To tell you the truth, few trust me now." For a few minutes and more, Svon rode on in silence. "Duke Marder's coming. Sir Able said so."

"I don't know him."

"I do, and he thinks he knows me. He was my liege, but he never trusted me."

Side by side they rode through the gate of Utgard, and out on the echoing bridge Toug had crossed on foot the night before, and recrossed with a war sword on his shoulder and Etela skipping after him.

"It's by bearing mail and sword that we become strong," Svon said, "and by bearing hardship that we become brave. There is no other way."

"I need to talk to you, Mani."

Mani nodded and sprang into my arms. "I require my place in your saddlebag. You'll oblige me?"

"Certainly." To prove it, I put him there.

"Now talk away, dear owner. Or do you want me to?"

"I want you to tell me about the Room of Lost Love. You mentioned it. Tell me everything you know."

"I haven't been in it." Mani paused, his emerald eyes vague. "I believe I said that."

"I'd like to hear everything you've heard about it."

"Ulfa probably knows more," Mani said slowly. "Pouk may, too. They were in Utgard longer."

Gylf made a small noise, half a growl.

"They aren't here," I said. "You are. How did you learn what you know about it?"

"Originally? From Huld. The Angrborn never love. I suppose everybody knows. It's the main difference between them and you. You're both very big. They're bigger, but you're both big and noisy. You don't think much, either of you. You both can talk. Which is good, I admit."

"Tell me about the room."

The last of the pack mules was being loaded. Marder and Woddet were already in the saddle, and as I watched Uns made a step of his hands to assist Idnn in mounting.

"Lost love's got to go somewhere." Mani was speaking slower than ever, and as much to himself as me. "People act as if lost things vanish. We cats don't. I used to have a house I liked, a little place in the woods and a good place for field mice and rabbits. I left—my mistress made me— and now I hardly think of it. But it's still there."

Gylf looked up, plainly expecting me to say something, but I did not.

"It hasn't gone away," Mani continued, "unless it's burned. I'm the one who's gone away."

I said, "I'm not sure I follow this."

"I'm like love," Mani explained. "There's a great deal of love in every cat. Not everyone believes that, but it's true. Dependency and fawning aren't love."

"I love Bold Berthold," I told him.

"There. You see? Now suppose you stopped. You'd feel a sort of emptiness, wouldn't you?"

"I suppose so."

"You certainly would, if you really loved Berthold to start with. That would be the space the love used to fill. It's like losing a tooth. If a tooth comes out, you throw it away. Very likely you never see it again. But it's still somewhere. A peasant digging might turn it up, or a jack-daw might put it in his nest."

I nodded absently. "Gylf, would you bring my lance?"

"Love is the same, and love tends to go where it is most needed. A lost cat goes to water, if it can."

"I didn't know that."

Cloud, who had been listening, filled my mind with the image of a pony splotched with white and brown, climbing hill after hill until it reached the foothills of the mountains.

"So lost love comes to Jotunland, where no love is, or at least very little—some poor slave whose cat is her only friend. Anyway, this is one of the places where it comes."

I took my lance from Gylf's mouth and mounted, swinging my right leg wide to miss Mani.

"It's stored in the Room of Lost Love in Utgard. Those who've lost love . . . This is what they say. As I told you, I couldn't get in. Those who've lost love can go in there and find their lost love again, sometimes."

Mani sighed, and drew his sleek black head deeper into my saddle bag. "I haven't lost love. Or if I have, I can't re-member what it was. Perhaps that's why I couldn't get in."

Riding alone, a long bowshot in front of the main body with empty fields and woods to either side, I found myself wondering whether that door would open to me.

"That's it," Toug said, and pointed. "That's where they made the picks and the shovels—all the tools." As he spoke, he heard the deep and sometimes rasping voices of Angrborn. A moment later one lumbered around the cor-ner of the house. He was carrying a mattock, but wore a

long sword like the swords with which Skoel and Bitergarm had fought.

Svon and Toug urged their mounts forward, but he
barred their way with his mattock. "STOP!"

Svon reined up. "We are on the king's business. You
halt us at your peril."

"The king's dead!"

"That is a lie."

The Angrborn raised his mattock.

Svon clapped his spurs to Moonrise and shot past him,
galloping toward the forge.

Toug laughed.

"You! Who're you?"

Toug took his shield from the pommel to display its
white griffin.

"One of them foreign knights."

"Since you call me one, I'll be a knight to you. Will you
engage?"

"A month back, I killed a dozen better'n you."

"Then we fight as we are and where we stand. Single
combat." Rising in his stirrups, Toug raised his voice as
well. "Put aside your bow, Sir Svon."

The Angrborn turned to look. Toug spurred his horse as
Svon had. The war sword—drawn with one hand, wielded
with both—caught the Frost Giant below the ribs, and
driven by Toug's strength and Laemphalt's thundering
speed sank to the hilt and was torn from Toug's hands as
he flashed past.

He wheeled Laemphalt and let his gallop subside to a
walk. The mattock lay on the road; the Angrborn who had
held it knelt beyond it, bent double above a pool of blood.
His hands were pressed to his side, and momentarily Toug
wondered whether he was trying to draw out the blade that
had pierced him or merely trying to ease his pain.

He fell, and Toug urged Laemphalt forward until smoking, seething blood bathed his hooves, dismounted, and wading in ankle-deep blood wrestled his war sword free and wiped it with a swatch cut from the dead giant's shirt.

An auction was in progress on the far side of the forge, attended by two score Angrborn, some of whom Toug recognized. For five minutes, he watched the bidding; then, having seen an open door and gaunt faces in the shadows beyond it, he spurred Laemphalt between two Angrborn and into the house.

"A horse." It was one of the blind slaves from the forge. "There's a horse in here."

"I'm riding him," Toug told him. "Are you afraid we'll get the floor dirty?"

"I'll clean it up." A worn woman came forward and grasped Laemphalt's bridle. "Who are you?"

Toug explained, and soon three blind, muscular men and two women were gathered around him. He cleared his throat. "Do any of you want to go back to Celidon?"

"Get out o' here?" "Not be slaves no more?" "What's this you say?" "Yes!" "It's a trick!"

The last had been from one of the eyeless smiths, and Toug addressed him. "It isn't a trick, Vil, but it may be tricky. To tell the truth, I think it's going to be. But maybe it can be done. We're going to try, if you'll help."

"They're supposed to sell us," one of the other men said, "after the rest's gone. Master's dead."

"I killed him," Toug admitted. "I had to. He was going to kill Etela and me."

"You got her?" That was Vil.

A woman said, "Her ma thinks she's back at the castle."

"She is. I took her there last night, and your master tried to stop us." Toug drew a deep breath. "Listen to me, because we're not going to do this unless you're willing. The king, King Gilling, can take slaves whenever he wants them. That's the law. He—"

"Here you are!" It was Svon's voice, and he strode in from another room, his shield on his arm and his sword drawn.

Toug said, "I thought you were at the sale out there."

"Schildstarr's taking care of it. We were supposed to keep an eye on him, remember?"

Toug nodded.

"So I did, and he's playing a man's part as well as I can judge, buying up a lot of tools, and the tools to make them. I came back to help you . . ."

"I think it's all right," Toug said. "They know I killed their master."

"Did—did a certain person help you? Today I mean."

Toug shook his head.

"I'll teach you the lance, and we'll get you knighted as soon as I can manage it. His Lordship might do it."

Toug was too stunned to say anything.

"I thought he'd chase me, or anyway I hoped he would. When he didn't, I circled around to surprise him. I'd left the road for fear of meeting another."

Toug nodded. "Sure."

"By the time I got back there—well, you know what I found. And you were gone." Svon stood straighter than ever, and squared his shoulders. "This is offensive, and should you challenge me when you're a knight, your challenge will be accepted. I thought you'd probably gone back to Utgard."

"I didn't even think of it," Toug said. "Maybe I would have if I had. I don't know. But I wanted to find you, and I thought you'd be here somewhere."

A gaunt woman in ragged black came out of the shadows, led by a smaller woman with floating hair; the smaller said, "Don't forget this one, Lord."

"Baki?" Toug did not try to hide to hide his surprise. "Is that Etela's mother?"

"Indeed, Lord."

"I hadn't known she was so tall."

Svon motioned to Baki. "Come here, maid. Are you a slave? You're dressed like one."

"Indeed I am, sir knight."

"No doubt that's why you call my squire 'Lord.' He's a free man, and any free man must seem lord to you."

"I am his slave, sir knight. Thus I name him Lord."

"I've seen many slaves since I've been here, and many of them women. Sometimes Utgard seems full of them. None I've seen have been as a pretty as you."

"Beware, sir knight." Etela's mother had taken Toug's hand, and her large, dark eyes held a question.

"She's back at the castle," Toug whispered. "She's been very good, and I haven't hurt her. Nobody has."

One of the blind men said loudly, "You said we might get free."

Svon raised his voice. "Listen, all of you. I speak here for the king. As of this moment you belong to King Gilling, all of you except the girl who belongs to my squire. We're taking you out of here and taking you to the market."

Voices were raised in protest.

"Not to sell you! We need to buy food to feed you once you get to Utgard, and I've got money for it. I'll buy sacks of corn and baskets of vegetables—turnips or whatever they have here. And we'll buy meat, and perhaps live animals we can drive before us. You'll carry the sacks and baskets, and help drive the animals. The point I have to get across is that you've got a new master, the king, and I represent him. If you're loyal and obedient, we'll take good care of you. If you're not, I'm not going to play the fool for you with reprimands and beatings. King Gilling wants good slaves, not bad ones, and there's more where you came from. Follow me."

Baki tugged at Toug's sleeve. "The sun is bright."

He nodded. "I understand."

"I fear she may wander away."

A woman said, "I'll take care of her."

"Do you think she might ride behind you, Lord? She is very thin. She cannot weigh much."

"If we can get her up here."

Etela's mother spoke. "Let me have your hands, maid."

"I do not think I am strong enough." Baki spoke to the other female slave. "One knee. Let her step on the other."

It was easier than Toug had expected; Etela's mother was soon seated behind him, her skirt hiked to her thighs while her pitifully thin arms locked his waist.

"The rest will be going out a window on the other side of the house, Lord. That was how the knight entered, and his steed is tied there."

"We'll join them," Toug said, and tapped Laemphalt with his spurs to signal that they were ready to go.

"She is an Aelf," Etela's mother whispered as they rode through the doorway.

"I know. How did you know it?"

There was no reply.

Once they were stopped as they rode through town, but Svon declared loudly that they were on the king's business, and the Angrborn who halted them grumbled and moved aside.

The market, when they found it, was larger and poorer than Toug had expected, its stalls staffed almost entirely by humans. After some inquiry and bargaining, they bought a large wagon, heavily made and nearly new, and four bullocks to draw it. When it was theirs, Svon began buying every kind of food and having the slaves load it.

A small hand found Toug's. "He's paying way too much."

His jaw dropped. "What are you doing out here?"

"Going with. I was afraid you'd get in trouble, 'n need help. I figured you'd come here 'cause you said, so this's where I came, too."

Shaking his head, Toug picked Etela up and stood her on a barrel. "You know you shouldn't have. I told you not to. You've been bad."

"If I got to be bad to help you, that's what I'll do. I'm not really little like you think. Give me your hand."

He did, and she put it to her breast. "Feel that? Mama says I'll be big any day now."

Despite his good intentions, something stirred in Toug.

"We slept an' you never touched me, only it wasn't how I was hoping. I wanted you to hold me, and maybe we'd kiss."

Toug gulped, "I think we ought to wait 'til—"

Someone—an Angrborn with tusks—was pointing at him and shouting at Svon. Quickly he turned and advanced on them with outstretched hands.

And fell. Svon's sword had struck too swiftly for Toug to see it, but half its blade was red with blood.

The Angrborn writhed on the trampled mud of the market, roaring, dragging himself with his arms, still toward Toug.

"We're going!" Svon shouted. "Slaves on the wagon, all of you. You women, one of you drive."

The barrel top was empty. Toug drew his war sword and severed two fingers from a huge hand that reached for him. Without thought he found himself in Laemphalt's saddle. A long whip cracked like the breaking of a lance, and he saw Etela's mother on the seat of the wagon with Etela beside her. An Angrborn with a sword fronted it, shouting for them to stop and catching a bullock by the horn. The whip licked his face, and he staggered backward.

Toug rode for him and drove the war sword home.

And all was confusion: Giants pouring from the houses

around the market; Svon clearing a path with horse and sword and deadly courage; booths tipped over, baskets spilled and warty brown roots rolling underfoot. Slaves scattering or screaming while others boarded the wagon.

"Marigolds and manticores! Marigolds and manticores!" A shrieking demon drove the wagon with a curling, cracking viper that struck and struck until it roused the bullocks to its own frenzy and they charged head down and bellowing, threatening to overrun Svon, then rushing past him.

They were in sight of the great gate when the wagon lost a wheel. Schildstarr and his followers saved them for the moment, checking their fellow Angrborn with their voices and their spears, and in that moment Garvaon cantered down the arch of the wooden bridge, trailing white-faced archers and men-at-arms.

Seeing them roused the Angrborn to new fury. Toug, who had felt that he had fought often and hard, learned that he scarcely knew what it was to fight—to slash and stab and have the stallion he loved die under him. To fight on foot, the arm that should have held his shield useless, voice gone and strength gone and nothing left but the knowledge that Etela was somewhere in the madness.

The knee before him was higher than his waist. He swung Sword Breaker with all the force that remained, and when the giant did not fall held her with both hands and swung again, though the pain left him half blind and he felt the grating of his broken bones.

"The castle!" It was Svon, and Svon was gripping his arm; the pain was excruciating. "Come on!"

Toug shouted, "Etela," but Svon was not listening and nothing Toug said afterward made sense even to him.

An arrow flashed, followed by another and another. A clear voice rang over the shouting and the clash of steel. "We are your queen! Hear us, all of you! Stop this! We command it! We, Queen Idnn!"

"Hot slut!"

The insult brought another arrow, and the arrow a scream that might have been the very stones of Utgard crying out.

Silence fell, or something near to silence. Looking up, Toug saw a gray mount above the Great Gate of Utgard, a gray that pawed air, its reins held by a knight who held a bow as well. A woman in a riding skirt sat behind him; and although we were silhouetted against the noon sky Toug recognized her.

"By the authority of King Gilling, we command you stop! Is that my husband's trusty servant Schildstarr below?"

"Aye!" roared Schildstarr.

"Restore order, Schildstarr! Hear us, you sons of Angr! He who strikes Schildstarr strikes us, and he who strikes us strikes the king!"

When Toug and Svon, with Etela between them, hurried through the Great Gate, the gross body of a Frost Giant stretched on the filthy mud of the bailey. Toug did not pause to look at it, although he was vaguely and weakly surprised. Crownless, clothed in bloodstained bandages, stripped of honor, it made little impression until he heard Svon's awed whisper: *That was King Gilling!*

CHAPTER TWENTY-ONE

A BARGAIN WITH THIAZI

You're young and healthy." I paused to study the wounded face turned toward the floor, the jaw set hard. "This will heal. The bone will knit. In a year or three it will be a lot easier to forget than that puckering scar on your cheek."

Mani sat motionless save for his tail, which switched

and curled and straightened again. I sensed that Mani, too, was waiting for Toug to speak; but Toug did not speak.

"The broken ends didn't go through the skin," I said. "Sometimes they do, and that can be bad. Fatal, too often. When they don't, the break nearly always heals." I wound another strip of rag around Toug's shoulder—pulling it tight, and knotting it more tightly still.

Etela said, "He can't die. Don't die, Toug."

"Do you hear us?"

Slowly, Toug nodded.

"Good. You have to understand the point of all this bandaging. Why am I doing it when you're not bleeding?"

"He is!" Etela exclaimed.

I nodded. A child at the edge of womanhood, I decided, and wondered whether Toug knew it, or knew what it portended.

Mani said, "The bleeding's not severe or serious. Just skin lacerations and a little from the old wound because the bandage was torn away."

"Cats can't talk!" That was Etela.

"This is actually the knight speaking," Mani declared smoothly. "The knight can throw his voice."

"I don't believe you!" Etela jumped to her feet.

"But you must," Mani told her. "Cats can't talk."

I watched Toug's lips, hoping for a smile. "Mani's right," I said. "The salve would be enough if the bleeding bruise were the only problem. Perhaps a pad to hold the blood. All these bandages, with the stick, are to keep the ends of the break from moving. If they move they won't heal, or won't heal right. Let them stay where they are, and don't assume they've healed because the pain is not as bad as it was. What's the moon, Mani?"

"Almost gone."

I nodded. "Let it go, Toug. Let it come back and go again. Then we'll see." There was moonlight in the eyes of the strange woman Etela called Mama; I wondered what those eyes would be like when the moon was full, and found myself hoping I would never see them by moonlight.

Etela said, "He can't fight, can he? They're going to come in here after us, but Toug can't fight them."

"He can fight," I said carefully. "He simply can't fight with his left arm. He can't hold a shield, or fight with a big sword like the one he used today. He's a knight, save for being knighted, and knights often fight in spite of their wounds. Toug could do that."

Almost imperceptibly, Toug shook his head.

"If you and your Mama were threatened. He may think he wouldn't. When the swords were out, it would be different."

To my surprise, Gylf licked Toug's hand.

"They know the king's dead," Etela continued hopelessly, "'n they'll come, too many to fight. Too many for anybody. 'N we'll scream 'n run 'n hide. Only they'll find us, one 'n then 'nother one, 'n kill us."

Toug raised his head. "Too many for Sir Svon and Sir Garvaon and me, Etela. Maybe too many for Schildstarr, too. But not too many for Sir Able. You'll see."

"Well said!" Mani declared.

"But I wish Baki was here." Toug's voice had dropped. "There's something I've got to tell her."

I stepped back. "It's a good thing she's not. You may want to think your declaration over before you make it."

"No, I know what I'm going to say. I just want to say it. I want to say you've got to stay here, stay with us. Baki wants you to go off someplace and fight somebody."

"Aelfrice." I supplied the words. "Garsecg."

"But you're here, and we need you. If you're not here we'll all die."

"You're both wrong." I seated myself on the rung of a chair. "You take too dark a view, and so does this girl."

"Etela, sir."

I nodded and smiled at her. "Etela. I don't blame either of you, but you're wrong just the same."

Speaking for the first time, the strange woman said, "I will not run or hide."

"Correct." I nodded. "You were slaves here before. Why shouldn't you be slaves again? The Angrborn would kill Sir Garvaon, Sir Svon, and me—if they could. They might kill our men-at-arms and archers, too, or most of them. They might even kill Toug, Sir Garvaon's squire, Lord Thiazi and Lord Beel. But why kill slaves? Slaves are loot, not foes."

"Nor am I a foe," Mani remarked, "or at least they won't think so. Do you think they'll kill Queen Idnn?"

I shook my head.

"Neither do I." Mani considered, his sleek head to one side. "I'll do what I can for her, and I feel sure she'll do what she can for me. We'll come through all right. She'll want to save her father, too, and perhaps we can."

I grinned at him, then at Etela. "So you see, Toug, Gylf, and I are the only ones present who're in real danger, and only Gylf and I are in much."

Gylf's growl was loud and very deep.

"He says *they* are in danger from *him,*" I interpreted, "and no doubt he's right."

"Is it all right if I pet him?" Etela asked.

"Unless he moves his head away."

Gylf did not.

"Let's get to the other things you and Toug said. Toug wants to notify Baki that he'll no longer honor his promise to persuade me to go to Aelfrice. He feels I'm needed here to protect you and your Mama."

"And me," Toug said.

I ignored it. "He's wrong, because there's no reason for him to sully his honor. I won't go to Aelfrice or anyplace else as long as you need me. You have my word."

Etela smiled and thanked me, but neither her mother nor Toug gave any indication of having heard.

"I want to go to Aelfrice, I'm—"

The oaken door (one of five doors of various woods and sizes) opened, and Thiazi stepped into the room.

I rose. "Your pardon, My Lord. This chamber wasn't locked, and I thought we might wait for you here."

Thiazi went to the largest chair. "You think I leave it unlocked so that my visitors may wait in comfort." A slight smile played about his mouth.

I shook my head. "I thought nothing of the kind, My Lord. Only that since your door wasn't locked you wouldn't object to my bandaging Toug here, if we did no harm."

"I keep it unlocked as a boast. It has been my boast that there was no one in Utgard so bold as to come in without my invitation. These two slaves," Thiazi indicated Etela and her mother, "presumably know nothing of me. Even if they knew, they can't have known this apartment was mine unless you told them. Did you?"

"No, My Lord. If I had I would've had to explain why I wanted them with me when we talked, and I wanted to bandage Toug instead. That was far more urgent."

"You have bandaged him now," Thiazi pointed out.

"I have, My Lord. This girl is Etela." I turned to Toug. "Is that right?"

Etela herself said, "Yes, sir."

"And this woman is her mother. I think I know her name, but it would be better if she were to introduce herself."

Etela's mother seemed not to have heard.

Etela said, "She don't talk a lot except just to me. Sometimes not even to me."

Thiazi made a steeple of his fingers and smiled above it. "An exemplary woman."

"Too much so," I told him. "Your art is famous. King Gilling was very near death, yet you would have saved him."

Thiazi's glance darkened. "I could not discern the identity of his assassin, thus I could not."

"I didn't mean that."

"He's under a spell of protection. There can be no other explanation. I safeguarded our king, but he left his bed . . ." The steeple vanished, and the great hands clenched. "He heard that woman, and rushed from his bed. Pah!"

"Toug thinks our situation grave. Don't you, Toug?"

Toug lifted his head. "I guess I do. They hate us. I don't know what we did, but they do."

"The Angrborn are descendants of those Giants of Winter and Old Night who had to leave Skai," I told him. "Those who forced them to go are our Overcyns."

"Mythgarthr was made from the body and blood of Ymir," Thiazi added. "It's ours by right."

Mani lifted an admonitory paw. "Gentlemen! Gentlemen! Surely you see that this quarrel is not in the best interest of either side."

"The Giants of Winter and Old Night," I said levelly, "take whatever they can by force and keep it. The Sons of Angr behave in precisely the same fashion."

"You wish to quarrel with me," Thiazi muttered.

"Why, no." I smiled. "Toug reminded us of our ancient enmity. Can we agree to set it aside? For the present?"

Thiazi started to speak, but fell silent.

"Toug believes that thousands of Angrborn will storm Utgard, butcher everyone and burn it to the ground."

Etela touched my arm. "It's rocks, mostly."

"So it is. Nothing of the sort will happen, of course. Those who would have set up a new king attacked Sir Svon and Toug, whose force consisted of themselves and seven slaves, three of them women and one a child. All fought like men from what I saw. Schildstarr and a few followers joined them, and the mob couldn't overcome them. Hundreds against one knight, a squire, some slaves, and twelve or fourteen of their own people. Sir Garvaon arrived with a few men-at-arms, and the hundreds who would have overthrown King Gilling couldn't keep his supporters—"

Etela's mother said, "Fewer than fifty."

"Right. They couldn't keep a scant fifty from reaching the gate. Queen Idnn appealed for peace, and by then they were eager to agree. Anybody who thinks they'll go to work tomorrow on a ramp knows nothing about war."

"I never said I knew a lot," Toug declared.

I nodded. "You fought to exhaustion and were wounded. Both have colored your thinking. You need to realize that."

"It was Queen Idnn that got you to come back?"

Mani's voice was smooth, "Indirectly, it was I. I moved my royal mistress, and she Sir Able."

Toug nodded. "I think I see."

I said, "Then we don't have to talk about it."

Thiazi shrugged. "I won't try to plumb your secret. I can do it easily anytime I think it important. You've told us what won't happen, and I agree. What will?"

"Will you seek the throne for yourself?"

He smiled bitterly. "Would you support me if I did?"

"That would depend."

"I will not. It is a dangerous seat, and I am by no means popular."

"Someone will. Someone popular or at least plausible. Probably not one of the those who instigated the attack."

Toug said, "The first one got killed."

"Then I'm right." I spread my hands. "Somebody else. If we're lucky, he won't surface before His Grace arrives. If we're not, our position will be weaker. In either case, we'll offer our friendship and our king's, and ask him to let us leave Jotunland in peace. Since he'll have everything to gain and nothing to lose by that, I think he will."

"What of me?" Thiazi asked.

"You'll serve your new king loyally and ably, just as you served King Gilling."

"He may have scores to settle."

"If he does, he won't settle them, though he may think he has. Every king requires a sorcerer, and somebody who'll take the blame for unpopular decisions. You're both. He'll ask himself why he shouldn't make use of you, at least at first, and congratulate himself on his cleverness."

"I congratulate you on yours, Sir Able. You make your speculations sound very plausible."

"That's because they are. Have I earned a boon?"

Thiazi nodded. "Several, if you want them."

"Swell. I need three. First, the division of slaves—"

"You wish to claim some for yourself? Or for our queen? You must speak to Sir Svon now."

Toug looked up. "You've divided them already?"

Thiazi shrugged. "You were wounded, and we saw no need of your presence. I acted for you, in your interests."

Toug started to speak, but Thiazi silenced him with a gesture. "First you should know that there were but six to divide, one having perished in the fighting. Another has an injured arm. Sir Svon got first choice, you'll remember."

Mutely, Toug nodded.

"He chose the sound man, naturally. I, acting for you, choose the other man. His name is Vil."

Etela gasped.

"A strong slave and a skilled one, from what I gather. When his arm heals, he should be a valuable possession. Sir Svon then chose one of the women—not this one. I, knowing your fondness for this child, chose her."

"I was his already!" Etela exclaimed.

Thiazi shook his head. "You were not, but you are now. Sir Svon took the other woman—understandably, I'd say— and I was left with your mother for this squire. Thus you and your mother belong to him, together with the smith Vil."

Toug said, "That's good. I—I never really liked you much. I was wrong."

"You failed to understand me," Thiazi told him, "as you fail now. I do my duty as I see it. Will you give a slave to Sir Able? If you do, Sir Svon will surely give one of his to the queen. All of them, perhaps, but we'll have to see."

"I don't want any," I declared. "I do want boons. This woman. What's her name, Toug?"

"I don't know. What is it, Etela?"

"Lynnet. I say Mama, only it's Lynnet really."

The strange woman whispered, "Marigolds and manticores."

"That's something she says," Etela explained. "I told Toug, 'n he said marigolds were flowers."

Thiazi added, "Symbolizing wealth or the sun."

Etela nodded gratefully.

I said, "Manticores are beasts the size of Gylf here. Their heads are like the heads of men or women, but they have the teeth and claws of lions. Their tails are like the tails of scorpions, though much larger, and their sting is fatal."

"Why does she say it, Etela?" Toug asked.

"I don't know. Why do you say why?"

Thiazi snorted. "I've a better question. What's the second boon you crave, Sir Able? I may grant it if I can."

"Can you heal this woman? Toug's slave?" As I spoke, Gylf looked up at me. From Gylf's look I knew Gylf knew I could have healed her myself, that such acts violated my oath, and that he was far from sure my oath had been wise.

"I can try," Thiazi said, "and perhaps I will. Whether I will or not depends on your answers to some questions. Can you tell me who stabbed His Majesty the night of the combat and who took his life? And what is the third boon you ask?"

I sighed. "May I sit, My Lord?"

Thiazi nodded, and I resumed my seat on the rung. "I

can't answer your first question. If you want my opinion, the assassin was the same both times, though I'm not sure even of that. Is my final boon—I didn't get the first—to be withheld?"

"You may not get the second, either." Thiazi rose to pace the room, looking as tall as a tower. His voice boomed from the walls. "I will not believe that a man of your penetration cannot offer a guess."

"I could offer a guess." I paused, sorting swirling thoughts. "I won't. I'm a knight, and a knight doesn't put the honor of others at risk. Suppose I did. Suppose I said that though I couldn't know, I felt it likely that the guilty party was a foreign knight, Sir Able of the High Heart. The accusation would spread as such accusations always do, and my reputation would never recover. Even if somebody confessed, people would say my character made the charge plausible."

Thiazi paused in his pacing to say dryly, "You were absent, I believe, upon both occasions?"

"I was. That's why I accused myself. Schildstarr has a friend with two heads. I don't know his name."

"Orgalmir is the left, and Borgalmir the right."

"Thanks. I don't say this, but suppose I did. I guess that Orgalmir wounded the king and Borgalmir killed him."

"Absurd!"

"No more so than lots of other guesses. You wanted a guess. Okay, you've got one."

"You risk your boons. Both of them."

Etela said, "My mama isn't—isn't always like I would like her to be."

"She was taken from her home," I made my voice gentle, "and enslaved here. She's an attractive woman, and she may have been used in ways you can't understand. The shock disordered her mind. Soon we'll go back to Celidon—your mother and you, Toug and Gylf and Mani and me, and even this Vil. Your mother will return home, and though the change may be slow, I think you'll find she gets better."

Thiazi, who had gone to the window, turned back to us. "I have not said I would not treat her. One of you—you there, sick woman. Put more wood on the fire."

Etela did it. "Toug says there isn't much more, 'n we got to be careful."

"Lord Thiazi believes things will return to normal soon," I explained. "So do I."

"Your boons . . ." Thiazi's voice filled the room. "Your boons depend on your answering three questions. Questions I will put here and now. Answer, and I'll grant them. Refuse as you've refused already, and I'll grant neither."

"You want me to talk," I said. "Okay, before I hear your other questions I'll say three things. My first is that I didn't refuse to answer your question. I don't know the answer and I told you so. My guess, if I made one, might be more valuable than this girl's. But would it be worth as much as yours? You know it wouldn't. You were here both times. Your opinion deserves far more respect."

"Do you accuse me?"

"Of course not. I won't accuse anybody—that's what you're mad about. I'm just saying you're bound to know more. What are the questions you mentioned?"

"I ask for your second and third remarks."

"Okay. I remark that you've bound yourself to grant both my remaining boons, though you don't know the last."

"If you answer my questions, speaking out without quibbling about what your honor requires, I'll grant it. Assuming I can." For a second or two, Thiazi's huge hands appeared to wash each other. "Whatever it is."

Toug said, "I have an idea."

Thiazi nodded. "We need some. Let us hear it."

"Like Sir Able said, he wasn't there when the king got stabbed the first time. He was down south in the mountains, fighting anybody who tried to come through a pass. This morning when the king got killed, he was pretty close, riding on the air with Queen Idnn. But all of us thought he was way far away. So maybe the person's afraid of him and wouldn't do anything except when he was gone."

"Possible, but unlikely." Thiazi paced the room again, an austere gray eminence, and his steps sounded even through the ankle-deep carpet. "Until today, he was here for no more than an hour or two. Sir Able, what is your third remark?"

"That though I lose my boons, you could lose more. Your foes, and even your friends, will accuse you of ingratitude."

"My friends accuse me of nothing, since I have none."

Etela said, "We'll be your friends, if you'll let us."

"My foes accuse me of ingratitude already, and worse. Here is my first question. I warn you that you must answer all three."

I nodded. "I understand."

"Did King Arnthor send Lord Beel with instructions to assassinate King Gilling?"

"No."

Thiazi paused in his pacing to glare at me. "A simple yes or no will not be sufficient. Explain yourself."

"Certainly, My Lord. I'm not King Arnthor's councillor, nor have I ever been. His reputation, however, is that of a hard but honorable man."

Thiazi snorted. "My second question. In what ways will King Arnthor benefit by King Gilling's death?"

"In none, My Lord. A king in Utgard could forbid the raids that lay waste to the north. No king can't. Besides, King Gilling took a share of the proceeds, which discouraged raiding. As long as there's no king, the raiders can keep whatever they get, and they'll raid more."

"While we war among ourselves, we'll have neither time nor strength to spare for raiding."

I nodded. "My Lord's wiser than I am, though many

may prefer profit to killing their relatives—still more, to being killed by them."

"My final question. You're to imagine that I am King Arnthor. I have explained to you my reasons for wishing King Gilling dead, and although they may not satisfy you, they satisfy me. I then confide that I've chosen Lord Beel to act for me. Would you approve my choice?"

"Absolutely, My Lord. When failure is preferable to success, the course of true wisdom is to choose the man most apt to fail. May I speak freely?"

"You may. In fact, I desire it."

"As I told you, I know nothing directly of King Arnthor. I've never seen him. But I traveled with Lord Beel through Celidon and the Mountains of the Mice, and some way across the Plain of Jotunland. I feel I know him well. For diplomacy, he's the man—levelheaded, courteous, and tactful, with few passions beyond family pride and a father's natural love for his daughter. If I were a king who wanted peace with my neighbor, I'd look for somebody just like Lord Beel. But for an assassination . . ." I shook my head.

Etela said, "Doesn't Lord Beel know magic, too? That's what Toug said. If he does 'n wanted to kill somebody, he'd do it like that."

Thiazi sat down and stared at Etela, who met his gaze boldly. At length he said, "Would I be a fool to treat a child's counsel as serious?"

I smiled. "A fourth question, My Lord?"

"Let us make it so."

Mani cleared his throat, a soft and almost apologetic sound. "You limited yourself to three questions, My Lord Thiazi. Allow me to answer that, and so preserve your honor. Wisdom is wisdom, and doesn't become foolishness in the mouth of another speaker. A child's counsel should be heeded if it is wise. But not otherwise."

"Could not the same be said of a cat's?"

"It would take a wise man, My Lord Thiazi, to discover foolishness in a cat's counsel."

"Just so." Thiazi bent toward Etela. "My child, we do not know that magic was not employed. It may have been used to render the assassin invisible, for example."

"I didn't know that," Etela said.

"Naturally not. You have a lively intelligence, but little experience of the world, and less learning. You must take both into account."

"Yes, sir. I mean, My Lord."

"Would you laugh if I were to tell you that an invisible creature has been seen in this keep?"

"No, sir, I wouldn't. Only I wouldn't understand 'cause you just said invisible."

"Invisibility is never complete," Thiazi told her, "as every grimoire dealing with topic asserts. Beings rendered invisible by magic are partially or entirely visible under certain circumstances. These circumstances vary with the spell employed. Rain and strong and direct sunlight are perhaps the most common."

Clearly impressed, Etela said, "Oooh . . ."

"Invisible entities sometimes cast shadows, more or less distinct, by which their presence may be detected. They also leave footprints in mud or snow, though that does not really represent a loss of invisibility."

"Invisible cats," Mani added, "are completely invisible only at night."

"I did not know that," Thiazi said, "and am pleased to have learned it. I repeat: would you be surprised to learn that an invisible being has been glimpsed in this keep?"

After a glance at Lynnet, Etela nodded.

"One has been, and the first glimpses followed Lord Beel's arrival. I would suspect this being of having stabbed our king, were it not that it seems to fracture the cervical vertibrae. For obvious reasons, invisible beings rarely bear arms. When our king was stabbed, five others had their necks broken. The fact has been lost to sight in our distress over the wounding of our king. Yet it remains."

I snorted. "Is this supposed to implicate Lord Beel? It seems to me it makes him less likely than ever. If the being is his—I don't think it is—and he wanted to harm King Gilling, wouldn't he use it? If it isn't, and it didn't stab the king, why are we talking about it?"

Mani raised a paw. "Well said. May I add that in my opinion you've answered Lord Thiazi's questions as required?"

Thiazi nodded. "You'll receive the boon you've asked—I'll do what I can for this slave, although I can't promise great improvement. What is your final boon?"

I had to think about things then; it was my last chance to turn back. When I looked up, I said, "I love a certain lady. Who she is doesn't matter, she's real and I can't be happy without her. I've returned here to Jotunland for her sake, from a far country."

Thiazi nodded.

"I've been told the Sons of Angr never love. If that's right, why did King Gilling rise from his bed and rush out to his death at the sound of Queen Idnn's voice?"

"You have been misinformed." Thiazi's words might have been the wind moaning through a skull. "We love. Shall I supply the fact which misled your informant?"

I shrugged. "If you please, My Lord."

"We are never loved."

"Not even by each other?"

"No. Your final boon?"

"All my life I've been aware of—of an emptiness in me, My Lord. There was a time when I acquired a new shield, and my servant, who's my friend too, suggested that it be painted with a heart." I hesitated. "I'm called Sir Able of the High Heart, My Lord."

"I am aware of it."

"Though I have never known why. My friend suggested

that a heart might be painted on that shield. I was very proud of it—of the shield, I mean."

Toug looked away.

"And it came to me that if a heart were painted on it, it would have to be an empty one, thin lines of red dividing, curving upward, and coming together at the bottom. I said no. I felt, you see, that my heart was filled with love for the lady whose love brought me here. Just the same, a heart on my shield would need to be empty, and I knew it. You've got a room, a famous room since I heard of it long ago, with Here Abides Lost Love carved in the door. Is that true?"

Slowly Thiazi nodded.

"From what you said, I understand why you've got it and why you value it. It can't be one of these doors—there's nothing carved on them. Another door in this suite?"

Thiazi said nothing.

"May I, only once and as a great favor, go in? It's the third boon I ask."

"You will have to come out again." Every word seemed weighted with double significance.

"I never thought I could stay there."

"I will grant you both boons." For a moment it seemed Thiazi would rise from his seat; he stayed where he was, his face gray, his huge hands grasping the arms of his chair. "But you must do something for me. You must take the slave woman with you. Will you do that?"

"Lynnet? Where's the door?"

By a slight motion of his head, Thiazi indicated one of the five doors, the narrowest, a door of wood so pale that it looked almost white.

"Through there?" I stood and took Lynnet's hand. "Come with me, My Lady."

"Manticores and marigolds." She rose, and her rising was neither awkward nor graceful, and neither swift nor slow.

I said, "She's sleepwalking."

Thiazi shook his head. "A terrible rage burns in her."

I looked at him. "I'm still a kid—a boy still—in a lot of things."

"We envy your good fortune."

"Is she really angry? At this moment?"

Etela said, "Mama never gets mad."

"I would not advise you to look into her eyes."

Toug cleared his throat. "I told you a little about the battle, Sir Able. She was—was fighting then. With the whip that came with the wagon we bought. I guess I didn't say the Frost Giants were scared of her, but they were. She was blinding giants with it."

I said, "I didn't know that."

"I know I didn't say I was scared of her, too. She was on our side, but I was scared anyhow."

"Yet you fought on."

Toug shrugged. "Then Sir Garvaon came with men-at-arms, and they were scared about having to fight, and I could see it. I saw how scared they were, and I thought you tough men, you don't know half, not even half."

Thiazi said softly, "Angr was our mother's name, Sir Able. We are descended from her, all of us. Thus we know something of anger. I tell you that this woman must control hers or destroy everything in her path. She seems a woman of wax to you?"

"Something like that, yes."

"You will have seen a candle stub thrown into a fire. Remember it."

"I'll try. Come, Lady. I'll open the door for you."

Thirty steps took us to the door Thiazi had indicated, and although it was narrowest of all, it was wide and high for me; I had to reach over my head to lift the latch. When I touched it, I saw the graceful script of Aelfrice in the pallid wood: WHERE LOST LOVE LIVES.

The door seemed to weigh nothing, and it may be that we stepped through without opening it.

CHAPTER TWENTY-TWO
LOST LOVES

Night blacker than the blackest night of storm enveloped us. I heard the rush of waters, as I had when I had breasted tides and dark, uncharted currents with Garsecg. There was a great pounding, swift and very deep. I tried to imagine what sort of creature might make such a noise, and the image that leaped into my mind was that of Org, green as leaves and brown as bark, alone in a forest clearing and pounding the trunk of a hollow tree with a broken limb. Under my breath I murmured, "What's that?" And Lynnet heard me and said, "It is my heart." As soon as she spoke, and I knew she was right and wrong, that it was my own heart, not hers. For a long time we walked through that dark, and I timed my steps and my movements to the thuddings of my heart.

The darkness parted, as at the word of the Most High God. What had been dark was pearly mist, and I saw that there was grass, such lush grass as horses love, underfoot; the mist spangled it with dew.

"This is a better place," Lynnet told me; perhaps I did not speak, but I agreed. Sunbeams lanced the mist, and as it had made the dew, so it now made a colonnade of mighty oaks. She began to run. "Goldenlawn!" She turned to look back as she spoke, and I have, on my honor, never seen more joy than I saw in that wasted face.

Beside Sheerwall, the castle would have been an outwork—such a gray wall as a strong boy might fling stones over, a round keep prettily made, and a square stone house of four stories and an attic. It was, in short, such a castle as a knight with a dozen stout men-at-arms might have held against fifty or a hundred outlaws. Nothing more.

Yet it was a place very easy to love, and made me think, all the while that I was there, of the Lady's hall in Skai. The Lady's Folkvanger stands to it as a blossoming tree to a single violet, but they breathed the same air.

On its gates stood painted manticores. Their jaws held marigolds as the jaws of cows sometimes hold buttercups, and there were marigolds at their feet, and to left and right of them more marigolds, not painted but real, for the moat was as dry as Utgard's and had been planted as one plants a garden, while manticores of stone stood before the gates.

There were servants and maiden sisters, fair young women who might have married in an instant, and anyone they chose. All were filled with wonder that Lynnet, whom they thought never to see again, should unexpectedly return; and after them, a grave old nobleman with a white mustache and the scars of many battles, and a gay gray lady like a wild dove, who fluttered all the while and moaned for joy.

"This is Kirsten," Lynnet told me, "dear, dear Kirsten who died when I was fourteen, and my own dear sister Leesha who died in childbirth. Father, may I present Sir Able of the High Heart? Sir Able, this is my father, Lord Leifr."

"Slain by the Frost Giants who stormed Goldenlawn," Lord Leifr told me, smiling, and offered his hand.

"My mother, Lady Lis."

She took my hand in both of hers, and the love in those fluttering hands and her small, shy face would have won me at once even if I had been ill-disposed to her and her husband. "May you stay with us a long, long while, Sir Able, and may every moment of your stay be happy."

Soon came a banquet. It was night outside, and snowing, and when we had eaten and drunk our fill, and sung old songs, and played games, we walked in a garden bright with light and summer flowers. "This is mother's grotto," Lynnet explained, "a sort of pretty cave made by our gardeners. The fashion at court was to have a grotto when my parents married, a place where lovers could kiss and hold hands out of sight—and out of sun, too, on hot days. My father had it built to please my mother before he brought her here."

It made me think of the cave in which I had lain on moss with Disiri, but I said nothing of that.

"Only I'm afraid of it, and I didn't know I was until I started talking about it, I suppose because my sisters and I weren't allowed in there when we were children. So I'm not going to go in, but you can if you'd like to see it."

She plainly expected me to go, so I did. It was not that I imagined I might actually find Disiri there—I knew I would not. But the memory the grotto evoked was strong and sweet; and I hoped that if I went in, it might be stronger still. Filled with that hope, I descended the little stone stair, stepped across a tiny rivulet, and entered the grotto. There could be no dragon here, I knew, nor any well reaching the sea of Aelfrice. Nor was I wrong about those things.

In their places I found a floor of clean sand and a rough tunnel that seemed to plumb the secrets of the hill, and then a familiar voice that mewed, "Sir Able? Sir Able? It's you, I know. I smell your dog on your clothes. Is this the way out?"

"Mani?" I stopped and felt him rub my leg. "I didn't know you were in here. This is a strange place."

"I know," Mani told me. And then, "Pick me up."

"Some of these people are dead, and it doesn't seem to make any difference."

He only mewed in response to that; when I picked him up and carried him, he was trembling.

I will not speak of the time I spent in the grotto. The time of Skai is not the time of Mythgarthr, nor is the time of Aelfrice. The time of the Room of Lost Loves is different again, and perhaps not time at all, but merely the reflection of time. Etela said none of us had stayed inside long.

Mani raised his head and sniffed. Hearing him (he was cradled in my arms) I sniffed too. "I smell the sea."

"Is that what it is? I've never been there. Your dog talks about it. I don't think he liked it much."

I said, "He was chained in Garsecg's cave under the sea. I'm sure he didn't like that."

"That's all right," Mani told me, "it's only wrong to confine cats." He leaped from my arms; soon I heard him ahead of me: "There's light this way, and water noise."

Before long I could see it for myself and hear the surge and crash of waves. I felt that I was coming home.

The gray stones of the grotto appeared to either hand, and I (recalling its mouth and the rivulet across which I had stepped) paused to look behind me, for it seemed possible at that moment that I had become confused and was walking back the way I had come. Faint and far was the mouth behind me. Faint and far, but not nearly as faint or as far as it ought to have been. I had walked the better part of a league; and yet I could see the rough circle still, and glimpse rocks and ferns beyond it.

"There's a woman here!" Mani called.

I knew then, and holding up Eterne I ran.

Parka sat spinning as before, but her eyes left the thread she spun for a moment to look up at me as she said, "Sir Able of the High Heart."

I felt that I had never known what that phrase meant until I heard it in her mouth; I knelt and bowed my head and muttered, "Your servant always, My Lady."

"Do you need another string?"

"No," I said. "The one you gave has served me well, though it disturbs my sleep and colors my dreams."

"You must put it from you when you sleep, Sir Able."

"I would not treat them so, My Lady. They tell me of the lives they had, and hearing them I love my own more."

"Why have you come?" she asked; I explained as well as I could, not helped by Mani, who interrupted and commented more often than I liked.

When I had finished, Parka pointed beyond the breakers.

"It is out there? What I seek?"

She nodded.

"I can swim," I told Mani, "but I can't take you. Nor can I take my sword or my clothes."

He said, "That mail would sink you in a minute."

It was not true, but I agreed. "Will you remain here with Parka and watch my things 'til I return?"

"Your possessions," Parka told me, "are not here."

Nevertheless I stripped, and laid my mail, my leather jerkin, my trousers and so forth on a flat stone, and put my boots beside them. Parka spun on, making lives for we who think we make them for ourselves.

How good it was to swim in the sea! I knew then that much of my sea-strength had left me, for I felt it returning; and although I knew Garsecg for a demon, I wished that he were swimming at my side, as he had in days irrecoverable. It is well, I think, for us to learn to tell evil from good; but it has its price, as everything does. We leave our evil friend behind.

To what I swam I did not know. Seeing nothing ahead, I swam a long way under water, then breached the surface and swam on, still seeing nothing. The bones of Grengarm lay in this sea, and somewhere in it dwelt Kulili, for the bottom of the sea of Mythgarthr (and I felt I was in Mythgarthr still) lies in Aelfrice. I resolved to go to the bottom before I was done, and come to land in Aelfrice, and search there for Disiri. For I did not know then that one finds none but lost loves in the Room of Lost Love, and my love for her—love fiery as the blood of the Angrborn, yet pure—could not be lost, not in the Valkyrie's kiss or the Valfather's mead.

Surfacing again, I saw the Isle of Glas. What love, I asked myself, did I lose here? None, surely.

For a time I was filled with thoughts of Garsecg and Uri and Baki. At last it came to me that had I been able to recall that love, it would not be lost. Lady Lynnet, in her madness, had forgotten her parents, her sisters, and her home, had remembered only marigolds and manticores and the fighting tradition of her family, which had been in her blood, not in her wounded mind. Thus it was that although her mind had failed, her hand had itched for a sword, and found one in the whip.

It is not the weapon that wins, no, not even Eterne.

The beaches of the Isle of Glas are like no other. Perhaps they are gems ground fine—certainly, that is how they appear. Nor are its stones as other stones. Its grass is fine, soft, short, and of a green no man can describe; and I believe that Gylf, who could not see colors well, could have seen that one. I have seen no other trees like those along its beaches; their leaves are of a green so dark as to appear black, but silver beneath, so that a breath of wind changes them to silver in an instant. Their bark appears to be naked wood, though it is not.

When I think back upon the moments I came ashore, it seems to me I cannot have had long to admire the beach, or grass, or trees; yet it seemed long then. The sun stood fixed, half visible, half veiled by cloud; and I, with all eternity at my disposal, marveled at the grass.

"Oh, son . . ."

It was a peasant woman. I had seen many fairer, though she was fair.

"You are my son."

I knew that she was wrong, and it came to me that if I were to lie upon the ground, and she to bend above me, I would see her in the way I had just recalled her. Then I understood that she was the fairest of women.

"You and Berthold suckled these breasts, Able."

I said he was not here, and tried to explain that he

would not have forgotten her, that he had been old enough to walk and speak when she vanished.

"Read this." She held out the tube of green glass.

Shamefaced, I admitted that I could not read the runes of Mythgarthr, only the script of Aelfrice.

"This is not Mythgarthr," she said, "it is the country of the heart."

I unrolled the scroll and read it. I set it down here as I recollect it. You will wonder, Ben, as I wondered, whether she was not our mother as well as Berthold's and his brother's. I think that she was both.

"Mag is my name here, and here I was wife to Berthold the Black. My husband was headman of our village. The Aelf cast their spell on it. Our cows birthed fawns. Our gardens died in a night. Mist hid us always, and Griffinsford was accursed. An old man came. He was a demon. I know it now, but we did not know then. I was big with child when he came.

"He said our Overcyns would not help us, and to lift the curse we must offer to the gods of the Aelf. Snari fed him. Berthold said we would not, that we must offer to our right Overcyns. He built an altar of stones and turf, with none but our little son to help. On it he offered our cow, and sang to the Overcyns of Skai, and Cli and Wer with him.

"A turtle with two heads crawled out of the river and bit Deif and Grumma, strangers were on the road by night, and there were howlings at our windows. The old man said we must give seven wives to the gods of Aelfrice. Berthold would not hear of it.

"The old man said I would never give birth until the gods of Aelfrice allowed it. Two days I labored with none but Berthold to attend me. Then I begged the Lady of Skai to take my life if only she would spare my child. I was able to bear him, and I named him Able because of it.

"The old man came to our door. Grengarm, he said, demanded seven fair virgins. There were not seven fair virgins in Griffinsford, and soon he would demand fair woman whether virgins or not, and children too, whom he would eat. I do not know that he told the truth, though I believed him. He told me he would take me to a place where Grengarm would not find me. I said I would go if I might take my children.

"I might take Able, he said, but Berthold was perhaps too big, and he offered to show the place to me so that I might judge if it was a fit place for them. It was not far, and we would return long before either woke. May the Lady and every lady forgive me! I went, thinking Berthold would rock Able if he woke.

"We went to the edge of the barley, and there the old man cautioned me that I must not be afraid but climb on his back. He went on all four like a beast as he said it. I mounted and he flew. I saw that he was a terrible lizard, that he had always been, and the kind face he showed was a mask. I believed him Grengarm, and believed he would eat me.

"He carried me to this island and stripped me naked. Here I remain, so the seamen I tempt may feed Setr and the Khimairae. There are other women, stolen as I was.

"We tempt seamen so the Khimairae will not eat us, but we hide when the old man walks out of the waves, and do not worship him as the Khimairae do. Groa carved an image of the Lady for us, but another came by night and broke it, leaving an image of herself by the pool, beautiful beyond women.

"Groa can write. She has taught me to write as we write here, tracing letters in the sand. This vase I found in the wreck, with the paper and the rest. O Lady of the Overcyns, Lady of Skai, you spared my life. Grant that these writings of mine will come to the eyes of my sons."

"Years have passed. I am no longer beautiful, and soon the Khimairae will eat me. I have caught Setr's poison in a cup. I write with it, and with a feather of the great bird. When I have written to the end, I will put this scroll in the vase, and stop it, and drink. None will touch my poisoned flesh for *fear*."

I asked whether I might take her scroll to read to my brother. She said that nothing I took from this place would remain when I left it, and cast her scroll into the waves.

After that we sat long on the beach, naked together, and talked of the lives we had led, what it was to live and what it was to die. "I was taken by the Aelf," I told her, "to be playmate to the queen, for the Aelf live on, but few children come to them and any child born to them is a queen or king, as if every Aelf of the clan were mother or father."

"You were a king to me," she said, "and to your father and your brother also."

"We played games in a garden wider than the world, and I sat at lessons with her, and talked of love and magic and a thousand other things, for she was very wise and her advisors wiser. At last they sent me into Mythgarthr. All memory of Disiri and her garden left me. Only now has it returned."

"You loved them."

I nodded. "Mother, you are wise. I knew I would not find Disiri here, for my love for her has not been lost. But those were lost—as lost as your scroll."

"Which is not lost. It remains on the Isle, where you found it." She took up the green glass tube that had held it as she spoke, and removed the stopper. "Do you want to see it again? It is in here."

The tube was empty; and yet it seemed to me that there remained something at its bottom, some scrap, perhaps, of paper, a pebble or a shell. I tried to reach in, although it was large enough to admit only two fingers. My whole hand entered, and as it sought the bottom, my arm.

I found myself drawn into a tunnel whose sides were green glass. At once I turned and began to run back the way I had come, troubled (until I caught and held her) by Eterne, whose weighty scabbard slapped my leg. Soon I found a pale door. I opened it, and had no more stepped through than I was followed by Lynnet and Mani.

"I thought you would stay in there a while, Mama," Etela said. Lynnet only smiled and stroked her hair.

Thiazi said, "None of you need tell me what you saw. Should you wish to, however, you will find me an attentive listener."

None of us spoke.

Toug said, "Everybody got to ask questions before you went in, or anyhow that was what it seemed like. Now I'd like to ask one and all of you have got to answer just this one question. There isn't one of you that doesn't owe me."

Lynnet nodded and took his hand, at which Etela looked astonished.

"Here it is. Did it work? Did you really find love you had lost in there?"

I told him I had, that I had found a mother whom I had forgotten utterly. To myself I added that her bones lay on the Isle of Glas, and I would not rest until I had interred them and raised a monument, as I now have.

"What about Etela's mother?"

I nodded, and was about to explain; but Lynnet herself spoke: "I did, and saw women dead and men who fell when the Angrborn came to Goldenlawn. I celebrated the winter feast, and danced the May dance, and cut flowers in our garden."

She turned to Thiazi who sat huge as a carven image in his chair. "Your folk destroy so much to gain so little."

He nodded, but did not speak.

"What about Mani?" Toug looked around for him. "I saw him come out."

Etela pointed. "He went out the window."

"That's too bad," Toug said. "I'd like to know if he found love he'd lost too."

Thiazi's voice was as dull and distant as the beating of the monstrous drums outside. "If he had lost love, Squire, he found it there."

I said, "Of course he had love to find—and of course he found it. If he hadn't, he would be here telling us so. He left because he's not ready to talk about it."

There was a frantic pounding at the door, and Thiazi roared, "Come in!"

It was Pouk, and though he did not look around I saw his living eye rest on me. "Lord Thiazi, sir," he began, "is my old master Sir Able in here, sir? I thought I heard him."

"He is your new master as well," Thiazi told him. "I give you to him now."

Pouk pulled his forelock. "Thankee, sir, an' I hope it sticks."

"I'm here, Pouk," I said. "What do you want?"

"Nothin', sir. Only I got news you ought to know. That Schildstarr, sir. He's got th' crown, sir, an' says he's king. He's fixin' to go out in th' town, sir, wit' all his men an' Thrym an' his guards."

Thiazi rose, "Then I must go with him."

I nodded. "First, Pouk, you mustn't talk of His Majesty King Schildstarr as you just did. If you're disrespectful I may not be able to protect you."

"Aye, aye, sir."

"Second, you're to go to the stable at once and saddle Cloud, and bring her to the entrance as quick as you can."

Pouk hesitated. "I ain't no hand fer horses, sir, an' that'n don't know me."

"Do what she tells you," I said, "and all will be well."

After that, I sent Toug to notify Svon and Beel, and armed myself.

Of Schildstarr's parade through the town I will say little. We human beings were kept to the rear—no doubt wisely. Garvaon, Svon, and I rode three abreast, with Beel and Idnn before us and Garvaon's men-at-arms and archers behind. The castle of Utgard might have been taken, for there was no one to guard it save Toug and Gylf and a few slaves. But there was no reason to fear it would be taken, though the crowding Frost Giants who cheered so wildly for their new king eyed us with hostility that was almost open.

When I saw their faces, I knew we would have to go, and go soon. I told Beel when we returned to Utgard. He agreed, but reminded me that he would need the king's permission.

A dark and silent figure waited outside the chamber Thiazi had assigned me. "They're in there. . . ."

Recognizing her voice, I bowed. "Who is, Lady Lynnet?"

"My daughter, another girl." For a moment it seemed to me that a frown of concentration crossed her face, that face which so seldom wore any expression. "The cat. And a man. They wanted me to . . ."

"You would be welcome," I told her.

"I know." It seemed that she would go; though I stood aside she remained where she was, her head erect, her hands at her sides, her lank black hair falling to her waist. "I will return south with you. Goldenlawn will be mine."

"I hope so, My Lady."

"Shall I have a husband then? Someone to help build?"

"I'm sure you will have your choice among a score."

"They are so eager, for a little land. . . . Five farms. Our meadows."

I nodded. "There are many men who are hungry for land, though many have land already. Others hunger for love. If you marry again, My Lady, you would be well advised to marry a man whose desire is for you."

She did not speak.

"There are many women, My Lady, who feel that a man who greatly desires them can't be good enough for them. That they prove their mettle by winning one who could couple with a lady more beautiful or more accomplished, winning him with land or gold, or by trickery. I don't pretend to be wise, but another lady whose name may not be spoken told me once how foolish that is, and how much of her time and strength was spent striving against it."

"You?"

"No, My Lady. If I'd been speaking for myself, I would have spoken less boldly."

She passed me without a nod or glance. I watched her erect back and slow, smooth steps until she vanished in the darkness at the end of the corridor. There are ghosts and worse in Utgard, as I knew very well; but no one was less apt to be affrighted than she, and it is possible that they (like us) thought her one of themselves.

Two girls, Lynnet had said, a cat—Mani, clearly—and a man. Little Etela would be one of the girls. The other seemed likely to be one of the slave women, somebody Toug had found to care for her. The man was presumably Toug himself, though I hoped for Garvaon.

Shrugging, I opened the door and stepped in, and saw that I had been right in some regards and wrong in others. The second girl was Uri, and not in human form but clearly a woman of the Fire Aelf. The man was neither Toug nor Garvaon but a blind slave, muscular and nearly naked, with one arm supported by a sling.

Etela said politely, "Hello, sir knight. We came to see you. Only I was here the first."

Uri rose and bowed, saying, "Lord."

Mani coughed as cats do. "She is afraid I will slip ahead of her, as I easily could, dear owner. I won't. I want to talk to you alone, after these others have gone."

The blind slave stroked Mani's back with a hand thick with muscle. "This is him?"

"Yes," Mani said. "This is he, my owner, Sir Able of the High Heart."

The slave knelt and bowed his head.

"It means he wants something," Etela explained. "That's how they have to do."

"We all want something," I told her, "and when I do I kneel in just the same way. What's his name?"

"It's Vil, and he was my old master's just like me. Only now we're Toug's."

I nodded. "Stand up, Vil."

He rose. Etela said, "Can I still go first?"

"Sure. It's your right, and I have another question."

"Well, I got a bunch. You can be first if you want to."

"No." I took off my helmet and laid it in the armoire in which I would hang my mail. "You were here first, as you said, and I came in last." The truth was that I hoped her questions would make my own unnecessary.

"I don't know where to start."

"In that case it probably doesn't matter." I unbuckled my sword belt, took my place on the hassock, the only seat of merely human size, and laid Eterne across my knees.

"Aren't you going to put that away too?"

I shook my head. "I'll hang it by my bed. Something may happen during the night, though I hope it won't."

Uri murmured, "I have often watched over you, Lord." I remembered then that seamen lured to the Isle of Glas had fed the Khimairae; but I said nothing.

"Is the new king going to hurt us? Mama and me?"

I shook my head again. "I would not let you be hurt, but I doubt that he intends you any harm."

"Toug doesn't want to be a knight. Not anymore."

"I know."

"Only I want him to be one, and he'd be a real good one, wouldn't he?"

This was addressed to Uri, who said, "I think so too."

"See? We're going to get married, Mama said, 'n we slept in the same bed already 'n everything."

Uri said, "I don't believe so, Lord."

"Yes, we did! We're going to do it again tonight, an' I'm all washed 'n everything. So he has to be a knight."

I nodded. "Which he is."

Etela's voice rose to a wail. "You said he wasn't!"

"I said nothing of the kind. You said that he didn't want to be one, and I told you I knew it. When I was tending his wound, I did my best to keep him from saying what none of us wanted to hear. I may also have said he was a knight already, though no one calls him Sir Toug. I think I did—and if I didn't, I might easily have done so."

She tried to speak, but I silenced her. "If Duke Marder were here—I wish he was—he'd tell you there's no magic in the sword with which he taps a knight's shoulders. Queen Disiri, who knighted me, might tell you anything, and she commands more magic than Lord Thiazi and Lord Beel combined. But no magic can make a knight. Not even the Overcyns can. A knight makes himself. That's the only way. Come closer."

She did, and I put my arm around her.

"Many people know what I told you. I learned it from a good and brave knight when I was a boy. Fewer know this, a thing I learned for myself in a far country."

Mani asked, "Where there are talking cats?"

I nodded. "Talking cats who draw a chariot. What I learned, Etela, is that a knight cannot unmake himself. A knight can be unmade. It's difficult and is seldom done, but it can be done."

Etela said nothing; her eyes were bright with tears.

"It cannot be done by the knight himself, however. If Toug ever ceases to be a knight, it will be because you've done it, I think. Though there are other ways."

"I never would!"

I told her very sincerely that I hoped she would not.

"But he doesn't want to, an' what can I do?"

"What you're doing. Be good, take care of your mother, and show Toug you love him."

"Well, I want him to ride a white horse, with a sword—" She sobbed. "An' one of those long spears an' a shield."

"I hope we'll leave this castle tomorrow. I'm going to ask the new king's permission, and do all I can to set Lord Beel and his folk in motion. If we go, you'll see Toug on a horse with a sword. His arm can't bear a shield, but the shield Queen Idnn gave him—the one that you saved from the fight in the marketplace—will hang from his saddle."

"Will you help?"

I nodded. "All I can."

"Mama's better."

"I know. She may never be entirely well, Etela. You must do whatever you can to help, every day. You and Toug."

"I'll try."

"I know. You must get Toug to help you. After all, she's his as long as we're here. Is there anything else?"

"No." Etela wiped her eyes with her ragged sleeve. "Only this girl is going to talk about me. She said so."

"Then go," I told Etela. "See to your mother, and get Toug to help if you can."

She would have remained, but I made her leave.

As soon as the door had shut, Uri said, "You might marry her, Lord. Do you think Queen Disiri would object?"

I returned to my seat. "Of course."

"You know her less well than you believe."

"Do I?" I shrugged.

"Or you might wed the mother."

I sighed. "When I refuse to consider that as well, will you suggest I wed them both? You may go."

"I may go whenever I wish, Lord, but I will not go yet. If you do not want to see me, that is easily arranged."

Vil, the male slave, grunted in surprise; I suppose he thought she might be threatening to blind me.

"When you speak foolishness, Uri, I don't want to hear you. Should I quiz you about the diet of the Khimairae?"

"That would be foolishness indeed, Lord. When I was a Khimaira I ate Khimaira food. Let us leave it so. You dined upon strange fare once, when you were sore wounded."

"I yield. You told poor Etela you were going to talk to me about her. Did you tell her what you meant to say?"

"No. Nor was I talking of her and her mother so much as of you, Lord. Would you not like a fair estate?"

"To be got by marriage? No." I laid Eterne on the hassock and went to the window to stroke Mani.

"A crown? That lout Schildstarr got himself a crown, and easily."

"So that I might sit a golden chair and send other men to their deaths? No."

Uri rose to stand beside me. "I speak for all the Fire Aelf, Lord. Not for myself alone. If you kill Kulili, we will serve you. Not just Baki or I, but all of us. If you wish King Arnthor's crown, we will help you get it."

I shook my head. "I have to get these people and more to safety, Uri. I have to do a lot of other things too. In Aelfrice, all these things will take only a few minutes."

"You want me to go back. In a year, Lord, you might be King of Celidon. In ten, Emperor of Mythgarthr."

"Or dead."

"You are dead!" Uri's eyes were yellow fireworks. "You know that and so do I."

"But Vil doesn't," I pitched my voice as low as I dared, "or at least he didn't. Which reminds me, I'd planned to ask Etela why she feared him. Why does she, Vil? What made her start when she heard your name?"

"She ain't feared, sir. Not really."

"She is. Before His Majesty's parade, Lord Thiazi told us about the distribution of slaves. You went to Toug, like Etela and her mother, and I saw her face when she heard it."

"I'm a conjurer, Sir Able, or used to was. I'd do things for her, just little things, you know, and tell her 'twas real magic. I guess she believed me, or sometimes."

To test him, I asked whether he had conjured up Uri.

"That's the girl talkin', I know. I listen, even these days when I can't see. More'n ever these days, really. No, Master, I didn't. I heard her and sounds like she's crazy, but I didn't have to do with that, neither."

Uri grinned like a wolf.

I am afraid I smiled, too; but I told him that he was not to call me Master, that Toug was his master, not I.

"I'm main sorry, Sir Able, it slipped out. It's square on my tongue. But you've the right of it, I belong to Master Toug now. Only he don't seem to have much use for me."

I told him that would change.

"That's so, Sir Able. Can I ask now?"

"No. When I've finished with Uri here, perhaps. But before I go back to her, what was it you did for Etela that frightened her?"

"Nothing, Sir Able. Just little things, you know. Took a coin out of her ear, and a egg once. Things like that."

Uri sniffed.

"Could you take a coin out of my ear?"

"Not now, Sir Able, 'cause I don't have one. Maybe you could lend me? Just for a moment, you know? Gold's best, if you got gold."

CHAPTER TWENTY-THREE

THE BATTLE OF UTGARD

I did, of course, in the purse Duke Marder had given me. Nevertheless, I turned to Uri. "Bring us a gold coin, and promptly. Any minting will do—whatever you can find."

"For this?" She sounded angry.

"Are you my slave, or have you dropped that pretense?"

She knelt as Vil had. "There is no pretense, Lord."

"Then do as you're told, and quickly."

When she was gone, Mani muttered, "She'll steal it."

"Of course she will."

Vil cleared his throat, his homely, sightless face not quite turned to mine. "Maybe now? My arm's got wrenched—"

"In the fight at the marketplace."

"Right. One hit me, maybe. I never done much."

"A blind man fighting giants."

"I can hear, and I can feel. I'm strong, too. I always was. In my trade it helps, but smithing got me stronger than I was when I come. Hammering, you know, and all that. So I thought maybe I could help, so I got one by the leg and threw him. Only the next one hit me or fetched me a kick and after that I couldn't do much. What it is, Sir Able—"

Uri returned, proudly holding a gold coin stamped with the features of King Gilling.

"Here is a gold coin." I handed it to Vil. "Now take it from my ear if you can."

"Ain't easy, Sir Able, conjuring when you can't see."

"I never supposed it was easy, even for the sighted."

"Is it real gold?" He bit the coin and swallowed it. "Not

bad! 'Bout twelve carat. From the taste, you know. Want me to try to get it out of my belly?"

Though he could not see me, I nodded. "If you can."

"I'll try." His hands groped for me. "I got to touch your ears, Sir Able. Main sorry for that, but I got to, so's to know where they is. Hope my hands ain't too dirty."

I told him to go ahead.

"Taller'n I thought."

It was somehow disquieting to have a face that showed evidence of many beatings this close to mine.

"You can hear me, can't you?"

I said I could.

"Ought to hear better in a minute. Where's that Uri?"

She said nothing until I told her she must answer.

"Come here, Uri. I can't see, so you got to be eyes for me. Look in his ear, will you? You see that gold in there?"

"Only his thoughts," Uri said, looking into my ear.

"Why, you're blind as me. Watch sharp." He displayed a coin. "Where'd that come from, Uri? Tell Sir Able here."

"From your ear, Lord." She grimaced. "So it appeared."

I said, "May I see the coin again, Vil?"

He handed me a large coin, much worn and tarnished.

"This is a brass cup of Celidon," I told him. "The coin you had just now was gold."

"No, it warn't, Sir Able. I know I said, but I didn't want you show you up in front of this girl and the boy that makes his cat talk. You see, Sir Able—"

"I do, and I saw it was gold. Produce it!"

He knelt again, his blind eyes upturned, his hands outspread. "Am I a man would lie to you? Not never! Truthful Vil's what they call me, Master. You ask anybody."

"And you, Truthful Vil, say the coin wasn't gold?"

"I do, Master. Look here." He held out an empty hand.

Uri said, "The coin I brought was gold, Lord."

I nodded. "I'm looking, as you asked, Truthful Vil. But there's no gold in your hand."

"There ain't?" He seemed genuinely puzzled.

"No. None."

"I can't see myself, Sir Able, being blind, you know. Only I feel it this minute—feel the weight." He clenched his fist. "There! I got it!" He opened his hand once more, and a shinning coin lay in the palm.

I took it. "This is a brass farthing, polished bright."

"I know, Sir Able, 'twas the coin I showed you, Master. A brass one, only I'd rubbed it clean."

"I had heard of conjurers, but until now I had never seen one. You must be one of the best."

He bowed and thanked me.

"Now I must require that gold piece of you. Uri and I will be through in a few minutes. When we are, she will have to return it to its owner. Do you know where it is, Uri?"

She shook her head. "You must beat him, Lord."

Vil raised his hands as if to fend off a blow. "You wouldn't hit a man what can't see, Sir Able. Not you!"

"You're right," I told him, "I wouldn't. But I'd cut one open to see whether he'd really swallowed my gold." I drew my dagger so that he might hear the blade leaving the scabbard. "No one calls me Truthful Able, but I'm truthful in this: what I say I'll do, I'll do. Produce that coin."

"I hid it under the cat, Sir Able."

Mani rose and took two steps to his left, and the big gold coin of Jotunland Uri had brought lay on the windowsill.

She picked it up. "Do you want to examine it, Lord?"

I shook my head. "If you're satisfied, I'm satisfied."

Vil said, "That's how we do, Sir Able. Only what we do is tell them it's a good ways away. Under that wagon over there, we'll say, or in the shoe of that man with the red hair. Him being, you know, the one that looks like he can run fast. If you've done everything right, why they believe it and look, and while they're doing it you run. Hide, if you can. I used to be good at it. Course I couldn't, now, but it's how I used to do anytime somebody fetched gold."

Uri said, "Surely you have seen enough now, Lord, to understand why the child fears him."

"Seen enough, but not heard enough. I'll do that later. You want me to come to Aelfrice at once?"

She nodded.

"To fight Kulili for you. Not long ago, Baki wanted me to come to Aelfrice to fight Garsecg. I won't do either one 'til I finish here."

"You say years would pass here, Lord, but the difference is not as great as you suppose. You may take a year here—ten!"

"I'll come when I'm ready. When I do, I'll fight Kulili as I promised. If I live, I may or may not lead you against Garsecg—no promises. Now take that coin back."

She faded as I spoke, and was gone.

Mani said, "Just between the three of us, and before she comes back to spy, do you think you can beat this Garsecg?"

I shrugged. "I killed Grengarm."

"And he killed you, dear owner."

I could not help smiling. "You see, you know more about it than I do, Mani."

"I don't even know who Kulili is."

"You won't learn it from me today. Do you know who Garsecg is?"

Mani looked smug as only a cat can. "He's a dragon."

"Who told you?"

"You did, dear owner. I asked if you could beat Garsecg and you replied that you had killed Grengarm. Grengarm was a dragon—Toug told me about your battle with him. Therefore Garsecg is another dragon. Elementary. You know who stabbed King Gilling, too, don't you?"

I shook my head.

"Of course you do. I heard what you told Lord Thiazi. You know, you just can't prove it."

"I don't want to," I told him, and turned to Vil. "Mani

here wanted to be the last to talk to me, and both girls have had their shot. What do you want to talk about?"

"Help, sir. That's all. Can I say first off nothin' I heard will go farther? I don't think you'd like me blabbing it, and I won't."

I thanked him.

"Master Toug's talked to me, sir. He says I'm his only I'll be free once we get south. That true, Sir Able? Seemed like he believed it."

"As far as I know. I don't know much more about our country than your master does. Less, perhaps."

"Well, Sir Able, I'm blind. You wonder why I fought 'em? Why we all did? I can't ever forgive it. Never. I wish I could, only I can't."

"Once I dreamed of returning here with an army and driving them out," I told him. "I doubt that I ever will."

"So the thing is, Sir Able . . ." He groped for me, and I gave him my hand.

"The thing is, how'm I going to eat when we get south? I know the conjuring trade and can still do it some. You see how I worked them coins?"

"No," I said. "I watched you closely, but I did not."

"Only I can't live like that no more. If I was to take their gold boy and run . . ." He laughed bitterly. "How far'd I get, you think?"

Mani murmured, "You told us you could hide. I do that at times myself."

"You got eyes. A man that can't see can't keep out of sight. If I was to try now, you'd laugh." Vil's face had never turned from mine. He seemed to collect himself, and said, "I got my new master, Sir Able. Only he wants to be a farmer like his pa. People like that, they don't have enough to eat. That's why I left to start with. What're they goin' to do with a slave that can't see?"

"I would hope them too kind to drive him out," I said.

"So I thought I might ask him to sell me while he's still

here." Vil drew a deep breath. "The others, they went to Sir Svon, and he's goin' to is what I think. That's Rowd, and Gif and Alca. He'll let 'em go cheap and raise what he can. The women ain't worth much, but Rowd ought to fetch a bit. Only there's the girl and her mother, Sir Able."

"Etela and Lady Lynnet? I don't think you have to worry about Toug's sellin' them."

"How it was at Master Logi's, Sir Able, was a woman for each man. Gif for Rowd, you know, and Alca for Sceef. So Lynnet for me, it was supposed to be. Only she wasn't right, Sir Able. Not right . . . Maybe I ought not say. Sometimes we did, you know? Only not often, and I never did feel right about it. But I tried to keep track of the girl. You won't trust nothing I say. I know that and don't blame you."

"That depends on what it is, Truthful Vil." Wearied by the hassock, which afforded no rest for my back, I climbed into the chair it served.

"I didn't touch her, nor let anybody. You take my meaning? It was gettin' worse as she got older. There's them that'll hump a pig. Maybe you think I'm jokin'."

"No."

"Makin' monsters, for what's born of such you wouldn't like to meet, and they live sometimes. So there's them that would've jumped her in a minute. I took care and kept her close, and spanked her, too, if she talked back or run off. Said I'd turn her into a doll to keep her close by. So she's feared, Sir Able, like you said. Only I . . ."

"Love her."

He coughed. "Yes, sir. And her mama too. Her mama's a fine, fine woman. A high-class woman."

"A noblewoman, the daughter of a baronet."

"Is she, Sir Able? I didn't know. You said I loved Etela, and you weren't wrong neither. Only . . ."

"I understand. What do you want of me?"

"Help, Sir Able. That's all. Etela, she'll stay with Master Toug if she can. But her mama can't look out for her nor for herself neither. I would if I could. But—but . . ."

"My owner is a kind and a chivalrous knight," Mani said; there was a note in his voice I had not heard before.

"If I could work for you, Sir Able? After we get south, I mean. I wouldn't ask no pay. Not a farthin'. Only that you'd help with Lynnet, and Etela too if she needs it."

"Lady Lynnet may not want your help," I told him.

"I know it, Sir Able. Only that's not to say she don't need it. She ain't right. And many's the time I've took care when she didn't want me, and Etela the same. You ask her, and if you get truth out of her you'll hear it."

"No doubt."

"Only she'll cry. It'll be a while, you know? Before she gets over that. Will you help me, sir? All right, I'm blind. But you ain't, you can see these arms." He flexed his muscles, which were impressive. "I'll work hard. If you don't think I'm working enough, you tell me, Master."

Mani muttered, "Work hard and steal."

"You tell that boy to swaller it, Master. Not from you, nor from Master Toug, nor any other friends you got I won't."

"All right," I told him, "you may serve me in the south, provided we can find nothing better."

He surprised me, not for the last time. Groping toward the sound of my voice, he found my feet, which reached the edge of the chair, and kissed them. Before I could recover, he was at the door. He turned, and where his empty eye sockets had been, there were two staring—in fact, glaring—eyes of bright blue. Then the door shut behind him.

"That was a trick," Mani said.

"I know. I wish it hadn't been."

"Pouk's was better." Mani sprang from his windowsill to the floor, trotted over to my chair, and with an astonishing leap caught the upholstery of the seat and pulled himself up. "Pouk made them think he was blind when he wasn't."

"He was already blind in one eye," I said. "He has been as long as I've known him. Was that what you wanted to talk about, Mani? The thing so private you wanted to speak last?"

"No." He settled into my lap.

"If you'd rather not say it, or prefer to wait . . ."

"I've helped you. Haven't I earned a few minutes?"

I agreed, and sat stroking him for some while. Gylf (who had gone to the stable) scratched at the door; Mani asked me not to admit him; I called to him through the door, asking him to look in on Toug.

"I ducked into that place with you," Mani began.

"The Room of Lost Love? I know."

"You went with the madwoman, but I wasn't interested in whatever love she might have lost. I went looking for my own. That was a mistake."

I continued to stroke him and said nothing.

"Once I was a free spirit. Once I was a normal cat, not troubled by lies." Mani spoke slowly, and as it seemed, mostly to himself. "The first is the finest of existences, the second the finest of lives. I have lost both."

He looked up at me, and there was far too much sorrow in his forlorn black face for me to find it amusing.

Schildstarr sat the throne that had been Gilling's as if he had been there all his life, and Thiazi stood beside him with his gold staff as if he had served Schildstarr's father before him. It was one of the times when I could see that the Angrborn were foreign, not just to us but to everything; the Valfather was not foreign to us at all: he was ours, as we were his.

"Your Majesty." Beel bowed almost to the stone floor. "I

congratulate you, not on my own behalf alone, but on my king's, upon your ascension to the throne of your ancestors."

Nor, I decided, were Uri, Baki, and the other Aelf alien in the same way. Kulili had modeled them on us.

"Hail King Schildstarr!"

"Hail!" Garvaon, Svon, and I, standing behind Beel and Idnn, pounded the floor with the butts of our lances.

Neither was Michael alien like that. He was, I think, what the Valfather himself might aspire to become, somebody good the way that a good blade is good, and one who saw the face of the Most High God.

Idnn's lovely voice rang even among the cloudy rafters of that hideous hall. "Your Majesty! We, Idnn, a Queen of Jotunland, most humbly beg a boon."

Even the dragons of Muspel belong to Muspel. They are demons to us, but not to themselves.

"Speak, Queen Idnn."

Those oversized eyes, bigger than the eyes of owls, were made to see through the freezing black of Old Night; and Old Night (I have been there, although only on its edges) is not any of the seven worlds. It is not that the Angrborn always seem horrible. You get used to them. It is that they really are, that being horrible is being like the Angrborn.

"Our king is dead. Our husband is dead as well, for they were one and the same. It is the custom of our people, of the people of the south, Your Majesty, to mourn a husband for a year, a king for ten. Thus you see us in black, and in black we shall go for eleven years. Far to the south, Your Majesty, stands the castle of our girlhood. It is nothing compared to this Utgard of yours, yet it is dear to us, for it holds the room in which we slept as a child. With Your Majesty's most generous, most compassionate leave we would go to that room, bar its door, and weep. To be at your court is glorious, but glory has no savor for widow's weeds and tears. May we go? And with Your Majesty's leave, may our father and his retainers give us escort?"

Beel bowed again. "My heart implores me to accompany my grieving daughter, Your Majesty. Equally my duty demands it. Our king dispatched me to King Gilling. I must apprise him of King Gilling's death, and of the dawn of your splendid reign. Thus on my own behalf—may we depart?"

Wistan and Toug had gone to ready our horses for a quick getaway, and to tell Master Egr to see to the baggage. While Beel talked, I could not help wondering how they were coming.

"Before you go," Schildstarr said slowly, "we might give you gifts for your king. How say you, Thiazi?"

He bowed. "I shall attend to it, Your Majesty."

"Then we have your leave?" Beel took a short step back. "Words cannot express our gratitude, Your Majesty. May peace reign forever between these realms."

Thiazi's staff thumped the floor, the signal that the interview had ended. At a whispered order from Garvaon, we knights faced about. When walking with lances, you have to keep step; otherwise the lance-heads hit each other, and the pennants get fouled. We had practiced half the morning, and did well enough.

In the courtyard, I found Wistan, Toug, and Egr ready to depart. "There'll be gifts," I told them. "Gifts for King Arnthor, and we must wait 'til they're presented. Get those saddles off the horses, and get them back into their stalls."

Wistan looked dismayed, Toug fatalistic.

"Don't feel that you've wasted your effort. You've located everything and cleaned it up. We should be able to leave tomorrow with little delay, and that's good. Now step closer. I don't like having to shout at you."

They gathered around me, even Lynnet.

"You're to stay with the horses," I said, "all of you. You must be here to take charge of the gifts. Lord Thiazi will present them to Lord Beel, and Sir Garvaon and Sir Svon will bring them to you. You have to stow them and protect them once they've been stowed. Except for Lady Lynnet and her daughter, not one of you is to leave without permission. Everybody understand?"

They nodded.

"Etela, you and your mother sleep in Toug's room with Mani. If you're not there when we leave, you may be left behind. Is that understood?"

Etela nodded solemnly,

"If your mother insists on leaving—"

Lynnet said, "I won't."

"Good. Thank you, My Lady. Etela, I was about to say that if she goes—if someone comes and takes her away, for example—tell me no matter how late it is. Or how early."

"Yes, sir, Sir Able. I will."

"Vil? Is Vil here?"

"Right here, Sir Able." He raised his hand.

"Fine. If you can't find me, Etela, tell Squire Toug or Vil. Is there anyone who doesn't know what he's to do?"

No one spoke.

"Good. Queen Idnn has a diamond diadem, given her by her husband. King Schildstarr's gifts to King Arnthor will have to equal or exceed that, I think. The danger of theft will be very great, and if anything is stolen it will go hard with all of you—and very hard with the thief."

Master Egr asked, "We leave in the morning, Sir Able?"

"I have to talk with you about that." I drew him aside.

Here I am going to have write more about things I did not see. Woddet and Hela told me most of it.

Daybreak had found Marder's party in the saddle. The War Way lay broad before them, nearly straight and spangled with frost. A league ahead it passed between boulders and heaped stones where it looked as if a rocky hill had been leveled. Beyond this low defile, they saw the towers of Utgard, towers so big you might think them shorter than they were, if it were not that their tops were so near Skai.

"We will eat our next meal in that castle," Marder told Woddet; and Woddet said, "Yes, Your Grace, if those who are there already do not make a meal of us."

Hela, loping beside him, pointed with the short spear she had made for herself from a broken lance. "Seeing that, admit that my father's is no mean race."

"I have never thought it was," Woddet told her. "Though I have never fought the Sons of Angr, I'm eager to. I'm told that in all Mythgarthr there are no foes more fell."

"Wounded as you are, dear Lord?"

"Wounded as I am," Woddet replied stoutly.

"Now have you your wish." Hela pointed again. "See you those stones? Do you, Duke Marder? And you, Sir Leort?"

The Knight of the Leopards said sharply, "They're in plain view, surely."

"Why no." Hela grinned, showing big yellow teeth like knives. "Not so plain, sir knight. There is not a stone to be found there, for I have been this near Utgard and nearer. What you see are the Sons of Angr, crouching or sitting, with their heads covered by their cloaks, all sprinkled over with dust from the road."

Marder reined up, his hand lifted so those behind him would stop as well. "They are waiting for us?"

Hela made him a bow. "So does it appear, Your Grace."

The Knight of the Leopards said, "I will ride forward and see how these matters lie, Your Grace."

"And perish, if Hela's speaking truth?" Marder shook his head. "Do you serve Sir Able or Sir Woddet, Hela?"

"Sir Able formerly," Hela replied, "and Sir Woddet presently, by Sir Able's leave."

"Sir Woddet. Is she to be trusted?"

Woddet smiled at her. "I would trust her with my life."

"Then let us not distrust her to Sir Leort's death." Wheeling his mount, Marder gave orders; and when his archers had ridden within bowshot of the stones, they spread over the fields beside the War Way, dismounted, and let fly.

Roaring, the Angrborn rose; and we, their intended prey, who had left Utgard before dawn at my urging, heard the sound of battle, and riding with all haste took them from behind.

Not since I left Skai had I fought as I fought then, charging down screes of air to drive lance or sword into the upturned faces of the sons of the Giants of Winter and Old Night. The blows before Utgard, if I described them all, would fill a hundred pages. I will say only that once Eterne clove the skull of a Frost Giant to the jaw, and that though I tried to sweep the heads of Orgalmir and Borgalmir from their necks with a single blow, I failed, and that giant who had been two-headed fought on with one, though blood spurted from the severed neck as though to dye Mythgarthr.

Upon that and other blood, the grim ghosts brought by Eterne's baring feasted, so that in the level rays of the morning sun they seemed no less than men, and their spectral blades rent palpable wounds, at which their owners grinned that cheerful grin we see in skulls, and slew again.

I have been writing too much about myself. Let me write about others. First, Marder. No one who saw him could have guessed there was white hair and a white beard under his helm. A lance and horse better managed I have never seen.

Beel fought too; and we who thought him dead found him under the corpse of Thrym, and gloried, laughed, and shouted to see him blink and gasp for air.

Toug, who had sworn never to fight again, fought and fell, and would I think have died that day were it not for Gylf—bigger than any lion, and more fierce—who stood over him until Wistan dragged him to safety.

As for the Knight of the Leopards, a leopard from his shield might have sprung to life. Lance broken and helm gone, he fought on; and I have rarely seen a brand fly that fast or cut that deep.

Wounded more sorely even than Toug, Woddet fought with Heimir to his left and Hela on his right. Three Angrborn fell to them, which should be one for each; but someone who swears that he knows (and should, since he watched from my saddlebag) said one was Woddet's and two were Hela's.

That I can well believe. The Lady stands shieldmaid to the Valfather, and I cannot compare Hela to her. But think of the goddess of a ruder nation, thick-limbed, tall as any rearing mare, with ravening mouth, flying hair, and blood-drenched spear. If I met Hela in battle, I might turn aside.

Marder and the Knight of the Leopards surprised me. I hope I have made that plain. Idnn surprised me too, plying her bow like the best, and taking cool aim when the battle was hottest. But no one surprised me that day more than Garvaon. I knew him for an able swordsman. I had thought him a prudent knight, careful and perhaps a bit cautious. He fought as furiously as Hela, with helmet and no helm, as he and Svon had fought King Gilling's champions. Unhorsed, he fought all the harder, caught a horse whose rider had fallen, and charged into the thick of the fight once more.

So we had our furious fighters; no doubt I was one. We had our rocks as well. The Angrborn would have killed Idnn and scattered her bowwomen a dozen times had it not been for Svon and the servingmen he led, and in all honesty I doubt that Toug would have gone into the fight without his example.

It was, in short, one of those rare battles in which nearly everyone fought (although Berthold and Gerda did not, nor did the blind slaves, Etela and Lynnet, and the slave women), and in which everyone who fought, fought well. That said, it seemed to me that without Garvaon and the Knight of the Leopards we could not have won, and it was only through the Valfather's grace that we won with them.

After the battle I took the rear guard—the Knight of the Leopards and his men, and ten of Marder's; thus I had no chance to speak with the rest until we camped. It was late, black night, for we had ridden far, fearing pursuit. Pouk helped me out of my armor and began to clean and polish everything while Uns (returned by Idnn as she had promised) cooked for us. Persuaded by Berthold and Gerda, I lay down, and half asleep heard the whisperings of my bowstring: the lives and deaths of many men and women, and children, too—lives of toil mostly, of poverty and hunger. Perhaps I had just closed my eyes. Equally, I may have closed them an hour before. In any case, I was roused by Beel's valet, who shook my shoulder calling, "Sir Able? Sir Able, sir?"

I sat up and asked what he wanted.

"It's His Lordship, Sir Able. He's—His Lordship would speak with you. His Lordship is far from well."

Still half asleep, I stood. "Dying?"

"Oh, no, sir! I hope not, sir. But he—he cannot walk far, Sir Able. I mean, he would try, but we won't let him. They won't, sir. He wanted to come here, sir. He wanted me to support him so he wouldn't fall. They wouldn't allow it, Sir Able. The Queen, Sir Able, and His Grace. And I had to agree. So I came." He paused, and cleared his throat. "If I give offense, sir, the fault is mine."

Uns was trying to give me a bowl of stew and a spoon.

The stew smelled delicious, and to silence him I accepted both and began to eat.

"If you would come, Sir Able . . . ? I—I am aware you owe me nothing, but—"

"Nonsense. You spoke boldly in my defense, Swert. Do you think I've forgotten that?"

"You recall my name, Sir Able? That is—is . . . Well, sir, I—I confess—"

"Have you eaten?"

"I? Why, ah, I don't think so, Sir Able. Not since we left that horrid castle, sir. I've—we've been caring for His Lordship, and there's been no time."

I gave him my spoon and what remained in the bowl, a bit more than half, and munched the piece of coarse bread quickly offered by Uns. Thus, both of us eating (and eating as fast as we could), Swert and I made our way through the discomfort and disorder of the camp to Beel's pavilion.

I had hoped to find him asleep, but he was awake and propped in his folding bed, with Idnn on a stool at his bedside and Marder in a chair eating porridge.

"Sir Able." Beel managed a smile, although I could see he was in a lot of pain. "Be seated, please. You must be tired. All of us are."

I looked to Idnn, and received a glittering nod. Marder nodded as well. Swert brought in a folding chair, and I sat down. "To see you sitting up and smiling is worth hours of rest to me, My Lord. I imagine Her Majesty and His Grace might say the same."

"I killed Thrym, the captain of the King's Guard."

"So I heard. I congratulate you, My Lord."

"I don't congratulate myself." Beel was silent for a moment, adjusting his position in his bed, his mouth twisted with pain. "You weren't present when he halted us outside Utgard, Sir Able. Neither was His Grace. But you may have heard of it. King Gilling had been told—though I can't imagine who his informant may have been—of Her Majesty's cat. You gave her that cat, I believe."

Idnn said, "We asked for Mani, Father, and he gave him to us."

"Exactly. Exactly. He wanted to see the cat, and keep us waiting outside. I stood there in the road, in the wind, and talked with Thrym for an hour. Trying to get us in, you know. He was a monster, the largest of them all. I was terrified of him and tried not to show it."

Idnn said, "Father, you weren't!"

"Yes, I was. Shaking in my boots." He smiled. "If you had told me I'd have to fight him, I would have slashed my wrists. If you'd told me I would win, I'd have said that all prophesy is moonshine, even mine. You know me, Your Majesty. I bounced you on my knee and played hide-and-seek. Am I a man of war? A knight, or anything like one?"

Idnn shook her head.

"Now I've killed the captain of King Schildstarr's Guard. That wasn't what we wanted to talk to you about, Sir Able, though it may bear upon it. But I did it, and I can't keep quiet about it. Killing one giant, even the captain of the Guard, can't mean much to you. How many did you kill this morning? A score?"

I shook my head. "I don't know, My Lord. I didn't count. Not as many as that."

Marder said, "You rode through the air. I'd heard about that from some of my men, but I didn't believe them. Today I saw it myself. You galloped on air as though it were a range of hills and your arrows—I've never seen so strong a bow. Never."

"It's my bowstring, Your Grace. I've had it since I was a boy, but I hope not to need it before long."

No one spoke, so I added, "As for riding on air, please don't fall prey to the idea that I do it. It is my mount who does it. I have a good mount."

Mani bounded into Idnn's lap, and she smiled. "And a good cat."

"A very good cat, whenever he's not Your Majesty's cat."

Marder dropped his spoon into his empty bowl. "I need to sleep. So does Sir Able—we all do. The first thing we wanted to say, Sir Able, was that after what happened this morning Celidon and Jotunland are at war. Border raids can be blamed on unruly vassals. This can't."

I nodded.

Idnn said, "And we wanted to ask you why—why King Schildstarr laid an ambush for His Grace's party." She gave me her old impish grin. "Knights aren't supposed to know much. You're to be fighters, and leave the thinking to us. We were teasing Sir Svon about it as we rode."

"Your Majesty is as wise as she is beautiful."

"Thank you, sir." She made me a mock bow. "We are Queen of Jotunland." (Some sound outside the pavilion told me we were overheard.) "But a queen without power is a queen without wisdom, we're afraid. Wise enough, however, to know who has it. Why did King Schildstarr want to kill His Grace and his knights?"

I said, "I don't think he did, Your Majesty. The ambush wasn't intended for them. They came on it from the rear, and were wise enough to detect it."

Marder said, "Sir Woddet's giantess did. I would have ridden straight into it."

"Hela?"

He nodded. "We were traveling without an advance guard. In retrospect, that was foolish."

Idnn's eyes had never left my face. "If the ambush was not meant for His Grace's party, for whom was it meant? Us?"

"I can only speculate. But yes. I think it was."

"We don't—we were bearing Schildstarr's gifts to King Arnthor. Why would he . . . ?"

"To get them back, to begin with." I glanced at Marder

and Beel."Do you want to hear this, My Lords? Her Majesty and I can speak privately if you want to rest."

Beel said, "I do. Very much," and Marder nodded.

"As you wish. Second, we aren't popular in Jotunland. Before he got the crown, we were an asset to Schildstarr, fighters he couldn't afford to lose. That's why he helped rescue Sir Svon and his party when they were attacked in the market. Once he was king, we were a liability. His people despise us, and he was associated with us."

Beel nodded. "It was one reason I was eager to go."

"So was I, and I hoped that if we left at the earliest possible moment there wouldn't be time to arrange something like we saw today. I was wrong, of course. He waited until his ambush was ready before turning the gifts he was sending King Arnthor over to you."

Mani rose and appeared to lick Idnn's ear, and she said, "Wouldn't it have been better to attack us piecemeal, while were still in Utgard? We wouldn't have had our horses, and some of us wouldn't have had weapons."

I shook my head. "It would have been a violation of the laws of hospitality—"

"We know. But Frost Giants?"

"I believe so, Your Majesty. While I was traveling with a certain friend not so long ago, we were attacked on our way to a castle belonging to giants. We fought them off, reached the castle, and asked for lodging. They lodged and fed us. And entertained us, for that matter. While we stayed there, it became obvious that they had been our attackers. We left stealthily, and so avoided the second attack they planned."

Slowly, Idnn nodded. "We see."

"It would have given Schildstarr an ill name among his people, something he can't afford. He was trying to wipe out the one he'd gotten already by associating with us."

Marder added, "From what you've said, he'd have wanted to do it in public, anyway. Kill you in a place where his people could know of it."

"I agree, Your Grace. But by waiting until his ambush was ready, he ran an awful risk—you might arrive, tripling our strength. He gambled, and lost only by a hair."

Idnn sighed. "To get back a few trinkets."

"Not really, Your Majesty. To humble the small folk who had beaten his more than once, pigmies they thought should be slaves or dead. Also to reclaim that diadem you wear. Gold plates, cups, and amber may seem like trinkets to you, though there are bold men and virtuous women who own nothing half so fine. But there's not a king in Mythgarthr who would think the diadem King Gilling gave you a trinket."

Beel murmured, "He's right, Your Majesty. You must be very careful of it."

"He loved us, didn't he?"

I nodded, and Marder said, "He surely must have."

"We didn't love him. We—we tried to do our duty . . ." She pulled a handkerchief from her sleeve and wiped away her tears. "Be a good ruler to our people. For those few short, short days we believe we were."

Gently I said, "He knew you couldn't love him. What he got from you was as near to love as Angrborn can ever come. Thus he loved you, and tried to show it."

Marder cleared his throat. "You yourself are not one of those bold men who own nothing as fine as a gold plate or an amber necklace, Sir Able. You have a good horse, as you say, and a good sword. I would have said I had those too, if I hadn't seen yours this morning."

"His bowstring," Idnn whispered.

I said, "Yes, Your Majesty. My bowstring, as you say and though no one would count my bow as valuable, I made it myself and I treasure it. I have the queen of seven worlds' swords as well, and the best of all dogs."

Mani made a sound of disparagement, which I ignored.

"But no squire," Marder continued, "now that Svon has become Sir Svon. And no land."

"No, Your Grace."

"When Lord Beel wanted to see you, we discussed the advisability of rousing you from sleep—and missing some ourselves. You've heard the questions Her Majesty and Lord Beel had. I didn't have any so urgent that I felt justified in keeping you up."

"I'm always at your service, Your Grace."

"Yes, I've noticed. Ahem! I can't offer you a new squire. Not here and now. I brought no boys, save my own squire. As for lands, well, the deed's at home, locked in a drawer. But the place is yours, and I'll give you the deed as soon as I can. Redhall's one of the best manors in my dukedom. Quite fertile, and nicely situated on the road to Kingsdoom. I see you've heard of it."

"It—" I could scarcely speak.

"It was Sir Ravd's. Reverted to me at his death, of course. I've a steward taking care of things. You may want to keep him on. Or not. Up to you."

I doubt that I managed a nod.

"I'll let him know you're coming, naturally, and give you a letter for him."

Idnn spoke for me, prompted perhaps by Mani. "This is most generous of Your Grace."

"Not at all." For a moment Marder seemed embarrassed. "I wish I could do more. No, I will do more. But I can't do it now, not in this wilderness. Later though. You'll see."

I left soon after that, and left abruptly enough to see a tall figure steal off into the shadows.

The next day we decided that the Knight of the Leopards should take the rear guard. We all agreed it was the post of greatest danger, and Svon, Garvaon, and he were all eager to command there. Garvaon led the advance guard, however, and Svon was wounded. That day I rode with the advance guard, and Sir Woddet with me.

The Plain of Jotunland is a strange and unsettling place,

as I have tried to make clear. One sees phantoms, at dawn and twilight particularly. One hears strange sounds, and finds inexplicable things—paths going nowhere, and sometimes broken pieces of earthenware pots that were once crudely beautiful.

Hela found such a pot about noon, running some distance from the War Way to pick it up, and exhibiting it to Woddet and me when she came trotting back. It had been broken at the lip, losing a segment of clay the size of my hand. The rest was complete. "Is it not lovely, good Sir Able?"

I agreed it was, but explained that I dared not burden Cloud with anything beyond the most necessary.

Heimir said that it recalled Idnn, which surprised me.

"It's red and—something like blue." Woddet took it from him and turned it so its winding stripe took the bleared light of the winter sun, azure, aquamarine, and royal. "I'd have said that Her Majesty's white and black, mostly except for the diamonds."

I said, "I suppose so," or something of the sort. The truth was that I was scanning the road ahead and had stopped paying much attention to Hela's find.

"Red lips, of course," Woddet finished lamely, "but her eyes are dark, not blue."

"Do you count her friend?" Hela asked him.

He grinned at her. "I don't like her like I like you. That's Sir Svon."

"And do you care for him, Dearest Lord?"

Woddet looked to me, baffled, and I said, "He does, but not in the sense you mean."

"I meant what I said. No whit the more." Hela tossed the pot aside. "Do you count him friend, dearest Lord?"

"More than that." Woddet cleared his throat. "He's someone I've wronged, Hela. Or I think he is."

I said, "So do I."

"There were rumors. I didn't like him, so I found it easy to believe them."

If Hela understood, nothing in her broad, coarse face showed it.

"Easy and a lot too convenient. It's wrong. It's something a knight shouldn't do. A man's honor is sacred, even if he's not a knight. You believe the best, until you see for yourself it's not right."

On that morning, the morning of the day after we had left Utgard, this talk of ours seemed no more significant than Hela's broken pot. I have re-created it, however, as well as I can; reading it over, it seems clear that I ought to have realized that Hela was planning to do Idnn and Svon some favor, and that her favor would prove no small thing.

CHAPTER TWENTY-FOUR

A RIDE AFTER SUPPER

We traveled all that day, the warmest any of us had enjoyed in some time. There was no sign of pursuit, but we agreed that there were surely Angrborn behind us, a war band formed around the survivors of the battle, strengthened from Utgard and gathering more from each of the lonely farms we had passed.

These Angrborn would (we thought) trail us like hounds until we reached the marches of Jotunland, then fall upon us. If we ran, only the best mounted would escape—and perhaps not even they. If we fought, we might prevail; but ruinous defeat was more likely. If we scattered, we would be hunted down, and those who escaped the true Angrborn would almost certainly fall to the outcasts the Angrborn called Mice.

We decided to fight, of course, if we could not outtravel them; but I, privately, resolved to ride back that night—not to see whether the Angrborn did in fact pursue us, but to hinder their march if I could.

The day grew warmer still, the sort of winter day one gets occasionally in Celidon, when it seems spring cannot be far behind, though spring is months away. The snow on the War Way softened to slush, and the horses' legs were muddy to the knees. Gylf panted as he trotted beside me.

"This will slow them, dear Lord," Hela said. "It turns me sluggard even now." Her face was streaming sweat.

Woddet reined up. "If you cannot keep the pace—"

"By all that I hold dear, Sir Woddet, I will never leave you." There was steel in her voice.

He seemed taken aback. "I wasn't going to suggest it. I was going to say that you and I—your brother, too—might go more slowly and join Sir Leort."

"I do not weary," Hela insisted; it was clear she did.

I told her such weather could not last.

"Nor can I, Sir Able?"

Discomfited, I said nothing.

"Know you . . ." Hela was panting in a way that recalled Gylf, her tongue lolling from her mouth. "Why you name . . . My sire's folk Frost Giants?"

"Certainly," I said. "It's because their raids begin at the first frost."

"Would they not . . . War rather . . . In fair summer . . . ?"

I tried to explain that we supposed they could not leave their own land until their crops were in.

"I'd thought . . . Might teach you better. . . ."

I slowed Cloud's pace, telling Woddet we gained too much on Garvaon. He agreed, though he must have known it false.

"They swelter. . . ."

I considered that for a time. Old Night, the darkness beyond the sun, is the realm of the Giants of Winter and Old Night, and it is ever winter there, as their name implies. Winter, and ill lit—for them, the sun is but another star, though brighter than most. Thus huge eyes, which like the eyes of owls let them see in darkness; and huge bodies, too, hairy and thick-skinned to guard against the cold.

Telling Woddet to go slow, I went to speak to Marder. "We needn't fear the Angrborn's pursuit in such weather as this, Your Grace. Hela and Heimir can hardly keep up with us, though they're of our blood as well. The greater danger is that we'll tire our horses. We used them hard yesterday."

"I was thinking the same. If they overtake us with our chargers blown, they'll slaughter us like rabbits."

"I agree, Your Grace. Wholeheartedly."

"Then stop wherever you find water and grass," he said.

We did and quickly, although we would not have found the spot at all if it had not been for Hela, who told us of it. It was some distance from the War Way, which was an added point in its favor—it is difficult for any but a hound to track by night, and if our pursuers were not sharp-eyed they might pass us by. If that happened, we would take them from behind the next day, while our mounts were still fresh. Uns and Pouk made our camp while I saw to Cloud, and Mani offered to climb a tree—tall ones are rare in Jotunland, but there were a few there—and keep watch; for cats, as he said, see by dark nearly as well as Angrborn.

Woddet's camp he and his men made for themselves, while Heimir and Hela stretched sweating on the clean, soft grass. We had camped so early that the pavilions were up and every rope tight while the sun was still a hand's breadth above the horizon.

Uns had gone to Svon's fire to borrow a light for ours, for it seemed that Vil was uncommonly clever at fire-making, which I thought extraordinary in a blind man. " 'Taint no trick, Master," Uns explained. "You'd look fer smoke. So'd I. Dat Vil smells hit, 'n blows, 'n feels fer hit."

Idnn came, with Berthold to carry her chair. I taught Uns and Pouk to drop to one knee, as one does for a queen, and bow their heads in the proper style. Gylf made his own bow, the dog-bow we are too quick to call groveling when it is in fact simple canine courtesy.

"Arise, good people." Idnn smiled on all of us. "Will you dine with us tonight, Sir Able? His Grace will not be there, nor Sir Woddet, nor Sir Leort. Our noble father may attend, though we'll discourage it if we can."

I had planned to be off as soon as I had eaten, and muttered something stupid about honor and my allegiance to Marder.

"That's what we thought you'd say—we'll dine with you instead. Have you royal fare, Uns? Answer us honestly."

Uns bowed again. "Ya knows me, mum. I does wat I can's aw, 'n li'l 'nough ta do wid."

"He doesn't," I said. "None of us do."

"Then there's no shame in providing a queen with what you have, Uns. Whatever you'd eat yourself. We assure you we're hungry enough to dine upon the bats of Utgard."

She turned to Berthold. "You may go. Go back to our pavilion and get what food and rest you can."

He bowed and turned away, feeling his way with a stick.

"Uns is to serve us, Sir Able?"

"He does normally, Your Majesty, but I would have the honor of serving you myself, if I could."

"It would not prevent you from eating? You're three times our size—if we're famished, you must be starving."

"If I may serve myself, too, I'll eat with a will."

"Good. We ask that Uns and Pouk, though we feel certain they're both good men, be kept out of earshot."

I told them to remain on the other side of the fire, and (there being small need of warmth on such an evening) to stay well back from it unless Uns' cooking required him to come closer. After that, I fetched two wooden trenchers and two jacks of wine that Uns had mixed with water.

"They'll tell you when the meat's ready?"

I nodded. "Yes, Your Majesty."

"We'd like bread. Don't tell us it's hard—we know."

I brought her half of one of the twice-baked loaves Svon had secured for us before war broke out in the marketplace.

"One needs a Frost Giant's teeth to bite this," Idnn said, chipping off a piece with her dagger. "They have massive jaws, all of them. Did you notice?"

I nodded and said I had.

"We asked our husband about it. We were telling him how handsome he was. You understand, we're sure. He said they most enjoy the bones. It was a pity, he said, that we didn't eat them. We explained that we eat the bones of larks and thrushes, and he smiled. We felt so sorry for him! We ought to have asked whether the jaws of the daughters of Angr were as strong as those of her sons, but it didn't occur to us at the time. Nor would it have been politic, perhaps. Do you know, Sir Able? You must have seen a few since we told you of them."

"No, but I've seen giantesses of the Giants of Winter and Old Night, Your Majesty."

"Have you really? What were they like?"

"In appearance? They change their appearance readily, Your Majesty, just as the men do."

"The men of the Giants of Winter and Old Night, you mean? They must be fabulous creatures."

Uns called that our soup was done, and I fetched it. When I had given Idnn hers, I said, "They are indeed, Your Majesty."

"You said you'd seen them, the giantesses, at any rate."

"I've seen the men too, Your Majesty. And killed a few. Of the women, Skathi is beautiful and kind, though so big in her natural state that feasts are held upon her belly."

Idnn laughed. "You set your table there?"

"Many tables, Your Majesty, and when we sing she

sings along with us, and when we eat opens her mouth so we can cast dainties into it. Yet at other times, she seems only a tall lady, with strong arms and many plaits of golden hair, her husband's shieldbearer."

"We think you mad, though there may be more wisdom in it than in the sanity of other men. What of the rest?"

"Angrboda is a daughter of Angr, Your Majesty, though she wasn't banished from Skai like so many of Angr's brood. I have seen her many times, though only at a distance."

Idnn smiled. "Do you fear her?"

"Yes, because her husband is Lothur, the youngest and worst of the Valfather's sons. If she attacked me—it's said she attacks all who come near—I would have to defend myself or perish."

"We understand."

"She's hideous, and they say that the time of her womb is a thousand years. When it's complete, she bears a monster and couples with her lord again. It may not be true."

"Yet you think it may be. You were long in Skai?"

"Twenty years, Your Majesty, or about that."

"But you saw no more than those two?"

"One other, Your Majesty." The memory darkened my mind, as it does even now. "Modgud guards the Bridge of Swords. If it were destroyed, no ghost could visit us, and there are those who'd destroy it. Thus Modgud, a giantess, protects it night and day. Because she does, the ghosts may come forth when Helgate stands wide."

Idnn spooned up a little soup. "We take it she's fierce and well armed."

"I don't know what weapons she may have, Your Majesty. She bore none when I saw her."

"Is she very large?"

I saw then that Idnn would question me until I told her everything; yet I hoped that by telling her much I might hold something back. "It's hard to judge the natural size of any of the Giants of Winter and Old Night," I said, "when one has seen them but once. When I saw her, Modgud was no larger than many Angrborn."

"And in form . . . ?"

"A maiden, fair-haired and slighter of limb than any Angrborn I've seen, small at the waist and not wide at hips, though womanly. Barefoot, and dressed as the poor dress."

"Yet she frightened you."

"Say that she impressed me, Your Majesty. In justice to her, I must add that she didn't oppose our coming in, nor our going out. Thunor blessed her and praised her for her care of the bridge, and she received his blessing and his praises graciously and seemed glad of them. Thunor was our leader." I cleared my throat. "Many think the Overcyns are always at war with the giants, but that isn't true. There's friendship at times, as well as strife."

Idnn nodded solemnly. "We know of that. Won't you tell us what we want to hear? The thing you're holding back?"

"Modgud's face is that of death. It's naked bone, save for a maiden's eyes. Perhaps it's just a mask. I hope so."

Idnn stirred her soup and sipped a spoonful. "We are glad it was you and not we who saw her, Sir Able."

"You will see her, Your Majesty, when you cross the Bridge of Swords."

"We hope for better." Again Idnn sipped, spilling soup from her spoon. "We didn't examine you to pass the time."

"I never thought you did, Your Majesty."

"Will you stand a few more questions? What think you of Hela? She was your servant once."

"Only briefly." My own soup was cooling; I tasted it while I considered. "She's an outcast, and knows she must always be one. Her brother's an outcast, but not sensible of it. Hela is, and there's poetry in her because of that, and sorrow. In the warm congress she's a slattern, and yet I believe she truly loves Sir Woddet."

Idnn nodded, her dark eyes on the glowing embers of our little fire, or perhaps on Uns and Pouk, who sat eating and talking beyond it. "Go on."

"He doesn't love her as I love Queen Disiri. Yet his tenderness is real—"

"And she warms her hands before it."

"Indeed, Your Majesty. Like every poet, she's a clever liar, but too clever a liar to lie much or often. I wouldn't trust her the way I would Pouk or Uns. But maybe I'm being too hard on her."

"It may be that we are as well. She came to us tonight, calling us queen, and asked what we knew of our subjects."

"About the Angrborn, Your Majesty?"

"So we thought. We told her we had no subjects, that the Angrborn follow King Schildstarr, that though a queen we do not rule. You're anxious to be off, to ride your wondersteed among the stars. So would we, in your place."

She had seen through me like glass. I pretended not to be surprised and said, "The stars are too far for Cloud and me, Your Majesty. Nor am I as eager to depart as I was."

"You may go soon. Where are the Angrborn women, Sir Able? The women who named us queen when we wed?"

"Your Majesty must know better than I do."

Idnn shook her head. "We stayed in a farmhouse on our way to Utgard. Our servant Berthold had been a slave there. You'll recall it, we're sure."

"I do, Your Majesty, though it seems very long ago."

"It wasn't. There were slave women, too, as Gerda was on another farm. But of the owner's own women, none. No wife, no sister, no mother. Hela says the womenfolk of the Angrborn remain our subjects."

I asked whether Idnn hoped that I could add to what she already knew about them; when she did not reply, I assured her that I could not.

"She said she'd bring some of our subjects here, and so saying went into the night. Do you think us in danger?"

"From your subjects? I can't say. We're all in danger from the Angrborn, Your Majesty."

"Of course. When Hela left, we called for Gerda. She's lived among them most of her life, and she kept her eyes. We asked where the women were, the wives of the Angrborn we see. We won't tell you all she said—much of it was foolish. She said she'd seen them from a distance, and they frightened her—that they have their own land, far away."

No doubt I looked incredulous. "Your Majesty once said the same, I believe."

"We did not, for that was not what they had told us. Our race would die out if we women lived in one nation and you men in another, and I know of no beast that lives so. Besides, if the females were so far away, how was it Gerda had seen some? So we popped her into the fire—you know what we mean—and wouldn't let her out 'til she'd told us everything. You see them early in the morning, mostly. Very early, before the sun is up. Or before moonrise. For more than our lifetime Gerda had to rise and dress by firelight, milk four cows, and turn them out to pasture. Do you know what frightened us? When we were at Utgard?"

"The place itself, I imagine, and the Angrborn."

"Only some of them, the ones with two heads or four arms. We don't know why, they were no worse than the others, but they did."

For half a minute, perhaps, Idnn gave her attention to her soup. Then she said, "Who killed our husband, Sir Able?"

I told her I did not know.

"We feel it was one of those monsters. There was one with a lot of legs. Did you see him? Like a spider. A big eye and two small ones." Idnn shuddered.

"There was one covered with hair as well."

"We hated him—hated the sight of him, we mean. He

356 ‡ GENE WOLFE

may have been a perfectly worthy subject for all we know, and he was a member of our husband's guard. But when you rode over them on your wonderful horse and slew a score—"

"Not as many as that, Your Majesty."

"A score at least with your arrows, and we were shooting arrows too, with the maids we'd taught to shoot—or anyway with the ones who had stomach enough for it—we kept hoping that one would be him, and we'd see him and put an arrow into his eye. It didn't happen, but that was what we hoped."

"I've wondered about these things," I told her. "The Angrborn were cast out of Skai because they were inferior. Not because they were evil—many of the Giants of Winter and Old Night were as bad or worse. Because they didn't measure up in some fashion. It may have been because they had lost the ability, which the Giants of Winter and Old Night certainly have, to change size and shape. Having lost it, they may have been judged unfit for Skai."

"You were there."

Seeing what was coming, I did not nod.

"Could you do that then? Turn into an eagle or a bull. Or—or be smaller than Mani."

I smiled. "Who'd catch and eat me, and serve me right, too. Can't you see how foolish this is, Your Majesty?"

"You were a very poor liar before you went to Skai. You aren't much better now."

I explained that nothing I had said had been a lie, that it would indeed be foolish to make myself smaller than Mani.

"Can you do it?"

I shook my head. "No. No, Your Majesty, I cannot. Am I lying now?" Setting my soup bowl in my lap, I raised both hands to Skai. "Valfather, be my witness. I cannot do either of those things."

"You're not lying, but you're holding something back."

No doubt I sighed. "When I came back, the Valfather required an oath, one I dare not break. I had to swear I'd use none of the abilities I'd been given there. I gave it. Do you think that was cruel of him?"

"We doubt that he is ever cruel," Idnn said, "but you must think him so."

"I don't. He's wiser than any mere man, wiser even than the Lady, though she's wise beyond reckoning. He knows how much harm such powers can do here. Remember Toug?"

"Of course."

"In his village, people worship the Aelf. It's a false worship, and it does harm to them and their neighbors. Isn't the Most High God as high as the Valfather?"

Idnn said, "We'd always understood he was higher."

"That's right. But there are those who say he's lower, inflicting on the Valfather such humiliation as they cannot conceive. If I were to use the powers he gave, there might spring up a cult to rival his, with worshippers claiming I was his superior. He'd be humiliated, and they'd be as far from the truth as those people in Glennidam. As it was, his kindness to me exceeded all reason. He let me take Cloud."

I set aside my bowl and rose. "We've talked enough, Your Majesty, surely. May I go?"

"Eat your meat and let us eat ours, and you may go with our blessing, if we may go too."

I must have gawked at her like a jerk.

"Are we so weighty? Your arms and armor will outweigh us by a stone, and your saddle's big enough for two, when the second's our size. Besides, Cloud's carried us before."

I fumbled for words, and at length managed to say, "Your Majesty will be in some danger."

She smiled; Idnn had always had a charming smile, with a hint of mockery in it. "Our Majesty is in danger here, Sir Able. Our Majesty will be in less on your wonderful horse's back, with you to protect us, than Our Majesty would be in here, with Sir Able and his wonderful horse gone."

"Sir Svon would not like to hear that."

Idnn nodded. "Nor need he, unless you tell him. But really, Sir Able. He is wounded, and not such a fool as to rate himself with you if he weren't. Do you think he has spoken to the Valfather as a knight to his liege? Do—"

"I hope he has," I told her. "He should have. Out of my ignorance I neglected his training when he was my squire. I didn't realize at the time how badly I was neglecting it, but I can't believe Sir Ravd neglected it at all. If he didn't, Sir Svon has talked to the Valfather as his knight."

Idnn rose; and though she was small, she seemed tall at that moment. "We are properly rebuked. Rebuked, we remain a queen. Take us with you. We ask a boon."

I knelt. "A boon that does me far too much honor, Your Majesty. I was . . . Your condescension stunned me."

"As your courtesy gratifies us. Perhaps it would be best if we mounted first, then took our foot from the stirrup. But here is our meat."

It was not quite as easy as that, of course. I had to call Cloud, and saddle and bridle her with Pouk's help.

"She'll be tired," Idnn said; and I thought that some small part of her regretted her decision.

"Not she, Your Majesty. She might be ridden in war a long day through, yet remain fresh enough for this." Cloud's thoughts had confirmed my words before I spoke them.

"May we stroke her?"

I nodded, and she caressed Cloud's muzzle very gently, as all who know horses do.

Uns brought my saddlebags; I told him I would leave them with him, since we would be returning in an hour or two. They cannot have weighed as much as Idnn, but they must have come near it, and I left my lance with Uns as well.

"If Your Majesty will do me the honor . . ." I knelt with linked hands to help her. She did, but sprang up so lightly that I doubt she required the least assistance.

Having mounted first, she sat before me. I would guess she had planned it, wishing me to ride as I did, with the perfume of her hair in my nostrils, embracing her when Cloud mounted that steep of air none but she could see.

Might I have had her? Few men know less of human women than I do, and it may be she only wished for me to want to. She did not speak until the steep ended and we galloped at a level, with Gylf running ahead and wood and plain unrolling beneath us. Then she said, "Oh, this is grand!" and breathed again, as my sword arm told me.

Of all the times I rode above Mythgarthr, I recall that one best: the unnatural warmth of the wind, and the glooming towers of the snow clouds to the west. Lesser clouds with the moon behind them, filling Skai with silvery light. A queen before me, and the Valfather's castle floating among the stars. Idnn's black velvet gown, her diamond diadem and perfumed hair. The soft pliancy of her waist, which made me desire her so much I took my arm away.

"Why do you ride to Utgard, Sir Able?"

"I won't, Your Majesty, unless it happens so. We're retracing the War Way in search of our pursuers."

"Shouldn't we have seen them by now?" She pointed. "On the horizon—those are the battlements of Utgard, surely."

I agreed, and urged Cloud forward.

Soon the wind grew chill. Idnn drew her cloak about her, and Gylf stopped panting. Twice we circled Utgard; a few lonely lights still shone, but we rode so high that no one there could have seen us. A little snow fell, and Idnn shivered and begged me to hold her again. I did, and drew my cloak around us both.

"We thought our velvet too warm all day, and too warm even by night, but wore it for its mourning color. Now— Why is your dog leaving us?"

Gylf's deep-throated bay had reached us, borne on the still air. "He's scented something," I explained, and sent Cloud after him.

"From way up here?" Idnn sounded incredulous. "He can't possibly sniff the ground!"

"I don't know what is possible to him, Your Majesty. But you've hunted deer and the like. Haven't you ever seen your hounds course with their heads high?"

"On a hot trail? Yes. Yes, often."

"That's because the scent is in the air. It's not a man's feet that leave the scent. If they did, the best dog in Mythgarthr couldn't track a man in new boots. It comes from the groin and under the arms, mostly. Some settles, and some hangs in the air and blows away or drifts, which is why even the best hounds put nose to the ground on a cold trail."

"He's lower than we are, but not much."

"Because he has to go no lower to catch the scent. I doubt that he's following one man, or even two or three."

"They didn't go by the War Way."

"No," I said, and it was my turn to point. "See that lighter streak? That was the road they followed, I think."

"Then they can have nothing to do with us."

I shrugged; she could not have seen it, but perhaps she felt it. "We're not camped by the War Way, Your Majesty."

"No. In the place Hela told us about." Idnn was silent a moment. "We see what you mean."

"I meant no more than I said."

"There they are! Look under the trees."

Far ahead Gylf had halted, and it seemed to me that he was looking at me. I shook my head, hoping he could see it.

"Are we going back now?"

"As soon as I get a closer look."

"You'd like to fight, wouldn't you? You'd surprise them while they slept, if we weren't here."

It was true, but I denied it.

"But we—we're glad we are. They're not our subjects, really. They won't obey us. But they were his, and we . . ."

"You're their queen, whether they'll obey you or not."

"Yes." She sounded grateful.

"We can wake up a few and tell them so, Your Majesty. It'll be dangerous, but I'll do it if you want me to."

She sighed. "They will only say that they serve King Schildstarr. No."

"I think you're wise. The time may come, but this isn't it." I whistled for Gylf, and we rode away.

"Did you count them?"

Reminded of Sir Ravd, I shook my head.

"We did, more than two score. There were probably more among the trees we didn't see."

I said, "We won't fight them unless we have to."

"You and Sir Svon and Sir Garvaon."

"Yes. Your father, too, and His Grace. Sir Woddet and Sir Leort, with the archers and men-at-arms. Also Heimir and Hela, and the servants."

"Against four score Angrborn?"

"Against whatever number we face. Gylf too. Gylf's worth a hundred good men, Your Majesty."

"We want you to promise us something, Sir Able. We want you to promise you'll let us talk to them first. Will you?"

"I will, Your Majesty." I felt my heart sink, although I knew that she was right.

"As you've helped us, we will help you. You're not the only one to give a pledge to the Wanderer. Remember what we told you about Hela?"

"That she'd bring your subjects to do homage? Yes, Your Majesty. I haven't forgotten that."

"That the women are still my subjects. What you told me of the giants in Skai did nothing to allay my fears."

I knew I could have said more and frightened her worse.

"Would Hela do it if she thought they might harm me?"

I laughed to think she expected me to fathom a woman's heart. "I can't say. I'll stand by if you want."

She shook her head. "If they are ours, we are theirs, and we must trust them."

Then I wished we were not in the saddle, so that I could kneel to her.

CHAPTER TWENTY-FIVE

LOST

The unnatural warmth had left us, and the air lay so thick with freezing fog that I could not see my outstretched hand. Vil came, found wood for us, and rekindled the fire. Pouk asked whether he should saddle Cloud; I told him no, to wait until the fog lifted.

Marder and Beel came. I offered the same advice, and they agreed; Beel said he thought the fog more than natural, to which I said nothing.

Marder said, "You don't think so, Sir Able? Tell us."

"I consider the fog wholly natural."

Beel shook his head. "You know more of wizardry—"

"No, My Lord."

"Than I, but I can't agree. Thiazi's magic has created it. I've tried to counter it. I admit I've had no success."

Marder tugged his beard. "I don't know you as well as I want to, but I know you well enough to feel sure you have a reason for saying what you do. What is it?"

"I rode back to Utgard late last night, Your Grace."

He nodded. "Her Majesty told us."

"There was no fog, but there were a few lights high in the keep, and one a bit lower. We liked the warm weather." Recalling Hela and Heimir, I added, "Or most of us did. But the warmth we liked too much to question was Thiazi's work, I would say. After Her Majesty and I returned, he ceased his effort and winter closed its jaws on us again."

Marder nodded. "Chilling the air. That would do it."

Beel nodded too, I think mostly to himself. "No wonder I couldn't counter him. He wasn't doing anything."

"Can you raise a wind?" Marder asked.

"Yes. Of course."

"That should clear it off." Marder stood up. "We'll wait here until it's gone, but we should be ready to leave as soon as we can see."

Together they disappeared into the blank gray around us.

"I'll be here forever if they mean it," Vil whispered.

I asked about Toug.

"Better'n he was. You think them ladies Hela's fetchin' might help, Master? They knows herbs men don't, sometimes."

"I agree, and maybe they can. But how is it you know about Hela's errand, Vil? Did she tell you?"

"No, sir." His empty sockets stared into an obscurity no adept could lift. "I wasn't, listenin' in, I swear."

"You would never do such a thing, I hope."

"Well, I might. Only I didn't. I was busy settin' up for Master Toug. He's mendin' like I said, only he's shamed, Master, to talk to you. He want's to come 'round, only he's that shamed. He won't hardly talk to Sir Svon, even."

Pouk cleared his throat and spat. "I been tooken aback meself, Vil. Who ain't? We might rag him now an' then, I mean Uns an' me might if we knew what 'twas, which I don't. Only we wouldn't mean no harm. Would we, Uns?"

"I woun't. Nosar! Him's Squire Toug, Pouk."

"If he won't come to us," I said, "we've got to go to him. But I doubt that it's kidding he's afraid of. Have you stolen while you were here with us, Truthful Vil?"

"No, sir!" Vil held up his hands. "Not nothin', sir. I wouldn't steal from you, Master. Ever. You can search me, or have your men here do it. Whatever way you choose."

I smiled. "Much good that would do. If you've stolen and your conscience pains you, you've only to bring it back. You won't be punished."

"I wouldn't never steal from you, Sir Able. You've my word on that."

"Then go," I said.

When Vil had gone, Uns asked what he had taken.

"I don't know, but I could see Gylf didn't trust him, and he knew about Hela's errand."

"Wot's dat, Master?"

Pouk answered. "Gone to fetch ladies is what he said."

I told them that I wanted my mail cleaned, and all the horse gear well washed with saddle soap, which put an end to their gossiping. When they were busy, I took Gylf aside and asked what Vil had taken; but he only said, "Don't know," and "Don't see"—this last meaning, I think, that his world was the world of smells and sounds. He did not say, "Ears up," as he often did, yet it seemed implied.

Svon came asking to speak to me privately. "There's no privacy here," I said, "less even than there is at night. We can't tell when others may be listening."

"Then promise you won't repeat what I say."

I refused.

"You are . . ." He seemed to find his words difficult. "The—greatest knight of us all."

"I doubt it, but what of it?"

"It's what everyone says. Sir Garvaon and Lord Beel, Sir Woddet and His Grace the Duke. Even Queen Idnn."

"I thank the gracious Overcyns for Sir Leort."

"Him too. I forgot him. I was your squire. Not for long, I know."

"Long enough for a journey that seemed long to us."

"I remember." For a moment it appeared he would say no more than that. "I didn't like you, and you didn't like me."

I agreed.

"You said once that you were the boy who threw my sword in the bushes. You can't have been, but you said you were."

"I am."

"But you're the greatest knight. In a month my leg will heal. Will you fight when it does? I mean to challenge you. I'd rather you fought gladly—that we engaged as friends."

"I will," I promised, "but not here in Jotunland."

Svon rarely smiled, but he smiled then. "It's settled. Good! Will you give me your hand?"

We clasped hands as friends should.

"Why wouldn't you promise to keep my confidence?"

"Because I had no idea what you might say. Suppose you said you intended to betray us."

"Or that I'd betrayed Sir Ravd, which is what everyone else says." The smile vanished.

"That would trouble me less. But if I'd given my word that I'd keep your secret, I'd keep it. If it were that you meant to betray us to the Angrborn, I'd fight you now and kill you if I could. But I'd never reveal what you told me."

Svon nodded slowly. "I understand. You really thought it might be something like that."

"I feared it. I didn't mean that your confidences, or any-one's, will be served at dinner like venison. But you don't have my word I won't reveal them, nor will you get it."

He seemed about to choke. "I love Idnn. Her Majesty."

"Is that another confidence? I knew it already, and there can't be many who don't."

"I think she—she . . ."

"She does, I'm sure."

"But she's a queen, and I—my father was a baron. . . ."

"But you're not, or at least not at present. This is why you want to fight me, isn't it?"

"It's part of it. Yes."

"Would you like me to lose? To yield to you? After a considerable struggle, of course."

"Certainly not!"

"What if I win?"

Svon held himself very straight. "I'll live or die, like other vanquished knights. If I die—in a way I hope I will—it will be with Her Majesty's favor on my helm."

I congratulated him.

"Though I engage the greatest knight in Mythgarthr, I won't be worthy of her. But I'll be more nearly worthy. Sir Woddet fought you. So did Sir Leort, and His Grace."

"You have given me part of your reason," I said, "will you give me the rest?"

"Because you took my sword. It unmanned me and you thought me a coward, if that was really you."

"It was."

His hard, handsome face (made human by its broken nose) was entirely serious as he said, "Then I must prove myself."

"You already have," I told him.

He shook his head, and as if eager to talk of something else said, "This fog—isn't it ever going to lift?"

I mentioned my concern for Toug, and Svon shrugged. I said, "If you could contrive some little errand and send him to me, I'd appreciate it."

"Certainly. As soon as I get back. He despairs."

Svon seemed to expect a comment, so I said, "I know."

"Etela helps him more than I've been able to."

"That's natural."

"Her mother, too. Lynnet. And Vil does what he can, showing him his tricks and getting him to describe what he saw, then showing him—sometimes—how the trick was done. He'll get over it. Boys always do."

I nodded, although I was not sure I agreed.

Svon turned to go. "I've been thinking . . ." He turned back. "I should tell you. All my life men have told me they were helped by this one or that one. No one ever helped me."

"Sir Ravd tried."

"Yes. But now someone has. You gave me the accolade—elevated me to knighthood. Were you really authorized to do it? By a ruler?"

"I was and I am."

"By the queen you say knighted you? The queen of the Moss Aelf?"

I shook my head.

"I won't ask any more. His Grace was surprised to find me a knight. At first he thought Lord Beel had done it. I told him it was you and expected all sorts of objections, but I was wrong. He just congratulated me. Then he asked if I'd given allegiance to you. I said I hadn't, that I had given it to Lord Beel. You were there."

I nodded again.

"It was very informal. I suppose we'll do it over when we get back, if we do."

I said we would, but that the ceremony would not take place. "Not because His Lordship will refuse, but because you'll ask to be released. Yours will be another liege."

"Idnn. Her Majesty."

I nodded.

"I've thought of that. I— She has no one, nothing, and I've land from her father. Swiftbrook. It's not much, I'm sure, but I might win more."

"You will."

"Thank you. Thank you for everything. You taught me more than you realize." He turned again, and was lost in the fog after a step or two. When I could no longer see him, I heard him say, "We'll engage when we get home. You agreed. Perhaps she'll accept me after that." From the sound of his voice, he was still quite near.

An hour passed, or at least a time long enough to seem an hour; when the sun is invisible, it can be hard to judge. Mani joined me, saying, "Do you like this?"

"Our fire?" I knew it was not what he meant. "No, not much. The wood's wet."

"The fog."

"No. It's wet, too."

"Neither do I." He jumped into my lap and made himself comfortable. "You know, dear owner, I wish you'd taken me along when you and the queen went riding."

"You were in one of my saddlebags, I suppose. I should have thought of that."

"As if you didn't! But if I'd heard you, I might be able to offer advice. Don't tell me you're Able, I know it."

"I don't make that sort of joke."

"Oh, no! No, really you don't. Yours are better, but often you think no one understands."

"And you," I said, and stroked his back.

"You haven't told anyone about the . . . About that room. Lord Thiazi's room."

"About your experience there, you mean? No."

"Thank you. I think about it. I think about it a lot. I'm not usually that way."

"Introspective? No, you aren't."

"Will I really be free when the cat dies? You said something about that—or somebody did—and Huld says it, too. That I'll be an elemental once more."

I was not sure he wanted an answer, but he insisted he did. "No," I told him. "No, you won't."

"She says elementals aren't really alive but just think they are, so they can't die."

I told him she was correct.

"So I'll be free. That's what she says."

"The elemental will be free, no longer having any share in life. You're not the elemental or the cat. You're both, and the cat will die like other cats."

"I'd like to think that I'm just . . . The other thing. The thing that talks."

"Then I'll cut off your ear and we'll see if it hurts."

"You would, wouldn't you?" Mani's voice, always fairly close to the mews and purrs of a common house cat, had become more so, though I could still understand him.

"No." I drew my dagger, and he vanished into the night.

Svon had promised to send Toug, and I waited some time for him, warming my hands and thinking of Disiri and the things I would have to do before I searched for her. I had promised to fight Svon—under the circumstances I could not do otherwise—and it was possible he might wound me badly, in which case my search would be further delayed. It was at least as possible I would kill him to prevent it.

At length it seemed clear that he had neglected to send Toug, or that Toug had been unavailable for some reason, and I remembered what I had said to Uns, that we would have to go to Toug if Toug would not come to us.

Motioning to Gylf, I rose. I knew which way Vil had gone, and made myself behave (as I picked my way through the fog) as a blind man would—walking in what I imagined to be the correct direction, groping the ground with my sheathed sword, and stopping every few steps to listen.

Soon I heard voices, followed by a deep grinding or grating that I could not at once identify. Someone (I was nearly certain it was Svon) spoke. Then someone else, who might perhaps have been Toug himself. The grinding came again, the sound one hears when one heavy stone slides on another, the sound that precedes an avalanche.

Another step; I heard the voice I now felt certain was Toug's say, "If you said you killed him, that might do it."

Never have I been so tempted to eavesdrop. I called, "Toug? Is that you?" and nearly choked on my own words.

"Master!" It was stone on stone; I knew then to whom it belonged. "Yes," I said, "I'm here, Org."

He was not the most terrifying creature I have seen, for I have seen dragons; but he was terrifying, and never more so than on that blind gray morning. It was all I could do to keep from drawing Eterne.

He knelt and bowed his head, repeating, "Master."

I laid my hand on it, and it was hot as fever, like the stones that are heated to warm a bed.

"Sir Able?" (That voice was Svon's.)

I called, "Yes." Less loudly, I spoke to the crouching monster before me. "Have you been bad, Org?"

"Many." He looked up as he spoke; there was unspeakable cruelty in his slitted eyes, but suffering, too.

"Did you kill King Gilling? Answer honestly. I will not blame or punish you."

"No, Master."

I nodded. "I never thought you did, Org."

Svon emerged from the fog. "He might easily have done it. Wouldn't you agree?"

"So might I," I said. "So might you or several others. But it's beside the point. He's an evil creature. We know it and so does he. Confess to having betrayed Sir Ravd!"

Svon took a quick step back. "No! I didn't!"

I shrugged. "You see?"

"You mean I'm an evil creature too."

"So am I. Why do we fight, if not to purge our evil? We're afraid to die and afraid to live—afraid of what we may do. So we shout and charge. If we were good—"

Wistan had come near enough for me to recognize him. "Where's Toug?" I asked him.

Svon said, "With you, I thought."

"You sent him to me?"

"Yes, with Etela, her mother, and Vil. She insisted."

When I said nothing, he added, "I thought you'd send them away if you wanted to talk to Toug alone."

Gylf whined, pressing his shoulder against my hip; I had not been aware that he had followed me. I said, "Let's hope we find them when this clears. Has Org served you well?"

"You overheard us."

"I heard your voices. Nothing of what you said."

Wistan started to speak, but Svon silenced him with a wave of his hand. "Do you want him back?"

Org himself said, "Yes."

"I should have thanked you for him. I mean, when . . ."

"When you shared your confidence."

Svon nodded. "Yes. Then. But I'm so used to hiding the fact that I have guardianship of him . . ."

"You must find it a heavy responsibility."

He nodded again. "I've done my best for him as well as for the rest of us. I've protected him from us, and us from him. Or tried to."

"I'm sure you have."

Wistan said, "This's my fault, Sir Able."

"What is?" I had guessed, but it seemed best to ask.

"Sir Svon was alone, except for the mad woman."

"Lady Lynnet."

"Her, and I didn't think she mattered. Her daughter had told me. Had told me enough, anyway. I said—I'm a friend of Toug's, and I think Etela thought Toug must have told me about Org. I saw him once or twice when we were in Utgard."

Svon added, "I suppose most of us did."

I nodded, feeling Gylf press my leg.

"So I thought it might help Toug if Org were to say—not to everyone, just to the ones that matter—that he'd killed the king."

This was an entirely new idea. I said, "You think Toug did it, and he's feeling guilty? I assure you, he didn't."

"No. Not at all."

Svon cleared his throat. "He was with Wistan the first time King Gilling was stabbed. Isn't that correct, Wistan?"

Wistan nodded.

"And he was fighting beside me when the king was killed, so it's quite impossible. But Wistan thinks others believe him guilty."

"Her Majesty."

Wistan added, "His Lordship, too. Her father. He won't say it, but he does, and thinks he can't believe Sir Svon and me because we're his friends. I'm—I am his friend. So it's true. If I thought he'd done it, I'd lie to save him."

Svon said, "I wouldn't. Why are you looking around?"

"The air stirred. It hasn't since this fog came. Gylf wanted to tell me something a minute ago, and I imagine that was what it was." My hand was on his head; I felt his nod. "It wasn't a breeze, but on a ship, sometimes, when you're becalmed, a sail stirs and everyone looks and smiles. Soon it stirs again, if you're lucky. The thing that stirs it isn't really a wind, only air that's been moved by a wind far away. But you're desperate for wind, and when the sail stirs you know one's on the way."

"May your words reach the ears of Overcyns," Svon said.

I had not thought him religious, and I said so.

"I felt they'd betrayed Sir Ravd and me. You're going to ask if I expected them to fight beside me. Yes, I suppose I did. I've outgrown that, or hope I have." He turned to Wistan. "Becoming a knight does it. That and wounds."

Wistan said, "He's trying to protect me, Sir Able, so I'd better tell you. Squires have honor to uphold too."

"Of course they do."

"I thought his ogre—could you send him away now?"

"He bothers you."

"Yes, sir. He does. Will you, Sir Able?"

I shook my head. "I'd sooner send you, Wistan. Say what you have to say, and go."

"I thought Org had killed the king. He says he didn't."

Weary with standing and weary with waiting, I leaned upon Eterne. "Go on."

"Anyway, I thought he had, and Etela told me he belonged to Sir Svon. So I went to Sir Svon and said if Org confessed to Queen Idnn and her father, and of course to His Grace, I didn't think they'd punish him, and Toug wouldn't think they thought he had done it anymore."

"You should say 'Her Majesty,' not Queen Idnn."

"I will, Sir Able. For a minute I forgot. Well, Sir Svon said he didn't think his ogre had done it, but we'd find him and ask him. So we went, you know, out here in the wood, and he called him, and—and . . ."

"He came."

"Yes, sir." Wistan gulped. "I mean Sir Able. I never had seen him up close. But he wouldn't say he did it, even after Sir Svon explained. So I wanted him just to say it, to tell them he did even if he didn't. That's when you came."

"I understand, but I wish you were half as concerned for Toug's safety as you are for the state of his feelings. He's lost in this with Lady Lynnet, Etela, and Vil, it seems, and the four of them may meet with something worse than Org—a nice steep drop, for example."

"I hope not, Sir Able."

"Or a bear, or any of a thousand other things. Would you like to meet Org when you were wandering in this?"

Wistan shook his head and backed away.

"Then return to the camp, directly and quickly. Sir Svon and I are about to send him away, as you asked."

Wistan turned and ran.

Svon gave me a tight-lipped smile. "He requires a bit of seasoning."

"He does, but he's getting it. Toug requires rescuing, apparently, and he's not getting that." My mind touched Cloud's, but she had neither saddle nor bridle. "Will you send Org to look for him? And Lynnet and the rest?"

Svon nodded and told Org to stand. He rose, and seemed larger than I had ever seen him. Uns had said he caught him young, but he had been so fearsome when I fought him that it had never occurred to me that he might not be full grown.

"Org," Svon said, "I know you were listening. I don't want you to harm any of our party. Nod if you understand."

Org nodded.

"I want you to search this wood for Toug, and for Etela, Lynnet, and Vil. If you find them, bring them back unharmed. Do you understand?"

Org nodded again. He had been dark, doubtless because Svon had told him to make himself visible; he grew fog-pale as Svon spoke.

"Go now."

Org vanished much more swiftly than Wistan had.

"He won't harm them," Svon said, "or I don't think he will. It may depend on how hungry he is."

I remarked that he had rescued Toug and Etela in the town beyond the walls of Utgard.

"He fed well there," Svon told me. "There was always killing, and he killed half a dozen Angrborn when Sir Garvaon and I fought their champions. Their friends buried them, but he robbed the graves. He says—do you want to hear this?"

I told him to go ahead.

"He says there's no better eating than a corpse that's been dead a week in a cold climate. Do you want him back?"

I shook my head.

"He's a useful follower, but . . ."

I said I understood, and calling Gylf to me asked him to cast about for Toug's scent.

"I should look for them myself," Svon said. "That's an amazing dog you have. He used to irritate me almost as much as Pouk, but I'd love to have him, or one like him."

I said, "I hope that someday you will."

"I doubt it, but it's pleasant to think about." The handsome, tight-lipped smile came and went. "Before I fetch my horse, will you answer one question? For old times' sake?"

I said that ignorance would prevent my answering many questions and honor many others, but I would not lie to him.

"Do you think I killed His Majesty?"

"Certainly not."

"I was fighting. Both times. Both times when he was stabbed, I was fighting. Had you thought of that?"

I shook my head.

"Well, I have." Svon looked troubled. "I've thought about it often, and even talked about it with Her Majesty. I could have done it so easily."

"Yes," I said. "I suppose you could."

"The first time, particularly, the night we fought his champions. My sword was in my hand. It was dark, and there was a great deal of noise and confusion. Pandemonium. Idnn has described it to you, I know."

I nodded and added that Toug and others had as well. As I spoke we heard Gylf give tongue; he had struck the scent. I listened for a moment (as did Svon), and said that if the fog had not deceived me, he was already some distance away.

"I'll get my horse," Svon said, and was soon lost to sight. Privately I hoped he would not become lost too.

For an hour I did my best to follow Gylf's voice, a deep-throated bay when the trail was plain, small sounds when some vagary of terrain made it difficult. Just before I caught up with him, I heard the silver notes of a trumpet, faint and far through fog that swirled and thinned as the wind rose, telling Marder's folk to put out their fires and saddle up. Overtaking Gylf, I warned him that we might have trouble catching up even if we found Toug.

More distinctly than usual he said, "Not alone."

"Toug? No, of course not. Lynnet, Etela, and Vil are with him, or at least I hope they're still with him."

"More." Gylf sniffed the ground again, and growled. I cannot say there was fear in that growl; but he grew larger and darker as I watched, and when he spoke again, turning to repeat that Toug and the others were not alone, his head was as big as my war saddle and his fangs longer than my hand.

"Nor are you," a voice behind me said.

CHAPTER TWENTY-SIX

SEA DRAGONS

The slope descended for whole leagues—so it seemed to me. And if it did not, if I am somehow mistaken, it is because I have made the distance less than it was.

How far to Aelfrice? No one asks, for all who know Aelfrice, even by repute, know that no man has found the league that will measure the way. How far to summer, sir? How many steps? How far to the dream my mother had?

The trees grew great and greater, until those of the wood we had left behind us in Mythgarthr seemed shrubs. The fog, which had been thinning, darkened from white to yellow. Gylf sniffed the air, and I did the same and said, "The sea."

"Does it please you, Lord?" Uri grinned at me, and I recalled all the fires we had fed together, the flying horror she had been, and the moaning Aelfmaid who had trembled in the lush grass beside the durian tree, red as sunset and too weak to rise.

I found I was smiling. "It would if I weren't needed in Mythgarthr. How much time has passed while I idled here in Aelfrice? A year?"

"Not an hour, Lord. You have only walked a few steps."

"But I'll walk many more before I find my friends."

"Not at all. Would you see them? Come with me."

She led us through trees where no path ran, and out upon a point of naked rock, with swirling fog to either side. I protested that I could see nothing, and Gylf backed away to shelter among the trees again.

"You will in a moment, Lord, when the fog lifts." Uri linked her arm with mine, perhaps to assure me that I need not fear the height, and I found her no Aelfmaid but a human woman, slender and naked, with a floating mass of hair like a smoky fire. A shower pelted us with rain—and was gone.

The fog parted; through the rent, I glimpsed the stone-strewn beach below, the white-maned waves that pounded it with every beat of my heart, and beyond them (where the water was no longer clear or green, but deepest blue) the head and shoulders, claws and wings, of a snow-white dragon greater than Grengarm. There are no words for the way I felt; if I were to say here that my heart sunk, or that I felt I had been gutted like a deer, what would that mean to you? Nor would it be true, since I felt far worse. Cold sweat ran down my face, and I leaned on my sword, fearful my knees would not support me. Uri spoke, but I did not reply. Nor can I recall what she said—her voice was lovely, but the singing of a bird would have conveyed as much or more.

The fog closed, and the white dragon was lost to view.

"*Bad! Bad! Bad!*" That was Gylf, barking from the shelter of the trees.

"Your master will not think so," Uri told him. "He has built his fame on the slaying of these creatures. Think of the joy in the Golden Hall!" Her arm held mine more tightly. "I had not meant you to see Kulili so, Lord. And yet—"

"You're glad I did, so you can bear witness to my fear and shame." I tried to turn to go, but she grappled my arm, and upon that narrow outcrop I did not wish to oppose her.

"Not glad. Amused. Kulili has defied armies."

"You would frighten me more, if you could."

"You are my lord." She turned to look me in the face; and her own held beauty beyond that of mortal women, though her eyes were yellow fire. "If you fear her you will not fight her, and if you do not fight her you will live. I have bantered with you often, Lord."

"Too often." I watched the swirling fog, fearful that it would part again. If I had seen the white dragon when it did, I might have thrown Uri from the precipice and fled.

"As you say. I am not bantering now. A second death for you, here, may mean oblivion. Do you think to ascend beyond your Valfather?"

I shook my head.

"Nor will you, Lord, if you die again—here or in Mythgarthr—you may perish utterly. This I hold is that part of the Able who was which survived."

"Sir Able," I told her.

"You demean yourself!"

I watched the fog in silence.

"Garvaon and Svon are knights. 'Sir Garvaon,' they say, and 'Sir Svon,' and bask in your reflected glory."

"As those who come after us will bask in ours."

"You're going to fight Kulili anyway, aren't you? You're going to fight her alone and perish from the world."

I did not speak; but in my mind Gawain knelt again, baring his neck.

"Did you see Garsecg and the rest?"

"No," I said.

"The Isle of Glas?"

That surprised me. I confessed that I had not, but only the white dragon. Nothing more.

"Then we must stay. Garsecg and some Sea Aelf wait on the beach, but we must remain until you see the isle, so you will know that Garsecg's words are true."

"He is a demon out of Muspel," I said.

"He was your friend, and would be your friend again if you would permit it."

"Baki wanted me to come here and kill him."

"I have seen, Lord, that you will not."

I did not believe then, and do not believe now, that Uri had power over the fog, which had been thinning as we spoke. Whether or not she possessed such power, the fog cleared a little. The white dragon had vanished beneath the waves. Far off I beheld the Tower of Glas, and its top (which had been lost in cloud when I had seen it in Garsecg's company) was just visible where it rose into Mythgarthr. At the sight I understood as never before that the land we walk on there, and the sea we sail on there, are in sober fact the heaven of Aelfrice. I saw the Isle, the tops of a few trees, and its beach. Five tiny figures waited there; and though they were so small, I knew that they were Vil, Toug, Etela, Lynnet, and another. One waved to me.

Perhaps I should write here of our descent of the cliffs to the beach below. I will not, because I recall so little. Disiri, Gawain, and Berthold swam through my mind, with the Valfather and many another, one of them a boy who had lain in the grass of the Downs and seen a hundred strange things in clouds, a flying castle among them.

Garsecg greeted us, in form a venerable man of the Sea Aelf, as I had first seen him and seen him most often. He embraced me as a father, and I him. "They have slandered me to you," he said, "and I dared not come to you. You would have slain me."

I swore that I would not.

"Uri and Baki told you I was Setr, and you believed it."

"They are your slaves," I said, "though they pretend to be mine. How could I not believe it?"

Another man of the Aelf (as it appeared) came near. "If

he denied it, would you credit him?" His eyes were end-less night, his tongue a flame.

"If he is Setr," I said, "Setr is not as I was told."

Garsecg nodded. "I am Setr. Let us leave these others, and sit alone for a moment. I will explain everything."

We left them, walking a hundred paces or so along the beach. When we had seated ourselves upon stones, I whis-tled Gylf to me.

"It would be better," Garsecg said, "if we were two."

"Setr cannot fear a dog."

He shrugged. "Setr fears interruption, as all do who must unravel complexities. It was I who taught you of the strength of the sea. Do you acknowledge that?"

"I do. I have never denied it."

"Not even to the Valfather?"

"Least of all to him." I wished then, and mightily, that he stood at my side. Not because I longed for his spear, but because I longed for his wisdom, which surpasses that of all other men.

"You have said you are my friend, Sir Able, and those words I will treasure always." Garsecg fell silent, staring out to sea, where mist mingled with white spume. "Let me unravel what has occurred here. There is much that is wrong, and I am to blame for much of it. I had plans. They went awry. Such things, I hope, do not befall you."

"Only too often they do." My eyes had followed his, and I was looking at the Tower of Glas; it seemed far in-deed, and I could no longer see the isle at its summit.

"I am of Muspel. So was Grengarm, whom you slew."

I waited.

"You are a man of Mythgarthr, and a good man. Are all the men of Mythgarthr good? I do not ask whether they are all as good as you—I know they cannot be. Only whether they are good at all."

"I would like to think there is some good in the worst of them."

"But on balance?"

I thought then of Master Thope. He had sought to save me when the duke's knights would have killed me. For that effort to protect the duke's honor, he had been stabbed in the back. "On balance," I said, "many who think themselves good are not."

"Just so. You have been to Skai. I have not. Let us leave aside the Giants of Winter and Old Night. They are for the most part evil as I understand it, and some say they are entirely so. We will not speak of them. Among the Overcyns, are there some in whom the worse part outweighs the better?"

I explained that there was said to be one at least, and that the rest—though they punished him—did not take his life for his brothers' sake.

"Here in Aelfrice?"

"The Aelf are worse than we, if anything."

"So in Muspel. There are many who are strong and very wise, though not good. Grengarm was neither the strongest nor the worst. They plotted to seize this fair world and despoil it. I tried to dissuade them, for the Aelf should be the objects of our reverence, as the Overcyns are yours. I tried, as I say. I failed." He sighed so that my heart went out to him.

"When I saw at last that it was no use, I determined to frustrate them. I came here." He spread his hands, mocking himself with a wry smile. "Humbly, I warned the Aelf of their danger. Some believed me, but most did not. They are divided into many clans, as you must know. I warned them that if they did not unite against us they must fall to us one by one. Those who had refused to credit me refused to credit that as well. Among those who believed, some would not merge clans with the rest. Your Queen Disiri was one of those. You see I am being completely honest with you."

"You were my friend," I told him, "when I was wounded

and needed one badly. Now I must ask about other friends, those upon the Isle of Glas. How did they get there?"

Garsecg shrugged. "They wandered into Aelfrice. So you did as a boy, not so long ago."

I nodded.

"My friends and I would have sent them home, but the white dragon—perhaps you saw it—snatched them from us and carried them to the Isle of Glas."

"You want me to fight that thing."

"Certainly not! Did I say so? You would be killed."

I looked at him sharply.

"You asked me how they got there." Garsecg laid a hand on my shoulder, a firm touch and a friendly one. "You should have asked how you yourself came here. I sent Uri to fetch you, realizing you would want to know of their plight. I intend to recapture my tower if I can. And if I can, I will mount to its top and see to their welfare. But events here move slowly, while time flows swiftly in your Mythgarthr."

"Which is where they are."

"Exactly. For them, decades may pass while I collect an army. You have influence in Mythgarthr. You might collect a force there and sail to their rescue. Such was my thought. If you would prefer to join us here, we would be delighted to have you."

I considered the matter for as long as it might take a man to pray, watching the farthest breakers so that I would not see Garsecg's eyes. My whole life, it seemed to me, was wrapped up in this—my knighthood, the Valfather and the Lady, even Disiri. At last I said, "You are a dragon of Muspel. Isn't that your true shape?"

Garsecg nodded. "It is, though my sire was a king in Mythgarthr."

"And your friends. Aren't they dragons of Muspel too?"

"Some are. Some are of the Sea Aelf, as they appear."

"Cannot several dragons defeat one?"

"We will try, leading an army of the Aelf. You have seen me as a dragon. Was I as large as the white dragon?"

"Not nearly. That was your true shape?" I took off my helmet as I spoke, and laid it on the shingle.

"It was."

I pulled my hauberk over my head; its links were so fine that I could store the whole of it in my helmet, and that was what I did, admiring it for what might well be the last time and wondering whether it was the wearing that brought its blessing or mere ownership. Grengarm had owned it, after all.

"Are you going to swim out there?" Garsecg asked.

"You know I am. I have sworn to fight Kulili." I undressed, and explained to Gylf that he would have to guard my armor and my clothing, and that he was to trust no one. He would not speak, but bared his teeth at Garsecg to show he understood.

No more than Skai is Aelfrice like Mythgarthr. I have tried to show you how different it is; but I know that I have failed. At this point in my story, Ben, I have to confess that even I had not known just how different it was until I drew Eterne.

The sound of her blade leaving the scabbard became a wind. (You cannot imagine this.) That wind snatched away such fog as remained. In Aelfrice, one never sees the sun. But there is light; and as the fog vanished, that light waxed until the whole sea flashed like a mirror.

Over it flew ships of the olden time, long ships with many oars like wings, and embroidered sails red and black and green and gold, and high prows and high sterns of painted wood. At stern and prow stood the knights of Eterne, real as I myself was real. Their armor, the blades of the swords they held (those were Eterne too), and their smiles gleamed and glinted in that light.

Still grasping Eterne, I dove into the sea.

* * *

It is no easy thing to swim while holding a heavy sword. I did my best, swimming mostly underwater with my legs and my left arm for oars. The advantage I had (and it was a great one) was that the water did not drown me, but received me graciously. I cannot say that I breathed it as I breathed air ashore—I was never conscious of breathing at all. Perhaps I drew breath through my skin; or perhaps breath was not necessary to me as long as I remained there.

Sharks came like shadows, swift and silent. One, then two, then three; the third was of monstrous size. I knew that though I might kill one, I could never kill all three if they attacked me together. Desperate, I slashed the nearest. Eterne's fabled blade severed head from tail, releasing a storm of dark blood and a dozen foulnesses. The remaining sharks fell upon it like hawks, and I swam for the surface as a dying man swims for Skai.

The ships of the Knights of the Sword were there and all about me, one not half a bowshot off. I had not thought them real, and had never supposed I might climb aboard one. But climb on board I did, and it was a wondrous thing to stand dripping upon the deck of such a ship, a ship rowed not by convicts but by bearded warriors in leather byrnies studded with bronze, men of mighty arms whose eyes flashed like ice.

"I am Sir Hunbalt," said the knight to me. "I welcome you to our company." We clasped hands and embraced.

Soon the white dragon surfaced. We went for it with arrow and spear, though I could do nothing until we closed. There was a ram beyond the prow; I stood on it holding the carven figurehead with my free hand while the oars beat behind me like the white wings of the griffin, and churned the sea to foam. *"Disiri!"* I shouted. *"For Disiri!"*

It was by this, I would guess, that the white dragon knew me. The ship on which her jaws had closed fell from her mouth. Our eyes met, and I saw the battle rage die in them as I felt it dying in my own. She sank beneath the sea, and I knew I must follow.

In Skai I saw grander sights than ever Mythgarthr or Aelfrice can offer, but none so strange as this. The dragon melted as I watched, so that I might almost have thought the sea dissolved it. It had been a dragon, great and terrible. It became a cloud, white, shimmering, and ever-changing. And at last the face of Kulili.

Will you spare me?

I could not speak as men speak in air, but I formed my thought as I had so long ago when I was young. "I will spare you if you yield."

We have not engaged. First you must follow me, and see the thing that I will show you.

I agreed, and in the dark abyss we men call the bottom of the sea, I saw that of which I will not speak—though I shall speak of it in time, I hope, to one mightier than even the Valfather.

Toug, young Etela, Lynnet, and Vil stood waiting for me on the beach at the foot of the Tower of Glas. Though Toug's left arm was in the sling still, that sling was crimson with blood, and Sword Breaker bright with blood to the hilt. Whom he had fought when they descended the tower I never inquired; but Etela let drop a hint now and again, as women will. It matters little to this tale of mine—and yet I shall never forget Toug's face, the eyes that started from their sockets, and the clenched teeth.

"They're coming!" Etela called, pointing. "We better hide!" Seven dragons—black, gray, turquoise, blue, green, golden, and red—flew stark against the luminous sky.

I shook my head and called the ship nearest us to

shore. When its keel ground upon the beach, I lifted her into it, and put Lynnet and Vil into it as well. Sir Hunbalt and I took Toug, who stood as if entranced, waiting to fight them all. When our words availed nothing, we lifted him bodily and carried him. The dragons flew low at times and high at others, swooping and diving, but never closed with us. They would have slain us all if they could, or so I believe; but something restrained them, and if it was no more than fear, then fear proved restraint enough.

"They wanted to kill us before," Etela explained, "only the white one scared them. Are you scared of the white one?"

I shook my head.

"We were. I was terrible scared, and Toug, 'n I think Vil would of been more scared, too, only he couldn't see it, you know. But it got us 'n it carried us way up where they couldn't get us. I shut my eyes, only then it went away."

"The claws shut 'round me," Vil muttered, and there was nothing of the showman about him then.

Sir Hunbalt shook his head. "He's blind, isn't he?"

"Yes, sir, I am," Vil said, "and it was better, maybe, to be blind just then. Little Etela was so affrighted me an' her ma thought she'd die. It was a hour I'd swear 'fore she stopped cryin'."

"Well, you were scared, too," Etela said, and turned to me, holding on to me as the crew pushed our vessel free of the beach. "I'm still scared. They wanted to kill us, the bad dragons up there did, 'n they 'bout killed Toug. The white one chased them 'n said don't be scared . . ."

She hesitated, and I said, "You couldn't really hear her, could you, Etela?"

"No, sir. Only she did. Then she grabbed me up, the first one. 'N she flew way up with me 'n I thought she'd drop me, 'n when we got way up there she did, only not hard, 'n then Toug said we had to go down where you was, and there was big snakes 'n Vil couldn't even see them, 'n a thing—I don't know—"

She had begun to sob again. Toug comforted her.

" 'N the nice one's gone, 'n the others are still here." She clasped Toug, trembling.

Vil said, "You're takin' her someplace safe, ain't you, Master?"

"I'm trying to," I told him.

Our ship was going about, the rowers on one side pulling while those on the other backed water. Sir Hunbalt touched my arm and pointed. The dragons Etela feared so much were coming to earth, and three had resumed Aelf form. I nodded.

Toug said, "I'll kill them." I was the first time he had spoken, and I was happy to hear his voice. Gylf, still guarding my clothing on the beach, clearly felt the same, standing and wagging his tail.

I drew breath. "If I fight beside you? Sir Hunbalt and I, and the other knights?"

Toug shook his head. "I just wish I had my big sword."

"Alone?"

"It doesn't matter."

Sir Hunbalt nodded approvingly, but I said, "They would kill you, Toug. Setr alone would kill you."

Toug only gripped Sword Breaker the tighter, freed himself from Etela, and went to the prow, looking out past the figurehead.

"He's a knight," Sir Hunbalt whispered.

I said that Toug himself did not know it.

"A young one, but a knight." Sir Hunbalt paused, and his voice, when it came again, seemed to issue from the grave. "What a man knows hardly matters. It is what he does." He turned away, and did not speak again.

Vil whispered, "Sick, ain't he?"

"Dead," I told him. "So am I."

"Not like him you ain't, sir."

Etela clung to Lynnet, no longer having Toug to cling to, and Lynnet stroked her and calmed her.

One of the crew brought a scrap of old sail, brown and having worked on it in white thread something that might once have been a feather. I tied it about my waist.

Ashore, two knights came riding out of the wood, one leading a mount I knew at once. Gylf barked greeting.

Garsecg called across the water. "Are these friends of yours?"

Etela wiped her eyes. "That's Sir Svon, isn't it? 'N Sir Garvaon."

That was; and when we had come nearer the mainland, I jumped from the gunwale, greeted them, learned that they had been searching for me for hours, and reclaimed my clothes and armor.

Garsecg said, "You will wish to take your friends back to Mythgarthr. At a later time, Uri can bring you again. Then we shall discuss the crowns I plan to give you."

I shook my head and spoke to Svon and Garvaon. "You come too late, both of you, for me to explain all that has happened here. Did you see dragons?"

"One," Svon told me. "A blue dragon, very large. But it's gone now. I don't know what became of it."

"It's here!" Etela burst out as she, Lynnet, and Vil followed Toug and Gylf ashore. "That's it!"

"It is," I told Svon and Garvaon. "But certain other things—the ships and the knights you see—are not here." I sheathed Eterne as I spoke; and it was seen at once that the Knights of the Sword and the vessels that had borne them had been illusions born of the light that flashed from wave to wave. "Sir Svon."

He looked nervous and a little frightened, but he nodded to show I had his attention.

"You seek to prove yourself. Because you do, I promised to fight you not long ago. Queen Idnn is not here to watch. Do you want to prove yourself to her alone? Or to yourself as well?"

"The latter." Svon stood very straight as he spoke, and I could see his hand itched for his sword.

Garsecg turned to his followers. "This has nothing to do with you. You may go."

One dove into the sea; two flew; the rest sauntered away grumbling, still in Aelf form.

"You are courageous," I told Garsecg.

"And hungry." His eyes were an emptiness into which whole worlds might vanish.

I remarked to Svon that his wounds had not entirely healed; he said it did not matter.

"As you wish. Sir Garvaon, you looked for death when we fought the Angrborn outside Utgard. You need not confirm or deny that. You know what you did, and I know what I saw."

Garvaon did not speak; but Etela said, "He was really brave. Toug said so."

"So was Sir Toug. We'll get to him in moment, Etela." Addressing Garvaon again, I said, "In a way, we come to him now. He has told me that when you led your men-at-arms out to take part in the fight that began in the marketplace, they appeared badly frightened. He thought it was because they were leaving the protection of the walls to war upon Angrborn. Yet they are brave men, they were led by a great knight, and they had fought Angrborn before and beaten them. I think they looked frightened because of something they had seen only a moment before."

Garvaon still did not speak.

"I haven't questioned them," I told him, "and I won't. What you did I judge to be no crime. Neither the first time nor the second."

Garvaon did not speak, but there was hope in his eyes.

I said, "When you left Lord Beel, did you offer to help Sir Svon search for his squire and his squire's slaves?"

"Yes. We went out to look for them, found your camp, and thought it would be well to bring your horse along in case we found you, too. Your servingmen were packing your things, and did not object."

"Thank you," I said. "I owe you a lot, and this is one thing more." I stopped to draw breath, not liking what I had to say next. "I must tell you that this blue man who speaks with us is called Garsecg. I dreamed of him, and you, once. In my dream he killed you. So it appeared."

"Go on," Garvaon told me.

"As you wish. If Sir Svon engages a dragon, and that dragon is Garsecg also, will you stand beside Sir Svon? You will have no help from me."

"I will," Garvaon declared.

Etela whispered, "They haven't seen them."

"They have," I told her. "They saw Setr as they rode up, and it is Setr they must close with. What about you, Toug?"

I do not think he had expected to be asked; he looked surprised.

"As the law would have it, you are merely Svon's squire. You have no duty to fight, only to save Sir Svon if he falls. You're wounded already, and the bone can't have knit in so short a time. Will you engage?"

For the space of a breath, Toug's eyes met Garsecg's. "I won't fight," Toug said. "Never again if I can help it."

"As you wish." I turned my back on him and pointed to Garsecg. "There is the dragon, Sir Garvaon—Sir Svon. He has been a friend to me, and I will not—"

Garsecg interrupted me; I think now that he spoke in order to have more time for the transformation, although I cannot be sure. "Did you fight Kulili? The white dragon? You swore you would."

"I did."

"Did you kill her?"

I shook my head. "I never swore to take her life, and I could not have if I wished to. I yielded, and she spared me."

Just then Etela shouted, *"Look out!"*

Garsecg had begun to change, his head lengthening and swelling. He dropped to all fours, and claws sprouted from his hands. He hissed, and fire and smoke wreathed his mouth and great leathern wings rose from his back. So swiftly did he strike that Svon had scarcely time to raise his shield. Setr's fangs pierced it even as his breath scorched it, and leather, wood, and iron were torn away.

I held Gylf, who would have rushed into the fight if I had not. As if in a dream I heard Vil demanding that Etela tell him what was happening; and she, with a trembling voice, struggling to comply.

Had either knight had time to mount, things might have gone differently. As it was, Setr went straight for Svon. Svon retreated, defending himself with his sword.

As he did, Garvaon attacked Setr's left side, keeping his shield between Setr's head and himself. Twice his sword rang on Setr's scales. A thrust found softer hide behind a leg, and Garvaon drove the blade in. What welled forth might have been boiling pitch.

Svon came straight for Setr then. I was proud of him, even as I knew his effort doomed. He thrust at Setr's eyes as Setr struck. His point missed by half a hand, slipping futilely along the bony plate that had been Garsecg's face, and Svon went down.

Garvaon fought on as few men fight, cunning and bold. Setr was compelled to keep a forefoot on Svon, who struggled against it and stabbed beneath its scales with his saxe. Setr's weight was insufficient to crush him, and his hauberk saved him (largely, though not entirely) from Setr's claws.

Setr's jaws closed upon Garvaon. That was a moment I would like to forget. At one instant, as brave a knight as woman has ever borne darted in to stab and slash, and out again before the dragon stuck. At the next, those terrible jaws had raised him high.

Only to open at once, so that he fell dying to the ground.

A monstrous figure to which I could put no name rode Setr's back. A moment more and that figure had broken, becoming Etela, who had slipped from Vil's broad shoulders and fled, and Vil, with a thousand hands about Setr's neck. No artist could paint it; but if one tried, he would show a chain of arms and hands, living and strong, that tightened until that scaly neck burst like a blasted tree.

Setr reared in his agony, and Svon rolled from beneath his claw. Setr trembled, and fell dead.

It was over. Rapture held me while sorrow groaned in a place too deep for words.

But not for tears. I did not know I wept until I saw them fall on Garvaon's upturned face.

"You knew," he said. "Tell her I loved her."

Toug was bending over Garvaon too, and Svon, and Etela. Cloud came as well; and what she felt filled my mind—that a great and noble rider had passed, leaving all steeds the poorer.

The air was as still as air can ever be; I heard a whistling wind nevertheless. Garvaon heard it, too. I saw his eyes turn upward. He smiled, that grim old knight. He smiled, and took the fair, white hand that had reached for his, and rose, leaving his stiffening corpse on the sand.

Alvit helped him mount, for she had not yet kissed him and his wounds troubled him sore. I wished them good speed. Alvit, too, smiled at that, while Garvaon waved farewell. She mounted behind him, the white stallion leaped into the air, and in less than a breath all three had vanished in that bright mist that is our own Mythgarthr.

"He's dead, sir." Vil knelt beside the corpse, his fingers on its wrist.

Etela laughed; there was hysteria in it, and I urged Toug to comfort her.

Svon said, "Sir Garvaon is dead, Vil, as you say. So is the dragon."

Vil said nothing.

"You went into battle with that child on your shoulders. You're a braver knight than I will ever be. So is she. I wouldn't have done what she did, not at her age or any age."

Vil said, "She told me it was like to kill you, sir. We had to do something."

"Without a sword and without armor."

"What I had was better." Vil held out his hand to me. It was empty, but when he had passed his other hand across it, my bowstring lay coiled in it. "Here 'tis, Sir Able. I know you must a' seen it. I filched it. You know when. You want to sort me out, ask Master Toug. Only you got the right to do anything you want to, an' I'll tell him so."

I took the bowstring from him and ran it through my fingers, feeling the lives of many, so very many, who dwell in America. I had passed beyond them, above or below them, and as they plowed and coded and traded, swept their floors and minded their children, we said our farewells. For a moment, my hands embraced them, and they embraced my hands.

Perhaps Vil sensed that in some unimaginable manner; perhaps it only seemed so. However that may be, he said, "There are tricks you can do with a string like that, Sir Able, lots o' 'em. Making things that ain't there, soon's you move your hands, an' lettin' 'em cut it, only it's not really cut, you know. Only when you do 'em with that'n it's all different." Although the air was warm, he shivered.

"No," I said. "Hold out your hand again, Truthful Vil."

He did, and I put the bowstring into it. "This was a gift,

when I began, from a very great lady. Men name her Parka, and she dwells in our own place."

"If you say it, sir."

"But she is of the world above Skai, the second realm. She is thus higher than the Valfather, who serves her. Do you understand?"

"I hope."

Etela exclaimed, "Well, I don't understand at all!" She was standing beside Toug, her arm about his waist. Seeing them I understood that she was no longer Little Etela, and that in sober fact she had never been, in the short time that I had known her. I said, "Vil will explain it to you."

We laid Garvaon's body across his saddle; Uri (silent still, and I would guess very frightened) guided us back to our own world.

CHAPTER TWENTY-SEVEN

REDHALL

We could not return Garvaon to Finefield, however much we wished to; but a grave in Jotunland seemed a thing of horror. We resolved to carry him south so long as the cold weather held, and inter him as near his home as Parka decreed.

The Host of Jotunland held the pass against us, as is well known. Fewer know that we interred Garvaon before the battle, fearing there would be too many to bury after it. We dug his grave and laid him in it, offered such sacrifices as we could make, and together sang our hopes for him. Hearing us, the Angrborn sent a flag of truce to inquire.

"Sir Garvaon is no more," Beel told the giant who carried it. "He was the bravest of my knights, and the best. We sing for his spirit, for we are not as you. And we have raised the cairn you see for him."

He looked for it, but could not discover it 'til Marder indicated it to him, for it rose higher than many a hill.

"You made that?"

"I alone?" Marder shook his head. "No, I could not. Nor could Lord Beel, nor Sir Able, Sir Leort, nor Sir Woddet. We all did, working together."

The Frost Giant leaned upon his sword. "I have to speak for those who sent me."

We nodded and said we understood.

"We're going to kill you and tear it down. There won't be two stones together when we're through."

"You must beat us first," Svon declared, and grinned.

"You know me?"

Svon indicated the giant's bandaged hand. "You are Bitergarm, and you were one of King Gilling's champions."

"That's my name," Bitergarm told Beel. "I fought them, him and Garvaon. You were there."

Beel said nothing; Idnn told Bitergarm, "So was I."

"I wanted to kill him myself." Bitergarm's deep rumble might have been a mountain's talking. "He was tough as your hotlands grow."

Svon and I agreed.

"So I'm sorry he's dead. That's for me. I'll tear it down along with the rest, only—" He had caught sight of one of Idnn's subjects.

Idnn herself advanced fearlessly and laid a hand on his arm. "I am their queen. Yours, too, Bitergarm."

"Schildstarr's the king."

"A king who'd have you war on your queen, your mother, your wife, and your sisters. I don't order you to fight for us against King Schildstarr. But I ask you, what sort of king is it who makes the right arm smite the left?

You're never loved, you Frost Giants. Not even by your mothers. I know it, and I pity you. But is the canard true? Is it true that you yourselves never love?"

He turned and left without another word.

They attacked by night, as we had feared they would; but our Aelf raised the alarm long before they reached our camp, and the fire-arrows turned them back with many dead, for all the Aelf see in darkness as well as Mani. We sent Org after them when they retreated, telling him to kill any who came to his hand, and to strike their rear when they fronted us once more.

The next day they held the pass against us, six of their grimmest shield-to-shield across the War Way, with a thousand more behind. There, in the pass I had held against the Black Knight who was Marder, those Mice they had driven out rained stones and spears on them until the sun was high.

Three times we charged them with the lance, and each time they threw us back and harvested their dead. At sunset I knelt for Idnn's blessing, and on foot led their own women against them. Eterne drank their blood to the hilt, and the Knights of the Sword drank it too, some with two followers or three, and some with a hundred.

Within an hour the snow began, and Baki's kin, with their bows and fresh fire-arrows, joined the Mice. The Sons of Angr broke and fled south into the mountains, where most who had not fallen, fell.

As for us, we struck off the heads of hundreds slain, and heaped them around Garvaon's cairn, one on another until they covered it; and Beel and I, recalling his victory when he was young and how he had dragged a head behind two horses, wept.

That night Idnn sent Hela for me. In the pavilion that had been Marder's, I sat with her (for she was gracious) and with Svon and Hela shared what little wine we had.

"You are an honorable knight," she told me. "Sir Svon is, we believe, the most honorable we have known. But when we charge him with it, he says he's but your image in that."

I did not know how to answer her, but Mani did it for me, saying, "To Skai this Mythgarthr we cherish is only likenesses and wind, Your Majesty. But a likeness cherished is more." His purling voice might have charmed a bird from its nest, I thought; yet I sensed that he meant all he said.

"Hela here and her brother have been of great service to us," Idnn continued.

"To us all, Your Majesty."

"As have you. No man and no woman has been of greater service than you."

"Kneel," Mani whispered; but I did not kneel.

"We are a queen." Idnn touched the diadem she wore. "You have led our subjects against the foe."

I remained silent, wishing that I might speak with Gylf. Cloud's mind touched mine; although it was filled with love, she had no advice to give.

"You have not seen the lands we rule," Idnn continued. "No more have we. Yet there are such lands, and they have been described to us."

Svon said, "We're going there when we leave the court. Her Majesty, my liege Lord Beel, and I."

"As a queen, we have power to give estates. As we have power to raise to the peerage, power we would have even if we had no lands to give. We will make you an earl, Sir Able, if you'll have it."

Hela murmured, "Take the title and the lands refuse, if you will."

"I will take neither," I told Idnn. "I know I can't refuse without insult, and I am loath to. But I must."

"Your liege consents."

"My liege in Mythgarthr, you mean, Your Majesty. He's the best of men. But no. I insult you because I must. Sir

Svon must be your champion. I've sworn to engage him when we reach the court. He'll avenge you."

Idnn glanced at Svon and shook her head, saying, "We wish to honor you, not to quarrel with you, Sir Able."

"I have wished to honor you always, Your Majesty."

Suddenly she smiled. "Do you remember when you came to my father to borrow a horse? You and Gylf and Mani?"

"It was long ago," I told her, "and I have forgotten it—once. I do not believe I will ever forget it again."

"It was in this present year," Idnn told me. "We don't think it's seen two moons. Certainly it hasn't seen three. But we want to say you've given Mani to us since, something we never dreamed would happen. Tonight we hoped to give you a great boon, for that and all your kindnesses, and for being an army on two legs. Instead, we're going to ask more. You know what Hela and Heimir have done for all of us. You let Sir Woddet have Hela, and she wishes to remain with him. You retain her brother. So he says."

I said I would not keep him against his will, and that I had seen little of him since Hela had gone to Sir Woddet.

"We'd like to reward Hela, and the boon she asks is that her brother be given to her."

Hela herself said, "He is my brother, and as a brother I love him, Sir Able. I fear he would fare ill without me."

"If he will serve you, you may have him," I told her. "If you have him, Sir Woddet will have him too. Though his tongue is lame, he's a first-class fighting man."

She thanked me; when she had finished Idnn said, "Since you will not leave your liege for us—you will not? Not for an earldom? We offer it again."

"I have to refuse it again. I beg you not to offer it a third time."

"Very well. We must have your liege here. Will you fetch him for us, Hela?"

"And Sir Woddet, Your Majesty? You know that I must

tell him all I hear, and he ask me. Would you send me out when I have brought the duke?"

Svon muttered, "I am with Hela, Your Majesty."

"Sir Woddet, too," Idnn agreed, "as quickly as may be."

When Hela had gone Idnn said, "We mean to examine you. Hela prompted it. The sister's mind is as sharp as the brother's is dull, we find. She's the edge of the blade—he's the back. We've given her mother to Woddet, too, and he's loaned her to us."

I smiled, and she graciously smiled in return.

"Sir Svon has told us of Aelfrice. How he went there with Sir Garvaon and found you with a fleet that vanished. About his squire as well—how Squire Toug had gone down a stair between worlds in a haunted spire, where fair women had been held to draw mariners to its summit."

"Sir Svon knows much of Aelfrice," I said.

Svon coughed. "You must wonder how I learned it."

"From Toug?"

Slowly he shook his head. "Toug will scarcely speak. When His Grace comes we'll ask about the matter you and I spoke of in the wood. I might as well tell you. It wouldn't be right for us to surprise you with it."

I said that I had surmised as much.

Idnn said, "We'd hoped to question you as a vassal. Your honor might not let you evade my questions then."

"It wouldn't, of course, Your Majesty, if they were questions yours let you ask me."

Svon said, "I've questions too, about Aelfrice. You told me you'd been knighted by an Aelfqueen. Remember?"

I shrugged. "It's true, though Sheerwall mocked me."

"When we camped by the river."

"You went to the inn. Pouk and I camped there."

He flushed. I saw that the boy still lived in him and liked him better for it.

Idnn said, "Do you mean the ladies mocked you? It was to get your attention. You may trust me here."

I shook my head. "I don't believe they did. Perhaps they pitied me. The men mocked me, save for Sir Woddet."

"Who's here with me," Marder said. "Did I mock you? If I did, I was drunk. We'll engage again if you wish it."

"You did not, Your Grace."

Svon yielded his chair and Hela fetched a bench.

Idnn said, "He will not answer us, Your Grace. You must ask him who killed our husband. We know he knows."

Marder frowned. "Do you, Sir Able? Yes or no."

"Yes, Your Grace."

He sat silent until Idnn said, "Will you not ask him?"

"Perhaps not. If he will not speak, he may have a good reason. I'll ask that instead. Sir Able, much as I respect you, I ask as your liege. Answer as you are a true knight. Why are you silent on this?"

I said, "Because no good can come of it, Your Grace. Only sorrow and wretchedness."

At length Marder said, "We might punish him, might we not? Or her. The guilty party."

"No, Your Grace."

"We could not?"

I shook my head. "No, your Grace. You could not."

So softly that it seemed he wished no one to hear but me, Mani said, "Wasn't it for love?"

I nodded.

Idnn made a sound but did not speak, and Svon filled the silence. "There's a question I've been eager to ask. I hope you'll answer. I never questioned you enough when I was your squire, and I hope you'll forgive that. I didn't talk with Sir Ravd as I should have, either. I hated him for trying to teach me, and for that I will never forgive myself. I'd like not to feel as bad about you as I do about him. I told you Toug would hardly speak. This was before the fog lifted."

I reminded him that he had just repeated it.

"Perhaps I did. It's like what you told us about the Aelfqueen. It's true, so why shouldn't I say it? But—but it's not entirely true. He said that when Sir Garvaon died, you saw something the rest of us didn't. He thought I might have, since I'm a knight too. He said—he said . . ."

Marder saved him. "That reminds me. Her Majesty's father is anxious to speak to you. It concerns young Wistan, Sir Garvaon's armor, and so on. He asked me to mention it."

I said that I would wait on him that night if he were still up, and the next morning otherwise.

Woddet coughed. "I'm a knight too. By the Lady, I wish to every Overcyn in Skai that I'd been there with you."

Idnn said, "Sir Garvaon would have lived, we're sure."

I said, "Don't you want to ask me why I didn't fight Setr? All of you? Go ahead."

Hela said, "Then I ask. It was not fear, I know."

Svon muttered, "He'd been your friend, you said."

"He had been. But there was another reason. It was because I knew Setr had to die." To change the subject, I added, "When heroes die, they are carried to Skai to serve the Valfather. Sometimes at least. That's what I saw, Sir Svon—what Toug saw I saw when he didn't and you didn't. I saw the Valfather's shieldmaiden descend, and Sir Garvaon rise and go with her. We humans—we knights, whether we're called knights or not—get to Skai sometimes. Suppose that one of us, the best of us, tried to seize its crown."

They did not understand; I waved Skai and its crown aside. "Setr had to die. For him to die, my friend Garsecg had to die too, because Garsecg was Setr by another name. Setr feared me. He could have joined me here any time, but he'd shaped me, like Disiri, and knew I could kill him."

Idnn asked, "Is that the Aelfqueen who knighted you? What are you talking about, Sir Able?"

I laughed, and said I did not know myself. The ghost of something taken from my mind had returned to haunt it.

Hela said, "It troubles him."

And Idnn, "Who is this queen?"

"She's Queen of the Moss Aelf, Your Majesty, and she educated and knighted me. She did what she did for a good purpose, though I don't know what it was. Garsecg, who was Setr, shaped me too, and thought his purpose good, perhaps. I was to fight Kulili—as I did, not long before he died."

Hela and Woddet wanted to ask about her, but I cut them off. "Having formed me nearly as much as Kulili had formed the Aelf, he knew I'd kill him if we fought. Because he knew it, he would never have fought me. He would have fled, and I don't believe even Cloud could have overtaken him before he got to Muspel. Grengarm was trying to get to Aelfrice when Toug and I caught up with him, but I had no griffin to chase Setr on. So I said I wouldn't engage him and set Sir Garvaon and Sir Svon on him, hoping they would be enough."

"We weren't," Svon said.

I rose. "I should've entered the fight in time to save Sir Garvaon. I thought he was about to rescue you. Before I could draw, he was in the dragon's jaws—the one I'd said I wouldn't fight. Every word of blame you lay on me I deserve. I'll redeem myself when I can." I addressed Idnn. "Have I leave to go, Your Majesty?"

"There will be no word of blame from us, Sir Able."

I bowed. "May I go?"

I left the pavilion and wandered alone, thinking about a death I could have prevented, and forgetting that I was to see Beel. At last I went to the fires of the Daughters of Angr, supposing that the women would be as conscience-less and violent as their husbands. I would goad them, all would fight, and I would leave Eterne in her sheath. Larger even than their men, they teased instead like girls and women everywhere. Having heard me shout Disiri's name in battle, they wanted to know whether I had kissed her, and a thousand other things. I ate with them, and drank the strong ale they spice with willow bark.

Marder joined me there, speaking of wars fought before I was born and knights who had served his father. After a time he said, "They wished to question you on a matter we both understand. I would ask about another matter, though it bears on the first. I ask no oath. You wouldn't lie to me."

I confirmed that I would not.

"You know the Aelf better than almost any man—that much is plain. Was one present tonight, when we spoke with that fair lady who rules these great ladies?"

I said, "There may have been, Your Grace, but if there was I wasn't aware of it."

We sat sipping ale and staring into the fire, a fire too great for any human cook to roast meat on, until Marder said, "In speaking of that other matter, someone whispered that it was done for love. The words were addressed to you, I think. Was it the queen who spoke so?"

I said it was not, and begged him not to examine me further, explaining that any answer would betray a friend.

"That being so I will not, Sir Able. I will ask one question more, however. I did not know this person present. Did Her Majesty, in whose pavilion we sat, know it?"

"Yes indeed, Your Grace. She was aware of it from the beginning, rest assured."

Then Borda, a fair woman as tall as the mainmast of a caravel, said, "The knight would leave our queen's matters to our queen. I know little of knights and nothing of dukes. Still it seems knights are wiser."

When I returned to my own fire, Pouk and Uns lay asleep; and a woman sat warming her hands while Gylf dozed beside her. I asked how I might serve her, and when she turned, I thought that it was Lynnet. "Sit with me," she said, and her voice was not Lynnet's. "No. You're weary and fuddled. Lie here with your head in my lap, and I'll talk to you."

I did, and she told me many things: her girlhood in America, how she met my father, and how they came to wed.

The journey south was long and slow, and one day I asked leave to ride ahead, explaining that I wished to see Redhall. South I galloped down the War Way, telling Wistan, Pouk, and Uns to join me when they could; and when Cloud and I were out of sight, we mounted into the air, higher and higher until the whole land spread below us like a map on a table and we saw the War Way as a thread, and the company—Beel's and Marder's and the Daughters of Angr whom Idnn was leading to the south—like a worm crawling along that thread. Ulfa's Glennidam was a dot by a silver stream, while on the margins of the Griffin I saw where Griffinsford had stood. Then the Irring, and ruined Irringsmouth where it met the sea. Behind us the mountains rose, a mighty wall with parapets of snow and ice; but Cloud and Gylf—and I upon Cloud's back—rose higher than they.

Until I saw a castle like a star. The Valfather stood upon a battlement, tiny and far but clear. One hand was lost in his beard, the other gripped his spear; on his head, in place of the broad hat he wore when walking the little roads of Mythgarthr, was the horned helmet that is his crown.

Our eyes met, and Cloud rolled at his glance, her hooves to Skai and her back to our world, so that the Valfather and his castle were far below us.

Had he indicated that he wanted us to descend, we would have done it at once. As it was we rose, although I felt that he wished—or at least invited—me to return to his hall. We climbed far before Mythgarthr lay below us again.

This I am tempted to omit: that I mistook another manor

for Redhall. Mistake it I did, and to its door came Cloud, Gylf, and I; and I hammered it with a great iron ring, and hammered again, for it was late. At last a servingman came. I asked if it was Redhall (it was on the road to Kingsdoom), and he assured me it was not, that Redhall stood some way to the south. He supplied particulars of the manor house and its gate, and offered me a bed for the night. I thanked him but explained that I was determined to sleep in Redhall. Even then I knew I would not spend many nights there, and I wanted to make them as many as I could.

Away we went, galloping hard, with Gylf running ahead as if hot on some scent, until (long after any horse would have been exhausted) I turned aside to ask again, for we had come far and I feared we had passed Redhall in the dark.

The gate was ruinous, the house beyond it more ruinous still. I was about to leave without knocking when I realized that the stone figure beside the entrance was a manticore. After that I knocked indeed, shouted, and beat the weatherworn panels with the hilt of my dagger.

The woman who came bearing a candle was old, bent, and nearly toothless. Knowing she might be frightened to find an armed man at her door so late, I gave my name and assured her that I was only a lost traveler who meant no harm.

"More's the pity. I hoped you had come to kill me."

"Only to ask directions," I said, "and bring good news. Is this Goldenlawn?"

She nodded in silence.

"And where stands Redhall?"

"A league and a half." She pointed south. "It has no lord. I doubt they'll open for you, and we've little here."

"It has a lord again," I told her. "I'm him, but I haven't seen it."

At that she stood straighter; and although she did not smile, it seemed almost she did. "The Frost Giants came at first-frost, years and years ago."

"Yes," I said. "So I understood."

"He was away, Sir Ravd was." She sucked her gums. "Off to the wars. He would've helped us. You going to stay?"

"In Redhall? For a few days, perhaps."

"Here."

"No, I'll sleep in my own bed tonight, though it's a bed I've never seen. I said I was Sir Able of the High Heart, I know. That's true enough—the name I've had for years. I have to learn to say Sir Able of Redhall, too."

"I wish you rest, Sir Able." Her door began to close.

"Wait," I said. "You haven't heard my good news."

"I thought that was it. What is it?"

"Your mistress, Lady Lynnet, is returning."

She stared at me so long I thought that she would never stop, and I backed away. At that she said, "You're an Aelf!"

"No. Sometimes I wish I were."

"Come to torment me!"

"I would never do such a thing. Lady Lynnet's coming to resume possession, with Mistress Etela. You must sweep the house, and make everything as presentable as you can."

"This is my house," the old woman said, "and I am Lady Lis." With that she shut the door; I heard her sobbing on the other side for as long as I stayed there.

No Angrborn had taken Redhall, or it had been repaired. Stone pillars topped with lions marked an entrance road of half a league, narrow but in good repair. It led to a broad gate flanked with towers in a wall by no means contemptible. The gate was barred, but a blast on the horn hung from it brought four sleepy men-at-arms. The eldest said, "You come late, sir knight. Early, rather. This gate closes with the rising of the evening star, and does not open again until a man can use the bow. Come back then."

"It opens when I want it to." I pushed him aside.

The bailey was pounded earth, wide and overlooked by a manor too lofty to blush before castles. The mastiffs who guarded it were scarcely smaller than Gylf, broad of chest and great of head. How they knew me I cannot say; but they did, and stood in turn with their paws on my shoulders to look me in the face, and fawned on me afterward.

"Who are you?" the oldest man-at-arms demanded. "What's that shield you bear? I must have your name."

I turned on him. "I'll have yours right now. Give it, or out sword and die."

To my surprise he drew. He was standing too near; I got his arm, wrenched his sword away, and laid him at my feet with his own point to his throat. Prodded, he gasped, "Qut. My name's Qut."

"From the south?"

"My mother—taken prisoner. Married and stayed."

The others had stood gaping all this while. I told them they had to learn to fight if they were to be men-at-arms of mine, and offered to engage their best then and there with Qut's sword. They knelt instead, three bumpkins with not a leader among them.

Taking my foot from Qut's chest, I said, "I am the new owner, Sir Able of Redhall."

The three nodded. Qut scrambled up to one knee.

"You." I pointed. "Take Cloud to the stable. Wake my grooms. She's been ridden hard. She's to be unsaddled and turned out to pasture. Tell them I'll know of any injury to her, however slight, and it'll be avenged in blood."

He took her reins and hurried away.

"There's a steward here?"

Qut said there was, and that his name was Halweard.

"Good. Wake him. Wake the cooks as well."

"It's barred, sir. I'll have to rouse somebody—"

A look and a gesture sent him. Our scuffle, brief as it had been, had ended any thought of sleep. I decided to eat—we had been on short rations, and I was ravenous—and stay up, retiring early the next night.

Which is what I did. I inspected Redhall, finding its

barns, fields, and larders in good order but its men-at-arms and archers undrilled and a little slovenly.

Next day we began contests for the bow. I gave a ham to the winner. (I had offered a piece of Marder's gold to any archer who outshot me; none did.) The one whose score was next to worst was to strike the one with the worst smartly on the bottom with his bow. He struck soft, so I had the next worst hit him for it. That was a whack that made dust fly.

My men-at-arms had been spectators to this and enjoyed it. Recalling the Angrborn, I decided to see whether they had profited as well. There were bows, as well as arrows by the hundred, in our armory. I gave each man-at-arms a bow and arrows, and had each shoot at very moderate range.

After that we held a contest (while the archers laughed and jeered) with the same prizes and punishment.

That evening Qut confided that there was grumbling among those who had done badly. The sword, they said, was their weapon—sword, partisane, and halbert. Thus on the third day we cut saplings for practice swords, as Garvaon and I had, and I drilled them all morning, and fought them that afternoon, knocking them about.

On the fourth day we cut quarterstaves, I explaining that the man who knew the quarterstaff would be a fighter to be reckoned with when armed with partisane or halbert. When I had beaten a round dozen, one knocked me sprawling with such a blow as might have done me real hurt had I not been helmeted. I gave him the promised gold, and engaged him again for another. The storm-surge returned in that match, and it seemed almost that Garsecg swam beside me. I broke his quarterstaff and knocked him to his knees when he tried to defend himself with the halves. After that I had him teach them first, and afterward set them against one another, with us to judge between them. Balye was his name.

That night I ate supper with Gylf. Halweard brought my bread and soup and ale, staying until I should dismiss him. "Winter's blast tonight, Sir Able," he said. "It was cold in the north, I'm sure."

I said it had been very cold at times.

"We haven't had it here, just a nip to ripen the apples. We'll get it good tonight. Hear the wind in the chimney?"

I was on my feet in a moment and back in my boots in two. Out the sally port we kept barred but unguarded, and across three meadows. I found her in the wood, and our hugs were sweeter than any wine, and our kisses more intoxicating. She showed me a shelter her guards had woven for us, and in it we lay on moss and kissed a hundred times, and kept each other warm, my fur cloak for her and her great cloak of leaves over us both; we talked of love, and all we said would fill a book thicker than this. Yet all we said was only this: that I loved her and she loved me, and we had waited long and long, would be parted no longer.

At last she told me, "I took you for my instrument, and filled you with the words I'd have you say to Arnthor, and to every king of human kind through all the world, and made of you such a man as might speak to kings, and thought that I did well. It was foolishness, all of it, and there is only love. I'll be your wife this moment."

As she spoke, she changed, her green skin white.

"No," I said, and made as if to rise.

"I'll be your wedded wife—or we'll tell men so—and live in shadowed rooms, and comb my hair by the pearl of your night, and perfume myself for you."

"No," I said again. "I'll love you in any shape you choose, but I love you best as you were here."

"Do not speak to the king. Promise me that."

I laughed. "I've faced an army of the Angrborn. Is there worse at Thortower?"

"For you? Yes."

I thought about that; and at last I said, "What about you? Are you afraid just for me? Would you be safe there?"

She wept.

I returned to Redhall with snow in my hair. Halweard had waited and brought me a pot of hot ale, which was kindly done. I told him I would leave in the morning for Thortower.

"Do you know it well, sir?"

I sat. "Not at all. I've never been there."

"It might be wise to find a friend to introduce you, someone familiar with the court."

I explained that until Beel came I had no such friend, and sent him off to bed.

That was where I should have gone myself. I did not, sipping ale that had been hot enough to hiss, staring into the fire, and thinking of what Disiri had said. She had not made me as Kulili had made her race; my parents had done that. Still she had made me in a sense, teaching me, and most of all teaching me what I was to say in Thortower. I shut my eyes and heard the cries of the gulls outside Parka's cave, the waves, the fluttering wings. What was I to say?

It was no ordinary message, clearly, since I knew myself no ordinary man. I had burned for renown and skill at arms, and had not known I had burned for them so the king would listen. Toug had met Disiri as well as I; but she had no message for him, and he longed only for the plow—for the slow turn of the seasons and the life his father had, in which ambition was the wish for another cow.

In Redhall I could live for years, shaping my men and overseeing the fields and dairy. If Marder called on me for knight-service I would go. But if he did not, I would stay, visiting Forcetti once a month and Sheerwall three times a year. Disiri would come; and if it seemed to my maids that a woman not quite human frequented our corridors, why, let them gossip. What was it Ulfa had called me? A wizard knight, though Gylf and Cloud were wizardry enough for any man. . . .

The darkest corner of the room, that point farthest from the fire, grew darker. I thought it no more than the failing of the fire, and told myself that there was small point in piling more wood on it; I would go to bed soon, and coals—and fire as well—would remain for morning.

Dark and darker. The hearth rug, the horns of the noble stag on the wall, and the pot that held my ale were lit as before. Yet night had come in and waited in the corner.

I called for Uri and for Baki, thinking it might be some trick of theirs, then to all the Aelf. Several clans were of that color, Mani had said, and they had often played tricks on Bold Berthold. But if the scraps of darkness there were Aelf, they made no reply.

At last I called for Org, although I thought him behind me with Svon and the rest. He answered from behind my chair. "Good Lord!" I exclaimed, and at that there was laughter from the corner, a laugh that made me think of ice in the northern caves, and the icicles that sang (as Borda had told Marder and me) if a spearhead touched them in the dark.

CHAPTER TWENTY-EIGHT

MORCAINE AND MORE MAGIC

She stepped from the darkness as you might step from an unlit room into a well-lit one. A moment before I would have said that no woman in Redhall was taller than I, though Hela was, and the Daughters of Angr were taller than her sons.

This woman overtopped me, and her gold coronet made her look taller still. She was willow-slender, and willow-lithe, long-necked, and long-legged. So groomed was her

jet-black hair, and so lustrous, that for a second I thought
she wore a velvet hood beneath the coronet.

"Don't you know me?" She laughed again; there was no
merriment in that laugh, then or ever. "We've met, you and
I, differently dressed."

I bowed. "I could never have forgotten such a lady."

"As stepped from a corner of your room? But you
have." The laugh came again. "You wore armor. I wore
nothing. Now I come to grant a wish, yet fully dressed. Do
you credit a Most High God?"

The question caught me by surprise. I said, "Why of
course," stammering like the boy I pretended not to be.

"I do and don't." She smiled, and the smile became her
laugh. It was music, but I never ached to hear it again as I
did Disiri's. Even then, I thought her less than human, and
that laugh was at the root of my opinion.

"I don't and do." She cocked her head like a bird.

I bowed again. "Just so, My Lady. We can think only of
creatures, of things He's made. Creatures are all we know,
and can be all we know until we know Him. When we think
of Him like that, we find we can't believe. He can't be like
a creature any more than a carpenter is like a table."

She nodded. "Wisely spoken. When I see how the world
goes, I know there cannot be a Most High God. And yet
that fiendish humor! Have you recognized me?"

"No, My Lady."

"Poor dear. If I took off my crown and gown, you'd
know me on the instant. You speak of *tables*."

She strode to the far end of the long serving table on
which my ale rested; her smooth, oval face held no fear,
but I sensed that she did not wish to come near Org. "Suppose I lay here, naked." One long white hand caressed the
wood.

"You were the sacrifice offered Grengarm."

"I was, and you my rescuer. Did you hope to enjoy me?"
I shook my head.

"There on his altar, or in some pleasant glade. I was in no mood to be enjoyed. I thought he'd devour us."

I explained that I did not blame her, and all the while Org whispered to me of stealth and broken necks. Gylf had appeared in a doorway and stood watching us, his eyes alert.

"I know your name, Sir Able. Much about you, too. That you stabbed King Gilling—"

My shock must have appeared on my face.

"You didn't? Or are you startled that I divined it?"

"I did not."

"That's well. I'd maintain that if I were you. Kings value themselves highly. Have you dredged up my name?"

I shook my head.

"Ah, such—such!—is fame. Suppose I had said that our king, my brother, values his blood far above that of the ruck of common men? Would you have known me then?"

"I've searched my memory, My Lady, but found nothing."

"What a pity. Well, well. Where are we to begin?" She removed her coronet, laughed, and put it on a stool. "It's why they have those points, you see? So that no one will sit on them and bend the gold."

"My Lady—"

She laughed. "I'm not, you know—anyone's lady. I'm a princess. Didn't you hear me say so? King Arnthor is my brother. Don't stare. I am Princess Morcaine, and the only princess our realm has—the only one it's liable to have, since the queen keeps her legs crossed." Morcaine shook out her hair, filling the air with musky perfume. "Will you free me from this gown? It's too tight."

"Your Highness, I love a queen. Not King Arnthor's. Not Queen Idnn of Jotunland, either. Another one."

Morcaine laughed again. "They're as common as ditch water, these queens."

"They're not, Your Highness, and she's like no other."

"Because she's the one you love. Haven't you wondered

about my underthings? I would've sworn I sensed that."

Not knowing what to say, I said nothing.

"If you won't let me show you, I'll tell you. That below is invisible, a cobweb put there years ago. It serves its function still—or I hope it does, though when things are invisible it can be hard to tell."

"I'm forgetting my manners. My servants are asleep—"

"Save these two." Morcaine laughed.

"Yes, Your Highness. The rest are sleeping, but I can find a glass of good wine, if you wish it. Some little cakes and dried fruits, too."

"A sip of your ale. May I have that?"

I presented the flagon that Halweard had brought me; she drained it and tossed it aside. "Now you've done your duty as Master of Redhall. We were discussing my under-clothes, were we not?" She laughed, belched, and laughed as before. "Wouldn't you like to see what holds these up?"

I shook my head.

"I've imps of lace for them. They bear them up as the giant on a map bears the world, and they will offer them to you like apples." She paused, weighing the objects in question in her hands. "No, they're bigger. Orbs. I like that. Orbs of ivory, smooth, firm, ruby-tipped. The king's orb is gold, but I like mine better. So will you."

"No, Your Highness."

"Of course you will. If not now, another time. For the dragon. I'm in your debt." Her face grew serious. "I repay debts. My father was a king in Mythgarthr, Mother a dragon of Muspel. My nurses were Aelf. Do you credit all that?"

"Yes, Your Highness," I said, "I know it to be true."

"I'm a good friend but a terrible enemy. You'll find that's true too. I've been watching you whenever I could find the time. Are those woman as big as they look?"

"Bigger, Your Highness. When I learned that their women lived separately, I wondered why the Frost Giants permitted it. When I met those women, I understood."

"You never quailed before them."

I shrugged.

"You're the greatest knight in Mythgarthr. I couldn't watch you in Skai, but I know you went there. You came back, too. You're going to need a friend in Thortower. It's what you said and why I came. It's truer than you can know."

"After speaking with one of those who live there, as I have been just now, I'm sure you're right, Your Highness."

"Do you think I offer myself to anyone and everyone? You couldn't be more wrong."

I struggled to explain that I thought nothing of the sort, but had to be true to Disiri.

"Is she true to you? You needn't answer—I see it in your face." Morcaine paused, and for the space of a breath white teeth gnawed her full lower lip. "I'm sorry. I never thought I'd say that to a man, but I am."

"Thank you, Your Highness. You're too kind."

"I've been accused of many failings, but never before of that one. Never again, I imagine."

Sensing that she was about to go, Org stirred.

"Are you sure, Sir Able? It doesn't have to be on the table. I merely thought we might like to pretend it was that altar. We can go to your bed."

"I'm tempted beyond endurance, but I can't. I won't."

She laughed for perhaps the twentieth time, and stepped backward until darkness lapped the edges of her gown. Her coronet rose as though it were painted wood and the air were water. It floated to her and settled upon her head.

"That impressed you, I see." She laughed. "In payment for your astonishment—you have visitors. Better rouse a servant if you don't want to answer your own door."

The knocker banged at the last word. When it stopped I said, "That will wake Halweard, if waking's needed."

Smiling, she took another step back; firelight returned, and I felt that the knocker had cut short a dream. Soon the door rasped on its hinges. Hearing voices and the tread of booted feet, I told Org he was not to kill people or livestock without my leave, but that he might take game in the park, and sent him away.

Gylf came to sit by me; I stroked his head. "Did you see her, Gylf? Did you see her eyes? Disiri has eyes of yellow fire, as all Aelf do. Hers were black, but how they blazed!"

"Ears up."

"Oh, yes. She's dangerous. I realize that."

In the corridor I heard Halweard say, "Sir Able's abed, I'm sure. We'll find you a place to sleep, and—"

I called, "In here!," and they trooped in: Halweard, Qut, Wistan, Pouk, and Uns. Halweard asked, "Is this your squire, Sir Able? That's what he says."

Qut added, "I thought it best to let 'em in, sir, but I come to the hall with 'em to make sure it was all right. We can put 'em out if you want."

"We's his folk," Uns began; and Pouk, "I signed on 'fore anybody, an' it ain't right if—"

I silenced them, affirmed that Wistan was my squire, and told him to speak.

"We rode after you, Sir Able. That's all." He cleared his throat. "I know you had to leave us behind, there wasn't any way you could've taken us with you, but you did. So I said we ought to ride ahead too, and maybe we could catch up. Lord Beel wanted us to stay, but Queen Idnn—I mean Her Majesty—said we ought to go, and after that His Grace did too and His Lordship said it was all right. *I* said for *them* to stay, but they wouldn't so I took them with me."

Pouk knuckled his forehead. "We has our duty, sir, I said, only Sir Able's—"

"You've got to tell them to obey me," Wistan finished.

I explained that he would have to earn their respect.

"I'll earn it with my sword next time." Wistan looked grim. "They insisted on coming, and bringing two mules."

I could see both wanted to talk, but I shook my head.

"It slowed us, but I kept driving them. I wanted to ride ahead. Yesterday I almost did. Only there might be bandits, and they wouldn't have had anyone to protect them."

Pouk snorted.

"So I stayed, Sir Able. Because of the mules."

"I've few possessions. Are these things yours?"

"No, sir. Or not much. I—"

Uns interrupted. "All yarn, onna mools. Loot, Sar."

"Gleanings from the Army of Jotunland, sir." Wistan looked apologetic. "It hadn't been divided when you left, but we did it the next morning according to the rule."

Not knowing the rule, I asked him to quote it.

"I think I can, sir. A quarter for the crown. Of what remains, one share for every person present, plus a share over for every gently born person not knighted." He touched his own chest. "Five for a knight, plus one for each man-at-arms and archer he brought, only the knight keeps those. Ten for each noble, plus five for each knight he brought. That meant fifteen for His Grace, sir, only they wouldn't hear of it because you're really His Grace's knight, it wasn't just Sir Woddet, and you did more than anybody, so they made him take twenty. And then—"

"Enough," I said. "I take it I got five shares, and of course you got two yourself, and Pouk and Uns one each."

"You got more'n that, sir," Pouk told me proudly, "When it were shared out Sir Woddet said you oughta have more—"

Uns interrupted him. "'N Sir Leort, sar. Him ta, 'n da queen. A peck a' 'um."

Wistan nodded. "His Grace said everyone who wanted to add to your share should line up, and we put yours on a blanket and everyone passed by and added what they wanted. Her Majesty was first, and she put down a big gold cup full of gold, and after that everyone put in a lot."

"Not you, I hope."

Wistan looked embarrassed. "It was a lot for me, Sir Able. Nothing in comparison to Her Majesty's gift."

"I understand, and I thank you. It's great to see you again, and Uns, too, and Pouk. Especially Pouk. You got permission to ride ahead, and you must have pressed hard to cover the distance as quickly as you did. What time did you set out this morning?"

"Before cockcrow."

I nodded. "It must be nearly midnight now, and I've ill news. We'll be leaving for Thortower in a day or two. I'd intended to go tomorrow, but you and your horses must rest. The mules and their loads can be left here."

I sent them off to bed as quickly as I could, and woke my grooms. The mules' packs I had carried up to my bedroom, where I glanced at a few things before I got ready for bed. I was nearly asleep when someone whispered, *"There is magic there, Lord. I feel it."*

If I had been awake, I would have questioned her about it and about Morcaine—about Morcaine particularly. As it was, I told her to leave so I could sleep.

In reading over this long letter, Ben, I see I have left out lots of things. One is how I have written it. I will not say much about that now, except that I have lots of free time (more than I want, because Disiri is gone so much), and that sometimes I walk all morning beside the sea, thinking about the facts I am going to write down, what other people said and what I said. Mani's voice, purring one minute and mewing loudly the next, Garsecg's glance, the soft warmth of Gylf's ears, and the deep love Cloud gave me. I would stroke her once I had unsaddled her in some lonely camp, and tell her that her horn was sprouting and that we must find a frontal with a hole for it, so that others would believe it to be an ornament. This we did when we reached Kingsdoom—but I am getting ahead of my story.

It had snowed a hand's breadth during the night, and there was grumbling among my men-at-arms and archers when I turned them out. I told them we had slept outdoors in worse weather in Jotunland, and when Wistan joined us he related his experiences. I had him shoot with the archers afterward, knowing he would talk of our fights with the Angrborn.

I myself endeavored to teach the men-at-arms the lance. The older ones I found proficient already, having been well schooled by Sir Ravd. The younger scarcely knew how a lance should be held, and though they knew the helm and chest were the best targets, they were more likely to stick the horse.

Jousting had to be given up in favor of the dangling ring; when every one of them had ridden at it twice (and missed it in most cases) I called Wistan, and with Cloud's consent mounted him on her, and had him ride at the ring. The wind came no swifter than Cloud with Wistan on her back, yet his lance took the ring both times. I was loud in my praise.

The light had begun to fade; but we made the most of it, finishing with practice swords in the snow and calling no halt until peeled wood could no longer be seen. We ate then, not they in their place and I in mine, but together in the wide hall, I at the head of the table with Wistan on my right. Pouk and Uns sat at its foot but were waited on by the servants just as my fighting men were. There was ale, bread, and meat in plenty, and cheeses, apples, and nuts afterward. While we cracked nuts, Wistan asked whether we would bring men to Thortower. I said we would not (which proved a mistake) for we came without hostile intent, and the road, which had proved safe for the three of them, would surely be safe for a knight, his squire, and two manservants.

It was not until I made ready for bed that I recalled the whisper of the night before. Then I unpacked the loads and looked at every object with care. Eterne was just such an object, to be sure; and yet Eterne seemed but a lovely blade until she cleared the scabbard.

There was a lot of coined gold, and I hesitated to dismiss it. I examined each coin, but though they were of five realms I found none that seemed different enough to arouse my interest. I dropped each into my burse and took it out again, without result.

How I puzzled over the remaining objects, turning each over and over, and wishing mightily that I had Mani to advise me! In the end I settled, with many a doubt, on three.

The first was a cup in which you could have washed a baby. It was, I felt sure, the one Idnn had given filled with gold. I thought it likely Gilling had given it to her; and since it was not unusual save for being red gold with good decoration, it seemed to me it might possess a secret virtue—that it might disarm poisons, or some such. I drank water from it, and a little wine, but felt nothing.

The second was a helm, old and not in the best repair. It was iron like other helms, and lined with leather somewhat worn and cracked. I suspected it because it did not appear a rich gift; yet it might have been worn by a hero and so bring glory to its owner. It was without a crest and undecorated save for marks about the eye slits. I put it on and looked about me, staring at the fire and peering out the window, but saw nothing unusual. After that, I polished and oiled it, oiling its dry leather also.

The last was a gold circle in serpent shape. It seemed to me it had been the finger ring of some fallen Frost Giant, although it would fit the arm of many a lady. It was too big for my fingers and too small for my arms. I looked through it and tossed it into the air without result.

After wasting some breath calling for Uri and Baki, I went to bed sorely puzzled, dreamed of the Tower of Glas, and woke thinking of the woman I had seen there with Lynnet and Etela. I built up the fire and slept again, dreaming of the raiders I faced long ago—we had captured their ship, which had something in its hold we dared not face.

For one more day I drilled the men; on the day following we left, Gylf, Wistan, Pouk, Uns, and I. I never saw Org on the road; but I heard him in the wood, although what I heard might have been no more than a branch snapping under the weight of the snow. We rode slowly, stopping at inns, and took more than a week to reach Kingsdoom, having traveled a distance Cloud, Gylf, and I might have covered in an hour.

Sheerwall does not stand in Forcetti but in a stronger place a league from the city. Not so Thortower—Kingsdoom surrounds it on every side, as the town called Utgard did Gilling's castle, also called Utgard. But whereas the town of Utgard is a mere huddle of barnlike houses, the city of Kingsdoom boasts many noble buildings. It being late when we arrived, we found an inn near Thortower and spent what light remained sightseeing around the harbor and along the broad thoroughfare from the quay to the castle.

Here I have to go back to the objects I described. I had brought them with us. Once we were snug in our inn, I showed them one by one to Gylf, then called Wistan, Pouk, and Uns to me. They could make no more of them than I could.

I called for Baki when they had gone, and she came. I hugged her, which I should not have. She gasped for breath when I released her. "Lord, I came to say I would come no more. Now—well, who can say? Do you love me?"

I said I did, and I had missed her greatly.

"And I, you, Lord. Always when I was away, and often when I was at your side. You have freed us—Uri and me. We are your slaves no longer."

"You never were. I freed you more than once."

"So you did. But called us at need, and sent us off when that was convenient, rarely with thanks. May I sit?"

"Of course."

She did, seating herself in my little fire. "We were yours

because we were Setr's. While Setr bound us, we could not go free."

"Setr is dead, you're free, and it was none of my doing. Vil slew him, though he could not have without Svon and Sir Garvaon, who occupied him while Vil got my bowstring around his neck. Your debt's to them, not to me. Still, I'm glad you're free and hope we can be friends."

"Prettily spoken." Baki looked at me sidelong. "You should do well at court."

"I must do better than that," I told her. "If you've ever wished me well, you must wish me well there. Have you really come to say good-bye?"

"I have! Soon—soon I will go, dear Lord, and you will never see me more. Nor I you. The parting is upon us, and that parting will be forever."

She spoke so dramatically I knew she was lying, but I feigned belief for fear our parting would become real.

"Will you not bed me, Lord? Warm the lonely Aelfmaid who served you so long in this cold world? Chilled though I am, we shall be fire and flame in bed. You shall see."

I shook my head.

"Then kiss me," she said, and stepped from the fire.

I kissed her, held her, and kissed her again; when we parted I said, "I won't try to keep you, Baki. But before you go I'll ask a question and a small service. In less time than it would take me to explain, you can do both."

"Then I will, for another kiss."

"Good. A few days ago someone whispered in my ear that there was magic among the gifts Wistan brought. Was it you?"

She shook her head. "Not I, Lord."

"Do you know who it was?"

"Two questions, so I earn two kisses. It was surely Uri, Lord. She is in terror of you, and does whatever she believes may stay your wrath."

I said I would not harm her.

"I know it, Lord. She thinks only of her long betrayal. I—they broke my back. You healed me. I cannot forget."

"I didn't, Baki. Toug did."

"He would not have, Lord, had you not fetched him, and told him to, and told him what to do." So suddenly that I took a step backward, Baki abased herself. "Lord, forgive me! I love you, and would win you if I could. Would win you if I had to share you with a thousand Disiris."

I raised her. "There's nothing to forgive—or if there is, I forgive it. Baki, I'm going to show you three objects. If one casts a spell, will you tell me?"

She nodded. "I will, Lord, if I can divine it."

I got out the gold serpent first. She took it, breathed on its ruby eyes, shrugged, and handed it back.

"Nothing? No magic?"

"It may be too subtle for me, Lord. But if it is, it is too subtle for Uri also. Or so I think."

I pulled out the old helm and held it up.

Her jaw fell. For an instant she stood like a statue of bright copper. Then she was gone.

Knowing it would be useless to call to her again; I called Uri and then Disiri, begging her to come. Neither responded, and at last I went to bed, thinking a lot about the old helm—and King Arnthor and his court.

CHAPTER TWENTY-NINE

LORD ESCAN

Wistan and I rode to the castle the next day. To describe all the people who quizzed us—some because it was their duty, others out of curiosity—would take more time than I want to give it. There were more than a dozen.

At length we were sent to a court I might have thought King Arnthor's if I had not been told otherwise. It was that of the Earl Marshal, a nobleman of many titles, who sat a throne a little smaller than Gilling's on a dais, attended by perhaps a hundred, most of them supplicants of one stripe or another and the rest servants and attendants.

He was busy with a matter involving the king's stable when we arrived, the borrowing of a stallion from a duke who was not Marder, the lending of one of the king's in return, a colt from a mare of the king's to be given the duke, a colt from one of the duke's mares to be given the king, and so on. The stallion to be borrowed had already been decided when we came; the one to be loaned in return was under discussion. So-and-so was the best, but the duke's man did not like the color. Another, white, was beautiful but savage; it was not to be ill-treated, although it kicked and bit. It was not to be fought for sport. The duke's man would not guarantee on his master's behalf that it would not be fought—they had not considered that. Very well, if it was . . .

And so on for an hour. I was impatient at first, but soon found much of interest in the Earl Marshal's questions, comments, offers, and suggestions. He was a formidable negotiator who if he had not been a nobleman might have made his fortune as a trader—subtle, patient, and ingenious. He was portly and gained advantage from his size, more from his jowls, the great pale dome of his head, and his eyes, which were perhaps the shrewdest I have ever seen.

At last the stallions were settled. For a moment those eyes were on me, and I expected him to talk to me or tell one of his bustling clerks to do it. An elderly woman was led before him instead. Seeing her infirmity, he asked whether she would not prefer to sit, and a chair was brought.

Her first husband, it transpired, had been a knight; it meant that she was formally addressed as "Dame." He had died in some long-ago skirmish and she had remarried, choosing a draper. Now he too was dead; she wished to resume her title, but her neighbors would not accord it to her.

"There is no question," the Earl Marshal declared, "that you ask no more than is yours by law. None but the king may expunge these honors, and I recall no case in which the loser was a lady. No doubt it has occurred, but the time would be prior to my birth and yours. If you require a declaration of your right, I make it—and publicly. If you ask a written one, a clerk can prepare it and I'll sign it."

Humbly the old woman said, "They know they wrong me, My Lord. They delight in it."

"And you," the Earl Marshal inquired, "do you yourself honor Sir Owan?"

"In my heart, My Lord. Daily."

"Harrumph!" The Earl Marshal's eyes rolled. "Hearts I leave to Skai, Dame Eluned. I cannot look into them. You are of means—your dress proclaims it. Are Sir Owan's arms displayed on your house?"

So soft was the old woman's reply that the Earl Marshal had to ask her to repeat it.

"No, My Lord."

"On the liveries of your servants—your manservants, if not your women?"

There was no reply.

"The favorable ruling you ask of me lies in your power, Dame Eluned, not in mine." The Earl Marshal made a gesture of dismissal, and at once his servants helped the old woman to her feet and removed the chair.

"I will have the knight next," said the Earl Marshal, indicating me.

The crowd parted, and I came forward.

"Do I know your mail, or does that but imitate it?"

I replied, "You know it, My Lord."

"It has been said to lie no longer within this world."

I made no answer, since no question had been asked.

"Was it in Mythgarthr that you obtained it?"

"No, My Lord."

For a moment his court was silent, a silence he himself broke by clearing his throat. "Harrumph! I move too quickly for reason. Your name?"

"I'm Sir Able of Redhall."

"Your allegiance is to His Grace Duke Marder, is that correct?"

"It is, My Lord."

"Yet you do not go to His Grace for justice?" The Earl Marshal raised a hand. "Peace. We shall come to that by and by. You ride a fine barb, Sir Able. One of my clerks called me to a window to see him. I will examine him more nearly when I have leisure."

"I will be honored to show her, My Lord."

The Earl Marshal's eyes opened a little wider. "Did I hear you say that animal is a mare?"

"She is, My Lord, though often taken for a stallion."

"I should like to see a stallion of her line."

"I've none to exhibit to you, My Lord."

"Has she been bred?"

"No, My Lord. She's still young, nor would the coupling be easy."

"She has not attained full growth?" He was skeptical.

"No, My Lord."

He passed a hand across his face. "I should like to see her grown. I'd like to see that very much. We will speak of this after."

"I'm at My Lord's command."

"You are one of His Grace's knights. He bid you hold a mountain pass for some months. Such was the last I heard of you, Sir Able. He has given you Redhall since, and so thinks highly of you. You held the pass?"

"I did, My Lord."

"Against how many?"

"Three, My Lord."

He chuckled. "Your fellows think well of you, too, or more would have come against you. You overthrew all three?"

"Yes, My Lord."

"Admirable. How may we serve you?"

"I need an audience with His Majesty, My Lord."

"And have no friend at court. I see. You wish to be presented?"

"We must talk, My Lord. I have a message for him."

"I see. From?"

"I'll keep silence on that, My Lord."

"I—see." The Earl Marshal motioned to one of his clerks. "Take Sir Able to the Red Room."

Wistan hurried forward to join me.

"Make that my library. You wish your squire to remain in your company, Sir Able? We will find entertainment for him elsewhere if you do not."

"I'd like him to stay, if it won't be too much trouble."

"Very well. You will desire refreshment. Tell Payn."

The Earl Marshal's library proved a snug room with a fire and a hundred books or more on shelves and tables. Payn (young and bald, with eyes nearly as shrewd as his master's) bid us sit and cautioned us about the books. "All these are priceless. You understand, I hope."

Wistan said we did.

I was looking at them, and took one from its shelf.

"Can you read, Sir Able?"

"No," I said.

"No more can I read that one. It's of Aelfrice, and the letters are very different from our own."

Wistan asked how the Earl Marshal had gotten a book from Aelfrice; the matter was complex, but Payn explained it at some length, ending with, "It's a history of the place, with an explanation of their laws."

I had been reading while he spoke. "They have none, and it's mostly a chronicle of the kings of the Stone Aelf. But this," I showed him the place, "is a spell to turn ghosts visible. 'By Mannanan and Mider, by Bragi, Boe, and Llyr, by all you hope from Bridge of Swords, I conjure you, appear!' "

The hag at the fire laughed, and by her laugh I knew she had been there the entire time. I heard the door slam, but I thought Payn alone had fled.

"Greetings, mother," I said. "I didn't really mean to conjure you. I'm sorry for my carelessness."

"You don't like having me around." She tittered. "What have you done with my cat?"

Hearing that, I knew who she was and said, "I left him behind me, mother, and I miss him a lot. As for you, you showed me hospitality once when I was in need of it. You're welcome to mine, whenever you choose."

She scooped coals from the fire, shook them together in her hands, and cast them onto the hearth. For a few seconds she bent over them, blowing on them to brighten their glow. "You fear the sister," she told me. "Fear the brother."

"Garsecg? He's dead."

She laughed, and vanished as the door swung back and the Earl Marshal came in, followed reluctantly by Wistan. "I was told there was a ghost here." The Earl Marshal smiled.

I bowed. "If there is, My Lord, we cannot see her."

"Just so." He pulled out the largest chair. "Won't you sit down, Sir Able? This is no formal hearing."

I thanked him, sat, and motioned for Wistan to sit.

"Payn rushed up to me with this young fellow. They said you had raised a spirit. I feared for my books and came."

I said I felt sure she had taken none.

"You did call up a ghost, Sir Able?"

"Unintentionally, My Lord." I closed the book, rose, and returned it to its place upon his shelves.

"Could you do it again?"

"I don't think that would be wise, My Lord." I went back to my chair.

"You're probably right—if you did as you say."

"I'd prefer, My Lord, that you think me mendacious. It will save a thousand difficulties."

"Can you read the book you were looking at?"

"No, My Lord."

"This youth, your squire," by the lightest nod of his massive head, the Earl Marshal indicated Wistan, "said you had found a spell in one of my books."

"That youth is no longer my squire, My Lord."

He sighed. "I share your difficulty. I won't dismiss Payn, but I should. You said you couldn't read that book."

"I did, My Lord."

"Are you saying that you said it or that you read it? It would seem we have fallen among conundrums already."

"Both, My Lord."

"Would you lie to me, Sir Able? I mean in matters other than that of the ghost, in which we agree on your mendacity."

"No, My Lord."

"So you read it, but can no longer read it? Why not?"

"It's shut, My Lord. I can't see the words."

"Tush." He raised a wide hand, damp with perspiration. "You read the character of Aelfrice. You need not say it, I know it. No wonder His Grace thinks highly of you."

Wistan coughed. "If I may, My Lord? As I am no longer Sir Able's squire, I may seek other service without dishonor. So it seems to me."

"And to me, young man." A slight smile played about the Earl Marshal's lips.

"I seek it with you, My Lord. Take me at my word when I say I wouldn't betray Sir Able's confidences. He's told me nothing in confidence, but I know more concerning him than most. I'll advise you in the matter, if you'll allow it."

The Earl Marshal chuckled.

"You've need of an advisor, My Lord. For years I served an ordinary knight-at-arms. He was as worthy a knight as ever drew sword, to which Sir Able will attest. But a common knight, however staunch. Sir Able is of is another ilk."

"I do not require you to tell me that, young man. What is your name, by the way?"

"Wistan, My Lord."

"You may advise me in this matter, Wistan, if you will."

"Thank you, My Lord. I am honored."

The Earl Marshal made a tower of fingers and regarded Wistan over it. "If your advice proves profitable, I'll take you into my service as you wish. If it does not, I will not. If I do, you must serve me better than you did Sir Able. If you do not, I'll dismiss you just as he did."

He turned to me. "Is he of good character, Sir Able?"

"Pretty much so, My Lord, though I've been trying to improve it."

"No doubt." The Earl Marshal turned back to Wistan. "You are my advisor, Wistan. This knight tells us that he bears a message to His Majesty—an important message, Sir Able?"

"I believe it must be, My Lord."

"He will not reveal its source. Do you know it?"

Wistan shook his head. "Know it? Not I, My Lord."

"Can you guess it?"

"I can try, My Lord. We were in the north when he left us, riding swiftly to Redhall. I joined him, bringing his servants and much treasure. Queen Idnn gave him that—"

The Earl Marshal's eyes narrowed.

"I mean much of it was her gift, My Lord, and she was the one who got the rest to give so much. So if he rode with a message, I think it must be hers."

The Earl Marshal looked to me. "Are we antagonists, Sir Able? I hope otherwise. I bear you no ill will."

"I don't bear you any either, My Lord."

"Until this moment, I'd have boasted that there was not a royal personage within a thousand leagues who was unknown to me." He laced hands on his belly, which was substantial. "Almost I am tempted to make the boast still. Is this a true queen of whom this stripling speaks? If she favors you, you must know her."

"She is, My Lord. She's Queen of the Skjaldmeyjar, the Daughters of Angr."

"By this you intend the wives of the Frost Giants?"

"And their daughters, My Lord."

"No man has seen them, Sir Able."

Wistan said, "I have, My Lord."

"So have I," I said. "So has His Grace and many others who were with us."

"This Idnn is their queen?"

"She is, My Lord. A good queen and a brave woman."

Wistan started talking, but the Earl Marshal silenced him, rose, paced the room, took down the book I had shelved and turned its pages, and at last sat again. "This past summer, His Majesty sent my old friend Lord Beel to Jotunland as his ambassador. Against my advice, for it seemed to me an errand too hazardous for any man. Lord Beel has a daughter, young and fair. These arms rocked her when she was still in swaddling clothes. I ask a plain answer, is this the Queen Idnn of whom you speak? Yes or no?"

"It is, My Lord."

"You have been with Lord Beel in Jotunland?"

Wistan said hastily, "We both have, My Lord. He was Sir Garvaon's liege. I was Sir Garvaon's squire."

"Was His Grace with Lord Beel as well? It was said a moment ago that he had seen the Frost Giants' women."

"Yes, My Lord. Sir Able brought him, My Lord, while we were in Utgard."

"Before Lady Idnn became queen of Angr's women?"

"Afterward, My Lord. Only we didn't know it then. We didn't know if there were any 'til Hela brought them."

"Harrumph!"

"Hela's Sir Woddet's maidservant, My Lord. Only she used to be Sir Able's. He gave her and her brother to Sir Woddet, My Lord, because they're friends and he wanted them. Sir Garvaon said not to trust them, so I tried to stay away from them. Only the Angrborn women are worse. They're bigger and I never liked the way they looked at me, only they helped us in the battle."

"There was a battle."

That was directed to me. I said, "Yes, My Lord. King Schildstarr's army tried to keep us from leaving Jotunland."

"By *us* you signify His Grace and His Lordship? Queen Idnn as well?"

"Yes, My Lord."

"Who naturally called upon her subjects. Did they fight with dashers and pestles? That sort of thing?"

"No, My Lord. With spears and swords."

"And they are of the size of the Angrborn?"

"Larger, My Lord. Something larger."

"Lady Idnn is their queen. Lord Beel's daughter."

"Right, My Lord. Lady Idnn married King Gilling. To be Queen of Jotunland is to be Queen of the Skjaldmeyjar."

"A King Schildstarr was mentioned not long ago."

"King Gilling's successor, My Lord."

"I see. Did King Gilling fall in battle?"

"No, My Lord. He was murdered."

"This is ill news." The Earl Marshal sat with pursed lips. "By some partisan of this Schildstarr?"

"I think so, My Lord," Wistan put in. "Some people thought Toug did it, but I know he didn't."

The Earl Marshal blinked, and asked me who Toug was.

"He's Sir Svon's squire, My Lord, and Wistan's right. Toug's innocent of the murder of King Gilling."

"Is this Sir Svon the Svon I know?"

"I believe so, My Lord."

Wistan said, "He fought the dragon in Aelfrice, My Lord. Only he wasn't killed, and Sir Garvaon was. I didn't see it. I mean I saw his body. The dragon bit him nearly through."

The Earl Marshal rose. "You offered to show me that, um, mare of yours, Sir Able. Let's look at her."

We traversed a dozen corridors and passed through four courtyards. I recall thinking at the time that in spite of Thortower's many lofty walls, soaring towers, and circles of fortification, it could not be defended by anything less than an army. It was too big to be held by a few hundred men—or a thousand, for that matter.

At last we reached the stables, and by pretending to quiet Cloud so the Earl Marshal could examine her, I was able to conceal the ivory dot that would become her horn. When he had stroked her muzzle, which she tolerated, he asked to ride her; and I was forced to say that he could not, that she would not permit it.

"I might tame her in time, I suppose," he said.

"No, My Lord."

"No one but yourself, eh?"

"I've ridden her," Wistan said, "but Sir Able's right, I wouldn't try it unless she likes you."

"My weight, perhaps. Well, she's a remarkable animal, Sir Able. I won't ask whether you'll sell her. I know the answer. It wouldn't be just in any event when you hope for an audience with the king."

I said, "I do, My Lord. Very much. I must get one."

"I understand. Some things, anyway. You've no friends at court? None? Ah. Your face says otherwise. Who is he?"

"She, My Lord. Princess Morcaine. Anyway I hope she's my friend, but I don't want to bother her unless I have to."

The Earl Marshal wiped his face with his hand, then wiped his hand on his coat. "That, I ought to have guessed long ago. This isn't one of my brilliant days. As to her friendship, who knows? It's the wind. I myself—well, I hope you don't find her friendship worse than her enmity."

It seemed a good time to say nothing, so I did.

"I ask you again. Who sends your message to the king? We'll send the boy away if it suits you."

"I think it better not to talk about that, My Lord."

"As you wish." The Earl Marshal gave Cloud a final pat, and turned away. "I like you, Sir Able. I'll do what I can for you, but there are risks I cannot take."

"He's no common knight, My Lord, as I told you." Wistan sounded older than his years. "You're wise to go carefully. You'd be wiser still to make a friend of him, if you can."

The Earl Marshal nodded as though to himself. "I will soon try. First, Sir Able, I can't ask an audience with the king at which you'll deliver a message of which I'm ignorant. You will not so much as confide the name of the sender. Will you? This is your final opportunity."

"I won't, My Lord." It was not as cold as it had been in Jotunland, but the stable was unheated and open in scores of places; I drew my cloak about me. "As for confiding the message itself, I can't. It is not in my power to do it."

"You are bound by an oath, eh?"

"No, My Lord. I don't know what it is."

"Yet you could deliver it to the king?"

"Yes, My Lord. I'll know it, My Lord, when we meet."

Wistan said, "There's but one way to discover it, My Lord, and if the words are ungracious you can't be blamed."

"You know little of the world." The Earl Marshal turned to me. "I can't run the risk of begging an audience for you, not with the best of wills. I hope you understand."

"I'm grateful for your good wishes, My Lord."

"I proffer two suggestions. The first depends on me, the second on you. Here's the first, if you wish it. When the time seems ripe, I will inform the king that a strange knight has come with news from the north, that he reports King Gilling fallen, and a new king in Utgard—with many marvels. It isn't improbable the king will ask that you be brought before him. Shall I do it? The choice is yours."

"I beg you to. I'll be indebted forever, My Lord."

"The second. You are a stout knight and overthrew all who challenged you in the north. There will be a tourney in three days, as always at Yeartide. You could enter those events at which you may excel. Those who greatly distinguish themselves will be entertained by the king and queen."

I vowed that I would strive to be among them, and he dismissed me.

CHAPTER THIRTY

MORCAINE'S SUMMONS

After taking my leave, I sought out the pursuivant of the Nykr King of Arms, as King Arnthor's herald was styled, he being charged with enrolling those who would enter the lists. He was away in the town; I waited until the short day was ended and rode back to our inn. That I was out of sorts I will not deny. I was curt with Pouk and Uns, although less so when I considered that I had gone far toward making a friend of the Earl Marshal, a most influential official of the court, that he was to speak to the king about me, and that I might hope to win an audience in the tournament.

I was making ready for bed when Wistan came. He bowed, apologized for his conduct, and declared I might beat him if I wished. I said, of course, that since he was no longer my squire I had no business beating him—that squires were beaten so they would be better knights by and by, and I was no longer concerned to make a knight of him.

"I pray you will reconsider, Sir Able. I behaved badly. I acknowledge it. Sir Svon told me he behaved badly when he was your squire. You never dismissed him, and before you left us, you knighted him."

"Sir Svon fought the dragon, Wistan." I made my tone as dry as I could.

Only his eyes reminded me that I had not.

"Reason and honor forbade it. You know I bear a dragon on my shield, perhaps you know also why it is there."

He nodded. "Toug told me. Is it really true?"

"Since I don't know what he told you, I can't say." I yawned. "You came so I could beat you? I won't. Now go."

He shook his head. "I came so you could take me back."

"I won't do that, either."

"You involve me in great difficulties, Sir Able." He looked frightened. "Would you see me hung up and flogged?"

I shrugged.

"It'll kill my mother. She's proud of all of us—I've got two sisters—but proudest of me. They'll say the king did it. It won't be true, but they'll say it and it'll kill her."

I said I doubted that anyone would do it. "Are you afraid, Wistan, that I'll tell the Earl Marshal you ought to be flogged? I won't. You have my word."

"He'll take me into his service, Sir Able. He said so."

"I congratulate you."

"I—I'd have nice clothes like Payn's. I'd live very comfortably. Good food and money. A warm bed."

"Then take it."

"I want to be a knight. Like Sir Garvaon. Like you."

It hung in the air between us until I hugged him. When I released him, he gasped like Baki. "I— Does this mean I'm your squire again?"

"If you wish it. Yes."

"I do."

I called Org, and he came forward to stand at my side.

"Is this to frighten me? I've seen him before, in the wood with Sir Svon."

"I know," I said. "You were frightened just the same."

Wistan nodded. "I still am."

"Then you see that you may be afraid without dashing out of the room."

He nodded.

"A knight's actions are governed by his honor," I said, "not by his fear."

"You said something like that before."

"I'll say it again, over and over, in as many ways as I can. Knowing it isn't enough. It has to become part of you. Why were you afraid they'd flog you?"

"They won't now. I'll tell you, but I need to tell you something else first. I told the Earl Marshal about going to Jotunland. How we set out and how you joined us. How you and Sir Garvaon rode down from the pass to fight when the giants attacked, and Utgard. Everything I knew."

"Did you tell him who killed King Gilling?"

Wistan shook his head. "No. I don't know. I said I thought it was Schildstarr or one of the giants with him, because I do. But I can't be sure. The important thing is that I told him about you. I told him Toug saw you die, but you came back to help us anyway. I told him everything I knew, and he made me swear to certain things. That was one, and Queen Idnn's bringing a hundred giant women was another. I pointed my sword to Skai and swore like he wanted, and he said the women would be the test—that when the women came he'd know I was telling the truth and take me. So he knows all that. Everything I know about Jotunland."

I nodded.

"He knows about Toug and Etela and Lady Lynnet getting lost in Aelfrice, and you coming there, and Sir Garvaon and Sir Svon. He already knows you can read that book." Wistan gulped.

"Of course he does. But can he read it as well? That's an interesting point."

"I guess so. He wouldn't have it if he couldn't read it, would he?"

"Of course he would. Books are extremely valuable. It takes a copyist years to copy one, and who know what errors he will introduce? Every book is valuable, and the older a copy is the more valuable it is. If the Earl Marshal couldn't read it, he might hope to find someone who could."

Wistan nodded again. "I'll try to find out."

He had suggested another test, and I called Uri. She stepped out of the fire, slender and quite naked. Wistan took it with more coolness than I expected and strove to keep his eyes off her—or when she spoke, on her face. She, who had always been beautiful, this night seemed more lovely than ever, willow-slender, graceful, and glowing; I soon realized that having learned she could not seduce me, she was exerting herself on Wistan. I told him then that he must leave.

He hesitated, his hand on the latch. "There's something else. I'll tell you when I come back, all right?"

"I'll be asleep. Tell me now."

"I had them put down your name for a lot of things in the tournament, Sir Able. I knew you'd wanted to, so I found the pursuivant and told him I was your squire and he did it. That's why I said they'd flog me if you didn't take me back."

"As they would have, I'm sure. You did well, however. What events?"

"Bow, halbert, joust, and melee."

"You said there were many. Only four?"

"Bow is two, really. Dismounted and mounted."

I nodded and waved him out.

As soon as the door had shut, Uri abased herself and pleaded for mercy. I made her stand, adding that I had not decided whether I would spare her life. That was a lie—I had no intention of killing her—but I felt it might be good for her to keep her in suspense.

"I have always loved you, Lord. More than Baki. More than—than anyone."

"More than Queen Disiri of the Moss Aelf."

"Y-yes, Lord. More than sh-she."

"This though she never betrayed me."

"She was no slave to S-Setr, Lord. I was."

"Baki was Setr's slave as well."

"Y-yes." She would not meet my eyes.

"When Baki's spine was broken, you would not bring me to her to heal her."

She stood a trifle straighter. "Another brought you, Lord, but you did not heal her. The boy did it. Not that boy. The other."

"Toug. I'm going to ask three things of you, Uri. If you do what I ask, I'll spare your life. Not otherwise. Do you understand? Two are just questions, and none are hard."

She bowed. "I am your slave."

"The first. Why did you come, when you knew I might kill you? You could have stayed in Aelfrice."

"Because you will not always be here, Lord. In Aelfrice you would have hunted me down, you with your hound," she gestured toward Gylf, "and the queen with her pack. I hoped to save my life by obedience and contrition."

"You talk bravely," I told her, "but your lip trembles."

"In fear of one it would p-prefer to k-kiss, Lord."

"We'll let that go by, Uri. You came. I appreciate it. It's a point in your favor, undeniably."

Org had edged nearer, and I saw that he intended to catch her if she tried to flee.

"Here's the second. The Earl Marshal has a book written in Aelfrice."

I saw that I had surprised her.

"I want you to discover whether he can read it, and what his connection with Aelfrice may be."

"I will try, Lord. I will learn all I can."

"Good. Here's the last, and the other question. It's in two parts. As I was getting to sleep, someone warned me there was magic in the gifts Wistan brought. Was it you?"

She nodded. "I will always seek to serve you, Lord."

"Why didn't you remain and tell me more?"

"I was in fear. That—that has not changed, Lord."

"Of the magic?"

She shook her head. "Of you, Lord."

"Is the magic in all my gifts? Or in one alone?"

"You ask what you already know, Lord."

"So you get an easy answer, and save your life."

Gylf raised his head and looked quizzically at me.

"In one, Lord. In the helm. You know it."

"But I do not know whose gift it was. Do you?"

"Yes, Lord. Borda gave it. I watched the giving."

"Have you any idea why she gave it?"

"No, Lord."

I studied Uri's face, although I could seldom pick up on her fabrications. "None at all?"

"None, Lord. Shall I try to find out?"

"Not now. I've worn the helm. Nothing took place. Do you know its secret?"

Uri shook her head. "I do not, Lord. If I discover it, I will tell you."

"Are you afraid of it?"

"Yes, Lord. As of you."

I glanced at Org, trying to tell him with my eyes that he was not to harm her. When it seemed he understood, I got out the old helm. When I straightened up, she was struggling in his grasp. I told her to be still, and put on the helm.

Org held a writhing thing shaped of flame and offal, of dung and blazing straw and such tripes as might be taken from a goat a week dead. Gylf snarled as if he saw it as I had, and he was a dog of gold with carnelian eyes.

Several days intervened between the night I saw Uri writhing in the grip of a monster of swarming vermin and the opening of the tournament. They held little of interest. Uri I let flee as soon as I took off the helm. I did not put it back on in that time, nor did I call for her again. If I must refer to any of those days as my account goes on, I will describe it when I need it.

The first day was for quarterstaff competition among churls. I could have entered, and I was tempted to. If I had, my participation in the joust and the melee would surely have been called into question. I watched with interest instead, as did some other knights. It was the custom of the castle to match the man thought most likely to win with the man thought least likely, number two in the standings (judged by the pursuivant) with a beginner, and so on.

Thus the first round, in which everyone fought at the same time, was over quickly, and quicker because no armor was allowed except a jerkin and a leather cap. In the second each pair fought alone, the pairing determined by the order in which each man had won in the first: the one who had won first fought the one who had won last, and so on. Speed and agility count a lot with the quarterstaff, so none of the matches were long; even so, some lasted longer than it might take to saddle a restive horse. In two, the fighters were slow to close. They were circled with a rope drawn tighter by the pursuivant's servants until one went down.

The second day was archery on foot. If I had still had the bowstring Parka cut for me, I would have won easily. I did not, and although my score was good, several others did better. One dined with King Arnthor and Queen Gaynor, but I did not.

The third was the day for mounted archery. We shot at a false target of braided straw, which held the arrows well and did not damage the heads. Gilt stood for the boss in the middle, and to strike the gold (that was how they said it) scored highest of all. Each rider rode full tilt at the false target and shot when he wanted to. Those who did not spur their mounts got a penalty, but many chose slow horses. I rode Cloud, and might have overtaken a swallow that flitted along the bailey. Fast though I rode, my first arrow hit the gold, and the onlookers cheered. As we trotted back to the starting line, I heard a dozen voices ask about the knight with a dragon on his shield—and Wistan's answer: "He's His Grace Duke Marder's Sir Able of Redhall, and I'm his squire."

For the second shot, I rode as hard as before, and that, too, hit the gold. No voices rose this time, but a silence louder than any applause.

Of the third I was completely confident. My first and second shots had struck gold. I had the feel of the exercise now, and Cloud had it as well. A third gold seemed certain. That night I would eat at Arnthor's table, deliver Disiri's message, take leave of her (a years-long leave dotted with ten thousand kisses), and go to the Valfather to beg some occasion when I could return to her, knowing that if I were gone a century it would seem to her in Aelfrice only a day or two. I rode—and my bowstring broke.

I had given Vil the bowstring he had stolen from me, and had begged another from one of His Grace's archers. Here I will spare the reproaches I heaped upon myself that day. I told myself a dozen times that I could easily have gotten a new string for the tourney, that I ought never to have been parted with Parka's string, and much, much more. None of it did any good. No one scored three golds, but three got two and a black. They dined with the king and queen, and I did not.

The next day was devoted to footraces, climbing greased poles, and catching greased pigs. Half crazy for something to do, I watched most of it. Wistan and I were leaving when we were stopped by a page who bowed prettily and informed us that the Countess of Chaus wished to speak with me. I said I was the countess's to command, and we followed him through passages and up and down stairs to a little private garden where a girl with hair like a bouquet of yellow roses waited in a snow-covered arbor. I knelt, and she invited me to sit across from her.

Although at a distance, I had seen the queen by then; and it seemed to me that this young noblewoman, with her high color and mixed air of boldness and timidity, resembled her closely. To tell you the truth, I thought she was probably a sister or a cousin.

"You are Sir Able of the High Heart?" She cooed; it should have been annoying, but it was charming. "I watched you yesterday. You're a wonderful bowman."

"A careless bowman, My Lady. I trusted my old string, and lost."

"Not my admiration." She smiled. "Will you wear my scarf for the rest of tournament?" She proffered it as she spoke, a white wisp of the finest silk.

"There's a dragon on my helm," I told her, "and they couch on treasures. Mine will couch on this."

When I had taken leave and Wistan and I were making our way back, he whispered, "That's the queen. Did you know?"

I stared.

"Countess of Chaus will be one of her titles. They do that when they don't want to be too formal."

Ready to kick myself again, I shook my head. "I would have begged her for an audience with the king if I'd known."

"You couldn't. That's one of the things it means. You have to pretend she's whoever she says she is. She would've been mad, and her knights might have killed you."

"I didn't know she had her own knights."

"Well, she does. She has the titles and all that land."

"How many?" I was still trying to digest the new fact.

"Ten or twenty, probably."

When we had ridden across the moat I asked, "If she has her own knights, shouldn't she give her favor to one?"

Wistan spoke with the weary wisdom of a courtier. "They want to give it to the one they think will win."

In my room I consulted Gylf. First I told him what had passed between the queen and me. When he understood, I said, "One point has me guessing. I should've told Wistan, but I doubt that he'd say anything helpful. Remember how the queen addressed me? She said of the High Heart. I've been calling myself Sir Able of Redhall here. I may have said of the High Heart once or twice, but I'm sure it wasn't more than that."

"Rolls?"

"Wistan signed. He would have written Redhall, I know."

"Who wouldn't?" Gylf asked.

"What do you mean?"

Gylf merely repeated his question, as he often did when he found me obtuse.

"It was Wistan who set my name down, so what does it matter who would've called me Sir Able of the High Heart?"

Gylf sighed, closed his eyes, and rested his massive head on his forepaws.

In bed, I thought about Gylf's question. He was a dog of few words, but they were worth hearing. Gaynor had called me Able of the High Heart; so she had spoken to somebody who called me that. It was possible Morcaine would, although she had visited me at Redhall. The duchess, His Grace's wife, could have mentioned me; but if she had known of me at all, it would have been while I was at Sheerwall, most people there had just called me Sir Able. Although I had no reason to think Her Grace was at Thortower, she might have come and gone while I was in the north.

In the morning it finally struck me that the queen need not have spoken directly with somebody who called me Sir Able of the High Heart, that she might merely have gotten her information from someone who had. I called for Pouk and Uns and learned that they had been quizzed by a well-dressed stranger while they watched the footraces.

"He says do ya work for him wat broke da string," Uns explained, "'n we says yessar, Sar Able a' da High Heart."

"I told him there ain't a knight here 'ud match you, sir," Pouk added. "So he sez Able o' th' High Heart, huh? We sez *Sir* Able an' off he goes."

I told them I would fight with the halbert that day, and asked if they wanted to watch. Both swore that Muspel itself could not keep them away; so the three of us and Wistan set out in company, I with my green helm on my saddlebow and the queen's white scarf floating from it.

I had expected that all of us would fight at the same time, for the first round at least. There being far fewer knights enrolled than churls for the quarterstaff, each pair fought singly. Hours passed before the Nykr King of Arms called my name. Just as I had to wait, so must this letter while I write about the combats I saw.

Halberts, many say, are the best weapons for defending a castle. For this reason every castle has a good store, some rich, others plain and meant for peasants and servingmen. It was with these we fought, because use in tournament requires that the points of pikehead and spike be ground away and the blade dulled. A helm is worn, and mail; but no shields are used, since both hands are needed for the halbert.

Like the quarterstaff, the halbert is grasped at the center and midway to the grounding iron, although other grips are possible and are favored by a few experts. The haft is Wistan's height or thereabout. The whole weapon, point to grounding iron, is the height of the wielder or a bit more. It is its own shield, and is a shield that does not blind the eyes. A strong man who knows how each blow can be parried cannot be struck if he is quick enough; but he must be strong indeed and parry so the edge does not hew his haft, although this is not likely when the edge has been dulled.

Most of the matches before mine were long, and the rope was not used. One might speak to one's neighbor and receive a reply, at times, between the blows, though at others they came fast and furious. As a knight new to Thortower, I was matched against Branne of Broadflood, who had gained the victory the year before. He was a goodly knight, tall and thick-chested, but he thrust too deep. I knocked his point aside, and stepping in struck the face of his helm with the haft of my halbert, tripping him with my left leg. He fell, and I had the win before most of the audience had given us their full attention.

In the second round I was paired with one of the queen's house knights, Lamwell of Chaus. He was smaller than I but very quick, and got in good blows before I laid him out.

For the third there remained eight knights counting me. I was sore under my arm and had a dented helm; those raised the storm, and I went for my man to kill him if I could, and had him down before he struck a blow. He was of noble blood like Svon, and a kinsman of his.

Four remained. I fought my man as I had the third and downed him quicker, for I broke his haft with my first blow. He was Rober of Greenglory, a good, brave knight who was to fight alongside me in the River Battle.

That left two of us. A hanap was brought with good

wine in it in which we pledged each other. He was as big a knight as I have ever faced; Woddet was no bigger. Gerrune was his name. He had no hall, but traveled from place to place and fought for pay, a free lance is what such knights are called. I thought it was his size that made him dangerous, because his halbert was half again the length of mine and the haft was thicker. I quickly found out that it was his cunning I had to watch out for; there was not a knight in Skai who knew more slights of arms. The blade of his halbert shone, and he caught sunlight on the flat to dazzle me. His blows began one way and ended another, coming thick and fast; it seemed that he would never tire, because he had no need to use his full strength.

He broke my halbert; I fought on like the man whose quarterstaff I had broken, and used the butt to parry, and struck with the head as if it were an ax, and stabbed with the pike-point, hit him on the knee and crippled him, and grappling him lifted him from his feet and threw him down.

I stood aside, and he doffed helm and loudly said he hoped we never fought again, and I was cheered.

But when the cheers had died away the trumpet sounded, and he—Sir Gerrune—was named victor.

"He bribed them!" Wistan declared; I shook my head, because I had seen his look of surprise.

That night Pouk knocked on our door. Wistan let him in, and he knuckled his forehead and said, "There's two below what wants to see ya, sir. I don't fancy their rig, only they give me this," he displayed a small gold coin, "if I'd tell ya. Can I keep it?"

"Certainly. Did they give their names?"

"Jus' the one, sir. Belos, he were."

"Warlike," Wistan translated (though I am not at all sure he was correct). "They could be assassins, Sir Able."

I said I supposed they could be, or merchants wanting to sell us feathers, or any other thing; but I knew of nobody who wanted me dead, and two seemed pretty thin for a knight and his squire, to say nothing of Gylf, Org, Uns, and Pouk himself.

They were slender men in hooded robes that carried the smell of the sea, and they seemed young. Neither pushed back his hood and neither would meet my eyes. "We serve a great lady of Thortower," said the first. "Her identity we will gladly reveal if you will send these servants of yours away."

Wistan bristled, and I had to explain that although he served a knight, a squire was not a servant.

"She wishes to speak with you, and it is to your own benefit. We will bring you to her, but you must go alone."

"You'll take me to her," I said, "but I won't go alone. There are thieves—I'd have no one but you to defend me."

They conferred while Wistan and Pouk grinned.

At last they separated. "We will protect you and take safe streets, and the distance is not great. Come, and we will see you back safe before sunrise."

"I must sleep before sunrise," I told them. "I'm weary, and tomorrow begins the jousting."

They promised I would be back before moonrise.

I pointed to Gylf. "May I take my dog? He'll be some protection for me."

One said yes, the other no. After wrangling, the second asked, "If you may take him, will you go?"

I nodded. "With Gylf, and with Wistan and Pouk. All of us now in this room."

The first said, "In that case we must return to her who sent us and report that you will not come."

I shook my head. "You must say I would've come, but you wouldn't agree to my conditions. And you've got to tell Her Highness I knew you were Aelf as soon as I saw you. Remind her that I was a friend of her brother's and refused to join my friends when they fought him."

They were backing away as I spoke. I added, "For your safety I warn you that I'll tell her all this myself when I see her, and that I told you to confess it."

They had vanished before I finished.

"They'll be back tonight," I told Pouk. "If they wake you up wanting you to take them to me again, say no."

Pouk touched his forehead, and I waved him out. Wistan asked whether the dragon Vil had killed was really Princess Morcaine's brother; I told him he was too clever by half and his ears would get him into trouble.

"But I need to know these things! You're going to take me with you."

"Because it's my duty to teach you. I've done precious little teaching so far."

"Have I complained?"

I yawned and said I felt sure he had.

"I haven't! Probably I was thinking and frowned or something."

"All right. The princess is the dragon's sister. She's human, as her father was, though not wholly human, since her mother was a dragon from Muspel. Dragons take human shape better than the Aelf. Do I have to explain that?"

"Please! Please, Sir Able!"

"Okay. There are seven worlds—if you know anything, you know that. This is the fourth, the one in the middle. This middle world is the most stable. There are some here who can change more than you and I can, but only a few and even they can't change very much. As you go farther, there's less stability. The Aelf look pretty human, and can look more human. They can take the shapes of animals and people but they can't go much past that or get bigger or smaller. Their eyes give them away. They fade in the sun and run away from sunlight."

"I remember from when they fought for us."

"Those were Uri's people. You saw her."

He nodded.

"They're Fire Aelf and were enslaved by Setr. Setr was the dragon. There's another brother—no doubt you realize that. We're not going to talk about him."

CHAPTER THIRTY-ONE

A SNACK WITH
LORD ESCAN

The jousting differed from our practice at Sheerwall largely in the splendor of armor and bardings, and the dress of the spectators. Our lances were supplied by the pursuivant, in order that there might be no difference in their quality, and to ensure that each would be topped by a steel crown of the same design. Heavy practice armor was not worn, but many used shields stouter than they would have carried to war.

Lists separated the jousters so that their mounts would not collide. One might strike the helm or the chest, if one could, but our lances were aimed at our opponent's shields, for the most part. Each pair engaged until one was knocked from the saddle or cast away his lance in surrender. I had but a single match that first day, against Kei, the champion of the year before. There was no nonsense about breaking lances with us. Each sought to unhorse the other from the beginning, yet we shattered six before Kei's mount went down.

Wistan and I would have been admitted to the sunlit stand near the throne when my match was done; I told him we would join Pouk and Uns among the commoners, I having more foresight in this instance than in most.

They came in less than an hour, not best pleased to have been sent by day. The lady of whom they spoke had relented. She would overlook my earlier refusal and consent to see me. I thanked them for their kindness in bearing her message, and told Wistan to follow me and bring Pouk and

Uns. Gylf had been exploring Thortower, for jousting held little interest for him. He joined us before we had gone far, and the Sea Aelf offered no objection.

She had a tower of her own, as His Grace's lady had at Sheerwall, and she received us in the great room of it, a room richly hung with black velvet in which censers strangely shaped hung smoldering. I did not like it and neither did Gylf, who sniffed behind every arras while she and I spoke.

"We are met again, Sir Able." She gave me her hand.

I said, of course, that I was thrice honored.

"Why would you not come alone?" This with some pouting.

"Your beauty, Your Highness, is such that I feared for my self-restraint."

"Liar. I would be your friend, Sir Able, if I could. You fear no magic."

"That's far from true, Your Highness."

"Don't toy with me. We both know—what we both know. If the dead walk at my command, what is that to you?"

"A lot, Your Highness. The dead aren't always to be commanded. I fear for you."

"As do I." Her chair was like a throne, and the dais it stood on enhanced the impression. She rose, stepped from the dais, and stood swaying before me, a full head taller. "Don't you think me a servant of the Most Low God, Sir Able?"

I shook my head. "He's no god, Your Highness. Nor do you serve him."

"You're right, though I've considered it. I seek to do good by my sorcery. You need not believe it. I'll prove it as the opportunity arises. You bent the knee to me."

"You're royal, Your Highness."

"I deserve it. Not because I'm royal—" She laughed. "But because I'm good. You wish audience with my brother."

"I do, Your Highness. Can you arrange one?"

"I could, but I won't. Riddle me this—why is Sir Gerrune a champion when you are not?"

I shrugged. "He was proclaimed so, Your Highness. Why I cannot even guess."

She laughed, beautiful and mirthless. "My brother ordered it. You wear the queen's favor, Sir Able; do you suppose his queen opens to every knave in the scullery?"

"Of course not, Your Highness. I would kill any man who defamed her in that fashion."

"Then you'll have to kill quite a lot of them. They tell my brother that and worse. He half believes them. Will he receive a knight who wears her favor, do you think?"

"Not often, Your Highness, though I try."

She took my hand. "Well said. There are few at court who love me, Sir Able, and none who trust me. If I were to tell my brother he must speak to you, it would go ill with the case you come to plead. Besides, you've worn his queen's favor in his great tournament. Will the Valfather help you?"

"I doubt it, Your Highness. I hope so."

"So do I, you need it. Meantime, I'll help if I can." Her voice fell. "So will the Earl Marshal, if he dares. Think of us as Skai's agents. It may comfort you." She spoke to Wistan. "Your education proceeds apace."

He knelt. "It does, Your Highness."

"One may stab with a bodkin, Squire, or throw it. Let's throw one. The dead walk at my command. So I told your master, and so it is. He warned me of the danger, it being a knight's business to protect the fair." She turned her head to let Wistan inspect her profile. "Do you think me fair?"

"Never have I seen a fairer lady, Your Highness."

She laughed. "In that case Sir Able will protect me." So saying, she turned her back, muttered something I could not hear, and mounting the dais again resumed her seat.

From the floor came the sound of a great door shut hard, and she smiled. "Perhaps you had news of our tournament last year, Squire?"

"I was here, Your Highness. I served Sir Garvaon. He shot, engaged with the halbert, and jousted too."

"What of the melee? So redoubtable a knight would wish to take part in that, surely."

"He did, Your Highness. But we couldn't. It's forty per side and the scroll was full."

"Sir Able is more fortunate."

"Yes, Your Highness."

"Do you know why?"

Wistan's voice dropped to a whisper, "Because I signed it. For him, only I don't want him to die. I know that's what you think, but I don't. You haven't seen him fight."

Morcaine turned to me. "This is your first tournament?"

I confessed that it was.

"There are knights, Sir Able, who know they've no chance in the earlier events. Was this Sir Garvaon a good bowman?"

"A very good one, Your Highness."

"Many are not, and do not wish to be humiliated. You knew something of humiliation when your string broke."

"Yes, Your Highness." Beyond Morcaine, Baki peeped from behind a black velvet curtain. Her face was stricken.

"Suppose all three had missed the straw. Many would stand no chance against Sir Gerrune with poleaxes, and less against Sir Kei in jousting. Yet they would be ashamed to come and take no part. So they fight in the melee. It is the most dangerous of all, but luck plays a large part."

"I understand, Your Highness." As I spoke I heard footsteps, heavy and slow, and Gylf growled.

"Weapons are blunted, and no mace may be used. Still, a knight or two is killed each year. Perhaps you didn't know."

I said I had not, but that it did not matter.

"Now if I've timed our talk correctly . . ." She laughed. "Sir Lich died in the melee, but his name—ah, here he is."

A trap in the floor rose. The knight who raised it and stepped forth was plainly dead, and had been dead for some time, his body stored in a dry place. There were maggots in his flesh, but they had not done great execution there.

"Would you fight him? In defense of my fair person?"

"Certainly," I said. There was a faint noise behind me, and Wistan tugged my sleeve.

"Bear in mind that you could not kill him."

"If he's a threat to Your Highness, I'll do what I can."

"He is none. Let's let him rest."

Perhaps she murmured some further word I failed to hear. The dead knight fell, his face striking the flagstones with such force that a maggot was thrown from it.

"Sir Able's servants have fled—what of you, Squire? Has your education progressed sufficiently for this day?"

Wistan's voice shook, but he answered that it had. The boy who had run from Huld's ghost was held in check.

"What did you think of the messengers I sent for you and your master? Didn't they set your teeth chattering, too?"

"No, Your Highness, they were Aelf, Sea Aelf, my master says. We saw Aelf in the mountains, Your Highness, and they helped us against the Angrborn." He finished bravely enough. "They were fine archers, Your Highness."

"You were unafraid?"

"Not—I was at first, Your Highness. A little."

"Sir Lich's worm affrighted you. I saw it. When next you meet my messengers, recall that they were made by worms. Sir Able, I asked you here so we might take counsel, knowing that my brother hates you for the queen's favor and knowing too that he will love you no better than me if you come under my auspices. If you've the ear of the Valfather, will you beseech him to grant my brother issue?"

The change of topic discomfited me, but I said I would.

"Beseech the queen as well. You've her ear." Morcaine had been bolt upright to that moment; she slumped almost as abruptly as the dead knight. "Our queen's a strumpet, he thinks, and I a murderess who would slay my brother for his throne. She is not, Sir Able. Nor am I."

I nodded and said, "I believe you, Your Highness."

"I thank you. He may kill me, fancying he defends his life. He may kill her to get a queen who'll bear him sons. She's no friend of mine." Morcaine straightened up, eyes blazing. "My brother is my brother, the playfellow of my childhood. I love few, but I love him. Do you understand?"

"I do, Your Highness. Better than you know."

"You mean him no hurt?"

"I wish only to deliver the message of the one who sent me, Your Highness."

"Who is . . . ?"

"In Aelfrice, Your Highness."

She sat in silence, her eyes upon my face. At last she said, "Will you deliver it in my hearing?"

"When His Majesty and I stand face-to-face, I know that message will fill my mind; and I'll speak it whatever it may be. I don't believe the presence of others—even yourself, Your Highness—will make a particle of difference."

"In which case I must be present. I offer this, the only help I can give. If you wish it, I will ask a boon."

I said, "I wish it, Your Highness."

She shook her head. "Not that you be brought to him. Hear me out. I will ask to name one of our dinner guests tomorrow. I will do it in the queen's presence, and if I know her she'll ask to name a guest as well. If my brother has granted my boon, it will look ill for him to refuse hers. You wear her favor in the lists, so she'll surely name you. My brother will have to receive you and speak graciously, though he will mean no word of it. Shall I do it?"

"I beg it, Your Highness. I'll be forever indebted."

"The odium will fall upon the queen." Morcaine laughed. "You realize that?"

"I will divert it to myself, if that's possible."

* * *

I had three matches next day, and won them all. Wistan and I awaited an invitation to King Arnthor's table after the third, but it never came. Long after sunset, I sent Wistan to the Earl Marshal to beg an interview. It was granted, and I told him I had spoken with Morcaine, and that Morcaine had promised to intercede for me with the king.

"I know." The Earl Marshal made a tower of his fingers. "You understand, I hope, that his sister is no favorite."

"I do, My Lord."

"When first we spoke, you said you hesitated to presume upon Her Highness's friendship. I thought it prudence." He pinched his nose. "Harrumph! You still wish an audience?"

"Very much, My Lord."

"You have distinguished yourself in the tournament as I advised, though apparently insufficiently."

"I strive to do more, My Lord."

"I wish you well in it. I've mentioned you twice to His Majesty. I believe I pledged myself to do it once? I have exceeded my pledge. He hasn't asked that you be brought. Was it for your sake Her Highness asked the boon?"

"I think it likely, My Lord."

The Earl Marshal sighed. "I'm keeping you standing, Sir Able, and you will be tired. I had hoped to finish this in a minute or two. Sit down. Would you like a little wine?"

I said I would, and motioned for Wistan to sit.

The Earl Marshal rang a handbell. "A boon was refused, Sir Able. Did you know it?"

I shook my head, feeling my heart sink.

"It's the talk of the court. Her Highness, lightly but politely, begged a boon of her brother. It was assumed, by me and I believe by all who witnessed this sad affair, that it was to be some trivial license. It was refused, and she

left the hall. I doubt she will tell you this. She was humiliated, you understand."

"I do, My Lord."

"He was shamed as well. Don't imagine, Sir Able, that
he doesn't know it. Our queen—is Idnn really a queen
now? You said so at our last meeting."

I began to explain but was interrupted by Payn.

"Wine," the Earl Marshal told him. "Not that swill, our
own from Brighthills. White or red, Sir Able?"

"As My Lord prefers."

"White, then. Some hot smoked fish, I think. Sturgeon
and whatever else you can find. Toast and herb butter. Your
Queen Idnn is a friend of Her Majesty's, Sir Able. Did you
know it? Girls the same age, you know, both at court a
good deal. These arms rocked Her Majesty in swaddling
clothes, however much you may doubt it."

The Earl Marshal's voice fell. "One reason Lord Beel
went, I think. The king sent him away to rob poor Gaynor
of a friend, I'd say. I'd say it, but don't you repeat it. And
Beel took the job, in part, to get Idnn away from the king.
It's dangerous to be a friend of our queen's these days. I
should know, for I am one. Don't repeat any of this."

Wistan and I swore we would not.

"I'm the king's as well, you understand. I'd bring them
together, if I could. In time I will, never doubt it. . . ."

"You've thought of something, My Lord?"

He shook his head, jowls wobbling. "A passing fancy,
Sir Able. A mere fancy."

He spoke to Wistan. "The great fault of intelligence,
young man. Stupidity is at least as valuable. Intelligence
causes us to overreach, much too often, and distracts us
with—harrumph!—mere fanciful notions. Is Sir Able
teaching you swordsmanship?"

"Yes, My Lord. He says I have a knack for it, too."

"That's well—that's very well. Strive to learn swordsmanship. But strive to learn stupidity in addition. The best knights are good swordsmen, but stupid men."

"Including this one," I declared, for I knew the Earl Marshal had hit on something but I had no idea what it was.

"Exactly. Exactly. You bear a message, but do not know it. A fine example. Why did the queen—?"

Payn returned at that moment, bearing a big silver tray laden with a carafe, cups, plates, and covered dishes.

"Noble! You're putting up at an inn, Sir Able?"

"Yes, My Lord."

"Good food?"

Wistan answered, "Tolerable, My Lord."

"We shall do something about that, I hope. Not tonight, but soon. After the tournament." (Payn had set a plate, a cup, and a towel dampened with hot water in front of each of us; as his master spoke, he filled our cups.) "Wouldn't you like to be a guest here at the castle? It could be arranged, though you'd be just as comfortable with a friend of mine in the city. Just as comfortable, and a good deal safer."

I said I hoped to leave soon after speaking to the king.

"Then I hope it for you. It's winter just the same, and plans change. Payn, I will speak with Her Majesty and Her Highness after breakfast if you can arrange it. Separately, you understand. You will present my humble request for an interview to each tonight. My visit will be brief, the matter is important, and that is all you know."

"Yes, Your Lordship. Shall I go now?"

The Earl Marshal nodded. "At once. Come back when you've spoken to both. As early as possible, but not both together, understand? Now be off. Taste this wine, will you, Sir Able? That we've had of late has been abominable to my own palate, though Payn thinks it not so bad as I say."

I sipped. "Excellent, My Lord."

"Have they better in Aelfrice?"

I sipped again. "It would seem impossible, My Lord."

He laughed, his belly shaking. "Not to be caught so easily as that. Well, well. Do you bear a message from a queen, Sir Able? Ah, a hit!"

"I think it better not to speak of that, My Lord."

"Your face spoke for you. The other day this boy said he thought your message came from Queen Idnn. I've been thinking on it, you see. What message Idnn might send the king so secret that the bearer was not to know it, and so on. A bearer who had clearly been to Aelfrice, and likely more than once from what the boy tells me. These women! Always sending messages and making trouble. You agree, I hope?"

"Why no, My Lord."

"You will when you're my age. Her Highness is drunk much of the time. Did you know it?"

"No, My Lord. I did not."

"She's very good at hiding it. Seriously now, what do you think of my wine?"

"Wistan is a better judge than I, My Lord."

He said, "Excellent, My Lord. I've never had better."

"Noble. We've toast here," he uncovered a dish, "and I believe this is cod, a favorite of mine. May I give you some of both?"

Wistan nodded eagerly. "With pleasure, My Lord."

"Your master must be served first, Squire, even when the server is a peer of the realm." The Earl Marshal heaped my plate with four sorts of smoked fish and added slices of bread that had been impaled on a fork and toasted before a fire, that being the custom of Thortower.

"Now then," he said, when we had both been served. "We must strike a bargain, you and I, Sir Able. When you first came to me, I offered you good advice, for which I made no charge. In addition I've twice mentioned you to the king, speaking of your knowledge of recent events—incredible events, some of them—in the north. I did these things because I like you, and because I thought them my duty."

I started to speak, but he stopped me with an upraised hand. "You think me angling for a bribe. So I am. But not gold. You have Redhall, one of the best manors in the north. I have four as good or better, and knights to serve me for them, and a castle. I say this not to boast, but to let you know that I am not much poorer than your Duke Marder. I may well be richer. You understand?"

I nodded. "Yes, My Lord."

"It's knowledge I seek. It's information." His voice fell. "I serve His Majesty, Sir Able. It's no easy service, yet I do it to the best of my ability, year after year. I couldn't stand against you with the sword."

I did not contradict him.

"Or even against your squire here, if you've trained him well. It is by thought that I serve my king. By the habit of reflection, and by knowledge." He sipped wine. "You have knowledge I envy. I'll have it from you. Do you understand? Leaving me richer, but you no poorer. I plan extraordinary steps tomorrow, steps that will bring you before the king without fail. Will you, in payment for this special favor I do you at the risk of my life, answer a few questions for me? Answering truly, upon your honor?"

He had not said that he would proffer no more help to me if I would not; yet it was in the air. I said, "There are a great many questions I can't answer, My Lord."

"Those you can. Upon your honor."

"Yes, My Lord. As much as I know."

"Noble." He leaned back in his chair, smiling, and ate a slice of smoked pike on a slice of toast. Taking our cue from him, Wistan and I ate as well. Both the bread and the fish were very good.

"My first question, Sir Able. How many times have you visited Aelfrice?"

I tried to recall, counting the instances on my fingers. "Five, I think, My Lord. No, six."

His eyes had grown wide while I counted. "Often enough to lose the reckoning?"

"Yes, My Lord."

"Time runs more slowly there?"

"It does, My Lord."

"Do you know the rule of it?" Seeing that I had not understood him, he added, "Suppose we went to Aelfrice for a day. There are days there?"

"Indeed, My Lord."

"How many would have elapsed when we returned here?"

"I can't say, My Lord. There is no fixed rule. A week, perhaps. Possibly a year."

"I see." He caressed his jowls. "I would not run too swift for reason, Sir Able. But I would run. If your honor does not forbid: is His Majesty's sister known there?"

"I have no certain information, My Lord, but I believe she must be."

"You never encountered her there."

I fear I hesitated. "No, My Lord."

"You did not?"

"No, My Lord."

"Yet you came near it, I think. Isn't that so?"

"I'm still a boy, My Lord. Only a boy, whatever you may think. You are a man of mature years and wisdom."

"Tell me."

I spoke then of Grengarm, without mentioning Eterne.

"The Aelf you speak of were bringing her from Aelfrice?"

"So it seemed, My Lord. I have no reason to doubt it."

"You saved her? The dragon would have devoured her?"

"I believe so, My Lord."

"Harrumph!" One fleshy hand wiped his face. "If she's not your friend after that, she's a most ungrateful jade."

"I've no reason to think that, My Lord, and some to think otherwise."

Wistan added, "We talked to her yesterday, My Lord, and she tried to help us. She's—I'm afraid of her. I don't like to say it, My Lord, but I am."

A smile tugged at the Earl Marshal's lips. "I believe you."

"Even if she's our friend. Sir Able's friend, and my friend, too, because he's my master. If she were our enemy, I'd be scared to death."

"I can't blame you, Squire. Let us retain her regard, all three of us. Our king loves and fears her, which alone would be reason enough." The Earl Marshal turned back to me. "You do not know what message you bear, Sir Able?"

"As I have told you, My Lord."

"So you did, and thought it unwise to reveal the sender. I ask now. That question and two more, and I'll be satisfied for the present. Have you sworn secrecy on that point?"

"No, My Lord. I didn't think you would believe me. You credited Grengarm—it was true, of course. All of it. You know something of the other worlds."

"I do." The Earl Marshal shifted his bulk in his chair and selected another piece of pike. "I have never visited them. As you have, I realize. I have spoken with the Aelf, however, more than once. I've done small favors and received small favors in return. Did Queen Disiri send you?"

CHAPTER THIRTY-TWO

TRIAL BY ARMS

My surprise must surely have been apparent.

"When we met," the Earl Marshal explained, "this young man suggested Queen Idnn as the sender. You flinched at *queen*, then relaxed. Queens are not so common as cabbages."

"No, My Lord."

"I thought it likely our queen was the sender. She would not have required the dragon, however." He took a bite of toast, chewed, and swallowed. "The Aelf are of many clans—nearly all ruled by kings. The Dryads, or Moss Aelf, are the sole exception. Possibly you know of others?"

I admitted I did not.

He spread his hands. "In that case, your message is from Queen Disiri. You see how simple it is."

I must have nodded, no doubt slowly and reluctantly.

"This is well. If you're asked, you can quite honestly declare that you did not reveal the identity of the sender to me. It may not be of importance, but if it is you have it."

"I appreciate that, My Lord."

"Then appreciate also—harrumph!—that you did not answer my question. You will answer the other two, I hope."

"If I can, My Lord. What are they?"

"The first. Why did Queen Gaynor give you her favor to wear in the lists?"

"I don't know, My Lord." I sipped my wine.

"You mean that she did not confide it. You entered the archery. Both events."

"Yes, My Lord. I disappointed myself, if I may say it."

"You will find that toast quite passable now, I think. But not if you let it grow cold."

"I will not, My Lord." I tore off a bit.

"You finished fourth, I think it was, in foot archery. You shot two golds in mounted archery. Your bowstring broke as you rode for the final shot. I was watching, like nearly everyone. Afterward, Her Majesty gave you her favor."

"Right, My Lord." I had eaten toast while he spoke.

"You didn't question Her Majesty. This boy might have. I wouldn't put it past him. But you? No more than I. One does not suject royalty to an interrogation."

Wistan said, "I didn't ask her anything, My Lord."

The Earl Marshal raised an eyebrow. "Still, you must have speculated. A dullard would not have, perhaps. You're no dullard. You have not visited Aelfrice with your master?"

"No, My Lord. Thank you, My Lord. I haven't, but I'd like to go, and Toug told me about it. So did Etela."

"I will forbear examining you as to her identity. For the present, eh? Let us return to our queen. You must have speculated. Let me have your speculations."

Wistan cleared his throat, a small, apologetic noise compared to the Earl Marshal's trumpetings. "I thought it fairly obvious, My Lord."

"Not to me, Squire."

"He's good-looking, My Lord. And mysterious, really mysterious to me, because I know so much about him. I've told you some of that."

The Earl Marshal nodded and chewed.

"He'd be mysterious to her, too, because he's never been to court. You mentioned his mail—this was the other day."

He smiled. "So I did."

"You can't have been the only one to notice that. Women love mystery, My Lord."

"I am aware of it."

"His string broke like you said, but he shot two golds first. A gold's any shot that cuts gold, but his were right in the center. Nobody else got two right in the center."

"I had not observed that," the Earl Marshal said slowly. "I was remiss, Squire. I'm glad that you were not."

"And he has the best horse, My Lord, Cloud. You know about her, because we looked at her. I take care of her, My Lord, and I rode her once like I said. It's not just that she's the best horse. I— This is going to sound silly."

"You're of an age at which it may be condoned. Let's hear you."

"If everybody fought with sticks, My Lord, and a knight came with a sword, they'd say he had the best stick."

The Earl Marshal smiled. "That's not silly at all."

"Ladies want the knight to win, My Lord, when they give their favor. A good horse is a big part of that."

"You're fortunate in your squire, Sir Able."

"Sir Garvaon chose him, My Lord. He was a knight of sound sense, as well as great courage."

"You yourself are a man of sound sense, Sir Able—"

I shook my head, knowing how wrong he was.

"One who must have thought on the queen's favor, as your squire did. Thought on it more, because you are more deeply concerned. Were your conclusions the same?"

"I came to none. It seemed to me Her Highness must have been at behind it, since we met before I came here. She may have urged it, thinking it to my benefit. Or—or she might have mentioned my name in passing."

"You will not say it." The Earl Marshal studied me with hooded eyes. "I will. Her Majesty may have learned that Her Highness intended to bestow her favor upon you, and moved to sequester you. That seems the likeliest explanation of all. Yet in strict justice I must rule that none of those your squire proposed can be wholly disregarded. They may have played a part, and may have played the whole part. I did not cross-examine you out of curiosity, as I hope you realize. I have a plan, though I shall not reveal it until it has been tried. Not then, if it fails."

"I'll be grateful for your assistance in either case."

He smiled. "I have hopes, Sir Able. I must persuade our royal ladies. Yet I am persuasive, or I would not stand where I do. Ladies like their knights to win, as a younger head than ours tells us, and even royal ladies are fond of intrigue. Nay, royal ladies are fondest of it. Thus we may hope. My last question. How am I to visit Aelfrice?"

I was taken aback. "You wish to go, My Lord?"

"It has been the dream of my life. I don't plan to take up residence, though sometimes . . . It is a perilous sphere?"

"It is, My Lord. Beautiful and dangerous. So is this."

"Well said. How may I go?"

"I may be able to arrange it, My Lord."

"After you have delivered your message."

"Yes, My Lord. I must put that first—I cannot do otherwise. I mean no disrespect."

"She is a queen. I understand. You will be here in the morning to continue jousting?"

I nodded. "We will, My Lord."

"It might be well to bring a serviceable lance as well."

Although I attempted to question him, I could elicit no further information. We ate and drank and talked, mostly of horses, and at last Wistan and I returned to our inn, where we found Pouk and Uns slumbering.

Another page stopped us the next day, saying the queen had urgent need of me. Wistan and I followed him, and as we made our way among the towers and strong-houses heard a roar from the crowd. I caught the page's shoulder and demanded to know what was happening.

"They've news from the Nykr King of Arms, I think."

"What news?"

"I don't know!"

I released him. "Does his news concern me?"

He nodded and only just managed to prevent himself from wiping his nose on his sleeve.

"Out with it!"

"I don't know, Sir Able. Really. She'll tell you."

Wistan volunteered to go back and find out. Sensing that I might learn more if he were gone, I told him to do it.

"I'll keep your secret," I said when he had left, "but I must know before I talk to the queen. What was the news?"

"They had a fight." The page whispered. "The queen and Her Highness. Everybody's scared of her. Of the princess."

"Small wonder."

"But they're going to fight. Only not really. Their champions will do it for them."

The queen was waiting in her snowy garden. I knelt, saying I hoped I had not kept her long in the cold.

"Oh, I'm warmly dressed." She smiled, and indicated her ermine robe. "I have to do this often. I can't have a man in my apartments, not even an elderly relative. His Majesty would not approve."

I was about to make some commonplace remark about warm rooms and fires elsewhere, but she swept it aside by asking whether I would like to disrobe.

"I would not like to sully Your Majesty's honor at any time or in any place."

She laughed merrily. "You're the knight for me. Or I hope you will be. I could order you to, but I won't."

"You need not," I told her. "Make clear what you wish, and it shall be done."

"Except disrobing." It might have been a dove's moan.

"Indeed. Except that."

"You know, this is fun." Her smile warmed me. "When I told Lord Escan I'd do it, I didn't think it was going to be. But it is, for me. You may be killed. I'm an awful person."

"Your Majesty's the only person in Celidon who thinks so. You are our glory."

She smiled again. "You will be mine, Sir Able. I know it! You'll fight Morcaine's champion for me, won't you? To defend my honor? We're doing this for you, really."

"I'd rather do it for you. If Morcaine had ten score champions, I'd fight them all for Your Majesty's sake."

"Hush! Hush!" The queen put a finger to her lips. "She may be listening. She's terrible about that."

"I've said nothing to you that I wouldn't say in her hearing."

"Oh, you Overcyns! Get up, please. I didn't mean to keep you kneeling in the snow. Rise."

I did, and her soft hand found mine. "I feel you're my friend. That you truly are. I've forty knights, and not one real friend among them. Did the Valfather send you?"

"Yes, Your Majesty. Or at least, he let me come."

She stared. "You're serious."

"Entirely, Your Majesty. When I talk to others, I try to conceal it. But I won't lie to you or the king. I won't even tell half truths, something I do much too often."

"You—I can't let you do this. You'll be killed."

"You have to let me do this, Your Majesty. I've worn your favor in the lists. I'm your champion."

"Oh, Lady! Dear Lady of Skai! It's . . ."

"Ordained?" I suggested.

Gaynor's eyes brimmed with tears. "It's for me, too. So the king will see that—that I'm not what he thinks. The Valfather will give the victory to the right, won't he?"

"That's what people believe, I know. It may be true."

"And she said something awful to my face. That I'm a slut or something. We haven't decided exactly what it was, and probably we won't have to. So I challenged her and it's at noon, and you have to die for me." She sobbed, hot tears rolling down smooth cheeks red with cold. "Only if you do, my husband will think he's right, and—and . . ."

"I won't, Your Majesty. You'll be vindicated."

"She's going to try to kill you." The queen looked around nervously, as if she thought Morcaine hiding behind a snow-covered rose bush. "She likes you, and she'll try to kill you anyway. You don't know her."

I said, "She'll naturally chose a champion whose courage and skill won't embarrass her, Your Majesty. I needn't know her inmost thoughts to know that. In her place, I'd do the same thing. Are we to fight to the death?"

"No." Gaynor had plucked a handkerchief nearly as large as a man's from sleeve. "It never is."

"Then he'll yield to me when he can no longer resist, and no one will die."

"It's not like the melee, with blunt swords and crowned lances. Don't you understand? Real weapons, real fighting."

"That's well. I had a bad bowstring, but I've got a good sword."

She rose, her lovely face no higher than the dragon on my chest. "Hear me, Sir Able. Girls aren't supposed to be serious at my age. Not 'til they've had a child. But I may never have one, I'm still a virgin, and I'm as serious as I'll ever be. I said it was fun, because it was then. But it's not now, because I like you and you'll die."

"All men do, Your Majesty."

"And all women. I know. But listen. She wants him to put me away and marry again. If she wins, he may. He could say it was what the Overcyns wanted." Gaynor took a deep breath, her inhalation loud in the quiet garden. *And I'd like that.* But I have a duty, and I love him. And I'm not sterile. It's just that . . . That—"

She had begun to sob. I held her and comforted her as well as I could.

At last she said, "You'll do it? For me? Champion my virtue before the king?"

"A hundred times over, Your Majesty." It was the truth, and the truth was that I would have done it a thousand times in order to speak to the king and claim Disiri.

Wistan was waiting when the queen dismissed me. "It's a Trial by Combat, Sir Able. The princess insulted the queen, and she demands satisfaction. Nobody knows who the champions will be." He gave me a searching look. "They all want to be the queen's, all the knights. A lot say Sir Gerrune."

He waited for me to speak, but I did not.

"Only a lot more say it'll be you, because of her scarf. Everybody knows whose scarf it is. Uns is boasting about you among the churls, and he and Pouk are laying bets."

I suppose I grinned.

"They'll be rich if you win. Rich for churls, anyway."

"What about you, Wistan? Won't you be rich too?"

"I haven't bet. Is it all right if I do?"

"Sure."

"Then I will. I got some gold up north, like we all did. The way Pouk and Uns are betting is they give odds you'll be her champion. Two to one. Then the other party has to give them two to one against you, if you are."

There are moments that remain fixed in memory, in some sense ever-present. Of all my fights no other stays with me like that one. I can shut my eyes and see the bailey as it was then—the winter sunshine, the cold air sparkling with snow, the pennants and banners snapping in the wind, a mad dance of bears and elephants, falcons and bulls and basilisks and camelopards, red, blue, green, yellow, black, and white. I hear the thunderous cracking of the great sea-blue flag of Celidon, with the royal Nykr embroidered in gold.

To my right sat the court, the king and queen in high places, Morcaine to the king's left, in a seat not quite so high. Around them clustered the peers and their ladies, proud men and gracious women in fur and velvet. To left and right the knights, muffled in thick cloaks, with here and there the gleam of steel. Facing them, the commons, half the town of Kingsdoom having turned out to watch, delighted on this winter afternoon to have a real fight to entertain them, a combat in which either knight, or both, might die.

For this I had practiced day after day in the golden halls and airy courts of the Valfather's castle. Not to fight the Giants of Winter and Old Night, nor to fight the Angrborn, sending arrow after arrow into their upturned faces as Cloud cantered over their heads.

The test had come at last, the deciding battle to which my

life had been directed, and I knew a joy whose price had been paid in sweat and stratagem and hard blows. This was the service of the Valfather, and his service was beatitude and exultation. The lance of spiny orange I had shaped was in my hand, Eterne at my side. A double-bitted ax bought in anticipation of the melee hung from my saddle, both edges ground and honed until they would split bone with a tap.

Cloud knew my mind as she always did, and arched her neck and pawed the ground. There was no barrier, as there is in jousting. This was not jousting but war.

Across the bailey stood her opponent, a stallion taller by two hands—her opponent, but not mine—and the horse cloth the stallion wore was black, the silver device on its sides that of no knight but Morcaine's margygr, a fanciful representation of her mother, Setr's, and the king's.

The Nykr King of Arms rode to the center, and with him a pursuivant who repeated his words so all might hear—so all might hear, I wrote, but so still was every tongue that there was no need of him. I will give the words of the Nykr King of Arms, and not trouble with the repetitions.

"This day shall be joined in trial by arms the gallant champions of Her Most Royal Majesty Queen Gaynor and of Her Royal Highness Princess Morcaine."

There was a little buzz of talk, soon stilled, as the younger man repeated what the Nykr King of Arms had said.

"Her Most Royal Majesty Queen Gaynor is the aggrieved party. Her champion upon this field is Sir Able of Redhall, a knight of Sheerwall."

As previously, the pursuivant bellowed the same words.

"Her Royal Highness Princess Morcaine is the aggrieving party." The Nykr King of Arms paused to look toward the riderless stallion. *"Her champion upon this field—and he come—is to be Sir Loth of Narrowhouse."*

To my right I heard one knight say to another, "Loth? He's dead." To which the other replied, "That was Loth of Northholding."

I knew then who my opponent would be.

He came soon enough, his dead face hidden by his helm, the charge on his shield a black elk on a white field. I put on my own helm at that point, with the queen's white scarf knotted about the black dragon that was its crest.

"At the first sounding of the clarion, the champions are to make ready. At the second, all save the champions and their squires must depart the field."

I looked then for Sir Loth's squire and saw a lad some trifle older than Wistan. He kept his back to the barrier, and seemed terrified.

"Upon the third sounding, the champions will engage. Neither their squires no any other persons may take part in their combat. Should a champion yield, his squire may succor him. Gentle right shall be observed. When a champion shall claim gentle right, his squire may help him to his feet and rearm him. Nothing more. Champions, raise your lances to signify your agreement."

We did so.

"Squires, your right hands."

Though the distance was a good bowshot, I saw the hand of Loth's squire shake.

That pursuivant who had repeated the Nykr King's words lifted a clarion to his lips and blew. I settled into my saddle, and tightened my grip on my lance. Should we engage right side to right? Left side to left (as in jousting)? Or mount to mount? These questions, which for a moment filled my mind, came from Cloud. I answered, *Left to left.*

The clarion sounded the second time. At my side Wistan murmured, "Thunor's blessing, Sir Able."

It may have been ill omened, for no sooner had he spoken than so dark a cloud veiled the sun that it seemed the dead knight and I engaged by night. Loth seemed to grow larger in the gloom. His white shield and white surcoat floated spectral above a charger almost invisible.

The clarion sounded a third time; I had no need to clap my heels to Cloud.

Loth's lance broke on my shield. Mine took him through the chest and plucked him from the saddle. I withdrew it as I rode; and it may be that most of those who watched did not realize what had happened.

He should have been slow, yet he was not. He remounted as Cloud wheeled, and drew sword. My point slipped from his helm, our mounts met chest-to-chest, and his was ridden down. Wheeling again, I charged a third time. I saw him standing like a ghost, the ichor of decay seeping from his wound, and tried to impale him again, thinking to leave my lance between his ribs to obstruct him, and to cut him down before he could free himself. It was a good plan, but none of it worked. His shield turned my point. His sword did what I would have said no sword but Eterne could, hewing my lance as a woodsman fells a sapling.

Then I feared for Cloud. In tourney, no true knight strikes the mount; in battle it is otherwise, and seeing that fell blade poised I knew what blow he intended. Cloud would have trampled him, and showed me so clearly I almost agreed.

He will take off a forefoot, I told her, *and you will be as good as dead.*

I slipped off her back, and met him toe-to-toe.

His sword split my shield so deeply that it was the mail on my forearm that stopped the edge. Turning as swiftly as I could, I wrenched the sword from his dead hand. My ax bit his helm, and he fell.

Fallen, he moaned aloud. All death was in it, lonely graves in winter, the wind that leaves beggars' bodies on the streets of Kingsdoom, and the howls of the wolves that tear the slain.

I turned and walked away, and seeing the Nykr King of Arms, with the pursuivant who assisted him, I told them that my foe claimed gentle right, which I would accord him.

Wistan came then with a new shield for me, one we had taken from Redhall, it having still its covering of cloth so that Ravd's golden lion could not be seen. I took it, and seeing that Loth's squire would by no means leave his place to rearm him, told Wistan that he must raise him, and give him some new weapon.

"I have none to give, Sir Able, save my own sword."

"Give it," I said; and when he ran to obey, I with the pursuivant's help took Loth's blade from my shield, although it was tightly wedged in the layered willow.

Wistan raised and rearmed Loth. White-faced and shaken he returned, and I gave him the sword that had been Loth's, a brand of watered steel. "This is yours," I told him. "See if your scabbard will hold it."

Returning to Loth, I made ready to continue the fight. He stepped back, raised the sword that had been Wistan's, and cried out again. Long ago I had heard fishermen hallooing from boat to boat, and though this was sad and that was not, I felt the purpose was the same, that he saluted others and called them to help him.

I thought little of it, or thought only that I had to close quickly and dispatch him before his help arrived. I tried to, and soon found that my ax had put out an eye and he was hard pressed to defend himself when I kept moving to my right. Yet he fought as skillfully as any live man, taking blows that would have killed a living man, and fought on in the darkness and flying snow, and although he lost the arm that had held his sword, he dropped his shield and snatched the sword from his own right hand, while his arm crept over the snow to close its hand on my ankle.

They came, the dead he had called, whether from the grave or tombs above ground I do not know, some new-killed, some so long dead that Morcaine could scarcely animate them. The onlookers fled, although I paid that little mind.

For I had thrown aside the ax and drawn Eterne; and my own help came, galloping out of the snowy sky. The cloud passed and the sun shone again, making the new snow sparkle, and dead contended with dead for the honor of a living queen. Wistan and Pouk and Uns fought beside me, and Cloud kicked and trampled my foes and would have gored them, save that her horn was still too small, and Gylf raged among them, greater and more terrible than any lion.

The sun was still high when the fight ended. I wiped Eterne's blade with such stuff as I could find, and cast the stuff away from me, for it reeked of the grave, and sheathed her at last. Arnthor sat his throne unmoved, with Gaynor fainting in his arms and Morcaine smiling beside him. Five knights with swords drawn stood before them; and I took note of them, for they were the bravest Thortower boasted, as was proved by what they did that day— Marc, Lamwell, Gerrune, Rober, and Oriel.

Morcaine called, "You have triumphed, Sir Able, and my sister-in-law with you. I own it, and her innocence." Her lips smiled, and her eyes held a dark and terrible lust.

Arnthor nodded. "You will share meat with us tonight? I would speak with you." His eyes, too, were the storm-black of dragons.

I dropped to one knee. "Gladly, Your Majesty."

CHAPTER THIRTY-THREE
UNDER THORTOWER

Uns had been stabbed; the wound sucked air until we bandaged it, and he seemed weak. "I'se awright, sar. I'se awright." That was all he said before his eyes closed. I could not heal him without betraying the Valfather, for I had pledged myself to do no such thing. Still I was sore tempted, and crouched by Uns and laid my hand on his head; and it may be that a little healing went out from me. I hope so.

We carried him back to the inn and left Pouk there to nurse him while Wistan and I made ready to dine with Arnthor and Gaynor, washing ourselves in water we heated on our fire and putting on our best clothes.

Wistan spent a long time examining his new sword, whose blade he wiped again and oiled, and whose jeweled pommel he held to every light, first to the declining sun and afterward to the fire and candles. When we were in the saddle, clean and sweet-smelling, he said, "When I'm a knight, I'll tell my squire how I fought the dead in the Great Bailey."

I nodded, and urged Cloud to trot.

"And how I fought the Angrborn in Jotunland in company with Aelf, and gained much wealth thereby."

"With more by betting," I said. "Those who ran today will be back tomorrow, and you can collect your bets."

He nodded absently.

"Pouk will collect for Uns, I suppose, as soon as Uns is well enough to leave alone for a few hours."

"I'll tell him about all this, and he'll think I'm the greatest liar under Skai." Wistan laughed.

"He'll soon grow older and wiser. How old are you?"

"Nearly eighteen. I'll be a knight soon, or hope I will."

"You're a knight now. It's only that no one calls you so, Sir Wistan."

"You said something like that to Toug."

"I did. Toug is a knight, though he doesn't want to be. It's not really a matter of choice."

Wistan nodded, but did not speak.

"I didn't understand that when I was younger. I wanted to be a knight, and I became one—not because I chose to be one, but because of the things I did and the way I thought. Good and evil are decided by thoughts and choices, too."

"Like the princess?"

I had not considered that. "Unlike the princess," I said. "She's chosen good, but it seems evil has chosen her."

We spoke more, before the bridge was lowered for us and after; but the only thing of note was said by Gylf as we were shown into the hall: "Ears up!"

He was right, of course; if ever there was a time to be watchful that was it; what was at least equally important was that he had chosen to speak in Wistan's presence. It was not that I had called Wistan a knight, or merely that they had fought side by side, but a combination of those things with something more. Gylf was a sound judge of character.

I had been in Gilling's hall in Utgard; Arnthor's seemed small in comparison; but it was better furnished, with chairs and benches with backs for his guests instead of stools. The walls were hung with shields, those of proven knights having the arms colored, those of less proven knights with the arms outlined but not painted in, and those of unproven knights blank. I had followed this custom when I chose a blank green shield, although I had not been aware of it.

Arnthor and Gaynor were to sit at a raised table, he with the queen to his right. I was to sit at Arnthor's left, as the page who guided us confided, with Morcaine to my left. This was made clear by the quality of the chairs, Arnthor's being gilt all over and set with gems, Gaynor's smaller and delicate, and the princess's gilt only at the top, although beautifully carved and furnished with a velvet cushion. Mine was plainer than these, but by no means contemptible, being large and boasting a well-carved Nykr on its back. Wistan was directed to a lower table, but Gylf sat by my chair.

"The trumpets will sound for His Majesty," the page

murmured. "Everyone stands until he says you may sit. As soon as he makes the motion, sit down."

I said I wished he could advise me as I ate.

"I will. Everyone at this table will have a page. I'll be behind you. Crook your finger if you need to talk to me. I'll help with the food or run with a message, if you want."

Other guests were entering as we spoke, I suppose about a hundred in all. I asked how I ought to conduct myself.

"Don't speak 'til they speak to you—not to anybody royal. His Majesty will be served first, then Her Majesty, then Her Highness, then you. Don't eat too much and don't drink too much. Don't laugh unless His Majesty does."

Then I wished that the Earl Marshal was nearer; I wanted to ask why Morcaine ranked behind the queen when she could claim the crown if the king died. Although he had taken a seat at the lower table, two diners separated us.

The nearer of these, thinking that I was looking at him, congratulated me on my victory.

I thanked him, calling him "My Lord," at which my page whispered urgently, *"Your Grace!"*

The duke in question ignored the page and my mistake, saying, "I'd like to know, Sir Able, how Her Majesty found a knight bold enough to stand against those you faced."

I replied, "There must be many in Celidon, Your Grace."

"I'm surprised she could find one. We'll have need of you when the Caan attacks."

I raised my eyebrows. "You expect war, Your Grace?"

"Yes, it's how one acquires the reputation for prophecy. Look wise, predict war, and you'll always be right. You're one of Marder's?"

"Yes, Your Grace. I have that honor."

"I'll ask about you when I see him. I'll be—"

The trumpets sounded. We rose, and those not facing the entrance turned to it. Arnthor came first, tall, erect, and walking fast, while the pursuivant who had assisted the Nykr King of Arms announced his name and titles: *"His Most Royal Majesty King Arnthor, Defender of the West,"* and so on. Gaynor followed. She was of course much smaller, but lovely in a white velvet gown and a crown of diamonds and red gold. Two pages bore her train.

"Her Most Royal Majesty Queen Gaynor, Duchess of Daunte, Countess of Chaus, Countess of . . ." A place I have forgotten, with a dozen baronies.

After Gaynor's lush beauty, Morcaine seemed mannish, as tall as her brother and richly dressed in black and scarlet, with a single page to carry her train.

"Her Royal Highness Princess Morcaine, Daughter of Uthor, Duchess of Ringwood . . ."

She smiled at me, the only one who did; I smiled in return, although I could not be sure she meant well.

And all this time I searched my mind for the message I had been given. Arnthor had spoken to me in the bailey, but no message had come. Here in his hall, I saw his face and he mine, but no message filled me. I searched, but found only the loving thoughts of Cloud, who waited patiently in the stables and assured me she was royally cared for and the object of much admiring attention from the king's grooms.

Arnthor took his place, sitting at once. Gaynor stood on his right; I thought her nervous and anxious. To my left, redolent of brandy, Morcaine came to the table as one who owned not only Thortower but all Mythgarthr, and stood there swaying, smiling as if she expected her brother's guests to cheer. He was indeed a king; but Morcaine was of the blood of kings. That thought was soon followed by another—that if she, more than he, showed the blood of their royal parent, then the blood he showed was that of a dragon of Muspel.

Garsecg, the brother of both, had been royal in manner, yet a dragon still. If there was anyone in Arnthor's hall who might breathe fire, it was surely Arnthor himself.

For a minute and more we remained standing. At last Arnthor made a trifling gesture, and we sat.

Food was brought at once, so quickly that it was clear the servingmen had been waiting at the lesser entrances. A chef put a great roast swan on our table, and at a signal from Arnthor split it with a knife not much smaller than a sword. Split, it could be seen that a goose had been stuffed into the swan to be roasted with it, a plover into the goose, a duck into the plover, and three lesser birds into the duck, all these save the swan having been boned.

The chef indicated the two smallest (I would imagine a quail and a thrush) to Arnthor, who nodded. The chef swiftly cut a bit from each, which he ate. Arnthor nodded again, and the birds were served him.

Gaynor was next, the chef indicating the lesser bird in the duck. She shook her head, and received the duck's breast instead. Morcaine declined all. I indicated the one Gaynor had declined, wishing to see what it was and wishing also to show that although she might fear poison, I was willing to run the risk for her sake. My bird proved to be a partridge, delicious and wholly innocent.

The chef having gone, Arnthor severed a leg of the swan with his own dagger, and held it up. "Here it is our custom to dine with our dogs in attendance," he said to me. "You know this, plainly, since you brought your own."

I nodded. "I was told that I might do so without offense, Your Majesty. I hope I was not misinformed."

"Not at all." He smiled. "You'll have seen my hounds."

"I did, Your Majesty. They're noble animals."

"They are." He whistled, and half a dozen boarhounds came to his chair, bristling and growling at Gylf. "Noble not just in appearance, but in conduct. I hunt boars, Sir

Able, and greater prey, when I can get it. Those who hang back are drowned at my order."

I said, "The chase is the noblest sport, Your Majesty."

"I'd have said war, and many here the melee. But it's a topic on which each man is entitled to his opinion."

Gaynor, who had looked frightened the whole time, had gone white. I would very much have liked to know whether Morcaine was still smiling, but dared not turn my head.

"Does your dog hunger, Sir Able?"

"I suppose he does, Your Majesty. He's usually hungry, in my experience."

Again, Arnthor held up the swan's leg. "You would not object if I were to present him with this? Some men, I know, do not like for others to feed their dogs."

"It would be an honor for him, and for me."

"As you say." Smiling, Arnthor tossed the swan's leg to Gylf, who caught it expertly in his mouth. The boarhounds swarmed him, snarling and snapping. He dropped it, set his forepaw on it, and roared to shake the hangings. Arnthor's boarhounds turned tail and ran. In the following silence, there was no sound save the breaking of the swan's bones.

I ate, and had half finished my partridge when Morcaine laughed. "They breed them tough in Jotunland, don't they?" At her words the king's guests began to eat and talk.

I said, "Perhaps they do, Your Highness."

"Didn't you get him there?"

"No, Your Highness. In the forests of our own Celidon. He was a gift from the Bodachan."

Her face became that of her brother, I cannot say how. I was not conscious of having turned, yet it was to him I spoke. "You see, I bear tidings from Queen Disiri of the Moss Aelf, King Ycer of the Ice Aelf, and King Brunman of the Bodachan. So it was that the Bodachan gave me a companion to help me in my errand."

"I've heard of no message until now," Arnthor said.

"Still I have one, Your Majesty. One that has occupied me most of my life, though it has been not so many years in Mythgarthr. I was to reach you, and not that alone, but to come as one to whom you would give ear. Seven worlds there are, Your Majesty, and so arranged that the highest, where the Most High God reigns and where no impure thing is, is larger than all the rest together. The world beneath that—"

"What? Have you come to lecture me in metaphysic?"

"Is less, yet greater than the sum of those remaining. The winged beings there are not perfect in purity, but so near it they are permitted to serve the Most High God as the nobles of your realm serve you."

"Better, I hope."

"Below is the one we name Skai. We of Mythgarthr, who think this realm spacious, think it unutterably vast, for its extent is greater than that of the four below it laid side by side. It contains many things and many peoples, but its lawful possessors are the Overcyns—the Valfather and his queen, their sons and their daughters, and their families. To them our hearts are given. It is them we reverence when we reverence rightly."

"I had a mind to question you concerning your victory today," Arnthor told me.

"Beneath them is our human realm. We are its legitimate inhabitants. Beneath us is the lesser realm of Aelfrice, smaller than our own yet beautiful. There dwell Queen Disiri and the kings whom I named, the monarchs whose messenger I am. In their realm the Most High God placed a numerous folk called Kulili. As we reverence the Overcyns, so Kulili was to reverence us, and did, and was revered by the dragons of Muspel. Kulili sought nearer subjects, and patterned them after us, the objects of her reverence, that she might be loved by the image she loved. She made them, and asked their gratitude. They refused it, and drove her into the sea."

By this time the whole royal hall had fallen silent to listen. Only Arnthor seemed of a mind to interrupt.

"In this way they became the folk of Aelfrice, holding it by right of conquest. The wisest among them revere us, knowing it to be the wish of Him Who Made Seven Worlds, the Most High God. The foolish, seeing our vanity, our avarice, and our cruelty, have turned from us to reverence dragons, by which much harm has come, for even the best of them are insatiable of power."

"You bear a dragon upon your shield," Arnthor remarked. "Have you forgotten that my genealogy bears another?"

"No, Your Majesty. Neither have I forgotten that your boyhood was spent among Sea Aelf, nor that you took the Nykr to honor them. Nor have the kings and queen I mentioned forgotten those things, which embolden them to speak to you as they do, imploring you to reshape our people. Kulili formed them, Your Majesty. They know that you might reform us, making us strong but merciful, and though merciful, just. May I speak for myself, Your Majesty?"

He nodded. "After what has preceded it, I welcome it."

"I lived in the northern forests, Your Majesty, not far from Irringsmouth. It is a city of ruins."

He nodded again.

"Outlaws calling themselves Free Companies rove those forests. They are as cruel and rapacious as the dragons; yet many cheer them because they rob your tax gatherers and try at times to protect the people from the Angrborn. Let those people have companies that are truly free, Your Majesty, and not outlaws. Teach them to arm themselves and choose knights from their number. Your tax gatherers come seldom; but when they come, they take all, for your people there are poor and few. Let them pay a fixed tribute instead, one not ruinous. Help and protect them, and you will find them richer and more numerous each year, and strong friends to your throne. Queen Disiri, and the kings who send me—"

"Have no claim upon your allegiance," Arnthor said. "I do. Are betrayal and sedition the reforms you would have me encourage?"

"No, never." His eyes told me I had failed, but I made a last effort. "The King of Skai rules as a father, Your Majesty, and because he does we name him the Valfather and count it honor to serve him even when defeat is sure. The Aelf ask that of you."

Arnthor held out his hand. "Take off your sword belt, Sir Able. Surrender belt, sword, and all to your king."

I heard Gaynor gasp but did as I had been told.

"Your spurs you may keep." He called two knights, and told them where they were to take me. Although they guarded me with drawn swords, they had no need of them.

"No royal banquet here," said the first of the knights who had escorted me to the dungeon. He sheathed his sword and offered me his hand. "I'm Sir Manasen."

The other gave me his hand as well.

A gaoler came up as we were talking, and Manasen told him he had to put me in a cell at the king's order but that he was not to mistreat me, adding that he would send a servant with food, blankets, and clean straw.

After that I was locked in a cell with walls of living rock, reeking, narrow, and very dark; and left alone there, I suppose, for eight hours. I entertained myself during that time by repeating those parts of my message I had succeeded in delivering, considering those that I had not, and trying to imagine how I might have spoken more skillfully.

Mercifully I was interrupted by the arrival of Manasen's servingman, with food, a great bundle of clean straw, and a jug of wine. After he delivered them, he argued with the gaoler, demanding that I be given a cell with a window.

This the gaoler adamantly refused, insisting that such cells were reserved for prisoners of noble birth.

I heard them with little attention, although with enough to resolve that I would obtain such a cell for myself as soon as I could. I had not eaten much at the king's table, and by that time was ravenous. The food Manasen had sent to me was simple—roast beef, bread, a slab of cheese, and an apple—but it was good and plentiful, and I devoured every scrap.

I was gnawing the core of the apple when the serving-man left and the gaoler came in. He was a burly man armed with an iron key not much shorter than my shin, but I knew I could overpower him if I wanted. He sat without being invited, put his key and his lantern on the floor beside him, and asked if he could have some wine. I poured him a good round tumbler.

"They think pretty well of you up there."

"Sir Manasen and Sir Erac spoke kindly to me, at least."

"It's good to have friends when you're down here." This was said with heavy significance.

I nodded. "It's good to have friends everywhere. I had many good friends in Jotunland and a good many more in Skai."

He passed over Skai without a thought. "The ice lands? Was you really there?"

"This winter. Believe me, I was glad to get out."

"Is everything big up there? Big cows and all?"

"No," I said, "only the people, and not all of them, because the Angrborn have human slaves. There's a dungeon under Utgard. I was never a prisoner there, but I went to look at it. I don't know how big your dungeon is here, but I'd assume it was bigger, since the prisoners were Angrborn. It was certainly worse than this has been up 'til now."

He gulped my wine. "I'd like to see it."

"Perhaps someday you will. It was a terrible place, as I

said, but there were few prisoners in it. I was told that King Gilling had generally executed those who opposed him."

The gaoler shook his head. "Not like that with us, only we're not full up, neither."

"Some of your cells have windows. I'd like one."

His manner stiffened at once. "We can't do that, sir. Just noble prisoners."

"I'm a knight."

"I know. It ain't enough."

"I would be willing to pay a modest rent."

"We was goin' to talk about that, soon as I'd finished this wine." He did, emptying the tumbler.

I poured what remained in the jug into it.

"You see, some's treated one way, some another. You take my meaning, I know. Now you, you got friends. When he come with straw and what you et, I never made no objection, you'll notice. I let him in nice as could be, didn't I?"

"Certainly, and I appreciate it."

"I knew you would. You're a knight and a gentleman, as anybody can see. Only I didn't have to. I coulda kept him out. I coulda said you get a order from the Earl Marshal, and we'll see. His master might have got such in a day or two, but if he'd told his lackey to, it'd been never."

I nodded.

"I'm a kindly man, but a poor man too. A poor man, sir, can't be kindly for free."

His lantern, as I ought to have said earlier, shone out through my door, which stood open behind him, casting yellow light on the wall opposite. For an instant something large, dark, and very quiet obscured that wall and was gone.

I asked how much his kindness cost.

"Only one scield a month, sir. That's not much, now is it, sir? For one scield—silver, mind—at the full of the moon, you'd find me kind, and helpful too, sir. Only I can't give you one with a window. Not for that nor more, sir. It's the Earl Marshal. He won't allow it."

"Yes he will. Does he come down here often?"

"Every fortnight, sir, and makes sure all's right."

"That should be sufficient. The moon is full now, isn't it? I believe I noticed a full moon the other night."

The gaoler licked his lips. "Yes, sir. It is."

"Then my first month's payment must be due."

"Yes, sir. Always, sir. Or I count from the dark of it, sir, or the quarter-full, or whatever."

"I understand." I nodded. "There's twenty-four scields in a scepter, I believe?"

"Course there are." He licked his lips again.

"Are you a man of your word? A man of honor?"

"Yes, sir. I try to be, sir."

"That's all any of us can say. I'm Sir Able—you know that. May I ask your own name?"

"Fiach, sir. At your service."

I got out one of the big gold coins of Jotunland. "This holds more gold than a scepter. Since I don't know how much, I'm going to call it twenty-four scields. Will you agree?"

"Not 'til I see it, sir."

I handed it to him. He polished it on his sleeve, held it so his lantern made the gold glow, bit it, and gave it back. "Seems right enough, sir. I'll try and get 'em."

I shook my head. "I'm going to offer you a bargain. You sell kindness at a scield a month, so this would buy two years' worth. More, but we've agreed on two years. I'll give you this for your kindness as long as I'm in here. For three years or five. But if I'm released in a week, you'll owe me nothing. The gold will be yours and we'll part as friends."

He shook his head.

"Why not?"

"We don't do like that."

I suppose I sighed. "You and the other gaolers?"

He rose, picking up his key and his lantern. "You don't understand how it is. You give me a scield."

"I haven't got one. I left small payments to my squire. He'll give you one if you'll let him in to see me."

He grunted, started to leave, and turned again. "Give me that, an' I'll fetch you the scields, like I said."

I shook my head.

"You think your friends'll stand by you. I know how that is. They'll come awhile. Then they won't come no more and we'll have it all." With his big iron key, he pointed to the burse at my belt.

I was tempted to say I would escape before any such thing happened. Perhaps I should have.

"You lick those dishes, sir, 'cause that's the last good food you're goin' to see for years."

I said nothing.

"You give me that, and I'll take it to a moneymonger. If he says it's good, you'll get twenty back. And kindness."

He paused, but I did not speak; and at length he said, "It'll be ours before the year's out, and I won't waste any more breath on you."

The door of bars crashed shut behind him, and I watched him twist his big key in the lock. I was of half a mind to call out to Org to spare him, and of half a mind to call out that he might have him; in the end, I did neither.

I heard Fiach walk away, six steps maybe, or seven; after those, the cracking of his bones.

When I judged Org's meal over, I got him to unlock my door and hide the key and went out to explore my dungeon.

CHAPTER THIRTY-FOUR
MY NEW SWORD

I slept in my cell that night, and wished (if the truth be told) that I had some means of locking it from inside. I was back on the *Western Trader*. (This was not the first time that dream had recurred since my return from Skai.) I saw the vicious, famished faces of the Osterlings and knew they meant to land on Glas and that my mother was there. I went to the captain and ordered him to put about; he did not hear or see me, and when I knocked the hourglass from his table, it returned of its own accord.

I woke shivering to find myself in the dungeon. Having no wish to sleep again until the dream lost its grip, I went looking for blankets.

At Sheerwall it was hard to get into the dungeon without going out into the bailey. It was different at Thortower; earlier I had found a stair leading to a barred door of thick oak. Now I climbed that stair again, took down the bar, and stepped into the castle kitchen, where a score of cooks and scullions snored on pallets. Clearly, the prisoners' rations were prepared here and carried down. I blew out my lantern, set it on a step, and shut the door as quietly as I could. A potboy woke and stared at me. I put a finger to my lips, and told him to go back to sleep; he nodded and slept, or at least pretended to. What he may have thought of a knight prowling the kitchen after midnight, I cannot imagine.

Beyond the kitchen was a hallway, by no means cramped, leading into the great banqueting hall in which I had sat with Arnthor, Gaynor, and Morcaine. It made me curious about the entrance they had used; I found it, and in it a mirror, the largest I saw in Mythgarthr. Here (I suppose) the king, the queen, and the princess checked their appearance before making their entrances.

It gave me an idea, and I filched a lump of hard soap from the kitchen, whittled a soap-pencil, and wrote on the mirror, "Your thoughts—our lives," first in the character of Aelfrice, and up and down the sides in the runes of Skai. Returning to my cell with stolen blankets, I slept again; and if dreams haunted my sleep, they were the merciful sort.

Underground as I was, I had no way of marking the rising of the sun; but I heard new gaolers come, and heard them call and search for Fiach, and judged that it was morning. I rose and asked one for warm water and a towel. He hesitated but at last refused.

"In that case, I'll get them for myself," I said.

He laughed and hurried off to rejoin the search; when he was well away I went to the gaolers' room, drew water from their cistern, warmed it on their fire, and carried it to one of the cells reserved for nobility. The gaoler's room had yielded a clean tunic I used as a towel; I washed with these and with the soap that had served me for a pencil, returned to my old cell, and carried my clean straw to my new one.

My window was small and high. Yet what a difference it made! Fresh air and winter sunshine found their way in; and although it was cold, the whole dungeon was as cold if not colder. Wrapped in a blanket, I was not uncomfortable.

Furthermore, I could see out by standing upon the basin. There was little to see but frozen, snow-covered mud and an occasional pig, but I watched these with some interest.

Aside from Manasen's servant, Uri was my first visitor. I called and she responded at once, standing very straight and meeting my gaze with frightened eyes. "You might be with Queen Disiri, Lord. Shall I guide you?"

I shrugged. "Equally, Queen Disiri might be with me."

"She is a queen, Lord."

"And I'm just an ordinary kid from America."

She looked more frightened than ever. "You are a knight, Lord. A knight of Mythgarthr."

"More than that. I am one of the Valfather's knights."

"I know n-nothing of that, Lord. As you say."

"I thought that when I had delivered her message to King Arnthor, Disiri would come for me. I lay in my cell waiting for her, and I hoped to see her this morning. I washed, and dressed, all in the hope she'd come."

"Y-yes, Lord."

"Is there unrest in Aelfrice that might detain her? The rise of another like Setr?"

"I know of none, Lord."

"I embraced her when I was at Redhall. It can't have been long in the time of Aelfrice, a day or two at most."

"Less, Lord. Come with me to Aelfrice, and we will see. I fear the queen but you will protect me, I know."

I shook my head. "We played together as children, Uri. Disiri and me. I remember now."

Her voice was tender. "Do you, Lord?"

"I do." Until that moment I had not known I remembered. "I thought they wiped those memories away, Uri, but they only hid them under the message. She had a palace, and big trees were its towers. Her garden lay around them, a garden of wildflowers, mosses, little springs, and rivulets. I was stronger than she was, but I was careful to take no advantage of it, and she punished me when she was displeased, striking me with her little hand." I laughed at the memory. "It was like being kicked by a bunny, but if I giggled she'd threaten me with her guards, Mossmen with swords who watched over us. They'd have killed me if she ordered it, but she never did."

"You will not ask me to carry a message to her, will you, Lord? Baki could do it. They would not harm her."

"I drank Baki's blood once."

"I r-remember, L-Lord."

"She said it would heal me, Uri, and it did. How would my life had been different if I hadn't drunk Baki's blood?"

"I cannot say, Lord. These questions—you are wiser than I. If you called me to trouble me with questions, I must endure it. But is there no other way I can serve you?"

I told her then that I was concerned for Cloud and Gylf. I asked her to find them, to free them if they desired it, and report back when she had done it.

My next visitor came so soon after Uri had gone that I wondered whether Uri had not fetched her. It was Morcaine, but she did not appear from the shadows as at Redhall; she came as any other might, save that she was accompanied by men-at-arms. These were not dead, but hard-featured axmen in brigandines and helmets who feared her as much as the gaolers feared them.

She sent five to each end of the corridor, so neither they nor the gaolers could hear us. "This was none of my doing, Sir Able. No revenge of mine."

I said I had never supposed it was.

"You refused me at Redhall. I've offered love to few men. Only two have declined." She laughed; it was beautiful and empty. "Can you guess the other? Answer, clerk!"

"No, Your Highness."

"You're a miserable liar. He was much better. Do you imagine that resentment smolders and flares within this fair bosom?" She pressed her hand to her stomach.

From her breath and her flushed cheeks, it was brandy that smoldered and flared there. I said, "Your Highness is too good a woman for that."

"You've no notion." She paused. "You might overpower me, ravish me, and escape in my clothes. We're of a height."

"I would never do such a thing, Your Highness."

"You'd rape a peasant girl—you all do it. What's the difference? It might save your life."

"No, Your Highness."

"I'd have to lace you up in back, but I would if the ravishing went well. I've been told that many men fantasize about lying with a woman of royal blood."

"As do I, Your Highness, though you are not the woman."

Morcaine laughed. "Neither is she. You'll find out."

Not wishing to contradict her, I bowed.

"I'll have you yet. You'll see. When I've finished with you, you'll crawl, begging me to take you back." Her eyes shone. "Then I'll remind you of this. I'll make you bring me the head of the Man in the Moon, and when you do, I'll refuse it and mock you."

She took my chin in her right hand. "Unless the Aelf try to feed me to another dragon, the little sons of worms. Then I'll scream oh-so-prettily, and you'll kill him for me and die again. You're dead, you know."

Although she still held my chin, I managed to nod.

"That Valkyrie's kiss did it. Did you know that? It's an act of mercy. They don't take you unless you're too badly hurt to live. And now—" Quite suddenly she kissed me, wrapping me in her long arms, her tongue gliding through my mouth and halfway down my throat. I fell to the straw, and she said, "Now you know how we feel."

I managed to say that I did not think I was capable of making any woman feel the way I felt then.

"Stand up!" She motioned imperiously for me to rise. "I'm going to ask my brother to free you. That's one of the things I came to tell you. I doubt he will. He doesn't like being told what a twisted little scoundrel he is, especially by the Aelf. The Aelf were our nurses—but you know that."

I was getting to my feet; she crouched beside me, surprising me again. "He caught little fish and killed them in ugly ways. Sometimes I helped him. They punished us for it, and he's never forgiven them. You dead obey me, Able. I bring you all to heel, even you difficult cases."

"I'm eager to obey, Your Highness."

"But I doubt that he'll free you, even for me." She warmed my hand between her own, and seemed to want me to thrust it between her breasts, though I did not. "You may have to wait 'til I'm queen. You'll be grateful then. Very grateful, because this is a terrible place and I'll make you mine, and lie with you 'til no part of you can stand, and cast you away, and send you after the phoenix's egg. You'll bring it, and beg and crawl." She belched. "And crawl, and beg, and in the end I'll take you back and we'll go where nobody knows us, young lovers forever."

I said, "You are kind at heart, Your Highness. I think I've always known that."

She nodded solemnly. "I'm a good woman, Sir Able. Fortunately everybody else is evil, so I get to treat them any way I want. It makes it much more fun. Help me up."

I stood and helped her rise; I do not think she could have without my help.

"I thought you'd like to know how all this is going to work out," she said, "so now you do. Brush off my bottom, I think I got straw on it."

I pretended to.

"Harder, and say I've been a bad girl."

Shortly after that she left, walking so well I might have thought her almost sober if I had not been aware of the effort she was putting into it.

One of my gaolers came in, bringing a basin of warm water, soap, and a towel. I laughed and told him to take them away. He did, locking my cell door behind him.

Hours passed. All the things I thought of then have filled this book, and might fill a dozen more.

At last two gaolers appeared. Addressing me through the

bars as "My Lord," they asked whether I knew what had become of Fiach, describing him. They had found boots as well as torn and bloody clothes; and although they were not sure they had been his, they were afraid they had been.

"Fiach refused to let me occupy this cell," I told them. "That's all you need to know. It is enough for you. Now leave me in peace and do your jobs." I had been on the point of calling for Uri when they had come to my door.

They begged and flattered, and at last threatened. No doubt I should have smoothed things over, but I was half nuts with inactivity and told them what I thought of them.

They left, but came back not long after with a third gaoler, opened my door, and came at me with their keys. The roar of the waves filled my ears. I knocked the first one into the two behind him before he could strike, wrenched his key away, and broke the shoulder of the second and the head of the third with two blows.

It had ended almost before it begun. (They must have felt they had lost before they had begun to fight.) The two who were still conscious prostrated themselves. I put my foot upon their necks and made each declare himself my slave forever—at which point Uri appeared, laughing, to remind me that she and Baki been forced to swear the same way. She wore no disguise, but was a Fire Aelf plainly, with floating hair like flames, fiery yellow eyes, and skin like copper in a crucible. I doubt that the gaolers heard a word she said; but her appearance, with a slender sword in one hand and its jeweled scabbard in the other, reduced them to gibbering.

"I'm keeping this key," I told them. "Since our king has seen fit to imprison me, I'll stay in this cell when I've no reason to leave it. I expect you to serve me loyally and faithfully, and I promise that your first lapse will be your last. Now pick him up," I used my key to point to their unconscious buddy, "and get him out of here."

It was easy for me to say that, but not easy for them to do it. He was a big, heavy man, and the one whose shoulder I had broken could not help the other much. I wanted to talk to Uri; so after watching the efforts of the one whose key I had taken for a minute, I picked up the unconscious one and carried him to the gaoler's room.

"I brought you a new sword," Uri said as we were walking back to my cell, "and you have not even looked at it."

I explained that I was a prisoner and was not supposed to have a sword.

"You can hide it under your bed."

"I don't have one. I sleep on straw, on the floor."

"But you could get one. Those men you beat will bring you one as soon as you tell them to. We could sleep in it, and you would have something to sit on."

I flexed the blade deeply between my hands; it sprang back straight and true.

"Do not cut yourself."

"I'm trying not to. Is this your work?"

"Mine personally? No. How about the bed?"

"I'll think about it, but you won't be welcome to sleep in it. I know what I'd wake up to."

She giggled, and I felt a sudden yearning for Aelfrice, for its crystal sea and the silent forest in which Disiri and I had run and shouted and tamed young squirrels.

There was no room to swing such a sword in my cell. I stopped outside the door, making cuts in air and thrusting between the bars. Its hilt of silver and snowy leather was simple, even chaste, its narrow blade written over in the character of Aelfrice with words too small and dim to read.

"I think it Ice Aelf work," Uri said. "It is old, no matter who made it, and I did not get it there."

"You stole it here?"

She looked at me sidelong. "I do not have to steal everything. You have seen this." She smoked, and in a few seconds she was smaller and not quite so slender, and her glowing copper skin had faded to white and peach, although her nipples stayed bright and looked too hot to touch.

"I have," I said, "and resisted temptation. Are you saying you sold yourself for this? I don't believe it."

"All right, I stole it." She held out the jeweled scabbard. "I refuse to tell from whom. You would make me take it back."

"If I could make you take it back, I could make you tell me where you got it."

"Please do not, Lord. Listen. The man who owned it will never know it has gone. Never, I promise you. He had locked it in an iron chest bound with seven chains and seven big padlocks. Do you believe that?"

"No," I said.

"Then you certainly will not believe he threw the keys into the sea, but that's what my friend told me. I reached up from Aelfrice—you know how we do—and pulled it down. He will think it is still in there until the day he dies."

I took the scabbard from her and examined it. I had expected turquoise, amber, and that sort of thing; but there were fine rubies, and the blue stones were sapphires.

"Soft wood, Lord, with thin gold over it."

I nodded and added, "And a white gold throat. Gold and silver mixed, I suppose. It's the only part that comes near to matching the sword." I sheathed it. "Though it fits well enough."

"The scabbard is your human work, I feel sure. You have better taste than we do."

I looked around at her. "I've never thought so."

"Neither have I, Lord, but you are above us."

"I no longer have a sword belt," I said, largely to myself, "the king took it."

"You can push it through that belt you are wearing now. It is not a heavy blade."

"I suppose so."

"Besides, I thought you would hide it in our bed. I mean, when you and Her Highness were not using it."

"You've been spying on me."

Uri grinned. "Only the tiniest bit. She is not bad looking for such a big woman, is she? A powerful sorceress, too. There could be a dozen pleasant surprises."

I went into my cell, shutting the door before Uri could follow; she slipped between the bars in her proper shape. "Unpleasant ones, too. Some sorceresses have teeth down here. You stick it in and they bite it off. Mani told me."

I hid the sword under my straw next to the wall. "You wouldn't know anything about that."

"About sorceresses? Why no, Lord. Or very little, though I talked with Mani about them once."

I sat and motioned for her to sit. "Morcaine and her brothers were reared in Aelfrice when their mother abandoned them. I'd think you'd know a lot."

"I do not. Shall I tell you what I know, Lord? I will not lie or make fun of you unless you interrupt."

I nodded.

"Whoever told you that deceived you. I was a Khimaira, but I have heard things, and know what makes sense. Their mother did not abandon all three. Setr was a dragon, so why should she? She kept him by her in Muspel, in Aelfrice, and here in Mythgarthr. He was her firstborn, and so the right king of this part of Mythgarthr, though I do not believe he tried to claim it."

I said, "I suppose Morcaine must be the youngest."

Uri shook her head. "Arnthor is, but males claim the throne first in this Celidon. Now stop interrupting."

She took a deep breath. "Second, Morcaine and Arnthor must have spent most of their childhood here. Otherwise they would still be children. And third, the Sea Aelf raised them, not my clan. We were Setr's slaves, remember? Loyal slaves, because we were terribly afraid. They were allies, or at least more nearly allies than we ever were."

"I understand. Is there anything else?"

"Yes. You will distrust it, but I will say it just the same. Is King Arnthor afraid of his sister?"

I shrugged. "He doesn't confide in me. Were you watching when I fought Morcaine's dead knights?"

"No. But I would like to have seen it, Lord."

"Nearly everybody fled. The spectators, I mean. But King Arnthor remained, and the queen, I think because Arnthor had her arm. And Morcaine herself, of course."

"Did he look frightened?"

I cast my mind back. "No. Resolute, if anything."

"Uh huh. You probably will not know this, either, Lord, but I must try. Is she afraid of him?"

"Yes, she is. Very much so." I paused, remembering. "It may be why she drinks. She loves him, but she's terribly frightened of him."

"In that case he is a sorcerer, Lord, a most dangerous one. You may trust me, though you will not. An older sister with magic at her command? She would jerk him about like a puppet if he were not. Setr had magic, a great deal of it."

I nodded agreement.

"So does Morcaine, from what I have heard, and you confirm it. Why should you think the youngest has none?"

"I shouldn't, I suppose. Here's another question. You stole that sword for me. A good one, made by Aelf long ago. Could you have gotten my own sword, Eterne, as easily?"

Uri shook her head. "I could not find it, Lord."

"The king took it."

"I know. Gylf told me. The king must have hidden it somewhere." She sifted straw between her fingers.

"You couldn't find it."

"No, Lord."

I reached out and touched her knee, I cannot say why. "That is a lie, Uri. You found it, but dared not take it. I'm glad you didn't. Arnthor's wrong, but Arnthor's my king. You've talked to Gylf. Where is he?"

"I do not know, Lord, though I can probably find him without much trouble. They had chained him up. I freed him, as you ordered."

I nodded. "He's gone into the wild, I suppose. What about Cloud?"

"She is in the stable, Lord, and well seen to. I told her you might soon be free, and she will wait for you."

"Have they tried to ride her?"

"Yes, Lord. Several of the grooms, without success."

"She may be in danger."

"There is a fat old nobleman who is interested in her, Lord. The grooms fear him. They dare not mistreat her."

"Have you seen Baki?"

"Lately? No, Lord."

I questioned her at length, but learned nothing more. If Cloud or Gylf had seen Baki, they had not mentioned it.

CHAPTER THIRTY-FIVE

DOWN

Time passed, until there came a day of excitement outside my little window, of men shouting and cursing, and horses and mules blowing and stamping.

Then silence.

I spoke to my gaolers, and the one called Ged told me Arnthor was to lead an army against the Osterlings. He was taking the other gaolers with him to look after prisoners, and Ged alone would be in charge of the dungeon.

"I wouldn't expect you to help, My Lord, but it's going to be a lot of work."

"You're right," I told him, "I won't help you with that. But perhaps we can find help for you just the same."

We began with the two barons whose cells were in the same corridor as my own. I introduced myself, which I had not done previously, explained that no menial work would be required of them, and offered to free them from their cells to supervise other prisoners if they would pledge themselves not to escape. Both agreed.

After that, we enlisted ten commoners, choosing the healthiest and strongest. We promised them clean straw, blankets, and better food; but when I got better acquainted with the misery the rest suffered, I gave them all those things. Their old straw, crawling with lice, we burned in the courtyard one night. One had been a barber; I stole a razor for him, scissors, and other things. He cut and shaved their heads and beards, and we burned the hair, too.

Wistan came, bringing my helmet and mail. "I'm sorry, Sir Able. They wouldn't let me in before, only Lord Colle did today. Is he really a lord?"

I said he was, and explained.

"Pouk and Uns are working or they would have come, too. They're terribly concerned about you. So was I. I— we don't really have to work. We've got some money."

I asked what they were doing, and Wistan said he was helping the Earl Marshal's clerks, while Pouk and Uns were working on a wall being built around the city.

Two men-at-arms were my next visitors, if they can be called that. They had come, they said, "To take me to the queens," from which I assumed that Gaynor and Morcaine were jointly charged with governing Kingsdoom. I was corrected, and told that there were Frost Giants in the city, huge women who frightened the good burghers.

Gaynor and Idnn received me in the throne room. I knelt and was allowed by both to rise. Gaynor spoke. "You were my champion, Sir Able. Are you my champion still?"

I said I would be if I could.

"You must think I abandoned you. So I did, because my husband ordered it. He ordered me not to free you while he was away as well."

"I understand, Your Majesty."

"Do you also understand why he gave that order?"

"I think so, Your Majesty."

"That is why I am seeing you like this." She waved at her courtiers: women and old men. "These are my witnesses. I believe you know Lord Escan?"

"I have that honor."

"He will speak on my behalf, my royal sister on her own behalf. You will be under guard the entire time, and will die if you try to escape." She made a small, futile gesture and cooed, "I hope it won't be necessary. I really do."

"If my escape would displease Your Majesty, I shall not escape," I said.

Idnn rose. "Come with me, in that case. Lord Escan?"

We spoke in the Red Room, a room of business that held a writing desk and a worktable, with a dozen or more bureaus for documents. An armchair with a footrest, prettily made, was carried in for Idnn; the Earl Marshal sat in the big oak chair that had been before the writing desk, and I on one of the clerk's stools.

"You should be free this moment," Idnn declared. "The way things are, it was all I could do to get my sister queen to order you brought up here. It's a—it's the worst sort of luck that you're a prisoner."

"For him it is," the Earl Marshal agreed, "for us it is good fortune. I thank Skai for it."

"I've seen him fight, My Lord, as you have not."

"I fled the sight, Your Majesty. Harrumph! He may help us now because he's not free. If he'd never been imprisoned, he'd be with the king and we wouldn't have him."

"I'll free you," Idnn promised me. "I'll contrive some slight. My sister queen is not unwilling."

"But fearful," the Earl Marshal added. "At the moment, however, we require your brains, not your sword. Her Present Majesty has persuaded Queen Gaynor—and me—that we ought to consult you. She was much impressed by you in Jotunland."

I said that I was honored, and meant it.

"Are you hungry? Lord Escan will order food for you if you wish it, I'm sure."

Thanking her, I declared that I was not.

"He's well fed, Your Majesty. He's the monarch of the dungeon, and gets whatever he wants. I've had to forgo my usual inspections, so I may say I saw nothing amiss. Perhaps Your Majesty would enjoy dainty fare while we confer?"

He rang, told Payn what he wanted, and turned to me. "I don't know how much you know of our situation, Sir Able. His Majesty is in the east with the army. Were you aware of it?"

I said I knew he had marched away, but no more.

"We raided them this fall, slew their Caans and gained much plunder. Now the Black Caan will have vengeance, if he can." The Earl Marshal smiled. "Every knight fit to ride has gone off with the king, and most of the nobility. His Majesty left Her Majesty in titular charge of his realm. I am her chief advisor. I am to supply remounts to his army, and fresh troops as they can be raised, and do a dozen other things. Among them, I'm to fortify this city."

Idnn said, "For centuries, Kingsdoom has boasted that the shields of its knights were its walls. Now the east is stronger than ever, and hungrier. The king sent my father to pacify the Angrborn so he might march into Osterland with his full strength. Surprise and a crushing defeat would leave the old Caan's plans in ruins—or so it was hoped."

The Earl Marshal nodded.

"The surprise was achieved as planned," Idnn continued, "the crushing defeat inflicted, and the old Caan killed. But Celidon's triumph seems to have united the Osterlings around his last son, the Black Caan, and hastened their attack."

I said, "A hasty attack may fail."

"We hope so. They've taken the passes, and that's bad. My father's gone to join the king. So has Duke Marder."

"Yet we're reinforced with a hundred Daughters of Angr," the Earl Marshal added, "Her Majesty Queen Idnn's bodyguard."

I said, "As long as the weather's cold, that's no small reinforcement."

"Lord Escan engaged men learned in such matters to plan fortifications." Idnn sighed. "They've presented the plan to my dear sister queen. It's an excellent plan, I'm sure, but will take years. You're no builder. I realize that. Do you know anything about siegecraft?"

I shrugged. "I was at the siege of Nastrond."

The Earl Marshal leaned forward, his eyes narrowed. "Where's that? I never heard of it."

Idnn overrode him. "We must have something that can be done in a month or less. If the king triumphs, we can make merry. But battle will be joined before the next new moon, and if he returns with a beaten army, the Osterlings will be at their heels. What can you suggest?"

"Nothing," I said, " 'til I've seen the ground."

The Earl Marshal shook his head. "I have maps."

"They'd mean zip to me. Most likely they'd lead me wrong. I need to ride around the city. A day at least, and two'd be better."

The Earl Marshal wiped his face and his bald head with his hand, but said nothing.

Silence filled the room, a silence none of us seemed willing to break. I rose and examined its crimson hangings, and the bureaus of waxed wood the color of wild roses, and their enameled fittings.

At last Idnn said, "I want to tell you about Lady Linnet and her daughter. May I? We may not get another chance."

I said of course that she might. Payn returned while she was speaking, carrying a tray loaded with dainties, a bottle of wine, and glasses. He filled them, and we ate and drank while we talked.

"She has reclaimed Goldenlawn," Idnn said. "This was

on our way south, of course, and we stayed there with her for a few days to help, all of us. She and Vil intend to rebuild it, and are wed. They— I'm sorry. You *will* win her."

I agreed and asked Idnn to continue.

"He's no nobleman, but what nobleman would have her now? He's Etela's father, too—or they say he is—and he loves her." When I said nothing, Idnn added, "Lynnet's still mad, though not so mad as she was. She talks more at least."

"That's good."

"She thinks there's another woman with her, a woman she calls Mag."

I cannot say how well I controlled my face, though I strove to remain impassive.

"A woman no one else can see." With a smile full of pity, Idnn spoke to the Earl Marshal. "Her husband's blind, so he says that there is, too."

I asked, "Are Berthold and his wife still with you, Your Majesty? I didn't see them in the throne room."

"No, I gave them leave to revisit their village."

"It's been destroyed."

Idnn shrugged. "I didn't know that. Doubtless they'll return quickly in that case."

"Perhaps it's been rebuilt. I wish I could go there and see. Did Bold Berthold believe in Lady Lynnet's friend?"

"Ah, I see." Idnn spoke to the Earl Marshal again. "Berthold is a servingman of mine. He's blind, too."

I said, "But did he say the woman was there?"

"I don't know, I never asked. Perhaps my sister queen could—could accept your parole. I'll urge it."

The Earl Marshal shook his head. "She will not dare."

I escaped that night, although I did not think of it as escaping. Cloud's thought guided me to her, and told me long before I reached her stall that Uns was with her; I woke him, and we soon found him a sturdy cob, saddled, and rode out. After circling the city by moonlight—it took a good three hours—we went to the inn, got Pouk, and ate breakfast.

They went to their work after that, and I went with them. A big ditch was being dug on the land side of the city for the foundation of the wall. Pouk and Uns were diggers, and it was already ten paces wide and so deep that ladders had to be used to carry the hard red clay out. We tied Uns' cob so he could return it to the stable after work, and I began the circuit of the city again, seeing by daylight what I had ridden over a few hours before. I had completed about a third of it when I met a patrol.

We fled, Cloud and me. An arrow struck her neck, and she turned on them, terrible as Gylf. Two died. I was trying to control her when I was knocked from her saddle.

I was taken to a guardroom in Thortower, kept tied up there for three days, robbed, and kicked when I objected. After that I was brought before Gaynor. She was in mortal fear of Arnthor, and ordered that I be chained in a cell on the lowest level of the dungeon.

Strictly speaking, her orders were not obeyed. Neither Ged nor the men-at-arms would go below the twelfth level; nor did they know how many might lie below it, for Thortower had been built upon the ruins of an older structure, and that twelfth level was as wide as Forcetti. A smith was brought, a silent, hard-bitten man who did me no intended hurt but would not speak to me. He puffed his charcoal, put gyves on my wrists and ankles, and welded them shut. Then began my true imprisonment, because I swore that I would make no effort to free myself until Thortower fell or Arnthor triumphed, if triumph was the Valfather's will.

As for him, not one hour passed in which I did not hope he would appear and free me from my oath. At first I felt sure he would, and I planned everything we would do before we returned to Skai—how we would set the whole world right.

Days passed in which I shivered, hour after hour, in the cold, and burrowed in Colle's straw, and at last had Org sit with me, savage and silent in my cell, so I could warm myself from his heat; he hungered, and I gave him leave to kill any man whose name he did not know.

From time to time he went out; and from time to time he returned with bloodied jaws to crouch and warm me as before. Until at length a day came when no one brought me food.

I waited, telling myself that at the next meal they would come again, and that if they did not come, I would call Baki and have her free me. They did not. I called her, and called again until I had called a score of times, and she did not come. And at last I realized that chained as I was she no longer feared me. The service she had entered on the stair of the Tower of Glas was done, and she whose love I had so often refused was free at last. She would live the life of a Fire Aelf now, and give no thought to me, dead in the dungeon of Thortower.

What I would have done then, I cannot say. I might have broken my oath and saved myself. I would like to think I would have come to that in the end. I might have died, as I resolved to; I was not much tormented by thirst in that cold, and hunger had ceased to trouble me.

I might also have asked Org to bring me whatever meat he could find and united myself with the Osterlings, who eat the flesh of their foes, and howled in my madness.

Lights in that utter darkness, and the clank of weapons. I told Org to hide himself, but it was already too late. My cell door opened, and the glare of torches blinded me.

A remembered voice: "By the Lady's crotch . . ."

The king's: "What's that by him?"

I laid my hand on Org's arm. "Something it were better you had not seen, Your Majesty." I choked, for my mouth was dry. "Go back up the steps. Return, and you won't see it."

There was excited talk, to which I paid scant attention. They left, and I told Org I had to have water. He brought a little, warmed in his cupped hand; I drank and sent him out.

The torches and the knights who bore them returned. I stood, fell, and stood again with Beel helping me.

The king looked me in the face, for we were of a height. "I love my queen," he said.

Perhaps I smiled. "And I don't. Your Majesty, I ask no leave to speak freely. Those who ask leave of you do it out of fear of your displeasure or worse. Your displeasure means nothing to me, and any torture you might inflict would be a relief. I speak for Aelfrice and myself. You are a tyrant."

"I love her," Arnthor repeated. "I love Celidon more."

"You treat them the same. You abandoned Aelfrice and taught your folk to. No doubt Queen Gaynor wishes you had abandoned her as well, and Celidon is blessed every moment you neglect her. You're of royal birth. Queen Gaynor is of noble birth, and your knights boast their gentle birth. I'm a plain American, and I'll say this if I die. Your villages are ravaged by outlaws, by Angrborn, and by Osterlings, because they've been abandoned too. The Most High God set men here as models for Aelfrice. We teach it violence, treachery, and little else; and you have been our leader."

He nodded, which astounded me. "You say you're of low birth. Are you not a knight? I let you keep your spurs."

I nodded. "I am."

The knights who had come with him stood silent, though I knew that if the chance came they would kill me. I smelled their torches, and saw in the hard, flat planes of

Arnthor's face, the cold and filthy cell where I had shivered so long and in which I shivered still.

Beel said, "I had hoped to free you, Sir Able."

If Arnthor heard, he gave no sign of it. "You are a knight. A knight of my kingdom?"

"I am."

"You worked wonders in Jotunland, and only wonders will save us."

"Strike off these chains," I told him, "and I'll try."

He spoke, and my chains fell clanking to the floor.

My story has almost ended; before I end it, I want to say that had it not been for Org, whom Arnthor glimpsed in my cell and whose terror was such that even Arnthor retreated, I do not believe he would have freed me.

I was bathed, dressed, and fed. "I'm to send you to His Majesty as soon as you can ride," the Earl Marshal told me. "Meanwhile, I'm to arm you. What would you like?"

"For you to leave. I've my helmet and mail, which our king lets me keep. My sword he lost trying to regain the passes, when the army was overwhelmed."

"Wait," the Earl Marshal told me, and hurried away.

In his absence I plotted against him—against Gaynor and Idnn, too. Plotted, and mocked myself for plotting, for I was too weak to stand.

Days passed in which boys waited on me, pages scarce old enough to hold bows. Once they asked whether the Osterlings would conquer us, and what would become of them if they did; I told them I had no doubt they would, but if they wanted to escape I would take them to the dungeon, where they would be devoured at once. "It would be better for Celidon," I told them, "if it were left to the trees. There's an isle called Glas. There the great dragon Setr put lovely women to lure seaman ashore. The women died, killed by one another or the seamen they tricked. The last took poison, and it's a place of beauty, silence, and clear light. Have you poison?"

Swearing they had none, they fled.

The Earl Marshal returned, bearing the sword Baki had found for me. He was as fat as ever, with fear in his shrewd eyes. "It does me honor," he said, "to give you this." He bowed as he held it out.

I took it and belted it on. "For this," I said, "we'll go to Aelfrice."

He cannot often have been surprised; but he was then, astonishment that showed plainly in his face.

"It won't take long," I promised him, "though time runs slowly there. Come with me."

He would have argued for an hour. I drew the sword he had just given me and pricked him with it, and although he shouted for guards, none came.

"The king has taken every man fit to hold a spear," I told him, "from the castle and the city too. Leaving you."

"Someone must be in charge," he said.

"Why, no. Where's Queen Gaynor, who sentenced me? The boys said she had gone, but they did not know where."

"She's with the king." The Earl Marshal's voice shook. "There's no one left to protect her here."

"Besides," (I urged him forward with my sword) "I'm free again, and he fears I'll lie with her. Move!"

"Where are we going?"

"To Aelfrice as you wished," I said. "To Aelfrice, as I promised. It's down those stairs, and you'll go quicker than your age and weight permit or feel my point."

I took him to the dungeon, discovering in the process that I was more afraid of it than he was. It seemed to close around me like the grave. If the Earl Marshal's face was white, mine was whiter; I kept him moving, so he could not see it.

Dandun had gone; Colle remained, locked in his cell. I freed him, and with his help freed such other prisoners as we could find until we had cleared the twelfth level.

"They don't go down there," Colle said, as the Earl Marshal and I started down. "There's no one there."

"That's not the same thing," I told him, and prodded the Earl Marshal with my sword.

"Please," he said. "I'm twice your age, and there is no railing."

"You're four times my age," I told him, "and there's no railing."

"If I had known the conditions under which you were being held, I would have come to your rescue, believe me."

"Sure you would have. You were careful not to know."

There was a fourteenth level, and a fifteenth below that. After it, I did not count; but we soon stepped out onto a rocky plain where the breeze smelled of the sea.

"There is a draft," the Earl Marshal said. "The dungeon must connect with caverns larger still."

"There's a wind," I told him.

"Didn't Lord Colle come with us?" The Earl Marshal looked behind us. "I thought he was coming, too."

"Only as far as the twelfth level. Walk that way."

"There are no more stairs." He sounded happy. He had been frightened as we descended and descended, and must have thought that having reached bottom we would go up again.

"There must be more stairs." I was speaking mostly to myself, and I prodded him again with my point.

"But there aren't!"

"This is Aelfrice," I explained. "So there are worlds that are lower still, Muspel and Niflheim."

"The realms of fire and ice." He sounded awed.

"You wished to go to Aelfrice," I told him. "You are here. It will soon be day."

We walked on and heard the lapping of waves. "Winds are rare here," I explained, "but there's a breeze at dawn and at twilight, near the sea."

"This is the air that I've longed to breathe," the Earl Marshal said; it seemed to me that he addressed me even less than I had addressed him.

Night was gray as we strolled down the shingle to the water's edge. I sheathed my sword, for I had no more need to prod him.

"Where will the sun rise?" he asked.

I knew he was thinking of the sea of Mythgarthr, in which he must often have seen the sun set. "It won't," I said. "We are their light. You'll see." His silence told me he did not understand. "The worlds get smaller as you descend. Aelfrice isn't as big as our world, though I think it must be bigger than Celidon."

"There is a geometric progression," the Earl Marshal told me, and tried to explain what a geometric progression was, a thing I could not understand and that I doubt anyone can understand. "The highest world, the world of the Most High God, is infinite. The world below his is one hundredth as large. But a hundredth part of infinity is infinity still, though so much smaller. The world below that—"

"Skai."

"Yes, Skai, is a hundredth the size of that, and so a ten-thousandth the size of Elysion. Still infinite. May I sit on this stone?"

"Of course, My Lord."

"Very kind of you, Sir Able. Harrumph! Kindness to a prisoner. Knightly. You got little yourself."

"I did the first time, My Lord, but not the second. I'd escaped—so Her Majesty chose to take it."

"We'd been defeated." The Earl Marshal wiped his face. "We have been, as I ought to say. They are less than human, those Osterlings."

"I fought them at sea, My Lord, and they are not. The

Angrborn often seem very human. King Gilling did in his love for Idnn. But they aren't. The Osterlings don't look as human as King Gilling, yet they're what we may become."

The air grew brighter. There is no air anywhere like the air of Aelfrice. That of Skai is purer than the purest air we know in Mythgarthr, so pure no distance can haze its crystal transparency; but the air of Aelfrice seems luminous, as if one breathes a great gem. Day came, and we saw before us the sea that is like no other, as blue as sapphire and as sparkling, stretching to island realms unguessable. A league overhead Mythgarthr spread itself as stars do on a cloudless night. Jotunland lay north, wrapped in snow. Above us was Celidon, where green shoots peeped from tree and field. All around us, Aelfrice, white where it was not green, rejoicing in the silver light, forests of mystery and cliffs of marble.

"I could stay here forever," the Earl Marshal muttered. "Give up fortune, castle, horses—everything. They're all lost anyway if the Osterlings prevail."

"Maybe you will," I said, because I was thinking of leaving him there; but soon I said, "Follow me," for I had spied a crevice in the base of the cliff to our left.

He did. "Where are we going?"

"To look at that, and go down farther if we can. I have—you don't understand my nature. I don't either, though I understand much more than you do. I can't use the powers my nature confers. I've given my oath. But I can't change this nature that neither of us understands. What do you smell?"

He sniffed the air. "The sea, and I think these meadow flowers."

"I smell sulfur, and I wish Gylf were with us."

We descended into the crevice, I eagerly, he more slowly behind me. Fumes billowed about us at times so that we could scarcely breathe, at others vanished, leaving air that would have suited the desert, lifeless, dusty, and scorching.

The Earl Marshal took my arm. "This is dangerous. We must be nearing Muspel."

"We're there," I told him. I had glimpsed a dragon in the darkness.

It seemed to hear the hiss of my blade and came at us, silent at first, then roaring. The Earl Marshal tried to flee and fell, rolling down the stony slope into darkness. The dragon struck at me, and I put my point into its eye.

How long I searched for the Earl Marshal I cannot say. It seemed a minute or two, but may have been much longer. No matter which way I turned, the ground sloped down. It grew cooler, then cold, and air as clotted as phlegm held pitiless white light that drew the color from the gems on my scabbard and the skin of my own hands.

"Able! Sir Able!" The Earl Marshal came waddling so rapidly that I knew he would have run if he could. "There's a—a giant—a monster . . ." He pointed behind him. "We—go. We must! It—it—"

I told him I wanted to see it, thinking it might be Org.

"No, you don't! Sir Able, Sir Able, listen. I—I—I've seen it." He fell silent, gasping for breath.

"Yes, you've seen it, My Lord. I want to see it, too." His fear had infected me, and I added, "and afterward go."

"I'll go now."

"And face the dragons alone? If you won't come with me, I'll go with you and save your life, if I can."

We started up the slope, walking easily. After some while I realized we were not walking up it, but down. I corrected our course. We reached a ridge, and had to descend or turn back. Great sheets of ice hung like curtains from a dark sky; the ground was hard as ice, and slick with frost.

"This cannot be Muspel," the Earl Marshal gasped.

A voice before, behind, and all about us answered him. "You call this Niflheim." It was weary, yet resonated with such power as no Overcyn possesses, not even the Valfather.

Trembling, the Earl Marshal fell to his knees.

"You wished to see me, Able. You have only to look."

It surrounded me. I cannot write it in a way that will

make it clear if you have not seen it. I was in it, and it scrutinized me from above as from below, huge and stronger than iron. Hideous in its malice. I tried to close my eyes, feeling that I walked in a nightmare. It was there still.

"Call me God, Able."

Pride woke in me; that pride did not still my fear, but shouldered it aside as the weak thing it was. I said, "Call me Sir Able, god."

"You come near the secret that lies at the heart of all things, Able. Worship me, and I will tell it."

The Earl Marshal worshipped, but I did not.

"Learn it, and you will have power such as men and gods scarcely dream of, easily obtained."

I said, "This lord is worshipping you. Tell him."

"You behold me as I am, Able. It may be the sight is too much." As it spoke, it no longer surrounded me. Instead there sat before me upon a throne of ice a creature grossly great. Toad and dragon were in it. So was the Earl Marshal, and so was I. "Worship me now. You shall know the secret."

I said, "I don't wish to know this secret, but to return to Muspel and from there to Aelfrice."

"Worship me!"

"Lord Escan is worshipping you," I repeated. "If you'd tell me, why won't you tell him?"

It lifted the Earl Marshal before I had finished, held him close, and whispered; Niflheim trembled as it whispered, and a sheet of ice miles long fell with a deafening crash.

"Now you know me," it said to the Earl Marshal, but his eyes were shut tight and would not look.

"I know you, too," I told it. "This is the seventh and lowest world, the final world, and you are the most low god."

"I will tell you, and you will worship me, seeing that it is right and good that you do so. Come nearer."

I did not, yet the distance between us diminished.

Its voice fell to a whisper, and that whisper was the worst thing I have heard. The voice of Grengarm was as pure as the wind beside it. "Know the great secret, which is that the last world is the first—"

Niflheim shook again. Its frozen earth groaned.

"You stand in Niflheim, and Elysion."

The tremors became more violent. A pillar of ice fell; and its ruin sent ice shards flying, and a cloud of sparkling crystals, like snow. The thing that spoke looked about it, and I glimpsed its fear.

"You see my face," it whispered, and seemed to hear my thought. "If you could see my back, you would see the Most High God—"

Niflheim broke as it spoke. A crack opened between the place where it sat and the place where I stood. I helped the Earl Marshal rise; I cannot say why I did, but I did.

Perhaps he could not have said why he rose.

"For He is me—"

Ice and stones rained all around the thing that spoke. A stone as big as an ox struck it.

"And I am He!"

Even as it spoke it fled, with the frozen earth rolling under its feet like the sea, and stones, ice, and fire of Muspel nearly burying it. I saw its back then, and the back of its head, and they were covered with lumps and running sores.

When we regained Aelfrice at last, we sat surrounded by its beauty, we two, and Aelf came from the forest and the sea with food and gifts. We ate, and an aged Aelf whose beard was of those fall leaves that remain streaked with green drew me aside and whispered, "Our queen is waiting for you."

"I know," I said. "Tell her that I'll come as soon as I have illustrated her message, as she and the kings wished."

I returned to the Earl Marshal and sat with him, and ate an apple and a wedge of cheese.

"You're wise," he said, "and I, who thought myself wise for so long, am a fool."

"By no means."

"I couldn't attain this world of Aelfrice. Harrumph! Not in thirty years. You did it easily, and followed the worlds to the end."

I nodded.

"I've never heard of anyone's doing that. No one but you. And I, because I came with you."

I said that someday I would like to go to Kleos, the world above Skai; but it would be years before I tried.

"I wish I could sit here forever," he told me solemnly, "watching these waves and this sky, and eating this food."

I paid little heed when he said it; but when we rose to return to Mythgarthr, I chanced to look behind us. There he sat with food before him, staring out over the sea, his face rapturous. I stopped to point, and he whispered, "I know." There are things in Aelfrice I still do not understand.

CHAPTER THIRTY-SIX

THE FIGHT BEFORE THE GATE

Even as time in Aelfrice runs more slowly than in Mythgarthr, so time in Muspel runs more slowly than time in Aelfrice, and time in Niflheim slower still. We had been away half a day. When we returned, Kingsdoom lay in ruins, the red rag floated over Thortower, and the season was high summer.

We found a woman begging food. We had none to give her, and our coins were worthless—there was no bread to buy. "The king's dead," she told us, "and Osterlings rule Celidon, eating those they don't enslave. I have a hiding place."

She would not show it to us, saying there was room for one and no more. The Earl Marshal asked about his castle of Sevengates, but she knew nothing of it.

"I'd like to go to Thortower," he told me. "Payn's my bastard. Did you guess?" He knew a secret way; and I told him I would go with him, hoping to find Wistan. He said, "I must have a sword. I won't see sixty again and was never a good swordsman. But I'll try, because I must."

I said, "That's all swordsmen do, My Lord."

We thanked the beggar woman, promised we would bring food when we had found some, and went to the inn. It was a grim business to walk, that fine summer day, and find cobbled streets choked with rubble, shops burned, and people gone. In a public square, the Osterlings had kindled a fire and dined on human flesh. Bones littered the fine paving blocks, gnawed and half burned. "I know of nothing more horrible than this," the Earl Marshal said.

"I'd a servant," I said, "who did the same, though he didn't cook his meat. Thus I'm inured. Is it worse to kill a child, or to eat it before the worms do?"

The inn was still standing, its windowpanes gone and its doors smashed. I called for Pouk and Uns. My shouts brought Uns to a fourth-floor window, but brought a patrol of Osterlings as well. Uns threw rubble from his window, and the Earl Marshal snatched the leader's sword as soon as I dispatched him, so we fared well enough.

We went up when the fight was over, meeting Uns on the stair. (It was on that stair that a thought from Cloud reached me. Lonely and wild, joyous at the touch of my mind; but fearful, too.) Uns had my shield, he said, and my bow and quiver; we followed him to the lumber room where he had hidden them. "'N dis, sar. Dis ol' hat. Ya fergit dis?"

It was the helm, old, as he said, and rusty again. I put it on, and saw Uns sturdy and straight, the Earl Marshal older, knowing, and because he was knowing, frightened.

"Pouk's gun ta see his wife," Uns told me. "On'y he's got some a' yar dings, ta. 'E's keepin' 'um fer ya."

I asked about Wistan, but Uns knew nothing; nor had he more news of the war than we had heard from the beggar woman. We held a council then, speaking as equals. The upshot was that the Earl Marshal and I would go to Thortower as planned while Uns collected the beggar woman we had promised to help, fed her (for he had some food), and packed such possessions as we could carry. We would meet again at the inn and try to reach Sevengates, which might still be holding out.

That decided, I drilled the Earl Marshal with his new sword. It was a saber whetted on the inner edge; he found it unhandy at first, but soon grew fond of it. I thought it too short and too heavy at the tip; but the blade was stiff and sharp, and those are the most important qualities.

We slept, woke after moonrise, and went into the broken lands east of the city. Bushes hid an iron door in a cliff little taller than a lance; the Earl Marshal produced a key and we went in, I fearing we would find we were in Aelfrice.

So it nearly proved. Hands snatched our clothes from the time we relocked the door behind us, and the thin voices of Aelf mocked and challenged us. When the end of the long, narrow tunnel was in sight, I caught one by the wrist; and when the Earl Marshal unlocked a second door and admitted us to the wine cellar, I dragged her into its lesser darkness and demanded her name.

She trembled. "Your slave is Baki, Lord."

"Who thought she'd have fun with me in that tunnel." I drew my sword.

"T-to t-take you to Aelfrice where you w-would be safe."

"Who abandoned me chained in a cell." I felt no rage against her, no lust for vengeance, only a cold justice that had pronounced sentence already.

She did not speak.

The Earl Marshal asked whether I knew "this Aelf."

"She's declared herself my slave a thousand times," I told him, "and I've freed her over and over, and neither of us believed the other. Would you like an Aelfslave?"

"Very much."

"She'll swear fealty to you, if I spare her. And betray you at the first opportunity. Won't you, Baki?"

"I was your s-slave because Garsecg wished it, Lord. I will be his, if you wish it."

I spoke to the Earl Marshal. "We're going up, aren't we? It's obvious that neither of them are down here."

Baki said, "There is a stair to your left, Lord."

"Thanks. I could kill you here, Baki. Cut your rotten throat. I'm going to take you where I can see to make a clean thrust instead. Want to talk about the blood I drank when I was hurt? Let's hear you."

Perhaps she shook her head—it was too dark to see.

The stair opened into a pantry, the pantry into a wide hall hung with shields and weapons. Night had fallen while we were in the tunnel, but candles guttered at either end of the hall, more than enough light for a good thrust.

"May I speak, Lord? I know you will kill me, and it will be no use to defend myself. But I would like to say two things before I die, so you will understand when I am gone."

Perhaps I nodded—doubtless I did. I was looking at her through the eyes of the old helm, a thing like a woman molded of earth, blazing coals, and beast-flesh.

"You have refused me a hundred times. I have been bold, and you have refused. I have been shy, and you have refused. I have helped you over and over, but when my back was broken you would not mend me yourself, bringing a boy to do it. I knew that if I came to your cell and freed you, you would refuse again. I hoped that if I left you there until you were nearly dead, you might feel gratitude. I would have come before you died. I would have demanded oaths before I fed and freed you. That is the first thing."

The Earl Marshal said, "I don't know whether I should envy you or laugh, Sir Able."

I released Baki and removed the helm; I had seen her too well, and the sight sickened me. "Would it help you to know I'm just a boy playing knight, My Lord? I've seen you as you are and Baki as she is, and if you saw me the same way you'd know. Men don't mock boys—or envy them either."

"Then I'm no man," the Earl Marshal told me, "for I've envied a thousand."

I turned to Baki. "Why don't you bolt? You might save your life."

"Because I have more to say. We pinched and tweaked you in the tunnel. How many of us could you catch?"

I had heard the soft steps of scores of feet; I made no reply.

"Only me, because I was trying to draw you to Aelfrice and safety while the others only wished to tease you."

I believe I might have stabbed her if I had been granted another second; Osterlings burst in, and there was no time. Baki snatched a sword from the wall and fought beside us, an Aelf, a maiden, and last a living flame. The sword Uri had stolen sifted our foes and drew me on and on, but Baki was always before me, cutting men as harvesters cut grain.

When the last had fled, she confronted me, her stolen sword ready. "Who carried the day, Lord? You?"

"No." I had on the helm but would not look at her.

"Will you meet me? Sword-to-sword?"

"No," I repeated. "I'd kill you and I don't want to. Go in peace."

Her sword fell to the floor; she had vanished.

"We'd better not stay here," the Earl Marshal said; I agreed, and he showed me a narrow stair behind an arras.

Describing our search of Thortower would be weary work—indeed it was weary work itself. We had to stop more than once to rest; and in the end I searched alone, and returned for him (hidden in his library) when I was sure that neither Payn nor Wistan were to be found.

"They are dead, I suppose." He rose stiffly. "I was trained with the sword as a boy. It had been twenty years and more since I'd handled one." He held his out although I had seen it earlier. "Do you know how many men I had slain with the sword?"

I shook my head and dropped into a chair, exhausted.

"None, but I killed four today. Four Osterling spears, with one the Aelf and I killed together. How long can such good fortune endure?"

"Until we reach Sevengates, I hope, My Lord. East?"

"Five days ride."

"Then three or less if we hasten." I was hopeful, for I thought Cloud might rejoin me soon.

"We'll be hurrying into the teeth of the army the Caan will send to recover the Mountain of Fire." The Earl Marshal wiped his face and stared at the ceiling. "If we take the direct route, that is. You know the north?"

"Tolerably well."

"So do I. It might be better for us to turn north at first, then east, then south."

This we set out to do, tramping away from Kingsdoom unopposed, although we had left Thortower in an uproar. The first night, while the Earl Marshal, Uns, and the beggar woman Galene slept, I lay awake staring up to Skai; once I believed I glimpsed Cloud among the stars, and sent urgent thoughts to tell her I was below. They cannot have reached her, for there was no thought from her.

Next day we encountered Osterlings everywhere. Twice we fought them. We had to leave the road, and when we returned to it, to leave it again. They had striped the countryside, burning every village and farm, and devouring people and livestock. That night we finished the bread and bacon we had carried; and although we continued to feed our fire when they were gone, we would much rather have fed ourselves.

"I have dined well throughout a long life," the Earl Marshal remarked. "I'll die now with an empty belly. It seems a shame. Do they eat well in the Lands of the Dead? Queen Idnn told me you spent some time there."

"Only as a visitor. No, My Lord, they do not."

"Then I won't go, if I can help it."

Galene looked at Uns, but he only grinned and said, "Ya feed dem Os'erlin's, if'n ya die, sar. Yar belly be emp'y, on'y not deirs, nosar."

"May I speak openly of the last place in which we were well fed, Sir Able?"

I nodded.

"Might we not go to Aelfrice again? All of us?"

"Are you asking if I could take so many? Yes, I think I might. But food is uncertain there, and we might lose a year while we ate."

"Better to lose a year than to lose our lives."

"We might lose those too. You didn't see the dangers, My Lord, but there are many. Dragons come there often, and there are many others, of which the worst may be the Aelf themselves. Don't you remain there?"

He nodded.

"Let that be enough."

Galene muttered, "You know nothing of hardship."

Uns corrected her. "Sar Able do."

"A knight, with servants? I don't think so."

The Earl Marshal told her to mind her tongue; I said

that if I could endure the swords and spears of our enemies, I could surely endure anything a woman might say—provided she did not say it too often.

"I don't know what you might have gone through, that's fact. Wounds and all. Fighting's a knight's trade, but the rest shouldn't act like it's just a trade like a butcher's. I been poor my whole life and what I had was taken 'cause you knights didn't fight enough. I'd a man. We'd a baby . . ."

"Many of those knights paid with their lives," the Earl Marshal muttered.

Uns put his arm around Galene and held her hand in his, which seemed more sensible. Looking into the fire, I saw Baki's face. She mouthed a word I could not catch, pointed to my left, and vanished. Excusing myself, I rose.

Deep in the shadows, a woman with eyes of yellow flame wrapped me in such an embrace as few men have known. I knew her by her kiss, and we kissed long and long. When at last we parted, she laughed softly. "The wind is in the chimney."

I agreed that it was.

"I had better go, before the fire burns too bright." I stepped back and she vanished, although her voice remained. "News or a promise—which would you hear first?"

"The promise, by all means."

"Unwise. Here is my news. Baki says you were looking for your squire and the fat man's clerk. If you still want them, they are defending a little place called Redhall. We last met near there."

I nodded, unable to speak.

"There are two hundred attacking it, and more coming. It is already full of women and children who fled them. You may know some of the women."

I asked who they were.

"I paid no heed to them, and would not have known the fat man's clerk if I had not spoken to the boy. Toug?"

"Wistan," I said. "Toug's Sir Svon's squire. Or he used to be."

"I doubt it matters. Do you care about the big women more than you care about me?"

"I care for no one as I care for you."

She laughed, delighted. "I enthrall you. Wonderful! My reputation remains intact. Are you going?"

"No! I'm going to Aelfrice with you, forever."

She stepped into the moonlight, naked and infinitely desirable. "Come then." Her hand closed on mine. "Leave the others to their deaths. They die soon in any case."

Until then I had not known we stood upon a hilltop; the ground ahead fell gently; jeweled air shimmered not far down the slope. "I can't," I said.

Disiri sighed. "And I cannot love you as you love them. Will you come if I promise to try? To try very hard?"

"I can't," I repeated. "Not now."

"I will tire of you. I know you know. But I will come back to you, and when I come back we will know such joy as no one in either world has ever known."

She must have seen my answer in my eyes, because she vanished as she spoke. The hill vanished with her, and I stood on level ground.

Uns and Galene were sleeping when I returned to the fire. "Wistan and Payn are at my manor of Redhall," I told the Earl Marshal. "It's besieged. I'm going to help them."

The old helm stood before the fire in the place where I had been sitting before I left it. I sat beside it, put it on, and removed it at once.

"How do you know?" the Earl Marshal asked.

"Disiri just told me."

He said something else then, but I did not answer and I no longer recall what it was.

I tapped the old helm. "I wasn't wearing this."

The Earl Marshal raised an eyebrow. "Of course not."

"I'm glad I wasn't. Very glad. Are you going?"

"To Redhall with you? The queen said specifically that Payn was there?"

I nodded.

"Then I am. I must."

I had hoped he would not, and had planned to send Uns and Galene away with him. I made it clear that I had no reason to believe Payn and Wistan were there beyond Disiri's assertion, and warned him that no Aelf could be trusted.

"I loved his mother," the Earl Marshal said. "I loved her very much. I couldn't marry her. She was a commoner, one of Mother's maids. I've never told anyone this."

I said he need not tell me.

"I want to. If I die and you find Payn alive, I want you to know. She became pregnant and hid in the forest, half a day's ride from Sevengates. I gave her money and bribed my father's foresters to bring her food. Sometimes I went to see her." His face writhed. "Not nearly often enough."

Setting the old helm on my head once more, I beheld such suffering as I hope never to see again.

"She was four days in labor. She could not deliver. A forester had fetched his wife, and when she stopped breathing Amabel opened her and took out my son."

I removed the helm. "You're torturing yourself. It's of the past, and not even Overcyns can change what's past."

"They adopted Payn for my sake, the forester and his wife. Their names were Hrolfr and Amabel, rough people but goodhearted. Payn was thirteen when my father ascended, and after that I was able to see that he received an education. When His Majesty raised me to office, I made him one of my clerks. I could've given him a farm, but I wanted him by me. I wanted to see him and speak to him daily. To advise him."

The old helm fascinated me. When I wore it, our fire was only a fire, but the stars!

"My wife has born no child, Sir Able, and I've had no lover save Wiliga. You understand why, I feel sure. I've never told Payn I'm his father, but I believe he must have guessed long ago."

Reaching Redhall we hid in the forest, weaving fruitless plans and hoping for some means of crossing the besiegers' lines and scaling the wall. While the Osterlings built catapults and a siege tower on wheels, Uns wove snares of vines and willow twigs. He caught conies and a hedgehog, and Galene found berries which were not poisonous, though sour. Without that food we would have starved.

The Osterlings were their own provisions. When they had nothing left, they attacked; those killed or sorely wounded became food for the rest. They used scaling ladders, and it was by these that we hoped to mount the wall.

"Darkness and rain would favor us," the Earl Marshal said, not for the first time. "It seldom rains at this season, but the moon is waning."

"So's us," Uns remarked dolefully.

"You can eat me when I die," Galene declared quite seriously, "but I won't die so you can eat me."

That decided me. I had given my oath to the Valfather indeed; I would break it, only by a trifle, and take whatever punishment he imposed. I spoke to Skai when none of the rest could hear me. Clouds arrived to blind the moon at my order, and autumn's chill crept south from Jotunland in servitude to me.

"Here you are!" Galene grasped my arm. "We've been looking everywhere. This's the time."

Stealthily we left the forest, the Earl Marshal behind me, Galene behind him, and Uns behind her armed with a stout staff. Rain pierced the blind dark, delighting us.

We were nearly close enough to steal a ladder when the gate of Redhall swung wide and its defenders rushed upon their foes. Tree-tall women overturned the tower on wheels, sending it crashing down on the huts the Osterlings had built. The ropes of catapults were cut and axes laid to their timbers. A great golden knight, a hero out of legend, led the attackers, fearless and swift as any lion. I shouted "Disiri!" as I fought, and saw the moment at which he heard my cry and understood what it portended, and his joy, and how he raged against the Osterlings then. His sword rivaled the lightning, and his shout of *Idnn!* its thunder. My blade rose and fell, slashed and thrust beside his, and as in Thortower, it seemed to seek, tasting the blood of each who fell, and springing away dissatisfied. I fought in our van at first, and afterward before our van, for that sword drew me forward, thirsty and seeking, slew contemptuously, and sprang away.

There came new thunder, a black storm that raged across the field raining blood. I knew his voice and called Gylf to me, as tall at the shoulder as any black bull, with eyes that blazed like suns and fangs like knives.

I would have said I was weak with hunger, and that the sea Garsecg had waked in me could lend me no strength. It was long coming, but came when a chieftan of the Osterlings barred my path. His armor was savage with spikes, and he wielded a mace of chains with three stars. They outreached my shield as a man reaches over a hedge and knocked me flat in the mud. I rose as the sea rises, saw him for the horror he was, and I drove the stolen sword into his throat as Old Toug might have dispatched a hog.

How many fell after that I cannot say; but the rest fled, so that what had begun as a sally ended as a victory, the first of Celidon in that war.

Dawn came, yet the storm still blew so dark we scarcely knew it. Every knight who reads this will say we ought to have mounted and ridden in pursuit of our foe. We did not. We had few horses, those we had were thin and weak, and we staggered with fatigue. I took off the old helm, for the sweat was pouring down my face, there in the rain and the cold; and by gray light I saw the field of battle for what it was not, mud and water before the gate of Redhall, littered everywhere with the leaves and sticks of the fallen huts, with chips and notched timbers and the pitiful bodies of the slain. And the rain beat upon their faces and the faces of the wounded alike, on men and women who screamed and moaned and tried to rise. Some went among the wounded Osterlings and slew them, but I did not.

Instead I looked for the golden knight who had led us. He had dwindled to Svon—Svon with half a shield still on his left arm, and half a swan on it, and a swan on his helm, a swan of gilt wood that had lost a wing in the fight. We embraced, something we had never done before, and he helped me get the Earl Marshal into the manor, with Gylf gamboling to cheer us by his joy, and wagging his tail.

Twenty or thirty people came crowding into the room, drawn by the news that a nobleman of high station had joined them. They hoped, I am sure, that he had brought substantial reinforcements; but they were gracious enough not to grumble when they learned that Gylf, Uns, and I comprised the whole. (Some may even have been relieved, for they were on short rations.) We made them stand back and be quiet, and finding Payn among them let him attend his father. Other wounded were carried in. The many women cared for them, while Svon and I with others went out to search the field for more, and collect such loot as the dead might provide.

Outdoors again, I asked Svon who commanded.

"You do, Sir Able, now that you're here."

I shook my head. "I saw Her Majesty among her guard."

"My wife will defer to you, I'm sure. This is Redhall, and Redhall is yours. Your duke is not present, and you are no subject of ours."

I congratulated him on his marriage, and he smiled, weary though he was. "It was my hope, my dream, to rise to the nobility. You remember, I'm sure."

"To return to it. Your sire was noble."

"I thank you. To return." The bitter smile I had come to detest in my squire twisted his lips. "I would have been overjoyed to die a baronet. Now I find I am a prince."

I congratulated him again, saying Your Highness.

"A fighting prince far from his wife's realm, who finds his experience as a knight invaluable. Do you want to hear our story?"

I did, of course. Idnn, as I knew, had taken a hundred young Skjaldmeyjar with her when she came south. They had astonished Kingsdoom and had attended the nuptials of their queen, attestation to her royal status—a status Arnthor had readily recognized, seeing an ally who might restrain Schildstarr. When he had refused to free me, they had fought the Osterlings, the most feared troops in his host, in the hope that he would grant Idnn a boon.

The first warm days had shown only too plainly that the dreaded Daughters of Angr could not continue to fight. Idnn had marched north with Svon, Mani, and a few others, but was stopped short of the mountains by the Caan's northern army, which had already ravaged Irringsmouth and was scouring the countryside for food to send south. Driven back, they had joined others who fled or fought, taking refuge in manors and castles that the Osterlings had quickly overwhelmed, and so come to Redhall. Of the hundred Skjaldmeyjar, twenty-eight remained before our battle, and twenty-seven after it. The unseasonable cold had made it possible for them to fight, and Svon had ordered the sally; but it was certain they would be unable to fight again until the first frost.

"Would you like to meet the leader of those who joined our retreat?" Svon asked. "He's over there." He gestured, the rain (warmer now) running from his mail-clad arm.

I said, of course, that I would very much like to make his acquaintance. In my own defense, I add here that the day was still dark, and the man Svon had indicated was wearing a cloak with the hood up.

"Sir Toug! Sir Able is eager to speak with you, and I'm surprised you're not at least as eager to speak with him."

Toug managed to smile at that, and gave me his hand. I asked about his shoulder, and he said it had healed. That was not the case, as I soon discovered; but it was better.

"I said I didn't want to be a knight, and you said I was one, that I couldn't help it," he told me, "and we were both right. The Osterlings came, and there was nobody to lead our village who knew fighting except me, so I had to do it. They didn't want me at first, so I led by being in front. We beat off a couple parties and a Free Company joined us. Our stock was gone and the barley stamped flat, so we went south. We got to where Etela was, but they'd only started fixing it back up. She's here, and her mother and father, too."

I asked whether Vil were her father, and Toug nodded. "They didn't want to say it 'cause they weren't married, Sir Able. Only now they are. He won't let you say *my lord*, though. He's still Vil."

"Quite right," Svon muttered.

"But I'm Sir Toug and Sir Svon's Prince Svon now. He knighted me—I was his squire up north. You did that."

I nodded again.

"So he did, and Etela and I are going to get married next year if we're still alive."

Gylf leaped up, putting his forepaws on Toug's chest and licking his face. It amazed and amused me like nothing else. I cannot help laughing when I think of it, even now.

"There's somebody else here I ought to tell you about," Toug said, "you always liked them. It's the old couple from Jotunland, the blind man that was a slave on some farm."

A thousand things came rushing at me then—the ruin of the land, Arnthor's eyes, the drunken smile of his sister, and the empty, lovely face of his queen. Sunless days in the dungeon, cold that was the breath of death, Bold Berthhold's hut, wind in the treetops—Disiri's kiss, her long legs and slender arms, the green fingers longer than my hand. Gerda young, as Berthold had remembered her, with flaxen hair and merry eyes. Mag in Thiazi's Room of Lost Love.

The Lady's hall in the flowering meadows whose blossoms are the stars, and, oh, ten thousand more. And I, who had been laughing only a moment past, wept. Toug clasped me as he would a child, and spoke to me as his mother must have to him: *"There, there . . . It don't matter. It don't matter at all."*

A rider came, the same Lamwell of Chaus who had played at halberts with me in the tournament, so worn that he could scarcely hold the saddle, on a horse so nearly dead it fell when he dismounted. The king lived—was in the south in need of every man. We held a council and I said I would go, that the rest might go or stay, but the king who had freed me had need of me and I would go to him. Pouk and Uns stood by me, and their wives by them; they must have shamed many. Idnn said she could not go, the Daughters of Angr could not fight in summer and could scarce march in it—they would have to march by night, and short marches, too. She and Svon would go north now that the enemy in this part of Celidon had been beaten, and hope for cooler days in the hills. They had lost three-quarters of their number in service to a foreign king, as she reminded us, and overturned the siege tower. We agreed, some of us reluctantly.

Afterward I spoke with Idnn privately; it was then that she told me of her visit from Uri and her interview with the Valfather. When we had talked over both, I asked a boon. "You may have any in our power," Idnn said, "and we'll stay if you ask it. But aside from our husband we shall be of scant service to you."

"You may be of greatest service to me, Your Majesty, at little cost to yourself. I gave Berthold and Gerda to serve you in the north. Will you return them?"

She did most readily.

And did more with it, creating Payn a baron of her realm—this sworn before witnesses. When it was done, the Earl Marshal declared that if he died, Lord Payn of Jotunhome was heir to his castle and lands, and all he had.

I would have left next morning, but could not. There could be little provision in the south. Two days we spent in gathering all we could. There was another matter, too. I hoped Cloud would join me. If she had, I would have left the rest and ridden straight to the king; she did not, though I called every night. She had been the Valfather's last gift, and it seemed to me that she knew I had broken the oath I had given him and was executing his mild justice. After we left Redhall, I called to her no more.

CHAPTER THIRTY-SEVEN
FIVE FATES AND THREE WISHES

We had two horses fit for war. Lamwell and I took them, but they did us little good; we could travel no faster than those we led, and most were on foot, though we had a decent palfrey for Lynnet and a gray donkey colt, scarcely big enough for a child, for Etela.

The badly wounded we left at Redhall with Payn, also the women who would consent to remain. I wanted Bold Berthold's counsel, which was why I had begged him from Idnn; Gerda would not leave him. It was the same with Ulfa and Galene—Pouk and Uns were going to war, and they would have followed us at a distance if we would not take them.

No more would Lynnet stay. "I'm of a fighting family," she said; and when I looked into her eyes I felt I was her son and could deny her nothing. Where she went, Vil and Etela must go too; they did, Vil walking beside Lynnet with one hand on her stirrup and a staff in the other.

We went to Irringsmouth, hoping to take ship; but the town was more ruinous still, and neither gold nor the sword could produce a ship. From there we marched down the coast by rugged roads or none. We were three knights with seven men-at-arms and four archers, mine from Redhall; we also had fifty-two armed churls, twenty of them outlaws and not to be relied upon. The rest were peasants who scarcely knew how to hold the weapons I had given them.

In addition we had the two blind men and far too many

women, some of whom would fight if led. Recalling Idnn and her maids, I had given bows to those who showed ability. The rest had staves or spears. Lynnet, still mad at times, wore a sword Etela said had been her grandfather's; and nobody in Mythgarthr brought a swifter blade to battle, or a wilder one. I had also Pouk and Uns; although neither was expert, both had some knowledge of arms and could be trusted to follow or to stand their ground. Lamwell was my lieutenant, with Toug second to him. Below them, Wistan (who had followed Idnn and was not much short of another knight), Pouk, and Uns.

There was one more with us, one some scarcely counted at all, though others stood in awe of him. It was Gylf; and I, who had seen him killing men like rats, knew he was worth a hundred spears. With us too at times were Aelf. Sometimes they brought food (never enough), and at others told us where we might find it or find horses.

For hungry though we were, we were hungrier for them. In Irringsmouth we had been able to buy two horses and a mule. We searched for more everywhere, paying for them when we could and fighting for them when we could not.

In this we lost a few of our company, as was inevitable; but as we went we gained more: ruined peasants, hungry, but hungrier for leadership and starved for vengeance. I spoke with admiration of their strength and courage, swore we would free Celidon from the Osterlings, and set Uns to teaching them the quarterstaff, and Pouk the knife.

Near Forcetti we met the first sizable body of the enemy, I would guess two hundred. Expecting us to run at the sight of the red rag, they were unprepared when we fell on them—no more than a hundred, but fighting as if we had a thousand behind us. The air was clear, hot, and still, with scarcely a cloud in the wide blue sky, and our bows had grand shooting when they took to their heels. We lost arrows, and arrows were more than gold to us; but we picked up others, and got more bows, too, with swords crooked and straight, spears of two sorts, shields, and other plunder. Duns joined us there; Nukara had been killed by the Osterlings who had looted and burned their farm. With us, Duns quickly learned that he could no longer boss his younger brother.

We fought foraging parties and heard from their wounded what had seemed clear already—the Caan was in the south, opposed by Arnthor. Some said the Mountain of Fire was still in Arnthor's hands, some that it had been taken, and one that Celidon had retaken it. I asked Uri; she went, and confirmed it. She also said that while they held it, the Osterlings had cast children and old people into the crater, theirs and ours, and for them three dragons of Muspel had joined their host. That was hard to credit, since it seemed Arnthor's army could not have stood against the Osterlings and three dragons. Vil suggested that the Caan had made dragons of wicker, which might be displayed on poles to frighten us; Uri insisted she could not have been deceived by such things.

Kingsdoom was deserted. We entered Thortower, although we had to fill the moat before the Great Gate, the drawbridge having burned. In the Rooks' Tower, we found Osterlings, barricaded and devouring one of their own number. We smashed their barricade and Lamwell and I went for them, with Wistan, Pouk, Uns, and Qut behind. One said they had been put into Thortower by the Caan, a company of his guard, to hold it until he returned. When he had gone, they had been visited almost nightly by an invisible monster. It carried away one, sometimes two, on each visit. Although they had fought it, it had seized their spears and snapped the shafts.

I sent the rest away, returned to the dungeon, and called Org. He had grown so huge I could not believe he had entered the Rooks' Tower at all; none of its doors had appeared large enough to admit him. By a few words and many gestures, he explained that he had climbed the tower and entered where a catapult had broken the wall.

"You may hold this castle for King Arnthor," I told him. "If you do, the Osterlings we've slain are yours, with any others who come here. Or you may come with me. There'll be battles to feed you, and it seems likely you can help us."

"Nort'?"

"No, south. Into the desert."

"Ru'ns? Leort say ru'ns."

I had forgotten that. I said, "Yes, it's possible you may find more of your kind there, though I can't promise."

I put Uns to his old duty again, and though he did not confide in Duns, he enlisted Galene to assist him. When we had gone some way south, I saw her floating as it seemed over the plain, borne up by a shambling monster more visible to my imagination than to my sight.

A week passed, and another; if I were to write all that happened, this would never end. We fought twice. Beaten by day, we came back at night with a hundred Khimairae and forty Fire Aelf. Org took our foe in the rear. A few days later we sighted a column of black smoke on the horizon, and three more brought the snow-clad peak of the Mountain of Fire.

We joined the king's host. He sent for me, and I found him wounded, with Beel attending him. "We freed you to fight for us," he said, "but you were too weak for it."

I agreed.

"But not too weak to vanish. To vanish, and to take Lord Escan with you. What did you do with him?"

"I saw to it that his wounds were salved and bandaged," I said, "and that Lord Payn, his son, remained to attend him. They are at my manor of Redhall."

"He has no son."

"Then it cannot be of Lord Escan that I speak, Your Majesty, since the man of whom I speak has an unlawful son who's a baron of Jotunhome. Doubtless I've mistaken another for your Earl Marshal."

Arnthor rolled his eyes toward Beel, who said, "These matters smack of gossip, interesting but unimportant. You brought reinforcements?"

"Fewer than a hundred."

"How many?"

"Sixty-seven men able to fight, with twenty-two women to bend the bow."

"And have they bows to bend?"

I nodded, and added that we needed more arrows.

"You bent a famous bow in the north. I have told His Majesty about that. Your shooting in the tourney, though good, disappointed him."

"It disappointed me as well," I told them. "Why don't we hold another here? Perhaps I can do better."

Arnthor said, "This is madness."

"I agree, Your Majesty. But it wasn't me who began this talk of tournaments. If you want me to command your forces, I'll take charge and do what I can. If you want me to fight as one of many knights, I'll do what I can still."

"We command Celidon. Do you think us unable to rise from this bed?"

"I wish you stronger than that, Your Majesty."

"We will be strong enough to stand when the time comes—to stand, and to sit a charger. We would make you our deputy if we could, Sir Able."

I bowed. "Your Majesty does me too much honor."

His smile was bitter. "As you say. You're not to be trusted. We know it. You are of Aelfrice, however you may look, and whatever you may say. So are we, and know our own kind." I believe he would have laughed as the Aelf laugh, but his wound would not permit it. "I was born in Aelfrice. My royal sister, too. Do you know the story?"

I nodded. "Your royal brother told me something of it, Your Majesty."

"He is dead. We have tried to call on him for aid, but he is no more. Did you kill him, Sir Able?"

"No, Your Majesty."

"Would you tell us the truth, Sir Able, if you had?"

"Yes, Your Majesty."

The bitter smile came again. "Would he, My Lord Beel?"

"I believe so, Your Majesty."

Arnthor's eyes closed. "I pray to Skai that the man who killed him join us, and quickly. We may have need of him."

I said, "The Overcyns have smiled on Your Majesty."

His eyes opened. "He is with you?"

Beel said, "The blind man? My son-in-law told me."

I nodded.

"Setr was our brother." Arnthor's voice was a whisper. "We used . . . It does not matter now. Nor will we avenge our brother upon a man who cannot see."

I knelt. "I speak for the Valfather and his sons, Your Majesty, having knowledge of both. It's well to triumph over foes, but it's better to deserve to triumph over them. No more than any other man can I predict whether you'll win the day, but today you've done more."

"Thank you." The king shut his eyes as before, then opened them wider. "This man is blind, you say. We are not. Do we not know your helm?"

I held it out. "It is Your Majesty's, if you want it."

"We do not. We say only this: you are not to wear it in our presence."

I swore I would not.

"We must hoard our strength. Tell him, Beel."

He cleared his throat. "I'll be brief. Duke Coth was second to His Majesty until two days past. With his death the position falls on your liege. I've counseled His Majesty to summon him and urge that he be guided by your advice. There would be no mention of you in the formal announcement, you understand. Would that be agreeable?"

I said it would, and so it was done, Marder giving his sword to Arnthor (he sitting in a chair draped with crimson velvet and made to serve as a throne) and receiving it back from him, this witnessed by such peers as remained.

When we were alone, I asked Marder the state of our troops, although I had seen something of it already, and little that had been good.

He shrugged.

"You drove the Osterlings from Burning Mountain."

"We did, with great loss to ourselves. We fought on foot. It was like storming ten castles. If the king had taken my advice, we wouldn't have fought at all."

I waited.

"We are crushed between millstones, Sir Able. Our men have no food, so we must fight while they can still stand. That's one stone. The other is that we're beaten. If you'd seen us at Five Fates . . ." He shrugged again.

He looked old and tired. His beard was always white, but his face was tired and drawn now. When I had waited for him to say more and he had not, I asked, "Is our hurry so great you can't tell me about it? I was in Jotunland."

"Where I had sent you. I used all my influence with the king to extricate you from his dungeon. He was immovable."

"The king himself extricated me. Why is the battle called Five Fates? Is it a place?"

Marder shook his head. "It's a tale for children."

"Well suited to me in that case."

"As you wish. The old Caan, the present Caan's father, had no lawful issue. Bastard sons, in which he differed from our king. But no lawful sons or daughters, for his queen was barren. It became apparent to his advisors that when he died his bastards would rend his realm into twenty."

I suppose I smiled.

"Would it had been so! He summoned a famous sorcerer and gave him a chest of gold. Perhaps he threatened him as well, accounts differ. The sorcerer assured him the queen would bear him boys, and went his way. She conceived, grew big, and dying bore not one son, or two, or even three."

"Five?" I suppose I looked incredulous.

Marder shook his head. "Six. In all my life I've never heard of a woman bearing six children together, yet six there were, like as peas. There was no question of succession, because the midwives had marked them in order of birth, tying a red ribbon about the ankle of the first, a brown ribbon on the ankle of the second, a white ribbon on the third, a gilt ribbon on the fourth, a blue ribbon on the fifth, and a black ribbon on the sixth and last. Ribbons of the first three colors had been provided for the purpose by the Wazir. The rest they tore from their raiment."

"And this is true?" I asked.

"It is, indeed. Our king has many ways of learning what transpires in Osterland, and all reported it. Besides, the young tijanamirs were clothed in those colors so they might be known in their order, and so they would know their places. The eldest was called the Red Tijanamir, and so on."

"And the five fates?"

"Were the fates of five tijanamirs. As you may imagine, the appearance of six heirs in one birth occasioned comment. Seers were consulted, and one prophecy was repeated all over the realm, though the Caan forbade it. The seer had been asked—perhaps by the Wazir—which would reign, and if his reign would be long. He rent the veil and foretold that all would reign, and all would die young."

I said, "That's very good news, if it can be credited."

Marder lifted his shoulders and let them fall. "Do you wish to hear the rest?"

"If it bears on the battle."

"It does—upon the name we give it, if nothing else. This seer went on to foretell how each would die. The Red Tijanamir, he said, would be crushed by a stone. The Brown would be trodden into the mire. The White would die at the hands of his followers. The Golden was to perish in a gold fortress. The Blue was to drown. And the Black Tijanamir was to be run through and through with the sword the Caan wore the day the prophecy was made. What troubles you?"

I waved my hand and begged him to proceed.

"As you like. This prophecy came to be known as that of Six Fates, the seer having foreseen the fates of all six. The Red Tijanamir succeeded his father when we killed him. You were in the north, but I took part in that campaign, and Sir Woddet won great renown."

"I want to see him. How did the tijanamirs die?"

"As the soothsayer had foretold, in every case. The Red Caan, who had been the Red Tijanamir, had removed his helm to wipe his brow. A slingstone struck and killed him, the first fate. The new Caan, the Brown Tijanamir, was trampled under the hooves of our chargers. That was the second. The White Tijanamir became Caan upon his brother's death. Not an hour later, a lance pierced him through. Sure to die, he tried to end his life but found himself too weak. He begged his friends to kill him, which they did. Thus, the third fate."

"I see."

"The fourth was the Golden Tijanamir, as you may recall. He wore a golden helm, just as his brothers' helms were red, brown, white, blue, and black. Sir Woddet's point entered the eye socket, and the Golden Caan died in that fortress of gold. I rewarded Sir Woddet richly for the thrust, as you may have heard. The king rewarded him more richly still."

I said, "I take it the Blue Tijanamir drowned."

Marder nodded. "The dagger of a man-at-arms pierced his lungs, so that he drowned in his own blood, the fifth fate. The sixth tijanamir, whose color was black, is the present Caan. This is because the old Caan, hearing of the prophecy, gave the sword he had worn that day into his son's keeping. We are told it is locked away in a sealed vault; it appears that as long as it remains there, the Black Caan is safe."

I had my own thoughts, but I nodded to that. "It seems the seer erred. He said all their reigns would be short."

"Seers err frequently," Marder said, "but suppose we defeat the Osterlings in a month or two. Might we not take their capital, open the vault, and retrieve the sword?"

"We might," I said, "if it's still there."

My inspection of our troops convinced me that winning was out of the question—our only hope was to march north, get as many more men as we could, and collect all the food we could find. If there had been any chance of terms and decent treatment, I would have told Marder and Arnthor to surrender. There was none; and although giving up Burning Mountain, won at such a high cost, shattered what little morale remained, we left it.

In the time that followed, there were days when I wished I were back in my cell. We marched north. The Black Caan, who must have known what we were doing very quickly, moved to prevent us and make us fight. We backed down the coast again instead, spearing fish in the shallows and scrounging mussels and clams. When our horses died (and more and more did) they were eaten at once.

I took the rear guard and had Woddet with me, and Rober, Lamwell, and others. There was scarcely a day in which we found no work to do, for the Caan's skirmishers were swift, and being eager to drive us from our dead attacked boldly again and again. Like ours, their archers were hard pressed to find or make arrows; but they had slingers in plenty, and there were stones enough to kill everyone in Mythgarthr twice over. A shower of stones, a few javelins, and a charge—it was a pattern we soon came to know well. Broad shields were needed to ward off the stones; even our lightly armed soon had them, woven of palm fronds when there was nothing else. We knights formed the first line and took the brunt of every charge, sometimes slinging our shields so as to wield our lances with both hands, more often with shield and sword, fighting morning and night when we were lightheaded with hunger.

Gylf saved us, finding game where we would have found none, and killing it or driving it to us. Marder told me, when the army took six hellish days to bridge the Greenflood, that our rear guard looked better than the rest. I went to see the rest, and he was right.

We had marched north of Burning Mountain before the Caan halted us. That night (how well I remember this!) we saw its sullen glow again: light the color of old blood staining the sky. A page came for me, a frightened boy; but before I tell about that, I must say that Gylf, who had fought like five score men and found food where there was none, had saved me in good earnest that day. I had fallen, and would have died had he not raged over me, killing every Osterling who came near. Marder heard of it, and asked to speak with me. That is why I went back and Gylf with me, to see the starved faces and empty eyes of a thousand men who had been strong.

"Sir Able?"

I had not known there were boys with Arnthor's army, save for squires who were nearly men; but he was a lad of ten. I was wearing the old helm, having no other, though I had little wish to see the truth it revealed; thus I may have seen his dread plainer than he showed it.

"Her Highness must speak with you, Sir Able."

I was angry at the condition of the men I had seen, and happy to have a target for my anger. "Morcaine has spoken to me before," I told him. "I say to you what I said to her. She left me to rot in a dungeon, from which the brother she fears so much freed me. My loyalty is to him, not her. If she wants my friendship, let her earn it."

He left but soon returned, more frightened than ever. "Her Highness says you don't understand, that she doesn't want to talk to you herself. She has company . . ." His voice had failed. He seemed to strangle, then tried again. "She does, too, Sir Able, something—somebody . . ."

His teeth had begun to chatter. While he struggled to control them I said, "The queen?"

"N-no. No, sir."

"The king, in that case. Why didn't she say so?"

The poor boy shook his head violently.

"All right, the Black Caan!"

He collapsed in tears. "I've *got* to bring you. She— she'll kill me this time."

"You will bring me," I told him. "Come on. I'm tired and want to get this over."

The Morcaine who greeted Gylf and me was a woman to the hem of her skirt, and a snake below it, the great, trailing serpent body prettily marked with runes of degeneration and destruction.

"Suppose you were king," she said.

I told her she was speaking treason.

"Not at all. Someone very important is waiting to see you." She gestured toward the rear of her pavilion, where a black curtain fluttered and billowed. "Still, we may have a minute to ourselves. My brother is sorely wounded. He is determined to take part in the next battle—he knows what happens to kings who don't fight. No one would regret his death more than I, but suppose he dies. Who rules?"

I said, "Queen Gaynor, I imagine," though I knew better.

"With you as her sword?"

I shook my head.

"I don't blame you. She thrust you into that dungeon and left you to rot. You, her champion. Nor is she of the royal line. Perhaps she betrays my brother—perhaps she doesn't. Guilty or not, my brother thinks her false and has told your liege and others. They might accept her in peace. Not now. Not here. Not three lords would stand by her."

"You then," I said.

"Better, because I'm royal. Bad still. I'm no warrior, and none of them trust me. Duke Marder?"

"He would have my sword."

"An old man without a son." Her laugh was weak and shaky; when I heard it I knew something had scared her sober. "Who leads this army? Who issues its orders?"

I said nothing.

"You would relish revenge."

I could not speak, but I shook my head.

"How could you avenge yourself better than by marrying me? You could rape me twice a night. Or thrice. You look capable of it. You could have a dozen mistresses and throw them in my face. You could thrash me with the poker, and all Celidon would call me disloyal if I said a word against you."

She brought my hand to her cheek. "How strong you are! How can you gain revenge if you *don't* marry me? Think about that. You can have Gaynor's head on a pike. I'm royal, but I'll be on the other side of the bed, in easy reach."

"No." I drew my hand away.

"Listen! We haven't much time. My brother will be dead in a month. No one will want Gaynor. Many will cleave to me for my father's sake. More will want you. Wise men like His Grace will fear a new war, pitting brother against brother 'til the Osterlings conquer both. Calling those who favor us together, we'll declare our intention to wed."

She paused, unable to see my face within the old helm,

but watching my eyes. Suddenly she smiled. "Curtain! It's what the jugglers say. Are you afraid to go in there?"

I shook my head.

"You should be." She tried to laugh again. "I would be, and I brought him. Think over what I've said, beloved, if you come out sane."

Perhaps I nodded or spoke; if so, I do not recall it. She or I or he pushed the curtain aside. I cannot describe the empty inferno there—there are no words. *"Take that off,"* he told me, and I could no more have disobeyed than I could have picked myself up by my belt.

The old helm gone, I recognized him at once, strong, sharp-featured as any fox, and crowned with fire—not the floating hair of the Fire Aelf, which only suggests flames, but real fire, red, yellow, and blue, snapping and crackling.

"You know me," he said, "and I know you. You called me the youngest and worst of my father's sons not long ago, and insulted my wife."

"I meant no insult," I said. "Would I insult two people I fear so much?"

"You boast of fearing nothing." He frowned at Gylf. "You've stolen one of my father's dogs. He won't like that."

"No," Gylf said shortly. "He knows."

"Then I don't like it." He smiled. "But I'll overlook it. You need me. I don't need you, not at all, except for fun. You know I have a kind heart."

I managed to say, "I know you say you do."

"I'm a liar, of course. I take after both parents in that. Not lying—I never lie—I offer help. For fun. Because it amuses me. Still, my offer is real."

I only struggled to master my fear.

"You people complain of us—the same things the Aelf say about you. We pay no attention, we don't care whether you live or die. What's the use of becoming a druid? Why pray, when nobody listens? All right, here I am. Do you deny I'm an Overcyn?"

Gylf spoke for me. "No. You are."

"Correct. Nor am I the least of us. Will I hear your prayer, standing here before you? I couldn't miss it if I put my fingers in my ears. Kneel."

I knelt, and Gylf lay down beside me.

"Excellent. If I told you to touch your nose to the carpet so I could put my foot on your head, would you do it?"

"Yes," I said. "I'd have to."

"Then we'll dispense with it. Pray."

"Great prince of light," I began, "prince of fire—"

"Never mind. We don't need that. Let's just say I'll grant three wishes. I know what they're going to be, but you have to say them. What do you want? Not two, and not four."

"Food. Enough for everyone 'til we fight."

"That's right. What else?"

"More men."

"Too vague. One man? Two?"

"Ten thousand."

He laughed, a terrible sound. "I can't do it, and you couldn't manage them. Five hundred. That's my best offer."

"Then I accept it." I had recovered some part of my self-possession. "And thank you most sincerely."

"You'll have to do more than that. The third?"

"Cloud. Your father gave her to me, but I lost her when the queen imprisoned me. I think she's been looking for me, and I've been looking for her."

"You've changed, both of you," he told me. "You met the most low god."

"Yes," I said.

"He grants wishes, too, but he grants them in such a way that you wish he hadn't. I never stoop to that."

I said I was glad to hear it.

"However, you may feel that I stooped to something of the sort after I catch Cloud for you. Send her away if you do. She won't cling like a curse, believe me. Still, she costs a wish. Do you want her?"

"Yes," I said.

"All right. When do you want the men?"

"Now."

"I can't do it. I'm going to need time to work."

"As soon as possible, then."

"Fair enough. You may stand."

I rose. He had been no taller than I when I knelt, but he had grown by the time I rose, so tall that I was afraid his crown would ignite the roof of the pavilion.

"Payment will be simple and easy, but fun. What's more you've already done it, as we both know. Break the promise you made my father. Again."

I could not speak.

"It's letting you off far too cheaply, isn't that what you're about to say? I'll like it just the same. He trusts you, and I enjoy salting his silly dreams with reality now and then. Will you do it?"

Looking up at him (for he seemed farther above me now than he had when I was on my knees) I could not help but see how handsome he was, and how shifty. "I'll do it," I said, "but you must give me the things I've asked for first."

"What!" It was feigned anger. "Don't you trust me?"

"I won't argue. Do as I say or do your worst."

"Which would kill you and every friend you have."

I scratched Gylf's ears.

"Do you think my father wouldn't forgive me for killing a dog? He's forgiven me far worse."

Gylf licked my fingers.

"He'd die for you, of course he would. Would Disiri? Would you want her to?"

I turned to go.

"Wait! I won't haggle, and I want to make that clear. Here's what I'll do. I'll get you the food and the men—half a thousand tough fighting men—as soon as can. Let's say it takes . . ." He stroked his chin. "Ten days. When you've got them, you'll have two of your wishes. Agreed?"

I nodded.

"At that point you must break your word to my father. Not just some technicality, three times and big and showy."

I said, "Suppose three times isn't enough?"

The truth, Ben, is that I had already decided before I went into that pavilion. If I could have pulled bread out of the air, I would have already. I could not. There were a lot of things I could not do, raising the dead and so on. But there were things I *could* do, and I had settled on them, although without Lothur I might have changed my mind.

Did he know it? Shape my payment as he did, because he did? It is possible he did, but I do not believe it. He is as clever and cruel as a den of foxes, and knows more tricks than a score of Vils; but his father sees far.

And very deep.

CHAPTER THIRTY-EIGHT

DRAGON SOLDIERS

Had the queen summoned me that night as well, I would not have been surprised; I knew she was Morcaine's ally, and that one might sift a thousand foolish women without finding even one fool enough to trust Morcaine. The queen would want my account of what had transpired that night, as well as hers.

I was surprised just the same, for the queen came to me, crouching beside me as I slept, while Lamwell stood guard. She touched my shoulder. I sat up and saw him—a small figure with a great crest of white plumes and a drawn sword.

"Here, Sir Able." It was as though a dove had spoken.

I turned. Her robe was dark, but her golden hair glowed in the moonlight and her pale face shone. "You've plighted your troth to my sister-in-law," she said. "That is well. She has remained too long—what are you doing that for?"

I had picked up the old helm and was putting it on. "I may need to protect you from the king's men, if not from the Osterlings." The moonlit woman shrank, her fair face younger still. "We're both kids, Your Majesty, and us kids have to stick together, or the wolves will tear us apart."

"You must hate me. She said you did."

"How could I hate you, when the king loves you?"

"Prettily spoken. May I pet your dog?"

"I could not match you in wit, Your Majesty. Nor would it be fitting for me to try."

She laughed softly, a delightful sound after Morcaine's laughter, and Lothur's. "I didn't think you'd understand that. There's more to you than meets the eye, Sir Able."

"Less, Your Majesty."

"Won't you take it off? So I can see your face?"

"Sir Lamwell's my friend, Your Majesty, and I've seldom known a truer knight. But if you were to order him to kill me, he would—or would try."

"But I won't!"

"You can't know that, Your Majesty, and I surely can't."

"My husband knows more of sorcery than his sister, Sir Able." Gaynor's coo, soft already, had grown softer still.

I told her I was aware of it.

"Few are. People don't like the idea of a sorcerous ruler. She shows it, shows off and draws their displeasure. He keeps his hidden. If you really know all this, you ought to know I don't have any such power. None at all. Do you?"

"Yes, Your Majesty."

"You don't know what it's been like for me." Her hand found mine and squeezed it. "Husbands are—are bad enough without that. His rages are terrible, and he could spy on me anytime he wanted. I was a queen. I am. A queen in a glass castle. I ran a terrible risk for you when I let you confer with Queen Idnn and Lord Escan. Do you understand that? Do you know how great a chance I took? The gaolers knew, and all those people, but I had to let them see there was nothing between us. Not then." She squeezed my hand again. Hers was small, and so white it shone in the moonlight.

"You didn't take it long, Your Majesty."

"No. No, I didn't. I couldn't. You went out on your own, and you were caught. They'd tell him when he came back. They were bound to and I couldn't stop them. Sometimes he spies and sometimes he doesn't, but—"

I said, "Suppose he sees us now?"

"He won't. I spoke to him before I came to see you. He—he won't. He's seen the future, Sir Able. And he dies."

"We all do."

"Before the new moon. He kills the Caan and the Caan kills him. Can that happen?"

I nodded.

"I'll be a widow. Your queen and the first of a new dynasty. I'll need a minister, a strong man who can keep order. I'll rule wisely and well, but only if they *let* me rule. And you . . . Can you be gentle, as well as strong? I've never had anyone gentle, never had anyone but him."

You know what I was tempted to say, Ben. I did not say it, merely saying that her husband was not dead yet, and I needed time to consider. If I had refused, she would have told Lamwell to kill me and I would have had to kill him. I liked him, and we could not spare a single knight.

Ten days, Lothur had said. Knowing they could not be hastened, I did not try to hurry our march south. We had to collect all the food we could along the way, and I had to plan the actions that would violate the oath I would break.

We met them on a cliff-side road overlooking the sea, stranger warriors than I had ever seen, dark, hard-faced men with little eyes. Their armor made them look like bugs, and their shaggy ponies like peasants. They challenged us; and I found that although I understood their speech, no one else did. There were three hundred, perhaps, with a baggage train so long that it wound away down the coast.

Wistan and I advanced under a flag of truce. Their prince wore gold armor; his was the hardest hand I ever clasped, and he the only man I have known who smiled all the time. When we met, I thought he simply wanted to assure us we would be well treated if we yielded. Later I learned that his men called him He-who-smiles. Wistan and I settled for Smiler.

He was accompanied by three ministers, middle-aged men of his own race. One carried a horned staff, one a whip, and one a sword with a blade of dragon shape. He would choose one or another of these ministers and whisper to him. The minister would confer with the other two and speak to me. It became tedious; I will abbreviate it as much as I can.

"You are to surrender to us." This was the minister with the sword. "Give me your weapons."

Wistan tugged my sleeve. "Why does he talk like that?"

I said, "Because he thinks we might, I guess."

"Might what? What did he say?"

"We won't surrender," I told the minister. "If you'll share your food with us, we'll be your friends and lead you to a great victory. If you won't, we'll take it."

The prince continued to smile, gesturing to the minister with the whip. "The Son of the Dragon fears you misapprehend this matter. He is sworn to conquer or die. With him we are all sworn to conquer or die. We conquer or die!"

"Then you'll die," I said.

Still smiling, the prince spoke with his third minister, the one with the forked staff. "You are a barbarian," this minister told me. His tone was fatherly. "You do not know us, nor the customs of civilized men. Do you wish to?"

I said I certainly did.

"That said, you are no longer a barbarian. We are the children of the Dragon, Sirable. For most, by adoption. For the Son of the Dragon, by blood. The Blood of the Dragon is his father." He fell silent, standing with head bowed. At length he said, "His Sons are Sons of the Dragon. Dragon Blood fills him each time he engenders sons in his wives."

I told him I understood.

"Each would rule. Is he not Son of the Dragon?"

Wistan was tugging my sleeve again. I told him to stop.

"A son may bow to his brother, and be cut. He remains. If no, they fight with magic. Our prince chose to fight."

Thinking of Arnthor and his sister, I said, "We have a lot of magic. If he contends with us, he will lose again."

The minister tittered. "No, no! He won. The winner leaves Home Throne to his brother. Do you not understand?"

I confessed I did not.

"It is his glory to extend the Realm of the Dragon. He is permitted five hundred warriors. It is honor to go. The Talking Table is consulted. Always the Talking Table says, 'Go north! Go west!' or 'Go south!' This is traditional. To east there is much water."

The minister with the forked staff retired, and the minister with the whip came forward. "Yours is the Land of the East. Obey the Son of the Dragon and prosper. Disobey . . ." He tapped his own hand with his coiled whip.

"You are in our country," I told him, though we were well south of Celidon. "You must obey our king. He is King Arnthor, a good and wise ruler. I speak for him now."

The minister who bore the sword came forward once more. "Will we fight here, on this narrow road?"

"Yes," I said. "Will you fight me now?" I knew I would have my point in him before he could poise his big blade.

He shook his head. "Our champions will fight. In such a place it must be so." His voice fell. "My son, you do not know our law. Let me make it plain. When one fights one, three victories are sufficient. Is this clear to you?"

I admitted it was not.

"The first two fight. We win. That is a victory."

I nodded.

"The first of our champions fights your next. That also is a victory, it is two."

I nodded as before.

"The first of our champions fights your third. That is another, it is three. You must accept the beneficent rule of the Son of the Dragon."

I said, "We will not."

"If you do not, every man will be put to the sword."

When we left, I explained to Wistan, who looked very serious. "I'll fight, Sir Able, but I'm not a champion."

I laughed, and slapped his back.

I was our first, though I had great difficulty securing the position. Arnthor wanted to negotiate further, and sent Beel with me to interpret. We learned more about the Dragon soldiers and their prince; but quickly discovered there was no hope of making them allies, as our instructions required. Neither would they share their food with us (although they boasted of its quantity) or even sell to us.

By Marder's influence and my own, Woddet was our second champion. Kei was the third. We did not think we would need more than three. As for me, I was determined that neither Woddet nor Kei would have work that afternoon. They looked imposing, and that was enough. Wistan and I made nothing like so good a show, although I learned afterward that the Son of the Dragon had been impressed by the gold rings in my mail, and by my speaking the tongue of his nation.

The Nykr King of Arms went with us to see fair play, the minister with the sword serving a like function on the other side. He objected to Wistan; we explained that he was there only to bear my lance with my pennant, to carry my helm and shield, to help me from the field if I were wounded or to guard my corpse. It was agreed that he would retire one hundred paces before I engaged.

Each of us retreated ten paces. The Nykr King of Arms raised the staff with which he would strike the roadway, and the minister with the sword lowered the sword he would raise. I could not see our pursuivant up on the cliff, but no doubt he raised his trumpet. At that moment Gylf howled. I had been obliged to chain him, for he had sworn that he would not stand by and see me killed; but he knew the battle was about to be joined, or so it seemed. His was the howl of no common dog, and I saw its effect on my opponent.

No sooner had I put on the old helm than I saw more. I saw that for all his fanciful armor and flat face my opponent was a bold knight who would add real force to our charge when we faced the Osterlings—force that would be forever lost if I killed him. I took my lance from Wistan.

My opponent, Ironmouth, cut through it at once; I have seldom seen so good a blade. I knocked that blade from his hand with the butt of my lance, tripped him, and almost pinned him. In a moment more he had nearly pinned me, for he was a fine wrestler. As we struggled, I caught sight of Lothur's inferno upon the cliff.

We parted, rushed at each other, and Ironmouth by an unexpected slight threw me down not a hand's breadth from a sheer drop. I regained my feet, but not quickly enough.

I snatched air, caught thick, coarse, white stuff—I knew not what—and clung to it for dear life.

A great thought, kind and warm and wonderful, filled

my mind, crowding out the fear; and the thought was this: *Can you not run on this as Gylf and I do?*

And I could have. It would have been a violation of the oath; but I intended to violate it.

I did not do it then, but climbed on Cloud's back, a back no longer gray; it was spangled with ice crystals as well, for she had been far above the clouds a moment before.

We are born dark, she explained. *We reach our true color with age. I am nearly grown now.*

Like a cloud, she rose into the sky, carrying me with her. The Caan had elephants; they were nothing before her. We talked. I told her of all that had befallen me since we parted, and she told me of strange adventures in the east, of her return to Skai, of what she had told the Lady there (for the Lady had stabled her), and what the Lady had taught her. Below, the sea-blue flag of Celidon snapped in the breeze, flaunting its nykr to the dragon that was Celidon's new foe, a dragon of red and black on a wheaten field. Woddet came forth to fight, and fell, and Hela bore him away.

"Lothur has promised us the victory," I told Cloud, "so we must prevail."

Given a mount and a stout lance, I would have matched Kei against a hundred; with the sword he was no match for Ironmouth. He fell, and I watched him die. After which, the Dragon Soldiers raised a great cheer, bellowing and beating their shields, and I saw the minister who bore the sword and the Nykr King of Arms come together, and the latter bow his head. Neither could have understood the other, but they had little need to as Cloud and I galloped down the sky.

With one hand I held her mane. With the other, I caught Smiler, and pulled him onto her back. "We're going to Skai," I told him, "where time runs fast. We'll find Lothur, or if not Lothur, Angrboda, and confront her together."

It did not prove necessary, for Lothur found us.

* * *

As I have said, we had crossed the Greenflood on our march south. When we turned back north we knew we must encounter it again. We had burned the bridge we built, a bridge that could not have stood another week in any event. More significantly, we had swept the sea-lands of food, buying or pillaging all its fishing villages had.

The minister who bore the sword (Stonebowl was his name) told us his men had found more inland; they had captured five towns, all well-stocked, and had taken the coast road only after gaining food enough to carry them to next spring. Beel agreed, pointing out that Osterland's raiders frequently harried the coast, sailing as far north as Irringsmouth or farther. This stretch would see them often.

Knowing that the Greenflood would be nearer its source, and unwilling to deplete our allies' stores more than we had to, we turned east as soon as we came upon a passable road, and engaged local people to guide us. Some were reliable, others less so. Too often we found ourselves marching south or southeast when we would have preferred to turn north.

Before long we gained a reinforcement of one knight and six men-at-arms; and though it was so small it cheered me, for it was the Knight of the Leopards. Sandhill had held off the Osterlings, who had failed to carry it by storm and been forced to lift a siege by thirst. Shepherds whose flocks we had bought had reported that the king was in the south, two days' ride below the river; and the Knight of the Leopards had gotten his father's permission to join us with a few men.

"Now I know we'll win," I told him. "There's a tide in war not even Overcyns can turn aside. It's making— I feel it in my blood."

He was looking up at Cloud. "If that grand beast obeys you, I do not matter. Nothing could stand against it."

"Don't you recognize her?" I said. "She's Cloud, the mount I rode in Jotunland."

"That's no horse!"

"Why no. She never was a horse. I doubt I ever said she was, but if I did, I lied."

Wistan could keep silent no longer. "We can ride her through the air. You can't know how wonderful it is, Sir Leort. She carried the Son of the Dragon, because Sir Able had taken him prisoner, but she didn't like it. He couldn't ride her alone like we do."

Leort wanted to know who the Son of the Dragon was, and I explained.

"He's going to carve out a kingdom for himself here in the south? He'll have a hard time of it."

"Of course he will," I said, "but he'll have help from Celidon. His Majesty has sworn it. A strong friend down here would be the Valfather's hand." I said nothing about Arnthor's prophecy, although I could not help thinking of it, and salved my conscience by telling myself I knew nothing beyond Gaynor's report; it might be a false prophecy or an ambiguous one, for many prophecies are. It was even possible—almost probable—that there had been none.

A matter you will readily guess troubled me much more. Lothur had promised allies and food on my own promise to break my oath. Cloud was to be returned to me when I had fulfilled my part of the bargain. By his generosity, she had been sent ahead of time. We had received the reinforcements he had promised, and I could not complain of their quality. We had food for a season, and every prospect of gaining more in Celidon when we overcame the Black Caan. All that, and I still had not fulfilled my promise.

Nor did I want to.

The Valfather is the kindest and wisest ruler, and the bravest. His son Thunor is the model for warriors, as is often said. A hundred times more is the Valfather the model for kings. In that time, when I thought about him often, it came to me with a shock that he was the model for fathers, too. I had told myself I never had a father. Far less than you, Ben. It was not true. He had been my father, and he had known it when I had not.

I would betray him, and my honor would be forfeit. Or if I did not, my honor would be forfeit still. Lothur is the model for thieves and murderers; he would kill us or help the Caan do it, and all I hoped to do with the power Skai had given me would never happen.

Wistan and I rode on Cloud's broad back, well ahead of the advance guard. Our leisurely pace was compelled by our baggage train, and by our army, too, men worn out who regained their strength through easy marches and whole days of rest.

Arnthor was gaining strength as well, though his wound had been almost fatal. Once when I was with him, someone complained of the rigors of the campaign, calling it (with some justice) the worst ever fought.

"Ah," said Beel, "you ought to have been with Sir Able and me in Jotunland, where our sharp-eyed bowmen were my daughter's maids, and my cook rode among my men-at-arms with a slaughtering knife."

Marder laughed. "Well said. Just don't forget that I was there before it ended, and at the Forest Fight."

So swiftly that it came and went like the shadow of a bat, Arnthor frowned as if he might kill him. I did not understand that look and was disturbed by it. Arnthor seldom showed his dragon side, but I had seen it plainly then. What more I might have seen had I been wearing the old helm I can only imagine; and I am glad I was not.

I sought out Woddet among the wounded that evening, telling him what had transpired and asking whether he had been at the second battle Marder mentioned.

"I was," he said, "and we had a bad time of it. We had

gone into the wood—run there, when it seemed certain the Osterlings would crush us all. There were so many trees you couldn't swing a sword. I had never used a mace since—never mind. I used it again, and dropped it wrestling two fellows Heimir brained for me. We had no time to look for it, and I used a saxe after that. I'd not thought it more than a camp knife until that day, but I learned what it could do. I'd hold it low and rush them with my shield up. Some had mail shirts, but their legs were bare. I'd put it through the thigh and cut my way out, and go to the next."

I asked whether we had gained the victory, and he said we had to retreat, but we had captured their camp and burned it. "The Black Caan thought to crush us, and win the war," he said, "but he slept on the ground that night."

Etela came—Lynnet was talking strangely. Etela felt I could help, so I went with her. Wistan, who had told her where she might find me, came with us.

Bold Berthold was seated at Lynnet's feet, with Gerda not far away. Toug stood behind her, watching. As we came up, Lynnet said, "Your father was a fine, strong man. Not tall, though he seemed tall. There must have been a hundred times when I saw him standing with another man and noticed, the way you notice suddenly what you ought to have seen long before, that he was no taller than the other. But if you listened to them, you understood that he was much bigger. It was something you couldn't see, but it was there. The other man looked up to him, and when he did, he was looking high. All the men looked up to him, and all the women envied me. Do you remember Daddy's name, Berthold? I won't blame you if you've forgotten after all these years. Not one bit."

"Black Berthold," Berthold said.

"That's right, his name was Berthold, and he was a fine, strong man. The strongest in our village. Once I saw him wrestle a bull. The bull threw him twice, but he jumped up each time before it could gore him. He threw it and held it down. It struggled like a puppy, but he wouldn't let it get its legs under it again. It frightened me so much I made him promise never to do it again, and he never did. I never knew him to break a promise to anybody."

Etela said, "I've brought Sir Able, Mama."

Lynnet looked up at me and smiled. "Good evening, Sir Able. I had a son of that name once. You aren't my son, I know, but I'd like to think of you as a son. May I?"

I had not noticed Vil until then, because he was farther from the fire than any of the others; but he stepped forward when she said that. Blindness had let him forget to control his expression, and it was a look of mingled hope and fear such as I have seldom seen. I sensed what he wanted me to say, I believe, and said it gladly. "I'd be proud to be called your son, Lady Lynnet, and proud to call you mother."

"My name's Mag." She smiled. "But you may call me Mother, or anything you like, Able. You've always been my boy, because I love the boy you were before I met you."

I sat at her feet beside Bold Berthold. "Something's troubling me, Mother. Perhaps you can explain it. Do you recall the Room of Lost Love?"

She shook her head. "I've never heard of such a place."

"What about the Isle of Glas?"

"Ah," she said.

"You recall it." I looked up at her. "Do you remember how I came there? How we met, and what you told me?"

Her smile saddened. "My son Able came to me in that beautiful, terrible place, Sir Able, not you. I was chained there, and though I would willingly—oh, very, willingly—have come away with him, I could not."

Although I often have strange dreams, I have tried not to pester you overmuch with them, Ben. Here I am going to make an exception, not because the dream in question seems specially significant, but merely because I remember it so vividly. Go to the next section if you are impatient.

I was in the Forest Fight with Woddet and the others. Either I had no sword, or I could not use it. Perhaps I had a dagger or Sword Breaker. I cannot be sure. There were green bushes and spindly trees all around me. I struggled to push through, afraid that the king would leave me behind. Frantically, I threw myself forward, striking the saplings that obstructed every step, and making leaves fly. As I went farther, I realized that I was not on the ground, nor was I obstructed by brush. I was in the treetops, fifty feet up. If the twigs and small limbs that held me back had not been so thick—if they had not been almost impenetrable—I would have fallen. No sooner had I understood this than I reached the edge, standing high in a great tree and looking out across the open countryside.

A pavilion of black silk had been pitched in a meadow. I knew that Eterne was in there. I also knew Eterne was my true sword; I bore no sword until I had her, and should have borne none until I got her back. I had taken another sword, and could never be shriven of that guilt.

Beyond the black pavilion was a highway. Cars, trucks, SUVs, and minivans—all sorts of vehicles—were traveling on it, going so fast that it seemed certain they would crash. There was a school bus, a red hook-and-ladder, a black-and-white police car, and a white ambulance. Those stand out even now. The ambulance rocked from side to side as it tore along with its light bar blazing and its siren screaming. I climbed down and went to the highway. The drivers would not stop for me, and I shouted at their cars, thinking how far the ambulance was getting ahead of me. Able—the real Able—was in that ambulance. I knew that, and I wanted to help him.

I woke up. "Baki?" Someone was stroking me.

"Guess again."

I thought it a better dream than my dream of the treetop and the crowded highway, my dream of the Forest Fight.

CHAPTER THIRTY-NINE
IT THIRSTS

From time to time Wistan and I met others on the road, often people fleeing the Osterlings. We spoke kindly to them, and though the news of the enemy they had was far from dependable we heard them gladly. That morning it was a fine young man, lean and dark, who fell to his knees. "Sir! Sir! Can you spare a scrap of food? It's been two days and three nights."

Cloud crouched, and I dismounted. "Tell me something of value, and you'll get a good meal. Are you from Celidon?"

Reluctantly he said, "This is my country. Here."

"Then your countrymen should feed you. Can't you work?"

He stood, abashed. "I'm a herdsman. Only—only . . ."

The dry brush stirred, and I knew we were watched.

"Only I never saw a animal like that, sir."

"Nor will you ever see another."

Wistan pointed. "How'd you get that scar?"

"A arrow. Sometimes people steal our cattle, or try."

I said, "You yourself never cross the river into Celidon to steal cattle, I'm sure."

"Would you kill me for it? Now?"

I shook my head.

"My children, sir, and my wife. They haven't had a

thing to eat. Not today, and not yesterday neither. If you'll give something, sir, anything we can eat, and tell us what cattle's yours? I'd never bother one head of yours. Never again." He looked up at me hopefully.

"Who has your herd?"

"Them from across the mountains. I won't never touch a animal of yours nor fight your herders. By wind and grass!"

"If I give you something now. Something to eat."

He fell to his knees again, hands outstretched. I doubt that he had begged before; certainly he knew little about it.

I made him rise. "Tell your wife and children to come out. I won't hurt them and I want to see them."

She was tall and graceful, darker than he; her eyes were the sky at moonrise. Their boys were about four and five.

"I don't have food," I told him, "but I can see you get plenty if you'll earn it. There's a knight behind me. Do you know what a knight is?"

He nodded, a little hesitantly.

"A man like me, with a painted shield. His has leopards on it. Tell him you've talked to me, to Sir Able."

The woman said, "Sir Able."

"Right. Make him the promise you offered me. Tell him you'll fight the men from over the mountains with us if he'll feed you and your family and give you weapons."

He grinned and rubbed his hands.

"They're close behind us, Sir Able," his wife said.

I promised her that she and her children would be safe with us if her husband fought for us.

We met the first at noon, a small group I thought was a patrol. Cloud charged, and I made good use of a new string while wishing I had Parka's. They scattered, we topped a ridge and saw the advance guard of the Host of Osterland—a hundred horsemen, a horde of famished spearmen, and two elephants. Cloud impaled an elephant and tossed it, men and weapons scattering the way water scatters from a trout. The other fled, and we returned to our own advance guard and sent a man to warn Arnthor that the enemy was at hand.

There was a brisk fight that afternoon. The open, arid desert is perfect for cavalry, but the Knight of the Leopards and I had few horses, and those we had were not in the best condition. The Caan's horsemen flanked us, charging our shieldwall and nearly breaking it, scattering when I charged from between our ranks and re-forming behind their infantry. Our bowmen made good practice, and each charge cost men and horses. When the last had been repelled, their infantry showered us with sling-stones. We advanced and were met with the kind of wild attack we had come to know so well.

The Knight of the Leopards and I fought on foot before the shieldwall, and though the questing blade Baki had found for me was not Eterne, it drank blood to its hilt, drawing me step by step in search of the life it was destined to end.

"I tried to keep pace with you," the Knight of Leopards said afterward, "and so did the men. They could keep up with me, but not with you."

"I was scarcely able to keep up with my own sword."

He laughed. "But you were Able. How's Gylf?"

"He'll live, I'm sure, if we can keep him from fighting 'til he's well. Wistan's with him, and I'll sleep by him."

"You thought he couldn't be hurt." It was said soberly, and was not a question.

"Yes," I said. "I suppose I did."

"Anyone can be hurt—*anyone*. That includes you."

"I've learned I can be killed."

* * *

To tell the truth—and I have tried throughout this whole account to tell you the truth, Ben, as I knew it at the time— I expected an attack that night. The Osterlings, I thought, would be eager to bring us to battle. In this I was misled by my ignorance of the early stages of the war and the battle on the wooded slopes of the Mountains of the Sun that came after. I had not experienced it as the Caan had.

Osterland had been beaten by Celidon (decisively, it no doubt seemed) at Five Fates, the battle that had cost him his father and brothers and made him Caan. He had regrouped, beaten Celidon at the passes, and pressed on, his army gorged on flesh and ready for battle on any terms— a battle he must have felt sure would be the last.

The result had been the Forest Fight, over which neither he nor Arnthor had exercised control. He had won in the end; but his camp had been sacked, and the war that seemed nearly over had become a long struggle. He had outflanked Arnthor and taken Kingsdoom and Thortower, had sacked them both and butchered thousands, and so regained the prestige he had lost in the Forest Fight; but Arnthor had refused battle again and again. Driven south, then west, then south again, Arnthor had yielded the Mountain of Fire, retaken it, yielded it again at my urging, retreated, and now returned renewed, proving a dangerous and persevering enemy. A night attack might have become the sort of uncontrollable clash the Forest Fight had been; and even if Osterland prevailed, a night attack would be more apt to disperse than to destroy us.

None of which I knew when I lay listening to Gylf's labored breaths and wondering whether I had cleaned his wound well enough. Knowing that even if I had, he might die.

"Able?"

"Yes," I told him. "I'm right here."

"Ears up."

"Are they coming?" I sat up. Some strident insect was singing. Much farther away, sentries bawled the numbers of their posts to prove they were awake and in position. Cloud slept; her dreams were of elephants and starry meadows.

"Ears up," Gylf repeated.

"What is it?" I asked him; Uns stirred in his sleep.

"Master," Gylf muttered. "He walks."

The insect had ceased buzzing, and the sentries fallen silent. No wind disturbed the dry brush or moaned among the naked rocks; and in that charmed silence I came to understand that Gylf was right. Someone far bigger than Heimir—someone far bigger than Schildstarr—had left the seat from which his single eye beheld Skai and Mythgarthr. His ravens flew before him, and their all-seeing eyes were his. His wolves trotted at his heels, winding the blood that had not yet dyed the Greenflood. I shivered with fear, and drew my cloak about me. Gylf slept, but it was hours before I did.

I dreamed of the Caan's sea rovers; my mind was full of them when I woke. The brave blood runs first, we say, and mean that someone who has taken a wound never fights boldly again. No doubt there is truth in it, as in many sayings; but I have never found it a good guide. The older a man is, the more cautious he is apt to be, but that is true whether he has been wounded or not; and it was slaughtering so many enemies, not wounds, that had sobered Woddet.

How did it feel to be a man as large and as strong as he, and to lie with a woman half again your size, a woman who could snap pike shafts? How did it feel, for that matter, to lie with any woman? Disiri had been human—or humanlike—for me so long ago.

Seeking any distraction, I rose and donned the old helm. Gylf was a sleeping beast far mightier than he had appeared, but wounded still; no strength was left in the jaws that had shaken men like rats.

* * *

Next day we advanced in good order, reaching the river at midmorning. The Host of Osterland was massed along the north bank. I sent a messenger to report it, and he returned (as I expected) with a summons from Arnthor.

The Royal Pavilion had been set up by the time I reached the rear; Beel and the three dukes were seated inside, with Stonebowl, Gaynor, Morcaine, and Smiler. Arnthor himself presided, wrapped in his purple cloak. I had not expected the women, although I tried not to show it when I knelt and was invited to rise and claim a chair.

Beel cleared his throat. "We've been conferring in your absence. His Majesty and His Highness think it best to ask your opinion before you hear ours. As we see it, there are three questions. First, should we attack at once? Second, if we do not, should we await an attack or retreat? Third, if we attack, in what order and with what plan?"

I was collecting my thoughts and did not speak.

"There are many other questions, granted. For example, should we parley? Should we go up or down the river and attempt a crossing at some other point? But His Majesty and His Highness—all of us, in fact—concur in thinking the three I have stated central. Do you agree?"

I addressed Arnthor. "I don't, Your Majesty. Most of the day is before us. Will Your Majesty and His Highness wait for sunset? If you'll wait, the answer to My Lord's questions is that we should attack. But if you won't, we should retreat."

A long silence followed this, and a whispered conference between Stonebowl and Smiler. When it was over, Arnthor nodded to Beel, a nod that seemed to me to give permission to say whatever he thought best.

"It is only just that I make you privy to our opinions now—that is to say, to the opinions we voiced before your arrival. His Majesty reserved his. His Highness and his minister insisted on your presence. Her Majesty thought we should retreat. Her Highness urged that we wait, and—"

Morcaine interrupted. "I said stay here." She laughed. "If they attack, let them try. I think we can beat them and I want to try sorcery, which takes time."

"They will be trying it, too, Sister." Arnthor gestured to Beel.

"Their Graces favored an immediate attack. So do I. It seems to us that our situation is more likely to deteriorate than improve. You disagree, and we would like to know why."

Stonebowl said, "The Son of the Blood of the Skai Dragon is in agreement with your worthy self, Sirable. He wishes you to know that he will support your decision."

I thanked Smiler in his own language.

Beel muttered, "I'd like to know how you learned their tongue," and Morcaine laughed.

"I have not learned it," I explained. "I understand it, but I've never learned it. It's not a matter of study."

Gaynor leaned forward as if to touch me. "You can never forgive me for imprisoning you. But won't you forgive me for trying to avert a battle that may end my husband's life?"

I said, "I bear no animus toward Your Majesty in that or any other matter."

Arnthor spoke for himself. "Whatever the outcome of our council, I will have a word with you after it."

I made him a seated bow. "I am yours to command."

"Then tell me how you can promise victory."

"In the same way Their Graces and Lord Beel fear defeat. They know the Caan will have called for more troops from the north. My Lord Beel didn't say so, but that was surely in the minds of all those who urged that Your Majesty attack."

I thought there might be contradiction, but none came. "Your Majesty, it would be folly to attack 'til we know more about the state of the river. I have two brave young men, Squire Wistan and Squire Yond, investigating it now—I gave the order before I came. We must know how deep it is, and how swift the current is. If there are shallow reaches, we must find them. Waiting until twilight will give us time for it. We should also bring up our supply train and the women and wounded, and set a guard on them. Waiting for twilight will provide time for that too."

I drew a deep breath, resolved to lie and make my lie come true. "Most signally," I said, "I can promise you a thousand archers at twilight."

Bahart, the youngest of the dukes, said, "Spun out of air in this wilderness? You're a wizard indeed if you can do that, Sir Able."

Marder murmured, "Wouldn't it be better to let them make camp and get some sleep? We can attack tomorrow at sunrise."

Thoas added, "If they're archers, their bows will avail nothing after nightfall."

I nodded. "I had thought their bows deadly by night, Your Grace. Doubtless you know more of Aelfrice than I."

Arnthor's eyes widened. "A thousand Aelf, Sir Able?"

"At least a thousand, Your Majesty. I hope for more."

Beel coughed. "We had archers from Aelfrice when we defeated Schildstarr of Jotunland at the pass, Your Majesty. I believe I told you of it. Two score, possibly."

I nodded again. "Those were Fire Aelf, Salamanders. It's a weak clan, diminished by their slavery—"

Arnthor said, "To one who need not be named."

"Your Majesty is wise. These will be Mossmen. Wood Aelf the ignorant name them, and the learned Skogsalfar." I turned to the three dukes. "Theirs is the strongest clan. We may get help from the Earth Aelf as well, the Bodachan. They are not warlike, but their aid is not to be despised."

There was a silence, broken only by the whispering of Stonebowl and Smiler. When they had finished, I spoke to them, repeating what I had told the others.

"You, Scatter of the Dragon's Blood, are my ultimate ancestor," Smiler said in response, "but let us have also the blessing of the Fox."

I thanked him for the compliment and agreed.

"I will endeavor to obtain it."

I rose too when the others rose to go, but I remained in the pavilion with Arnthor. He sent his servants away, saying they were not to return until I sent them to him.

"Your messenger said you wished to speak with us. Do you think us cowardly, Sir Able?"

I shook my head. "Never, Your Majesty."

"Yet we are. The blind man you told us of killed our brother. Who will kill us?"

"I hope it will be Time, Your Majesty. I hope you will die, when you must die, full of years and wisdom."

"We know better. Nor have we any wish to perish as you suggest. A thousand lovely virgins wait upon the Valfather."

I did not speak.

"We know who and what you are. Do not feign ignorance. We do not fear death. We fear that not one of the thousand will stoop for us—that we will be driven over the Bridge called Swords."

"If I could promise a Valkyrie, I would," I told him. "I can't."

"Nor did we think it." He studied me. Some instinct told me it might be dangerous to meet his eyes. I did not; yet they probed deep. "You did not lie with our queen."

"Nor have I sought to, Your Majesty, knowing the effort would be fruitless."

"Pah! You might go in to her tonight. She'd receive you with open arms. And legs. Will you?"

"No, Your Majesty. That I will not."

He was silent again, searching me. At length he said, "It is not enough to die with courage, Sir Able. One must die honorably. Since we're to die and know it, we have taken thought upon our honor. It is not unstained."

"Nor mine, Your Majesty." Although my thoughts raced, I could not imagine what he was getting at.

"We imprisoned you without cause, but we freed you and have raised you to honor. What more can we do?"

I said, "I did not ask to speak with you privately to beg a favor, Your Majesty, but to make you a gift. I feared you'd refuse it, as I still do. Thus I hoped to give it when no one else was present."

"The gift of death?" He threw back his cloak and spread his arms. "Strike!"

"Never, Your Majesty."

"You could not if you wished to, since we will not die by your hand. We wear no armor; you just observed it."

I was more puzzled than ever.

"We wear a sword belt. Perhaps you observed that, too. We did not lie when we told you we had lost your sword. It was with our baggage, which was captured."

I cannot write down all the hope I felt at that moment, or my gratitude to the Valfather, who orders such things.

"It was retaken in the Forest Fight and returned to us." A little shakily, Arnthor stood and unbuckled his sword belt. "You say you bring a gift. We've none to give here. But we return what is yours and reclaim our honor." Suddenly he smiled. "The scabbard is nicely decorated. And the hilt, though primitive, is beautiful. We could not judge the blade, because we were never able to draw it. Did you not wonder why no one described the spirits of men long dead fighting beside us?"

I could not have spoken had I wished to. He handed me Eterne; and I felt that part of me, long lost, had returned. My hands acted of themselves.

Then—oh, then! Ben, Ben, how I wish that you could hear what I heard: war cries no live man knows, and the hoofs of chargers dust a thousand years. The whole pavilion, big as it was, was thronged with fell men in armors of antique mold, knights with shining faces and eyes to make a lion cower. They knelt to Arnthor, and one said, "Do you learn in this hour, O King, why the span we cross is called the Bridge of Swords?"

"We do." For an instant Arnthor, even Arnthor, seemed to hesitate. "You may not speak the secrets of Hel."

They nodded.

"We ask a question, even so. We hope its answer will not be among them. Though we could not draw it, we too bore the blade. Is it possible we may join you?"

Phantom voices whispered, *"It may be—it may be."*

"Sheath it," Arnthor told me.

I did and the knights faded, their deep voices still whispering, *"It may be . . ."* when nothing else remained.

"You owe us no boon," Arnthor told me, "and we owe you many. We ask a boon nonetheless, for that is the privilege of kings. Centuries ago, an ancestor of ours wished to honor a certain knight above all others. He had already given him nobility, broad lands, and riches—so much that he refused more. They exchanged swords, the king wearing the sword that had been that knight's forever afterward, and that knight wearing the sword that had been his king's. We have not given you our sword. It was your sword, the sword we took from you, the sword you won from a dragon if the tales are true. Yet it's the one we've worn since the Forest Fight returned it, and you have it. Will you give the sword you wear now?"

I saw then how Parka shapes our fates, and took off my sword belt, and the sword Baki had found for me. "This is the gift I intended to give Your Majesty. I give it gladly. Wear it tonight, and I'll be honored above all others."

He took it from me and put it on. "May we draw it?"

"You may."

He did, and the brand gleamed in his hand as it never had for me, filling the pavilion with gray light.

"It thirsts." His voice had fallen to a whisper. "We have heard of such things. We never thought them true."

"Most often they are not, Your Majesty."

"Yet it does," he said. (I doubt that he had heard me.) "It walks in the desert and dreams of a lake of blood."

CHAPTER FORTY
THE RIVER BATTLE

Wistan and Yond had found two points at which the river could be forded, although only with difficulty. The west crossing was the better of the two; I gave it to Arnthor, as well as the best fighters—the nobles and nearly all the knights, and Smiler and his Dragon Soldiers. I planned to take the east crossing, charging on Cloud (who would scarcely wet her belly). Toug and Rober were to ride behind me. After them, such wounded men-at-arms as could draw sword, the peasants, the Free Companies, and such Aelf as might be. We would attack first and draw the Caan's strength.

It was a sound plan. Arnthor had agreed to wait until our attack had begun before he began his, and his men would be in the rear out of sight, giving us about fifteen minutes more. I told him that under no circumstances would we fight before sunset. In point of fact I meant to attack sooner, feeling that the more pressure I put on myself the more likely I was to succeed. It is always good to have a plan before battle, so I have found; but once battle is joined, the plan is liable to vanish like morning mist. So it was in the River Battle.

Although Arnthor's force was to assemble out of sight of the river, I thought it prudent to station sentries along the bank, particularly at the fords, in case the enemy tried to cross; Sir Marc had charge of these. He was inspecting his men when a captain of the Osterlings shouted some insult. Rather than letting it pass in silence, Marc returned one of his own. The captain waded into the river, challenging Marc to meet him. Marc did, the captain's men attacked him when their captain fell, Marc's sentries ran to support him, and the fighting spread.

All that I learned later. At the time, I heard shouts and the clash of weapons; Etela ran to tell me the Osterlings had reached the south bank, where Arnthor and his knights had met them. "We'll cross the river," I told her, "to take them from behind. Get to safety."

She did not, although it was some time before I knew it. I asked Cloud to crouch so I could mount.

She looked Skaiward instead, pricking her ears to catch the voice that rolled upon Mythgarthr. I heard it too, and when she sprang into the air, cantering up a faint breeze, no thought of mine came to trouble her. I could have tried to turn her back; I knew it was impossible and did not try.

I should have taken a horse. I did not, but waded out alone. Arrows struck my hauberk. More whistled past my ear. I had been holding Eterne out of the water; I drew her.

They came from all directions, or so it seemed to me, faint to the eye but loud to the ear. Their blades could not yet kill—we were in full sun, although the sun was low. But it was no small thing to feel the bite of those swords, no phantom touch or tickle. I heard the screams, and saw men drop their spears to clutch wounds that did not bleed.

More substantial help followed: Toug and Rober mounted, with the wounded men-at-arms behind them also mounted. After them, the outlaws and peasants, running and shouting, all on foot. I had been afraid both groups would hang back, and had done all I could to support leaders who seemed eager for war; both fought far better than I expected.

Wistan and I were at their head, by no means shamed by our men. Men and women, I ought to have said, for although the women who had come with their men were not many, they fought bravely. I shall come to that later, Ben, or try to.

The last of our mounted men had passed before I climbed out of the river, soaked to the waist with my boots full of water. I had meant to lead them in a wide semicircle, and to take the enemy in the rear, as I had told Etela. Now they had Toug and Rober to lead them. Both were brave, and even Toug, young as he was, had some knowledge of tactics. They might do as I had planned; but if they did not, there was nothing I could do about it.

As for me, I had this ragtag band on foot, and had to do the best I could—get Celidon a victory as cheaply as might be. For us no semicircle was possible. I decided to move left along the bank, rolling up any Osterlings we met and hitting the flank of those fording the river.

We had crossed without much opposition, in a mass that was on the way to becoming a mob. I halted it, and got them to form ranks as they had been trained to. The archers had of course held their bows above water and kept their strings dry. I put them in a line on our flank, where they could keep off slingers and bowmen. The charge of a dozen horsemen would have scattered them like starlings, but no such charge came. The horsemen had work enough already.

I put those with the best shields in front, with pikes behind them to thrust between the shields. The rest were massed behind the pikes, with Wistan to keep order and see that someone picked up the pike or shield when a buddy fell. I stayed six paces ahead, marching boldly and turning every few steps to shout orders or encouragement. We needed flags. We needed trumpets and drums. We had none, but someone (I could guess who) got the women in back singing and shouting and clapping, and maybe that was better than trumpets and drums. *"Step out!"* I told them. *"Step out lively there!"*

And step out we did. *"Disiri! Disiri! Disiri!"* Some Osterlings had come to know that shout; and whether they knew it or not, we were many. If we were half trained and worse armed, it cannot have been apparent to those who fled us.

We had gone a surprising way west along the river when we met a hundred or so determined to make a stand. Their captain had one of those pole maces they favor. Eterne hewed the iron chaps behind the head and left him with a stick. He flung it at me and tried to draw sword, but I took off his arm at the elbow before I split his helm.

A score of his men were at me like terriers. I remember cutting through two spears and putting my blade in the belly of one tall fellow who looked as if he had eaten nothing but grass for the past month. I recall wondering whether Wistan had sense enough to see to it that the weapons of the men I was killing went to those who needed them. Other than that, almost nothing. It is well to strike hard; but it is better—much better—to strike quickly. Garvaon had taught me, and I struck as quickly as I could, not thinking of Garvaon or much of anything: cut, cut, cut, thrust. Get the shield in front of the eyes. Fast! Fast, before another comes to help. Thrust under it. Thrust hard and deep and very fast, before he gets it down. His leg's out—kick the knee, fast and hard. Slash before he recovers. I caught one Osterling in his dirty fangs with bottom of my shield, and saw a pikehead in his chest before I could follow up.

They were running, and the riverbank much too far to my left, and ahead a great cloud of boiling dust in which a flag and a few plumes were visible, a cloud so thunderous that the trumpeting of an elephant sounded small and lonely, like the crying of a child. We would take the cloud—the cloud that was an army—in the flank. We would damage and delay it, and that might be enough; but whether it was enough or not, it would turn and crush us. I ordered my brave, desperate, untrained, badly armed troops forward, and ran ahead of them shouting, *"Disiri!"* Our arrows raked the cloud. It might do some good. Better to die than not fight and know that Rober and Lamwell would have fought like the heroes they were.

And then the dragon roared above us belching flame, and wheeled in air (I had stopped to look up) and came at us so low its wind stirred the parched dust, and straight for me. Its flame washed over me, and its jaws closed on me, burning; but the sun's last rays were sapping its reality still. It could not lift me or crush me, and our arrows flew through its scales and into its vitals.

It rose with a wild cry that swiftly became a cry of triumph. The sun was setting, and the blazing breath that had been weak as a candle in sunlight strengthened every second. It circled, skimming the Osterling army it had made its own. The shadows that had been sharp when we crossed the river were vanishing, melting into a general darkness. And the dragon, Ben, was as real as I, as real as Setr had been in Aelfrice, a monster of jade and jet.

I had failed to think of Garvaon earlier, and I failed to think of him then—and of Svon, who had fought Setr and lived. There was no time. No time for anything but to shout nonsense at the men who followed me, wave my sword above my head, and dash to meet the dragon.

Knights in antique armor galloped past me. The dragon roared to shake the earth, but they shook it in cold fact. I felt it tremble under the blows of a hundred iron-shod hooves. Lances shattered on the dragon's scales; two struck home in the fiery mouth. That was when I did the thing I had hoped to do when I spoke with Arnthor, the thing Michael had done beside the pool. All that I had told Toug became true for me; and the Aelf, even Disiri, were less than dreams—only thoughts to be created and dismissed at will. I called for them as a god, and my call compelled them.

The Osterlings before me and the men behind me halted, and in the sudden silence I heard a humming overhead, as if a million bees had taken flight. I looked up, and the sky was full of arrows.

Disiri had come, and two thousand with her: Mossmen and Mossmaidens, Salamanders, Ice Aelf, and the little Bodachan who have in them no delight in war but fight (when they do) because they must, asking no quarter and giving none.

There are songs and tales of that battle, Ben. I know you cannot hear them and I cannot equal them; I will outline it here, but nothing more.

Toug and Rober took the Osterlings in the rear, as I had hoped. We struck the flank—the Knights of the Sword, the Aelf, and those who followed me. The Osterlings held longer than their Caan had any right to expect, fighting the bravest knights the world has seen in a sleet of arrows. Arnthor spoke, their dragons turned on them, and they broke and fled; those south of the river, seeing the battle had been lost behind them, fled too. Great execution was made among them. Greater still when they halted to hold the north bank. They were the best that Osterland had to show, the Spahis and the Caan's own war band, and few lived.

Beyond that, I can only give some incidents. When we were attacking the flank and everything had been thrown into confusion, I saw as if in a fever two blind men wielding staves, directed by a half-grown child and a woman with a sword. You will have guessed the identity of these four. You will not have guessed that Bold Berthold took a spear in the belly before the moon was high.

Once I fell, and the chief who had stunned me stood over me to strike again. He knew who I was, I think, and hoped that I would beg for my life so that he might boast of it afterward. The scarecrow who saved me had been shaped of moss and mud, of twigs and bark and fresh green leaves. I knew, and taking off the old helm I embraced lovely Disiri there on the battlefield.

Arnthor met the Black Caan at water's edge. The Black Caan fell, and though the weight of his mail sunk his body, the current bore it away and it was never found. Arnthor lived long enough to learn that we had triumphed, but not longer. Marder and Bahat covered his body and let no one see it; it was burned that night on a pyre of broken lances and arrows, and shattered shields. If I had seen it, I might explain why Gaynor so adamantly refused him. I did not, and offer no guess.

He lacked his brother's magnetism and vaulting ambition, and it was well he did. He was inclined to brutality and avarice, but kept both in check better than most such men. He was courageous, and just without mercy—or at least with little. His line had provided Celidon with wiser kings and better commanders, but none more cunning. He never unbent, and if he had many willing servants, he had no friends.

There was another incident later. I will tell you that in a later place.

When the battle was over and I had sheathed Eterne, I assembled those I had led. It was only then I learned of Bold Berthold's wound and realized that he would surely die. Otherwise I might not have chosen as I did.

Toug and Rober were there, and old Gerda, who had helped with the wounded until she could scarcely stand. So were Lynnet, Etela, and Vil. Wistan had a bandage over half his face, put there by Ulfa, and Uns attended him in a way that showed he thought Wistan might faint or die. I made them sit nearer the fire, and sent Pouk for Gylf, whom we had double-chained in the rear to save his life. I did not say much or do anything before they joined us.

"Friends," I said, and I tried to look past the nearest to

the exhausted faces farther from the fire. "I owe you a great deal. I can't reward you as you deserve, and it may be you will never be rewarded for having saved your country. What I can do is tell you the truth, and let you see what I'm going to do—what I'm going to keep doing 'til I'm stopped. Which will be soon."

They stirred, but no one spoke.

"First, the truth. I had thought to lead you on Cloud. I had lost her. You will recall that I did not have her on our march south, not 'til we met the Dragon Soldiers. In his goodness, Lothur restored her to me. He may have thought I'd break an oath I gave his father in payment. That would've been the end of me, as it will be very soon. I didn't, but at the worst possible moment his father took her back. It did us great harm, and the fault is mine. I confess it to you now."

Several muttered objections. I silenced them.

"That was the truth, and you have it. Here is more. In Skai, the Valfather, the greatest and kindest of all kings under the Most High God, gave me power. Years later I begged to return here. He consented on the condition that I not use my power here, and I swore I wouldn't.

"I'm an oath-breaker, since I broke that one when the Osterlings were besieging Redhall. Some of you were there, and will not forget the storm I raised. Tonight I'm going to break it again, openly and for as long as I can."

Exhausted though they were, that stirred them.

I called to Bold Berthold. He could not stand, but Pouk and Uns helped him. I tore away his bandage and healed him.

"Kneel," I told him, "and Gerda beside you."

He was exploring the spot where his wound had been, but he knelt; Ulfa brought Gerda and had her kneel too. I put a hand on each head and felt my power flow out. It took a lot to restore the thing he had left in a pond so long ago.

When I opened them again, they were kneeling still. I

wondered at the silence, because I expected a lot of noise, but the others were watching by firelight and could see only their bent backs. Bold Berthold's hair was black once more. Gerda's was the color of ripe corn. Yet my hands were still on their heads, and even the closest could not be sure.

I told Bold Berthold and Gerda to rise. They did, and Bold Berthold exclaimed, "I can see! I can see!" Gerda embraced him and they wept—this though she was fair and young again, with laughing eyes.

Etela tugged my sleeve, weeping too. I knew what she wanted, and had Ulfa bring Lynnet to me. "You are not my son," Lynnet said, "and yet you are. Will you make me go?"

"Never," I told her. "But I cannot make you live again. That is beyond me. Kneel. I don't have much time."

She knelt. The derangement of Lynnet's mind was deep and hard, so that I felt I was picking a knot with my nails and my teeth; I loosed it at last, and I had her stand. She smiled, and I at her, and we embraced. "Mag is still with me," she whispered. "She came on that sea isle. You won't make her go home?"

"No," I said.

Gylf next, and swiftly and easily. And then I knew, for I saw *him*, standing behind those farthest from the fire. I thought he would speak when I called for Uns. He did not.

As for me, I found I could hardly whisper. I laid my hand on Uns' hump, something I had never done before. "Stand straight."

How slowly he rose! He thought it a dream—I saw that in his face. He thought he was dreaming, and feared at every finger's width gained that he might wake. Toug came to stand by him. Toug was crying, and so was I.

Wistan was almost the last. Before I healed him, I thought of how he had fought with Toug in Utgard; that was long over and he had served me faithfully.

"You were there in the beginning," I told Pouk. "It is not right you should be last now. I hope I have time."

"I got a eye, sir. Take Vil."

I had forgotten him, and had Pouk bring him forward. For a moment or two, I felt I lacked the strength. He took my hand when it was over, and put something in it, a thing that buzzed and sang with many voices. "I want to pay, Sir Able. Ain't enough, but it's what I got. When I got more, you'll get that too."

"My bowstring."

"Yes, sir. Yours again."

I was exhausted and very happy at that moment, Ben. I made Pouk come to me and blew into his blind eye. He said, "Thankee, sir! Thankee!," and I hugged him and he me, and I knew that he too had been healed, and I could heal no more. I wanted to sit, but the tall man in the wide hat was coming and it was impossible.

"You have done, Drakonritter." It was not a question.

I bowed my head.

"You are shamed." His eye gleamed in the dark. "You would end your life if I asked, and will end it in any case."

"I will, Valfather." My hand had found my dagger.

"I forbid it! But I expect no obedience from you. You will die when Winter and Old Night whelm us. So will I. So will my son Thunor, who does not believe it. Meanwhile, I thank you for mending my dog. Shall I return Cloud?"

"No," I said.

"I'll give you another, younger, of the same breed."

"No," I said again.

"You thought my son Lothur kind and generous. He is neither. What you saw as his generosity was only groundwork for betrayal. If you had known him as others do, you would have seen it at once."

Something kindled in me, and I raised my head. "I

never entreated your son for help, nor did any act of mine deserve his gratitude. He told Morcaine to summon me and offered his help. We were starving and too weak to face our foes. He brought us food and men. I will make no complaint of him—never again."

"Others he has treated better have spoken worse." There was a smile in the Valfather's tone. "Are you coming back?"

I said nothing.

"Few have been asked—Sir Able. Even once."

"I am not Able," I whispered.

"You are. I'll summon Cloud, and you and I will mount. Together we will ride to Skai."

I could not talk, Ben. I have sometimes when I found it so hard that I wondered afterward how I did it. This time I could not. Etela took my hand; her face was wet with tears, but she was not crying then. "He's afraid she won't come with him," Etela told the Valfather.

"She would not, child." His voice had become remote and severe. "She cannot." He turned away.

Disiri had been watching and listening. She stepped out of the shadows.

The Valfather gestured to Wistan. "You've served your knight faithfully. You must do him one service more. Bring his helm and set it on his head."

Wistan did.

Lovely Disiri became a puppet of mud and leaves. That was horrible, but I had expected it. Two other things I had not expected and cannot explain. The Valfather was a bright shadow. Nothing more.

And Bold Berthold, who had been sitting beside Gerda, vanished. She was the same lovely young woman, but Berthold was gone and you, Ben, sat in his place. As I say, I cannot explain these things.

"You see what you are surrendering," the bright

shadow told me, "and know to what it is you go. What will you do?"

I drew my dagger, pushed up the sleeve of my hauberk, and cut my arm. "Drink," I told Disiri, and she bent and drank of my blood. Not a few drops, as Aelf often do, but great sobbing gulps while I clenched and unclenched my fist so that human life flowed freely, never stopping until a small, green-eyed woman stood beside me.

When I looked for the bright shadow again, it had gone. Soon Disiri and I went, too, I leaning on her, for I had lost much blood and was weak.

Here is the third incident I promised. We went slowly, and twice I fell. By the time we reached the river, fresh sunlight had dyed the clouds a thousand colors, though the sun's face was still below the eastern mountain. I stopped at the edge of the water, not sure I could make the crossing. A beautiful young woman supported the knight I saw reflected there; but that knight was not a boy but a grim warrior whose eyes gleamed from the slits of his helm.

I took it off and cast it into the river, and when the ripples had subsided, Disiri and I were just the same.

We live in Aelfrice, and for whole days we are children again, as we were the first time I came. Children, we run and shout among the groves and grottoes of an endless wood more beautiful than any you will ever see. Children, we go to the sea I love, to splash in the shallows and play with kelpies. She has given me a new dog, a white puppy with red ears. I call him Farvan; and at night we speak to him of the play now past and the play to come and he tells us puppy things.

But we are not always children, and sometimes we lie upon our backs in fine green grass to watch the world above where time runs swift. There we saw Marder knight Wistan and Bold Berthold slay Schildstarr. Soon time will ripen, and we will come again.

Michael has found me at last, and that is why I have